HOMAGE

CHRONICLES OF A HABITANT

ALSO BY SHIRLEY BURTON

UNDER THE ASHES
Book One of the Thomas York Series

THE FRIZON
Book Two of the Thomas York Series

ROGUE COURIER
Book Three of the Thomas York Series

SECRET CACHE
Book Four of the Thomas York Series

RED JACKAL

SENTINEL IN THE MOORS

shirleyburtonbooks.com

HOMAGE

CHRONICLES OF A HABITANT

Shirley Burton

To John,
Shirley Burton

HIGH STREET PRESS
CALGARY

HIGH STREET PRESS
Calgary, AB, Canada
highstreetpress.com
shirleyburtonbooks.com
First printing 2017

This book is an historical fiction. Names, historical characters, named families and persons are largely based on research, and with some embellishment; incidents, conversations, and some activities and events are fiction.

Printed in the United States of America.
Available in eBook formats.
Cover photos Public Domain: Chateau de Dissay, Louis Boudin 1699; Breaking Lent (A Friday's Surprise) Cornelius Krieghoff 1847; The Blacksmith's Shop, Krieghoff 1871.
Editor and design Bruce Burton

Library and Archives Canada Cataloguing in Publication

Burton, Shirley, 1950-, author
Homage: chronicles of a habitat / Shirley Burton.

Includes bibliographical references.
Issued in print and electronic formats.
ISBN 978-1-927839-08-9 (softcover).--ISBN 978-1-927839-09-6 (hardcover).--ISBN 978-1-927839-10-2 (PDF)

    1. Title.

PS8603.U778H66 2017   C813'.6   C2017-903152-X
                                              C2017-903153-8

". . . these are the actions and language of a thousand people of merit, who deal with the affairs of New France with as much courage, if not more, as they would with the affairs of the Old France."

—Father Paul LeJeune, Jesuit Father, 1600s

Introduction

The journey of the French passion from the Province of Poitou to ports of the St. Lawrence is more than a voyage of body and heart. It's a determination of the soul and indelible spirit of the descendants of New France.

This historical journey follows the tribulations of ten generations over four hundred years, from Dissay, Poitou in France, to Charlesbourg and the village of St. Andrews in Québec.

The Pasquier family is real and based on research, and the stories of their lives are presented as fiction, representative of all those that sailed from the ports of France to life in North America.

Following the footsteps of the Pasquiers of Brie, our characters depart from the ancient harbor of La Rochelle for the Atlantic journey, on a quest for free land and opportunity.

Over many years, the author has researched to understand the struggles and joys endured. War, birth, death and marriage are not the only milestones of these generations, but are enhanced by what we glean from their experiences—adventure, vision, survival, love and faith.

Through research for this book, I never came across an expression more poignant than that of Father Paul LeJeune, Jesuit Father to the missions around Tadoussac during the time of Champlain. Let your heart read these words, and become part of this journey of the stalwart habitant.

"To leave one's parents and friends, to abandon one's acquaintances, to leave one's sweet homeland and its traditions, to cross the seas, to defy the ocean and its storms, to sacrifice one's life to suffering, to leave behind all present belongings, in order to throw oneself blindly forward for the sake of distant hopes, to convert the traffic of the earth into that of the heavens, to want to die in Barbary, is a language that is not spoken in the school of nature; and yet, these are the actions and language of a thousand people of merit, who deal with the affairs of New France with as much courage, if not more, as they would with the affairs of the Old France."

I am grateful for the path of historians, uncovering facts and traditions for the sake of future generations, sharing opinions and etching their research, whatever their nationalities.

This narrative commences in the 15th century in the midst of the Hundred Years' War battlegrounds of England and France as kings were looking beyond their borders to expand their wealth, and with intent to take control of trade.

It was the time following Christopher Columbus' discovery of the Americas, declaring that the world is round. Then, Giovanni Verrazano's navigation and expeditions of the northeastern seaboard of the Atlantic and into the Carribbean incited a race to stake claims in the New World.

In France, the family of d'Amboise becomes interwoven from the late 1400s with the Pasquier family of Paris and Brie and the open doors to commissions sanctioned by the kings of France. Although others travelled before Jacques Cartier, he becomes our eyes to this new land, then followed seventy years later by Samuel de Champlain.

On one side of the Atlantic, we see hardships of the vassals strip farming in favour of the royal court—and on the other, we are led to the indigenous people of the St. Lawrence in their Garden of Eden.

Natives inhabiting the New World before Champlain's explorations had inbred respect for the land and the spirits. They believed that the land's resources were gifted to the abiding peoples, with nature to be shared, long before the greed of foreign continents would interfere, bringing new hostilities.

Both the French habitant and the native tribal member stand out as protectors of heritages that become blended into the richness of the Québecois. The development of relationships between the habitant and the Huron and Micmac was pivitol; without it, explorations might have dwindled into obscurity from scurvy, disease and lack of survival skills.

The Québecois love their culture, their rich heritage and their Roman Catholic faith, and have a deep gratitude to the native society who guided them through the woods and taught them wilderness skills standing shoulder to shoulder in war and in friendship.

Relationships developed between the Five Nations Confederacy, between natives and French, French and British, Americans and British, natives and British, Loyalists and Québecois, and the unity of Canadians. Each is a unique story, exposing emotions and characteristics, among them the fortitude of Adam Dollard.

Thousands of years before the imagination and vision of explorers, the migration began, transplanting cultures. Although the Amerindians moved north from the Columbias and Spanish lands, the aboriginal tribes of Canada had arrived from Eurasia, journeying the Beringia land bridge joining the continents. On the rim of the north Pacific, the land eroded, leaving the route divided by the Bering Sea.

The cultures and aboriginal language of these pre-Columbian civilizations—from the Mayan and Aztec to the Inuit, Algonquin, Iroquois and Micmac tribes—divided Amerindians who fought against each other for centuries. The South American Andean influence brought rich art and history that melded with the pre-Spanish and Portuguese colonization, before the natural resources were pillaged by European explorers.

Far away, the great European continents played monopoly, seeking routes to the Orient's riches, while remnants of the mindset of Roman cultures emerged in battle from the North Sea to the coast of Africa. Land was dealt by Treaty back and forth as a commodity, and war tested the might, pride and patriotism of England, France, Spain, Portugal and Italy.

This collection ventures to understand Québecois patriotism from its French foundation to the 21st century, with emotions from cultural changes, expectations of wars, laughter and tears from family celebrations, from births to passings. In some degree, all immigrants share the history and experiences depicted in this journal.

Before exploring new worlds, the French were warriors defending faith and their homeland. Life was unyielding in France as plagues ravaged towns, with families torn apart as husbands spent months and years defending the king. In spite of the leadership of Joan of Arc, the embattled troops saw little dawn of the horizon.

The enticement of free land in the new world changed the aspirations of the oppressed vassal, and one by one the people of Poitou and the Loire valley ventured to the ports as engagés.

We follow their passion and heroism, facing an unknown future in a rugged wilderness, reconciling unexpected hardships of starvation, hostile Iroquois, harsh winters and scurvy, but surviving through devotion, inherent faith and optimism.

The core people of initial settlements of the St. Lawrence were from Carignan-Salières Regiment who came as engagés. As Louis XIV saw the imbalance between men and women, he introduced the program of the King's Daughters, bringing descendants from parishes around Paris, with generous dowries and enticements for farmers to stay on the new land.

Our habitant treks across the ocean, becoming at home at the rivers and thick woods, rural villages and towns of Québec and Montréal, until settling in the quiet village of St. Andrews East in Argenteuil, in the Eastern Townships of Québec. His life becomes integral in fur trading, farming, merchant development, timber, roads and canals, ship yards, churches, schools and the fruition of a new patriotism. Progress and inventions unfold for him and the lives of his descendents.

Wars bring anguish to families as they had in France, but now with British, French, American and natives, at times with families split by loyalties.

Coinciding with life in New France, we parallel the British who had inspired literary writers to flourish, railways to burgeon, unions to defend the foundry worker, and parliamentary reforms that eventually secured pensions and benefits to keep the struggling class from the poorhouses. Growing pains of the Industrial Revolution were creating a working class a world away from the habitant farmer.

The 21st century finds our habitant in disagreement with politics, misunderstood by the British, and overlooked as a unique people. The Pasquiers/Paquettes had been craftsmen and sportsmen since the time in Dissay in the 16th century, and remain, with each descendant line a result of heredity and environment.

As the book comes to conclusion, my joyful habitant is a blend of characteristics made up of Métis, French, British, and American Loyalists, rich in qualities that define the Québecois.

One

Sulpice I, Seigneur of d'Amboise, Loire Valley – Conversations with a swallow of obligations & patriotism – Soldiers & Cannons, Hundred Years War – Henry II Betrays Thomas Becket - Hugues Chaumont 1075-1129 – Hugues II inherites first House of d'Amboise - Battle of Agincourt, 1415 – Pierre III of d'Amboise appointed Lord, 1422 – Introduction of Anne de Bueil, 1428 – Hundred Years War & Seige of Orleans – Joan of Arc, people's heroine – Charles VII grants Pierre II the Seigneurie of Disset-deBourg – Royal Château built at Dissay for Pierre d'Amboise – Chance meeting at Clos Luce with Leonard da Vinci.

d'Amboise, France - Fifteenth Century

CHIRP, CHIRP. THE DISTANT CANNONS MUFFLED, THEN echoed across the valley. Through the morning stillness, a white-throated sparrow made a cheerful plea and waited for a starling to serenade a throaty warble in reply.

Spring puddles and dried creeks permitted high banks of wild grass. A wandering young man lay on his back, his gaze following the shapes of clouds, drifting toward a new world that had never yet seen the turmoil of war. It was impossible to block out the constant thudding sound of the cannons; he had always known about battles, and the Hundred Years War had drafted his allegiance and the Amboise courage.

The lords, dukes, counts, barons and French noblesse found it convenient to support the king who claimed the throne of France, even if he were English. Otherwise, they had learned it meant the burning of their lands and the pillaging of their families and estates.

"Ah, it feels so good to rest my weary bones, whilst I look upon the heavens through the glory of sunrise. I shall not be missed at the palace before this dew is sucked into the sky. Away from the sounds and smells of battle, away from the disdain of royal obligations."

He stretched his arms behind his head, and placed a staff of sweet grass in his mouth. Since a small lad, he had heard nightly talk of the heroics of the Amboise family and their loyalty to the kings. He rolled onto his side to lift his head.

"From my lofty perch above the Loire River, I look down at the valley blessed by our first seigneur, dear Sulpice I, who engraced himself with the Counts of Anjou and invited royal courts into our château. This is the valiant call that I am to defend."

The young man jolted upright. With angry blood coursing, he called out aloud upon the heavens.

"Count Fulk V enticed my grandfather[1] to join the First Crusade to Jerusalem, to protect the pilgrims of Israel travelling to the Temple of Solomon. You did not shield him from war, yet you bring Thomas Becket, Henry II's[2] own administrator, into our home to trick into treason. If Becket had not betrayed Henry II, he would not have burned our ancestral home in his ire and turned Chaumont into ashes. But Amboise does not die. My noble father rebuilt his castle."

The echo of the artillery moved closer and his stead neighed in objection. He raised himself to one knee and stretched his neck toward the horizon to filter the sound. The calm of the cornfields became drowned by the thundering hoof prints of a stallion scout in the area, then the urgent flapping of birds rising from the orchards. His own black horse, languishing under the shade of budding russet trees, reared up, then settled back to feast on the rich grass.

Pierre's ears tuned to the clomping of foot soldiers, marching behind horses and crippled wagons up the narrow road between Orléans and the

---

[1] Hugues Chaumont 1075-1129 joined religious crusades commanded by Fulk V, Count of Anjou. His body was returned to his widow, Elizabeth de Sauvigny for burial at Amboise. Hugues II of Chaumont inherited the first house of Amboise.

[2] Henry II married Eleanor of Acquitane. Having conquered Normandy, he privileged himself of apartments at Amboise. In 1162, sequestered in a tower room, the King met with Thomas Becket and his new Archbishop. Becket questioned the supremacy of the ecclesiastical courts, vowing loyalty to the church laws, confirming his own death warrant.

château. Remaining low and still, he waited for the sound to recede, then slowly crept to his knees. In the silence, a pair of red-rumped swallows caught his eye, as they sipped from the trickle over the creek bed.

"Hello, little bird, are you loyal to the King? If not, I shall slit your throat. But have no fear, little one. I will spare you because you keep my secrets."

Pierre laughed at himself, straightening his britches to tuck in the ruffled white shirt.

At the creek bed, he inched a hand-sized boulder from its place on the bank. With a stick, he dug a deeper hole, then removed a small package from his pocket, and buried it under the rock.

Up on the stallion, with the wind in his face, Pierre galloped to the castle, home of his father Hugues VIII of Chaumont and Jeanne de Guenand.

"Such treachery is our fault; our burden hast taken the blood of my father. Our Holiness demands my soul; our Generals demand that we march to battle; and what remains belongs to d'Amboise."

The castle rose behind a tree line and he eased to a canter in the lane. Excitement surged at the sight of the glistening black royal carriage arriving in front of him at the Loire Castle. Assigning his horse to the hands of the stable master, Pierre skipped ahead, hoping for a chance to see the king's favoured black stallion. The horse, a gift from the Duke of Savoy, was rumoured to be mean of stature, with only one eye.

"They say he is feared, but I shall peer into his one angry eye and see the dread in his soul. We shall become friends and Monsieur Bageau will let me help to groom him."

Looking up, he saw that the standard of King Charles VIII had been raised from the Minimes Tower. House staff were whispering and scurrying to become obscure, and knowing the back stairs and invisible rooms behind the casements of stone, Pierre schemed his way into the great rooms reserved for royalty.

As fresh as if yesterday, Pierre heard the voice of his father on the eve of battle in 1415. But it had been many years before at the Amboise castle, when he had listened from behind the tapestry of the castle's great room.

On that day as a boy, Pierre feared that his hiding location would be revealed by the house beagle that came licking at his boots.

"Shoo, Sergeant. Go find Georges." He instantly regretted his kicking reflex as the pup tugged his pantaloons in confusion.

Pierre spied the hemp sock that the hound preferred for play, and edging out from his hiding place, he caught it with the toe of his boot. Grasping the sock in his hand, he tossed it through the open window. Sergeant's legs spun down the polished corridor, intent on retrieving it in the jousting courtyard.

Suddenly the door of the great room thrust open and a contingent of a dozen men entered. Six royal military officers marched in formation, wearing tunics over long-sleeved smocks and royal sashes. Each soldier had a sabre at his side in a leather sheath.

Last to enter was King Henry V himself, pompous with authority and raising his head to project a booming voice above all others.

Pierre stiffened up and affixed himself to the wall behind. For a cool October day, a light breeze drifted through the tall mullioned window casements, yet Pierre found it stifling and almost suffocating behind the heavy tapestry.

He imagined that the sound of his own breathing echoed into the great hall, and he covered his face with his hand. Drawing a pick knife from his knee garter, he intruded through the curtain to cut an eyehole and pressed his eye against the tapestry until his lashes conflicted, lest he could be involved in the event taking place.

King Henry walked over to Hugues' grand case of polished longbows, gleaming silver sabres and heavy wooden muskets mounted in the arms case. The room was silent, waiting for any words from the King.

"M'Lord Chaumont, you have a fine collection of armour. Most commendable," Henry announced, and strutted with his hands positioned appropriately behind his back. "Is that the gilt emblem of your father engraved on the stock?"

"Merci, your Highness. Do you wish to prize a piece?"

"Non, non! I will remember they are here."

Once the King was seated, the round of dignitaries relaxed. Pierre thought how fine his father looked in his green velvet shirt and woolen beret, with a brilliant purple thistle pin of gold affixed at the front of his tunic. His wavy golden locks were trimmed, not to exceed his jawline, where they met with a reddish-blond beard.

"We will advance on Calais at dawn," Hugues III said to Henry V's royal lieutenant, drawing a routing on a parchment on the table. "We have learned from Harfleur of the flaws of the English army and the skills of the French feudal army. We will march from the River Somme to Calais."

"The king's troops are nearing Agincourt as we speak," the admiral interjected. "We have over 6,000 crossbowmen ready to go."

"Here . . ." The men leaned in to focus on an 'X' drawn on the map. "This farmer's field is where we will take them by surprise. We will not retreat without victory."

Pierre heard a fierceness in his father's voice, and he trembled, wanting to call out to him. But that was a long time ago, that his father, Hugues VIII of Chaumont[3], walked out the door into the night. That was the last that Pierre saw of him. Now he only had faint visions of the hero, but that night burned in his memory forever. Days later, when the English troops arrived at Amboise with Henry's flag, Pierre knew it was time to become a man. After Hugues' funeral, his cousin Bertrand Duguesclin recalled the tragic events to Pierre while visiting at d'Amboise Château.

"With my own eyes, I saw death. French soldiers and knights stood in the fields as far as the eye could behold, yet the British came with axes, mallets, spears, and horses without mercy. French archers and knights braved the battle for days before retreating, leaving the wounded to be hacked by the English, and to die in a river of blood."

"Tell me, Monsieur Duguesclin! Tell me of my father!"

He hesitated and placed his hand on Pierre's shoulder. "Pierced through the chest by an English sword, he was a valiant and brave soldier, but succumbed on the battlefield defending the freedom of France. Your father was a hero."

In 1422, Pierre himself went to the battlefield, bow and arrow, shield and sword, to accept the responsibilities of his birthright, loyal to the King of France. Inheriting the title of Pierre III, he assumed lordship over the d'Amboise fiefdom of Blesoes, Berry and Touraine. With his title of Bishop of Poitiers, he was a member of the military.

---

[3] Hughes III of Chaumont, husband of Jeanne Guenand, died at the Battle of Agincourt on October 25, 1415.

As other kings from the House of Valois had done before, Charles VII often took up terms of residence at Amboise, hoisting the king's own royal banner with the figure of a golden salamander. The d'Amboise family shield was always present, with three red stripes and three vertical of gold.

The Château d'Amboise was an extension of opulence not seen outside Paris until Versailles. Terraces, casements, drawbridges, fortress walls, St. Hubert's chapel, horsemen towers, exotic gardens, and all signs of royalty sprawled over lands greater than a townsite.

Damask curtains, Flemish and French tapestries, Turkish carpets, arts of the masters, and luxurious velvet chairs crafted with imported walnut were demanded to provide a royal environment for guests of the King of France, partaking at the medieval round tables.

Requesting a visit with his mother at the château, Pierre promptly attended at her rooms, resplendent with a grand balcony watching the Loire River, where she could ignore the semblances of battle.

"Mother, I wish to speak."

"Yes, my son, what is troubling you?"

"Are you well, dear mother?"

Jeanne waved a handkerchief, nodding in agreement.

"Do you feel well enough for a walk in the gardens?"

Pierre offered his hand, as his mother placed hers on his, and they walked from her apartments through wide marble halls to the glass patio doors. He kept pace with her slow, short steps as they strolled through the manicured gardens. They were silent, but using the precious time together to admire the long rectangular maze of hedges that were groomed to perfection each day. They stopped to touch the marble of the fountains and statues, and to inspect the patios of roses, spring lilies and hyacinths.

"Ah, the lavender smells good. I forgot to come here," Jeanne mumbled, stopping to pick a sprig and savour the aroma. "Have you seen your brothers? Charles was here a short time ago."

Pierre bent to show respect and kissed his mother's hand. Her heavy velvet gown was elegant, with a train trimmed with rabbit fur, and her coiffeur was pinned under a coned garden hat, with a flowing veil attached to a button on her wrist.

Of course I can't hug my mother, she'd fall over.

"Yes, I saw Charles a short time ago, and Emery too, but Charles is too involved in his governorship of Île de France. Georges spends most of his time in Milan. We are a large enough family."

Pierre smiled kindly at his mother's fading memory. "Mother, do you believe the visions of the young girl from Barrois? She claims the Archangel Michael has been chosen by the saints to protect the King's royal army. They say she is not more than ten."

She stopped again. "Some say she is a heretic, while others believe she may be the one to save France. Villagers are rallying with great enthusiasm to follow her visions. I have not the answer, but we have pledged our loyalty to the King and that cannot be changed.

"We have sent young boys into the battlefield since the time of William the Conqueror. Will there be no end?"

Jeanne looked sadly into a distance that wasn't there. Pierre didn't wish to pain her further and turned to more pleasant conversation.

"I understand the king has discussed my taking the title of Lord of Chaumont. It will be a great honor."

"Yes, indeed. Your father would be pleased; you inherited his wisdom."

"Dearest Mother, I would like to invite Dame d'Aubijoux to the château to meet with your approval. She is Anne de Bueil[4], daughter of Jean IV de Bueil. They attended the royal ball held here last year."

"Oui, Pierre, I do recall. She is a lovely girl and I would be most anxious to meet her. Her family is well regarded at court."

Months after Pierre's marriage to Anne, the tensions came to a peak between France and England.

King Henry VI of England dispatched the Earl of Salisbury with more than six thousand troops, landing across the English Channel at Calais to invade Normandy again.

The English army built viewing towers as they advanced southward, and erected a base at Les Tourelles with sights on Orléans. The Château

---

[4] Anne de Bueil married Pierre d'Amboise on Aug. 23, 1428, daughter of Jean IV de Bueil and Marguerite Dauphine d'Auvergne, Countess of Sancerre. Anne and Pierre had seventeen children, many received in royal appointments.

d'Amboise, located southeast of the city, feared that the swelling English troops would cut off supplies and reinforcements and considered the possibility that the walls could be breached.

Pierre d'Amboise and his cousin Louis fought side by side with the troops of King Charles through the cold winter of 1428 and into spring of 1429. Receiving appointments in the king's army, they fared better than recruitments, occasionally finding a warm bed and a hot meal in the towns en route, as hostilities continued to rise.

"Louis, if the battle lines close on Orléans, Amboise will be next. We must protect our birthright."

"We will not let that happen, Pierre. Orléans is a walled city with thirty-four manned towers; they will be protected. The king has agreed to permit a passionate young woman from Domremy to lead his army."

"Yes, she is only seventeen, but already she leads an advancement from the south. Our king is desperate, it seems." The pair chuckled, knowing their amusement was strained at least, perhaps terrifying.

Within weeks, Louis and Pierre found themselves under the Duke of Alencon, charging reinforcements toward Château Chinon, residence of Charles VII, then toward Joan of Arc. Alencon had served five years in prison and recently obtained his freedom, becoming passionate to defend his bloodline to the heroine and serve as Saviour of France.

Disguising herself by cutting her hair, Joan of Arc dressed as a warrior. Professing that God was leading her, and with visions of the Archangel Michael, Saint Michael and Saint Catherine, she was the self-proclaimed Saviour of France. The garrison commander, Robert de Baudricourt, relented, providing her a horse and a limited convoy of soldiers.

Forging across farmlands, woods and valleys, her enamored troops pursued their leader with burning passion. Volunteers were eager to join the campaign toward certain victory. Approaching Les Tourelles from the east, Joan of Arc led the attack, barely penetrating the English lines.

In May of 1429, she was wounded in the shoulder and removed from the battlefield; without her leadership, the French faltered and talked of retreat. Alencon gave his promise to continue the campaign.

Joan was defiant with the taste of victory, and although wounded, she charged with the French flag to the front lines. She incited battle cries from the beleaguered French, and the troops rallied with a surge of fierceness and patriotism, bursting through enemy lines and victorious in battle.

Joan of Arc was captured in May 1430 and handed over to the English. In the courts, she was convicted of heresy and condemned to death by fire at the stake. She surrendered life in 1431, in Rouen, France at the age of nineteen. But twenty-five years later, the charges would be debunked and she would be declared innocent and a martyr.

In 1434, Pierre was designated as Chamberlain to Charles VII. A royal envoy arrived at Amboise with scrolls, sealed by the King's own insignia and official escort.

The new castle in Dissay would be exquisite, built of stone in Gothic Renaissance style. Word went out that servitude to the new castle and its Bishop would require skilled tradesmen—charpentiers, métiers, masons, menuisiers, and jardinières. Craftsmen had already long been in the favour of the royal courts, where the highest skills were sought to perfect their castles to exhibit a gentlemen's stature.

Trade masters were selected and skills taught to farmers who previously toiled to turn woods into arable land with only their bare hands and oxen.

With loyalty and optimism, they rushed to clear the new land and establish the hamlet of Dissay, centred by the imposing, new castle.

Moving to the castle, Pierre and Anne raised seventeen children, passing the magnificent structure down to their next generations. Under Louis XII, Pierre was appointed Ambassador to Rome and Bishop of Poitiers, and on his death in 1473, the distinction passed to his son, Pierre.

In the purple cornflower fields outside the Château d'Amboise, Pierre III was stopped by the greeting of a long-haired man whose voice spoke from through the bushes. The man was hunched over on a rock stubble.

At first glance, Pierre didn't recognize him as Monsieur da Vinci, but was instantly glad to see him, with his paints spread onto a small table as he viewed the vineyards of Clos Luce Manor.

"Bonjour, Monsieur da Vinci. It is a fine day for painting."

"Bonjours, Pierre, mon ami. God changes the colours every day, they are never the same. Nature is a silent guardian to keep our souls seeking beauty beyond what we see."

"I never thought of nature in thèèat way."

Château de Dissay, by Louis Boudin 1699, French artist and engraver,
Castle of Pierre d'Amboise, Bishop of Poitiers, granted from Charles VII.
Gallica Digital Library. Public Domain ⊛

Charles VII, King of France, House of Valois,
The Victorious
Grants to Pierre d'Amboise,
sons of Hughes III of Chaumont for
His Distinguished Service and Military Gratitude
Land and Seigneural Rights for Dubourg-Disset, Poitiers,
Poitou, on the Seine River,
north of Poitiers in the Provence of Poitou-Charente
By order, construction of a castle is to be built this year
including moats and ditches, defence walls, drawbridges,
corbeils and mullioned windows.
Dated: August 3, 1484, Chinon, France.

"It is not simply nature, it is how our souls connect with it. I come here daily to watch for the woman who seeks wild berries. The season is short, but she comes each day. I am grateful that she agreed to allow me to take her depth and beauty to my canvas."

"Is this someone that I know from the château?"

"I certainly understand your curiosity, Pierre, but the mystic of the natural spirit would be spoiled if I mention her name."

Pierre blushed, realizing he was at the point of being an intrusion to the great man, Leonardo da Vinci[5] (1452-1519).

Pierre knew much of the Italian, well aware of his crazed artistic and scientific mind, vied by aristocracy. He wished solitude to allow his prolific ideas to develop, with his driven desire for portraits of humans and human anatomy. His inventions would in time rank into the thousands including parachutes, helicopters, rudimentary tanks, and scientific discoveries beyond the imaginations of any era.

In his later years, da Vinci thrived in the serenity of the vineyards and Château at Amboise and died at the castle.

---

[5] Leonard Da Vinci, died May 1519, at Château d'Amboise, assumed to be buried at the Chapel of Saint-Hubert. Franceso Melzie, his long-time companion was executor and heir to his vast collections. The Masterpieces 'Last Supper' and 'Mona Lisa' are at the Louvre Museum in Paris.

Two

Pierre III d'Amboise, Governor of Touraine, 1530 – Stephen Pasquier landowner of La Ferlandière, Brie attends Palais de Justice, Paris – Discussions with d'Amboise over rumors of New World explorations – Discontent of the Vassal System - Jacques Cartier of Saint-Malo – Introduction of Étienne Pasquier b. 1529 - Pasquier, the Attorney, defends Labertine in the Stolen Milk Case – Demonstration in the Courtroom of Benevolence – Repentence – Don't Let your Left Hand Know.

Stephen Pasquier of Ferlandière, Brie

PIERRE III D'AMBOISE, GOVERNOR OF TOURAINE IN 1530, had only an honourable motive in wanting to see Stephen Pasquier, a wealthy landowner from Ferlandière in Brie[6], a lush commune in north central Île de France. With his small entourage, Pierre journeyed to Paris to meet with his old friend Stephen.

Paris was like an artist's palette in springtime, with the sun languishing on the avenues and spires of great cathedrals and palaces, and the centre of everything at the magnificent Gothic edifices of Notre-Dame and Sainte Chapelle.

Standing in the very place where King Charles VII stood celebrating the victory of his royal troops in retaking Paris, passion broiled in Pierre's heart for his country.

---

[6] La Ferlandière at Brie, halfway between Poitiers and shores of Bordeaux, once owned by Dames de Poissy and Lordship of the Chatelet. Granted by King Louis XII to Stephen Pasquier, of Héricy.

Although Charles VII had no official royal residence, he spent much of his time at Château Chinon and travelled regularly to Paris to meet at the Palais of Justice. The hallowed halls echoed the slightest whisper through its arched painted ceilings and polished Italian marble floors.

Since the building was used by the Courts of Paris over ancient Roman ruins, the centre of politics was berthed here. An adjoining dining hall was availed to lords and earls at their pleasure. Here, Pierre and John d'Amboise delved into discussions with the Brie landowner, Stephen Pasquier, about the New World, debating King Francis I's passion to discover the passage to the riches of India.

"The fiefdom is tiring—have you not worried, my friend?" Pasquier asked Pierre. "The vassal system will not be sustainable in years to come. I know this from the farmlands and vineyards at Brie. The vassals are not content with soccage of uncertain render. The soil of France is weary and our grazing pastures are torn by war. What good comes from a rotting field of cabbage?"

Stephen Pasquier, Seigneur of Ferlandière, dared with caution to criticize the king, not in attendance. "Indeed, our king's ambition across the Atlantic has dampened his fierceness in battle and turned his attention to the gentry's taxation. Vassals at Brie are indeed discontent and disheartened with fealty for their leaseholds." The gentlemen were silent, and Stephen thoughtfully added, "God bless the King of France."

John d'Amboise spoke with urgency. "Yes, the French need to take the new lands, before the overbearing English plant their dragon flag on the mossy barrens of Newfoundland."

"Have you heard of the mariner from Saint-Malo? He has travelled the ocean before, and I hear that he is fervent to receive a commission," Pierre said.

"Yes, I know," Stephen said. "You talk of Jacques Cartier. I was privy to an expedition report by the Italian explorer, Verrazano, and he boasts of the young man's skill at navigation and cartography."

"Adventure, discovery and knowledge represent our bequest to our children. The borders of the mind are boundless while life expectancy is measured."

Pasquier was of the same mind. "I am blessed with sons and grandsons; my youngest, just a babe, shares my name 'Étienne' (1529-1619)."

"It is the future of our children's generations and theirs to come. We have a responsibility as Frenchmen."

The Stolen Milk, Paris

IN 1540, even as a lad, young Étienne was exquisite in his finery, attending the courts of Paris with his esteemed father, Stephen Pasquier. A crude wooden cog wagon passed by as they walked briskly to the Paris courthouse located on the Île de la Cité, on the Boulevard du Palais. The Pasquiers had rooms a few blocks away in the upper class district of Place Royale, however Stephen preferred to be picked up by a hired horse-drawn carriage.

"Papa, it is a beautiful day. Shall we walk and listen to the birds singing? I'll use Grand-père de Montaguerre's walking stick and I'll keep up with you."

"But of course, Étienne, it is the way in spring. Yes, we shall walk."

With his head straight, back erect, chin firmly in line and hat adjusted, he practised twirling the stick. Stephen laughed at his peacock stature and proudly walked with his son. Any Frenchman dreamed of the day his own son would follow in his footsteps and enter the sacred halls of the Judicial Building.

It was typical, on a Tuesday morning, to see a prisoner shackled in weighted chains, cowering in wagons from the jail to the courthouse to await his fate. Unfortunately, a culprit were presumed guilty unless he had evidence to the contrary, and the acquaintance of a respected attorney. Lined with fishmongers and poor farmers selling their chickens and eggs along the avenue, Stephen and Étienne walked past smartly, avoiding the window buckets.

"Ah, see Étienne, this is why I prefer the set out. Stay clear of windows above."

"I will be a lawyer just like you, father."

"Yes, you are old enough to study under the great professors. I will be proud someday to face you in court."

Taking a second glance at the victim in the prisoner's wagon, Stephen recognized François Labertine, from Brie. He had a small farm not far from the brook at Ferlandière that forked off toward Héricy. Only a fortnight before at the Three Heads Inn alehouse, they had ranted and laughed over the hypocrisy of the noblesse and the seigneural lands.

Pasquier was royally attired in a heavy, dark green coat with satin lapel, and his high starched white cotton shirt braced his neck with a ruffle held high by a padded vest. He agonized over the fifteen feet between himself and the cart. Moral justice served him best.

"Monsieur Labertine!" Stephen waved and started toward the wagon, but was warned off by the gaoler, then by a rock thrown from the chanting mob.

"Down with him—and the wig too!"

The words came from a poor hag, in scant sackcloth, a woolen cape and kerchief. Her vacant smile paraded a row of decaying and missing teeth as she spat toward them.

Ordering young Étienne to stay where he was, Stephen adjusted his silken waist-coast and nudged his top hat. He caught up to the wagon and walked behind, approaching the dissipating throng. From the Quai de l'Horlage, he could see the domed roof of the courthouse as they rounded the corner.

"Excusez-moi, Madame," he called to the hag.

She jabbed a wooden stick toward his face. "What do you want with the likes of me?"

"God bless you, Madame. Please find a spot of empathy for Monsieur Labertine. He is a man unjustly accused."

Her eyes looked hungry and he shoved half a crown into her nimble palm. "Please pray for us all," he said.

Cursing, the shrew disappeared with a scornful laugh, absorbed among the baggers and pick-pockets loitering outside the jailhouse. "There's no mercy in heaven or among the kings," she flared. "Pray for yourself!"

Entering the grand, three-story stone edifice of the Counsel d'État, Stephen passed through the arches. A court page acknowledged him without delay, opening massive double doors to a hall where men wore silk cloaks and powdered wigs. The air was stuffy with dignity.

At the Magistrate's bench, he was handed a dossier to defend Monsieur François Labertine for the simple theft of milk from his neighbour's cow. Nausea overwhelmed him, knowing the judicial cost to his friend and his own personal conflict. They had stood shoulder to shoulder in battle years before.

I wonder if Monsieur Labertine is here because he is a Huguenot or only as a man trying to feed his own. How can I judge the qualities of man who simply borrowed the cow for milk to feed his children? The cow was returned and the consequences to me are a heavy heart. Is there a commandment 'that shalt not borrow'?

Young Étienne sat in the back row, watching the anguish of his father. The lad thought his father to be a masterful giant defending moral values, and marvelled in his defence of M. Labertine.

"Your Honour and our noble Prosecution, the only crime that Monsieur Labertine has committed was being born into an unfortunate time, finding himself in a position of too many children to feed, a poor crop and nothing in his pocket."

Stephen stopped and looked directly at the victimized neighbour. The courtroom was silent in anticipation.

"I believe that our society is to blame for this pitiful situation. Each of us here who languish in comfortable homes and dine heartily . . . we are the cause."

Many in the audience gasped at such audacity and forthrightness.

"Do you wish to call a witness, Monsieur Pasquier?" The judge hastily wanted to move away from the unpleasant scenario the lawyer portrayed.

"Oui, Honorable Judge, I would like to call Monsieur Chabot.

The prosecuting attorney jumped up in objection. "It is not Monsieur Chabot that is on trial, it is Monsieur Labertine. Monsieur Chabot is the one victimized. This is improper."

Sighing, the judge nodded for the victim to enter the witness box.

"Merci, Monsieur Chabot," Stephen began. "Thank you for allowing us an opportunity to clarify what crime Monsieur Labertine has committed."

"Oui." Chabot looked into the eyes of the inquisitor.

"Monsieur Chabot, do you sell your milk at market?"

"Oui."

"How much milk do you keep to feed your family in a week?"

"Four gallons a day." Chabot's face flushed. "I have eight children."

"Eight children. It must be hard some days to feed a full house, when perhaps you have lost a cow or given one to your seigneur for taxes."

"Oui, we make adjustments."

"Do you regularly attend mass, Monsieur Chabot?"

"Oui."

"Have you heard a sermon preached about loving your neighbour?"

"Oui, but the milk I sell helps me to buy other food. I cannot afford to feed my neighbours too."

"And we don't expect that of you, Monsieur Chabot." Pasquier glanced at the jury and continued. "How much money did you lose when Monsieur Labertine borrowed your cow for milking?"

"Half a crown."

"That's quite remarkable." Pasquier smirked. "On my way to the courthouse I encountered an old woman throwing stones at Monsieur Labertine. As a good Catholic, I did not curse her but I gave her half a crown."

Pasquier reached into his pocket withdrawing another half-crown coin. Placing it on the ledge of the witness box, he walked back to his bench, but turned once more.

"By the way, Monsieur Chabot, Monsieur Labertine is very sorry for the inconvenience he has caused you. He and his wife, Sophia, and his sons William, Stephen, Godfroy, Samuel, and daughters Maria, Thérèse, Caroline and Geneviève are grateful to you. On the day that Monsieur Labertine borrowed your cow, his wife was delivering another child. The cupboards were bare and Monsieur Labertine saw desperate hunger in the eyes of his family. Perhaps if you had known the situation, you might have been charitable and offered the milk."

Stunned silence enveloped the courtroom during a long pause. The judge ordered the prosecutor and the defender to a sidebar.

Pasquier and the prosecutor negotiated that Labertine should serve two days in the stocks with a sign around his neck, 'Voleur de lait de vache.'

They approached the judge with their proposal, but he raised his hand in wisdom.

"Since Monsieur Chabot has been paid in full for the milk in question, the court requires that ten public lashings in the galley will be sentence enough."

Hiring a carriage to take them from the Counsel d'État, Stephen whispered to his son. "When we get back to La Ferlandière, I want you to take our best milker to M. Labertine's home."

"Oui, Papa, but we should keep it quiet. The Lord commands us to give to the needy, and not let your left hand know what the right hand is doing so that it may be secret."

Stephen Pasquier welled with pride. He would see that Étienne would be well-educated, and sent him to study as a legal scholar at the University of Padua in Italy and the Collèges des Dorman in France. He looked forward to the day when his son would take his place in the courts of Paris.

Three

Manor Limoëlou at Saint-Malo, Cartier's Home – Jacques des Granches, Knighted by Francis I – Jacques Cartier marries Catherine des Granches, 1520 – France focused on finding trade routes to Far East – Jacques Cartier commissioned by Francis I on *Grande Hermine*, 1534 – Voyage across Atlantic – Scurvy & Starvation Threat at Sea – Off shores of Newfoundland run aground on cod banks – Cartier staked his first cross at Havre Saint-Servan – At P.E.I. meets Micmac – Trade with Chief Panounais – Negotiate to take Donnacona's sons to France – Next commission of three ships, 1535 – Settlement at du Cap-Rouge, later Charlesbourg – Cartier dies in France 1557.

Saint-Malo, France to Stadacona, Québec

T HE BREEZE SPLASHED SEA SALT SPRAY ONTO JACQUES Cartier's face as he stood on the beach of Saint-Malo in northwest France. Looking outward was the ocean, but turning the other way, he gazed up at the Brittany seaside estate that he shared with Catherine. He was torn between his devotion to her and the hunger in his soul that could only be satisfied by the sea.

Since Giovanni da Verrazano's death in 1528, Cartier had continued studies at Dieppe in cartography, astronomy, navigation and the discoveries by those that previously crossed the Atlantic to charter the new world.

As a seaman's apprentice, Cartier had travelled as far as Brazil and the coast of Newfoundland. The vision of the lush banks of Labrador now controlled his thoughts and stirred his imagination.

VUE DU MANOIR DE JACQUES CARTIER.

Cartier's Manor of Limoëlou at Saint-Malo. Source Histoire des Canadiens-Français 1608-1880. Artist Sulte, Benjamin. Original at British Library ⑨

His father, James Cartier, understood his son's destiny to be a mariner, and a great one at that.

When Jacques married the elegant Catherine des Granches in 1520, daughter of Jacques-Honore Guyon des Granches and Françoise Du Mast, the Cartier family was already established among the bourgeois.

The cherished seaside estate, known as the Manor of Limoëlou, was close to town. The grand two-story main house rose above the forest, with a high garret, a lone turret and thatched roof extension.

The elaborate dining hall and grand kitchen were envied with their polished red clay floors hosting feasts for the noblest families of Saint-Malo including Jean le Veneur, Abbot of Mont-Saint-Michel.

Jacques des Granches, father of Catherine, and chevalier du roi and constable, was a frequent guest, always doting over his daughter and two grandsons. His only son, Jean Vicomte de Beaupré, was already established in society and his other daughter Françoise had married well. Knighted by King Francis I of France, Jacques des Granches was honoured to introduce his son-in-law, Jacques Cartier, into the courts of Paris and the King.

On Cartier's previous return from Brazil, the Italian captain granted high praise for his apprentice's determination and skill in manning the ship during a threatening gale. Commissioned under the French flag, he took the initiative to introduce Jacques to King Francis I, whose early priority was to plant the French flag across the Atlantic before the English.

The kings of France, England, Spain, Italy and Portugal knew the competitive urgency of selecting and indenturing experienced explorers to seek these new trade routes to the riches of the Far East. Cartier was a superior candidate.

Catherine, with a woolen shawl around her shoulders, stood on the stone terrace overlooking the sea. Jacques saw her and waved his hat as he started toward the house. He had forgotten time in his dreaming, that the Bishop of Saint-Malo, Jean le Veneur, was invited to dine with them that evening.

Jacques was tall and lean, with a pointy Vasquez beard and moustache that he fiddled with in thought. Legend suggested that he preferred his hair properly cut and groomed rather than the common tied tail of sea farers. A dark cap with a narrow brim sat on the crest of his head, giving the effect of a backward point, an appearance suitable to greet a king.

Catherine affectionately greeted her husband at the main door and touched his cloaks with her palm. She held the coat close to her face then brushed her cheek against the lapel, cherishing the senses that she could hold in her memory. Knowing that Jacques would be leaving again for the sea, she lingered now to make it last.

"Jacques, the Abbott came by this morning. He seemed burdened with thought and wished to speak with you."

"Did he leave a hint? What would he want?"

Catherine didn't answer right away.

They sat together in front of the floor-to-ceiling hearth, one of two chimneys the house could boast. Whenever Catherine asked for something, Jacques made sure she got it, and had only recently ordered French bevelled glass windows with squared frets, to be custom made in Paris.

"Catherine, I received word today that your windows will be arriving next week."

"It's not my windows that I think about, dearest. It is only you. I heard from my father that the Abbott has been promoting you to the King, for your own sea commission. I expect he will bring news at dinner tonight."

"I heard rumors myself, dearest. It would only be for a few months."

"I have always known that the sea is your first love, but darling, you are mine." Catherine was stoic and didn't permit tears to come. "I will miss you greatly and wish you safe passage."

"You are my salt of the earth, Catherine. Wherever I am, I long to return to you." Jacques eyes became soft and she knew his soul was torn.

The door knocker announced the arrival of the Cartier's dinner guests: Abbot Jean le Veneur, accompanied by one of his priests from the citadel; Monsieur Macé Jallobert (Catherine's brother-in-law); Madame and Monsieur Beaudoin and the aging widower Jacques des Granches.

A musician sat on a velvet chair in the foyer and guests gathered and marveled in curiosity at her three-stringed instrument and bow. "The sound . . . as if it's from heaven," said Madame Beaudoin. She closed her eyes. "The strings play such high sweet notes."

Catherine gushed with pride, "It's a violini from Milan, a rare new invention for orchestras. It's not ours of course as they're so rare, but we arranged it for each of you, as our special guests."

The five-course feast was regal, starting with pigeon soup, then stuffed quail and rice accompanied by wild samphire, black truffles in sauce, poached artichoke thistle, and Lyonnais potatoes sautéed in butter and parsley. The conversations were lively with humour and laughter, and the party wound down with pickled pear and port followed by cheese and more of France's finest wines.

Late in the evening, M. Granches-Guyon convened with the Beaudoin's to confer over Duchess Anne of Brittany's marriage to Louis XII.

The Abbott nodded to Cartier, who understood it was time for a discussion, and they retreated to the conversation area by the veranda.

"Monsieur Cartier, I speak frankly of my purpose," the Abbott began.

"Ah bien. I have great respect for directness and discretion."

"There is much excitement about coastal land claims in the New World since Columbus' discovery of 1492. England, France, Spain and Italy are anxious to stake their flags. Explorations to the Strait of Belle-Isle have whet the appetites. We must not only exert our patriotism and independence at home, but the coast of the Atlantic must be penetrated to seek a passage to East Asia."

"Yes, I was with Verrazano when I saw the banks of the Carolinas. The Spanish are preoccupied with the gold treasures of South America. The Brazilian gold was so heavy that the galleons sank before they were plundered. I have studied the Atlantic route and the voyages of John Cabot sent by Henry VII, thirty years ago. The Tudor standard was planted on a place called 'Kahnawaye'. Cabot confirmed that there is habitation and lucrative trade with the Tuscarora natives."

"I am glad you have the taste for adventure and new found fortunes. Your previous journeys put you in good stead for consideration to a commission."

"It is not fortune that I seek. The sea is in my bones. I desire for navigation and exploration of new waters. Do you know of commissions offered by King Francis?"

"Precisely, my dear Jacques. He has already sent seven expeditions and hired Italian explorers. The king longs to see the royal banner of the fleur-des-lis planted in the New World by a French patriot."

"Why do you tell me this, my dear Bishop?"

"I am privy to the king's court where we have talked of his desire for another exploration. Basque whalers are swarming the coast and the king's desire has become urgent."

The Bishop paused to look out into the darkness.

"You will meet with King Francis next month to discuss a voyage. I have agreed to send one of my priests to join you as ship's chaplain."

The walled city of Saint-Malo was perched on the British Channel, named Oceanus Britannicus by the geographer Ptolemy in the second century, and later called the English Channel.

Its harbour was filled with galleons on the day Cartier departed on April 20, 1534, with their own two small ships loaded with provisions. The foul smell of the water was forgotten in the quest to be underway, and the moorings at last loosened.

With a sad heart and left with her sons to carry on at Limoëlou, Catherine bade adieu to her husband. Straightening her bonnet, she stepped back into the throng of wives and townsfolk sending off the ships.

Standing at the helm of his ship, the *Grande Hermine,* Jacques Cartier watched until Catherine was barely visible as a dot on the pier. The crew was fully occupied pulling in ropes and anchors and securing stores, but Jacques' eyes remained on Catherine in the distance, knowing she would be a faithful sentinel. She remained, while the others dispersed back through cobblestone streets to their homes.

The masted carrack was stocked with provisions. As Cartier and sixty-one men from Saint-Malo sailed beyond a rocky island at the mouth of the Rance Estuary, the northwest coast of France disappeared past the ramparts.

At seventy feet in length, the *Grande Hermine* was considered a small ship and was accompanied by her sister vessel. Both had three squared sails on each mast including the masthead, two crow's nests, and a spire at the front with a furled flag of France. The tri-colour banner of the Ancient Regime represented white for clergy, red for nobility and blue for the bourgeoisie.

The magnificent power and depths over the green rolling waves and surf of the sea inspired the crew in their early days. The cold wind gusts against Jacques' face and the spray dampening his hat were welcome at first, new unexplainable thrills that vibrated and enhanced the mission at the outset.

On the eighth day out, Cartier's ships faced a two-day gale, with the erratic sway of the sea roll keeping the sailors off balance. All hands were required on deck, fighting with the masts during the grey and blackest hours of night. Thankful that daybreak brought calm and filtered sun through the clouds, young Gaeten of Brittany joined Cartier at the wheel.

"Sir, I have watched throughout the storm; it was a magnificent one at that. When the ocean roars its head to have a look at us, that's when I feel a true seaman. It receives defiance from me each time. The compasses and traverse boards have been reset. It should be another two weeks and hopefully our bad weather is behind."

Jacques looked down at an image of himself. "Do you hunger for the sea, Gaeten?"

"Oh, yes, Sir. I hope someday to have my own commission."

"Hoist yourself and tell me what you see."

The lithe youngster shinnied up the mast pole to the nest, squinting with his hand above his brow.

Cartier mused.

He has the disease.

"Ahoy, Captain. Five knots south, there is a whaling ship on its return to France or Spain. Must be coming from Red Bay where they have those magnificent right whales and bowheads. They hunt with harpoons and spears. Have you ever seen them?"

"Yes, I've seen the Basque ships. Blubber oil is precious in Europe, but you'll have to sign on another ship if that's what you want to see."

"No, Sir."

After three weeks at sea, the salt barrels were empty and starvation was on the horizon, wherever that would be. Scurvy was making its rounds, crippling even the strongest sailors.

Cartier recognized the hollow look in the eyes of his crew—not just hunger, but flashes of hopelessness.

"Ahoy, Capitaine! Land ahead." Gaeten's first sighting from the crow's nest brought all hands on deck with a renewed energy.

Taking the helm, Cartier studied the spy glass, and returning to the captain's cabin, he made navigational measurements with the traverse board and compass rose. Gaeten's last peg in the nautical board corroborated their position according to their sea charts.

Coasting at half-mast in pea soup fog, a dark shadow of land loomed ahead at last. In a calm silence, the crew heard cawing from seagulls ready to scavenge debris from slaughtered whales.

"Drop the lead line to record our depth," Cartier called to his assistant, Jehan Poulet.

"Shallow waters, 300 feet deep. Looks like we are entering the Grand Banks."

Poulet ordered the knotted line to be reeled in, and joined Cartier in the map room, anticipating a fine cognac. The adjoining captain's cabin had portholes on both sides, high above the rudder, and Cartier stood at one to ponder the arrival.

On May 10, the high banks were in sight, guarding Saint Lawrence Rivière, and beyond that was only a barren land mass. As the thick fog closed in, Cartier could barely focus. The crawling ship began to drag slowly by the surround of weight in the water.

Cartier shouted to his weak, disgruntled crew, "Man the sails! We're stuck on something! Keep us moving!"

Two deck hands leaned over the side, checking the surf to see if the ship had run aground. "Poisson! The water is thick with fish, that's what's dragging us down."

"C'est bien!" The captain gave a sigh as he leaned to the rail. He'd never seen so many fish in a bed on the Atlantic Ocean. "Hail to the King! It is manna from Heaven."

Rowboats were dropped, and nets packed with cod for the salt barrels. In less than an hour, the boats were listing at dangerous levels, and were rowed back to the ship. Netting was strung across the bow in tight layers, drying the fish in the sun to prevent spoilage.

"Is this the gold of the New Found Land?" one of the sea-journeymen shouted with a taste of sarcasm.

Cartier called to the men. "Les poissons have come to us! We can fish every day and never go wanton or waste.

"It has been claimed that this land is abundant with beaver and deer, skins that bring a King's ransom. We will hunt well on land and sea ahead of the snowfall, and before the English come again."

Sea monsters sighted offshore in the deep waters were none other than 50-foot humpback whales that the men had heard talk of in France. Cartier watched their playful greeting, thrashing and spouting.

The longboats were dispatched to find the shoreline with their load of cod, and to begin building spruce cellars for winter stores.

Returning late, their cargo was empty and the bow light in the water.

"Come aboard lads. Tomorrow we'll get more fish and continue until the ship floats freely in the water and we can sail free."

One hundred miles west of Belle-Isle, Gaeten sighted a larger known ship. From the foremast, he recognized it from the French port of La Rochelle, their first encounter with Frenchmen in more than two months. Together, the crews sang and danced and feasted on cod, consuming the last beer barrels from their stores.

Cartier sent a long letter back with the other ship, to be delivered to Catherine at Saint-Malo, journalizing the voyage and sharing his lonely heart in prose.

The rewards of summer made navigation easy in June and July, scouring the north coast, and documenting descriptions of the geography, terrain and channel plotting. Cartier staked his first cross with a French flag at Havre Saint-Servan, honoring the first Roman-Gallo city of Brittany.

Disappointed by the expanse of rock, the crews disembarked on a barren rock-ribbed shore, with shear natural stone monuments standing in the water.

Cartier confided to his officers, "It's been three weeks seeking arable land suitable for a new habitant settlement. It's time to push onward; this is the land of Cain."

Discouraged, Jacques' nightly thoughts returned to Catherine. Bending beside his cot, he prayed for courage to continue, wisdom to lead his men, to protect his home and family, and to survive the unknown destiny of his mission.

This did not look to him like the gates to Eastern riches, and he knew his crew was weakening further with disease. Staking another cross at Île Brion they continued to the Îles-de-la-Madeleine, the Magdalen Island archipelago in the St. Lawrence.

He gathered the men. "This must be the mainland! Poulet, send a crew to investigate beyond the rocks and forests."

"Oui, Capitaine. Overhead the sky monsters circle. The fish carcasses must be deceiving the sea banks."

After several days, Cartier was again dejected, but satisfied that this was, at least, an island at the mouth of the St. Lawrence.

The *Grande Hermine* and its sister ship sailed southwest to the lush gardens of Prince Edward Island on June 29. Studying navigational notes, Cartier knew this was the land of Micmac, an island from the 'Great Spirit'.

Cartier logged the entry: Île aux Oiseaux, Island of the Birds.

"Seek the bushes for game or fowl. Les oiseaux are plentiful and easy to shoot down. Bag what you can. Build winter cellars with cedar below the permafrost and mark their locations for our return."

In spite of bagging an extraordinary quantity of birds including Great Auks, the deer and beaver that the natives had talked about with eloquence remained elusive.

The ships sailed onward to the Strait of Belle Isle off the coast of Labrador. Unfortunately, Cartier overlooked the mouth of the St. Lawrence, thinking it to be only a bay, and didn't penetrate the waterway farther.

Cartier Meets the Micmac Chief Panounais

JULY WAS sunny and the waters calm, when Cartier sailed along the north side of Chaleur Bay.

Two scouting parties set out, rowing in the longboats. Not more than a hundred feet ahead, past a wooded cliff, was a convoy of birch bark canoes entering the cove.

"Micmacs!" Cartier raised his hand for his boats to halt.

"Monsieur Jallobert, a white flag please."

"Oui, Capitaine."

Jallobert handed him a pole with two flags, one for white surrender, tied above the fleur-de-lis of France.

The Micmacs were equally hesitant, and each party sent one boat forward with apprehension.

Forewarned by accounts of Jesuits and earlier explorers[7], Cartier knew that extending a handshake with the natives was not as simple as it seemed.

He understood there were invisible boundaries, with a new culture to be learned, and methods of respect that would be scrutinized by the natives.

Walk slowly and walk backwards.

---

[7] John Cabot, Italian explorer, claimed the coast of Nova Scotia for Henry VII of England in 1497. Although they didn't have contact with the natives, they found campfires and trails.

Grande Hermine, Petite Hermine and Émérillon, 1535 in St. Lawrence
Source 'The Mariner of St Malo', 1914, author Stephen Leacock. Ⓢ

On land, Cartier slowly moved toward the Micmac Chief with his hands outstretched, holding a European blanket as a peace offering.

"We come in peace."

The Micmac Chief wrapped himself in the blanket, smoothing the fabric, but refusing to smile. After a long, penetrating gaze, he invited Cartier and a small party of his crew to share pipes in his village.

The camp was encircled with two large wigwams, housing up to twenty natives each including the Chiefs, and six smaller wigwams for families and children up to twelve people. On a cooking stove near the campfire, Cartier saw a copper kettle and nodded at it. "You've met John Cabot?"

The chief responded by pointing to the compass hanging by a chain from Cartier's breast pocket. "Please accept this as a gift." Cartier slowly removed the instrument and offered a half bow to Panounais.

Chief Panounias' face bore the paint of his status in the tribe. The Micmac dialect of Restigouche was difficult for Cartier to understand, but through motions he praised them for their agricultural techniques.

The children's eyes were frozen on Cartier's plumed hat. As they giggled in turns, Cartier removed it and knelt to their level. He held the hat out, then topped off their excitement with a looking glass. Their laughs changed instantly to silent bewilderment as they absorbed their reflections in disbelief.

The Frenchmen were hungry, and the Chief directed the women to bring pemmican, salted smelt, and bowls of dried beans, corn and squash in hollowed pine bowls, with torn flat tortilla to wipe the remains.

Cartier bowed respectfully in thanks for their hospitality, and the grateful men devoured the feast as the natives sat cross-legged to watch.

Chief Panounias passed out long smoking pipes to bind a circle of friendship, showing with his hands how the puffs and swirls rising to the Heavens were in fact taking prayers of the aborigines to the Great Spirit.

Instantly, Cartier felt ill from the tobacco, coughing and feeling faint, but insisted on accepting the customs of his new friends. The outcome was more than the Frenchmen could wish for, and they left with the understanding of a truce with the Micmac Chief.

Among the Micmac with Panounais was a tall Membertou saqamaw chief, quietly observing the meeting with Cartier. He thought the curious Frenchman to be a man of distinction and liked the musical lilt to his strange language. Returning to his village, he told his wife, Marie, of the encounter with the great boats.

Sailing south, Cartier camped at Gaspé Bay. After their third encounter with natives, Cartier joined a group of Iroquois on the north shore of the bay. Planting a thirty-foot cross, he declared 'Long Live the King of France', and claimed the territory with a stake.

The Iroquois were dubious of his actions, unlike the Micmac. The great chief Donnacona protested Cartier's claim and took a small party, prepared to board the *Grande Hermine* to demand the cross be removed.

Unbeknownst to the local tribes, it was the beginning of encroachment that would take centuries to repeal and return native rights over their natural resources. The Chief of the Iroquois was supported by its nation, as they watched the power and greed of the Europeans ravage their sacred hunting grounds.

Cartier's diplomacy prevailed as he negotiated with Chief Donnacona to take two of his sons back to France on the return voyage. After drinking and feasting, the Iroquois Chief unfortunately agreed to allow his sons to leave for the trip in exchange for a mere gift of an axe.

The French party considered it a hostage taking, as security in exchange for safety for the small settlement established by the crew that would remain, and the chaplain the Abbott had sent from Saint-Malo.

Integration of activity initiated in the settlement, with French crewmen joining the tribe on occasional hunting trips, securing venison for their stores. French influence appeared among the natives as well, as maidens chose to use gift beads and baubles in their needlework, instead of the long aboriginal custom of shells and quills.

Bitter August winds whistled as the sugar maple foliage turned to shades of yellow, amber, red and purple, an unfolding palette of nature's change of season. Cartier recorded notes of the sweet maple sap. The stores of the French ships were almost filled by now for the journey, with meat and fish, dried beans, pummeled corn, sweet water, seal oil, and an impressive quantity of deer and beaver skins.

When the ship was ready, Cartier gestured with kindness to the Chief's sons, "Come, Domagaya and Taignoagny. We have made room for you as guests in the Officers' Quarters."

Cartier was disappointed that he hadn't found the gateway to the great river, the passage to India, nor had gold been discovered. But from Donnaconna's sons, he had learned about routes he'd missed, and he vowed to return. As the sons' French language communication improved, Cartier was astounded at the knowledge he freely shared.

The *Grande Hermine* arrived back in France before winter settled in. On the approach to Saint-Malo, the ship's masts could be seen from high ground. A thrilled lad on the docks ran all the way to Limoëlou to tell Catherine.

"Thank you for alerting me, young man. Shall I pay you dearly, if you would gather my carriage and we will return to the harbour?"

"Yes, indeed, Madame Cartier."

Catherine's eyes were glued to the waterscape as the carriage bumped along the rutted road to town. She had endured great loneliness and the loss of her dear father. Even a glimpse of the ship made her heart skip a beat.

"There he is, Madame," the boy pointed with excitement.

"Yes, my dear boy, I see it too. May I ask who your father is?"

"My father is dead, but my brother, Gaeten, rides the main crow's nest for Monsieur Cartier. He will be a captain someday too."

Madame Cartier smiled with kindred understanding.

Second Royal Commission of Cartier, 1535

JACQUES CARTIER was granted a second royal commission in 1535, taking three ships from Saint-Malo: *La Grande Hermine*, *La Petite Hermine* and *L'Émérillon*. The expedition would be charted to Stadacona, later to be Québec. Reports of the first expedition extended hope to Francis I for a passage leading to copper and gold. Besides the new commission, Cartier was given a generous bonus of three thousand livres.

The *Grande Hermine* was piloted by Thomas Fourmont as ship's Master; the *Petite Hermine* by Guillaume Le Breton Bastille and Jacques Maingard, and *L'Émérillon* by Macé Jallobert and Guillaume Le Marie.

Cartier met with Jehan Leveillé, the registrar of the Abbey of Saint Jehan to compile the list of over a hundred crew and passengers.

"Monsieur Leveillé, I wish to appoint François Guilault as the ship's apothecary. The Micmac have a resilience that only an educated man of medicine can interpret. Perhaps he will find the cure for scurvy that creeps among our crew."

"Oui, Monsieur Cartier. We have no objection, and perhaps he will wish to remain in the settlement to assist with habitation."

"Yes, and we have much to learn still from the natives."

On May 19, 1535, the three ships set sail with over a hundred men, including a contingent of Cartier's relatives: Antoine des Granche, a brother-in-law, Macé Jallobert another brother-in-law, Étienne Noël, nephew, and four Maingarts.

For fifty days, the ships tossed on rough waters before reaching the coast of Newfoundland. By mid-August, they sat at the mouth of the St.

Lawrence. Two natives from Hochelaga willingly guided them up the river from salt to fresh water and on to the rapids of Saguenay.

Cartier left the ships behind and took thirty men in longboats to the fortress at Hochelaga, where a miraculous event took place. The Iroquois, eager to hear of the French gospel and passion for Christ, sat within the walls, listening to Cartier and his native interpreter. With a stick in the dirt, the natives drew a map for Cartier to the Saguenay where they expected to find the gold they sought.

Cartier's men constructed a fortress at Stadacona to prepare for a cold winter, but hypothermia and disease became rampant among the men. Lack of Vitamin C made them weak with swollen joints and rotting flesh, and he knew that without a remedy, he faced devastation of losing his entire crew.

As the crew dwindled, Cartier faced a new challenge. The small fortress must always present the appearance of being fully armed, to prevent a native attack through intimidation. The remaining able-bodied crew responded by running from post to post, giving the outward appearance of a strong contingent of healthy men.

By November, Cartier resorted to convincing a native interpreter to show him the secret of the natives to cure scurvy. He observed that a young maiden, called Maga, had followed the tribal leaders whenever they conversed with the explorers. Listening intently, she whispered translations back to the Chief.

Quietly at a campfire, the men tormented amongst themselves over the rampant spread of scurvy, fearing for their own lives. An oarsman in ill health, François Guilault was blunt, "Captain, why is it that just *our* crew that suffers the evil of scurvy, and not the natives?"

"I have wondered that myself," Cartier replied. "We thrive on a great deal of salted fish and meats, yet the natives do not use salt in their pemmican and dried meats. Perhaps it is time to send a scout to follow as the Iroquois hunt and bring back food. Do I have volunteers?"

"I would go myself, Sir, but I can no longer walk," François said.

Cartier looked around the campfire at his ravaged men.

"Macé and Regis, you will come with me. There is word that a hunting party leaves for the forest at sunrise looking for game. Be ready." Ice had covered the rivers, and winter hunting would be by land, more difficult than spring when natives would again paddle the river banks for beaver.

Maga, the interpreter, was the sister of Domagaya, who had gone to France with the previous expedition. She had spent a winter at a Jesuit Mission at Montréal learning the language. While grinding corn into a powder, sitting on the floor with a wooden bowl and stone pestle, she turned her attention daily to new French words and soon understood their conversations.

Her tresses were twisted into long braids, wrapped in strips of leather around a small animal bone, and she wore a plain deer skin tunic. Her headband was painted by porcupine quill, with images of a deer and beaver with a lone partridge feather laced to the back.

At sunrise, Cartier's men approached Maga in the forest as she foraged for winter berries. With their acquired broken language, they begged her to show them the cure for the winter disease.

"Maga, we come in peace, needing your help to save our men who suffer painfully."

Cartier acted out a limping man with a severe headache and she laughed, displaying pearly teeth and twinkling brown eyes. She replied in French.

"Not now, Monsieur Cartier, but tomorrow morning, we go to find medicine. Oui?"

She assured them she would come alone and not tell the Chief of her secret visit.

Cartier and his scouts followed Maga into the forest. Her soft moccasins blended with the silence of the snow, averting attention from birds or animals. Bending to gather a feather of a male grouse, she froze, then raised an arrow. The arch of the arrow whirred through the air and caused a stir in the brush.

Maga nodded to the crew to retrieve the bird for their camp, but the feathers would be hers. "Great white man, why do you bring your men? Do you not trust me?" Maga asked with a puzzled gaze. Her long braids fell over her shoulders.

"We are ready to learn your secrets of healing from you and your brothers." Cartier knelt on one knee in the snow and held a leather pouch in his hands. "This is to show our gratitude."

Maga inched forward to take it, and tapped the coloured stones and gems into her palm. With a smile, she tied the pouch to her belt and motioned for them to follow. Snow chunks fell from the straps of deerskin tied around her ankles as she created a new path in the deep banks.

With their trail filling in behind with heavy drifts, Maga marked the route with notched branches. In the shelter of a thicket of white cedar trees and silver birches, they dug through the permafrost to find suckling roots of a giant spruce. Cutting out the fine stalk, they gathered strips of bark, frosted leaves and needles to take back to camp to be boiled into a precious healing remedy.

Maga heard a branch crack to break the silence. She raised her head as an arrow whizzed past them through the woods and burrowed into a tree trunk not far from Cartier.

"I must go. My brothers have seen me—this was their warning to you. Return and tend to your stricken crew." Before Cartier could reply, Maga blended into the white forest.

The crew returned through the covered tracks, following the notched signs to the winter settlement. Those with scurvy drank the tea with hope and desperation, and poured the healing water over their wounded joints. The potion worked as magic for many and enabled a slow recovery for others. Spirits lifted as fewer graves were dug in the following weeks.

As preparations for the return voyage to France commenced, trading became brisk with the natives. Metal goods were exchanged for bales of prized deerskins and beaver pelts, with rough fur softened by the body warmth of natives to produce a soft, wearable fur.

By spring, the thick ice was swallowed into the St. Lawrence. The winter had taught much to the French, including the Micmac and Iroquois languages and new awareness of the culture.

The Europeans observed that the comfort level and familiarity was changing for the natives, as groups of Micmac pelt traders often arrived at the French camp asking for baubles and liquor.

Tribal elders also watched the behavior, harbouring a growing concern about the rising boldness of their braves, as drunkenness became more common.

Abandoning the *Petite Hermine*, a small crew remained to work with the natives, as Cartier's ship plied the St. Lawrence to face the angry Atlantic.

Before departing Québec, Cartier's men cunningly captured Chief Donnaconna, joined by interpreters and a few natives. With a guarantee of safe return the following year, Donnaconna agreed to sign his testimony before King Francis and learn customs and language from the French.

After fourteen months away, the *Grande Hermine* arrived in Saint-Malo in July 1536, with intentions to return to Québec as they promised. However, a new commission from King Francis I was postponed when war broke out between Francis I and Charles V of Germany over dominance of Italian lands and the wavering Hapsberg-Austrian House.

Four years passed before King Francis I returned his attention to explorations again, commissioning Cartier in 1540. He was assigned fifty prisoners, to work and slave among the tribes of Saguenay.

But the plan changed, out of Cartier's control. Before he set sail, La Roque de Roberval was given full authority over the colonization, usurping Cartier's leadership in the St. Lawrence.

In May 1541, Roberval dispatched Cartier with his shipmaster, Thomas Fromont, and again enlisted two of Cartier's brothers-in-law and a nephew.

Jacques Cartier left Saint-Malo with a fleet of five ships and fifteen hundred men to New France, arriving in August 1541. He was welcomed back to Stadacona with exuberance by the natives. He relayed the sad news of Donnaconna's death in France, assuring them that he had enjoyed great wealth and happiness.

Relations with the natives soured quickly, and Cartier left to establish a settlement at the mouth of Rivière du Cap-Rouge, that he claimed as Charlesbourg-Royal. Cartier was ordered back to France in the summer of 1542, and as his ships departed, the settlements were facing growing unrest among the Iroquois.

On return to his seaside village of Saint-Malo, he resumed teaching students Portuguese and cartography, publishing detailed records of the voyages. Cartier contracted typhus and died at his Limoëlou estate in Saint-Malo in 1557. His dear Marie-Catherine had predeceased him.

Four

Étienne Pasquier Scholar of Odet de Turnebe – Opposition to Jesuit Indoctrination of Universities, 1554 – Étienne marries Françoise Belen de Montmaine from d'Amboise, 1557 – Étienne writes at Brie & Château d'Amboise – Suffers Long-term Illness from Poisoning – Publishes Reserches de la France, 1560 – Political Unrest in Paris – Pasquier's success in high profile cases returns him to royal favour – Admiral Gaspard de Coligney leads Huguenot march on southern France – Castle of Dissay Stormed in 1569 – Pasquier returns to disfavour of Henry III – Henry IV returns Pasquier to the Advocate General – Pasquier Resigns, 1604 – News of Samuel de Champlain's Voyage, 1603.

Étienne Pasquier - King's Historian 1529-1615

T HE YOUNG LAD FROM THE BACK OF THE LABERTINE trial, Étienne Pasquier, long remembered when his father pled 'Not Guilty' for his client and successfully freed the accused with a light sentence. He longed to absorb the law himself and challenge the avenues of justice. Now, ten years later, he was ready.

Étienne was born in Paris in 1529, privileged to be not only the son of Stephen, a Court Justice, but also nephew of the notable scholar Odet de Turnèbe. A student of Collège des Dormans and later at Toulouse under Jacques Cujas, his passion for knowledge led him to an early acceptance at the bar, soon competing for crown cases.

Passionate about the judicial and parliamentary systems, Étienne wrote at an early age of his theories, with ambitions to succeed in Henry II's court. Sitting on the well-worn walnut university bench, he ran his fingers around the lectern, envisioning himself before the Grand Jury.

Aspiring to become Advocate General in Paris, he opposed the Jesuit Order when they attempted to legally indoctrinate the universities in 1554 under Pope Paul III. They demanded a charter, vowing poverty and chastity, with goals of censoring education.

Absorbed in his works and writings as an historian, theorist and poet, Pasquier avoided courtship and marriage, but it changed on meeting the alluring young widow, Françoise Belen de Montmaine. After successfully defending her in a lawsuit, she determined to repay him by offering herself and her wealth in a proposal. The enticing and wealthy client from Amboise charmed him into marriage in 1557, and in the following year, Theodore was born.

"Dearest Étienne, you know how I love to go with you to Paris."

"Yes, and I love to have you with me."

"Our family is growing quickly and the children need to be in the country to run and play. Do you mind if I prefer to stay at either Ferlandière or Amboise?"

"Your mother will be pleased to see you at Amboise, and the children will be delighted to see their grandmother and Chaumont cousins. I can join you there in a few weeks when the courts adjourn."

"So, Amboise it will be. That's excellent and I will long to see you, Étienne." Françoise enveloped her arm in his and walked him to the door. But several weeks later Françoise was summoned to Brie. Étienne had been moved from Paris to his Ferlandière country estate, weak from eating suspicious mushrooms.

"Françoise, he must remain in bed with plenty of rest if we hope for a full recovery," the doctor said.

"How long will it be before he can return to his beloved writing? He is highly regarded in the courts and will be missed in Paris as well."

"Poison takes time to run its course. Use broth and tea, and plenty of it. I've seen cases like this go on for years, but your Étienne is a fighter." She knew that.

"I will tend his bedside day and night."

"Here is a bottle of laudanum and castor to be given as needed. Do your best to keep his fever at bay."

In 1562, Pasquier was incapacitated from his work in law at the Palais de Justice in Paris.

First he convalesced at Brie, where Françoise oversaw the vineyards. After a second attack, he rested at his mother-in-law's at Amboise in the Loire valley, where he began writing the famous *Les Recherches*.

When his mother-in-law died at Amboise, Étienne attended to matters of her estate.

Les Recherches de la France

AT THIRTY-TWO, Étienne Pasquier published the first book of *Recherches de la France* in 1560, with the literary work becoming a critical essay reviewed by students, universities, his critical peers and mentors.

Beyond being a humanist and historian, he was a defender of Joan of Arc and an antiquarian. He had a mission to reveal the truth of France, expressing a passion of religion and the place of the Papacy, the protestant church, and the Jesuits in the New World.

In the course of his political research, Étienne came into possession of one of the four transcriptions of the trial of Joan of Arc, persecuted as a heretic, with a death sentence that was pardoned twenty years later. A priceless document, this remained in his personal archives.

Regaining enough strength to return to the den of the court houses, Étienne was surprised that the King's favour had turned to others. His seat at the Counsel d'État had been replaced, but he vowed to regain his former stature.

A tempest was brewing between the University of Paris and the Jesuit Order, demanding accreditation and input on the course curriculum, and Pasquier's intervention avoided a lawsuit against the University and the crown. Ramat, a jealous opponent, foresaw the fame to be had in this victory, and threatened Étienne with grievous harm, but he remained stalwart in his convictions.

Pasquier's delicate handling of religious issues gained him approval from the papacy, raising the name of Étienne Pasquier to become a hero among Frenchmen.

The Jesuits pledged their allegiance to the Pope as a means to their end. Their society benefited from several clergy bequests including a town house that was converted into the Collège de Clermont, a Jesuit school. Francis II objected to the school's claim to be the 'Society of Jesus' and their teachings, as did Pasquier.

A polished black carriage, led by a pair of sleek stallions, trod through the cobblestone streets of Paris from Étienne's apartment to the Palais de Justice. A sentry guarded the wrought iron gates of the Court House, opening into a fine courtyard. Étienne smiled to himself at the pageantry, and lowered himself from the carriage.

Entering the grand stone building of the Counsel d'État, he strode through the heavy doors, ahead of the arriving Justices. At the four arches, soldiers stood in regal uniform and spit polished boots, with rifles and bayonets.

Easing into formalities, he permitted the couturier in the magistrate's cloakroom to garb him in the black, silk robe with long, loose sleeves.

"Eh bien. I have regained my due."

Pasquier straightened his back to reach his full height, and donned a heavy powdered horsehair wig.

Étienne Pasquier's[8] eloquence and illustrious show of passion heightened recognition among the elite class, as he continued to win high profile murder cases, such as d'Arconville. His reputation landed him the defence of the Duke of Montmorency, and he succeeded in achieving the man's release from the Bastille.

During the Third Religious Wars of 1569, Pasquier lectured at the University of Poitiers. While sojourning at the d'Amboise Castle at Dissay, he met often with his old friend Pierre, the great-grandson of Pierre d'Amboise III.

Pierre lamented, "King Charles IX assigned the leadership of the royal troops to his younger brother, Duke d'Anjou, but I'm concerned, Étienne.

---

[8] Throughout Étienne's illustrious career in the courts, he defended the Duke of Lorraine, the City of Augoulême, and the Guise Family through colorful observations and indulgence in philosophy, resulting in his clients being returned to the good graces of the King Charles IX.

The Huguenots are amassing mercenaries numbering fourteen thousand, marching on Limousin. I know that it is just a matter of time before Dissay is next."

"It is the Admiral Gaspard de Coligny (1519-1572) who leads the Huguenots," Étienne said. "Dissay and La Rochelle will fall under attack soon, as we don't have the defences to save ourselves."

"The Catholics and the Huguenots are relentless in their march through southern France. Those who have survived have been forced to join or be killed. I fear as well for the land of our ancestors," Pierre said.

Their premonition was right, and the Castle of Dissay was stormed by Admiral de Coligny and the Huguenot army in 1569, leaving the town ravaged and the castle in ruins. The damage was ordered repaired, and a church was built high on the hill within view of the castle turrets. At the highest peak of a cobbled road, lined with ancient houses, the sanctuary of Saint-Pierre was dedicated by the Bishop of Poitiers.

In 1574, the royal throne of Charles IX was succeeded by Henry III. However, just as the Kings enjoyed the country castles, Pasquier thrived at his rural sojourns at Poitiers from 1567 to 1579, then Troyes in 1583, where he renounced his position as Advocate General, of the Cour des Comptes.

Henry III was a corrupt King, and the cabinet of Paris quickly challenged him. During Henry's alienation from the French, Pasquier's popularity on the bench was tainted. His home in Paris was confiscated and he was stripped of his crown appointments.

For several years, while Étienne and Françoise lived in exile, his wife's ailing health became a grave concern. Henry III was ultimately pressured to extend an olive branch to Pasquier, and he returned to Paris for a symbolic appearance at the opening of the Chambre des Comptes.

Henry III was assassinated in 1589 after a tumultuous reign. It was too late for Françoise Belen, and in exile, she succumbed to ill health and died the next winter.

Nicholas, Maître des Requêtes and Lord of Ferlandière, the second eldest son of Étienne Pasquier, took over the Château and lush countryside of the Brie estate, keeping the lands in the Pasquier family for another generation. Late in life, four years before her death, Françoise bore Étienne another son, taking a legacy of his father's name.

Henry IV, the Protestant king, renewed France's royal interests in explorations across the Atlantic, and in 1594, Pasquier returned to his position on the judicial bench, resuming his opposition to the Jesuit Order.

Étienne, the historian, studied the reports of Samuel de Champlain's conquests through the great St. Lawrence and the persistent campaign of the Jesuits to set up missions in New France. As the king's former historian, he was enthralled with maps and records of the settlement at Québec, with fortresses built and land cleared. But he was alarmed that the population was dwindling from disease and native attacks.

"Ah ha, it is women that they need—nurses to attend to the sick, nuns to teach, wives to tend to the farm and family. What is a man's life worth, if he has no sons? The extension of love and obedience is the natural course of life."

In 1604, Pasquier offered his resignation in Paris, with his imprint as one of the most renowned historians of France etched in history. Étienne's oldest son, Theodore, succeeded his father as Advocate of the Chamber of Accounts in Paris. But Étienne pined over the future of his children and grandchildren, and they reciprocated with adoration.

Despondent, he returned to his country home in Brie, before throwing himself into his writing again. He was at home in the loneliness of the enormous stone farmhouse, often found talking at the hearth to Françoise, after her death.

On many days, Étienne paced the lanes of the vineyards, always crouching to inspect the spring buds on the grape vines. When the Chardonnay harvest was near, he longed to belong to his land once again.

From a wooden rocker on the porch of the manor house, the aging Étienne grappled for his beech walking stick. Accepting physical limitations, he allowed his manservant to lift him up onto the seat of the small umbrella cart. As the narrow vineyard path was not sufficient for the oxen, a nanny goat was harnessed to the lead and walked with objection toward the field, guided by the headmaster.

At the perimeter of the vineyards, Étienne was lifted to sit on the ground. He rubbed the underside of the grape leaves and slowly dug with his arthritic fingers into the roots. A world away from Paris now, his pleasure was in taking a clump of grapes, to hold, sniff and taste to savour.

Ferlandière Farm, property of Pasquiers in Brie in 16th & 17th centuries, including scholar Étienne Pasquier. Painting 1944, La société d'histoire du Châtelet-en-Brie. ☺

"Hmmf." Étienne rose to his knees smelling the black soil, then letting it fall through his boney fingers. "You must learn to taste the soil, my dear vintner."

After a long two minutes, his terse growl broke the silence. "Down here! You'll learn nothing standing up there with an air of superiority."

"Oui, Monsieur Pasquier." The overseer scrambled to his knees until his own nose touched the soil. With his index finger he took a taste.

"What do you taste, Monsieur?" Pasquier asked.

"It is nutty and pungent, I think."

Étienne pointed to the tip of the overseer's nose. "Excellent! Capture that for next time, to improve the quality of the grapes. A little more goat dung!"

Demand continued for academic lectures from Étienne. In reaction to news of native hostilities attacking French habitant settlements, he addressed a spellbound audience in a Paris lecture hall, hungry for information about the Jesuits in New France. The wars between the Huron and Iroquois were pressuring the French to take sides, and in response, France sent a company of Jesuits with Jean de Brébeuf from Normandy, in a campaign to convert the natives to Christianity.

Back in Ferlandière, Étienne expounded to Nicholas, "I have heard that the Pasquiers of Dissay are considering joining the Carignan to the New World. It would be a proud day for our family to plant our name in New France for generations to come."

During the native uprisings, explorations in the New World subsided for several decades before resuming with the quest of Samuel de Champlain, returning to the St. Lawrence in summer 1603.

Five

Champlain, son of Captain Antoine de Champlain born at Brouages, 1574 – Adolescent Curiosity in Navigation – Sailed with Gravé Du Pont, 1598 – Champlain Royal Geographer & Cartographer to Henry IV – With Gravé Du Pont, 1603 – Meet with Saqamaw Henri Membertou – Chief Panounais killed in Iroquois Wars – John Duval's Plot to Assassinate Champlain – Mutants Arrested – Harsh Winter & Scurvy – First Church built at Québec, 1608 – Louis XIII cancelled Champlain's royal pension – Du Gua de Monts received trade monopoly of New France – Plans to build Fort Saint-Louis – Hurons align with Champlain during Beaver Wars – Champlain weds Hélène Boullé, 1610.

Samuel de Champlain of Brouages, 1574-1635

A HUNDRED MILES NORTH OF BORDEAUX, IN THE QUIET fishing village of Brouage, young Samuel spent hours observing the ships in the port, including that of his father, Captain Antoine de Champlain[9].

From his birth in Brouage in 1574 on France's west coast of the Gulf of Saintonge, the ocean was always in Samuel's sight. His mother, Marguerite Leroy, was from the port of La Rochelle, thirty-five miles north again. As a lad, he climbed the ropes to the crow's nest and shinnied the mast of his father's military-commissioned ships in the port.

"Father, are you certain the world is round?" The young Samuel knew, but from his perch half way up the mast, he watched the Admiral with

---

[9] The baptismal register held by the Province of Québec indicates Samuel Chapeleau was born to Antoynee Chapeleau and Marguerite Leroy at La Rochelle, France, August 13, 1574.

admiration, waiting for an answer. Antoine had only arrived back in port that day and was anchoring his ship, with the boy already on board. Samuel had gone daily for the past weeks, to sit on the walls of the fortified town, looking out to sea in hopes of seeing his father's ship.

The Capitaine quizzed, "Can you not see from up there?"

"No, I can't see that the ocean goes on, but I feel in my bones that it comes back from the continent on the other side. If I listen carefully to the breeze, it calls my name."

"Ah, you have the makings of a sailor. Perhaps one day you will captain my ship."

Samuel beamed until he felt his toes tingle.

As a boy, Samuel was led to investigate not only the stars, but celestial observations of distance above the ocean. In the evenings, his mother found him perched on the roof with his father's spyglass, searching the heavens and drawing maps chronicling measurements and mathematical calculations. He believed the stars could be seen from all points in the world, with sea tides chartered by proximities to the moon.

Brouage was a vital manufacturing hub and port for salt trade, bringing ships into the seaport. Salt marshes along the gulf were abundant and a commodity for the town.

The Champlains were held in the highest regard, propelling Samuel to mingle with admirals, cartographers, military generals, Abbotts and Cardinals, and local politicians. His passion for the sea was welcomed by many willing to share their knowledge. Often, as a ship became visible on the horizon, Samuel rushed to the harbour for its arrival, to sketch the galleon, ever patient to discuss the journey with the tired seamen.

"Ahoy, Master Samuel, have you come to unravel my nets?"

The delight was reciprocal, as tired sailors unfailingly welcomed the lad to jump into the fray. "Sir, indeed I have. Permission to come aboard?"

As a young adult, Samuel at last raised it to Capitaine Antoine at dinner.

"Father, sir, I have been a loyal patriot of France since birth. I have fought in our civil wars, studied the heavens, recorded the history of Brouage and cataloged the ships coming and going. I have not been educated by a tutor and haven't entered the Universities of France and

Italy, but rather I've acquired knowledge through first-hand experience and encounters with those well-versed."

"Indeed, you made that your accomplishment. Europe is overcome with a desire to conquer the riches of the West Indies. I've heard that the Spaniards have chartered a French ship to attend those islands. Many have gone before, but I could put in a word for you based on your term as quartermaster for the French Army."

"Yes, father, the fascination will not abate. I am meant to follow your footsteps."

As a dutiful Frenchmen, Champlain served in battle for three years in Bretagne, accepted when barely old enough for enlistment. With inherited connections to nobility, his uncle offered to represent him in negotiating his navigation skills to join the Spanish fleet as a mariner. Grasping the ropes of navigation and sailing, he joined the command of François Gravé Du Pont in 1598 on a French ship, casting anchor at Vera Cruz. By native boat, he sailed to the Gulf of Mexico, then traversed inland to Mexico City for a month to study the people and culture.

Back in France two years later, Samuel was granted a modest state pension as the royal geographer and cartographer, representing the French flag. Henry IV was taken with the detailed accounting of the voyage and sketches of natives and ports, and granted 'de' to Champlain in recognition of his initiative and abilities.

Champlain's Voyage to Tadoussac

FOLLOWING THE accounts of Jacques Cartier sixty years before, Gravé Du Pont sailed again from France in 1603 on the *Bonne-Renommée*. Introduced by an acquaintance, Aymar de Chaste, Samuel signed on to the upcoming voyage to Tadoussac, as a member of the fur trading expedition.

Champlain's role as captain of the mission was enhanced by his skill as a cartographer, recording astrolabe measurements of the coastline.

His rolls of parchment were never far from his being, and he conferred with his native friends to accurately mark inland routes.

Champlain Trading with the Indians, Charles W. Jeffreys (1869-1951),
Oil on commercial canvas board 1911. Library and Archives Canada Ⓢ

Sixty-five years before, Saqamaw Henri Membertou had watched the arrival of Cartier. He since learned the French language and converted to Christianity, requesting baptism and receiving his Christian name 'Henri'.

Now, as the Mi'kmaw Chief, he received Champlain. Samuel was fascinated at once with Henri's detailed construction of a birch bark canoe, and sketched as he watched.

Henri slowly peeled the bark in large sheets. "Monsieur, patience with the bark is important. Next, we seek the finest white cedar strips, close to the root so they are pliable. We'll soak until ready while I prepare the sticky mash."

Henri looked up with a broad smile, at the humour in the words.

"Sticky mash? Shall I record that in our journals?" The two burst in laughter at the sudden degree of their new comradery.

"Yes, sticky mash. Write it. A good glue will enable the canoe to carry a heavy burden on the river. And if you go overland, the canoe is light to carry. Good, yes?"

Samuel breathed deeply, admiring the coast of Cape Breton from the hilltop of the Annapolis north bank. His compass and navigation sextant were in his pack, with his sketching tools and journal.

He watched as a gull swooped to catch a fish breakfast, then set his sights on Goat Island. The day was brisk and the sun glimmered over the rippling river.

Below and in his sight, his ship, the *Don de Dieu*, was drawing a surge of habitants to unload provisions and construction tools for the new Habitation being built at Port Royal. Taken by the surreal autumn landscapes and colours of the heavens, Samuel stayed on the stoop, relishing the scene and sketching scenes that would become valuable records.

Combining his cartography with artistry, he transferred his visions into an accurate map of Acadia, with exquisite lead etchings and dabs of earthen water colours.

Etching in his historic journal, Champlain wrote of Port Royal:

We began to clear the ground, which was full of trees, and to erect houses as quickly as possible, nicely protected from the cannon. Everybody was busy at work. The habitation was completed in short order. Here I will build a summer house and stock my pond with trout, that I might enjoy the fresh air.

He turned his head at the crackle from the tree line, producing Chief Henri Membertou, with two of his sons behind.

"Bonjours, Henri!"

The chief's face broke to an ear-to-ear smile, displaying an impressive set of teeth for a well-aged man.

Lore in time would carry future tales of this legendary saqamaw, reaching nearly one hundred years, and seeing the beginnings of Québec settlements. His thin straggly beard showed only a hint of grey and his demeanor remained youthful.

But the smile faded as he faced Champlain.

"I am once more called to bury a great Micmac chief. Panonais has been killed in battle with the Armouchiquois. First, I will bury my friend, and then I will take five hundred of my warriors and seek revenge."

"Henri, I heard that you converted to Christianity. Your new found faith must give you a different answer, does it not?" Champlain asked.

In Algonquin, Henri replied, "Monsieur Champlain, it does, but I must lead my people in the way of our ancestors."

Several days later, Membertou invited Champlain for a somber face-to-face, in private and away from his crew. Samuel saw his troubled look.

Henri looked to the ground. "Monsieur, I listen and understand well the language of your men. Also, I am like a frozen rabbit in the woods and sometimes I choose not to be seen."

He hesitated at the depth of his concern.

"I have heard some of your men talk of assassination. Your pilot Tetu has told me himself."

"Assassination? Who?" Champlain lowered his voice, yet the surprise was deep and genuine.

"I can show you. Four men—they plan to kill you and your loyal men so they can take over the settlement. See over there at the fortress wall, they talk in whispers. The plotter is John Duval, a Norman locksmith."

Champlain clearly saw the tête-à-tête.

"When is it to be?"

"Tonight, when you are in your bed. They plan a distraction to bring you from your tent, and they will be ready with guns. Tetu says they have already agreed with the Basques and Spaniards to do this in exchange for turning over the fortress of Tadoussac."

"I am indebted to you, Henri. You are a good friend."

Champlain gathered a crew of men, of sound loyalty that he'd never doubted, and told them what the Saqamaw relayed.

The first mate jumped to his feet. "They must be arrested immediately. This is mutiny—treasonous."

One of the conspirators, Antoine Natel, was eager to absolve himself and cooperate with Champlain, providing details to entrap Duval. With his men, Natel delivered an invitation to meet at Tadoussac and celebrate that the plan was in play.

Instead, Champlain and his trusted crew waited and took the deceived men into custody. Without discussion, the ringleaders were placed in irons. Each was given a fair trial and Duval was sentenced to death by hanging in Québec, a swift punishment.

The event was entirely distasteful to Champlain, but it had to show leadership to his remaining crew.

"The others will be held as prisoners and returned to France's bastilles."

The French inhabitants learned to embrace the four seasons, preparing for the tempering crops. It would be folly to go into winter hibernation and not enjoy the sunshine across the drifts of snow—to snowshoe, toboggan, tow a traverse, and skate on the ice. The aboriginals had taught them to tap the sweet water of the sugar maples, and the natural irrigation of the seasons became indicators of a promising harvest.

The ship's crew hunkered onboard with whatever skins they could trade for, but aware their food and fuel were insufficient to bare the coming harsh winter winds and blankets of snow. As the spring thaw produced new saplings and sprouts, the remaining habitants salvaged the remnants of corn and tobacco fields, as the Iroquois had abandoned their settlements around Tadoussac.

As the supreme medicine man of the Micmac, Membertou readily recognized the symptoms of scurvy, seeing Champlain's able-bodied crew weakened by the bone-eating disease. He guided the French to find edible roots, white spruce leaves and bark, and brought food substance, with plentiful traps of rabbits and squirrels.

Escaping the winter at Saint Croix, Champlain relocated the settlement to the shelter of the Bay of Fundy, where he stayed until 1607. Before returning to France, he mapped explorations south to Massachusetts Bay and inland to Lake Champlain. Thirty settlers remained at Québec, having earned the trust of the natives.

When Gravé and Champlain returned to Québec in 1608, the defensive habitation fort was well under construction, having survived thanks to the medicinal tea of the natives. The Hurons and Algonquins were camped close to Québec, learning from the explorers and teaching agricultural methods. Woodcraft skills were passed to the settlers, carving maple bows and shaving stone points for hunting, and skills for spear fishing and netting smelt to support their food needs.

The ship's Huguenot crew established the first church in the lower town of Québec in 1608. Champlain was enchanted by the singing of the Psalms in French, but received a stern message from Pierre du Gua who had replaced Aymer de Chaste as Lieutenant-General of New France.

"Your men must cease the singing of music. Tadoussac is not Huguenot, nor a proclaimer of the Psalms. Let the natives believe in their Great Spirit. You are a fur trader."

Samuel replied, with respect and understanding. "As you wish your Lordship. My men will confine their music to the Don de Dieu."

Champlain restricted his men, forbidding that their music should not be heard onshore; but daily prayer and singing remained a routine onboard to keep their boosted.

Receiving a recall to France, Champlain raised a pole with the French flag over Stadacona, now referred to as Kébec. Inspired by Samuel's vision of the great walled city, those who remained were diligent to build as many houses, churches, walls, ditches and gardens as they could in his absence.

In an unexpected twist, King Louis XIII cancelled Champlain's modest pension of six hundred livres granted by Henry IV, forcing Samuel to beg for reinstatement a new commission. His hopes for robust mercantile trading then stumbled upon the laws of the North West Company that was vying with the Hudson's Bay Company to control the fur trade.

The British were ravaging the beaver hides, great grey wolves and elk. Samuel was convinced that trade was vital, but subscribed to the theory that 'every great empire must be built on farming'.

Pierre Du Gua de Monts, of France, held the trading monopoly, and presented Champlain with blueprints for a quadrangle of wooden buildings, surrounded by moats and a stockade atop the towering cliff.

Stone walls and foundations were laid in 1608 for the Fortress of St. Louis, high above the stock houses and merchant buildings along the shore where the great ships plied and rested. Completion of the wooden structure would take five years, using carpenters and stone masons sent as early crew members to repair ships and build fortifications.

In no time, narrow streets, bearing the names of Champlain, Couillard, and Hébert, became lined with shops and stone houses. The settlement was the early economic base for the St. Lawrence, at the head of the estuary where the river narrowed.

Champlain was drawn into a reluctant battle ensuing in the Five Nations. The blood-thirsty Iroquois and Onondagas were disgruntled as winter lands were taken from them, but the Algonquin relied on European trade in seeds, tools and arms at the expense of their indigenous farming and culture. Later, when the French would fight the British or the New England colonies, the Huron and Algonquin would paddle and take up bows alongside Champlain's men.

In 1609, Champlain's party joined with the Algonquin, Innu, Wyandot and Huron to ambush a Mohawk and Iroquois raiding party. The Battle of Sorel introduced muskets, bayonets, metal arrow heads, and the long-barrelled firearm arquebuse, surprising the Iroquois who retreated south of Lake Champlain.

This was the beginning of the Beaver Wars, inciting the Iroquois against natives allied to the French. During these wars, Membertou caught dysentery and died in September 1611. In his final days, he asked Champlain to bury him among the French, instead of by his own ancestors.

Returning to France, Samuel married Hélène Boullé[10] in 1610, only twelve years old and the daughter of a Huguenot. Born in a Calvinist household, her flaming, red hair and rosy cheeks charmed Samuel, and she delighted in his stories of the natives.

Champlain came back to New France as appointed Governor in 1612, and a stockholder in the trading monopoly. He stayed long enough to see the fruits of his efforts, but returned to France in 1615 as the Iroquois raids became more vicious. His next return to Québec would be with Hélène, five years later.

---

[10] Hélène Boullé, daughter of Nicolas Boullé, Lord Chamberlain, and Marguerite Alix, married in Paris, Dec.1610. The arranged marriage gave Champlain £6,000 and required that Hélène stay with her family for 2 years while Champlain returned to Québec.

Six

Étienne Pasquier of Brie meets nephew in Dissay, 1614 – Discussion of Philosophy & Reminiscents at Poitiers – Death of Étienne Pasquier, 1615 – Étienne of Dissay inherits his grandfather's royal cape & trunk – Hélène Boullé travels to Québec, 1620 & 1624 – Construction of second Habitation, 1626 – French & natives exchange skills – Anglo-French War of 1627-1629 – England hired Kirke Brothers to blockade French supplies in the St. Lawrence – France cedes Newfoundland to Kirke – Treaty of 1632 returns lands to France – Company of One Hundred Associates inhibits free trade of serfs – Coureur des Bois integration – Champlain's death at Québec, 1635.

Pasquier of Poitiers meets Pasquier of Dissay

THE KING'S HISTORIAN, ÉTIENNE PASQUIER, RECEIVED a message from his namesake nephew in Dissay, requesting a visit when the elder would be lecturing at the University of Poitiers. It was during the reign of Louis XIII, in 1614, and Étienne Pasquier was an aged man.

Hungering to hear of the historian's account of Champlain's flourishing settlements in New France, the two Étiennes detoured to the Black Stag alehouse, a walk from the University. The pub doors were wide open on the warm afternoon to allow the stink of ale and tobacco to escape. Outside, in the centre place in town, the echoing sound of a six-string hurdy-gurdy instrument, la Vielle-à-roue, delighted the crowd.

Young Étienne was honored to share his uncle's name when his own father had lived at Brie, and had spent many summers at Ferlandière with his cousins.

After the historian's brother lost his in life in battle defending Henry IV, he watched over his nephew, inviting him frequently in his early years to the Brie estates, and to Poitiers and Château d'Amboise.

The visits became less frequent after the elder Étienne was widowed, yet each encounter remained a treasured memory for his nephew, building his curiosity of politics and the new world.

"How is Ferlandière, Uncle Étienne?"

"I spend my time in my Paris apartments, mostly writing. Nicolas is now Lord of Ferlandière and the king has granted him additional lands at Brie. Perhaps you heard of the death of my dear Jean at Meung-sur-Loire. I remain a man rich in family and knowledge.

"I love the Loire Valley and the Seine, and spend time at the Amboise Château where my mother-in-law had a suite of apartments. I recall seeing you there when you brought a set of oak doors carved with the Amboise family crest. They keep them well-polished as an entrance to the great room. It bears your sign."

The aged scholar fumbled in his cloak before speaking as young Étienne waited in patience. Withdrawing a clenched fist, the tassels of a delicate velvet pouch fell from his grip.

"My dear nephew, these gold medallions were emblems of honour gifted to me by the good King Henry's court, for the valour and bravery of your father in his defence of our homeland on the battlefield. They no longer belong to me, but to you, as I was simply entrusted to their care. My brother would want these to remain in your bloodline."

The arthritic fingers fell back to an open palm, and he tapped out a handful of fine gold coins with the unmistakable royal insignia. The dazzle of gold was unlike anything Étienne had seen before.

"Dear Uncle, I am indeed honoured to receive this. My father would be proud that they were in your care these years."

"Your father was a prince in my own eyes." An awkward watery run made tracks down old Étienne's cheek.

"Indeed, you are my dear uncle to say such a kindness. It is with great sadness that we offer condolences to you regarding Jean. He was brave and courageous."

Succeeding an awkward pause of respect, Étienne of Dissay spoke.

"It has been too long since we shared of your insights, sir. I have read your writings, *Les Recherches de la France*, and found it both enlightening and complex. Your philosophy on the place of religion and education in our government extends to all of us, whether Protestant, Catholic or Huguenot. Since Martin Luther's Protestant Reformation eighty years ago, France has been in turmoil.

"The teachings of John Calvin challenged the throne and the Catholic cardinals. The massacre on St. Bartholomew's Day under Charles IX, influenced by Catherine de Medici, will not be forgotten nor forgiven. Whose Bible do you believe?"

Étienne of Dissay waited hungrily for the historian's answer.

"I am indebted to the French throne, and for a time the Huguenots had a reprieve until the assassination of King Henry; and now Louis XIII wrestles power from the regent and her Italian supporters. All Frenchmen believe in God, no matter their faith. Our hearts are free to worship, but whose principle or matter of faith is proclaimed is decided by royal blood. The Reformation of the Church has brought out factions throughout Europe long festering now, such as the Palatines. Does your heart not belong?"

"You know my parents raised me in the Catholic Church, the Church of Saint-Pierre et Saint-Paul in Dissay. I attended seminary and my principles are ingrained in that faith."

The aged Étienne looked into the depths of the younger man's eyes. "You are wanting to ask me something else, young man, and not prattle about religion."

"Yes, you have perceived me as a wanton shadow. I hunger deeply for knowledge of the new world—of the Champlain settlements. I feel a burning need to satisfy my soul, that my bones will be buried under the ground of the French flag in the new world, devout to my God."

"The king demands skilled tradesmen—and you, my dear nephew, are a master charpentier. The adolescence of the settlements has yet to come. I was privileged to be in Paris after the ascension of Louis XIII and met with the explorer Champlain. He has chronicled his voyages in a recent publication, *Des Sauvages*; he is an excellent artist and cartographer. You would be astute to study his explorations."

"Yes, my wise uncle. I have time before me. I pray you leave for Ferlandière in good health. Adventure to the New World is the future of the Frenchman. God speed."

A few years later, on August 31, 1615, Étienne gathered together his family, knowing death was imminent at eighty-six. Early the next morning, he passed to be with his Heavenly Father, leaving his mark in history.

Confidants at Ferlandière had come to know that a small metal box rested under the floor boards of the master bedroom, not to be opened until Étienne passed on, and his will read.

Étienne's oldest three sons were well-established in position, title, and landholdings before their pre-mature deaths. He often bemoaned, 'a parent should never outlive their children' and boasted that his children had honored him by calling him 'sir' and the sweet name of 'father'.

A solicitor from Paris took young Étienne to La Ferlandière at Brie in October, after his uncle's passing.

"Étienne, I have the esteemed honor to be entrusted by your uncle. He was a complicated, yet brilliant man. He confided in me, that your own father left a trust for you under his discretion. The family pact of the Seigneurie of Ferlandière may not provide for you. Another has already received the birthright of the manor, however there are a few things for you to attend to as residual from your own father's estate."

"I want to remember my uncle for the great work he has given to the world, not for his wealth. Advantage does open doors, but it is hard work and loyalty that make you a man."

"I see you are more like your uncle than you think."

The grandeur of Ferlandière looked different on this day. It had become home to others and less welcoming.

"The gentleman of the house has arranged with the butler that we proceed according to his will, in his testament. Come with me to the master bedroom."

Étienne observed the room and its furnishings.

"It is clean and sparse, but I see nothing that I want."

The solicitor took a letter opener from the desk and pried in between floorboards, withdrawing a metal box.

"This, Étienne, is from the estate of your father, and your portion of his bequest, so that your children will remember to follow greatness."

At the desk, he raised the lid of the box in silence. Inside was a letter from his mother, addressed from Château d'Amboise. He unwrapped six tiny silken folders.

The first was a bronze medallion struck when Jeanne d'Arc was first declared a heroine, fifty years after her death. One by one, he held and admired the others—two gold ducats with the emblem of Charles d'Amboise, Governor of Milan, and three variant florins with a profile of Henry IV engraved on the face.

The parchment note in his mother's pen and ink reminded him of the parable of the gold talents, but he showed disinterest and closed the box.

"One more thing, Étienne. Your father's bequest requires that his trunk be taken to your place of residence. The cape your uncle wore before Kings is also now yours to be treasured."

"Thank you, Monsieur. I will do as my father and my uncle have asked."

Étienne rifled through some papers of his uncle, with particular interest in notes of Samuel de Champlain and New France, recalling the inspiration of their meeting at the Black Stag and the discussion of explorations.

Champlain Returns to Québec

At twenty-two years, Hélène Boullé accompanied her husband to Québec in 1620, endearing the natives with her warm and infectious personality. Many bore welcoming gifts in respect.

Sitting on a stump in a gathering, she enamored young children with her picture books from France. In adoration they called her 'White Princess'. On a summer day, Champlain found her here and retrieved his journal to sketch the endearment of this moment for his scrapbook.

Hélène's last visit to the French settlement came in 1624.

"Samuel, wouldn't it be lovely to have a party for mon frère, Eustache. He has been in Québec with the Order of Minims for many years and I yearn to see him again."

NOTRE DAME DES VICTOIRES.
Site of Original City.

*Notre Dames des Victoires, Stadacona (Québec), engraving on wood,
Artist W.T. Smedley, Engraver W. Mollier, Picturesque Canada, Vol. 1, 1822.*

"Dearest, to see Eustache, we will need to go inland to the Mission. Do you wish to travel over rough land and through native territory?"

Hélène placed her arm in his, her brown eyes sparkling like topaz. "Oui, I trust you will protect me."

"Then when the weather is good, I'll send a scouting party to lead us."

Confined to the wooden fortress, Hélène made trips to the nearby Algonquin village, learning to craft with beads and quills. She allowed the women to braid her hair while they giggled together in the looking glass.

"Wait until Samuel sees me. I've become a tribal squaw, most certainly."

With the temperate weather, Hélène stood out on the parapet overlooking the St. Lawrence, pondering her Québec residence. After long thought, she went in search of Samuel who was overseeing the placement of cannons on the cliff.

She stretched her arms wide and raised her eyebrows. "Mon cher mari, you need to build the vaulted basements and walls even thicker than the length of Monsieur DuPont lying on his back." Hélène refrained from smirking at her description.

"Oui," Samuel agreed. "That will protect from dampness and rotting of the wood, and the ceilings will be low, but strong."

Construction of the second fort began in 1626, to fortify the ramparts at the top of the cliffs, and Hélène was pleased with her contribution.

Champlain proudly entertained Hélène with the finest luxuries that were available in the settlement, to appease her homesickness for Paris. But after four years of trying to adapt without such culture, gaiety, ruffles and finery shops, she decided to return to France, leaving Samuel behind, heart-broken.

She pleaded, "My dear, my souls stays with you, but I long for my family and the way of the French at home. I have tried to endure, but you can see for yourself that I have grown despondent."

Samuel held her in his arms.

"My love follows you in the wind, Hélène. I will come to you again in France."

France and England Battle over Québec, St. Lawrence

AS QUÉBEC settlements grew, so did the skills of the Europeans, adopting birch bark canoes, snowshoes, toboggans and moccasins; and in lands abandoned by the Iroquois, the French now farmed tobacco and corn.

Champlain agreed to take on Savignon, a Huron brave, to gain knowledge of their ways and lore, and in return enabled Étienne Brûlé, a young man, to affiliate and learn from the aboriginals and share his passion of the Jesuits. Brûlé lived with the natives and moved inland as the first explorer to see the Great Lakes.

Quickly, Savignon learned the carpentry skills required by the stone masons to bring materials to the Habitation. When not labouring in Québec, he accompanied Champlain inland to Trois Rivières, mid-point to Montréal. As Champlain's explorations spread—south to New York, north to Ottawa, and west to Georgian Bay, the Great Lakes, and the Trent waterway—the native braves, Savignon and Antoine, followed faithfully as interpreters. Champlain is credited with negotiating an alliance of Huron and Algonquin into a peace agreement with the Iroquois Confederacy.

Savignon had a near death experience on the Saint-Louis Rapids and was saved by his brothers. Champlain blamed himself for not being more vigilant, but it was a parting of the ways for the explorer and his Huron companion.

Battle was raging in Europe between France and Britain over English support of the French Huguenots at La Rochelle, a diversion to the events on the St. Lawrence.

During the Anglo-French war between 1627 and 1629, England dispatched war ships to New France, and Charles I of England hired the Kirke Brothers to cut off supply ships to the French settlements and take Tadoussac.

Admiral Roquement, with four French supply ships, attempted to bypass the Kirke position; but British military easily overtook the merchant ships, reinforcing the British fleet that was desperate for supplies.

In 1629, Champlain had no choice but to surrender to Kirke, who ordered the French to return to their homeland, and staked the English flag on the settlement.

Spending the next three years in Paris with Hélène, he was employed by King Louis XIII to stabilize the economy and to plan a strategy to overcome the British.

Champlain's plea for illegal occupation eventually led to the 'Treaty of Saint-Germain-en-Laye' in 1632, when Québec, Acadia and Cape Breton were returned to the French as just compensation for their losses. Kirke took English claim on Newfoundland, becoming the Governor.

Champlain truly understood the needs of the habitants and sent Louis Hébert, a French apothecary and herbalist, to Québec. Hébert, with his son-in-law, Couillard, delved into cultivation, tilling and reaping at Port Royal. Hébert brought his wife, Anne, and children Guillemette and Guillaume, along with Claude Rollet, his nephew, to assist, clearing land in hopes of a deed on the Saint-Charles River.

In 1633, Champlain returned to the building of Québec, but fell ill there and succumbed on December 25, 1635.

The following year, the *St. Jehan*, one of the earliest passenger ships from France, departed La Rochelle on April 1, 1636, bringing entire families and relatives. Stopping in Acadia, before Québec, a contingent was forced from the ship. Travel was not easy on the leaky ships, as workers replaced rotten boards and reinforced the masts. Morning rounds brought oakum buckets to seal leaks and wedge hot tar into the cracks. It was a common sight to pass the wreck of an old hull off the North Atlantic shores.

The first sprouts on the Hébert farm surfaced in August and a full crop matured by the end of harvest. Using native methods, bumper crops of wheat would soon need water-powered gristmills to dispense and distribute its yield.

Company of One Hundred Associates Inhibit Free Trade

CARDINAL RICHELIEU'S monopoly, named as the Company of One Hundred Associates, controlled merchant trading in New France, sending supplies on its ships. In turn, the habitants were restricted to trade exclusively with merchants of the Associates.

But along with goods and necessities, the European ships were bringing rats and influenza, infecting the pristine new land and its indigenous people.

The third fort as envisioned by Champlain, was built at Québec by Charles Huault de Montmagny, the new Governor of New France. Entrenching broad ditches with a stone foundation, the fort was fit for royalty, with elaborate storehouses, wine cellars, scullery kitchens, butlers' quarters, ice refrigeration and china shipped from France.

As stonemasons constructed Saint-Louis Forts, disdain was growing by habitants and natives against the Company of Associates, who were negotiating to improve trade. In 1645, they overcame the obstacles and established their Community of Habitants, forcing the surrender of exclusive trading privileges and an agreement with the Associates of Montréal.

Private trading in goods and furs outside designated trading posts was illegal and punishable by imprisonment, or banishing the culprits to France on rat-infested prison ships. English merchant ships did not accept this proclamation without resistance, sparking a three year trading war. Jean de Lauson, Governor from 1651 to 1657, monitored the British merchants, commanding buffalo and beaver pelt trade under the Hudson's Bay Company, controlling Indian fur traders, and enacting laws to inhibit free trade by the serfs and farmers.

As early immigrants, Louis Hebert with Augustus Chaumin were conflicted between trading with the Hudson's Bay Company and his friends, who had become coureurs des bois. The quiet rivers surging their waters to the Atlantic were trafficked by canoes porting pelts, and soon they were forced inland to avoid the river routes used by marching British soldiers. The ecology of the land was changing to the distress of natives.

Outside Charlesbourg, Hebert and Chaumin and a winter hunting party and came upon a camp of a coureur des bois that they recognized from French immigrant ships to Québec.

"Anomgyme, mon ami, how goes the trapping?" Hebert asked.

"It is difficult because the King of France insists I pay a penalty to his coffers for catching a muskrat or mink. It's a matter of principle that the natives and trappers be able to thrive on the land without interference. I have made the choice to live with my wife and children among the Algonquin and find my living as a native." The coureur des bois' physic did not blend well with the natives—he was tall with golden braids yet dressed in deerskin and beaver hat like his adopted tribe.

"I will not judge you, my friend nor will I trade you my furs."

"I don't ask that of you, Chaumin. You are a noble man and your leadership value to the settlement is known even among my new community."

The woods crackled with movement and Louis Hebert and Augustus Chaumin feared Iroquois attack upon their hunting party. "Those coming. Are they friend or foe, Anomgyme?"

"My friends—but perhaps your foe. They have come to help me ford the rapids with the weight of our pelts. We have found ourselves too close to Montmorency Falls and must move inland before nightfall. We must travel over the rapids to portage the overland canal."

"Journey well, Anomgyme."

Several Algonquin braves appeared on the shoreline carrying a portaged canoe laden with furs. The river crashed against the jagged rocks as the birch bark canoes were eased into the chaos. Skillfully, the Algonquin party moved onward into the white water rapids.

The coureurs des bois easily integrated into native villages, slipping in the back door without being noticed, and shunning the Company of One Hundred trading rules.

It was logistically difficult for the French government to completely control native trading. The coureurs des bois were the soul of fur trading, and the French recognized their value in contrast to the English, that sought only the furs. When Dutch and Spanish ships came up the coast, they brought rum from the West Indies, contributing to the corruption of the natives.

An enormous stepping stone in history was left by Champlain on the shores of the St. Lawrence, a place and people he loved. Following his death in Québec in 1635, Hélène, childless, found widowhood difficult. She took vows with the Ursuline movement and entered a nunnery outside Paris, where she died in 1654 as Sister Hélène de Saint Augustin.

In an expression of devotion to the people of Québec, Champlain bequeathed his estate to the Notre-Dame-de-la-Recouvrances as heir to all his property. Hélène denounced any part of the will to honor her husband.

Médart Chouart des Groseillieres continued the work of Champlain between 1654 and 1660, reinforcing to France the need for a larger influx of arms and aid.

Seven

Étienne Pasquier has War Shield Repaired – Treachery of War – Étienne Meets Jeanne Poussarde in Paris, 1620 – Love Succeeds over Dowry – Étienne Pasquier & Jeanne Poussard Marry, 1620 – Sheep Farming on Seigneurie of Dissay – Étienne as Charpentier & Jardiniere – first son, Étienne, baptized at Dissay Church of Saint-Pierre et Saint-Paul, 1621 – Thirty Years War, England vs. France – Night Run for Docteur Arnoux to assist Jenne in childbirth – Another is buried in the church courtyard – Jeanne Poussarde dies 1633.

Étienne Pasquier of Dissay (1585-1638)

THE ACRID SMELL OF HOT MOLTEN IRON SINGED Étienne's nostrils as he entered into the blacksmith's stable in Dissay. Knocking chunks of mud from his boots, he waited for Gilles to look up from his work. The man's smile bared rotting teeth, as he was glad to see Étienne.

The town forgeron's bare arms shimmered with sweat as he raised his hammer to the ceiling, then descended with enormous weight onto the deformed iron on an anvil platform. The forge was fueled by wood and coal into a white hot tempest as the bellows fed the fire. With another strike, the metal flattened into a plate, then three more hammers swung before his arms rested.

"Ah bien, this is good."

The smithy turned to a rack of boards resting behind, and pulled out an abused shield of armour.

Gilles raised it as he spoke. "Such treachery we have endured for centuries—first the Vikings, then the battles with England after Norman's

Conquest. Our blood boils with passion and pride for our country, yet this is all I can offer."

Gilles pulled his barrelled chest closer to the anvil to continue working with the metal, leaving his legless pants folded under him.

"Our children will at least have their land and patriotism to will to their children," Étienne reassured. "We cannot defeat the kings and queens of history, yet we can kill our English, Spanish and Portuguese neighbours and sleep well. And that is all well and good with our royal guard."

"C'est dommage, mon ami."

Gilles wiped his hands on a gritty apron, then extended a firm handshake to his friend.

"My Petronille sews the chain link with wire, and promises to be finished next week. This shield will protect you better against the arrows of the English and the Spaniards."

Étienne fingered the newly molded plate, distressed by war. He was fortunate to have armour, unlike many of his comrades who walked into fields with meagre protection—some only behind an undisciplined spear or axe with a rusted blade at his waist.

"Please extend my gratitude to Petronille for her nimble fingers; she has done a fine mend. Ma mère always sends her best."

"I will tell her," Gilles said.

Étienne contemplated and added, "The call to battle peals across our farms both day and night and echoes to the Dissay castle, our only fortress. Contentment comes at a great cost."

Gilles protested. "Henry III and then Henry IV proclaimed themselves the Kings of France, but my heart knows to whom I belong. They took my legs and my sons, but never my passion. Now we have a new monarch, Louis XIII, and he has a taste for war. He's determined to quash the Protestant Huguenots."

"Victims pass through the Paris courthouses to no avail," Étienne confided. "The Crown will win every time without a murmur of gratitude for spilt blood, but our religion we are born with."

"Merci, Étienne. God speed." Gilles locked hands with him. "If a man is not scared, he is not a soldier."

"Oui, oui. That I know is true. I am both scared and scarred from battle and so is the inheritance of my children."

Étienne was a worthy foot soldier, knowing his might had improved with his reinforced shield and sword. He rubbed his shoulder, where clothing concealed a clot of distorted flesh, from an English axe.

For an instant, his mind returned to the gold medallions for his father's service to the king. *I would rather have my father's breath and life than his medal.*

Doubting he would see the smithy again, he took his charge toward La Rochelle, where Louis XIII blockaded the Huguenot rebellion at the port.

On a visit to cousins in Paris in 1620, Étienne first met the lovely, fair-haired Jeanne Poussard. Blonde ringlets hung below her wide-brimmed hat adorned with silk flowers and feathers of a scarlet tanger, accenting a hooped dress he thought to be remarkable. Struck by her beauty and sky-blue eyes, his imagination instantly created occasions to bring about another chance meeting. His uncle suggested a literary reading.

In her shy manner, she described the pleasure of her Sunday walks in the park. He listened to the sensitivity of her words, describing the serenity of resting by the pond as ducks played in the water.

On Sunday morning, Étienne was also walking early in the park at a leisurely pace. Beyond the pairs of parading parasols, he spotted her at last, and as they walked closer, he noticed she showed delight on seeing him.

"Mademoiselle Poussard, may I accompany you to the Hôtel de Rambouillet tomorrow evening for the readings of Madame La Fayette?"

Étienne's heart took an extra beat, wondering if he made the appropriate invitation to the lady, and he added a gentleman's bow.

"Monsieur Pasquier, I would be most pleased to attend with you, however, my aunt will require that my cousin attend with us," Jeanne replied.

"Yes, of course. How rude of me not to have mentioned her name. Give my regards to your aunt and your cousin too." He flushed with embarrassment.

"Here is my calling card with my address." Jeanne reached into a tiny silken sack at her wrist.

Her eyes followed his as he noted the address. She wondered if he would find her to be below his class and regret the invitation.

Étienne's eyes. "I'll look forward to meeting you at seven tomorrow."

The park's entertainment included other literary readings beyond Madame La Fayette's, and their stroll on the promenade stopped at a bench away from the crowd. Jeanne was burdened to tell Étienne that her dowry would not be agreeable to a man of his stature.

"Mon dearest Étienne, it is time that I tell you of my truth. I am not of a notable family. I live with my cousin and aunt and we do share the Poussard name, but my father was never a man of great wealth. Maintenant, we are not."

Jeanne's face flushed and her eyes faced the ground. "I am simple, without a handsome dowry."

"The great writer and poet, Étienne Pasquier, is my uncle. My father didn't chose the way of the courts and the Palais de Justice in the footsteps of my uncle and cousins. And I have chosen to remain a master carpenter and not fall on education for favors. It is I who have deceived you, ma chère. I am simply a vassal from the commune at Dissay." For a moment his thoughts returned to the metal box, then dismissed it.

After the posting of banns, Étienne Pasquier and Jeanne Marie Poussard married at Dissay, Poitou in 1620 and settled in the quiet commune outside the castle.

Étienne vowed that his own sons should not have the gift of a silver spoon, but earn the rewards of the vassal and the accomplishment achieved in master carpentry. They were faithful patrons of the hilltop church Saint-Pierre et Saint-Paul.

At the same Dissay church, their first-born son was baptized the following year. Carrying the name of Étienne Pasquier, it was a natural succession that the family pastured sheep on their strip of seigneurial land, and his skill in carpentry and gardening should find favor with the seigneur.

Growing up facing the fear of battle every day during the Thirty Years War, the youngest Étienne stuck close by his father whenever he returned to Dissay from the battlefields.

Class was earned in battle, along with favor of the King. Spanish troops had captured the Archbishop Elector, inciting Louis XIII to war with the Spanish and Portuguese, but as the wars raged, government coffers dwindled and Cardinal Richelieu recommended desperate measures to collect taxes.

The tax collectors had been to Dissay and taken all that the Pasquier family had, leaving them with farm implements, a pair of oxen and a lone cow. Their sheep in the shared pastures dwindled, leaving the commune habitants little to perpetuate.

Although Étienne's father had chosen a path apart from Ferlandière and his wealthy relatives at d'Amboise, he was not a foolish man. When the hardships of poverty enveloped his family nearing starvation, Étienne journeyed to Tours to see the gold dealer. Nagging guilt was overcome by the hunger he felt outside the shop, but without bartering, he was handsomely reimbursed for one of the gold florins from his inheritance.

"Thank you, Father in Heaven, and my Father from this earth for this reward. I will invest wisely in the strength of my family and in your service, just as my mother taught me the story of the talents."

He had never declared to Jeanne the full truth of the trunk beneath his carpenter's bench, but determined that on his return to Dissay, she should be privy to the secret of the compartment.

Every day, Jeanne took down her Bible and read to her family the instruction of her faith.

'And the barrel of the meal wasted not, neither did the curse of oil fail, according to the word of the Lord which she spake to Elijah.'
   —I Kings 17:16.

His son, young Étienne, as a lad of five, stood on a stool to run his fingers over his father's bow and arrow, high on a hook behind the kitchen larder.

"Papa, did Gabriel protect you at war?" the boy said. "I asked for God to send his best angel to be with you."

Étienne Sr. bent beside the boy and whispered, "Yes, Gabriel was with me, but if you don't tell anyone, I will appear even braver to your Ma." The boy's eyes widened.

"How old will I be before I get my own arrows?"

His father's eyes burrowed into his, and he bit his lip.

"Étienne, soon you will need to use a bow and arrow to hunt rabbits and grouse, but we shall pray that you won't need a shield and will never go to war. We fight the Kings' Wars between England and France, but this is not a war for little boys."

"Have you ever killed an Englishman?"

His father tousled his hair and kissed his forehead, then left the room.

Heavier chores were left to Étienne while his younger brother, Mathurin, was still a toddler, and the new baby, Marie-Étiennette, incapable of contributing.

In the dark of early morning, his mother called to him. "Étienne, it is time to collect the firewood and start the hearth." He tumbled from the warm bed and nudged Mathurin to get into his boots.

Mathurin's voice replied in the darkness. "I am here, brother,"

Étienne lit the barn lantern. Behind the house was an animal shelter where they kept a lone cow, pigs and a pair of oxen in an open stable. When the milking was done, Étienne reached for the pail, as Mathurin was struggling with its weight.

"Non, non, Mathurin. You will spill it. Our milk is too precious. I will carry it."

As soon as they stepped into the kitchen, Mathurin got his own grip back on the handle and hollered. "I've got the milk!"

His sweet mother gave him a knowing wink.

The deep voice of his father shook him from his sleep. He was alarmed but firm.

"Wake up, son! Étienne, your mother needs the doctor!" He rustled the boy to his feet.

"Oui, Papa, I'll run my fastest to bring him."

Étienne was seven now, and ran his heart out through the streets of Dissay. The doctor's residence was uphill, adjacent to the church of Saint-Pierre et Saint-Paul. Without a lantern, he stumbled in the slippery darkness as rain pelted his head.

A mangy German shepherd joined his chase down the final lane to a heavy door that he recognized; he'd been there when he broke his leg in a groundhog hole while rabbit hunting.

He knocked twice, then pounded harder, and the urgency couldn't be missed.

"Please docteur; c'est ma mère!"

His heart throbbed in his chest, but through its beating he heard a shuffle inside the house. The flame of a lantern lit up in the window and the docteur pulled on his boots.

"Étienne? What is it, boy?"

"C'est ma mère—she is in great pain and Papa fears for her and the baby. We need your help!"

Docteur Arnoux clutched his medical bag and jacket and followed the boy back down the cobblestone hill, with the dog behind.

Étienne reached with impatience. "I'll take your satchel, sir, and you can walk faster." The man stepped up his pace to stay with the boy.

The night shutters on the cottage were latched, but slivers of light alerted the street that the house was astir.

Étienne Sr. had a fire glowing and a pot of hot water boiling on the hearth. Mathurin sat frozen in a corner chair, while the petite Marie-Étiennette rushed between the kitchen and their mother's bed with hot cloths she drew from the pot with a poke.

Docteur Arnoux displayed a grave look on his face, and Papa was fearful, muttering prayers as he wrung his hands.

Étienne stood at his father's shoulder with his hand on the great muscles. "Papa, if we pray, will our dear mother be alright?"

"Oui, Oui! You are turning into my little man."

"Please, Étienne, I need your help!" Docteur Arnoux called sternly from the bedroom.

The room became silent—their mother didn't cry anymore and neither his father nor the docteur spoke. He listened for cries that didn't come, but the tears of Mathurin and Marie-Étienette were muffled as they clung together in the corner.

The docteur made her comfortable with some magic medicine but she refused to give up her weak little bundle. It was another son, but the docteur offered comforting words.

"Jeanne, your little one is in Heaven. You must regain strength for your three thriving children. Stillbirths are common, and perhaps next time, if the child is carried longer, he will have a better chance in this world."

Étienne crept into his parent's bedroom to peek at the infant swaddled in his mother's arms. The next day, the little bundle was buried in the Dissay church courtyard.

The Dissay cottage was built of stone, with an infested thatched roof and earthen floor. Étienne had breached childhood when he took his father's carpentry tools to make a four poster bed with a canvas tied to the four corners. It was a grateful shelter for his dear mother from the leaky roof.

Gathering local stone, they expanded the cottage. Hand-hewn timbers braced the interior, and they packed the crevices with sand and lime, and built a sloped clay shingled roof with a ridge. The aged hearth still stood in the kitchen, and Étienne and Mathurin reinforced the chimney.

The boys were taught by their mother and father to read, write and study the political ambitions of the French Kings and the teachings of the récollets. As young boys, the Catholic Church was the center of literacy and education, bringing local, school-age children to the monastery for classes.

Throughout Jeanne's birthing years, the survival rate of her infants was her greatest disappointment. She toiled daily beside her husband in the planting and harvest fields, but some days she simply longed to be a child again, far away from the canons.

She reminisced of happy days with her family on the farm in Sarthe, running with Jacquette to collect wild flowers.

The boys worked from dawn to dusk with the crops, and ventured in off hours into the countryside in search of rabbit, grouse, squab and ducks. They could only imagine wild game hunting of deer and large animals, as that was reserved for nobility—a sport with hounds exhausting the prey before the bow and arrow kill.

Young Étienne Jr. knew his parents had ambitions for him, and often overheard them discussing such options.

"Perhaps Étienne should have education in Paris, where he can learn from philosophers and historians," Jeanne suggested. "France is changing quickly, and King Louis has turned his attention to explorations in the New World."

Jeanne's face flushed as she stammered, fighting to hold back words that needed to be said.

"Perhaps . . . about the trunk. I am a wise woman who has married a wise man. Should not our children benefit from their ancestors?"

"Dissay is his home, and this is *his* land when I am gone. We are French and loyal to the king—this is the land of Pasquiers, from Paris to Bordeaux. King Louis has demands for artistic furniture and even offers bonuses for master craftsmanship. There will be plenty of work for Étienne here at the grand château of Dissay. I will take them, myself, more often to the University and teach them to love books."

Jeanne said, "I see you are weakening, my dear, and you wish to be sure of your sons' future. In due time, they will receive the true inheritance, the wealth of a loving family, the love of the land, and education."

Étienne reached for Jeanne's hand. "You have lost weight and I see you in pain every day. It is time to see the docteur."

Young Étienne was twelve years when his mother passed away in 1633. Jeanne was buried in the courtyard at Dissay's ancestral church on the hill above the castle. The pain was greater than Étienne had felt before. He was old enough to know that she was not with Gabriel, but his father reassured him that they would all meet again.

Standing in his father's field, he was entranced by the clouds floating through the peace of the blue sky, wondering if he would still recognize his mother in Heaven. He chose not to cause any pain to his father by asking.

Turning his passion to education as his mother wished, he poured himself into the Jesuit College and the annals of the University at Poitiers. Most times, his horse walked outbound on the three hour journey of twelve miles over the flat land from Dissay to Poitiers, but often sped to a trot on the return.

It was at the University that he poured over *Les Reserches de la France*, written by his great uncle and namesake. On his return to Dissay, young Étienne queried his father about the historian.

"Dear son, the time has come that I share his secret with you."

"Secret?"

"Your grandfather was a great and generous man, just as your great uncle was. I was sent away to study in Europe and did not share the family life I so much longed for. Without my mother, and with my brothers much older and settled in the king's courts, I vowed to myself that at all costs, my sons would be raised with their family."

"We are a family, father."

Handwritten register (bottom left) of the funeral of Étienne Pasquier, at May 21, 1638 Church of Saint-Pierre et Saint-Paul, Dissay, France. Photos Shirley Burton 2013

"Indeed we are. When it is time for me to join your mother in Heaven, you will be the man of the house. The responsibilities for the future of your brother and sister are great. It may surprise you, son, but we are not paupers."

"Why have we lived so?"

"There is a price for everything in life. I chose to give you the wealth of parental love and the sense of accomplishment at the end of a hard day's work. Your grandfather left us a treasure of gold coins and your great uncle's royal cape. We have never gone hungry or suffered impoverishment."

"I know the trunk and I have seen the cape, but never the gold coins."

"I am a skilled carpenter and, of course there's a deceitful bottom built in the trunk. Underneath, you will find a metal box."

"The box will stay, but your wise story we will pass on. I am far richer in Dissay than any child raised in Paris. I will take care of my sister and brother in the same way."

"Yes. You are wise like your mother."

Étienne's father was not an old man when he died in the spring of 1638[11] and was buried at Saint-Pierre et Saint-Paul, the same church where Étienne Jr. was baptized in 1621.[12]

---

[11] Death Register at La Mairie, Dissay, France records Étienne Pasquier's burial on May 21, 1638, spouse of Jeanne Poussard.

[12] Baptism of Étienne Pasquier in 1621 recorded by Direction Regionale des Affairs Culturelles, Fich No. F86-132 of Saint-Pierre et Saint-Paul, Dissay, France.

The three Pasquier children were orphaned before Étienne was eighteen, Mathurin[13] just fourteen, and Marie-Étiennette an adolescent.

Taking responsibility for his father's farm and his siblings, Étienne toiled days at the seigneurie, and by the night hearth, he produced intricate craftsmanship suitable for recognition by Louis XIII. Perfecting grape wood scrolls, inlays, and artesia techniques, his work was praised at castles as far as the Vienne, Poitou-Charentes, Seine and Loire Valleys.

Journey to Poitiers

ON THE route, Étienne observed the cultural contrast, from the humble clusters of dwellings he passed, to the grand villas and châteaux with charming lavender and rose gardens.

In the last miles, he slowed to observe the Gothic churches and auberges near the livery in Poitiers. Dusk had fallen, and he hired a stableman to take his horse. In the noise of the evening, he meandered the cobblestone streets, avoiding drunkards and angry soldiers that had been thrust from the alehouses.

Upstairs over the Black Stag, Étienne paid for a bed in a common room on the third floor, lined with cots, bales, and ticked mattresses. Inebriated soldiers, behaving badly, had already taken charge in the inn, and the stench of stale lager, perspiration and smelly clothing consumed the entire floor.

"How is this suitable for a nobleman?" Étienne grunted and returned to the alehouse matron demanding more fitting accommodations. For an additional compensation, the owner offered a shared boarding room in the family quarters on the second floor, already occupied by another man.

"Bonsoir, garçon. Je m'appelle Étienne Pasquier de Dissay. Which bed shall I take?"

"It is good to have your company, sir."

---

[13] Mathurin Paquier, son of Étienne Pasquier and Jeanne Poussarde, is recorded in the Baptismal register at Saint-Pierre in Dissay as April 24, 1624.

The gentleman introduced himself simply as Claude, and gestured to a single bed behind the door. "What brings you to Poitiers, Claude?"

"I am on my way to La Rochelle to seek enlistment following the route of Champlain."

"Aha, oui! The route of Champlain!"

Leaving the Black Stag at sunrise, Étienne strolled the boulevard, looking for an inn offering gruel and journey cakes. Walking in the back lanes past the herb gardens and brick ovens, he met Madame Trudel, outside her door, struggling to balance fresh loaves on her oven boards.

He went to her aid, and it was the polite, reciprocal thing for Madame Trudel to offer him to come inside for bread in return for his kindness.

"Merci, Madame, for the bread and your delicious sweet butter. A bachelor rarely encounters such privileges."

She replied, "Sir, I have lived in Paris all my life and outlasted a few of our Kings. The explorations in the new world now bring back treasures and delicacies for our kitchens."

She hesitated. "Do you hear that?" Étienne listened to a kettle on the stove, with a glass hub perched on the top. Bubbles started popping as he watched, then became vigorous, emitting a strong aroma and whistle.

"We have allowed ourselves to sample the Mexican savoury they call coffee. It is strong and bitter at first, but you can use milk until it is just right."

Madame Chabot poured a metal mug with the dark liquid and set it before Étienne.

"Yes, it is delightful—Mexican coffee." He nodded.

"Are you from Poitiers?" she asked.

"Non. Dissay. Mon père et ma mère sont décédés. I tend to the family land at the seigneurie with my brother and sister. I am a charpentier. I could repay you with some repairs for the coffee."

"Très bien!" Madame Chabot respected his courtesy and dragged a three-legged chair from her pantry and a wooden bucket with sundry tools.

Boulevards and stone fences skirted the lines of medieval fortifications of the ancient town of Poitiers, in the heart of the Provence of Poitou-Charentes. Étienne followed the winding cobblestone streets toward the University of Poitiers that had been chartered by Charles VII.

Étienne entered the sanctum of the conservatories and great study halls. Straining his eyes momentarily, he adjusted to the dim lighting and the reverent echo of sacred halls.

Distant whispering echoed from the atrium, and music of a lute and muffled harp floated down from the conservatory. Double doors to the library were closed, securing the reverence of volumes of wisdom, lest it escape or succumb to time.

Étienne pushed the door and slipped through the widening crack, easing it back. Fingering the scrolls, censored scripts and leather bound law books on the hallowed shelves stirred a new passion in Étienne's soul, a desire for learning and to open windows of prospect for himself.

He flashed back to a meeting here with Urbain Tessier from Anjou, some years before. They had delved into topics of feudalism, the charismatic power of the lords and new lands, and the struggles of the Jesuits.

Not only were Catholic religious principles administered under strict control of the Church at the time, but also art, poetry, literary writings, and even the 'Lettres' of historians and Jesuits of the New World were endorsed within the web of Catholicism.

Neither Étienne nor Urbain had ever known freedom of the purest sense, and both agreed then that the new world could bring opportunities they dared to dream of.

A dream they shared.

Eight

Old friends debate New World opportunity – Engagés & Carignan Soldiers Recruited – Zacherie Cloutier signs with M. Giffard of Beauport, 1642 – Urbain Tessier engaged to Montréal, 1648 – Regular Carignan Regiments sailing from Bordeaux and LaRochelle – Urbain Tessier Captured by Iroquois – Jeanne Manse Recruits in France for Nurses at Hôtel-Dieu, 1642 – Black Plague & Quarantine throughout Europe – Étienne & Isaac Pasquier of Dissay Debate New World – Pasquier Inheritance Passed to Mathurin.

Louis XIV Recruits Soldiers to Québec

ENGROSSED IN LEATHER-BOUND LEDGERS OF SCRIPT, Étienne hauled out voluminous accounts of expeditions by Cartier and Champlain to the new world, documenting topography, missions, native hostilities and lists of ships that had departed from La Rochelle.

Near him in the corner, engrossed in conversation, were Zacharie Cloutier, a master carpenter from Mortagne and Thomas Pageau of Sarthe.

"Étienne, mon ami, come and join us!" Zacharie insisted, rising from his chair. "My dear friend, it is good to see you. We are telling of accounts from the returning exploration ships."

"Indeed, the stories are food for the soul."

"Not more than one hundred and fifty years ago, Columbus found the new world, then Magellan confirmed that the world was round. But now, New France is an eruption of possibilities."

"What brings you from your homes?" Étienne asked.

"Robert Giffard, a renowned surgeon and apothecary from Tourouvre, has been awarded the Seigneurie of Beauport in New France. He left from Mortagne in 1634. He now looks among us to build palisades and fortresses, and cultivate crops with primitive plows. For each harvest, a portion of crops are paid back to Monsieur Giffard," Zacherie said.

"Do you plan to go, mon ami?" Étienne asked.

"Giffard's enthusiasm and his vision of lush farmlands and skilled craftsmen is infectious. He asked that I go as well, to take my carpentry skills. And also Jean Guyon as a stone mason," Cloutier said.

"How much land did he offer you?" Pageau asked.

"At first it was three hundred arpents, but my family is imbedded in France and felt I should resist. I talked with Jean long hours and we decided to decline." Zacherie hesitated and his brows betrayed his distress.

"I can see you are troubled," Étienne said.

"I was. But now, Giffard sent me another offer that I cannot refuse. We are destined to a life of battle in either place, whether France or Kébec. In return for three years of service in the Carignan-Salières regiment, and turning my allotted land from trees to crops, I will receive a deed and freedom. I am considering signing the contract."

Zacherie removed a ragged hand-written map from his coat, displaying the range of lands encompassed in New France, including settlements along the St. Lawrence River, Mississippi Valley, Louisiana and Acadia.

"Here, Thomas. Read this description for us."

Zacherie passed a rolled parchment to Pageau, to read aloud.

"The seigneur establishes each habitant with a few head of cattle and oxen, providing a ration of food and crude lodging. After two or three years of mandatory labour clearing virgin forests into arable farm land, the engagés repay their passage and dues. As well, a small portion of the one or two thousand arpents of land they toiled is deeded to the settler.

"During the engagé's tenure, he can hunt and fish freely, but may not trade outside the designated trading posts, nor marry until the term of his contract is satisfied."

Étienne burst in objection. "Who is this who tells me I cannot marry without permission? I am a widower of forty-five years."

"Mais Étienne, you can still be a widower in New France, working on your own land." Thomas laughed, but Étienne was less amused.

Pageau continued, "They want both muscle and skill, with heavy labour clearing thick bush and roads, and loading at merchant ships. Artisans, masons, carpenters, métiers, tisserans, and meuniers[14] are still needed too."

The ancient manor house of the Seigneurie of Monsieur Giffard was designed in 1642 to display an opulence of wealth in its fixtures and artistic accoutrements. It later became known as Aubergine de Fine Gueule of Château-Richer.

Several years passed before Zacharie Cloutier married his sweetheart, Madeleine Barbe Émard, in 1648 back at La Rochelle, France. After the wedding, they embarked for Montréal in July, and at a large home at Château-Richer, they raised seven children. Later, Zacherie built the estate of La Cloutierie[15] at Beauport, with a distinguishable four-sided, sloped mansard roof.

Urbain Tessier, Voyages to Montréal

AT TWENTY-THREE years of age, Urbain Tessier left Anjou of Touraine in 1648 and voyaged to Montréal under contract to Monsieur de Maisonneuve.

In Québec, Urbain married Marie Archambault from Aunis, barely thirteen, with Robert Giffard as witness. Notably, he was deeded the ninth grant given to any engagé or farmer on all of Île de Montréal.

Urbain Tessier and his father-in-law, Jacques Archambault, working with fifteen men on farmlands outside the walls of Ville-Marie, fell prey to a surprise attack by more than two hundred and fifty Iroquois. The habitants were greatly outnumbered, and the attack was violent, with an account sent back to La Rochelle for delivery to King Louis XIV.

---

[14] Translation of occupations: cordonniere – shoemaker; chapellier – hat maker; charpentier – carpenter; ecuyer – horseman or stabler; meunier – miller; tailleur – tailor; soldat – soldier, and tisseran – weaver.

[15] *La Cloutierie*, estate of Zacherie Cloutier at Beauport, has withstood over 300 years of history.

Urbain Tessier of Anjou reports of rugged land and savages. Settlements were fenced for protection but the farming lands in long strips in a circular fashion remained vulnerable to attack:

'Last year, when the Iroquois rampaged, they raided my settlement outside Montréal. I had the fortune to achieve ranks of great respect and was allowed with three others to stand guard at night. It was during this watch when the savages attacked my house, burning it to the ground. Although my wife, Marie Archambuault, and children were spared, I was taken captive with four others. My family feared I was dead.

'We were tortured for a year and a half, but I managed to negotiate the release of our men. Marie Archambault was glad to see my return, albeit sans une digit.'

After the conflict, only four farmers remained on the field, and the others, including Urbain, were taken captive. Urbain and his peers marched a long distance. Blindfolded, they weren't able to say where they'd been taken, but it was among barbarians.

A later account reported that a man named Lavigne had one of his fingers detached by the Iroquois, and that the release of the Frenchman was negotiated by Father Simon Lemoyne, a Jesuit. Urbain Tessier was thereafter known as Urbain Tessier dit Lavigne.

Ships continued from Bordeaux and La Rochelle in the spring and summer, bringing needed soldiers for reinforcement against the marauding Iroquois, along with migrating engagés to clear land.

Settlements were flourishing at Montréal, Québec, Château-Richer, Montmorency, Ste. Anne and Beauport, with burgeoning demand for craftsmen. Louis XIV demanded an annual accounting of the habitants in Kébec; in 1650, the population was reported at 750, but he also wanted statistics levied by the natives.

A comparison of marriages, births and deaths by Iroquois ambush was a deepening concern to the king, also displeased with the rising records of Frenchmen marrying sauvagesses in Acadia.

Adding to the colonies at Tadoussac, Kébec, St. Joseph, Trois Rivières, Fort Richelieu and Montréal, a settlement was established at the mouth of the Saint-Charles River known as Cap-Rouge, built due to hostile encounters with native tribes. Land there was farmed in groups, under the watch of a native scout.

Before 1650, habitants easily traded for pelts in return for weapons and cheap liquor, called firewater. Natives along the St. Lawrence traded five beaver pelts for one musket, two pelts for a blanket, and three beaver hides for eight pounds of gunpowder.

Within the walls of Québec, on four acres at the corner of rue St. Paul et rue St. Sulpice, a foundation was laid for Hôtel-Dieu in 1642. It would be a secure mission hospital, operated by Jeanne Manse, an Ursuline nun and the first nurse in the new colony, administering to battle wounds and illness.

Jeanne was inspired by Father Charles Lalemont and Father Saint-Jure and readily drew the attention in Paris of charitable women committed to the new works in Québec. Among them was Angelique Faure, widow of the French Superintendent who shared Jeanne's vision. Jeanne returned to France to recruit nurses and nuns, and the Order of Religious Hospitaliers of St. Joseph was established. Fund raising continued until the stone structure began to rise many years later in 1688.

Deadly Quarantine Strikes Dissay

UNDER LOUIS XIV's stable government, there was no protection from the rampant plagues that were invading the European continent. Disease travelled by ship, port to port, village to village, and country to country.

Towns along the southern coast of France were quarantined at the first fearful sign of sickness from the Black Plague. Merchant shops were closed, trading ceased, crops were abandoned, and magistrates ordered the doors of afflicted homes locked, in an attempt to restrain its spread.

Parisians kept windows uncurtained for daily guard inspections, with each household member standing before the window to prove his health. The status of health or a death was recorded and if all the occupants perished, the home would be burned.

At Dissay, the commune was in quarantine and access to the castle prohibited. Marie-Étiennette nursed her brother in the family home at Dissay, forbidding Étienne entry lest he fall victim to the plague.

In every city, town, village, valley and countryside, families buried their kin. Slowly Mathurin regained his strength, but Marie-Étiennette was so weakened, she became another victim.

Pasquier: Patriotism of a Dissay Soldier

A PASSION about the New World continued to eat Étienne. With some urgency, he went to Bordeaux to hear more of the ships and of Rémy de Courcelles, the new Governor. He was intrigued that twenty companies of ships and men would leave France the next year.

Isaac Pasquier of Dissay told Étienne he had signed as an engagé to the La Motte Company scheduled to leave La Rochelle.

"Étienne, you should come. The Carignan regiment is looking for recruits," Isaac said, finding Étienne in his fields. "The Treaty of Pyrenees, a few years ago, liberated the regiment to take on mercantile adventures. There is fur trading and land, you just reach for it. I beseech you, my cousin, meet my friends tonight at the tavern."

Étienne debated against his instincts.

"Isaac, the land that the French take from the Iroquois is the same land the British try to take from the French. It is no different. Whether here or there, we fight under the flag."

Hours later, staring into the heavy lager, Étienne pondered this news. He looked down at his hands, calloused and scarred.

Isaac said, "There are other families from Dissay ready to leave. Gilles and Antoine Galipeau are among those signing onto the Carignan. Soon we will all be going to La Rochelle."

But Étienne didn't hear, as his eyes were far off. "I have nothing to hold me to France," he said. "Mathurin can take over the farm, and the rest of my family lies in the church courtyard. Years ago, I was married, but she didn't survive the plague. I was away in battle when the dreaded Black Death found my home and destroyed my family. The Bills of Mortality posted outside churches and hospitals are endless, yet every day I see the name of a friend or neighbor.

Original Five Pioneer Families from Dissay to New France 17ᵗʰ Century Plaque at Dissay, France. Photo Shirley Burton 2013

"The king talks of bringing boatloads of brides to the new settlements. It will be much better for you, Étienne. The New World has its own demons but they do not have the plague. Join us!"

At dawn the next morning, Étienne collected his nag and went in search of his brother. Tapping quietly on the door, he hoped Mathurin would be up. He stepped back to look at the house, built by his father's hands, and repaired with chink every year. Several years before, Mathurin had taken a wife, and two little ones were now in the loft where Étienne once slept.

Lighting the lantern, he fell asleep on the bench by the hearth, as embers still glowed from the day of cooking. Someone upstairs stirred.

Mathurin nudged him on the bench. "Your bed is upstairs, just as you left it, brother."

"No, Mathurin. This is your home and your farm. I've decided to go with La Motte Company that's preparing to sail. Tomorrow I'll travel to

La Rochelle. Life has not been good to me in France since the deaths of Patience and our stillborn child. In this very house, I am haunted by their ghosts."

"I've seen the passion burning in you, Étienne."

"My decision is firm, but my heart is wounded to leave you here in Dissay, the home of my father and mother."

The two men talked into the night over the midnight oil, entering an enlightened understanding of one another, knowing that Étienne's departure from La Rochelle would be imminent.

Looking into Mathurin's soul, Étienne saw a brief glimpse of his father. Quietly, he reached into his satchel and withdrew a metal box.

"Mathurin, this is yours now. It belongs in France. I have a story to tell you now of our grand-père and our father."

In the dimness of pre-dawn, Mathurin slowly opened the lid.

"Mon Dieu! What is this?"

"Shhh." Étienne put his finger to his lips.

"Father asked that we not want for fortune, but he gave us his own wealth, his heart and soul. Keep this a secret treasure and someday what remains may provide for your own children. It is Pasquier and belongs in France. Mother told me it was Elijah's oil."

Tears trickled down Mathurin's cheek. "You know, Étienne, I would trade this to keep you near, but I love you too much not to let you go."

Nine

Étienne Labours in Farewell to France – Confides with Toussaint Girould over Vassal Life – Serf's Birthright a Destiny of Subservience – Defensive skills required in a Barren Land – Adam Dollard des Ormeaux defends Long Sault against Iroquois – New France become a Royal Province in 1663 – King Louis XIV proposes plan with New France Intendent, Jean Talon to Recruit King's Daughters.

Étienne Pasquier's Tug of War to Leave France

THROUGH THE EARLIEST MORNING MIST, A MIDNIGHT blue riding cloak flapped in the wind, as a patriot stood at dawn on a Poitou hilltop. It was a gentleman's cape, delicately sewn in a three-quarter silk circle with gilt embroidery. Mathurin asserted that Étienne take it from father's trunk. Surveying the land from under the great gnarled oak, Étienne allowed his horse to graze nearby, then knelt by a small cross.

"My dear Patience, my golden angel, and my only son who never took even a breath of life—I fear I must take leave of you and this evil black death that consumes our country."

With his silent prayer, he bent to kiss the ground. Sighing heavily, he committed his heart; this was the day of decision. Mathurin would grow old in Dissay, his parents were buried in the church courtyard, and the prosperity of the new world burned in his desire.

His loose, sandy brown hair was drawn together in a clasp of leather, releasing a cascade of curls below his shoulders, inherited from his mother.

At this moment of struggle between his roots and destiny, Étienne welled up with pride, not only of his Pasquier heritage, but also of his Poussard ancestry.

Methodically, he stroked a narrow pointed beard that had grown long with decades of weariness, then rubbed the indented scar on his jaw, a souvenir of Italian wars. The other hand held the brim of a gentry's plumed hat, a gift from his uncle in Paris.

This was a favourite spot for Étienne, observing the horizon of Poitou, nestled in the valley north of Poitiers, and encompassing the Clain River. In the distance, were the turrets of the fifteenth century Castle of Dissay, where the Bishop of Poitiers, Pierre d'Amboise, had lorded over seigneurial lands.

The valleys below held grazing herds of cattle and roaming sheep. Scanning the lush vineyards ripening in the rising sun on the hillside, he watched Mathurin, with a hand plow and his only oxen, in view beyond the stone fence.

Mathurin looked back up, removed his Pa's ragged hat and extended a vigorous wave. It warmed Étienne's heart to see him working the beloved fields that his father endowed to them.

"Have I forsaken them? Dear Lord, I pray that you grant mercy to Mathurin and his family, give him courage and strength in battle, wisdom of his calling and protection from that over which we have no power. I leave him in your hands."

An unwiped tear trickled down Étienne's cheek. His chest was tight and he swallowed hard.

Toussaint Raphael Giroux, Linen Weaver (1633-1716)

MORE OF his friends talked of signing indentures to go to the new settlements; Toussaint Girould was one, respected by Étienne as a man of integrity and patriotic passion. Soon, the Girouxs and Godards would be leaving together from Mortagne.

From the crest of the uphill terrain to Mortagne, near Orne at Perche, Étienne saw Toussaint working far off in his pasture. The Giroux cottage, 'Bignon', was an impressive fieldstone two-story château, with a steeped tiled roof, imposing windows and plank doors. In the massive barn, bleating sheep beckoned a rescue from their shearing. The room already had mounds of wool tied in bundles, across from the weaver's carding shop and bench loom.

Hearing the approaching gallop of Étienne's steed, Toussaint stepped out of the barn with his younger brother, Thomas. He wiped his calloused hands on his apron.

Étienne called from his horse, "I wish to speak with you before your sailing."

Thomas disappeared with the aprons, leaving Toussaint alone in the paddock. They met in a firm gentleman's embrace, then stepped back to assess one another before Toussant spoke.

"Ah, bien! C'est bon, mon frère. Nous vivons dans des mains de Dieu."

Toussaint put a strong arm on Étienne's shoulder, to lead him down the footpath. He unlatched the gate, and their footsteps led to the harvest kitchen and its welcoming aromas.

Toussaint's widowed mother, Margaret Quilleron, was lifting a cauldron of rabbit stew from the hearth to the plank table that had been handcrafted by Étienne's own father. Marguerite, Toussaint's sister, placed a mound of baked bread and a slab of cheese in front of the men. Toussaint sat at the table's head with a worn, open Bible, and offered prayer for the blessing of food, friendship and strength.

"Dieu bénissent le roi."

Talking late into the night, Étienne and Toussaint enjoyed prized wines from the vineyard with Thomas and Antoine, who listened astutely and held onto every word.

"Will reformation of French feudalism be eternal? Can France and England come to an everlasting truce? My hopes are dim, Toussaint."

"Feudalism is a way of life in the new world, Étienne, but there is hope that the Jesuit influence will survive the Catholic Church. In Québec, we will rub elbows with the British and the Amerindians, as one injustice is traded for another. But there is opportunity to own large farms, and our children can look forward to freedom under that rainbow."

"Where do you plan to go in Québec?" Étienne asked.

"We have friends that settled near Montréal and others at Charlesbourg. I will go where I have promise of a deed."

"In France, peasant farmers toil as tired beasts in our fields from dawn to dusk, yet the serf's inherent birthright is a destiny of subservience. Before Louis XIV, we pledged allegiance to the King, the Roman Catholic Church, and our seigneur," Étienne expounded. "The circle of homage is unbroken."

"Over and over, my grand-père told stories of the Celtics, Pictones, Romans, Vikings and Huguenots, history that left us shrouded in scars of revolt, pillaging, plagues and famines," Toussaint said passionately. "But whatever strife was brought to bear, my ancestors held sacred to their faith."

"Since the Hundred Years' War, England and France fought barbarically with whatever weapons or tools they could find. The dominance of the two countries is tiring."

"I hear that cod banks stretch from the Atlantic coast of Newfoundland, thick enough to sink a ship. The navigation maps at the University chart ships to fortresses at Cape Breton, Montréal and Québec. From Trois Rivières inland, many settle at Charlesbourg. No battles with the English there, but I've heard of skirmishes with the natives," Étienne said.

"You must be prepared to be a fisherman, a hunter, and a trader, all of those, to survive. I have heard talk of great beasts—of bear, beaver and moose. But yes, Étienne, you are a masterful carpenter, and there's a need for that in Québec. I will have much work myself as a weaver tisserand-en-toille at Beauport. My friend, Michel Baugis, tells me it's in demand too."

"Well, if it is the favour of our King, then it must be."

Antoine's face reddened as his teeth gritted. "You both talk of free land and adventure," he retorted, "but I've listened well to stories of wounded soldiers they bring back on rotting ships. The Europeans have armed the New World natives with weapons and ammunition, and traded cheap brandies for furs. Don't you see that the French are planting the seed of decay among the natives, destroying their dignity and culture?"

Étienne replied, "Jesuits have written that the Huron and Mohawk fought shoulder-to-shoulder with the French against the British, and in turn the French defend them against the Iroquois."

"Well, I prefer to stay where I can see my enemy and not have an armed native at my back," Antoine said sardonically, hoping to end it playfully.

"Perhaps you'll change your opinion, Antoine, when I send back a prized beaver cloak for you that has been softened against the body of a friendly native. The bartered price will be a few glass beads or 'rassades', to adorn their garments along with porcupine quills," Toussaint said.

Antoine and Thomas left the room disturbed with thought, but Toussaint and Étienne talked on heartily, continuing by candlelight, telling more stories they heard from the French colonies.

Four weeks later, Toussaint Girould, a twenty-one year old linen weaver, signed as an engagé under the name of Toussaint Raphael Girou-dit-Tisserant and departed from Mortagne for Beauport. Soon after, he married Marie Godard at Notre-Dame in Montréal.[16]

Adam Dollard des Ormeaux, Hero of New France

IN THE SUMMER, on the road from Montréal to Trois-Rivières, Toussaint stopped to visit old friends at the Huron mission, and learned of the death of their heroic and great Chief Anahotaha.

"Toussaint, dear brother, we are saddened at the loss of our leader. It was vengeance that led our tribe to attack the Iroquois, but we raised the wrath of the devil," his Huron friend said.

"Yes, I heard that the Iroquois retaliated with ferocious anger."

---

[16] Toussaint Girould and Marie Godard married at Notre-Dame, Montréal, Sept. 29, 1654. Toussaint bought forty-two square perches of land from Jean Toussaint and deeded land in Fargy at Beauport, Mar. 22, 1659.

"But we had the miracle of a young lad with us, Adam Dollard des Ormeaux. It's true he was only of twenty-five years, but had the bravery of a wise man. With Anahotaha and forty of our Huron allies, Sieur des Ormeaux was forced into battle at the Long Sault[17]. He had only seventeen militia of his own, and Mitameg added six Algonkin warriors to defend as greater numbers of Iroquois attacked their fort."

"Dear brother, I know of the fortress and it would have been difficult to defend the garrison from the Iroquois," Toussaint said.

"In the moments before the final assault, one of our Huron braves escaped and viewed it from the bush. It lasted for five days, defending with only muskets, stones and old cannons. The Iroquois tomahawks, bows and arrows showed no mercy."

"Then Anahotaha and Dollard died with great courage."

"Indeed. But their beleaguered battle gave the Iroquois reason to consider the strength of French warriors, and I heard they detoured from their planned attack at Montréal," Toussaint offered. "So Dollard may have saved more lives than he knew."

Small bands of Iroquois continued to harass and ambush villages and towns isolated from the fortresses, but the mass campaign was over. The Iroquois had been forewarned of the eternal fortitude of the French.

The loss of Dollard was demoralizing to the habitants and to France. However, Louis XIV was heartened that the French spirit and culture flourished, as habitants gathered more frequently for soirées, singing and dancing. The Amerindians found it fascinating and participated eagerly.

Québec's government unfairly portrayed Hurons as inferior people, lacking in culture, and justifying the French advancement. They frequently overlooked the value of traditional native skills—even finding fire, hollowing oak stumps into canoes, or pounding corn and grain into meal. Instead, they were exploited through trading.

---

[17] Paralleled in history only to the Alamo, the bravery of Dollard in 1659 spent five days fighting to overcome 700 Iroquois. Mohawk reinforcements swooped in on the tired company on the eighth day of battle leaving no prisoners.

King Louis XIV declared New France to be a royal province in 1663, and appointed Jean Talon as Intendent two years later. Talon's priority was to bring prosperity to family life in the settlements, focused on the King's Daughters and census tabulations. Many engagés completed tenure with deeded land, but no families. Prospects for settlers demanded that new skills be acquired as craftsmen—coopers, masons, sawyers, carpenters, tinsmiths, wheelwrights, textile merchants, carvers and glass makers. The new age spurred an urgency for doctors and nurses, and nuns to host the hospitals.

The earliest settlers were bachelors and tradesmen, and later it was favourable to hire illiterate farmers who sometimes toiled without ambition, content to stay on the farm rather than take trades to merchant centres. Each habitant received from forty to a hundred and fifty livres per annum, proportionate to their skills.

Ongoing recruitment in France still sought out master tradesmen and soldiers to clear the thick woods, and searched diligently for eligible brides to send to Québec.

Many Pasquiers from around Poitiers, in Poitou, sailed as engagés and soldiers during the years of immigration of habitants—Étienne, Mery Pasquier, Jean Pasquier, Isaac Pasquier, Philippe Pasquier and others.

From the village of Dissay, five families left to join settlements in Québec; these pioneers and adventurers were Gilles and Antoine Galipeau, René Plourde, Antoine Tesserau and Étienne Pasquier.

Ten

Étienne Pasquier confers with amis over engagé contracts – Wagon along the road to La Rochelle taking eligible women to ships – Étienne Agrees to join Contingent of Five Families from Dissay – Tavern Stop-over Relieves Étienne of Royal Cape – Henriette Rousseau seeks counsel of Prefect in Paris – King's Daughters Organize with heirloom chests and dowries provided by Louis XIV – 800 girls enticement for soldiers to remain in New France – Carignan-Salières under La Motte depart LaRochelle on *L'Aigle D'Or*, 1665 – Étienne Pasquier is engagé of Robert Giffard.

La Motte and L'Aigle d'Or Sail from La Rochelle

MATHURIN RODE TO ACCOMPANY ÉTIENNE SOUTH through Poitiers and onto the Bordeaux road toward the Atlantic at La Rochelle. It was a four-day ride, stopping only for sleep and hot meals at wayside inns.

Soldiers marched on foot and wagons bumbled by, carrying frightened girls with trunks of their lives' possessions. Drivers were dispatched from the docks to pick up another group of eligible women destined for adventure.

The sun was hot and at least eight parasols waved over each wagon. Étienne's eyes were drawn to a damsel of chestnut brown hair and dark eyes, and she looked back at him with what he thought to be both fear and pleading. Continuing on his way, Mathurin teased Étienne to ask the lady for her name.

Étienne winked at his brother. "I'll marry when I have earned my land. When I get to Québec, the docks will be overflowing with fair damsels.

Toussaint Girould wrote of the King's Daughters who will surely be of the best stock able to work in the fields and bear sons. Those are the lasses that come with dowries.

"It is fortunate that we can travel from Dissay with the Galipeaus, Tesserot, and René Plourde. We'll need shelter somewhere before winter, and I hear that the snow and cold is harsh. The winds blow the sounds of the wolves and night ambush."

"Aren't you afraid?"

"Non, mon frère." Étienne's hand brushed against the deep scar on his cheek. "I have already battled the English, the Spanish and the Italians. Nothing can be worse."

It got the intended laugh from Mathurin, but Étienne knew the reality.

Light from the lanterns shone through the trees as they approached a hamlet alehouse, their last stop before La Rochelle. Rowdiness had overtaken the back corner, with a handful of soldiers drowning their sorrows in a dark lager. Étienne recognized a pair from Poitiers.

"What do you say, Mathurin? One nightcap and perhaps a weight of knowledge."

Mathurin shrugged and followed Étienne's tall frame to the corner.

"Bonjours, mes amis—I'm Étienne Pasquier of Dissay. In the morning, I intend to enlist with the Carignan at La Rochelle. Let us join you for a nightcap."

A Frenchman, with a long, dark beard and squinty eyes, pulled back his cap for a better look at Étienne. "Ah, oui, I remember you, I've seen you in Poitiers. You're the sheep farmer that brings wool to town."

"Oui, I am a sheep farmer, but I am also both a charpentier et jardinière." Étienne didn't wait for a response and continued to the pair of Carignans. "Where did you enlist? La Rochelle?"

The men all nodded.

"You won't have any trouble finding the recruitment office. A kid walks on the road toward the docks with a post about it. And that gentleman's cape won't get you any favours; it's best to sell it before you get to the Carignan office."

The squinty man shoved his hands into a pocket and threw some coins on the table. "I'll take it off your hands." He pulled at the cape and shoved the change toward him to seal the deal.

Étienne was taken aback by the abrasive move and the sudden departure of his grandfather's treasured cape. His muscles tightened, but it was not a time to make enemies. Mostly, he remembered the words his mother had said one day when she gave her warm shawl to a street urchin shivering in the street. 'God bless the man who comes in from the cold and you give him warmth.'

"Dear sir, treat it well and stay warm," Étienne offered.

The morning sun penetrated through holes in the thatched roof. The ale house garret provided sleep for eight others with them.

Surrounded by boots and hay, Étienne rose to his feet. Stooping under the slant of the ceiling, he nudged Mathurin. "The house matron is baking fresh loaves—can't you smell them?"

At the outdoor oven, others had already received some morning bread, and the Pasquier men passed the matron to find their steeds in the barn.

Étienne called out, "Bonjours, Madame. Merci beaucoup. We slept well." As he touched his hat, she stopped to wipe her hands.

"Wait only a moment," she said. Her palm was raised, then she shoved a chunk of bread and brie into a patch of burlap.

"Journey well, lads. If my sons had survived our wars, they too would be going."

Her eyes carried sadness and also wisdom of acceptance.

The King's Daughters Organize in Paris

DURING ÉTIENNE'S years of contemplation, Jean Talon, the colonial administrator for King Louis XIV negotiated the expanded immigration campaign of the King's Daughters. Recommendations were accepted from parish priests, poorhouses and orphanages, for sturdy, hardworking girls of child-bearing age, without families of their own, from Normandy and Île de France. The streets were also swept for orphans, widows, prostitutes, and criminals, to dually cleanse Paris of a dependent class of women.

Earlier groups of girls from orphanages and asylums did not have the fortitude and knowledge of farming, so later selections were more astute, with a special collection for military officers.

The crown put pressure on parishes to offer such eligible young women from all regions of France: Bourbonnais, Bretagne, Gascogne, Normandy, Picardie, and Poitou.

In the Paris 5th Arrondissement of St. Nicolas, the eleventh century Roman Catholic Abbey of Saint-Nicolas-du-Chardonnet had assisted orphans and refugees for generations. But in contrast, within view across the Porte Saint-Antoine Bridge, were the eight towers of the Bastille, housing criminals and prostitutes.

At twenty, Henriette shared a room in a boarding house near the bridge with her two sisters, Anne and Jeanne. Her parents, Jacques Rousseau and Jeanne Arnoult, had country property in Coutances, Manche in Normandy, leaving the Rousseau girls under the auspice of Saint-Nicolas Church in Paris, with hopes that they would prepare well for marriage.

Henriette and her older sister Anne were prime candidates for the King's recruitment. Having come from the family of a gentleman, the parish priest considered them a Capitaine's choice.

At eleven, Henriette had lost her father in 1657. Her mother wore black for several years, but had recently yielded to the kindness of François Bernon. He had children of his own and a home in Argent-sur-Sauldre, north of Bourges.

Life was hard in Paris for the girls. Henriette was a chambermaid in the early mornings, and worked at Madame Gauthier's seamstress shop, stitching fine work for the haberdashery, a skill considered a prized possession in Paris.

To each bridal prospect, King Louis provided an heirloom chest and a dowry from thirty to three hundred livres, dependent either on their stature or lack of it. Ships of 'filles du roi' continued routinely between 1663 and 1673, often with marriages within days or weeks of disembarkation.

The prospect drew the interest of the Rousseau girls, but Henriette was tormented between her loyalty and her desire to see the new world. She hoped that if she went, her mother would remarry before she left.

As soldiers and habitant farmers in Québec greatly outnumbered unmarried women, men were beginning to return to France. King Louis XIV's plan was accelerated, to send eight hundred girls, and news of the arrival of the King's Daughters became an enticement to stay.

With ships leaving soon, Henriette couldn't delay her decision. On a rainy spring morning, she slipped out of the rooming house with her bonnet tight over her long locks. With her brolly, she scurried through the slippery, cobbled streets toward the spires of the Church.

Ahead was rue des Bernadis, where it converged with rue Saint Victor. Stepping through the main doors, she sighed and amassed new courage. With formalities, she went directly to a confessional booth for a priest.

"Father Prefect, my heart is burdened. It's whether to accept fate in the new world or continue my obligation to Madame Gauthier. I have two more years in my agreement with her."

"My dear child, you have struggled in Paris for many years now. The King has made a generous offer to women such as yourself. I cannot tell you what your soul already knows."

"Will you grant me forgiveness if I leave my employer without her agreement, and leave my family in Normandy?"

"Talk to Madame Gauthier. I know her as a compassionate woman, and she's always been ready to help with refugees when they have no place to go. You underestimate her reaction."

A long pause ensued for Henriette to digest his wisdom.

"Father Prefect, will you bless me as I turn my back on my country, and follow the wishes of our King?"

"Of course, Henriette. I knew your parents for many years; they married in this very church. It was difficult for them, when the economy of Paris faltered and the noblesse found homes beyond the city walls. Jacques Rousseau would wish a better life for you than working night and day to subsist."

The Prefect stopped, to sense her reaction.

"Thank you for telling me, Father."

"Go dear child. You are in the hands of God. It is assured that you will seek a fine Frenchman, and I pray a thriving family of your own in Québec."

With an unburdened heart, Henriette barely noticed the spitting skies. Grief and worry was giving way to anticipation and a joyous song in her heart.

> Now when the sun says good-day to the mountains
> And the night says hello to the dawn
> I'm alone with my dreams on the hilltop…
> Quand le soleil dit bonjour aux montagnes
> Je suis seule, je ne veux penser qu'a toi.

La Motte Sails with the Carignan-Salières

ÉTIENNE WALKED down the planks to the army's enlistment room, breathing the salt air from the Bay of Biscay. Above him, gulls circled over the port of La Rochelle, calling in unison as if to him. His leather bag carried his worn Bible and few other possessions, as his life was otherwise packed for the new world in the shipping trunk.

As Mathurin secured the wagon and horses, Étienne hired a boy to drag his belongings to the pier. Stowed in the wooden trunk were his father's carpentry tools, some seed, warm clothing and his battle bayonet.

Stretching tall at the desk, Étienne signed his name in servitude to the Carignan-Salières, to the Company of La Motte, and the King of France, under the red and blue flag with a white cross in the middle.

The Carignan was named after Colonel Thomas François de Savoie, the Prince of Carignan, who proudly raised the flag in 1644 at Piedmont in Italy.

Seven ships were dispatched to the new colony before La Motte's posting, an Étienne had the fortune to be assigned with his cousin Isaac Paquet aboard *L'Aigle d'Or.*

Pride surged as he received issue of the official uniform of the Carignan: a flintlock musket with bayonet, powder horn and pouch of black powder, gloves and a side sword.

Officer and Men of the Carignan-Salieres Regiment
Artist Charles William Jeffreys, 1868-1951. Library and Archives Canada

His farm-weathered hands fingered the brown and grey uniform and his new neatly-pressed, ruffled, white shirt, then a black, wide-brimmed slouch hat of felt, with a narrow chin strap, and black leather buckled shoes, knee socks and britches to hold them up.

With his own clothing in a sack, Étienne stood smartly in the uniform and walked with others to join the parade on the main deck. Clenching the rough, planked handrail, greasy from sea algae, he steadied his foothold. The stench of garbage and dead fowl on the pier was a test of endurance, and a picnic to the bold seagulls, diving and scouring near his feet.

With his comrades, Jean de Roy, Pierre Brunet and Antoine Bazinet, Étienne marched to the great wharf, beyond the three fortress towers. The impenetrable walls of St. Nicolas and the Chain Towers stood on each side of the harbour entrance, and the ramparts of the medieval Lantern Tower rose in their roles to protect La Rochelle from invasion from the Atlantic.

A fishing village from the tenth century, La Rochelle had already been an important port and a trade route to England, Spain and Africa for goods, the likes of salt and wines, and at one time served as a slave trading port, smuggling Africans to labour on ships.

Étienne looked up to the turrets of the St. Nicolas Tower, recalling stories that prisoners of war had been held there in the Seige of La Rochelle in 1628 when King Louis VIII and Cardinal Richelieu suppressed the protestant movement.

With heartache, Étienne signed away his life, his blood and his sweat to Monsieur Giffard of the New World.

King Louis XIV promised an annual pension to new habitant families if they raised large families. Three hundred livres to be granted for families with ten or more children, and an additional one hundred livres when the family increased to twelve children. Each land grant provided four arpents wide and forty arpents long, in strips emanating from the central compound to form a circular pattern. Restrictions were placed on eligible bachelors, barring them from hunting, fishing and trading.

Étienne secretly envisioned his land, his farm, his wife, and children in Charlesbourg. In the distance, he looked back at Mathurin and waved, hoping he'd be seen. The men filed the plank to board.

With a final look back, he saw Mathurin wave. He knew this would be the last time. Lowering himself into the ship, he allowed the sea air to fill his lungs. He was ready to see Québec.

On May 13, 1665, *L'Aigle D'Or*, meaning 'golden eagle', set sail under Captain Sieur de Villepars. The regiments of Grandfontaine, La Frederie, Salières and La Motte travelled together, accompanied by the freighter, *La Paix*.

Twenty-four companies under the command of General Alexandre de Prouville, the Marquis of Salières, sailed on the four hundred ton *L'Aigle D'Or*. The fluted ship, with three masts, two bridges and an arsenal, was built at Brest, and set with arms at Brouage in 1664. Loaded with crew and supplies, the ship drafted at twelve feet.

La Motte company, commanded by Captain Pierre de St. Paul and 1st Lieutenant Philippe de Carrion, was comprised of Étienne Pasquier, Antoine Bazinet, Louis Bolduc, Jean Bricault, Pierre Hudon, Jean Soucy, Jean-Vincent Chamaillard, Germain Gauthier, Jean Laspron, François LeRoy, Hilaire Limousin, Honore Martel, Pierre Menard, Philippe Defresnoy Carion, Antoine Forester, René LeMeunier, Eustache Prevost, Jean René, Jean Roy, Isaac Pasquier dit Lavallee from Dissay, and others.

Étienne recalled reading *Relation des Jésuites*, as Father Paul Le Jeune described the fears of the New France pioneers and their sacrifices:

> 'To leave one's parents and friends, to abandon one's acquaintances, to leave one's sweet homeland and its traditions, to cross the seas, to defy the Ocean and its storms, to sacrifice one's life to suffering, to leave behind all present belongings, in order to throw oneself blindly forward for the sake of distant hopes, to convert the traffic of the earth into that of the heavens, to want to die in Barbary, is a language that is not spoken in the school of nature; and yet, these are the actions and the language of a thousand people of merit, who deal with the affairs of New France with as much courage, if not more, as they would with the affairs of the Old (France).'

Back in Paris, Henriette Rousseau was watching the Bastille from her fourth floor window of a stone tenement in the shadows of the St. Nicolas Tower.

Packing silken finery in the trunk that the Prefect had sent, her head filled with dreams of the future, wondering about the man who would become her husband. In the imaginations of Henriette and Anne, their lives were about to take on a wonderful, romantic adventure.

They understood the incentives and motivation for both male and female French migrants, with bonuses paid to men under twenty selecting a bride, and to girls who wed before sixteen. On the marriage ceremony, the girls would receive fifty livres if they chose a soldier or a farmer, or one hundred if they opted for an officer.

Eleven

L'Aigle D'Or at Sea Endures Three Months at Sea – Cramped Dank Quarters, Rules & Regulations – Québec Harbour in Sight – Days of Unloading Cargo at Charlesbourg – Soldiers met by Huron scouts – Mission of Fortification of Jesuit Missions – Overland Winter Trek into hostile Iroquois territory – Carignan attacked by Mohawks – 400 soldiers completed their 3-year engagé contracts – 1668 King Louis XIV recalls Carignan regiment to France – Many soldiers return to France included numerous wounded soldiers – Étienne Pasquier accepts offer of compensation & rations to stay at Charlesbourg.

One Hundred and Ten Days at Sea

FOR MOST OF THE HUNDRED AND TEN GRUELING DAYS, *L'Aigle D'Or* feared shipwreck as the ocean battered the creaking hull. Étienne yearned for days when the rain might abate and the seas would become calm. On rare clear mornings, he went up on top to search for a sign of the horizon beyond the waters. On the deck, the salt wind stung his sunburned face, but only reinforced his spirit as he anticipated his new life.

Onboard rules were strict, and everyone knew that any nature of disrespect was punishable. All aspects of life were there, as the Carignan-Salières regiment had enlisted men from criminals to labour, each taking shifts to man the oars when sails were insufficient.

Étienne found the basic rules to be easy enough: if you don't bring your mug, you won't get rations; be on time for prayer or lose rations; miss a watch and lose a full day's rations.

The crew witnessed the punishment of one poor sot, caught stealing a silver match box from an officer and losing fifteen days of ration. Another lad caught dysentery and defecated on the gangway, paid for by fifty lashes tied to the cannons. Étienne saw that it was Jean-Baptiste of Normandy, and as the man weakened and fell to the ground, Étienne stepped forward to take the man's final twenty lashes. The request was granted.

After supper as dusk settled in, Étienne joined Isaac Pasquier, sitting on the soggy deck with his back to the rails. "Memories of Dissay and those we left behind become sweeter each day. So I am glad to travel with kin, my dear cousin."

"Oui, Étienne," Isaac said. "I no longer remember the plague, nor the battle, but I well picture in my mind the cornfields and green pastures."

On that evening, smoking pipes and dancing on the quarterdeck was permissible.

"See, Isaac! The stars lead us to home, whether it be at Dissay or a Québec settlement. The Italian astronomer, Galileo, mapped our constellation, and Newton's Law of Motion helps us calculate our progress on the waters. In France, we marvel at inventions and explorations, and although we're leaving behind us the progress of Europe, we become part of the exploration, creating a new history," Étienne said.

"Oui, but the discoveries of the sky belong to everyone. It's far too big to be claimed by Italy." The two roared heartily and puffed their pipes.

The wind, reborn in the darkness, purged itself into a gale, and the night crew slept on deck to be ready to jump to the whims of the sails. Étienne threw his full body weight into pulling the great ropes, lest the slightest release cause a masthead to break. On this night, like others, several sailors were lost overboard into the murky guts of the Atlantic.

Sunset always brought dread to passengers confined to the bowels of the vessel. Thin canvas slings were anchored to iron rings in rows three tiers high. Soldiers remained in these cramped quarters until dawn, when the hatch was released and they rose to daylight.

The dank ship's hold carried a musty stench from the stores of rationed, rotting potatoes, and three months at sea left the sailors weak and malnourished, some now suffering effects of scurvy.

Bells and drums signaled the time to rise from the pitch black of the hold. Mornings began in prayer on deck, followed by breakfast, gnashing on hard sea biscuits with stale Bordeaux, never enough to fill a hungry belly.

The evening meal was a meagre feast of biscuits, wine, and measured portions of peas or broad beans, dolled from a large cauldron. Those that were weak and ill had salt fish, chicken or mutton from the Captain's stores. Special meals were served to ship's officers, docteur, any chaplains or nuns, or merchants having paid passage of 150 livres.

Since the sighting of seagulls the previous day, the soldiers and crew had new life, with renewed chatter and vigour.

Étienne climbed high to the crow's nest, extending his spyglass telescope. Fixed on a rocky shore rising toward the red bluffs of Québec on the skyline, he saw the mouth of the St. Lawrence that seemed to him to be ready to swallow their ship. Giant, icy mountains rose out of the sea, the likes of which the crew had never seen.

"Those are bergs, with a treacherous reach of deadly ice below the tip of their glory," the Captain blustered, always delighting the crew with his boisterous laugh. "We will steer away but if any man can sink one, he'll dine at my table tonight." The men howled in laughter and celebration.

Volleys of musket fire chipped away at the iceberg, at last breaking a small floe. The Captain and his crew were sufficiently entertained and invited several men to feast that evening.

Étienne Pasquier's Arrival at Charlesbourg

BOTH SHIPS, *La Paix* and *L'Aigle d'Or*, dropped longboats to fish on the cod banks, enhancing their dwindling food supply. The cod was laid on a canvas blanket across the bow to be dried and salted before packing in the barrels. The catch was plentiful and the crew savoured the sweet taste of cod with peas and wine that evening.

The oars directed them to the north shore port of Québec at the convergence of the Saint-Charles River. On August 18, 1665, *L'Aigle d'Or* arrived at Charlesbourg, with *La Paix* a day behind.

An emerald backdrop of glades of pine and fir climbed above the rocks, with a stunning kaleidoscope of autumn colour blanketing the Laurentian hills. Fall foliage displayed unspeakable glory as the yellow afternoon sun projected itself on crimson sugar maples, burnt walnut, amber oaks, elms, and golden birch.

Beyond the palisades of Québec lay sunny cornfields, wild vineyards, and terraces of long cultivated farmlands. Montmorency Falls, a few miles east of Charlesbourg, was a natural monument itself, muffled by the thundering of green waters over magnificent cliffs, then transformed into majesty of spray and foam.

Étienne watched navy galleons and frigates resting in the bay, as French corsairs and merchant trading ships waited their turns in the harbour, with riggings taut and masts furled with the fleurs-de-lis.

It was still the season for large rafts and barges, fishing boats, steamers, and skiffs to be vying for anchor near the merchant piers. The great wooden docks moaned, as heavy hemp ropes cast anchor at the deep water wharf.

Carefully folded, the brass and leather sextant was returned into its small wooden casing and returned safely to the Officers' Quarters.

In haste, the Captain bellowed out from the ship's helm, "Open the belly of this ship's hold and lay the planks."

The seamen opened the hold to begin letting animals find freedom from their confines.

"Yes, sir, here come the oxen . . . and now sheep and cattle. But they can barely stand from their cramped quarters and meagre rations." The soldiers knew only enough meal, hay, or moldy oats and water to survive had been provided.

"Herd them to the docks," the Captain said.

With bleating and neighing, the livestock obliged. The rancid smell revolted the stomachs of the dockworkers. A Huron scouting party was ready to give cedar bark tea from a cauldron to strengthen their bellies and treat scurvy.

Étienne held out his ration cup for a hearty dose of tea letting the medicinal aroma fill his nostrils and invade his lungs.

Pulleys hoisted crates of artillery and munitions from the innards of the ship to the dock, where heavy cannons, flanked by regiment guides, rolled down the gangplank. Next came sacks of potato and corn seed, coffee, sugar, and bales of blankets for the trading posts. Wagons came from within, carrying kegs and barrels of salt, salt-pork, dried cod, and cases of tools, hand ploughs, and farming implements. The soldiers laboured into the next day, until the ship listed in empty respite.

Townsfolk and merchants lined the lower docks, hoping to see a familiar and friendly face from France. Others waited, eager for the deck master to hire them to haul storehouse goods up to the habitation, or to load the outgoing vessel, for a few coins.

They were not the first Carignan-Salières in Québec, as several months before, four companies had arrived in June 1665. Hardships of winter took a toll, then they faced the marauding Iroquois, who didn't fight in an offensive line like the British. Instead, they attacked by ambush in the woods, in canoe convoys from the rivers, and with arrows in the forest.

After a few days' rest, the Commanding Officer, Henri de Chastelard de Salières, ordered the soldiers to load the vessel with barrels of salted cod and bales of pelts of bearskin, beaver, caribou, and fine mink and fox furs. The ship was recalled to La Rochelle soon after with its full recruit, including stowaway rats, and a dismal passenger list of returning and wounded soldiers, some Jesuits, and a handful of discontented habitants.

When *L'Aigle D'Or* pulled away from the dock, the listing hull of an earlier Carignan ship was scaffolded, ready for repairs to its rotting boards. Settlements around the habitation offered charpentiers to do the work, including Paul Chalifour and his father-in-law Jacques Archambault.

Québec had an immediate need for fortification on its trade routes and to build bastions on the Richelieu River, to forewarn and defend the settlements. Fort Chambly had been completed the previous year, with more amibitious plans underway by the Governor, Daniel de Remy de Courcelles.

The enlistment campaign continued through the late 1660s until King Louis XIV recalled the regiments. Over four hundred soldiers completed their three-year terms of service and remained in Québec awaiting the arrival of the King's Daughters.

With the growing demand for brides, matrons from an upper class Québec family were selected by Jean Talon, the Intendant of New France, who also recruited noblesse women in Paris to organize suitable girls.

La Motte Company received an official military inspection on arrival, and pledged allegiance to France. Each soldier lined up to receive an issue of a flintlock musket and a pouch of gunpowder. Oxen, yoked to wagons loaded with tools and munitions, were led on foot to the garrisons at Charlesbourg, west of Beauport in the Richelieu valley.

First Winter in Québec for the Carignan

AFTER FOUR months of winter preparation, the Carignan was ready to regain strength in their sea legs for an overland trek.

"Soldiers of the Carignan, it is time you travel through dangerous Iroquois territory," the commander of *L'Aigle D'Or* ordered. "You will be led by Huron guides. Leave your trunks and burdens here to lighten your travel, as each man must carry a portion of the rations and supplies."

Isaac whispered to Étienne, "I heard news of massacres and merciless random attacks along our route."

"Yes, we must always keep up our guard," Étienne replied. "Settlers from settlements on the Richelieu River will join us in combat during the Indian uprisings. They have no choice, it is the king's command."

Étienne hoisted his leather sack to tie to his back.

"We will come to a Jesuit mission soon," Isaac said. "There, we'll rebuild the Regiment's fortresses that were destroyed in Iroquois offences, and replace our fallen soldiers."

"Then it's a good thing we are carpenters from Dissay," Étienne joked.

Walls and forts were erected around Jesuit missions during the winter, before they turned back and began to clear their own farms.

Fieldstone was cleared from the terrain, for masons to build churches at Notre-Dame, and leave the soil cultivated for spring seeding. With winter near, they stockpiled firewood, scavenged for berries and roots, and dried carcasses of meat and fish. Their food supplies would be rationed, as the threat of scurvy would come like the north wind.

With both courage and trepidation, Étienne fought as part of La Motte's company against the Iroquois and Mohawk tribes in the winter of

1665-1666. The Governor was alerted that the soldiers were ill-prepared, without snowshoes, ice picks, shovels, or warm clothing.

Nevertheless, Étienne's unit was sent at the end of a freezing January. Travelling in a group of five hundred soldiers, two hundred habitants, and a loyal troop of natives, they marched for three weeks into the wilderness. Étienne's feet were numb with frost yet he trekked onward with his unit.

The Huron scout that preceded them returned to them from Schenectady with alarm.

"The Mohawk village near the Anglo-Dutch settlement has been viciously attacked. It was bloody with many scalps taken. The woods ahead breathe with angry warriors."

Étienne's troop secured themselves under brush and thickets covered by snow, and the Huron scouts swept away their footprints to a smooth surface.

"They are clever—they fly with the wind and call with the birds. You cannot see them but they are near," the scout warned.

Within an hour, a pack of sixty Mohawk warriors stepped from the woods in a rowdy surprise, attacking the regiment with hit-and-run agility. Feet from Étienne, a marauding Iroquois warrior leaped in silence in midair, about to swoop down on Jean Bricault as he reloaded his musket. In the instant, Étienne was forced to a choice between fear and bravery and brought him down with his axe.

Returning to Saint-Louis Forts, the limping French troops left more than four hundred graves in the woods and brought back more wounded than the surgeon could see. Gangrene from frozen feet left many crippled for life.

By spring 1668, a majority of the Carignan-Salières soldiers returned to France, but Étienne remained committed, accepting one hundred livres and a year of rations as enticement to stay. He bonded into his community at Bourg Royale with his acquaintances from France.

Jacques Archambault still teased, "Just you wait, Étienne. There will be a fine damsel for you from the King."

Twelve

La Motte's troops at Fort Ste. Anne under Iroquois Attack – Wachinksapa, Huron Guide and translator – Pasquier Learns Skills of the Woods – Étienne Pasquier completes tenure with Giffard, 1666 – Jean Talon holds first Census at Charlesbourg, 1666 – Pasquier is deeded land at Petite Auvergne – King orders construction of Saint Gabriel Manor – Three ships commissioned to carry King's Daughters from France, 1668 – King's Daughters at Sea – Henriette Rousseau taken ill aboard ship – Simeon LeRoy takes his bride, Claude Blandina DesChalets, 1668 – Étienne waits & watches and agrees to contract with Françoise Barbary – Contract Annulled – Étienne Pasquier attends at Saint-Gabriel to court Henriette Rousseau.

Carignan-Salières Depend on Huron Scouts

WITH FACES REDDENED BY FROSTBITE, THE SALIÈRES snapped to attention and saluted in unison to await instruction. "We have day scouts, fortress guard positions and a night watch. Each of you will take turns," ordered Monsieur de Courcelles.

"Yes, sir." The volume of their unison pleased de Courcelles.

Étienne joined three hundred of La Motte's troops at the fortress at Ste. Anne on the Richelieu River, supported by Hurons who allied with the French to defend Québec and Montréal from the Iroquois attacks.

Étienne was attached to join a Huron scout to search the surrounding area for Iroquois movement. Wachinksapa knew broken English from the Jesuits, and between spoken word and hand signals, they bonded quickly, perceptive of the other's actions and stealthy in their investigations.

Étienne was respectful in his need to learn, and appealed to his friend, "Wachinksapa, teach me your skills of the woods."

The Huron grinned with his finger to his lips, and whispered, "Shhh. No sound. Mark your trail as I do, so you will know the direct path of retreat. Silence is your best partner."

The Huron man crouched low to the ground. He waited and listened, then motioned to Étienne to hide behind a tree.

"Someone comes." He placed an arrow in his bow.

Étienne had seen the Iroquois during raids on the fort, and braced himself for the marauding natives.

"Must be just like battle with the English," he whispered to himself. Loading a volley into his musket, he raised it to his shoulder, watching for his unseen target.

Eventually, a white shadow came into sight in the thick ahead. A chorus of birds took flight, with flaps and cries proclaiming a disruption. Sounds of thrashing continued to approach, then increased to heavy plodding.

"Ah bien, Étienne. It is only a lost oxen," Wachinksapa whispered without rising from his crouch. "We'll wait to see if he has been sent to expose us, or if it has only lost its way."

The beast moved within a few yards of Étienne and rambled on.

"Shall we take it back to the fort to toil?" Étienne asked.

Fortified by Hurons and peasant farmers, the Carignan advanced southward on foot under de Courcelles and Sieur de Tracy. Huron guides forged ahead diligently for vantage points, returning before dawn to sketch maps on the beach sand.

Étienne's adrenaline heightened as they crawled through the wooded riverbanks parallel to their boats that drifted in silence along the shore. He paralyzed himself at any sound—the cracking of a branch, a whistle of ambush signals in the pines, or the hoot of an owl.

Wachinksapa will not always be my guide, but if I can learn to think like a native, I will know when to expect an ambush.

He lowered his head to the ground to listen for vibrations.

Descending on the Iroquois, La Motte's company was seven hundred strong, thought to be sufficient, knowing that the Indians would not fight with battle lines.

Suddenly, with furtive cunningness, bows and arrows, tomahawks, and muskets came from all sides, and painted faces, emblazoned with daunting fierceness, closed in on their prey with curdling war cries.

Étienne felt surges between courage and the urgency of survival as he fired his rifle again and again. The time to reload seemed an eternity, and in one of those moments, he was overtaken by a lunging brave, swinging a tomahawk into his shoulder.

Searing pain flooded his body, and he raised his rifle's bayonet to wrest the life of the young brave. War meant one life or the other.

Many were lost that day on both sides, but the strength and numbers of the Carignan claimed victory. Medics cleansed their wounds with liquor rations and bandaged the injured, and those that couldn't walk were loaded into bateaux. Étienne, weakened from loss of blood, had his wound sewn, then packed with a poultice and bound in strips of cloth. With a sling, he joined the foot troops back to Fort Ste. Anne.

Winter in Ste. Anne was bitter as expected, and brought widespread hunger and sickness. Étienne was content with a straw bed in the corner of a one room cabin, crammed with soldiers.

With fever and weakness, he couldn't find strength in his legs and was taken to the Jesuits for healing; by the grace of God, he was soon on his feet again to do small chores. Supplies came by river, but when access routes to the fort succumbed to ice, their stocks depleted, and disease and scurvy became the enemy rather than the Iroquois.

In the spring, Étienne travelled to the seigneurie at Charlesbourg and completed his indenture as manor jardinier. The new task was an honour to him, designing and cultivating gardens for Seigneur Giffard who held an upper class ranking among feudal lords.

Jean Talon's 1666 census of Charlesbourg, recorded 3,125 habitants, showing Étienne as unmarried, as a jardinière voluntaire, residing near his friends Toussaint Girould and Marie Godard and their four children. The same enumeration recorded Zacharie Cloutier and Xantes Dupont, Olivier Charbonneau and Marie Garnier, Urbain Tessier dit LaVigne and Marie Archambault, Jean LeRoy, Vincent Cloutier, Jean Guyon, Mathurin Roy and Marguerite Bire from Aunis, Paul Chalifour and Jacquette Archambault from Aunis.

1666 Census of Charlesbourg (list of unmarried inhabitants):
1. Étienne Pasquier – 45, jardinière voluntaire
2. Philipes Guyon – 34, voluntaire
3. Antoine Chevasse – 30, voluntaire
4. Simon Chauvert – 30
5. Jean Jouy – 45, habitant
6. Nicolas Matte – 26, habitant
7. René Bruneau – 22, tisserand en toile, habitant
8. Jean Tiberge – 25, mueniere habitant marie en france
9. Bertrand Coutois – 21, habitant
10. Jean Lauson – 24, voluntaire

At last, Étienne was deeded a large plot of land on Seigneurie de Petite Auvergne. A few miles west of Charlesbourg, the farm rested on the bank of the Saint-Charles River, beside the seigneurie road that connected the waterway to the inland feudal fields.

From first daylight, he worked the rough land to clear the trees, burn stumps and fertilize the soil from ashes and fish remains. For three years as an engagé, he laboured, reaping crops of peas, beans, squash, corn and wheat. Although the harvests were meagre, he earned his land a few lots east of the Jesuit seminary in the farm neighbourhood of the Belangers, Montels, and Roussels.

Henriette Rousseau Arrives as King's Daughter

IN 1665, shiploads of livestock had arrived, with the horses needed to speed the clearing of land and increase crop output.

The natives had never seen a horse before 1647 and referred to them as the 'Moose of France'. The Governor intended for every farmer to have at least one.

Wars between the French and the Iroquois continued with a vengeance through winter 1666. The Carignan moved south under Commander Prouville, destroying native crops and villages, and in 1667, the defeated tribes relented to a peace treaty. This was good news to France, as the recruitment of unwed women was showing success.

Louis XIV ordered construction of a large estate near Fort Pointe-à-Callière, named Saint-Gabriel, with manor houses, barns, and gardens. It was run by nuns, with Mother Marie de l'Incarnation coordinating the dispatch of arriving brides. The land oversaw the banks of the St. Lawrence, with thirty acres of arable land. Selected brides were invited to move to the country house to prepare them to be good wives, learning all aspects of farming and foraging.

The French monarchy commissioned three new ships to be crafted and launched at Toulon in spring 1668. These grand vessels, the Royal Louis, Dauphin Royale, and Monarque, would transport the King's Daughters, but were also fitted to forge battle at sea, each armed with more than a hundred guns.

On the maiden voyage of one of these ships, the Rousseau sisters travelled to Québec, including Henriette. King Louis ordered suitable quarters on board to accommodate women of class. From a shared cabin with Anne and two other women, Henriette had a glimpse of the swells of the ocean, and fresh air when the wooden slatted window was open.

Henriette was raised to be charitable and compassionate, with no qualms about taking over assignments of the weaker girls, as society's class distinctions from France applied equally at sea, even to menial duties of scrubbing decks and peeling potatoes. On a blustery morning in the third week, Anne found Henriette, in her crinolines, on her knees, scrubbing seagull poop from the captain's deck.

"Dearest Henriette, here you are. I've looked high and low for you. You missed breakfast, you know," Anne said. "I hid a biscuit in my skirt pocket for you. Here, you must eat something or you'll be the one that is faint."

"Thank you dear sister. At sea for so long, I've had time to read my Bible and contemplate my place before God as we near an unknown land. Papa taught us to be benevolent. Geneviève was taken from an orphanage in poor health. This work has been too grueling for her."

"The Captain can assign another able body," Anne insisted.

"I don't do this for the Captain," Henriette said. Closing her eyes for a moment, she recited, "And as yet would that men should do to you, do ye also likewise." She reached to Anne for help to get up. "I do it because God commands me."

"You stand and eat, and I will take Geneviève's place. Your face is burning already from the morning sun—go and take fresh water."

Relenting, Henriette stood on wobbly feet and went for rest, feeling the weakening effects of sun stroke.

Henriette's place was again empty at the dinner table, and Anne returned to the cabin with a bowl of watery stew with boiled potatoes.

One of the nuns attended to Henriette lay prone on her bed. "Dear, what is the complication?" The nun leaned to distinguish her incoherent mumbles, and touched her blue lips. "Tell me what you feel."

"The sea is rolling in my head and my ears are painful inside, as if my head will explode."

Sister Marie dispatched Anne for a basin of water to cool Henriette's burning forehead. She still hadn't opened her eyes. The nun patiently dabbed water on Henriette's face, neck and forehead until the redness of her skin began to fade.

"Henriette, you are weak, but you must sit and sip on tea and some broth. The tea is specially made for nausea and will help to fortify you."

Anne stayed at her side for the next two days only leaving for meals and tea, and the nun returned every few hours. Reading from her treasured book of poems, Anne recited all fourteen verses of Remy Belleau's song of April until slumber came to them both.

April, pride of woodland ways, Of glad days,
April, bringing hope of prime, To the young flowers that beneath
Their bud sheath Are guarded in their tender time;

April, pride of fields that be Green and free,
That in fashion glad and gay, Stud with flowers red and blue,
Every hue, Their jewelled spring array;

April, pride of murmuring Winds of spring,
That beneath the winnowed air, Trap with subtle nets and sweet
Flora's feet, Flora's feet, the fleet and fair;

Three days later, Henriette gathered enough strength to walk on the deck. Young Blandina DesChalet, leaning on the rails with Claude Decheurenville, stopped Henriette to speak about a matter.

Blandina, a seventeen-year-old orphan from the parish of Notre-Dame de Fortenay-le-Comte, was on board with two of her sisters, all hopeful to find husbands in Québec. Claude was twenty-two, born in the same parish as Henriette.

"My dear Henriette, you are so pale. I've known of your illness and prayed for you. I'm delighted to see you on your feet again at last," Blandina said.

"Thank you, Blandina. Yes, I'm gaining new strength finally and they say the sea air is good for my lungs." She laughed. "Is that true or just reason to get me outside? Did I hear that someone has spotted land in the distance?"

Claude interjected, "You are such an optimist, Henriette. There hasn't been sight of a land bird or warm water sea life. Nothing to give us hope."

"Claude, we all have hope. I heard that the Captain spied another ship on our same course. Just a few more days, I feel, then we can parade down the walkway in our finery and parasols and pick our husbands as if we were marveling over a candy jar."

"Perhaps we will even recognize soldiers from our own provence," Blandina chipped in.

"Oh, yes!" Henriette giggled. "We'll look out for them."

Waiting for a Bride, 1668

THE NEWS spread rapidly in September 1668 of ships arriving in Charlesbourg, and that others were enroute to Montréal. Eager habitants still outnumbered the few dozen new women by a ratio of six to one.

The King's Daughters were dressed in fine taffeta, hooped skirts, petite coats and crinolines, silk blouses with pearl beads and lace, and couturiers' French bonnets, with powdered curls and ringlets framing porcelain faces.

Jean Talon and François de Montmorency-Laval await arrival of King's Daughters in Québec in 1667. Painting by Eleanor Fortescue-Brickdale (1872-1945). ⑨

Prospective husbands vied for first glimpses of the women at the docks. Eligible men waited with hats in hand, and the impatient ones vaulted to the boardwalk.

Étienne attempted to move to the front of the jostling throng. Rugged men converted on the spot into gentlemen suitors, pairing off with their best efforts at charm and chivalry, and as the crowd dissipated, the remaining girls were taken by carriage to the nunnery.

Simeon LeRoy[18], a carpenter from Créances in Manche, the same region as the Rousseau family, was smitten at first sight by the lively Claude Blandina DesChalet[19] from Maillezais, Vendée, Poitou, who arrived with her orphaned sisters, Madeleine and Elizabeth.

The girls were taken to quarters at Saint-Gabriel, where suitors could be interviewed. If a girl's French parentage were known to established habitants, she would be taken in as a boarder. The royal treasury paid for

---

[18] Simeon LeRoy, born Oct. 1, 1637, at St. Trinity, Créances, son of Richard LeRoy and Gillette Jacquet of Créances, Manche, Normandy.

[19] Claude Blandina DesChalets, born 1651, Poitou, France; married Simeon LeRoy on Sept.3, 1668, at Notre-Dame, Charlesbourg, Québec.

their food and lodging expenses until an agreement was made with an eligible bachelor. A notary then prepared a contract with the ensuing marriage to take place within thirty days.

In October 1668, the last ship before winter arrived, and Étienne was dockside, hoping for a bride. More than five hundred maidens had found husbands and settled around Québec, and Étienne felt greater urgency to find a wife.

A few dozen women stood at the ship's rail, each hoping that her groom would be at hand, but prepared for the pain of rejection. Étienne, in his elaborate French waistcoat, pantaloons and plumed hat, searched the railing.

Henriette Rousseau reflected a graceful poise, and Étienne's head turned to admire her grey-blue eyes, her milk-white complexion, and the chestnut curls set along her forehead.

But it was vivacious Françoise, the négresse daughter of a master florist Rollain Barbery from Paris, who slipped her arm into Étienne's. He was charmed by her confidence, her creamy brown complexion, flashing brown eyes and the sway of her skirts and crinolines. When he turned back, he had lost sight of Henriette in the crowd.

Soon after, Étienne and Françoise agreed and signed a marriage contract in front of the notary Leconte on October 9, 1668. When the couple waivered, the contract was annulled the following month.

Meanwhile, Anne Rouseau accepted the proposal of another Carignan soldier, Pierre Jouineau, and they married at Notre-Dame in Montréal.

Courtship of Étienne & Henriette

ÉTIENNE HADN'T forgotten the instant he'd noticed Henriette on the platform that first day. His eyes followed her refined features as she gestured her hand for assistance of a suitor to steady her footing and carry her parasol. As Françoise had drawn his eyes away, a Carignan officer reached from behind Étienne and seized Henriette, swooping her away.

Curious about the girl from Normandy, Étienne strolled often outside the Saint-Gabriel boarding house[20] in Québec where she'd been billeted. Each time, he hoped for a glimpse of the chestnut curls.

A few weeks later, as Étienne passed by the Nuns House, he stopped and tipped his hat to several of the women in the garden. At forty-six, he was handsome with his dark brown hair carrying an insistent wave, and clean-shaven, directly from the barber.

Near the stone fence, Henriette pruned some thorny bushes, with a basket of flowers and garden herbs over her arm. Her bonnet fell to her shoulders and curly wisps brushed across her cheeks. When she raised her hand to brush the curls aside, she left a smudge of dirt from her gloves.

Étienne nervously touched his hat and lowered his head without leaving her eyes. 'Bonjour, Mademoiselle," his voice cracked.

"Bonjour, Monsieur. It is a beautiful day for gardening." She shyly raised a white daisy to sniff the fragrance.

"Do you like gardening, Mademoiselle?" Étienne thought it to be a suitable starter.

"Ah, oui. I grew up in Normandy and loved to walk on the beaches, gathering shells from sand dunes, and running in fields, collecting daisies and buttercups. My family moved to Saint-Germain, near Paris, when I was a child. My name is Henriette Rousseau. Please call me Henriette."

"Merci, Henriette. I am Étienne Pasquier from Dissay, south of Paris."

"I know of the town, not far from the University of Poitiers. Did you come from a large family?" She removed the basket and set it on the lawn.

"Would you like to take a stroll, Henriette?" He dared to look directly into her sparkling eyes, blue as the sky.

"Very much. Wait here, I will ask the sister."

Returning, her face blushed. "The sister requires some questions of you, Étienne, before I am allowed to walk on town streets. Come, meet Sister Thérèse; she is kind, and likes a gentlemen with caring eyes such as yours."

Étienne waited anxiously on a stone bench for Sister Thérèse to make up her mind, feeling her scrutiny.

---

[20] At Montréal the girls were taken to Marguerite Bourgeoys, founder of the Congregation de Notre Dame and were housed at St. Paul Street and another house at St. Paul and Dizier Streets.

"Monsieur Pasquier. I understand you had already made an agreement with another of the brides. Did you not know what you were looking for?" Sister Thérèse asked.

"I was taken in by flirtatious eyes and creamy skin, but soon agreed with Mademoiselle Françoise Barbary that we were not meant to be. I know I am seeking a good women of virtue, who is kind and gentle in spirit, but strong and sturdy on the land. I see qualities in Henriette that speak to my heart. I have not arrived here by coincidence; I come every day and watch from afar to see her fair face. I cannot now look at another, without feeling unfaithfulness to my soul."

"Merci, Monsieur Pasquier." The nun smiled. "You have not asked of Mademoiselle Rousseau's dowry. That is admirable on a first stroll. But of course, you understand that since Mademoiselle Rousseau comes from a family of gentry in France, we will want assurances of your background. Should she select you, where will your home be?"

"My heart has chosen. Whatever dowry King Louis has given Henriette will be gratefully received. In turn, I offer my home and farm at the Seigneurie de Petite Auvergne, a stone cottage on the Charles River that I have built with my own hands. My parents are Étienne Pasquier and Jeanne Poussard of Dissay, and I am skilled as a master charpentier, favoured by the King. I came to Québec with the Carignan."

Étienne took a folded parchment from his pocket listing his complete assets, and handed it to the Directress.

"You will return her shortly then, Monsieur Pasquier." Sister Thérèse rose to conclude her questioning.

Henriette's eyes twinkled as she took his arm. Étienne observed her blushing cheeks, finding her shyness appealing. He had heard a rumour that a Carignan Officer proposed to Henriette days earlier.

"I have watched you in the garden many days. Each time, I am pleased you are still here and not off to the Notary's office."

"Me, as well, Monsieur. I see you walking by, each time in your fine gentlemen's suit. I am pleased that you stopped this lovely morning."

"If you are not committed to another, I would like permission to court you, Mademoiselle Rousseau."

There, the words were out. Étienne looked at the ground waiting for her reply. She didn't say a word but held tighter to his arm.

They walked the first block in silence, then Étienne began. "I am an engagé to Monsieur Giffard. I travelled two years ago with the Carignan in La Motte's regiment. My first crop of corn and wheat came up this spring, but I still have a lot of land to clear. With the native skirmishes, I am often called to defend the settlements."

"Yes, there are many soldiers here at the docks, but it is you that I have waited for. On the day the ship arrived, I saw you waiting. Not pushing to the front, but observing timidly as a gentleman should."

Henriette's eyes locked with his, hoping he would rescue her from such a bold comment.

"You wore a beautiful dark red dress, with lace and crinolines. Your hat had a plume of red feathers. I was sure I would not have a chance." Étienne paused. "And here we are."

They both laughed and she squeezed his arm tighter, wondering if she had found 'home'.

Thirteen

Coins versus Script in Québec – Dowry of a King's Daughter – Marriage of Étienne Pasquier & Henriette Rousseau, 1668 – Farming on Seigneurie of Petite-Auvergne – Sowing & Reaping – Rider Warns Habitants of Iroquois ambush – Habitants Race to Seigneur's Block House to defend against the attack – Women and Children Join in Defence of Walls – Muskets & Arrows – First Child of Étienne Pasquier born 1670 – Another daughter for Pasquier then son, Philippe, 1673 –King Louis XIV's incentive for successive children provides bonuses.

Marriage of Étienne Pasquier & Henriette Rousseau

LIVRES WERE PAID IN SILVER COIN TO SOLDIERS FOR services and to King's Daughters for their dowries.

Ships from France carried the silver coins to Québec. Meanwhile, repayment vouchers were accepted by merchants, instead of actual coinage. Once traded, the chits as credit vouchers were accepted for goods and services. The official formalized voucher would then be returned to France and adjusted in silver.

Henriette brought a generous dowry of three hundred livres[21] from the king. Her heirloom trousseau carried silk and silver, a taffeta handkerchief and shoe ribbons, a comb, sewing needles, four spools of white cotton thread, pair of scissors, two knives, a box of a hundred pins, socks and

---

[21] Livres or leaves is a currency of silver coin established to pay Québec military. Until the silver coins were returned from France, a substitute paper livre circulated in barter, its value in direct proportion to the earnings of a soldier (30 livres or 50 French pounds).

gloves, a bonnet, four lace braids and a bolt of taffeta and two broadcloth. Most trunks also held several pieces of silver coin. Of the silver allotted, ten pounds were intended for winter clothing for the crossing and the first winter. Henriette rated an extra gift of a velvet lined trunk, with brass corners and a locking key. Part of her dowry included ten livres for personal moving expenses, thirty for her passage and another sixty to provide for clothing.

Étienne and Henriette married on November 6, 1668, at Notre-Dame in Montréal, with the contract signed in the presence of Honore Martel dit Lamontagne and Marguerite L'Admirant.

> Étienne, his of Étienne and Jeanne Poussard, from the borough of Boussais (Two-Separate) diocese of Poitiers in Poitou, it signed from there another with Henriette Rousseau, daughter of Jacques Poussard and of Jeanne Arnould of the Saint-Germain suburb of Paris. The marriage was célèbre in the church of Québec on November 6, 1668.

After their marriage, Étienne was deeded his forty-five arpents[22] of land, by Governor Jean Talon, on the edge of the Saint-Charles River that skirts Saint-Jacob.

"Come, Henriette, it's time to survey our land."

Étienne took her hand and led her to the river. The morning dew had not left yet for the sky. Henriette felt the excitement in her husband's hand, but asked nothing. She knew this was land originally granted to the Jesuits, but later conceded to feudal land.

"See Henriette! See that pole, we will walk south in search of another. The land tapers from the central point of Bourg-Royal and tapers back toward the river. Forty acres are now Pasquier land. Our home, our farm."

Picking her up, he twirled her in a semi-circle, and she delighted in his strength and broad shoulders.

"We will count five poles, until we come to the town. We will add to the fieldstone house in the village. Jacques Magnian's land is to our east, and Charles Bourre to the west."

---

[22] Arpent is an old French unit for area and lineal distance. One arpent is the equivalent of approximately .85 of an acre or .35 of a hectar; one league is 84 acres or 3.1 miles, equaling 5 kilometers.

Henriette stayed briefly in quiet thought.

"We have both a meadow and a forest."

"Yes. We begin by pulling the stumps and stacking firewood for the winter. There is time to plant your spring garden from the King's seeds. The Chalifours have invited us to stay in their cottage until ours is complete with windows and doors."

Étienne uses Surname of Paquet

USING THE NAME Paquet, Étienne took employment as a gardener at the Giffards. His own cottage was at Petite Auvergne, a humble one-story home with a loft of hewn pine beams, and obese masonry walls of grey, whitewashed stone. French accents of steeped, red clay roof tiles and wide window dormers let in the day and kept out the night. From the hillside, they gathered fieldstones in the mornings for a grand hearth and bread oven, to establish a fine kitchen.

Beyond the fortress wall, narrow plots of land stretched from the riverbank in strips, forming a circle with a common fenced pasture for livestock. Habitants built simple barns or sheds as temporary homes, then constructed cottages in a parallel row along the river, directing irrigation ditches to the crops, and always maintaining a defensive position.

The seigneurie was five miles north of Québec. East was Beauport, and the Huron Jesuit settlement of L'Ancienne Lorette was west.

The narrow road in front of the cottages was wide enough for the wheel ruts of a barn-board wagon with a lone oxen, and the curves of the rivers led to a roadside chapel and sacred cemetery.

Étienne tended his animals and planted wheat, flax, corn and barley hoping for a prosperous late summer harvest. Reaping and threshing the grain took long days of scything, pounding and flailing in the hot sun.

When not in the fields, Henriette crafted tallow candles and carding wool. From the wild orchards, she gathered spruce boughs to pack salt fish, and foraged for edible berries, roots, and fruits. In the mornings, she drew water buckets from the stone well and chopped firewood for warmth.

When dusk descended over the fields and Étienne hadn't come for supper, Henriette felt a familiar ache. Frightened to walk the tree line at night, she carried her axe, never sure when or where natives might appear. Far in the distant field, in the shadow of the moonlight, she knew his silhouette, and always hastened her step as her heart danced.

In the warmth of her garden frock, she quietly stepped close to Étienne, to begin hoeing with her axe, content and proud to be at his side.

Henriette planted a handful of seeds in uniform rows in the herb garden at the back of the house. On tethered racks, she dried the fruits and herbs, and dug a cellar behind the kitchen to store apples, potatoes, corn and the hunter's yield. King Louis had generously provided them one horse, an oxen, chickens, a cow, two pigs, and two barrels of salted meat.

Close to the cottage, she kept a poultry coop and running pen of wild turkeys, a few laying chickens in a crude henhouse, and whatever wild squab or pheasant they acquired from the bush. Each day before coming in from the fields, the Paquet harrowers bowed their heads in the night air, thankful for their bountiful blessings.

With the day's work done, Henriette settled on the porch with her sewing basket, mending and making Étienne's work shirts, or manifesting cotton and woolen scraps into rugs and quilts. Sitting next to her with his tobacco pouch, Étienne puffed on his clay pipe full of Indian weed.

As moonlight cast itself on the river, she sensed that the trees whispered the secrets of today, and the heavens bore witness to their good works.

Young Henriette wondered if Étienne had yet noticed her swelling belly. Cradling her arms over the child within, she rocked beside him, anxious to share her news.

Henriette's First Encounter with Iroquois

IT WAS EARLY December and only a skiff of snow swirled across the fields, leaving white hats on the bales of hay as far as she could see. A clear night sky was over them and a frigid blew from the north. Henriette tucked a beaver rug over her legs and a thick knitted shawl around her shoulders.

Étienne's instincts were on edge. The hair bristled on the back of his neck and he craned his view through the trees.

After only a few puffs of his pipe, he extinguished it. "Henriette, it's time for you to go into the house. Ready my travel satchel." She looked into his worried eyes, knowing that the satchel meant a revolver and ammunition.

She was on her feet in an instant, almost tripping in her haste. Although her chest throbbed with fear, Henriette kept a clear head, grabbing a sack of gunpowder from behind the front door.

An owl hooted on its barn roost preceding the silence, then frantically broken by a crescendo of pounding from down the road, with the clapping of charging horse hooves. The thunderous approach of the lone horseman was a signal itself to Henriette.

Étienne ran to the barn to tack up his Percheron, and reached for his loaded flintlock, bracketed over the door. In a hasty return, he hoisted Henriette onto the horse's back, as his neighbour Étienne Dauphin galloped to the barn with his torch blazing.

Dauphin came to a sudden halt.

"Une petite partie de guerre de Iroquois était en baisse le fleuve venant de cette façon—courez au blockhaus.[23]" Étienne Dauphin didn't wait for a reply and continued down the road to the next farm, the Chalifours, at breakneck speed.

Étienne called after his friend. "I'll take the river fork and alert the Girouxs and Pageaus on our way!"

Dauphin didn't reply but waved his hand high.

"You will know what to do by your instincts, Henriette."

The seigneur's manor house was more than a mile down the road in the opposite direction of the war party. Henriette clasped her arms tightly around Étienne's waist and the old nag was asked for her best. They didn't hesitate or look behind until the manor blockhouse came into view.

Pleased to see Toussaint's wagon ahead, Étienne allowed a tough swallow of nerves and veered to the right fork toward the Pageau farm. Dauphin's torch was out of sight as the fork went behind a divide of trees.

---

[23] "A small Iroquois raiding party has been seen coming up river—hasten to the blockhouse." The blockhouse is within the manor compounds to protect women and children from Indian attack.

Étienne recognized Marie Morin, Étienne Dauphin's wife, with her children huddled in the back of the wagon, covered in hay. Julien Brosseau was coming up behind as they entered the walled compound, with torches glowing outside the manor walls. Women secured the children in the safety of the blockhouse, as men armed with rifles and muskets took positions at the parapet of the stone walls.

It seemed that too much time passed, before Étienne Dauphin rounded the bend with a young boy saddled at his back, with other riders and wagons clamoring behind in a cloud of dust.

This was not the first alarm and as each knew panic could be their enemy, they moved quickly and orderly through the gate. The compound grew strong with farmers, Hurons, and habitants, many that were formerly Carignan soldiers.

Women and children rushed to safety inside, as men took up sentinel positions on the palisade. Hoping to deceive natives of their small defence, women and boys were sent to safe locations to fire arms, and the repetitive gunfire confused the Iroquois of the numbers within the seigneur's manor walls.

Henriette, still a young bride without children, ran to the munitions house and gathered rifles and gunpowder. Following her husband to the parapet, she sat low and tight in the corner. Looking toward Étienne with fear in her eyes, she determined that he should have no doubts that she was by his side, ready to fight.

With a gunpowder pouch from the folds of her skirt, she replenished his arsenals. The open field between the riverbank and the manor was swarming with moving bushes, with habitants signaling their positions as they lay in wait.

"We are scared, Étienne, but we are not naïve," Henriette said and nodded to an approaching bush.

Étienne smiled. "Don't underestimate the cunningness of the Iroquois, my darling. The more distance between us and them, the better off we are. They don't know that more than half our defence is women and young lads, shaking in their boots."

Henriette was buckled over the lens of a rifle. "I have good aim at a sycamore, Étienne. Can I take it?"

"Steady your stance and your arms and wait for the first arrow to fly from the bushes. Keep your elbow high and steady."

"You are a good man, Étienne. God has our fate in his hands." Henriette's voice was controlled and her face taut.

The moonlight shimmering on the river was disturbed by shadows, and the sound of rippling water should not have been heard. The silence was haunting. A shrill bird call was recognized by the Huron guide who joined the Frenchmen. He nodded, knowing this Iroquois attack signal. Étienne focused on a cluster of shrubbery moving toward them.

Étienne and Henriette heard the whiz of an arrow and replied with gunpowder and musket balls from a revolver and a rifle. Rapidly, Henriette kept reloading and lining weapons at Étienne's feet between her own steady shots.

Carignan soldiers took advantage of the first attack and raised a volley toward the advancing party. A war cry echoed from below as painted Iroquois rushed from the riverbank and woods like a swarm of ants. Munitions were not spared and anyone able to handle a weapon had a post.

Young Charles Giroux, Toussaint's youngest son, was barely ten years, but had seen enough Iroquois to make him a man. Henriette saw his fierce determination as he sat beside his father. Every few minutes, he rested his musket on a niche in the wall and fired into the advancing throng. Henriette knew it would be inevitable for her own son to do the same.

Wayward arrows flew through the sky and the few warriors that succeeded to the wall were bludgeoned back. In the background, Étienne heard the yelp of a boy, not far from his post. One of Dauphin's boys had fallen with an arrow in his shoulder, and Henriette crept low to him, ripping strips of apron to tie his wound.

A Jesuit priest mounted the ladder to the parapet to attend the stricken boy. Reeling in pain, he gritted his teeth as the arrow was removed, with Henriette's apron tight over his flesh and joint.

Within an hour, the canoes disappeared as the Iroquois retreated, astonished at the resistance of the relentless habitants. With no victory celebration but only silent thanks, the wounded were attended and the stockade replenished in the quiet night air.

"Henriette, we'll stay at the stockade until morning."

Étienne looked from the fortification toward his farm. It didn't appear that the raiding party had gone that way, otherwise the fiery blaze of a house or barn would be left as a calling card.

In the morning, the Pasquiers walked into the comfort of their stone cottage at Petite Auvergne. Henriette sighed her relief and brought Étienne to the table.

"What is it, Henriette?"

"Étienne, my dear, do you think you could build a cradle for us? We will be needing one late in the winter."

The Iroquois did not return to Charlesbourg that winter.

February 1670 was temperate, but brought persistent heavy winds, lasting for weeks. Étienne was worried about Henriette's ill health and the impending birth of their first child.

In the morning, he took on his haying chores in the barn, milking cows and bringing in eggs, then planned to ride to Saint-Louis Forts to help with the construction of a bastion along the waterfront at Québec. Cannons and a royal battery were being placed along the shores to defend the stronghold of the fort and for security of the naval ships in port.

Making a soft bed for Henriette by the hearth, he hoped Marie Godard would visit, as she was Henriette's planned midwife for their first delivery.

Henriette gripped his shirt tightly and begged him not to leave her alone as her labour became more intense. Étienne bathed her face with cool water and propped pillows behind her back. He hadn't heard the sound of fear evoked by his wife before.

Duke, the family sheepdog, wore a path between Henriette and the corner behind the stove. He licked her face, sensing her pain, and retreated to a safe corner when she cried out.

In the early evening, Henriette announced it was time.

"Marie Archambault told me that every delivery is different. She should know. They have thirteen children, and she is with child again. Urbain is even skilled as a midwife." Henriette tried to laugh. "All I really remember about birthing is hot water and clean towels. I left the towels and a blanket on the bedroom trunk."

"Yes, I see them. I'll leave you for just a moment to check that the water is boiling."

From the kitchen, Étienne heard her heavy breathing. Returning quickly to her side, he took her hand to press to his cheek.

"I can barely push anymore, my dear Étienne. I will need your strength." Her blue-grey eyes penetrated his with pleading and she clung to his hand, digging her fingers into his flesh.

"Ma chérie, God will guide us."

The last howl of wind echoed Henriette's final groan, before the cry of a baby filled their home with the safe arrival of their first daughter, Anne.

A half hour later, Toussaint and Marie were at the door.

"Bonjours! We have a new girl." Étienne embraced Toussaint, then Marie, as she rushed past to the bedroom.

"Oh, blessed be, Henriette. Your daughter is beautiful. She has your eyes and Étienne's nose. There is no mistaking that she is a Pasquier. That is certain."

By the time Anne learned to walk, Marie-Étiennette[24] arrived, then two years later, their first son, Philippe, in 1673. Philippe's baptism took place at Notre-Dame de Québec on a cold November morning, surrounded by his relatives Philippe Casolier, Hilaire dit Limousin and his spouse Antoinette Lebvre.[25]

Although Louis XIV provided incentives to populate Québec, Étienne and Henriette met only the first condition—having a child within the first year of marriage. Families with ten children would receive an additional three hundred livres a year and at twelve increased to four hundred.

Making it on the land was an early milestone for the Pasquier family. Clearing their wilderness land, they endured the harsh winter, foraging and hunting to feed their family. They knew they had been blessed in avoiding native skirmishes while others around Charlesbourg were not so fortunate.

The Seigneurie of Charlesbourg dominated the emerald Saint-Charles River valley. To the west, the village of L'Ancienne Lorette was nestled in a lush basin. Above it, the wilderness reach of the mountainous terrain of the Laurentians held babbling brooks and streams with secrets of tribal

---

[24] Marie-Étiennette Pasquier was born Nov. 24, 1671, Charlesbourg, Québec.
[25] Philippe Paquet's baptism on Nov. 20, 1673, with two nuns attending, officiated by P. Henri Desberriers, at Petite Rivière Saint-Charles, Charlesbourg, Québec.

culture. Jesuits established a seminary in Charlesbourg, barely in the reaches of Québec.

In spite of historical differences, the Jesuits were deeded seigneurie lands and contracted to clear the woods, secure native fur trade, and build the settlement village for over two hundred Hurons.

Although remaining allies of the French, the natives had been pushed back to their reservations, except for the Métis, who succeeded in moving into French settlements at Montréal and Québec.

Fourteen

Iroquois Confederacy – Nomadic Hurons – Jesuit Mission at Lorette integral for Pasquier – King Philip's War, 1675-1676 – Stop Throwing Stones – Rise of Coureur de Bois – Joseph Giffard succeeds as Seigneur of Beauport – Étienne uses Clover & Fallow Land Developing 3-Year Farming Rotation – Jean Talon suppresses Middle Class – Habitant Taxation – Company of One Hundred Associates become Hudson's Bay Company – Haying at Bourg-Royale – Mother are you Missing Me?

The Inheritance of the Seigneurie

HIGH ABOVE THE VALLEY, THE RED CLIFFS PROVIDED A fortress that overloooked emerald green pastures and golden fields of grain. Woodlands, rocky mountain ledges and steep crags gave a natural protection from the threat of ambush, and the reaches of new villages extended farther from the manor house.

The Treaty with the Five Nations, encompassing the Iroquois confederacy, became the threshold of peace with settlers for the next ten years. The truce of the Mohawk, Oneida, Onondaga, Cayuga and Seneca tribes, ceased attacks and lifted the trade embargo on Algonquin pelts.

Abandoning canoes, the nomadic natives kept mobile with portable wigwams and teepees, in contrast to the Hurons, with family-oriented birch and cedar longhouses in the old settlement at Lorette.

Deeply religious, the tribes centred the feasts and ceremonial rituals on the spirits. Medicine men, witch doctors and chiefs were held in esteem, with a democratic choice of leader, respecting voices of men and women.

Étienne's visits to the mission at Lorette became more frequent to trade furs. As he befriended Huron braves, he learned their dialect and refined his hunting and planting skills, making a lifelong pact of brotherhood.

Although skirmishes and native raids subsided around Charlesbourg, Henriette kept the satchel ready in the event of a race to the blockhouse.

Her youngsters had seen the curse of angry Iroquois, but Henriette scolded them for playing 'cowboys and Indians' in the farmyard.

"The day will come, my children . . . this will no longer be a game you laugh at. All natives are not our enemy—it is just the Iroquois, and when they are angry with the British. Now stop throwing stones at each other."

Volunteer militiamen were banding together with the Hurons to secure ramparts in towns and villages along the vulnerable Ohio and St. Lawrence Rivers. Provisioned with weapons, they scavenged for food supplies, and commandeered lodging during their campaigns.

The son of Massasoit, Chief of the Wampanoag, adopted an English name of Philip in the 1660s, becoming known as King Philip.

The uprisings initiated by the New England colonies led to the death of Wamsutta, with Philip's brother provoking the Amerindians.

The ensuing King Philip's War raged in 1675 and 76, and the fury of the natives escalated to guerilla warfare, burning towns and villages, and killing men, women and children without discrimination. Fear and unrest ran the gamut of the eastern seabord settlements.

The English pushed the natives from their lands in these wars, and the French observed it from an armchair position, until called to the aid of the Hurons, Algonquins and some tribes of Iroquois.

The Tax Man Cometh

FROWNED UPON by France, the coureurs des bois had become a significant organization, with men marrying and raising children in the tribes of the woods. Louis XIV knew he was denied his taxation of trades, and a year later he decreed a ban on fur trade with the coureurs des bois and private trappers.

In 1668, Robert Giffard, seigneur of Beauport, was succeeded in death by his son Joseph, Lord and Earl of Beauport. Joseph was immediately generous in ceding small parcels of land to the community for public use.

Serfs of Bourg-Royale at Charlesbourg hunted only for food, curing hides for domestic use until winter when they were went into the woods. When food sources waned, the Paquets needed pelts to trade for essentials.

Feudal taxes were due to the seigneur immediately after the fall harvest on St. Martin's Day, with a minor percentage of crops, new calves, pigs, and chickens delivered for accounting to the feudal manor.

As wheat was ground, an extra sack was set aside for the seigneur; as bread was baked in the central ovens, a loaf was provided in payment. Any withholding or unauthorized trading was not tolerated, with the habitant fined severely.

With pride, Étienne groomed the cedar hedges and rose bushes at the manor, and tended the raised beds of herbs, mustard, parsley, blue borage and medicinal plants that blended in a colourful medley. The expanding apple orchards provided a robust fall yield, to be collected for the seigneur.

As Étienne returned from gardening at the manor, his neighbours, Paul Chalifour, Nicolas Belanger and Jean Bergevinm waited for him outside the cottages. "We're disappointed with our own crops, Étienne," Nicolas said. The others nodded and smoked on their pipes.

"Mais oui, I have been concerned also," Étienne said. "I tendered an experiment on a patch of land at the back of my fields—I gathered cow manure, mixed it with ashes and dead leaves, and planted sweet clover. I waited a few weeks then stripped a row of rye and flax."

"Clover! What do you want with clover?" Nicolas Belanger laughed, and the others joined him.

"The land rests and brings bees for fertilization. My rye and flax were the best I've had. Next year, I'll reverse the technique, so each harvest I have fallow land, but the growing crops will flourish better than ever."

"Overseeding, eh? Well, I'll be." Paul Chalifour slapped his knee at the idea and the other two chortled between puffs, unsure what to think.

"Yes, indeed. I had an early *and* late harvest on the same land. Corn was at knee height when climbing beans and squash were introduced to the planting mound, reaching a surprising balance of soil enrichment."

Within a few years of experimenting, the others adopted a three-year rotation—the first year rye and winter wheat, second year spring oats and barley, and the third to let the land fallow without crops.

The trading posts were providing improved farming implements to trade for deer hides and beaver pelts, but the efficiency was putting greater pressure on the ecology of the rivers and creeks around Saint-Charles.

The affluent seigneur imposed his right to bind the sons of the serfs to him, becoming a self-ordained godfather—and thus Philippe Pasquier's godfather was Joseph Giffard.

Although the soil belonged to the seigneur, the minerals and all rights under the crops remained as royal land. Jean Talon, under the king's orders, made sure a class of landowners could not rise up, and the seigneuries stayed small, with land grants under eighty hectares.

Land clearing was mandatory, with an annual rental payment from all serfs, and an additional ten percent of the growth of the land, crops and animals to be paid back to the Crown. Habitants were indebted to improve lands and maintain the seigneur's manor including its gardens and flour mill, and a church for their common use.

At the same time, the Jesuits were given vast tracts of land to build missions, and encouraged intermarriage among the natives. As powerful protectors for the Roman Catholic Church, the Jesuits built churches, convents and hospitals that constituted the roots of Québec.

The historical sagas of French Canadian habitants never altered their passion or feigned their integrity. The old habitant sitting on his stoop, smoking a pipe, singing ballads of cultural lore in the seventeenth century, is the same habitant silhouette of the eighteenth century, a compassionate people with intense values of heritage and never a loss of humour.

Pipes, lutes and fiddles were at every gathering, with favourites *Le Clair de Lune*, a sleepy song of moonlight, *Psalms 137* and *L'homme Arme*. Music shops in Québec and Montréal were importing instruments for the wealthy, and music academies flourished for the talented and those just curious. A renewal of French culture sprang forth with vigor.

The Hudson's Bay Company, formerly the honourable Company of One Hundred Adventurers, was granted authority over all trade, with rights extended to lands drained by Hudson Bay from the Connecticut

Charlesbourg, Beauport, Québec Map, 1709, subdivided land and owners' names.
Author: Gédéon de Catalogne; Source Bibliotèque et Archives Nationales du Québec

River to Delaware Bay. Charles II gave authority over these lands to James, Duke of York and Albany in 1665.

Their forts, each strong as an arsenal, served as trading postings. With pelts for trade, the Iroquois were tough negotiators, wanting guns, kettles, blankets and liquor.

The seigneurs were displeased with the trading impositions as the French had no choice but to interact with the Hudson's Bay trading posts, usurping the power of feudal lords, and signaling the end of seigneuries including the Petite Auvergne.

With winter land barren, the men packed up and moved to lumber camps in the woods with Huron guides. With Étienne gone, Henriette took over the barn chores with the help of young Philippe.

It wasn't until late March that Étienne returned. With deep strokes, his paddle thrust the canoe, surging each time through the swirling currents. Encumbered with a cargo of beaver, deer, muskrat, wolverine and wolf skins, the keel of the boat plowed low in the water, crashing the swollen current and soaking their faces. The native steersman and his party forged onward, down the river toward Lachine, taking the winter's gains to the official British trading companies.

Philippe toiled unwavering by his father's side until he was seventeen. Étienne thought back to his younger days, when he too stood steadfastly by his father toiling in the fields at Dissay. Philippe shared a bond with him of quiet, mutual admiration, contemplating dreams of a prosperous future, and never entertaining thoughts of one working the farm without the other.

As they laboured, Étienne repeated his motto to Philippe that he'd said often on days like this, "Hard work is good for the soul."

Philippe would always laugh, with the identical reply.

"Oui, Papa—we have very large souls."

The large maple beside the house was shedding its colour, and the autumn morning in 1686 was like most others. Henriette toiled at the laundry, plunging shirts and aprons into the warm, sudsy water, bent over the oak wash bucket near the back kitchen stoop. She stood tall and stretched her neck to watch Étienne and thirteen-year-old Philippe, haying the field and loading bound sheaves into the box wagon.

From a distance, their movements mimicked one another, and over the usual pang of pride, she felt a rush of jealousy and loneliness at their closeness.

Reproaching herself, she knew she loved each of her men deeply and that she was equally adored as a wife and mother. As much as she cherished both of their daughters, Henriette was grateful to have given Étienne a son. In the ensuing years, childbirth had brought more heartache as infants were buried at the Church courtyard.

She stayed mesmerized by their silhouettes until her silence was broken by a soft voice.

"Ma chère mère."

It was Étiennette-Marie, bringing another kettle of water. Henriette gazed at her with fondness, and the loneliness faded. As the innocent, blue-grey eyes looked up from the soft fair-skinned face, Henriette thought it was as near to an angel as she would see.

"Mother, are you missing me?"

Little arms reached up.

Fifteen

Simeon LeRoy marries Claude DesChalets, 1667 – LeRoy & DesChalets Disfavour in the Courts – Henriette Rousseau called to testify regarding King's Daughters Voyage – Claude & Madeleine DesChalets repent for Insult to DeClerc – Simeon Buys & Sells land, ending up in Montréal, 1682 – LeRoys moves to Albany with Huguenots – William Penn brings congregation from Holland to N.Y. – Port Royal, Acadia captured, 1690 – Iroquois Align with British Americans – Employment Boon for Château Saint-Louis – Simeon LeRoy dies at Pauper, 1710 – Frans François LeRoy inherits N.Y land patents.

Simeon LeRoy, Immigrant to Ulster County, NY

S IMEON LEROY DIT AUDY, WHO HAD BEEN RAISED IN A monastery at Créances, Normandy was a long acquaintance of Henriette's parents, Jacques Rousseau and Jeanne Arnoult. Simeon immigrated to the new world in 1667 as an engagé and master carpenter at the Seigneurie of St. Joseph. His bride, Claude Blandina DesChalets from Poitou, came to Charlesbourg with the King's Daughters in 1668.

Simeon was distinctly handsome, of medium height with broad shoulders and a square jaw. His dark brown eyes twinkled with mischief on his introduction to the DesChalet sisters, captivating Claude, who was a natural beauty.

A month after their marriage, they purchased two arpents of river frontage from Guillemette Hébert, with the dowry of Claude Blandina. In 1671, Simeon acquired two additional arpents, with forty feet in depth, from Simon Daunes dit Jolicoeur of Beaupré. With the help of his brother-in-law and neighbour Jean Giron, who had married Madeleine DesChalet, Simeon built his house, and raised eight children with Claude.

Obliged as a serf on the seigneurie on the banks of Saint-Charles River near the Pasquier cottage, Simeon rented land from M. Herbert-Couillard de L'Espinay. But Simeon and Claude were not always in favour to their church, family or local courts, as he wheeled and dealt lands and mortgages to the harsh disapproval of authorities.

Controversy rose when Claude and her sister Madeleine were brought before the Québec court for engaging in scandalous gossip and unladylike pushing of the wife of Michael Riffault. By other accounts, it had occurred onboard the king's ship on the Atlantic.

Henriette Rousseau was called for questioning before the Sovereign Council at Québec, as a witness to the alleged DesChalets incident, and Henriette's solemn demeanor and poise bode well for the prosecution.

Étienne watched in pride from the back of the court room as Henriette was ushered to the box. She wore the same burgundy dress that captivated him on the docks the year before.

The wigged attorney paraded and strutted before Henriette as he spoke.

"Madame Rousseau, it is true you travelled on the King's ship from France with Madame DesChalet?"

"Yes, I was on the ship."

"Did you witness unladylike behavior from Claude Blandina and Madeleine DesChalets?"

"I'm not sure exactly what you mean by unladylike."

"Did you see either Madamoiselle Claude Blandina or Madamoiselle Madeleine DesChalets shove Françoise LeClerc?"

"No, sir."

"Did you hear them insult Madame LeClerc and ridicule her, saying she was a prostitute?"

The attorney paused, allowing the courtroom to gasp, then continued. "Both Claude Blandina and Madeleine further spread rumors, that Madame LeClerc gave birth to an illegitimate child on the ship, and then murderously destroyed the infant."

Henriette toiled with her moral judgement for the answer. Simeon LeRoy did nothing to be brought into the face of shame nor did the other defendant's husband, Michael Riffault.

The three orphaned DesChalets girls were used to a life of struggle in orphan houses, where bullies had survived. Henriette's heart went out to the hardships that Claude Blandina endured while protecting her ten siblings, bringing out the qualities or faults she lived with.

"I heard other rumors to that effect, but I cannot say I was present during the scene you describe."

The barrister gave Henriette a disappointing look and dismissed her from the court. Françoise's husband, Michael Riffault, was subsequently called to verify the purity of his wife upon their marriage.

The two DesChalet women were assessed fines and required to apologize for unsuitable behavior, standing in a public court and begging for pardon. In spite of their plea of forgiveness, they found that their friends and neighbours shunned them.

Simeon doubled his land holdings in 1680 by forty arpents at Saint-François du Bois-Brûlé, a chance to contract his woods for the cutting of planks. Local businessmen, Antoine Guibord and François Duard dit Laliberté, jumped on the opportunity to pay him forty livres per every one hundred planks over the next three years.

Domestic issues forced Simeon to sell his first concession at St. Joseph to Jean Giron for two hundred and fifty livres, and his family moved to Montréal in June 1682. However, financial finagling caught up to him and he confessed to owing the Seminary of Montréal ninety-five livres; his only recourse was to mortgage the property at Bois-Brûlé.

Two months later in August 1682, Simeon purchased a small house in Montréal with only a cellar, storeroom and living room, between the Bissots and Duponts. With negotiation, his indebtedness was covered by carpentry work for the Sisters of the Congregation of Notre-Dame in Montréal.

Later in the year, Simeon moved south to Albany, New York, with Claude Blandina and eight children born at Québec: Oliver, Jean Audy, Augustin, Marie Anne, Leonard Treny, Pierre, Charlotte, Jeanne and Maria. Infant Marie was left behind in a quiet cemetery near Montréal.

Son Augustin, at merely eleven, was apprenticed to Adam Winne for six years to master rope-making, and Simeon sent his second son Jean, nine, back to Charlesbourg to live with Jean Girou, his godfather. Simeon

LeRoy's family grew by three more in Albany: Frans François[26], Sarah and George.

The LeRoy's eldest daughter, Marie Anne from Charlesbourg, married a German, Hugo Freer. Hugo and Marie purchased a land patent from Anthony Crispell in New Paltz, NY to be paid in wheat and flax. The Freer family holdings included buildings, houses, orchards, gardens and yards at Daniel Hasbrouck's mill in northern New Paltz. Respected in town, Hugo became Deacon of the Old Dutch Church in Kingston, Ulster County. All of the Freer children married Huguenots or Protestant Hollanders, every one dedicated to the church community.

New England Colonies Butt Heads with Frontenac

THE SUCCESSFUL colonization by Frenchmen attracted greater attention across Europe, with settlement in New England appealing to immigrants from Holland, Denmark and Germany.

Boatloads of entire church congregations, none more renowned than William Penn's, travelled from New York to bring immigrants from Holland. Pledging allegiance, Penn received a large grant of land from the British King, Charles II, to repay a debt owed to his father.

The parish priest provided a schoolmaster and a Quaker church for the Dutch immigrants. Settlements began in Philadelphia, then spread to Maryland and northward. Penn saw the value in developing trusting relationships with the natives, nurturing a peace agreement.

In Québec in 1690, Governor General Louis de Buade de Frontenac was reeling from the capture of Port Royal in Acadia by the New England colonies, as the British rose up to challenge supremacy of the St. Lawrence. Once again, colonists from Massachusetts Bay saw trade advantages and seaway benefits to Montréal and Québec.

---

[26] Frans François, born Oct. 17, 1683, Albany, NY; married Celetje Celia Damen, born Oct. 7, 1683, Breucklen, New Utrecht, NY, d/o Jan Cornelisen Damen of Utrecht, Holland and Fytje Sophie Martense of Flatbush, NY.

Major John Walley led an offensive on Beauport, where Frontenac was ready with his troops. Walley defiantly offered Frontenac a concession appeal to graciously cede his fortress.

Frontenac was livid at the offer. "I have no reply to make to your General, other than to be heard from the mouth of my cannons and muskets."

His lieutenant agreed. "Yes, sir. Phips will *not* have victory over our Frenchmen. We have heard that Captain Schuyler brings a hundred and fifty militias from Albany, supported by Iroquois. They intend to canoe and portage overland on their way to Montréal."

Frontenac scoffed, "They mistake our spirit. We'll be ready for them when they arrive."

"The Huron scouts are following them overland, and their whereabouts are known to us. Schuyler was overheard to declare that the cowardly French would be easy bait for their hardy troops, including the Iroquois."

"I'm not surprised. I see they scheme . . . to take our fortress in the middle of harvest. Make sure habitants are forewarned of ambushes by Schuyler's troops. Fortify them all with muskets."

The ill-prepared Boston troops suffered smallpox, shortages of food and medical supplies, and then mutiny among Schuyler's lieutenants. A weak attack on farmers in their fields outside Montréal's garrison took the lives of fifty habitants; but in retaliation, Québec batteries bombarded the New England fleet that was cut off due to a calamity of errors under Phips' command.

On October 22, 1690, the New England militia made a full and hurried retreat, as musket fire and cannons chased them from Beauport's palisade, and they returned in haste to Boston.

Simeon and Blandina worried about Augustin and Jean in Charlesbourg, who would undoubtedly be called to defend the fortress at Beauport during the colonist attack at Saint-Charles. Soon after the Americans were repelled, Simeon heard about the marriage of Jean Audy LeRoy, the son he left with his Uncle, Jean Giron.

In the aftermath of the Battle of Québec, Frontenac recruited masons, carpenters and construction workers to enclose the city with a wooden palisade, the entire distance from the fort at Château Saint-Louis to the Saint-Charles River. Major Provost, the town overseer, saw the construction of eleven stone redoubts to protect the walls from cannon fire.

Jean Charlebois, François Charbonneau, Joseph Charbonneau, and Jacques Tessier acquired work building the fortification, leaving their farms at Pointe Claire, Laval, and Montréal to apply their skills.

The Legacy of Simeon LeRoy dit Audy

IN ALBANY, Hugo Freer was appointed executor of his father's will in 1697, with extensive obligations to his numerous children, including lands, barns, animals and household distribution.

Falling on hard times, Simeon LeRoy, Hugo's father-in-law, rented a home at Kingston from Jochem Hendrickse. But he struggled to pay rent, and when Claude Blandina DesChalet died in February 1708, the Kingston Council extended him poverty courtesy, providing him a pair of shoes, a load of firewood, and a paid pauper's funeral for his wife. Two years later, Simeon's death was recorded as a pauper on the Ulster County tax rolls.

Frans François LeRoy, Simeon's second youngest son, a converted Protestant of French descent, and Celetje Celia Damen, of Brooklyn, married and settled at the stockaded village of Kingston, Ulster County.

On an upbeat Sunday, when the Freer family gathered for dinner, Marie Anne LeRoy confronted Frans François. "Frans, when the militia talks of the need to quash Beauport, are you not torn for our brothers?"

Frans said, "Oliver is dead, yet Jean has deeded his own land and raised a large family in St. Joseph's. He has his Uncle Jean Girou and is rooted in the community. He must fight for his country and we for ours, dear sister."

"Is this the likeness of Cain and Abel? Shall our French brother take up arms against our Dutch brother?"

Frans dug deeper to defend his position. "*Our* duty is to our country of allegiance. All my children are christened here in Poughkeepsie where we are part of New Amsterdam. Religion and patriotism define our battle lines—not our bloodline."

"I am sad for your soul, Frans. I pray my children never have to take arms against their own kin, and that our blood does not flow as the Hudson River travels."

"Dear sister, I am sorry that we have disagreed. I will continue to love my kin, but I belong to New England not to France."

Land patents, in Ulster County on the Hudson River, were ordered to fence their farms and provide labour to build palisades at Kingston to defend against native attacks. The Iroquois had banded with the English, and the Huron and Algonquin sided with the French against the colonists.

Sixteen

Étienne Pasquier tires of Habitant Journey – Memories of old Dissay – Visit from old friend, Toussaint Girould – 'Je me souviens' – Passages of life – Burial of old Étienne, 1690 at Charlesbourg – Lachine Massacre, 1689 – Traumatic Recollections of Elizabeth Brunet – Louis de Buade, Governor Frontenac – Unrest among the Five Nations – Philippe Pasquier treacherous journey into high country with Hiroons – Coaxing Anabelle across the Charles River – Reminiscent of Great Spirits – Wolf pack endangers camp – Challenge of Hunter rather than Hunted – Rescue of Hurons ravaged by Ague – Snow Hut Survival – Friendly Hurons frequent Woman of Pasquier – Exchange and trade become reliable – Gratitude.

Étienne Pasquier at Charlesbourg

AT SIXTY-EIGHT YEARS OF AGE, ÉTIENNE WAS WEARY from his habitant journey. He was ready now for peaceful times, able to toil in the fields with Philippe less often.

Instead, he rested on his porch on late summer afternoons with his clay pipe. His brown eyes had become grey and hollow, and his arthritic hand trembled as he fumbled with the flint.

Henriette worried, seeing his spirit fading and body withering from the tower of strength he'd been. He had survived English swords, Iroquois tomahawks, winters of near starvation and scurvy, seasons of small pox and typhus. But now, without resistance, he was yielding to time alone.

With a puff from his pipe, he reflected to Henriette, "I wonder about Mathurin, the old Castle at Dissay, and the Seine Valley. I am glad there is a Pasquier in the sheep pastures. You know my dreams take me back."

"Yes, Étienne, wisdom and reflection is our due. You have toiled hard, fought well, and served your family and friends."

"That is not enough. I remember a time with Ononthio when he called out to the Great Spirit. I could feel the warmth of the heavens come down to greet us."

"Why do you talk about the heavens?" Henriette fretted.

"It is a time in life, dearest, it will soon be time to rest."

Henriette was overwhelmed with a sense of grief, but didn't want Étienne to see it on her face. She rose in silence and went to the house, returning with a folded warm quilt.

"Put this over your lap, Étienne. Cover your legs. Let us sit in the quiet and watch the crested blue jay on our porch. Let us listen to the bullfrogs in the creek, and the call of the sparrows from high in the trees. We are blessed with the fullness of life."

"God sends a message to me, when the willow leaves turn silver just before a rain, and to see the beauty of his lands and bountiful crops," Étienne said.

"Dearest, you have blessed me with twenty-two years of marriage and three wonderful children. I have had a good life."

Toussaint Girould Visits Beauport in Twilight Years

LONGTIME FRIENDS, Toussaint Raphael Girould and Marie Godard, from Orne, France, came regularly from Beauport in their carriage to spend time with Étienne and Henriette on the willow armchairs on the porch, always sharing grand stories.

This time they talked of patriotic France and not of adventure, but of memories—not of prosperity and dreams, but of their beloved homeland and the wisdom of ancestors.

"Je me souviens de mon père et la mère walking up the hill to the little church in Dissay."

"These are memories on which you built your own life, Étienne."

Their silent thought stretched for a moment. "You know, Toussaint, they are buried in the courtyard there, but no one goes to visit or say a prayer anymore."

Étienne whispered from his heart, then said aloud, "France, my dear France, I shall not see you again."

"Ah, Étienne, you are a Frenchman. It does not matter the land you stand on—it matters in your soul. We have toiled well; we have raised fine children. God is proud of our perseverance and the nurturing of his lands."

"My Huron friend told me the other day that it's time for me to go into the winter woods to share of the spirit. I hear of native skirmishes beginning again. They are troubled with the treaty and say they're robbed of their birthright. Frankly, I agree with them. Life is too much taking and not enough giving back," Étienne said.

Standing behind Toussaint, Henriette tried some amusement to break up the sobriety. "Mon dear Toussaint, did you tell Étienne how the children swing on ropes in the barn rafters?" She laughed awkwardly at the silence, knowing they were in a different place. Her heart pained to see two old friends talking of life's passages. She brought them a cassoulet of venison and peas with a crown of bread and a wild berry tart.

Wine and cheese were laid out but the glasses did not empty this time, and the singing of folk ballads were not called.

Instead, on this night, the kitchen was abandoned when Étienne, Henriette, Toussaint and Marie followed one another to the porch. In the mellow paleness of moonlight, they listened and allowed their souls to share comfort without words.

The sombre night sky and whispering trees became silent. In the stillness, a lone loon sent his song as a droning echo from the shores of the Saint-Charles, and waited for a distant reply from across the river.

In the morning, when Toussaint and Marie prepared to return to Beauport, hugs took longer and seemed more meaningful. Toussaint braced his old friend and in a stronghold leaned into his ear.

The rough wool of Étienne's jacket itched his cheek at the touch of his unshaven whiskers, and the lingering aroma of his pipe that clung to his hair.

Toussaint knew he'd remember this finest embrace for a long time.

Habitant and Snowshoes, Engraving on wood, Artist W. Raphael,
Engraver Edit Cooper, Picturesque Canada, Vol. 1, 1882

Tipping his hat, Toussaint nodded as they rode in the lane with sadness in his heart and only a brief glance back. From the lane, Étienne watched his friend for the last time. Within weeks, Henriette's letter arrived.

Nous partageons la peine de nos coeurs dans le dépassement de notre Étienne aimé. Il est allé de pair avec la grace de Dieu à un meilleur endroit. L'une des dernières choses que mon amour m'a indiquées était "disent Toussaint qu'il ne devrait pas être triste."[27]

---

[27] "We share the sorrow of our hearts in the going beyond of our beloved Étienne. He went hand in hand with the grace of God to a better place. One of the last things, which my love indicated to me, was "tell Toussaint that it should not be sad."

Étienne Pasquier was buried in August 1690 at the Charlesbourg Church cemetery, with Philippe standing in support of Henriette where his father belonged. Étienne was predeceased by his oldest daughter, Anne, and survived by his widowed daughter Étiennette and his son, Philippe.

Henriette wept and allowed herself to rest on her knees in prayer before kissing her rosary beads. Philippe grasped her elbow and helped her to her feet. From a basket, she placed a posy of garden roses at the footstone carved by René Langlois, stonemason of Beauport. Lingering, she fingered the name 'Étienne' on the stone.

Her focus took a moment through tears as she looked up into Philippe's face, and she breathed out relief seeing the strength of his father and the same kind eyes. She knew he would take Étienne's place in the field, but nothing would fill the grief in her heart.

The Lachine Massacre & the Iroquois, 1689

THE FRENCH villages knew to expect an attack, but were unprepared for its size and viciousness. The British incited it on August 5, 1689, and the Iroquois made their surprise ambush of Lachine at nightfall. An approach came from Lake St. Louis at first, then bolstered by a second wave of raiding parties from the bushes and riverbanks.

The Iroquois numbered over fifteen hundred, swarming like wolves upon the farmhouses. Villagers had little chance of survival, with screams too late to warn neighbours. Striking with a vicious vengeance, the ambush killed and burned all in their path, lighting the horizon to become a silhouette of flames. Spreading like locusts through the night, they showed no mercy.

At dusk, the survivors ventured out in search of friends and neighbours, to find and bring home the wounded. Instead, they found over fifty dead villagers in the embers and ashes. Almost a hundred were missing— farmers, women and children—with the grievous fate of being tortured and burned alive at the stake.

Half of the prisoners' lives were spared only by the grace of God, while the rest perished. The horrific events of that night were etched in witnesses' memories and passed on in history.

Seeing distant flames rising from villages and farmhouses, families fled for their lives. François Brunet and his wife Barbe Beauvais bundled their twelve children in the darkness and fled to the town of Lachine, in the background of flames and eerie war cries. Their daughter Elizabeth at six years was vulnerable to native kidnapping.

François never liked to speak of the night of the raid. But as Elizabeth got older, she horrified her classmates with recounts of fire, angry painted faces, screaming and consuming flames as their neighbour's home burnt to the ground.

It gave Elizabeth temporary strength to face the reality of the trauma. In graphic detail she told about the mother and two little ones buried in the yard. When a small girl in her class fainted, the schoolhouse teacher forbade Elizabeth to tell her stories again.

After that, she contained the agony inside, allowing with cries and screams only in her dreams, and never vanquished of deep emotional scars that she'd withhold.

The signing of the Great Peace of Montréal between thirty-nine First Nation tribes and the French Colonial government was a short relief, and French forces conspired with native break-away tribes to turn on the Americans coming across the Great Lakes.

Governor Frontenac, Louis de Buade, had been revoked and recalled in 1682 by Louis XIV to France. But the deceitful Cavelier de la Salle, as subsequent commander of the colony, led to an English invasion in 1689. After the massacre at Lachine, Frontenac was reclaimed as Governor. In July 1690, unrest was renewed among the five nations, with a hundred habitants attacked during the Battle of Coulée Grou, and French pioneer, Jean Girou, and others of his party burned at the stake.

Philippe worried greatly about his mother, who was often alone at the farm at Petite Auvergne as the natives fought amongst their tribes over winter land.

Philippe Pasquier's Trek with Hiroons

AFTER A LONG discussion, Henriette agreed that Philippe should make the trek across the St. Charles River before the ice came. Before he left, a pair of Huron hunters arrived, barely alive from an Iroquois ambush, having hidden their families high in the woods to await rescue.

The elder brave said his wife was very ill without medicine. Philippe knew the woman he spoke of—Madeleine the MicMac, the granddaughter of Henri Membertou, shaman and prophet of great respect.

True to his father's spirit, Philippe volunteered to climb with a native guide, experienced as a highland scout, to tend to the sick family and traverse them down before the river froze.

"Mother, I fear leaving you now, when the winter winds blow so harsh. I will pass by Étiennette's and ask Adrien Nivelon to come and feed the cattle while I am gone. Father would insist on that."

Philippe expected his mother would protest, but she smiled knowingly and went about preparing a supply pack.

"Be assured Philippe, I am a strong woman or your father wouldn't have chosen me to help clear the land," Henritte said.

"Indeed, he chose well, but you are not as young as you were in your settler days. You must learn to accept help."

"I'll try to do that, so that you don't carry undue burden in your thoughts."

"I need to take basics to attend to the sick—healing teas, salt, fortifying dry meal and beans, dried salted meat, bandages, and a small cache of whiskey. I'll get my axe head, bow and arrows, snowshoes, ropes and whatever else from the barn. I will need to take Anabelle, the pack pony, to carry the load."

Philippe struggled to keep the door from slamming from its hinges as he fought the howling wind. Henriette cleared a round of frost from the kitchen window to watch her son forge head first into the wind.

When Philippe returned, he was accompanied by a Huron brave by the name of Hiroons. The young man had fierce brown eyes under the brim of his beaver hat, and he bowed to greet Henriette.

"Good Pasquier woman!" He bowed again, having befriended Étienne.

Hiroons helped attach Philippe's backpack and tucked Étienne's rifle, bedroll and the axe head into a strapped canvas.

"No, Hiroons, the rifle must stay with my mother for protection." Philippe returned the wooden barrel to its roost over the door and removed two revolvers and a sack of ammunition from the cabinet.

"We go now," Hiroons said.

With a final hug for his mother, Philippe disappeared on snowshoes into the blustery wind with his friend and Anabelle. Henriette peered out through the frosted glass, but there was already no sign of them, and the pony's tracks had filled in with snow.

Philippe pulled down his rabbit fur hat over his forehead and tied several rounds of a red scarf over his face and mouth. He had an advantage over Hiroons, as he walked with Anabelle and stayed close to the warmth of her nuzzle.

Hiroons caught the sense of a passing Iroquois raiding party and they diverted to a longer route to the river to avoid notice, not resting until dusk had darkened the sky.

"River not far. Go or sleep?" Hiroons asked.

"Let's go, then we can dry over a campfire."

"Guns and supplies must be held high, as the river is starting to freeze. The pony will be able to cross as she is sure-footed and it is not too deep here. I will lead her."

Behind the scout, Philippe's body felt the shock of icy pain as he stepped boldly into the surging river. Momentarily frozen, he stopped to catch his breath and remembered that the lives of the Huron family depended on his success, while the undertow reminded him of the force of nature.

"Come without stopping, Philippe. Must go quickly!"

Anabelle needed coaxing, but soon knew there was only one way forward. Balking and snorting, she finally did her best as shards of ice floes sliced at her coat, but she was encouraged by surer footing on the rocks. The scout was tentative to her every step.

"Climb! Come on pony!" Hiroons urged her toward the north bank as her withers spasmed with resentment. Stepping from the swollen river, frosty breath rose from their beings.

"Slow down your breathing Philippe, it will confuse the cold air attacking your body," The native cautioned, as his friend was panting and fighting for respiration.

At the first shelter they came to, Philippe tied Anabelle to nibble on spruce boughs as he dug a hole with the axe head to scratch below the permafrost. Gathering armloads of hemlock boughs, he laid them in the hole and dug fronds of fir into a lean-to shelter.

Hiroons had the campfire burning and a blackened kettle boiling for tea and to soften a few beans. Philippe spread his coat on nearby branches to dry out while he wrapped himself in a dry blanket from the overhead pack.

"Thank you Hiroons. You are an excellent guide. Tell me about your family and the battle you've fought."

Staring into the flame, it was as if Hiroons saw a spirit communicating with him.

"The Huron come from a great nation, long before the white man came on the waters to build homes on our land. It was hard at first, when the Great Spirits told us to fear this new invasion from the place you call Europe. Then we found sanctuary in the missions, healing, teaching and new language. Our lives grew wide with knowledge, not only of the Heavens and Mother Earth, but of a new culture.

"But I'm sad that it brought baubles, whiskey and firearms in return for our blood in battle, sometimes against others of our own color."

"I am sorry, Hiroons, that the white man has taken so much from your people. I am grateful for your friendship, your scouting skills, and how you teach me of the Heavens and the talkings of the soil. The French people are indebted for the sacrifices and loyalty you give in friendship. My own father fought with the Hurons by his side, and my mother told me many times of the first occasion when my parents outraced a blood-thirsty raiding party to the seigneur's blockade."

"I don't understand why we fight," Hiroons said. "The land is much and we are willing to share, but it is the British who want everything from us and from you too. I learned as a brave to respect the land and nature, and that would be enough if we learned hunting skills and fording rivers. Why do explorers care so much about where their flag is planted?"

"You are a wise man, Hiroons. For me, I only want to provide for my family and live in harmony with my neighbors. Tonight it is the harshness of winter than opposes us. I am sorry that your friends—the friends of Membertou—are suffering in the high country, pushed from their homes and hunting grounds by the Iroquois.

"I have heard legendary stories of Henri Memertou and Jacques Cartier and the stalwart Samuel de Champlain. You know that each came in friendship."

"My father and his father before told us stories of the great ships arriving at the mouth of the Charles River. It was later—when the British wanted all the lands the French had conquered, and our tribes were considered nothing more than a barter in battle. The Iroquois were hungry for bloodshed and used the British as their own cover. The Great Spirits were not pleased as the five great nations splintered."

As the campfire embers reduced to glowing, red ashes, Hiroons poked his stick deep into the coals.

"You sleep Philippe, I take first watch and keep the fire to warm us but not high enough to alert others in the woods. I go for water from the river for the pony."

Long after midnight, Philippe was awakened from slumber as Hiroons shook him gently.

"Quiet! Don't move quickly. Over there I see the eyes of wolves in the woods watching. They are trying to circle our camp and the pony is skittish."

Philippe instinctively eased toward his rifle that leaned against the hemlock boughs. Hiroons held his hand up in caution as he watched pairs of stealthy eyes through the darkness, aware that low seething growls had surrounded them.

The neighing of the pony increased and she suddenly reared onto her haunch in terror. The wolf pack could smell her fear and inched closer.

With torches, Hiroons and Philippe surrounded Anabelle, but it was soon apparent it was them or the pony. The painful screaming and neighing went on for what seemed an eternity before she died. The distraction of the wolves of their fresh feast allowed Philippe and his scout to climb high trees to wait until the glow of sunrise on the horizon.

The wolves had retreated into the woods. The remains of Anabelle were buried under a collection of branches and rocks and the pair shifted the pack weight onto their shoulders. Thrashing through the brush they found a trail, but didn't speak of the events of that night.

Grey skies reduced their guiding shadows, and Hiroons checked the moss and climbed a tree to calculate their direction.

"I see markings where my people have come. We're a day and a half out." The scout placed his ear to the ground for vibrations. "Nothing is following us."

At dusk, they made camp, stashing their packs high in the branches. Philippe took the first shift while Hiroons rested, but Philippe knew the scout had one eye open. Again at an early hour, they heard the wolves and retreated to the trees until dawn.

"Philippe, we need to become the hunter instead of the hunted. Surely some wolf skins would please the trader? Hone sticks into spears and I will prepare traps for tonight. But we will not cook to entice their hunger." He passed a piece of dried pemmican to Philippe to suffice.

That night, Philippe heard yelping from outside the camp, followed by another. The growling became more distant and in the morning they found a giant-fanged black wolf impaled in Hiroons trap, and a young female pup. A pitiful wail echoed from the forest, and bloodied prints to the woods said another had been injured.

On the fourth day, the scout saw an indication of distant rising smoke from the victims' makeshift shanty. "That is good, Philippe. Someone keeps fire going. We be there by nightfall."

The snow was deeper as their snowshoes trekked in the higher terrain. Again they picked up wolf tracks but forged ahead in spite of dusk.

Bursting through the door, they were appalled to see Madeleine slumped by a meagre hearth cradling an infant that was obviously deceased. On a cot, an old man was barely breathing and a young girl with sunken eyes stared into space.

Hiroons was swift in his assessments.

"Philippe, make a broth and tea to fortify these people."

The scout consoled Madeleine and wrapped the babe gently in soft blanket shreds. The wolf pelts would warm the survivors as they were force-fed a watery concoction of Henriette's meal. Philippe found a vial of his mother's herbal medicine to add to the bark tea.

Two days later, they buried the baby and old man in the woods and prepared the mother and daughter for travel. Philippe didn't know how they'd make it back through the woods and across the river escaping tragedy, and without Anabelle.

Hiroons built two traverses and harnesses from strapling roots. The women were wrapped securely and laid on the poles, tied into a sort of sled to be pulled behind them.

"Philippe, I fear a storm is coming from the mountain. We must go."

"It is good that the bears are asleep for winter and the snow may draw the wolves back into their dens."

On the second night, Philippe thought he could go no farther. Out of rations, the elements were a painful foe. He thought of Henriette waiting at home and the fortitude of his father before him, and rallied a second wind as they came upon the river. Fortunately, the waters had frozen over and Philippe prayed that it would hold the traverses.

Across the river, the two rescuers collapsed in weakness on the bank. Philippe could see that Hiroons face was red, and worried he'd be too weak with flu to rise again.

"Hiroons, have you taken the ague from our friends?"

"I'm alright." But his eyes were closed and he shuddered violently.

"I'll build a snow hut. I'll make better speed if the three of you stay here and wait for me to bring horses and a wagon."

Hiroons was feverish, lying in silence unable to answer. Philippe dug beds with for the three under a cluster of pines. With branches to form a teepee, he covered the enclosure with fir and a wall of packed snow.

Forcing the last of the medicinal tea past feeble lips, Philippe reluctantly departed, leaving scraps of pemmican and a canteen of water in reach.

Following the markings from the outbound trip, Philippe made it half-way into the last day when the flu finally attacked him with unforgiving vengeance. His strength had departed from his legs, and with frozen feet he crawled on his belly using the axe head for leverage.

If it had only been himself, he would have yielded to nature and death, but he was strengthened by thought of Henriette, Hiroons, and the two natives in his charge. His entire body was racked with indiscriminate pain and life became oblivion, but his will took him several miles until his body collapsed.

In those moments he came to terms that the only value in life was his family, with the land, the motherland, battles and bartering insignificant.

The following day, a small Huron party found Philippe covered in snow and carried him to the Pasquier farm. Henriette barely recognized his frozen chapped face but he kept mumbling incoherently.

"Snow hut . . . get the others. I must take you."

Will forced him to a sitting position. But too feeble to lead the party, he scratched a map on the ground, remembering the three tall red pines. In the morning, word was delivered that Hiroons and the young maiden were in the care of the shaman at Lorette, but Madeleine had succumbed in the elements.

Habitant brick oven, common in New France.
Artist unknown. 'A Country by Consent'

Henriette Rousseau and her Huron Friends

FORTS AND VILLAGES were again flourishing and springing up along the St. Lawrence and south at the Ohio River. Fewer native skirmishes threatened trading routes, and friendly Hurons came often by canoe to the Pasquier farm, trading venison for milk, potatoes, a few eggs and Henriette's fresh loaves of bread.

The first time, only four braves ventured onto her farm.

As three waited by the water trough, one entered the kitchen, tapping Henriette gently on the shoulder. She was removing hot bread from the brick oven, and froze at first. But instantly, she recognized the Huron band on his forehead and his dark braid. Behind a necklace of colourful beads and bear claws, his brown chest was bare and scarred, and a wampum belt hung loosely at the hip of the buckskins.

With characteristic shyness, the man pointed at the bread, then to his mouth. Henriette relaxed her shoulders, smiled broadly and reached for a cloth from the table.

The Huron took the warm loaf under his arm and stepped back, but she saw hunger in his eyes and imagined his family. With her hand raised, she went to the larder for a piece of Oka cheese that she'd bartered for in exchange for eggs. She carved out and wrapped a large chunk, and handed it with a baked apple pie to the native, now standing by the door.

He nodded with appreciation in silence and disappeared with his parcels. The king-fishers charged from their roosts and a deer sprang from the woods as the canoes disappeared. At her door, Henriette heard a shrill call back from the river. It was the sound of gratefulness.

On their return visits, the Hurons sang a melodious canoe ballad as they approached, so Henriette would not be startled. When she saw them, she went about gathering eggs, cheese, potatoes and fresh garden vegetables, a few herbs, and always her morning bread. She found herself looking forward to the exchange for pemmican, or a few bagged ducks or fresh game, dried buffalo meat, or a surprise treat of bannock.

The familiar Huron brave, waiting by the larder, picked up an apple from the kitchen table and smoothed his hands over a tin plate then scooped his hand to pretend eating.

"You are asking for tarte au pomme?" Henriette laughed.

"Tarte au pomme!" he spoke slowly to understand the expression, then joined her in the comedy of the new words.

In her old age, Henriette gained new life, purpose and energy with the satisfaction of giving. Even waking with aching bones, she always fired up the bread oven. In the harsh cold of winter, the men still came on snowshoes, bringing fresh meat, cornmeal, dried mulberry and cedar bark chips for making tea. They brought in firewood, tended the horse and cattle in the barn, and broke the ice in the well to drop buckets to raise fresh water.

She was called 'woman of Pasquier' and when they departed with their few loaves of bread, she felt lonely, yet intensely grateful.

One winter day in February, the Hurons brought her a birch bark jug filled with sweet water. The brave stirred and fed hot coals in the hearth and poured the liquid into her black cauldron, then a small piece of venison was added and simmered before removing the meat, but allowing the potion to continue in its brew.

The brave tore a piece of meat and raised it to Henriette's lips; it tasted so succulent and sweet she responded with "mmm" that made him laugh. The liquid thickened and the Huron went out the door returning with a pan full of snow. The syrup was poured over it and quickly hardened.

Both Henriette and the brave became giddy as they pulled and twisted at the soft toffee, with buttered hands. Standing at the plank bench, the brave pushed the plate of maple sugar candy toward her, and gave a nod and wave that he was leaving.

She reached for his arm to wait, and went to the mantle where Étienne's pipe had rested since his passing. She fingered its familiarity once again before bringing it to the brave in gratitude. He smiled and was touched, but folded her hands around it pressing it back to her. With a broad smile he left.

Seventeen

Huron secrets of wilderness survival – Mission of Notre-Dame-de-la-Jeune-Lorette at Wendake – Adventure with Ononthio, 1697 – Craft of a birch bark canoe – Campfire chant of Father Jean Brébeuf's ballad – Flutes & Pipes – No Whiskers! – Spoils of a Fortnight Adventure – Étieniette Pasquier brings family to Henriette – Heroine of Madeleine de Verchères – Philippe Pasquier consigns with Julien Brosseau for waistcoat – Spanish Interest in trade routes – Treaty of Ryswick returns captured lands to British and French – Philippe Pasquier wed M- Geneviève Brosseau, 1699 – Great Peace Treaty with natives of Montréal 1701 fails.

Philippe Pasquier's Inspiration in the Wilderness

PHILIPPE WAS EAGER TO LEARN MORE SECRETS OF THE forest and survival skills from his Huron guide, Ononthio, since his near-death adventure with Hiroons. Onothio had an instinct and motivation to find the sweetest fresh water streams, to gather medicinal herbs from the underbrush, and to attend to the native way of tanning. Together they made beaver tail snowshoes and split the hides of thick white birches to build canoes.

Ononthio, already a grandfather, was from the longhouse village tribe of Hatindia Sointen at Lorette, five miles northwest of Québec. Village land had been granted to the Jesuits by M. Robert Giffard many years before.

Many of the light-brown skin Hurons, with shiny black hair, gathered at the missions for education and literacy, and could serve as interpreters.

While acquiring habitant farming techniques and French customs, they also retained the aboriginal ways.

Much of their clothing was of deerskin, with beaded decorations for ceremonial wear, and beaver skin coats for winter. Braves wore deerskin loincloths or pants, with a goat-hair blanket, and always a pipe, tomahawk and club in hand.

The Catholic mission of the Jesuits and Recollets was named Mission of Notre-Dame-de-la-Jeune-Lorette, operating as a trading post for the Huron community of Wendake.

Before the sun had risen, Philippe was waiting for his friends at the edge of the forested hills near Lorette. The October snow had already blanketed the ground for days. He recognized their silhouettes approaching against the orange sunrise—Ononthio, Philippe Casolier, and young Thomas Pageau from Charlesbourg. Together they would hunt and learn skills from Ononthio in the solitude of the woods. The river hadn't frozen yet, and two carried canoes for the fortnight adventure.

Ononthio built a fire to camp here that night, and the men gathered around to watch his demonstration to repair gunwales and seal the canoe seams.

"Your hunting knife must always be sharp," he said. "We'll go now to gather cedar spines for rolling, then willow branches for soaking, and birch ribs for carving."

With patience, some spruce roots were soaked for bindings, and Ononthio nimbly sewed birch panels using a fine bone needle and root straps.

"You make it look easy, Ononthio," Philippe teased.

"The hardest parts are watching . . . and then patience."

Over white-hot ashes, a cooking vessel boiled a concoction of animal fats and drippings mixed with gummy tree sap, then adding chunks of petrified coals until the brew was thick. When it had cooled, it was packed into each birch bark seam to secure the water tightness.

As dusk fell, the four hunters sat near the roaring flames, cooking perch wrapped in fragrant spruce and tied over the heat. Into the pot of bubbling water, Philippe added a fistful of dried beans and simmered it into a hearty mush.

His Huron-Wendat friend sat late into the night, his legs neatly folded under him, with his head bowed and eyes closed in prayer.

Swaying slightly, a soft moan came from within, and his rhythmic chant rose with the sparks and smoke.

Philippe knew the tune as Father Jean Brébeuf's ballad *Twas in the Moon of Wintertime* that had been taught by the Hurons.

Both Philippes and young Pageau began to slowly sway, allowing the moaning to come up from their own bellies, and not wanting to disturb ceremony or show disrespect. Straightening their backs, with hands resting on their crossed legs, their sounds surprised them from within.

A wayward wanderer passing in the woods that night would have been in awe at the reverent worship, hearing the most beautiful singing of men, one chanting "Jesous Ahatonnia" in the language of the Huron and a duet of tenors humming and mumbling in a melodious French mixture with broken Huron.

Twas in the moon of winter time, when all the birds had fled,
That mighty Gitchi-Manitou sent angel choirs instead;
Before their light the stars grew dim, and wondering hunters heard the hymn:
Jesus your King is born, Jesus is born, in excelsis gloria.
Within a lodge of broken bark the tender babe was found,
A ragged robe of rabbit skin enwrapped his beauty round;
But as the hunter braves drew nigh, the angel song rang loud and high:
Jesus your King is born, Jesus is born, in excelsis gloria.
O children of the forest free, O sons of Manitou,
The holy child of earth and heaven is born today for you.
Come, kneel before the radiant boy, who brings you beauty, peace and joy:
Jesus your King is born, Jesus is born, in excelsis Gloria.

In the clear sky, Philippe fixed on an especially bright star, and a tear escaped down his cheek.

"Oh, Papa, you would like this," he whispered. "I know you are looking down at us with a joyful heart, yet a pain of yesteryear. I know how you loved to hunt in the woods and feel the spirit of the land talk to you. You share my soul with me; you are not forgotten."

A gentle breeze brushed the back of his neck.

On the last chorus, Philippe Casolier took a reed flute from his tunic and repeated a soft lullaby that carried in the silence. Ononthio removed a long, carved bone pipe from his leather pouch and stuffed it with tobacco. After long, slow puffs, he passed it to the others.

The men rested on beds of aromatic spruce boughs and awoke early, cold and wet, with the stars still visible in the black sky. Ononthio brewed a blackened pot of coffee, then emptied a pouch of flour into leftover greases. With water he worked the dough with his hands.

Thomas and the Philippes were sent to gather cooking sticks for the lumps of dough, and returning to the fire they watched the coals as the rotated biscuits turned golden brown.

At the creek, Ononthio splashed cool water to his face and fumbled in the mud for clam shells. With two sharpened shells he stared into the glassy water and tweezed out two lone whiskers.

"Hey, my Huron friend, what are you doing?" Philippe Casolier asked.

"Do you not notice that Hurons do not have beards and moustaches for many generations before? It seems that our ancestors came across the continent from the north, called the Bering Sea. We find carvings in the rocks and pictures."

"Well, I'll be. Ononthio, what's the secret?" The French crew unconsciously fondled the long tresses from their own chins.

"There's no secret—it's just that Hurons are different than you Frenchmen. From time to time we grow a few annoyances, but the clasp of a clam shell takes care of that." The native rubbed his smooth chin and smirked at his friends.

The forceful current of the Saint-Charles River had not given way yet to freezing. Light snowfall and grey skies with clouds forewarned the woodsmen to pack the spoils into the canoe and launch downstream to Charlesbourg.

With a farewell salute, Ononthio vanished to his woods. Philippe knelt on one knee at the bow, and sank his paddle into the rushing waters, with Thomas at the stern. Twenty feet behind, Philippe Casolier steered the other canoe with effortless momentum as they forded the river.

A bird call echoed from the woods, and Philippe knew it would be Ononthio.

Life for Henriette Rousseau at Petite-Auvergne

Toussaint Hunault, from Île de Montréal, was enamoured with M-Étiennette Pasquier at once, and the courtship took only a few months before they married on July 2, 1691 at Notre-Dame in Québec. The lovely widow, Étiennette, was fair-haired like her grandmother, Jeanne Poussard, and was known to have the determination of her father. The Hunaults settled at Rivière-des-Prairies, Île de Montréal, and soon brought home grandchildren, delighting Henriette.

During the spring thaw in 1698, Toussaint and Étiennette gathered young Gabriel, Marguerite, and Marie-Angélique, for a wagon trip to surprise her mother Henriette.

Étiennette held a pie at the door, and the children each knocked and pranced on their tiptoes, waiting for Henriette.

"Our trip is spontaneous, dear mother, but it is so good to see you."

Collecting the young ones in her arms, her face showed elation.

"Mais oui, Étiennette. They give me such joy, but it is better to see your own face here before me. I miss you very much."

Henriette took her daughter in an embrace. "My dear, are you with another child?"

Étiennette giggled and blushed. "Ah, Toussaint said you would have the mother's instinct to know as soon as you saw me. The child will come at the end of the summer."

The children were pulling at her apron, with arms stretched for more of their grandmother's attention.

"Gabriel, do you wish to help your father and Philippe with the hay? The wagon is ready to leave." Henriette waved to Philippe in the yard to halt, and boosted the gleeful boy onto the buckboard between the men.

Returning from the field, Gabriel's eyes were wide, with fantastic stories playing in his mind. "I saw an Iroquois in the woods! Papa killed some coyotes in the cornfield and uncle bagged rabbits for dinner. I want to watch them being skinned."

His blue eyes flashed with excitement. "How old should I be before I get my own pitchfork?"

Étiennette held her mouth in alarm and looked to her husband.

But Henriette raised a palm and chuckled. "Gabriel, do not fear the natives around our farm. They are Huron; they're kind and will not harm you. Next time, take something to trade—it will make them happy, and you might be lucky enough to get a bear's tooth in return."

Philippe howled with enjoyment as the boy scrambled into the larder for something to trade.

"Toussaint, it's time you take Gabriel into the woods for wilderness learning. Soon he can be hunting and building canoes."

Henriette's eyes went to Philippe. "Remember your own experience years ago with Ononthio?"

"Ah, avec Papa, how could I forget?"

"Ononthio is our friend," she said. "But the children should be cautious and learn to guard themselves from the Iroquois. I could tell them stories of when I rode with your father to the stockade and fended off the arrows of a native raid. Wait until Gabriel is older. There is time for those stories."

Henriette looked at her son with great respect as head of the household now. "Philippe, did you hear of Madeleine de Verchères?"

"Oui, a magnificent heroine."

"Tell your children of her courage and bravery in defending her father's fort, but not of the cruelty and massacres. She defended the fort with an old man, two soldiers, and a cannon, while rescuing the Lafontaines and bringing in a herd of cattle."

"Yes, she deserves to be a heroine for my children and theirs as well.

Courtship of Philippe Pasquier & Marie-Geneviève Brosseau

PHILIPPE STOOD tall for his fitting at the tailor's stone house on the Seigneurie of Beauport. Julien Brosseau, from Bretagne, France, was not a stranger to him, as the respected maître tailleur de l'habits had been a longtime friend of his father. Monsieur Brosseau maintained a proud reputation for his finery and craftsmanship, providing designer textile creations to priests of the Jesuit mission and habitants at Beauport.

At twenty-four, Philippe needed both a gentlemen's coat, or justaucorps, and a waistcoat vest. On his last occasion in Beauport, he met the tailor on a social visit, mostly discussing the weather and the coming harvest. But when parting, Julien insisted that if Philippe ever needed supreme tailoring, he would be glad to fit him.

From the door, Philippe noticed the Brosseau girls waiting in the wagon and tipped his hat to the fine Marie-Geneviève.

The next morning, Philippe secured the Percherons in the barn and chose his best lone quarter horse for a journey back to the Brosseau cottage to contract tailor services.

Julien Brosseau and his wife Simone Chalifour had three daughters and five sons, and over their childhood years, Philippe had become better acquainted with Pierre, Joseph, Nicholas, Julien, and Charles than the three girls. Marguerite, the eldest daughter, had married and left home, leaving two young daughters on the farm—Marie-Geneviève, sixteen, and Simone, thirteen.

As Philippe entered the lane, Julien walked across the grass to greet him with a firm handshakes.

"Bonjours, Monsieur et Madame Brosseau."

"Oui, mon ami, you have come for a fine suit?" Julien inquired.

Simone rose from behind a picket fence at the side of the house with a toddler, Charles, in tow.

"Philippe, you must stay and join us for dinner."

"I would be grateful to accept if it is not an inconvenience."

"A Pasquier can never be an inconvenience."

Philippe and Julien surveyed the crops and fences, then discussed and complimented the livestock. Meanwhile, Marie-Geneviève and Simone fussed in the kitchen with dinner preparations.

Enjoying the environment of the large family at the enormous table, Philippe soaked in the camaraderie, but with a pang of envy. His father had been gone for nine years, and Étiennette had a family of her own.

"How is your mother, Philippe?" Julien asked. "We haven't seen her since your Papa's funeral, but we heard stories of her bravery with the Hurons. Is it true?"

"Oui. Our mother is a brave women. She takes great pleasure in the native visits, and they look out for her when they know she's alone at the farmhouse. She's generous in portioning cheese and bread for them, and they keep returning, always in friendship. Lately though, she spends most of her time in the rocker on the porch, as she is thin and weak. It would do her good to get into town more to see her friends."

"Well, bring her the next time you come. Simone's good food and our family cheer will be medicine for her."

After the meal, the women withdrew to the kitchen as serious talk ensued between the men. Smiles and formalities were soon dismissed.

"Philippe, did you hear that Spain and Britain are at war again in Europe? Soon, the conflicts might overflow to Québec, as the Spanish want routes to California and the riches of the Gulf of Mexico."

"Does this mean we will be called to war to defend the Mississippi River simply as a trade route?" Philippe asked.

"I fear the worst," Julien said. "The fickle Spanish pretend to be allies with us against both the natives and the British. The son of Brolet went to Spanish Florida and said the Spanish and the Amerindians were wiped out. The French seized land as far south as Alabama."

"Mon dieu! When I was a child, it was war that I feared most. Do I love my land more than my father, my brothers and my future children? That is between me and God, but we leave in disagreement," Philippe said.

Julien raised his hands in exasperation. "Incredibly, the French now control lands as far as Lake Superior and south to the Gulf of Mexico. What more do they want?"

Philippe said, "I was at The Hudson's Bay post last week, and heard from Jean Charlebois that there are rumblings from the New English colonies. My father fought with the Carignan-Salières for years, hoping for peace and freedom. And now, decades later, it seems we are back where we started, but with more enemies."

"C'est dommage!" Julien sighed.

He blew his coffee steam to curl in the air. "You know the Treaty of Ryswick returned all captured territory between the French and English. Does that give valour to the soldiers?"

"I am sorry, Monsieur Brosseau, to have troubled you with this unsettling news. Perhaps it is time to enjoy friendship and family. I pray for your family and my own, for Québec, and of course for Philippe de Regaud de Vaudreuil, our new Governor."

"Then we'll go to attend business."

Philippe followed Julien to the ten by ten foot tailor shop behind the summer kitchen. From a shelf above the worktable, Julien brought down paper packages, and the woolen fabrics were laid out. Philippe selected a dark brown wool for the waistcoat and an ivory linen for a broad sleeved shirt.

Calculating funds in his head, Philippe managed to buy one more white cotton dress shirt and a wool cravat. Julien retreated to a tall cupboard and returned with a wooden chest and selection.

On the tailor's insistence, he opted for a lace neck ruffle and heavy black hose for his knee-britches. With measurements and business completed, they returned to the parlour to settle in overstuffed chairs with their pipes.

Philippe found many reasons to pass by the Brosseau house or stop for visits in the succeeding months as the courtship of Philippe and fair-haired Marie-Geneviève continued.

One Sunday after church, he brought Henriette along for a visit to reminisce with her old friends. In mid-afternoon, he rose nervously to excuse himself from the living room conversation, and all eyes followed with pleasure as he invited Marie-Geneviève to spend the afternoon along the river.

Henriette watched from the garden as they walked back up the lane. In her heart, she knew Philippe was ready for a family of his own.

Philippe and Marie-Geneviève were married on February 9, 1699, in the Paroisse Saint-Charles-Borromée Chapel at Charlesbourg. Henriette was too feeble to attend, but stood in joy to watch the buggy and lone horse came back to the house. She embraced her daughter-in-law with all the love she had stored for so long. Marie-Geneviève leaned to give Henriette a kiss.

"Mother, you must have these lovely flowers that Philippe gave to me. As long as they last, you will remember this day, and long after."

Henriette didn't live to see her first grandchild—a boy, born in August of 1700, named Julien after his maternal grandfather. Sadly, he died before his second birthday. The following year, they welcomed Marie-Madeleine, a delightful and clever girl, the pride of her father's eye.

The French now had peace with the Iroquois, Hurons and Algonquins, and in 1701, the Great Peace Treaty of Montréal was signed by the Iroquois and French. Native descendants mingled inside the walled city of Québec, but the Iroquois relationship with the British remained tenuous.

In February 1704, the French forces and native allies attacked Deerfield, Massachusetts on the Connecticut River valley. Commanded by Hertel de Rouville, as part of Queen Anne's War, the raid demolished homes and captured over a hundred American colonists. Although the French returned home victorious, New Englanders also claimed a revitalization of American spirit. Philippe Pasquier remained as a guard at the palisades of Charlesbourg and Beauport.

Louis XIV decided that there was no choice, the French *must* assert superiority in battle over the English. Focusing on Boston in particular, he ordered a barbaric scourge. So fearful were the Iroquois of obliteration, they ceded their territories to the British.

Across the border, Captain Frans LeRoy served with the New York militia during Queen Anne's War of 1702 to 1713 between France and England, and their Indian allies. Frans was assigned to various posts along the Hudson River throughout his military service. As the new Americans were torn in allegiance, so was the LeRoy family.

Eighteen

France sends more soldiers to quash Iroquois – Jean Charlebois favoured scout under Marquis de Crisafy - Coureur de bois bloodlines – Jean Charlebois marries Marthe Perrier – Jacques Charlebois married M-Françoise Danis, 1716 – Louis XIV expands shipbuilding in Québec of Royal Fleet – 1681 Montréal Census – Jacques Charles Charlebois negotiates a Barter – Marie Archambault first Métis in Québec – Levesque Tavern habitant meeting place – Relentless Raiding parties at Charlesbourg – Philippe Pasquier continues carpentry craft in seigneurie – Vincent Giroux marries M-Angelique Boutillet.

Jean Charlebois joins French Habitant Army

GRUMBLINGS GREW AMONGST SOLDIERS ABOUT THE urgency for reinforcements, and their rush of hope and relief came in 1685 as trained soldiers arrived from France to help quash the Iroquois. Members of the new garrison were provided uniforms, firearms, food and lodging, but were otherwise unpaid, contrary to the earlier Carignan Regiment.

Forming an auxiliary force, French colonists rallied to support the movement of cannons. Transporting supplies by canoe to parallel the advancing route of the troops, these volunteer voyageurs were respected as an integral part of the military.

Among the fighting soldiers was Philippe Pasquier's friend Jean Charlebois, a labourer de métier from St. Macaire, Gironde, France, who had served under Marquis de Crisafy, from the order of Malta. At nineteen years, he arrived at Montréal with his regiment. Immigration records showed derivatives of his name Charlebois, as Bouet, Brisebois, Joly and Jolibois. Crucial supplies were under guard at Fort Onondaga, when Jean Charlebois arrived to join the scouting party.

Marquis de Crisafy, highly regarded by Governor Calliere, was appointed King Louis XIV's lieutenant of Montréal in 1697 and given the land grant of a noble without rights of justice. As a favoured scout of Crisafy, Jean Charlebois was ordered to the colonies to participate in thwarting eight hundred Iroquois from the fort at Sault Saint-Louis. From the coureurs des bois, Jean quickly learned the Objiwa dialect, guiding as a translator for French inland explorations.

The coureurs des bois were Métis, having married into the local tribes, living as nomads for months at a time and raising families in their villages. Maintaining the French language and characteristics, they adapted to a different way of life in the woods, trapping, hunting, and trading against the laws of Nouvelle France.

Jean Charlebois and his brothers had the instinct of skilled hunters, and their wanderlust led them to settle first at Bellevue, then Lachine, St. Anne, Montréal and on to Pointe Claire. Their acute senses could anticipate a hunter's prey and forge to the woods with stealth, not to disturb the nest of a sleeping eagle.

At Notre-Dame in Montréal, the early church on the site of the later Basilique Notre-Dame, Jean Charlebois married Marthe Perrier-Lafleur. They raised their first five children there, before moving to St. Joachim at Pointe Claire.

Jacques Charles Charlebois, the fourth son of Jean Charlebois, married M-Françoise Danis in 1716, at Notre-Dame. Skilled tradesmen were in demand in the cities, with tides of bourgeois, merchants, and upper class families arriving from France.

Jacques Charles apprenticed in the trade of his father to produce weaponry fittings, then found employment with one of the large shipping lines at Montréal and Québec, tasked with building the royal fleet. Planing oak planks, he inhaled the sweet aroma of freshly hewn logs, as his saw sang and his plane slid over the beams.

In New France, word of the Congress of Utrecht treaty negotiations in 1713 wore heavily on habitants. The British had usurped economic powers and infiltrated control of their resources and trade.

With devasting losses to his navy in the English Channel, Louis XIV needed new ship construction to rebuild the fleet; but instead of having wood hewn in Québec and shipped to France, he bypassed the boycotts by ordering shipyards to be adapted in Québec, and new yards were built to prosper at the Saint-Charles River in 1732.

Jean Tessier and the Métis

Away from the river, farther up the hill from Jacques Charles' cottage in the French quarter of town, was rich farmland where Jean Tessier lived on the land of his father, Urbain Tessier, neighbouring the Archambault farm. Jean Tessier came from a large family, and as a youth at eighteen years, the 1681 Montréal Census had recorded his father, Urbain Tessier, living on 36 arpents with eleven oxen and steers.

Jacques Charles Charlebois spent weeks handcrafting a chair of honey oak for Jean Tessier's wife, Marie-Catherine DePoitiers, who'd recently given birth to their first son, Louis. Jean contracted Jacques for the work on a recommendation from Toussaint Girould, from a visit to Beauport.

By September, the chair was ready. Jacques Charles stepped out the door of the back kitchen to inhale the woodsy air. It would be a long morning's drive by wagon along the rutted road to the Tessier farm.

The rocking chair was covered in canvas for protection from elements, and tied on top of the buckboard. He could smell the polished plank boards as he drove.

"Good day to you, Jean," Jacques Charles called out, barely in earshot, spying his friend in his cornfield.

Tessier was always eager for a chin-wag. "Mighty glad to see you, son. Should I hope that the lump of canvas in the back will please my wife?"

"Indeed, we both hope it does."

"Come sit a while on the veranda. Marie-Catherine has cold cider to cool us from the morning heat. Our russet apple orchard has abundant fruit this year, the best yet."

"Ahhh. Mighty fine tasting."

"I sell it to the British in town for twice the price that I give to Hurons," Jean chortled.

"It's their own fault for inflating the value of the livre, then running a royal treasury to look after a postage system. My own pa was in a tirade when he heard that."

"I don't doubt that he was. How are your ma and pa?"

"They're still healthy. The youngest of the kids now goes to the English school at Pointe Claire during fallow months."

Jean said, "It is the law now that we send our young ones to learn the British ways, but at home I teach my children about the Métis and their rich ancestry. I found out that my mother, Marie Archambault, is shown in records at the longhouse registry as the first Métis in Québec of the Tessiers."

"That is good. But I know that the English openly boast that aboriginal blood is a disgrace," Jacques Charles replied. He scratched at his reddish brown beard that struggled to make an appearance.

"The French bourgeois now also look down on me and my family for our heritage, that's rich in French ancestry and also enhanced by traits of the indigenous people we live with every day," Jean said.

"The French, Métis, Hurons and Algonquins have all fought shoulder to shoulder for this land," Jacques replied. "The natives taught us to survive, and we've done fine so far."

Jean said, "The story that passed down through my family claimed that Jacques Archambault married a sauvagesse or maiden soon after he arrived from France, and had at least one daughter." He stopped with a puzzled brow. "My grandmother, Françoise Tourneau, claimed to also be from Aunis, and married in Lucon, Poitou in 1628. But Papa avoided telling me about my Archambault ancestry."

"The church will have records if you know where to begin, Jean."

Jean stumbled over his words as he tried to unravel his ancestry. "The other Tessiers in Montréal say they are Métis. I just accept that church records don't lie. I'll admit we are darker skinned that some of our Parisian friends, with straight black hair and high cheekbones, but everyone is unique because of their personal heritage—yet we all descend from Adam and Eve, bien?"

"Bien! Métis is a blend of culture of those who founded our country. French, coureur de bois, Huron—we are all habitant. Our children should be proud, no matter what the truth is."

Marie-Catherine DePoitiers heard it from the door and came to rest her hand on Jean's shoulder.

"Marie-Catherine is expecting again," he announced, with his arm around her thickening waist. "This time, I am sure it will be a boy. I guess being Métis is the reason for my good looks and rugged skin."

Enjoying his wit, Jean winked and gestured for Jacques to follow him to the barn.

"Look over here, Jacques. It's my new Jethro Tull seed plough from New York. The Dutch farmers use this invention in the New Netherlands. We can plant early without the backbreaking task of sowing seed from a basket and bending. The summer weather was good to farmers this year, so I have reaped well and can pay you in script for the rocker."

"Perhaps a small amount, but I was looking forward to bartering with you, Jean," Jacques Charles teased, flashing to a moment as a youth with his father, discussing trade. With hearty laughs, the men tossed to each other the sacks of grain for the back of the wagon, to prop the loose bushels of apples and vegetables.

At the house, Marie-Catherine waited with a posy of fresh herbs and a jug of maple syrup to be sent back to Marie-Françoise. From the road, Jacques waved from the wagon, satisfied with his barter, and Jean returned the script to his pocket and patted himself with contentment.

Libations with Monsieur Tourangeau

The Lévesque tavern was a frequent stop enroute to Charlesbourg for the elder Jean Charlebois and his son Jacques Charles, and was especially welcoming as their wagon became disabled with an unbalanced load.

The horses stood in relief as Jacques got down to inspect it. "The load of wagon wheel hubs has shifted," he said. "I'll secure it and join you inside."

Barely inside, Jean spotted Jean-Baptiste Tourangeau at the bar. The Frenchman wore a fringed deerskin vest, and braids under a knitted toque. But it was the jovial voice that Jean recognized, booming across the room.

"How is my friend, Jean-Baptiste? Come and join us. My son is with me too."

"I'm well, my friend. And your family? We will soon need to learn to be English, eh?" J-B laughed but Jean recognized the biting sarcasm.

"Never," Jean started. "Even though we're a mere fraction of the British colonies, we have the French heart. I heard it said in Montréal that we are now twelve thousand Frenchmen." They raised their glasses in a toast to that, as young Jacques arrived.

"Have we not fought well enough?' Jacques posed. "It has not even been fifty years since our fathers and grandfathers came to the new world, claiming it as New France and staking the flag of the fleur-de-lis."

Jean-Baptiste became red-faced with emotion and his arms began to flail with animation. "Oui. Louis has reigned longer than I have had years in Québec. Perhaps he turned a blind eye to the extortion of trading and canoe exploration, and is content sending seigneurs and lords to rule the Québecois. We are a new people, yet our government is shipped from the shores of our mother country—most often a reward to a noblesse for military service in Europe."

Jacques said, "Since the death of William III, the French seized opportunity for expansion in Europe. With support of the new English king, Louis invaded the Rhineland, opposing the Palatines when they thought the Netherlands had turned their sights in another direction."

"God save our King," J-B said. "He has been victorious many times, but invading other countries is pointless. Every time, what has been ceded in battle is returned in a Treaty. That's the way I see it!

"We are no longer Ville-Marie, but the Governor has declared us to be the city of Montréal. And he's ordered a new stone wall to surround us; I guess it provides work for the masons and carpenters," Tourangeau quipped.

Stretching his back against the chair and reaching his arms a full length of the table, he surveyed Jacques Charles. "You must be all of sixteen, eh lad?"

Jacques started to reply, but his father interjected, "He's a wise man already, and a good carpenter, like his father and grand-père. Youth and wisdom is a grand combination."

The three men clinked glasses again.

"Jacques Charles, soon you must stop by our place. I have too many daughters for one farmer," Jean-Baptiste teased, then Jacques Charles watched his face tighten to seriousness.

"As a matter of fact, Monsieur Tourangeau, I *will* be coming your way next week with a furniture delivery."

"Please come for supper. My wife and daughters will want to see you, as they always do." Tourangeau leaned in closer. "My favourite is Marie Françoise, my eldest."

Jacques Charles smiled without it being noticed. He had seen the lovely fair-haired Marie Françoise from a curious distance and was heartened by the opportunity to see her again.

Ageless Instincts of Pasquier Men

Relentless raiding war parties were causing alarm, and Philippe Pasquier and Marie-Geneviève Brosseau moved to the safety of Charlesbourg to raise their young family. Philippe plied his trade as a joiner and carpenter, but also worked the farm with a few of the Chalifour and Brosseau boys.

From the wall of the barn, Philippe lowered his father's often forgotten worn satchel. He laid out the tools of a master carpenter from Dissay, having belonged to his grandfather and his father.

His hand ran down the smooth handle of the plane, a perfect fit in its wear from use, and he imagined the history it knew back in France. His carpentry shop was at the back of the house. When he opened the door, the smell of wood shavings and sawdust reminded him how he loved to work with fine dove-tail grooving and the feel of a lathe in his hands.

With the tools from Dissay, Philippe would establish a reputation beyond Charlesbourg for his tables, dressers, chairs, trunks, sleds and wagons.

*St. Louis Gate, Québec, Engraving on wood, Artist F.B. Schell,
Engraver J.E. Sharp, Picturesque Canada, Vol. 1, 1882*

Like his father, Philippe was using the name of Paquet, with the English meaning 'old French package'. Next to the Laviolette's farm, he purchased another strip of land in the Bourg Royal, planting corn, wheat, potatoes and vegetables and a length of orchards to the end of the acreage. He was gratified to use the seigneur's mill for harvest, with a portion of the crops returned in flour.

Seigneurial traditions continued as a condition of life, requiring Philippe to work three days of each year for the Giffards to build and improve roads and bridges in Charlesbourg. During fall harvest, serfs labored in the vineyards and seigneur's orchards to ensure adequate wines for his cellars. Even the sport of fishing in the rivers and creeks returned to the seigneur one of every eleven caught.

Philippe and Marie-Geneviève raised fourteen children. The youngest, François, born in 1720 at Saint-Jacques-La-Misère, Charlesbourg, would leave his name to the same land at Petite Auvergne that was cleared by his grandfather.

Sad word reached Philippe in the fall of 1732 that Toussaint Girould's wife, Marie-Thérèse Dauphin, died in childbirth. Philippe joined Jean Tessier for the journey to Beauport to bring condolences to the widower, remembering that Toussaint's father had shown the same respect when Étienne died. Marie-Thérèse Dauphin was not yet sixty years of age and had given life to fifteen children, although six died as infants. Grief and hardship was too often the way of life for habitant women.

European diseases diminished the population of both natives and habitants in the early 1700s. Threats of scurvy and dysentery were replaced by smallpox, consumption, and plagues. Quarantines didn't spare afflicted families and slowly one child after another succumbed.

Marie-Thérèse was not the only mother to sit by the deathbed nursing children without avail, until they had given of all their strength and yielded their fate. A journey to the graveyard was often followed with news of another child on the way.

When Philippe and Jean arrived to see Toussaint Girould, they found he had aged in appearance and was now despondent, but he still did his best to light up on greeting them. He was left with nine young children, and all but one of his brothers had predeceased him. Toussaint's youngest son, Vincent, was born in 1709 at the family homestead. For the next few years, the youngest went to live with older sisters when they married, or to close family friends on the seigneurie.

At twenty-two, Vincent married Marguerite-Angélique Boutillet, settling at Chambly, twenty-five miles south of Montréal on the Richelieu River. Vincent took up farming on the Seigneurie of Jacques de Chambly, the original site where Samuel de Champlain began the stone wall construction of Saint-Louis Forts.

Nineteen

Thomas Pageau, grave digger – Fête de Noël, Charlesbourg – Joseph Pageau weds Madeleine Bosme, 1715 – Building and canning bees – Reminiscent of Ononthio, wilderness native – Urbain Tessier died 1719 – Stumble on a Grizzzly Feeding ground – Survival in the woods – Congress of Utrecht Treaty negotiations, 1713 – Tavern tales – France concedes Acadia – Toast to Robert Giffard.

Joseph Pageau weds Madeleine Boesme

THOMAS PAGEAU, A MASTER STONE MASON FROM ST. Aignan, Sarthe, France, and a wilderness companion of Ononthio and Philippe Paquet, settled with his wife Marie-Catherine Roy in the paroisse of Saint-Charles-de-Borromée, Charlesbourg.

During the winters of consumption, he took a second occupation as the local grave digger, in addition to being a tailleur for the Jesuit mission.

Later, Étienne Roy would take the role of grave digger for Thomas Pageau's own passing in 1706, when his son Joseph was only eleven. Born at Charlesbourg in a family of eleven children, Joseph was raised on the family farm close to the Paquet and Brosseau families.

During the Fête de Noël in Charlesbourg, Joseph Pageau stood with other young men at the barn wall, watching jigs and dances of the lone farmers and trappers. Most came to town with hopes of finding a damsel, and Joseph felt the awkwardness of his own situation.

Across the room, Madeleine Boesme and her sister Marie-Anne swayed to the tempo. As her eyes met Joseph's, he knew it would be impolite not to at least attempt a greeting. With anticipation, he steadied himself and readied his words.

"Madamoiselle Boesme, may I have this dance? My name is Joseph Pageau from Charlesbourg."

But his gesture to Madeleine coincided with the approach of a bachelor from Charlesbourg, nearing her. Joseph edged forward and she reached her hand quickly to him, ignoring the rejected suitor.

She blushed. "My name is Madeleine." He knew already but didn't say.

The short bow fiddle music was playing in eight bars for the step dance, four to the right, then to the left, with community dancing impacted by a growing local Scottish influence, often with quick footwork, arms at the side and eyes focused on the other.

Joseph's mother's instruction rang in his thoughts.

A young suitor must never touch the waist of a young unmarried woman.

The jigs became faster and livelier, keeping with the fiddler's pace. Madeleine was bumped from behind and took the chance to grab Joseph to stabilize herself. Their eyes locked as he embraced her.

Joseph Pageau wed Madeleine Boesme in the winter of 1715 at the Boesme residence, where her unmarried brothers lived with their aging widowed father. He pushed the kitchen tables and chairs back to form a circle, and as friends and relatives arrived to celebrate, cassoulets, stews, cakes and pies were laid out surrounding a bowl of punch mixed from cold cider.

The priest arrived by carriage from the Paroisse de Saint-Borromée to officiate for his fee of three livres, that Joseph had frugally saved.

Madeleine had a small dowry plus a ten livre note from her father. Many guests brought supplies for the couple's shelves, with sacks of beans, coffee, flour and cornmeal. Craftsmen contributed samplings of their works, collecting a chair, candlesticks and an oaken bucket for the couple.

The wedding frivolity past the midnight hour, with dancing, fiddles and the priest's flute. Long before, the children found corners and a sofa in the parlor to snuggle and sleep.

Bleary eyes and morning exhaustion greeted those still there in the morning, quiet over a hearty ham and egg breakfast, then hot baked potatoes at the door to warm their hands for the journey home. An overnight skiff of snow covered the roads along the banks of the Saint-Charles, with ice piled against the rocks.

Pageau constructed a single story house that summer, hewn from his choicest pine timbers from the back woods, with neighbours rallying with food, sewing and a gift of gab. Men hammered and sawed, as women carried canning and cakes from the wagons, and scurried to the kitchen for the bee. When Joseph ventured in to ask about lunch for the men, he couldn't be heard over excited jibber-jabber and laughter.

The Christmas snow was silent, but the house lit up with the warmth of the fireplace and decorations. Joseph gathered the smallest ones around his chair to tell stories of his father and Philippe Pasquier. Eyes widened about the kindly native, Ononthio, who taught Joseph about the soul of the woods and the spirit of the skies.

"My dear little ones, I want you to remember as I do about a great adventure your Grandpa Pageau took one winter. He learned to survive with nothing—no snowshoes or canoe, and little food; but the priceless gift of a Huron."

Ignace's eyes danced. "Tell us more, Papa."

The dramatic inflections of Joseph's voice presented the story as an adventure, mesmerizing the children and relieving him of the spirit of Manitou.

In a soft, then crescendo tone, he visualized and portrayed the spiritual hunting grounds, and the talking winds and whispering trees. He paused and looked down at Ignace who was sitting tight on his foot.

"Yes, Papa. I will tell my own children too," Ignace said. "They'll need to know.

Charles-Joseph was the eldest of Joseph's sons. He bent down and picked up the sleeping Marie-Françoise, a toddler at the time, and carried her to a cot, but not before he put a gentle hand on his father's shoulder and nodded.

Louis Tessier and the Bear

AS A PIT SAWYER, coppersmith, farmer and carpenter, Urbain Tessier acquired new land at Côte Saint-François, and as his sons married, he deeded parcels of it to them. Marie Archambault outlived her husband, Urbain, by thirty years, as well as many of her children, before retiring to Pointe-aux-Trembles near Montréal where she died in 1719.

Legendary stories of Urbain lived on through his children and grandchildren in Montréal and their descendants.

In late spring of 1725, the river levels were running high with strong currents. Jean Tessier, son of Urbain, had business to settle at the Montréal shipyards, and felt it safe to attempt the trip by canoe and simply portage over the Chutes. Although warned of the danger, he felt the calling of Ononthio's spirit and persisted.

At the Charlesbourg trading post, he purchased a native canoe suitable for the trip. His son, Louis, paddled at the bow, with Jean at the stern. Soon into the first day, the currents became too difficult to advance, and they took land on a barren slope and secured the canoe.

Creating an adventure for the boy, and with the confidence of his own father, Jean went so far as to guarantee Louis the capture of a great creature, hoping for a bear, common along the shore. Scouring the site, he found bear scat and paw prints, but knew the animal had already passed through.

"We'll camp here tonight, Louis. In the morning, the anger of the water will abate and we'll continue. Bring the tarp and the beans to the clearing there near the barberry."

Nearby rustling froze Louis as he rooted in the woods for firewood. Turning to call, he realized they were in a feeding area for a family of grizzlies. He imagined hot breath at his back and swore later there was heat from a looming body.

Bear Trap, engraving on wood, Artists Schell & Hogan, Engraver Edith Cooper,
Picturesque Canada, Vol.1, 1882 Belden Bros. Public Domain

"Louis! Walk slowly backwards to the water's edge. Reach for the axe."
Jean Tessier spoke firmly in a calm voice, for his son to hear him from
twenty feet. The boy crept low, close to the bushes. As he gripped the
handle, the grizzly reared high on its haunches. He knew there was only
one chance, one axe, and one grizzly.

The roar echoed as the boy swung, and the bear thrust and fell forward
onto his father, thrashing and heaving. Then silence.

"Papa!" Louis refused to allow the tears to escape, knowing Papa would
need him to be strong, whatever happened with the grizzly. His jaw
clenched and his fists gripped until his nails indented his hands. He bent
beside his father, under the bear.

"Mon Dieu! Papa!"

Under the weight, Jean was helpless until Louis rolled the bear a few inches, enough to pull his legs free. Splattered with blood, Jean heaved the bear and crawled to freedom.

In an afterthought, Jean remembered the bear trap, still stowed in the canoe. Even in rusted state from past winters, it could have been the difference of survival.

He limped to the hunting cargo and yanked the rusty trap.

"Look, Louis!"

"Let's hope there will be another then," the boy said, to Jean's pride. "Papa, do we dare take the trophy head home, so they will believe our story?"

Jean was already putting on his father's old leather hunting gloves.

"Don't try to set the trap without me, Louis," Jean warned, and reached to it, snapping off his thumb. Ignoring the searing pain, he secured a wrap around the wound and didn't mention it further, coming to terms that his pride was greater than his pain. "I have nine more," he said.

"Shh! Look down the river."

A quarter mile upstream, three Iroquois canoes were gliding toward them. "Louis, there's no time to skin the bear. Come quickly . . . here's a lone claw; that will be your souvenir."

The two headed into the forest, keeping parallel to the river. An arrow pierced the tree next to Louis, but with their agility they outpaced the raiding party.

After resting in a mossy ravine, they back-tracked to their canoe, satisfied with the day's events and the stories it would bring.

Tavern Stories

PHILIPPE PASQUIER relished his social circle in Lower Charlesbourg, fraternizing at every chance at the old Lévesque Tavern. He squeezed a chair in next to Jean Tessier, who was already surrounded by eager ears leaning close for new fantastic stories of his hunting trips.

As Jean's voice rose and his tales were embellished, they responded with shouts of exhilaration and encouragement.

"You have never seen a grizzly as large or so blood-thirsty," Jean said. "His great foul-smelling fangs drooled soapberry saliva onto my face—I was that close. But he wasn't a match for my cunning and strength."

Jean searched the wild eyes of his companions, satisfied with their awe and acceptance.

Philippe slapped the table in laughter. "Well, mon ami, I will be wanting to see the trophy itself to confirm that the story is true. I met Running Bear in the woods near the old farm and he told me a similar story."

In a flash, he met Philippe's gaze, and it took only took an instant to reach an understanding.

Trading of stories continued in turn around the table, and erupted when young Charlebois brought his comrades to tears of laughter as he chased a cranky, wild boar and wrestled it down.

The tavern pact avoided politics and economics. Still, when a couple of British soldiers entered, the revelry stopped and the hush in the bar was resounding. Philippe looked up at the newcomers and leaned to his cohorts.

"I just traded pelts at the Hudson's Bay trading post and overheard those Brits talking about some treaty of the kings and queens in Europe, deciding our lands and quashing French authority. France conceded Rupert's Land, the Acadian colony and Nova Scotia yet again. I don't care much that they gave away some Caribbean Island called Kitts, and the Spanish can take the South Americas and its gold treasures. Let them fight it out around their tables, while we are the ones to face disgruntled natives and poor crops."

"Can this possibly be true?" Jean Tessier asked.

"Oui, and it gets worse. Those European representatives, who never set foot on New France, deem that Britain should have the trading monopoly and control Iroquois pelts. Who's going to tell the natives?"

The habitants were silent in disbelief, then young Charlebois spat his acrimony.

"When are they coming to take my farm?"

In anger, Philippe stood and thumped the table, prepared to be overheard. "France receives a pittance for conceding our explorations and toiling. Île Saint-Jean (P.E.I.) remains under French authority as does the Isle Saint-Pierre et Michelon, and Cape Breton. The cod banks remain in French control."

"Well, hurray for that." Jean leaned back in his chair, his hands in the air in surrender. "God save the King!"

Philippe called to the bartender. "Bring us a bottle of the seigneur's nouveau wine."

The room fell silent until the wine arrived.

"To Seigneur Giffard!"

Twenty

John Law creates General Private Bank – Philippe II granted Law a charter – Devaluation of French livre – 1716 Paper Issue of Script – Law takes control over cartel of the seas – 1720 Law's Bank destabilized – False values devastated Québec economy – Coin must support 95% - Dutch settlements at Ulster Co., New York – African slaves used in colonies – French Huguenots escape religious persecution in France – Frans François LeRoy increases wealth in N.Y. – Simeon LeRoy, son of Frans, inherits Wappinger Creek – Beginning of French-Indian Wars.

John Law's Mississippi Company

GOSSIP SPREAD QUICKLY OF THE CONTROVERSY, THAT a Scottish millionaire gambler and known murderer, John Law, had created the General Private Bank, establishing printed currency. His keen economist skills, inherited from his banker father, left him with a healthy estate that he successfully gambled away in London and Amsterdam.

Before the age of twenty, he'd been convicted in the courts for killing a man in a duel, supposedly defending a lady's virtue. But escaping jail, he headed across the Atlantic, beyond the reach of the English noose.

Law had an extraordinary mind, believing he had a fantastical purpose in gambling with economics, and recruited the support of Philippe II, Duke of Orléans of France, who reigned as regent until Louis XV was of age in 1723. Reluctantly, Philippe II granted John Law a charter.

Before leaving Paris, John Law knew politics and the royals well, having advised Louis XIV on economic issues before the king's death. Facing an enormous debt borrowed by the deceased king, he orchestrated a devaluation of the French livre, driving old coins out of circulation. The offenders of the devaluation scheme were eventually rounded up and exiled to the Bastille.

Philippe II realized the economic distress of France could be salvaged in Québec, and granted Law the charter to manage royal trading revenues. For Monsieur Law, it was the right to issue paper money or script, with the intention of providing Québecois the ability to pay taxes based on 25% coin and 75% in script.

Law established his bank in 1716 and quickly found that his paper issue was preferred by traders, amassing some control of natural resources and precious metals.

With eyes on the lucrative French colony of Louisiana, he was granted a monopoly on trade in the Americas. The riches of the West Indies were in his sight and his already immense greed was burgeoning. Soon he had greater control of the French economy, raising capital by selling stocks at an exorbitant value while discounting the paper issue.

The novel and now acceptable sport of speculating expanded quickly to the sale of tobacco, gold and silver refining, wines and liquor, dry goods, livestock, grain crops, farm implements, value for services and imported luxury items.

Extending beyond the French soil of the St. Lawrence, Law took control over the cartel of the seas, merging La Compagnie des Indes Orientales with Compagnie de China, resulting in the Compagnie Perpétuelle des Indes in 1719.

King Louis XV assigned control of government supported notes to the Banque Royale in France, allowing Law to guarantee Mississippi script. Paris thrived, while the folly of Philippe II was to justify that backing the issue with twice as much cash would double his treasury.

But Law gambled on issuing unbacked script while the king's sights were elsewhere. A stock exchange frenzy arose for a short time, before a French prince's greed sent three wagons full of script to Law's bank, to be exchanged for coin.

Law reluctantly sent him away with the three wagons, but regretted fulfilling the demand and ordered two wagons of coin be returned. As word spread of the situation, financial opponents demanded coin for issue en masse in 1720, destabilizing Law's bank.

In retaliation, Law declared coin illegal and his issue was the only value trade currency. Parliament responded by proclaiming that coin, by law, must support ninety-five percent of script value. Law was stripped of his authority, and as a hunted and hated man, fled to exile in Venice where he returned to gambling.

Québec settlers had thrived in their barter system, but the new taxation required payment in notes, valued even higher than the circulated coinage of the Banque Royale. False values rose on rents and land, luxury items, stock investments and livestock bought with script.

When Law's bank collapsed, so did the real value of habitant investments and savings. Fortunately, habitants regarded their toil greater than the piece of paper the economy was based on. Yet habitants and settlers as far as the Mississippi and north to Québec were reeling in economic devastation.

Script Becomes Worthless in Québec

Marie-Geneviève Brosseau heard the news from Marie-Thérèse Dauphin in Beauport, that Toussaint and their son Louis Giroux had suffered a loss on his wheat crop and was concerned for their own financial status.

"Philippe, have we traded much with paper?"

"Marie-Geneviève . . ." Philippe swallowed hard on his pride.

"Whatever it is then, we will overcome." She laid a reassuring hand on Philippe's shoulder.

"I need to go into town. I ordered a seed driller at the mercantile. I will not oblige him to provide me with something I have not truly paid for. It's a matter of honor."

"Yes, indeed," Marie-Geneviève stated with pride.

"I must go into Charlesbourg now, in fact." Phillipe rose from the kitchen table.

"Perhaps Pierre might like to go with you."

"So I should teach him the respect of paper?" Philippe laughed sardonically.

"He will soon marry and have his own land. We pray that this never happens to our children."

"Then yes, I will take Pierre."

Marie-Geneviève removed a tin from a shelf in her larder and clutched a handful of coins.

"Here, Philippe, buy your tobacco."

Philippe and Pierre returned in the afternoon, smiling and in laughter. Marie-Geneviève saw the paper package under Philippe's arm, and her daughters wanted her to ask about it, but she knew some things take time to be revealed.

Gathering at the table, Philippe untied the packet. Each of the children received sarsaparilla or horehound candy stick, and Marie-Geneviève opened a floral roll of yard goods and a length of ribbon.

"Where is your tobacco, Philippe?" she said, as her eyes welled up.

"Another time, my darling."

Frans François LeRoy Amasses Land in Dutchess Co.

South from the St. Lawrence, the Hudson River wanders through rolling hills and orchard groves into Dutch settlements around Ulster County, New York, with steamboats and trading vessels from the Mohawk River.

Self-esteemed, landed gentry from England were squeezing into farming areas surrounding the Hudson and conventional Dutch communities, with grand brick mansions from river clay beds, and stone manors with paned shuttered windows and typical English gardens.

By 1728, the List of Freeholders for Ulster County recorded the majority of Dutch and German settler surnames. While the Dutch freely employed the use of domestic and African slaves, the German Quakers were opposed to the principles of slavery.

French Huguenots were now escaping religious persecution in France by the Roman Catholic Church, and although some fled to Canada, the majority found their way into the New England colonies.

In Dutchess County, New York, the 1714 Census recorded that Frans LeRoy had eight children and one male slave under sixteen, and two female slaves. The next year, he added ten acres east of his farm at Fishkill. As a respected member of the Dutch community, Frans was appointed Assessor for Dutchess County in 1719. Quakers objected to his allowing thirty slaves to be inherited or bought as agricultural labour before 1720.

As landowners became affluent acquiring land, some didn't have enough able-bodied children of age to absorb the work, and others left the cultivation of plantations to slaves, while they entered the more lucrative merchant and economic system.

Like cattle, slaves of African descent were brought from the south, with public auctions and whippings common by unscrupulous traders. Branding, ear notching and castration were ignored by the colonists—the same people that filled the churches on Sunday mornings.

The Quakers' opposition to the sale and use of slaves became the catalyst in the eighteenth century of an alliance leading to the Underground Railroad, a network of routes and safe houses for slaves to escape to free states and Canada.

Frans LeRoy was the only LeRoy descendant that hired slaves, and as respected in his community, the naïve conclusion was that he treated his servants with kindness. Other LeRoys, Peter Lasink, and the Schoutens had no slaves in their households before 1720.

Frans, formerly Ensign in the British militia at Albany, served nobly as Captain under the command of Colonel Barent VanKleek's pre-revolution military force of Dutchess County. After the Treaty of Utrecht, the New England colonies enjoyed nearly thirty years of relative peace. His stature as Captain placed him in a position of leadership in the community and the Dutch Reformed Church, as deacon and later as elder in 1739.

Frans LeRoy and Celetje Damen's second son, Simeon LeRoy married Elizabeth Van Kleeck in 1736. The Van Kleecks, LeRoys, and Freer families had many marriages in Ulster and Dutchess Counties among their descendants.

Simeon and Elizabeth had two sons before she passed away, in the following spring, Simeon married Blandina Freer at Fishkill.

At Captain Frans LeRoy's death in 1762, his will divided his property between six surviving children and to his granddaughter, Frances, daughter of his deceased son, Frans Jr. Simeon and Blandina inherited family lands that included black slaves at Wappinger Creek in Rumbout Precinct, Poughkeepsie, now grown to become the core of trading north of Philadelphia.

King George's Wars were raging in North America, extending into the French-Indian wars with battles between the French, the Five Nations and the British in New York, Massachusetts, New Hampshire and Nova Scotia. France unsuccessfully tried to retake Annapolis Royal, Cape Breton, Nova Scotia; the Americans, led by Governor William Shirley of Massachusetts, attempted to take Fort Louisbourg, which eventually fell to the British.

The French organized with Micmac and Maliseet allies to take Saratoga, New York, where more than a hundred American habitants were killed and villages destroyed. Exacting retribution, the Iroquois joined with the British Americans to attack Québec ports and cut off supply routes to their outposts.

In turn, French and Indian forces retaliated in the Hudson Valley, attacking Fort Massachusetts and Schenectady, New York, with sieges that continued the next few years without resolutions or treaties.

Like many families, the LeRoy descendants were strongly divided in loyalty—some supporting the British and others the American colonies.

Twenty-one

Landscape of Montréal's shoreline – Cultural inventions of harpsichord & spinets elevate bourgeoise – Marie-Catherine Portelance and the Watchmaker – Cogs, gears, gauges & chronometers – Louis Roy Portelance buys Quare Repeater – Periwigs and sweet perfume – Montréal's Mercantile District – Great Fire of 1734 destroys Portelance Residence – Salvaging Porcelain Antoinette – Jacques Ambroise Charlebois helps to rebuild – Jacques Charlebois & M-Catherine marry, 1745 – Charlebois descendant Louis Joseph.

Montréal's Mosaic – Merchant, Artists and the Affluent

THE FLAT TERRAIN OF MONTRÉAL'S SHORELINE WAS ideal for its huge wharfs and rows of warehouses, customs offices, and fish markets. Lengthy cascades of wooden stairs ascended to the town above the stone walls, and as passageways rotted they were replaced with stone.

Rising behind the port, the skyline was growing with Catholic cathedral spires, magnificent Notre-Dame towers, tin roofs of Orthodox churches, and domed Citadels on the mountain.

On lanes and cobblestone boulevards, parallel and perpendicular to the river, the finest houses were under construction with cut stone and metalworkers' ornate cast-iron fences, imported French bevelled glass and window grates.

Bonsecours Market and wharves, Montréal, QC, about 1870,
Alexander Henderson, McCord Museum, Public Domain ©

Decorative iron grills guarded great casements that opened like gates to gesture an impression of affluence. Lace finery fluttered through windows, and passersby might hear the angelic music of a Cristofori's Italian harpsichord or spinet echoing to the streets.

Grand, gaily painted houses were wedged one into another, but a few streets away, lanes narrowed, with tall wooden structures and Irish tavern facades lacking in upkeep and paint.

The mosaic of society brought together Métis, who adapted to town life, along with skilled tradesmen, poor French artists, local merchants and the affluent.

Business was conducted from carts that moved up and down the streets of Ville Marie, loaded with barrels of goods and sacks for Bonsecours Market.

An appetite for finery by a new bourgeoise was creating demand for more trades—carpentry, masons, tinsmiths, ironmongers, carriage makers, weavers and tailors.

Scavenging seagulls circled the docks, with their noises drowned by the horns of merchant ships entering the harbour.

The Watchmaker & Marie-Catherine Portelance

Louis Roy Portelance released his daughter's hand once inside the shop. Marie-Catherine, a full six years of wonderment, followed her father to the counter. She had insisted they pass the other quaint shops along the market road, as her heart was set on the charms of Rochon & Sons Watchmakers.

The plank door creaked and the overhead bell jingled to announce their entry. Inside, with the street din muted, a melody of timepieces ticked loudly and echoed through the store in metronome rhythm.

"I love this store so much," she gushed, but carefully out of range of Monsieur Rochon at the back.

The store had become renowned to residents and visitors as a crafter and supplier of intricate pocket watches, pendulum clocks[28] of finely carved oak, and French porcelains and alabaster adorned with gold leaf.

Workshop sounds of clanging, pinging, gonging and ticking permeated the shop, and even entering was a solemn experience.

Marie-Catherine looked down at her black, polished shoes and smoothed the ruffles on her dress, before the clockmaker appeared from a curtain. Brushing his soiled hands on an oilcloth apron, he offered an apologetic handshake and warm greetings. Conversation would always come first before any business transaction. He straightened his nose spectacles.

"Bonjour, Marie-Catherine, comme une petite demoiselle pour visiter ma boutique. J'ai quelque chose de très spécial pour vous montrer, quand ton papa a fini d'affaires."[29] She pulled tight to her father's side and the clockmaker winked.

---

[28] Pendulum clocks first invented by Gallileo, the Italian astronomer. Later the Dutch scientist, Christian Huygens, refined the compact workings for a watch.

[29] "Hello, Mary Catherine, like a little lady to visit my shop. I have something very special to show you when your papa finishes business."

Laying a square tapestry on the counter, the craftsman drew from his drawer a wind-up in a simple gold casing, elaborate with etchings of a ship under sail, and with bold, raised face engravings in Roman numerals.

Marie-Catherine's eyes were instead on the wooden case with the glass top at the counter's end. The velvet-lined box was open, with an array of maritime compasses, nautical gauges, chronometers and bare workings of miniature wheels, cogs, gears, and hammers. As she balanced forward on her tiptoes, a dozen gongs and chimes began in unison on the walls and shelves, and she nearly lost her balance.

Monsieur Rochon and her father turned to watch her innocent surprise and confusion, and as the bells echoed, all three erupted into laughter.

"This is a lot of noise, Papa."

"It is the sound of time."

Each pendulum had precision timing, unique to the regulators and tall clocks. The English Graham began the outbreak, and each took turns pealing the arrival of ten o'clock. The patient chorus of chimes seemed to last longer than the count of ten, to Marie-Catherine.

"Ah, now it is ten o'clock everywhere," Monsieur Rochon reassured the little girl.

"Everywhere!" she repeated in her soft voice.

Louis lingered over the pocket watches and agreed to a Quare Repeater from London, assured by the watchmaker that it was a wise decision. Louis exchanged paper livres, and observed the merchant's care as his package was wrapped in a soft cloth pouch. When Monsieur Rochon finished, he attended to an intricate German-made cuckoo clock, hanging with long strings on the wall. Making an adjustment to the timing, he signaled Marie-Catherine to come closer.

Her fixation was on the miniature red doors, when suddenly they popped open and music started, with tiny carved people holding hands and dancing in a circle before disappearing inside the doors. A painted bird on a roost above the door chirped, "Cuckoo, cuckoo," and Marie-Catherine gasped in delight.

"Oh merci, merci, Monsieur," she squealed, coming down off her tiptoes. Louis Roy Portelance, with Marie-Catherine in hand, opened the creaky door, nodding to Monsieur Rochon, as if they were now old friends.

A few doors down, they passed Mignier's Navigation shop, intrigued at its magnificent window, filled with brass meters and gauges, optical prisms, armless pince nez, lorgnetts, monocles, silver and ivory sextants, pocket telescopes, barometers and code mirrors. Parisians wanting sophistication in Montréal frequented the shop, along with locals willing to pay for the appearance of prestige.

Marie-Catherine came to an abrupt stop, as a door flew open in front of her. A towering man in finery stepped forward in a way that scattered women and other children from his path.

The pompous Parisian stood tall and arched his back like a peacock. Powder was noticeably caked on his face and he smelled of sweet perfume. His colourful plumed hat topped a white wig of measured ringlets. As they watched, he drew a timepiece from his waistcoat, peering down with a pointy chin, to assess the time through his acquired pince nez.

The statuesque man had chosen from an elaborate choice of lens fittings imported from France, England, Germany, and Italy. Before he left the shop, the clerk adjusted the Lord's armless spectacles with a thin wire that could be hooked into the ringlets of his wig and rest above the ears.

"Behold, child, you are in my way," the man reined up.

Marie-Catherine took a step backwards and whispered to her father. "Is that indeed the king, Papa?"

"No dear, just a rude man. But dearest, it is also rude to stare at people who are a spectacle."

"What's a spectacle?"

Overhearing her innocent query, the Lord huffed at the insolence, and stretched his walking stick forward with long strides up the wide avenue. Louis Roy Portelance patted his daughter's hand with a smile at the lesson.

The Portelance family was recorded in the 1731 Census in Montréal's eastside, with six children, on a lot fronting on rue de Notre-Dame, their stone house in the centre of a bustling area near the citadel. Louis Roy worked his craft as a silversmith.

Nearby, shiny black carriages with felt-coated drivers in silk top hats courted manor ladies and gentlemen to haberdasheries, milliners, and chemists' shops for les maux de tête. Sunny afternoons brought them to the streets to stroll the shops of tobacconists, vintners, tailors, cobblers of ladies buttoned and laced shoes, tapestry weavers, and writing houses.

In graceful queues, the carriages moved east and west on Rue de Saint Paul, with hooves smartly clapping with a sound of superiority, away from the Citadel toward Jacques Cartier Square just beyond Rue St. Vincent.

The upper class came to the mercantile district as a place to be seen, and to admire the finest of silk, velvet and taffeta gowns from Paris, or perfected design copies made in Montréal. At the nearby docks, merchants congregated on the arrival of each ship from France, bringing bales of new dry goods and latest fashions.

Montréal habitants had become fashion conscious, with higher societal expectations from Europe. Although selections were largely limited to woolens, cottons, a few linens and silks, they were colourfully in vogue with Paris. Vegetable dyes from beets and berries produced vibrant reds and pinks, blueberries for indigo, carrots for orange and taming of browns; yellow weed blossoms were ground into brilliant mais, and grass mulch delivered nature's green. Each outfit became a unique masterpiece, competing with embroidery accents and hand stitching.

Periwig had been invented in Paris in 1630, in the form of toupées required of magistrates and esquires, and the craze found its way to the new colony, crafted with horse hair sewn into rows and ringlets. French culture and the status of a higher education were bragged about within the walled city. Artists and musicians were in demand by the elite, reflecting both an appreciation for culture and a separation in social class.

The Great Fires of Montréal, 1721 and 1734

MORE THAN A hundred wooden structures were crushed to ashes in the fire of 1721 in the borough between St. Nicolas Street and St. Dizier, creating hardship and trauma beyond imaginations of the families.

In response, Montréal magistrates quickly set building ordinances requiring stone foundations and limiting houses to two stories. Chimney sweeps were contracted to comply with new regulations to maintain roofs and hearths at a new standard, requiring monthly chimney cleaning and visible ladders on rooftops.

This was still not enough to prevent an alleged arsonist from setting the town ablaze thirteen years later, in 1734. The tragic blaze burned a quadrant of Saint-Paul, with many older wooden structures. Without an organized Fire Department, residents were helpless to quash the raging inferno, and lost over a hundred houses at Hôtel-Dieu.

Buckets, water barrels, and shovels were handled by volunteers, and the nearby streets were filled with awed onlookers. By the time the fire died to embers, an old historic church and several streets of homes had perished.

In the blaze, Louis Roy Portelance and his wife Angélique Allaire and their family lost their home. The skeletons of tall buildings smoldered for days, leaving families in search of accommodation. As many exterior walls were stone and mortar, they remained a tribute to the tragedy for years.

The Portelance family found shelter in a nearby church, with the children scared and confused, losing everything at such an age. As Louis searched the ruins of his home for anything to be salvaged, he encountered Jacques Ambroise Charlebois, a strapping youth at sixteen, who had come to help with rebuilding.

Little Marie-Catherine Roy, the same child who loved to stare in the watchmaker's window, was eight years old now. She watched the strength of Jacques Ambroise Charlebois as he lifted mortar and bricks, and called to him when he found her favourite doll, intact but seriously singed.

"Merci, Jacques. Antoinette is my special doll, and I'm so glad you found her. I will fix her burns," she said.

Jacques Ambroise was six feet, with broad shoulders and muscular arms from labouring. Bending down, he picked up the little girl and gave her a kiss on the cheek.

"You are a lovely girl. Someday you'll make some man very happy."

"Why can't he be you?" She leaned to his shoulder with a giggle.

Rebuilding homes, Jacques Ambroise worked side by side with Joseph Jean-Baptiste Charbonneau, who was also a victim of the Montréal fire, and brought his skills as a master carpenter for the Jesuits.

Jacques was also building a home for himself, a tall, narrow stone house, high on the hill of St. Vincent de Paul at Laval, lodged between two three-story tenements. On completion, it would become his family home, with space for his widowed mother, siblings and grandmother. With demand for housing, he furnished an extra room for boarding, and they took in a young Irish char girl.

"Jacques Ambroise, my mother insists you have dinner with us tonight. I told her you were an orphan. She laughed, saying she never heard of a Charlebois being an orphan," Joseph said.

"I learned long ago never to turn down a home cooked meal; so yes, I would be honored."

"We stay in temporary rooms at the convent, but my mother is welcome in the kitchen there."

"Soon enough you'll have your own home again," Jacques Ambroise reassured. He was in thought as he planed a velvet finish on the elm plank.

Jacques had no memory of his father who died before he was two years old. As a young man, he assumed the surname of Charlebois dit Jolibois and toiled as a labourer wherever he could find work.

When he finished the rebuilding of the Portelance home, a quaint cottage on St. Louis Street, Jacques moved across town to work with the Charbonneau boys. He hadn't crossed paths with Louis Roy Portelance for several years.

One day while at the Viau residence in St. Laurent, Jacques Ambroise was surprised to see a familiar young face.

"Could that be the little girl, Marie-Catherine, now a captivating woman?" he astounded himself.

She looked up and with a moment's hesitation greeted him shyly.

"Bonjours, Jacques Ambroise. It has been a long time. Are you fine, my friend?"

"I am good, Marie-Catherine. I've been labouring in my brother's fields, with building and carpentry when I can. May I inquire if you are now married?" He lowered his head as his nerves diverted from her eyes.

"Non . . . but do you remember when we met after the fire? You said I would make some man happy someday. I asked if that could be you."

Her voice trailed off, waiting for rejection.

"The Portelance girl, with the beautiful blue eyes, how could I forget? And how is Antoinette?"

Jacques Ambroise Charlebois married M-Catherine Roy Portelance on January 7, 1745 at Montréal, settling at Saint Anne-de-Bellevue. Their first-born, the first grandson of Louis Portelance, was Louis-Joseph, born on November 10, 1745. His grandfather arrived early for the christening, surprising Marie-Catherine on her porch rocker with the new babe in arms.

"Dear, I often recall and treasure the day we bought the Quare Repeater from Monsieur Rochon. Do you remember?"

"Oh yes, indeed, father. It was a magical place and time in my life."

"I know you cherished that moment. You are my oldest daughter and I want you to have this; and when the day comes, you will give it to Louis-Joseph." He pressed the pocket watch into her hand.

"Il toujours se rappellera à quel point le temps précieux est et le rendra dernier avec de bons contrats."

Soon after, the couple moved to Lachine to take up a small farm. Marie-Catherine was a devoted mother to Louis-Joseph, and sadly took ill in the spring of 1748. She struggled through a still birth, too much for her petite body, and passed away after only four years of marriage.

Jacques Ambroise Charlebois, as a bereaved widower, moved to Saint-Benoît with young Louis-Joseph. He would marry three more times and moved again to be a carpenter at Pointe Claire, Québec. At eighty years of age, Jacques died at St. Benoit as a widower once again, but grandfather to many.

Twenty-two

Philippe Pasquier revisits Spirit of Ononthio, 1728 – Dual of great red stags – Winter Migration & Hibernation – Geese have Families Too - The Grizzly Entrapment – Rendezvous at Lorette with Valin family – Tall Tales for Inquiring Minds - Fall Harvest Collection – Searching for Black Trumpet & yellow Chanterelles in the Woods – François Paquette rescues Marie-Josette lost in woods – Searching for Papa's Knotch – Harvest Feast shared by Paquettes and Valins.

François Pasquier Returns to the Woods

IN 1728, AT SIXTY-TWO, PHILIPPE PASQUIER RETURNED TO his hunting grounds near Lorette, nostalgic for the spirit of Ononthio who fell in battle years before. In his autumn tradition, he ventured out by canoe with his sons, Pierre, Jean-Baptiste, Philippe Bernard, and François.

Pierre, the oldest, issued a rifle to Jean-Baptiste, and fitted the boys with hunting knives for their belts. With a sack on his back, he dragged the canoe ashore to cover with underbrush at the shoreline. Up the steep incline, they gathered green saplings to whittle spears for Jean-Baptiste and François. Words were saved as they listened to the whisper of the wind, then the crack of twigs that echoed from the bush as a pair of antlered deer bounded away.

Philippe took lengthy strides, notching the north sides of trees, and snapping back branches to mark their path. Following the river's turns, they rooted the edge for beaver dams, looking for tail-markings or saw-toothed gnawing at trees, hopeful of a sighting.

François, the youngest, was born at Saint-Jacques-La-Misère in Charlesbourg, where Philippe had been deeded land the year before. His adrenaline was high with the thrill of this first hunting trip with his father.

He closed his eyes to envision a legendary grizzly charging from the woods. With a thrust of his spear, he'd easily fell it and would wear its claw around his neck for the rest of his life, a symbol of his bravery. His face beamed and the winter sun stung his face as he looked up to the sky, listening for the spirits of the land to call through the wind and clouds.

Philippe found a clearing to set up camp before nightfall. "Pierre, quickly while there's daylight, catch us a wild hare or partridge for supper, or bring down a duck. Jean-Baptiste, build a roaring fire and the young ones can gather wood and spruce boughs."

The forest was brisk with sounds and movements surrounding the two boys, when echoes of groaning and thuds startled them. Taking cover in the brush, they watched a herd of deer moving away. In the foreground, two magnificent red stags with massive antlers dared each other for supremacy. The Paquette boys knew the duel was a battle for life and death as the competitors locked horns and pawed the ground to prepare for the charge.

Philippe and Jean-Baptiste ran to them at the noise. "That is the Great Red King! He is legendary in these woods, but there's a time in life when the younger, stronger generation must take charge."

Bellowing, the opponents pushed and pulled for an advantage until the great one lost its footing. Mercilessly, the young stag dragged and prodded for a rematch. Instead of a final death charge, the new champion moved away followed by the herd, leaving the disgraced, bleeding king to limp into the woods.

"Well I'll be, I never thought I'd live to see this day," Philippe said. "Now remember boys, the reigning champion has supremacy of the woods. Take a good look at him, at the large scar on his front withers. When you draw your arrows next, choose another, and let this one make his own legend. This will be a good tale for the Charlebois boys."

Distant honking was now overhead, migrating southward in endless V's of black-hooded geese, with patches of white and regal ringed necks. Their recruiting efforts didn't abate, with leaders yielding to the back to scout for stragglers. The wonder enthralled the boys, and Philippe reached for his rifle and aimed steadily toward the sky.

François' stomach sank, weak with the urgent realization, and hoping his father's aim would fall short. He stepped to offer a distraction. "Papa, ne sont-ils pas les oies magnifiques, ils voyagent-ils dans les familles?[30]"

The gun was lowered and Philippe smiled and ruffled the boyish curls. "Mais naturellement, François, familles sont précieux. La fois prochaine nous attraperons le vieil oncle.[31]"

Flames danced as rising ashes sparked and disintegrated. The driest embers crackled loudest, stoked by wind gusts that breathed it life. Forked branches supported a spit of two rabbits, and as the meat roasted, pink juice oozed out, sizzling onto the flames. In the flickering light, Philippe showed the boys how to clean and hang the rabbit pelt.

The cleaver portioned the feast and the hungry boys tore at the morsels, gnawing the last flesh from the tiny bones, then drew close to the fire as the wind nipped at their ears.

Crossed-legged around the embers, they listened to Philippe's tales in hushed tones, of the Great Spirit of Huron honour. With demonstrative hands, he talked of nature and respect to the chiefs, then imparting the saga of the sons of Manitou, he fell quiet. His fingers stroked his thick, peppered grey beard, and he removed his woolen toque and rested back on a bed of spruce boughs.

"Boys, look up into the stars and you will see Tabaldak, the windmaker, and Gluskap, the great myth of the Wabanaki."

His eyelids closed as he spoke. "Stay silent and focus on the spirits; they will give you peace. Only then will you see the great eagle take flight in the enormous span and power of his wings."

A dusting of snow covered the slumbering bodies, and the only sound was from campfire coals, crackling with spurts of steam into the night. Shivering, Philippe rose to stoke the fire, and huddled close, poking hot rocks from the bottom with a branch. Wrapping them in hunting bags, he laid them at the feet of his boys. As dawn appeared, he was still nursing the flames.

---

[30] "Papa, are they not beautiful geese; do they travel in families?"
[31] "But of course, François, families are precious. Next time we will catch the old uncle."

Indians trade furs at a Hudson's Bay Company trading post in the 1800's,
Artist unknown estimate 1800; from Hulton Archive. Public Domain Ⓢ

With ten days of adventure behind, of fording rivers and bountiful hunting, they paddled to the village of Lorette to trade their prized beaver pelts, and a rack of muskrats, mink, and red foxes. On the return journey, their second canoe was packed with winter meat and hides.

Pierre stayed at the river's edge with the canoes and Philippe took the boys to the longhouse village with the skins. At the trading post, Philippe recognized Charles Valin and his wife, Louise Darveau-Langoumois, whose family had now remained on the Valin homestead at L'Ancienne Lorette[32] for two generations. Charles' parents, Nicolas Valin and Anne Trudel, were both from Picardie, France, and had been friends of Philippe's parents.

Philippe hailed the Valin wagon with a hearty wave. "Charles! Bonjours, mes amis!" Charles reined the team to a halt and alit with enthusiasm, raising his arms high for an embrace.

"Mon dieu, mon ami. Combien de temps l'a été puisque nous nous réjouissons dans nos familles? Il est bon mon frère pour vous voir dans la bonne sante[33]."

"These are my sons—Jean-Baptiste, Philippe Bernard, and François." Although François was a full head shorter than his brother, his attitude was equal, and he stepped to the front.

Charles gestured to a brood of little ones on a hay bed in his wagon. "Charles Jr., Marie-Louise, Jean-Baptiste, Nicolas, and Marie-Charlotte."

Louise held an infant in her arms and surveyed her own family with pride. The Paquette boys helped the Valin children down to stretch their legs as the parents conversed.

François saw an audience and his opportunity.

"We have just come from the woods where we survived night and day, only by our instincts."

He winked at his older brothers, to permit him a little Québecois amusement.

Charles Jr. and Nicolas Valin closed in to hear it all, gathering their heads together.

"One night around the campfire, we heard the whistle of an Iroquois brave signaling an ambush. I feared for the safety of my father and brothers, and crept to the tree where my bow and arrow stood."

François watched their faces and gained confidence and encouragement from the awe of the Valin children.

---

[32] Jesuit Pierre Chaumonot built chapel for Hurons at Lorette in 1674. By 1697, the Huron tribes of Wendake abandoned the village of Ancient Lorette. Patriots of the Jewsuits continued to teach their native language and medicinal skills in exchange for educating the natives in French and instructing the Roman Catholic religion.

[33] "My God, my friend. How has it been since we rejoice in our families? It's good my brother to see you in good health."

"I knew we were surrounded, but that I would be fast with my agility. We were encircled, and I sensed their presence without seeing their eyes."

François heightened his story, with a pause to add drama in his voice.

"What . . . happened?" Nicolas whispered.

"One lone arrow took off the feathers of their leader. They turned on their heels and fled, knowing we were protected by the spirit of the great Huron Ononthio and the cunning archery of the Pasquiers. We didn't see the signs of Iroquois again."

The Valin children were hushed and enthralled, and François didn't want to lose their concentration, in spite of Pierre's smirks. His eyes shifted back and forth to invoke anticipation.

"We hunted enormous elk, watched the battle of the great red stags, trapped beaver, and of course our encounter with a giant grizzly was the prize of our take."

"A grizzly!" Four year old Marie-Charlotte gulped.

"We had just brought a catch of fish from the creek, when I spied the great brown hulk standing on the riverbank. He rose to his full height, taller than a house. When he opened his jaws to roar, I saw his fangs, drooling with fresh blood. But he wanted more, he wanted us."

"That's true." Jean-Baptiste added his support to his younger brother. "Larger than a house."

"Was he going to eat you, François?" Marie-Charlotte asked with wide blue eyes and soft, frightened words.

"No, he was not about to eat Paquette men. My father and my brothers loaded their muskets, but the bear's sights were on me. I knew my aim was good, and I picked up a rock. It stunned him on the head, enough for me to pick up the spear Pa had whittled for me. I ran at him, knowing that it was him or me. First lunge went straight into him. You've never heard such a curdling cry as that giant grizzly when he realized he was done for."

The families listened in amazement and considerable amusement as François told tales of the adventure far larger than life.

"See this, Marie-Charlotte." François moved close and pulled a bear's claw tied on a leather string from under his shirt, a gift from a native. "This is only his baby finger."

"Ooooh."

Marie-Charlotte tugged at François' coat and looked up with wide eyes, imagining a boy of such bravery must have legendary stories to tell. François winked at his father, and Phillipe tempered his rebuke.

"Charles et Louise, come to Saint-Jacques-La-Misère to partake of Fête de Noël. Marie-Geneviève will be disappointed if you don't come," Phillipe said.

Charles and Louise were grateful to accept, and Marie-Charlotte jumped in anticipation of seeing her newfound hero again.

"Hurray! Hurray!" Marie-Charlotte kicked her feet in delight.

Lost in the Woods, Charlesbourg

Since the days of Champlain's explorations in the early 1600s, the feast at the end of November coincided with harvest and the start of Advent or the Feast of Saint Andrew. Celebrations stretched for four resplendent weeks before the Twelve Days of Christmas—a time for bachelors' match-making, children's pageants, dancing and social gaiety. Weeks before, fruits and berries were dried, apple ciders brewed, and shelves in the root cellar stocked with puddings, plum cakes, and a buche de Noël.

With limited days before winter would take hold, Philippe and the older boys worked daily until dark to harvest the last of the grain and bale hay stacks, returning wagon loads to the rafters for feed.

Before the sun, the girls were awake and chattering in excitement, and Marie-Geneviève already bustled in the kitchen, ready for their help.

"Tomorrow, Marie-Catherine will come from the Lessard farm with her three little ones. The party will give her needed cheer since losing the baby. She'll bring wild blueberry pies, and cider from the orchard."

"Yum. I can't wait to show her the dress we're sewing for my wedding," Marie-Agnes, one of the older girls, said.

"Just make sure Joseph Martel doesn't get a peek."

"Don't worry, Ma."

Marie-Geneviève called to the larder, "Marie-Josette, find François and take him to the rocky slopes for wild berries, any kind you see—

blueberries, gooseberries, currents, or barberries. And wear thick sweaters for protection from the barbs."

At the door, François hoped for recognition. "We return through the woods, Ma, and I'll bring balsam and cedar boughs too."

Out of sight of the farmhouse, behind the orchard, the bushes were still laden with wild juicy berries near the rocks.

"François, you're eating more than you pick! Stop or we'll never have enough for pies!" With no denial, François showed his broad smile of blue teeth and lips. When Marie-Josette was satisfied with the basket weight, they turned toward the woods.

"Come on, Marie-Josette," François said. "I know where to find the black trumpet and yellow chanterelles that Ma likes. It's back in amongst the thick trees, where it's darkest and damp."

"It's getting too cold, François." She hoisted the basket to her hip and followed closely over the roots and leaves. Two years older than François, Marie-Josette was daydreaming about treasures in the forest, as he scraped at the ground roots for mushrooms.

"I can't find the yellow ones, just the black trumpets," he conceded.

"François, it's dark! Let's go—now!" Marie-Josette shouted, with panic in her face. "We've been too long. Do you even know where we are?"

"Oui, oui!" François turned in circles, but each direction looked the same to him, thicker and darker by the minute. Every sound was now magnified, and they crouched together, as a doe chased its mom nearby with a thunderous noise.

Instinct told him to remain calm and remember the wilderness skills his father had taught him on his first hunting trip weeks before.

"It will be alright, Marie-Josette; stay close to me. I notched the trees like Papa taught me. The sun stays at our backs."

"I can't see the sun," she whispered.

"Look high above the trees, it is still there."

She looked up to the grey stillness. The forest floor was soft with pine needles and moss, and François searched for their footprints or any natural path out of their dilemma.

He thought that distracting her could only help. "Marie-Josette, take these balsam needles and cedar branches. Ma needs them for her potted jelly."

"I don't care, François! I want to go home."

A dusting of snowflakes covered their footprints, and a frosty wind rushed the tree tops and retreated again. Marie-Josette licked the snowflakes from her lips and pulled her wrap tighter.

Listening to the quiet of the woods, he heard a soft echo of a jabbering stream. Marie-Josette stopped suddenly in her tracks. "I found it! I found it—I found Papa's notch."

They reached a familiar clearing as dusk fell. In the distance, on sight, they knew the silhouettes of Philippe and Pierre, working with an oxen and a flat wagon, stacked high with hay.

Marie-Josette dug her heels, and announced with authority, "Papa, we found your notches."

Philippe and Pierre looked at François to interpret, and he shrugged his shoulders and looked at Marie-Josette as if she were a wimp.

They waited for Philippe and Pierre to finish loading, then the four led the oxen to the barn, labouring with the weight.

Sweat glistened off the men, and they stopped at the well for a ladle of water. It was clear to François that Philippe was weary, and he took the reins from his father's hands. With the oxen dismissed to the paddock, the wagon was abandoned beside the shed.

The smell of baked bread drifted to the field, and the hungry men headed to the house. Kicking off their boots at a bench beside a wooden stoop, they filled a bucket and tin basin; then with a chunk of lye soap and a wiping rag, they washed off the day's dirt that had built like thick badges of honour from their labour.

Marie-Josette swung her basket and sang as she skipped ahead to the kitchen. "Look, Ma, at what I have gathered!"

Marie-Geneviève stopped everything, and bent to cup her hand around her daughter's face. "Thank you dear. I'm so glad you remembered the balsam." She kissed her small forehead.

Marie-Louise fussed at the table, setting loaves of fresh, baked bread, boiled yellow potatoes, garden bean cassoulet, and a spit of crisp roasted wood partridge. Her mother prepared a bowl of quail eggs in brine and a slab of strong cheddar.

"Bring chairs for all of us," Philippe called to the boys.

Benches and chairs were pulled to the pine harvest table, enough for eleven hungry farmers. Talking and laughing, they ate until there wasn't a scrap, with juices wiped from the plates by the last crusts of bread.

Philippe shaved a brown pear and russet apple into slices and passed the pocket knife to François, who had taken an apple for himself. The fruit was ripe and juicy, and dribbled onto his chin for his and everyone else's entertainment.

Twenty-three

Fête de Noël, Charlesbourg, 1732

A T THE LONG ANTICIPATED EVE OF FÊTE DE NOËL AT Bourg Royal, Marie-Geneviève took on her role as self-appointed headmaster of assignments in the Paquette household.

"Boys, we still need a wild turkey or even a boar. Marie-Agnes and Marguerite, please collect more winter apples from the orchard."

Philippe teased, "Well, if you're sending the lads to do my hunting for me, what's left for me?"

"I was getting around to you." He tried a hug, but she waved him off. "I've got work to do—but Jean-Baptiste has gone for late corn and pumpkins from the patch. Can you meet him with the wagon? And before you go, the cleaver needs sharpening." He got the hug and left.

The household livened with the three oldest daughters—Marguerite, Marie-Catherine and Marie-Agnes—bringing grandchildren to the delight of Marie-Geneviève. Later, Marie-Madeleine arrived, with her five children under the age of six and another on the way.

Habitants 1852, painting Cornelius Krieghoff (1815-1872),
Library and Archives Canada Ⓢ

François knelt to his nephew and three nieces. "Alas, you have come to work with me?"

"I'm too old to be with the girls," little Pierre Allard said. "Can't I work with Grandpa?"

"But Pierre, I would be outnumbered and I need your strength."

"If you need me . . . I can lift a whole bushel of apples now without dropping any." François tousled Pierre's blond locks, as he remembered his pa doing to him at that age.

"Grand-mère needs yellow and sweet potatoes from the bottom of the bin. I think you'd get your clean shirt soiled; but come and I'll find you a man's apron."

"We want aprons too," the girls chimed.

The smallest had been plopped on a kitchen chair to dig into the flour bin. Pierre brought in the butter churn, then returned for firewood and to chop stumps into extra stools.

Philippe had been gone too long and Marie-Geneviève finally stepped outside, relieved to see him nearing the veranda. Over his shoulder was a young pine tree that he would try to squeeze through the front door.

"I'm glad you won't drag needles through my kitchen," she said, then stopped herself in a panic.

"Pierre-Bernard!" she called out, unable to hide her distress at his pale face. "Please help—it's your pa! Look at him."

The kitchen hushed as Pierre supported him to an overstuffed armchair in the parlor. With Philippe's eyes closed, Marie-Geneviève loosened his collar and sat close with a cool cloth and a tumbler of water.

"Don't worry—I'll be alright. I get excited in my heart at Christmas just to see my family all gathered."

Philippe tried to smile but he couldn't deny the pain in his chest. "I chop trees like I'm still a strapping lad."

Marie-Geneviève brought him a balsam tea and stayed until his colour returned. "Just rest and watch the children dress the tree. No need to do a thing; our house is full today of our strong and healthy family."

Pierre hammered a wooden cross to stabilize the tree base. "Is that right, Pa?"

Madeleine placed her hand on Pierre's shoulder, as their toddler, Michel, gripped her skirt.

Bowls of dried cranberries and apple rings were sorted on the floor with sugar and ginger cookies shaped like stars and angels, to adorn the tree. The children's cards from scraps of paper, wool, porcupine quills, and beads would go on the boughs last.

For the Christmas feast, they'd be hosting Vincent Giroux, a bachelor from Beauport, Joseph Pageau and Madeleine Boesme, Germain Mignier and Marie Daery from Charlesbourg, and Charles Valin and Louise-Darveau-Langoumois from Lorette.

The Paquette household was up before dawn, with the first voices of excitement in the children's bedroom. The crackle of the flame in the kitchen hearth drew everyone from their rooms, and the clay brick oven outside had a robust blaze, and the smell of warm loaves.

Giant hubbard squash, pumpkins, and winter apples lined the table, and before breakfast, Marie-Geneviève had pumpkin and cinnamon apple pies in the oven, filling the environs with the warmth of herbs and spices.

Returning with planks from the barn to extend the table, Philippe was stopped for his wife's scolding. "You are the director today! You have sons and daughters, grandsons and many sons-in-laws. Today you *must* rest."

"I am indeed blessed. But we must never lose track of the parables of talents and the feeding of the multiples. It is our duty before God that no friend or foe shall be hungry."

Their feast was enough, according to Philippe, to feed a small village, that this year included the neighbour's farmhand and a bachelor ferrier from town.

The Pageaus arrived after lunch, then the Migniers, all with gifts, and some jugs of wine from the Charlesbourg vineyards for the larder. By mid-afternoon, the tables were filled with baskets crammed with sweet jams, biscuits and cakes.

"Anyone without a kitchen job must go outside," Marie-Geneviève announced. "François will organize games for the kids." Soon, troops of children chased and dug in the packed snow, as the men went out to tether and brush the horses.

Charles-Joseph Pageau, tall for twelve years, spotted shy Marguerite Meignin, alone on a snowy stump, and enticed her to join their Blind Man's Bluff. In awkward silence, she gathered her scarf at the collar of her full-length coat, but within minutes, the shyness had passed and she was in full laughter with the boys.

In the lane, the Valin wagon stopped for theirs to scamper to the yard games, and Marie-Charlotte found François directly with a few of the boys. Her small heart was pounding, hoping he'd remember her.

"Hello François."

"Have you come for another story, Marie-Charlotte?" he teased.

Never ashamed to perform to an audience, François embellished the tale of his adventure in the woods, collecting chanterelles with Marie-Josette.

He looked around to ensure his sister wasn't listening, then proceeded. "As the sun vanished, the wind howled in the trees. I knew Marie-Josette was terrified, as she cried inconsolably. Then we came upon juniper bushes and soapberries, and I knew that was bear food. I didn't tell Marie-Josette, but I listened to the heavy steps of the largest black bear I'd ever seen."

François crouched and pounced, with his best drama.

"Then it crashed through the trees, a mother bear. We were between her and the cubs, feeding in the berry patch. Her instincts were to protect her cubs, and mine was to save Marie-Josette."

Marie-Charlotte held on to every word.

"The bear growled and panted, then charged with drool flailing from those enormous jaws. Fortunately, I had a green sapling spear, and I aimed directly into the savage breast of her matted, black fur. A curdling roar echoed through the woods as she fell not more than a foot from my moccasin. It was too dark to skin then, but I planned to go back to take the claws and fur."

"But what about the cubs?" Marie-Charlotte's brow tightened. "Who will look after them?"

François was quick witted to escape the conundrum. "These cubs were older . . . almost adult."

"Oh, François—" Frozen in awe, Marie-Charlotte hadn't taken a breath. Seeing her fear, he tasted sympathy and with some shame. He'd be more careful next time.

"It will be okay, Marie-Charlotte. If you are ever in the woods, I will protect you."

The joie de vivre spirit was always bigger than life at festive gatherings, bolstered by tales, chansons and fiddles. After the meal, the makeshift orchestra started up, some out of tune. The first requested was the canoe ballad *En Roulant Ma Boule* that every farmer knew.

> En roulant ma boule roulant,
> Rolling my ball…
> En roulant ma boule

Next, some danced to the lively *Sur le Pont d'Avignon* from the fifteenth century, then a fiddle played *A La Claire Fontaine*.

In the tradition, the children were politely quiet as Philippe brought his father's Bible and read of the 'Sower'.

"Philippe, as the oldest, you should read from Luke, Chapter Two, of the birth of Jesus."

". . . And Joseph also went up from Galilee, out of the city of Nazareth, into Judaea, unto the city of David, which is called Bethlehem, because he was of the house and lineage of David. To be taxed with Mary, his espoused wife, being great with child. And so it was . . ."

Silence fell as Philippe stood with a soulful prayer of thanksgiving and grateful blessings, then lit the first Advent candle. He no longer told the story of the Huron blessing, but his thoughts went back to those times, and to the loss of the three children of his own that predeceased him.

With plates empty and cookies gone from the tree, the fiddles played again. By the tree, everyone sang *O Little Town of Bethlehem, Joy to the World* and *God Rest Ye Merry, Gentlemen.*

When Vincent Giroux produced his wooden pipe recorder, François didn't miss the opportunity; he wouldn't disappoint the others, so stood in the centre of the room, drawing in all the girls to jig to a fugue carol.

"Marie-Charlotte, take my hand, in this circle. Follow what I do."

Stumbling one direction, then the other, the children bashfully nudged into the circle, rotating partners. Some adults joined, and those not dancing, clapped, hummed and tapped their feet.

Retrieving a reserved Jesuit brandy from the cellar, Philippe raised the bottle in the air.

"I never drink fine brandy alone. Who's in?"

Matchmaking from the Fête de Noël led to the marriage of Charles-Joseph Pageau and Marguerite Meignin on a winter day at the Saint Borromee parish church. Settling on a farm near the Pageau's, the couple welcomed a daughter, Marie-Geneviève Pageau.

That was not the only match. Nicolas Valin took Marie-Josette as his wife in 1745, after becoming a widower. Then there was the anticipated courtship of François Paquette and Marie-Charlotte Valin.

The Pasquier Torch Carried by François Paquette

PHILIPPE PASQUIER died on November 6, 1735 at his home, bequeathing divisions of his land at Saint-Jacques-La-Misère to his sons. Of fifteen children, three had predeceased him and the others were married, except for two daughters and the three youngest boys. Young François went to live with his brother and sister-in-law, Pierre and Madeleine, where Pierre worked a strip of Philippe's land.

François continued the family trait in carpentry, always carrying the tools of Étienne Pasquier of Dissay in the worn leather satchel. His favourite works were fine church pews that he created with Pierre Godin.

Ambling out of Charlesbourg with François, Pierre Godin said, "There is so much employment now while the government builds the Chemin du Roy from here to Montréal. They say it will take four years of labor, with thirteen bridges; but travel will be reduced to only four days."

"Oui, Pierre, I was with my father at the outpost when the British talked of expanding commerce. Many new inventions now in Montréal haven't even come to Charlesbourg. Like turbine steam, air pumps and barometers, to make foundry furnaces more efficient."

"When were you last in Montréal, François?"

"Ask me next week, and I'll tell you–last week!" François said, with a glint in his eye. He slapped his knee to add speculation to his quip. Come with me. My friend Jean Tessier passed away and his family struggles. When we're there, we'll sign on to the road crew for the Chemin du Roy."

Wagons with kegs and fish barrels wended their approach to Montréal's warehouses, with lads in woolen pantaloons and bartered shoes chasing to haggle with drivers over baskets of fish.

François watched with amusement as the boys returned uphill with handcarts to the market to sell their new inventory of freshwater bass, perch, trout, Atlantic sturgeon and eel.

"Hold up thar' boy," François called.

"Freshwater fish, sir, good price today. I just caught them myself from the Atlantic."

"I see—you must have a fine boat to handle the Atlantic!"

"Do you want fish or not?" The impudent boy replied.

"Actually, do you know where the widow of Jean Tessier resides— Marie Catherine DePoiters?"

"Yes, I know where. She lives with her son, Louis, at Ile de Montréal."

"How much for a basket of your prized fish?"

The taller boy leaned and whispered. "What do you want to pay? Give me an extra tuppence and I'll deliver it."

François sealed the deal and continued with Pierre to the roadway construction office where a queue of men waited for assignment. The pair was sent to join the work underway at Trois-Rivières.

The Giroux, Paquette, Charlebois, Pageau and Brosseau women were elegant for the Summer Fête of 1736, in colourful outfits. Beside them, the young girls looked almost mature in ruffled dresses over corsets and hooped bone panniers. Coiffed in Parisian hairstyles with tiaras of flowers and feathers, and carrying lace parasols, they were a regal parade, equal to those strolling the Grand Cours of Paris. Decorated masks on delicate holding sticks covered the eyes of young maidens as they danced.

François Paquette had recently mourned the passing of his father, Philippe, and he preferred to think of himself as his father's favoured son.

When in Charlesbourg in the weeks that followed, friends and neighbours poured on condolences to François, and his heart was not yet into celebrating. Yet as he worked his way through the crowded streets of Québec, he was glad to encounter Louis Tessier. "Bonjour, mon ami," he said with a slap on the back and a laugh in the manner they'd always shared. It did his heart good to see his trusted friend.

"François, I am so happy and content to see you today. But I'm very sorry that you wound from the loss of your père. My own papa had only great respect for him."

"Merci, Louis, your words are kind, and it's hard that you also lost your papa only last year. He was one of the great woodsmen, and your children will well remember to tell their own children about him."

La Fête de la Saint-Jean, 1875, Artist Jules Breton,
Philadelphia Museum of Art, Wikimedia Commons, Public Domain ☺

"Oui, it is true. Papa always said that a man is valued for what he gives and not what he receives. The Québecois have inherited great wealth in our families and friends and passion for our people. Ma mère was on the porch last summer when a lad came from the market with a basket of fish. The boy refused to say who sent it, but Ma insisted on a description. He was about your age, also with blond hair and mischievous blue eyes. Do you have a twin that we've not heard of, François?"

"And do you like freshwater fish, Louis?"

"'Twas a feast, mon ami."

"It couldn't have been me, my friend, I was working on the Chemin du Roy last summer."

Montréal merchants brought new energy to the business sector with its summer trade fair. The Tessier, Charlebois and Monderie children showed handiworks, livestock and woodwork in exchange for ribbons, and neighbours produced lace tatting, quilting, and linens.

Local tinsmiths, millers, weavers and carpenters vied for the coveted blue ribbons, and the recognition and customers they might bring.

In the spring, merchants stocked up with imported purses, French buttons, stockings, caked powders, and sweet smelling perfumes. The market's popularity grew each year, bringing trade and cash for natives' beadwork, bone pipes, hair combs, and moccasins.

But partying was the biggest draw, with feasting and drinking starting well before dark, then street dancing and singing under garlands of flowers strung between parading torches.

From old trunks, they brought out wooden flutes, heirloom fiddles, bright costumes and feathered masks, adding to the gaiety.

François and Marie-Charlotte

FRANÇOIS HADN'T stopped thinking of Marie-Charlotte. He had observed the content family life of his young friend, Vincent Giroux, married to Marguerite-Angélique Boutillet dit Saint-Amour at Beauport eleven years earlier in 1731, and already with three children.

Delivering a load of pews to the Lorette mission, he made a side trip to the Valin's cottage. Standing at the front door, he moved nervously from one leg to the other, gripping a dozen loose white daisies tied with a store-bought ribbon.

He knocked and waited and the few moments seemed like forever. Marie-Charlotte's mother, Louise Darveau, recognized him immediately and was pleasantly surprised.

"Hello, may I request the honor of speaking with Monsieur Valin?"

In the awkward moment, François stretched his arm forward with the flowers, realizing he must offer them to the mother rather than the daughter.

"Please, Madame Valin, these are for you."

"It's very sweet of you, François, but I think these should be for Marie-Charlotte." Louise leaned to smell the daisies still in his hand. "They're lovely. I trust your mother is well."

Seeing the Paquette wagon, Charles Valin climbed down from the barn loft.

"Hello, François. A fine day. How is your family?"

"Bonjours, Monsieur Valin. Ma mère is good. She has divided off the farm and now lives with my sister in Charlesbourg. She sends her good wishes to you and yours." Conscious of his nerves, François knew he must be stammering.

"François, are you here to see Marie-Louise?" Charles tucked his thumbs into his suspenders, slightly enjoying the painful anguish he relegated to the young man.

In his best Sunday suit and with slicked hair and an overly starched white collar, François had practised over and over what to say, but still felt the dreaded nerves setting in. He didn't expect his intentions to be misinterpreted toward Marie-Louise.

"Marie-Louise is a lovely girl, Monsieur. You are blessed with several beautiful daughters, but I was hoping to ask your permission to court Marie-Charlotte, if she does not object. Or if you and your wife don't object."

The daisy stems were cutting into his hands as he twisted and turned them in his grip.

"You understand, François, that Marie-Charlotte is not yet sixteen, and she is the apple of her father's eye."

"Will she not be sixteen in a few weeks?"

Charles looked at François from his head to his toes and pondered.

"Your parents are dear friends of ours and we have seen you raised well in Charlesbourg. I suppose you will want to take my Marie-Charlotte to Charlesbourg in a few years when she is older."

"Older! How much older?" François' voice cracked.

"François, I must apologize. I am pulling your leg. I should be ashamed to toy with matters of my daughter's heart. Stay here. I will go and get her."

Stepping through the doorway, Marie-Charlotte hesitated at first in her shy demeanor. Her hands were behind her back and her head tilted down, but François could see her face was flushed.

"Marie-Charlotte, it is good to see you. I hope you don't think it bold of me to ask your father's permission to court you."

Taking a step toward him, she smiled—not like a child, but as a beautiful woman. "I think it is very romantic. Should I ask what your intentions are?"

François thrust the drooping daisies for her to take, and the words blurted out before he could control them. "I plan to marry you."

He was stunned to hear them outside his head and wished he could start again without the awkwardness. But Marie-Charlotte didn't laugh. She gently put her hand on his arm.

"Shall we take a walk, François?"

They married in 1745 at L'Annociation de Ancienne Lorette, and settled near the family homestead at Charlesbourg, then moved to Lorette around 1751. They raised seven sons—Jean-François, Pierre, Jacques-Pierre, Joseph (died an infant), Joseph, Augustin (died an infant), and Godfroy.

Twenty-four

National festival on streets of Québec – Plays, chansons, & races – Hunting excursion with Running Bear, 1758 – Louis Tessier and the Newhouse Trap – Beavers & muskrats – Second Château of Saint-Louis – Louise Cloutier apprentices at Hôtel-Dieu – Grey Nuns assign Louise to critical patient – Victim of hunting tragedy – Joseph J-B Charbonneau at the Timber Wolf – Joseph Bouchard's Mushers – Debates at Chartrand's Mill over Lightning rods & seed drills – Americans eye St. Lawrence routes – Industrial Revolution in Europe.

Zacherie Cloutier, Montmorency Fiddler

SAINT-JEAN BAPTISTE DAY WAS ANTICIPATED BY EVERY class, with religious and formal ceremonies and celebrations in the streets. Bonfires were lit along the string of villages of the St. Lawrence, stretching from Québec, and as inspiration, candle lanterns were perched in every window.

Bystanders and curious natives proved capable of dropping anything important for games on the street, and especially the feasts, plays and chansons.

In the centre of the road stood Zacherie Cloutier with his grandfather's fiddle, showing off his Québec birthright of song and dance. No one in ear shot would want to escape his levity and enthusiasm.

A sudden game of Blind Man's bluff broke out, and Zacharie had no problem rallying even the most timid youngsters. "It's easy," he said to the skeptics. "We blindfold and rotate the loser. The one in the middle reaches out to catch one of the others circling."

A lad whined, "I'm scared," as Zacherie pulled him in.

"But I wanna play," one of Zacherie's own said to help. "You'll never catch me."

He pulled a polished apple from his pocket. "The winner gets this prize. Last year a Tessier took it home, but I won't let that happen again!"

Others played tag or lined up for three-legged and sack races. The politics of the French and British were benign during these celebrations, allowing a full-hearted Brit to join the marauding circles without ridicule.

Zacharie was married and widowed within two short years, leaving him with two young daughters. His first wife died in 1731, and months later he took Marie Madeleine Brisson from Rivière-Quelle as his new bride, to be a companion and raise his children.

His grandsons, René and Luc, both found winter masonry work on construction of the bombardments and foundations at the Château Saint-Louis, fortified at the cliffs of upper town Québec.

Annual Hunting Expedition, 1758

"Come hunting with us, Joseph," Louis Tessier said at the Pageau's gate. You can't say no . . . your bush is clear and the maples have shed. François Paquette says he'll come too."

"I'll be back from Montréal on Saturday if that will be fine? I have business at the shipyards."

Preparing tack, François called to his son in the yard, "Jean-François, you need to come too. It's time you sail down the Saint-Charles River in a dug-out canoe built by your own hand." It seemed too good to be true for the young boy.

"I have heard your stories. Can I really come, Papa?"

"Gather a bedroll and our gear. We will be gone many weeks, and Louis-Antoine Tessier will be coming with his pa."

"Yes, yes. I know Louis-Antoine. He once took down a grizzly just as his father and grandfather had done."

François laughed at the remembrance of the tale. "As long as you stay ahead of Louis-Antoine, you will be safe."

Ready for big game, Louis Tessier brought his trap, with grizzly bears in his plan. It promised to be the strongest made, able to hold the strength of a cougar, moose, or especially a bear. He measured the spread of the jaw at sixteen inches, and swung its forty pounds up to the stump to examine it meticulously. Louis put on his father's old leather hunting gloves.

"An inexperienced hunter could take off his hand just setting the dang thing. In fact, my father lost a few fingers in this."

Louis had barely said the words, when they all turned at a grotesque snap.

He roared at them, "It's only a couple of twigs. I was just testing it."

"I've a good mind to send you back to your ma. Wilderness trips take skill and cunning. No shenanigans, Louis-Antoine!"

The sullied boy lugged the trap to a tree, and with a stick he scratched out a hunter's map in the dirt.

"This is the way my father showed me."

The day before departing, François added one more, his native friend, Running Bear. The party of five needed three canoes to return their planned loads of precious meat and trading furs, and they rallied in the woods to fell large pines that would be light and easy to work with. Working as a team, they sang canoe songs with a rhythm as they dug into the front core to hollow out the pine. By nightfall, they were transformed into crude vessels.

The third day, their yield was successful, with wolves, rabbits, a beaver and fox finding their way into the new fandangled traps. They snared two small bears on the fourth, and their marksmanship brought down two deer.

Louis-Antoine Tessier and François Paquette tackled the creek in the mornings, with their eyes out for clusters of muskrats and beaver dams.

"Beaver pelts will be worth a fortune, Louis! Ah, this is the life we were meant for. Et vous, mon ami?"

"I suppose." Louis-Antoine raised his arm and pretended a claw. "These beavers have vicious tentacles that can take your face off, and a tail to whack you to the woods. I once saw one with her cubs swimming back with sticks. I had my shot but couldn't take it for the sake of the cubs."

"Better a beaver than a wolverine."

A cranky wild boar ventured within feet of their campfire at the smell of dinner, and with dramatic art, François brought his comrades to tears of laughter as he chased it on all fours and wrestled it down.

Over the fire, they made a pact to take these hunting trips every November. François nodded toward the sky.

"I hope it will be the same for my Jean-François when I am gone. I will be waiting."

Hôtel-Dieu at Québec

Before Christmas, Luc Cloutier and Paul Chaumin enlisted to the long-term building of the Second Château of Saint-Louis at Québec. Paul's Tessier cousins hadn't yet returned from the hunting expedition. He arranged for his sister, Louise St. Jean, to apply at the Saint-Louis, the Governor's residence, but she had greater ambitions to become a nurse with the Grey Nuns.

"Louise, if you work in the Governor's cellar kitchens as a scullery maid, listen well but say nothing," Paul said. "Grand-père Archambault taught us long ago that it's the best way to wisdom."

"Mais oui, Grand-mère that was the wise one but it was Grand-père that boasted of it," Louise quipped.

"I've heard that the Governor's house has an excess of imported luxuries and wines, in spite of France's economic state,' he said. "I've even heard mention of fine porcelains from China."

"I'll just pretend they are my own and take great care," she snapped quickly. In unison, her eyelids closed and her tightened chin raised.

But Louise was mostly determined to secure hospital work at Hôtel-Dieu, as she'd acquired skills at the Huron mission tending wounded soldiers and sick tribesmen. Paul walked with her to the entrance.

"I'll take leave of you here. One of the sisters from Hôtel-Dieu will greet you shortly for the interview. Perhaps you will return to Pointe-aux-Trembles in the spring."

She gathered her beaver coat tight to her chin and tied her scarf to cut the wind. With her hands in a muff, she waited patiently, with a carpet bag at her feet that held her possessions.

Two nuns in grey wool coats crossed the common toward her.

"Louise St. Jean?"

"Oui, dear sisters." Louise was uncertain if she should bow or offer her hand in greeting.

Under the auspices of Sister Jeanne-Marie, one of the Augustine nuns, Louise had risen only to become guardian of the shelved cabinets, and as she rarely ventured far from the château, she appealed for more varied work.

"Sister Jeanne-Marie, since our Governor Philippe de Rigaud of Vaudreuil died, the call for grand dinners has lessened. Perhaps I might help from time to time in collecting herbs from the palace garden?"

"We are part of a great institution. From the days of Governor Frontenac, the plates have been dusted and the silver polished every day. It is not our concern how much use they receive."

Louise hid the embarrassment of her rejection and was not prepared for further words on the matter. "Oui, sister, and I enjoy my work very much."

"But Louise, tomorrow I tend to rounds at the hospital. Would you like to walk with me? Perhaps, I could use your opinion on our herbal gardens."

Louise was certain she grew a full inch in confidence alone as Sister Jeanne-Marie spoke. "Oui, oui, it would be my honor. I will see that the china and crystal is entrusted in my absence."

"Sister Ouimette insisted on writing details for you; read them to be clear. You will meet me at Hôtel-Dieu for early Sunday morning mass. It's the ominous grey building looming at the end of Côte du Palais.

Footprints in the snow led the way for Louise, and at the door, she was met by a nun in a crisp white apron and nurses' cap. With a quick look up and no smile, she shoved a board with paper at Louise.

"Bonjours, Mademoiselle St. Jean. Suivez-moi. We have many patients suffering from the plague and others with hunting and war wounds."

The nun walked at a clip and turned her head sideways to speak, expecting Louise to keep astride.

"A woodsman is here named Louis Tessier. There is no hope for him. Somehow his friends brought him from the woods on a sled, but his body was badly torn apart by a grizzly. Do you have the strength to sit by him and read from the Psalms?"

"Of course, sister."

The patient was wrapped in blood-soaked rags, and Louise couldn't help but notice his hand, sans thumb, twitching in pain.

"Bonjours, Monsieur Tessier . . ." Her words trailed off as she sank to the floor.

Awakening to salts, Louise stirred and her eyes opened to the ceiling.

"Mon dieu," she said. "Pardonnez-moi maintenant. This is my own cousin. He went to the woods with his usual hunters."

Hearing her voice, a pale and stricken François Paquette arrived in the room from a chair in the austere hall.

"Bonjours, Louise, I'm so sorry for you to see him like this. He died just now, without regrets, and I have no doubt there are many a hoot and holler in the Heavens. Shortly before the attack, he was boasting of a previous tangle with a black bear where he had the thing by the tail and flung him far into the woods."

Louise couldn't stop the smile of remembrance.

"He could tell a tale, that's for sure, dear Louis. He knows well enough that bears don't have tails. I trust the rest of your hunting party was spared this tragedy."

Joseph and the Timber Wolf

Joseph Jean-Baptiste, François Charbonneau's first born son, married Marie-Anne Chartrand in 1745 at Rivière-des-Prairies. The two families became hunting partners too, with Joseph a friend to her brother, Pierre.

Frozen elements and blizzard winds wouldn't stop their excursions, and on a hunt in 1752, Joseph and Pierre followed the tracks through knee deep snow. Pierre halted to listen to whimpering, then started again against the whistling wind, pushing toward the sound. At a felled giant oak, the animal's tracks stopped, with blood oozing onto the fresh snow where a fallen tree was wedged. Joseph bent toward the heaving animal.

Speaking softly, he cleared the frost away from a young timber wolf, only a few month old, with an arrow in its shoulder. Joseph knew their habitat, to den in areas of thick timber, in packs not larger than eight. They could easily attack a range of prey, including their own as they become sick and feeble; but this cub showed no aggression, abandoned to die a slow death in the forest.

The men skirted the site for a sign of others. As the wolf shuddered, Joseph made forbidden eye contact, staring into its steely grey eyes, deep as a black prism. Stroking his head, the pup relaxed its muscles and resisted a struggle.

Joseph held its body firm with one arm, and a swift courageous yank pulled the arrow out, to a piercing yelp. As its sustained cry faded in time, the cub rested its muzzle on Joseph's hand. Within minutes, his eyes sealed tight in pain.

"Pierre, I know this pelt would bring a good trade, as the nap of such young fur is softer and more valuable. But I won't surrender this baby to such a fate." Pierre knew his friend, and nodded.

Cleaning the wound, Joseph bandaged the gash with a cloth binding. The quivering wolf was secured on their toboggan and pulled to Rivière-des-Prairies, where Joseph Bouchard and Madeleine Marie Thibault maintained barns for wagons and horses. Hearing the story, Joseph agreed to keep and nurse the cub and try to domesticate it.

In a fortnight, Joseph Jean-Baptiste was back with a handcrafted pine trunk for Madeleine as barter for their trouble. This time, he was freshly shaven, with his hair slicked back, hoping to make a distinct impression on young Marie-Catherine Bouchard.

"Has the wolf recovered?" he asked.

"Yes, he's strong now and I've named him Lucius. Suits a wolf, I think. He'll be a good musher and I'll pair him with my five-year old husky, Aggie, for training."

"Perhaps . . . could I go out with you when they're ready for trial?"

"In a couple of weeks, Joseph, we'll try them for a run with the sled. Already, he follows Aggie wherever she goes, so she'll remain the lead dog. We'll get them ready for the sled and musher races on the river."

Lucius curled at Joseph's feet for a jowl rub. "I guess it's true that even a wolf doesn't forget his rescuer," he said.

At ten years of age, the lead, Aggie, began to fail, and Lucius became despondent with her absence. His loneliness was projected into the dark of night, in a moaning howl that reached the forest and brought an echo in reply. The grey wolf still excelled with the sleds.

But one day years later, Lucius returned to the woods and was never seen again. Joseph Jean-Baptiste went many times to the site of the first rescue in hopes of a reunion with a long-time friend.

Oui, Lucius, it was the call of the wild. Rest well.

Steam and Inventions Come to Charlesbourg

WITH WIND in the community of the new farm invention, François teamed up the wagon to head to the Charlesbourg mill, sure that Monsieur Chartrand would know more. The Charlesbourg stone grist mill was built on the Jesuit estates in 1740, ahead of other Saint-Charles mills. The downstream current, where the river rushed to the St. Lawrence, provided enough power to churn its paddle wheels, with perpetual motion to rotate the cogwheels.

François jumped down for a customary handshake and didn't take long to pry it out of Monsieur Chartrand.

"Yes, François! It's true—the new steam engine is due in Charlesbourg in a few days. It is said that boiling water creates the steam that powers the engine. Like magic, the wheels move. Won't that be dandy if we don't have to plow by hand and oxen?" Chartrand mused.

"What could be next?" François added.

"The Franklin[34] fellow invented lightning rods to stop our barns from burning down in a storm. A metal rod deflects it, they say."

---

[34] Benjamin Franklin (1706-1790) writer, inventor and politician. In 1783, he negotiated the Treaty of Paris, ending the Revolutionary War.

The Cloutiers would have been glad to have that last year."

"And it must be expensive," François suggested.

"Cheaper than a new barn. They talk about steam to run tractors for planting and haying."

"Jethro Tull's seed drill works fine for me," François said. "I'm not keen on change. Can't afford to have a big, complicated machine break down in my fields. Old Beatrice and Claude do the work just fine."

"François, you won't need your oxen anymore. If you sell them, you'll have enough for the tractor."

Chartrand spread out a mercantile catalogue of farm implements, and dug his pince nez spectacles from his pocket. François watched him struggle to settle it tight on his nose.

"The watchmaker sells a modified lens you wear around your ears. Gervais Cournoyer got a pair and he can now see the print on his Bible. So you see, sometimes change can be good. Time you try them out, Jean-Baptiste."

"If that's so, I'll see the watchmaker to have a look for myself."

Chartrand retreated to his wagon and returned with the Weekly News, fresh from the printer. He read for a moment before he spoke. "François, have you seen that British battle ships are nearing the Saint-Charles?"

"Yes, that's a worry—we could be involved in another war, I say. The Brits have treated the Acadians badly. I heard they rounded them up like cattle and cast them from their farms, instead giving the land to the British."

Chartrand ad-libbed as his eyes glossed over the newspaper.

"They say that this fellow, Montcalm, will take back the land the British and Americans are stealing from under our noses. They want our St. Lawrence, our trade routes, and our shipbuilding facility on the docks, to build naval fleets."

"Last year, he captured Fort Henry on Lake George, and Fort Oswego. If we can keep control of the waterways, at least our trade and supply routes should be safe."

"But France needs to come to our defence," François complained. "Europe brags about their Industrial Revolution, but the French and the English take their pretty time bringing it to Québec."

Twenty-five

Québec Navy ships under command of Montcalm – Habitant soldiers defend Chemin du Roy – French Indian War begins 1754 – Abercrombie attacks Ticonderoga – British vie for control of Newfoundland fisheries – Acadians stripped of civil rights – Britain declares war against France, 1758 – Wolfe leads British to Beauport – Sounds of cannons echo over Jacques-La-Misère – François Paquette joins French troops – Battle of Plains of Abraham, 1759 – Québec capitulates during Siege of Québec – Montcalm mortally wounded – Dead Lists posted at churches around Charlesbourg – Ambush on banks of Saint Charles River, 1762 – François Paquette killed in battle, 1762 – Treaty of Paris, 1763, followed by Sugar Act & Stamp Act.

The Seven Years Wars - 1756 -1763

AS THE CONVOY ARRIVED, THE REGALIA OF THE NAVY ships was heralded in the city, knowing it was bringing Louis-Joseph de Montcalm to Québec.

Two gunned corsairs, the 'Marquise de Vaudreuil', and 'La Hurault' had been completed at the shipyards to coincide with Montcalm's arrival, and were ready to be launched to join the naval fleet.

In military costume, a drum and pipe band preceded the ceremony to unleash the corsairs into the St. Lawrence. Every citizen on the docks that day spoke about the pending war—with battle imminent between Great Britain and France.

Now it was inflicted on the new world, in the St. Lawrence and Ohio Valley, with both countries claiming ownership. Even the Spanish were determined to control the wealth of the southern states.

By 1750, habitants of Montréal and Québec were required to become soldiers, with patriot recruits trained to defend the towns and the Chemin du Roy, a key route uniting the two cities.

The war-weary French lost their offensive position when the French and Indian War began on May 28, 1754, in a great game of chess played between Britain and France on the eastern seaboard. At Halifax, a fortress was built, forcing Acadians to flee to Prince Edward Island or inland pockets of Québec.

In 1758, James Abercrombie rallied 15,000 British and American troops to attack Fort Carillon at Ticonderoga, then turned on Louisbourg to secure a port for the British.

Kingston's Fort Frontenac, at the mouth of the Cataraqui River, was another strategic vantage point, built as a fortress with limestone walls and parapets for the French army.

The British set sights on controlling Newfoundland fisheries and encouraged settlement of New England colonists northward, threatening ten thousand Acadians in Nova Scotia and New Brunswick.

The Acadians, a unique culture of Métis-Indian, Micmac, and French had such strong patriotism to France, they could not be rehabilitated to the British regime, and were stripped of civil rights, persecuted and banned from owning land.

Oppression of the Acadian community became a hotbed of British consternation, and many expelled habitants were too weary from conflict and political musketeering to find contentment in maritime life.

Attacks on French forts from the Ohio Valley north to Lake Erie and Lake Ontario needed a strong command, and Montcalm was appointed Commander-in-Chief over the French regiment on March 1, 1756. In response, Britain named John Campbell, Earl of Loudoun, as commander.

On May 18, Britain declared war against France. French General Montcalm from Nimes forged ahead capturing the British Fort Oswego. Meanwhile, Britain's naval fleet in Nova Scotia was destroyed in a severe storm, leaving the British position vulnerable.

Siege of Québec 1759

AS THE BRITISH plan to cut off supplies to the French troops went awry, Major General James Wolfe dispatched over nine thousand men up the St. Lawrence River from Nova Scotia.

Planning to rendezvous at Québec, Montcalm amassed sixteen thousand men along the shores of Beauport and the Saint-Charles River. Québec's supply routes were blockaded and the ill-prepared French fleet weakened.

French Regiment troops were uniformed in collarless pale grey coats, with blue cuffs lined with woolen flannel or serge, and battalion hats identifying their Company. Underneath were blue waistcoats trimmed with lace, and grey britches and garters with brass or pewter buttons according to rank.

Each soldier or habitant carried a cloth haversack across his back to afford meager food rations and ammunition supplies. Small escorts of women from local farms served as laundresses, cooks, and nurses. Sons of habitants too young to fight, but desiring to follow their fathers into battle, became errand runners and munitions aides.

As support, Huron and Algonquin tribes from the Saint-Charles River to Montmorency Falls rallied to help their neighbours and oppose the Iroquois, who were allies of the English from their position at Beauport.

As Saint-Jacques-La-Misère in Charlesbourg was a strategic target of the war, the habitants came to their own defence, offering up husbands, brothers, sons and grandsons to the battle grounds.

At the kitchen table, Marie-Charlotte was sobbing when François found her. "My dearest, what it is?"

"What right does the King of France have to take our children? For what? Another piece of land or more taxes."

"You needn't worry, our children are much too young to send to battle. Jean-François is only twelve."

"They sent one of the Brosseau boys who was barely the same age. My heart can't bear it, François."

Her pleading eyes tore at him for an answer.

"I will take you to stay with the Girouxs or Tessiers in Montréal. You'll be within the stone walls, safe and secure."

"It won't be safe to travel the Saint-Charles."

They both stopped. Keeping silent, they listened.

"François, I heard it too—the sound of cannons."

Marie-Charlotte stood and wrapped her arms around her husband. "I'll not go to Montréal or Trois-Rivières. This is my home. If you can take down a grizzly, you can protect us from cannons."

They tried to laugh.

François said, "Nicolas Jacques has organized a militia regiment from Charlesbourg. Many Frenchmen from our seigneurie are following his footsteps. I gave the handshake of my agreement, but I'll be back as soon as I can."

He took his uniformed jacket off the wall. "You know I must go."

Without a word, Marie-Charlotte filled a sack with dried beans, cornmeal, pemmican, cheese and a chunk of bread. She held François long and he kissed her goodbye before he turned away.

She watched, with Augustin hanging to her skirt, as François departed down the lane to join straggling soldiers on the road at the back of the line.

Across the field, the queue fell into an organized march, and she heard his voice. "Come on men, we're French not British, some enthusiasm and pride."

Young Daniel Turgeon was marching sprightly at the front, playing the old victory tune of 'Marseilles' on his piccolo.

> To arms, oh habitant, Form up in serried ranks,
> March on, March on, May their impure blood
> Flow in our fields.

On an unsuspecting farmer's field outside the walls of Québec, on September 17, 1759, an infantry of thousands marched at the spectacular Battle of the Plains of Abraham, with the bloody incursion testing the military prowess of both sides.

The French established battle lines of thirty-five hundred troops, while more than fifteen hundred habitants and Indians took positions along the flank and from the bushes.

The first volley of artillery was deadly for the French, and the second had them scattering. As cannons roared and muskets flashed, clouds of smoke and death covered the fields.

The British seized the naval weakness at dawn the next day, and with powerful swiftness they ascended the treacherous, steep cliffs of Québec. The British grenadiers were in black and red, with white shirts and leg britches, each armed with a sword, musket and bayonet and an ochre coloured waist belt that carried a box of ammunition.

Ahead were sounds of war echoing through the damp sky, and in their sight was grey smoke rising across the river.

The battle was vicious, with the 78th Regiment of Fraser Highlanders, a British and Scottish unit, swooping forward with bayonets and swords as French battalions pushed back across the Saint-Charles. Arriving by battleships and with an Iroquois contingent, the British attacked from the shores of the St. Lawrence orchestrated by Major James Wolfe.

Commanding the Royal Naval fleet with more than twenty ships and ten thousand soldiers, Wolfe set up batteries to take Lower Town. The French organized an encampment of sixteen thousand soldiers on the northern bank, but the superior British navy made the battle quick.

François Paquette huddled behind a rocky row of trees with a lieutenant and a dozen privates. With one eye shut, he focused on a British cannon battalion moving up the road. The Brits were using a ruse of loose shrubs to cover artillery as they moved, but it didn't deceive the Huron scouts. A squad of six men had two at the wheels, one to do the cannon worming, another to perform sponging, a trigger master and a corporal to give the command. Signaled by the wave of a flag, a row of cannons fired simultaneously.

"Lieutenant, I've got a shot on the corporal," François said.

"Wait for my command, Private Paquette," Jacques ordered.

"Yes, sir."

It seemed like forever, and François knew he only had seconds left before he'd lose his focus. His index finger wavered over the flint.

"Fire!"

François felled the corporal, and a rush of French troops surged from the bushes with muskets and bayonets, and cleared the British firing line. Not anticipating the ambush, the British receded, abandoning their cannons.

"Seize the cannons, men! Paquette, Parent, Duclos, Chaumont and Morais—form one unit!"

The habitants charged to the nearest relic, seizing the equipment and powder. François tied a small fleur-de-lis flag on the fore, claiming it as seized regiment property.

Speaking proudly to the private marching beside him, he said, "I have never felt such loyalty to King Louis as I do now."

"Victory is such a sweet reward, yet it seems so far away," Chaumont replied.

"Many of my friends are in the Berry Regiment, marching ahead of us as our human shield. It does not make me feel good," François said.

"Who do you know?" Joseph Chaumont asked.

"Jacques Lavigne and his brother Pierre; Nicolas and Pierre LeRoy. And in the Sarre unit are my relatives Joseph and François Tessier. Others I know from Québec and Montréal went to fight on the ships in the great river."

"The surgeons are equally busy, just as we battle with shovels, hammers, rusty muskets, slingshots and bow and arrows."

François sighed. "It's true. Behind us come the wagons carrying the wounded to Hôtel-Dieu and then the dead to the graveyards. Ahead of us go the cannons and artillery. I'm grateful I have not yet needed the surgeon."

For months after, attacks continued at Point-aux-Trembles, Montmorency, as French regiments defended Beauport.

However, in the dark hours of September, British troops beached at L'Anse de Foulon, on the banks of the St. Lawrence, with four hundred light infantry and thirteen hundred regulars. During a three hour period, forty-eight hundred British soldiers then landed an aggression on the walls of Québec.

Battle of Plains of Abraham, A view of taking of Québec on September 13, 1759 1979 engraving based on sketch by Harvey Smyth (1734-1811), General Wolfe's Aide-de-camp during siege of Quéec. Library Canadian Department Natl Defence

François Paquette, uniformed with the regular Québec Regiment in the Troupes de Terre de Nouvelle France, saw battle there during the fall of Québec in 1759, walking shoulder to shoulder. Bloodshed sickened him as he helped to clear the dead and wounded on the Plains of Abraham, praying each night for the safety of his own family on the Saint-Charles River.

Montcalm assembled his troops back from positions at the walls, the flanks and bushes. A slaughter had begun of many French troops, pushing them back to the Saint-Charles River, and both the English Admiral Wolfe and the French Commander Montcalm were mortally wounded on that day.

A stretcher bearing the fading Montcalm was carried from the battlefield along Rue Saint-Louis to the old red and white inn of François Jacquet, a prominent businessman in Québec. A trio of St. Augustine nuns tried in vain to stabilize his wounds, but the last rites were administered by the militia's chaplain.

The following morning, on September 18, 1759, Governor Vaudreuil ceded to the British, and retreated to Montréal.

The white flag with the French fleur-de-lis was lowered from the fortress of Québec and exchanged for the British red St. George's Cross ensign.

The next spring, the English launched a plan to take Montréal, the final French stronghold. After a mere three days of assault and cannon battery in September of 1760, the French aborted their offensive and the British flag was raised in victory.

Many lives were lost at Saint-Foy in 1760, and wounded soldiers filled the wards of Hôtel-Dieu at Québec and in Montréal, with the list posting their names. By June of 1762, François Paquette had still not returned to Charlesbourg for more than a few days.

A Dead List was posted and reposted on the yard outside the church at Saint-Borromée in Charlesbourg, and Marie-Charlotte went each morning, dreading to see François' name. Names of many habitants and soldiers from Charlesbourg were written, and through tears for others she knew, Marie-Charlotte sighed with relief each time when François' name wasn't there.

Augustin clasped his hand in hers. "Mother, when is Papa coming home? I hate war."

"Soon, Augustin. Soon." He kicked his worn shoes in the dirt.

"But you said that yesterday. When does soon come?"

Peering into his brown eyes, Marie-Charlotte bent to her knee and held his shoulders. "My dearest son, your Papa has gone to work for the king. It is important work and we cannot rush him."

"I suppose the king will take good care of him."

The words pained Marie-Charlotte.

"While Papa is away, you are my little man. It is time that you start to help Jean-François and Pierre in the barn."

"Oh, yes, Maman. I would like that."

Taking his hand, she led Augustin back along the farm road to the Auvergne cottage. Walking by the river, it looked to her that the water she knew was no longer sparkling blue as in the past, but crimson with the blood of Frenchmen.

Augustin appeared not to notice, in his dedication to gather buttercups for his mother, and she was glad of his innocence.

After a day of fighting, the French troops rallied around a campfire sharing their meagre rations. Spirits had begun to lift after the success at Sainte-Foy, and François was at last able to return to Charlesbourg for a few days.

But it was for too short, and soon it was time to rejoin his troop, to say goodbye yet again to Marie-Charlotte. It was too much to be stoic once more.

One night, after a sobering day of bush fighting, François stared alone into the campfire flames, trying to release his mind of the visions of the British soldier he had killed that day.

How can I ever banish such a memory?

Kneeling beside a stream, he washed his bloodied hands in the mud, but the last haunting look from the British lad lingered the next day and again the next.

"What's troubling you, my friend?" Jacques Terrebonne asked.

"Grand-père talked of the battles the Pasquiers had seen in France. Every morning the farmers prepared for battle, and in the afternoon they tended their crops and animals. It was that desperation that brought old Étienne from Dissay to the New World.

"But *this* is not freedom," he mused "I'm neither British nor American. I am born of French blood, and the passion of my country is in my soul. I've never met this man, Montcalm, who died as our valiant leader, yet I am ready to die.

"Governor Vaudreuil will not thank me for my service, nor tell my wife of my passing. My name won't survive history, nor concede my death as one of a thousand. Yet my soul cries."

Jacques said, "We fight not for ourselves or for the king, but for our children. I have hope France will succeed and we will have our autonomy."

François Paquette heard the moaning of a wounded soldier, crossed his chest, and whispered a prayer.

He knelt beside the private, holding his hand, repeating the Psalms aloud, "Yea though I walk thru the valley of the shadow of death I will fear no evil. Thy rod and thy staff comfort me."

Minutes later the soldier passed to the angels. François placed a coin on the man's eyelid so the surgeon would know when he came that it was too late. He turned back to his comrades.

"Do you have a wife and children, Jacques?"

"Oui, I have left them in Sainte-Rose-de-Lima with my parents. Do you know of the place?"

"Mais oui, my friends are there; la famille Charbonneau. Joseph Jean-Baptiste Charbonneau married one of the Chartrand girls. Marie-Jeanne, I think, was her name. They are in Laval now."

"Oui, I know of Joseph Chartrand."

Death of François Paquette, 1762

FOR MONTHS, François continued on foot patrol with his regiment, always with his father's hunting rifle, but now reinforced with a bayonet from a dead soldier, and with a Huron blade at his belt. In the silence, his unit awaited an expected British attack at Montmorency Falls.

Huddled in the woods as the British passed, François spotted a friendly native canoe convoy, led by the great chief, Pontiac[35].

Thirty-nine Brits were caught off guard and slaughtered before they could organize an ambush.

The French troops refilled their pouches and cinched them into their belts. Waiting for the native scouts to return, they listened to the battle in the darkness. They knew about war's sacrifices and the distant echoes of death, but remaining calm, they talked about families and better memories.

At forty-two years, François set out on a rainy August morning to defend against an ambush. The British outnumbered them three to one, and by the time he saw them, it was too late—two British soldiers and their Iroquois companion were almost upon him.

---

[35] Pontiac (1720-1769) was Grand Chief of a native coalition. Tried to repel British by mass attacks at fortresses in 1763. In 1766, he agreed to a peace treaty. In 1769, he was stabbed to death by a Perorian native.

They were too close to fire, but within reach for the revenge of a bayonet. With a surge of adrenaline, the thought of Marie-Charlotte and his children flashed before him. In a great clash of victory, a peaceful light, beckoning before the hand of God, reached down and released his spirit.

François Paquette succumbed to these battle wounds during the French and Indian Wars on August 26, 1762 at Saint-Jacques-La-Misère, and was buried at the Paroisse Saint-Charles Borromee, Charlesbourg.

It was neither Vaudreuil nor his commander who arrived at Marie-Charlotte's doorstep to offer condolences, but the humble private.

"Mademoiselle, let me introduce myself. I am Jacques Terrebonne." She covered her mouth, and her eyes watered in the knowledge.

He lowered his head and she watched his lips mouth the words of sorrow. Jacques reached out and she clasped the small book that François had read from each night, then held tight his sash of the fleur-de-lis.

"I was proud to fight beside François as my most valued friend. He talked about you and of his beloved family and ancestors. I knew that this rifle was passed down from his grandfather, and that he would want it to be given back to his family."

The unannounced arrival of the soldier was too overwhelming, and in the humble moment, Marie-Charlotte trembled with grief and fell into Jacques' arms. Predeceased by two of his little boys, François Paquette left Marie-Charlotte with five sons, the oldest only fifteen and the youngest a mere five years. The following year, his widow married Pierre Bernard, a widower, who had six married children of his own.

Jean-François was now fourteen and went to live for a while with his aunt, Marie-Jeanne and her husband, Jean-Baptiste Dufour.

The Treaty of Paris, 1763

ON FEBRUARY 10, 1763, the Treaty of Paris was inscribed at Versailles, returning to British control all fortresses and trading routes from the St. Lawrence gateway down the Mississippi to New Orléans.

Montréal was about to lose some of its colourful French heritage, and would serve as a trading post and lighthouse of the St. Lawrence. In the same way, the British assumed authority over the growing lumber trade in the Ottawa Valley.

British colonization introduced years of civil laws and taxation, and an influx of settlers from New England. In 1764, The Sugar Act was imposed on imports of sugar and coffee, then The Stamp Act of 1765 levied fees on documents and newspapers.

The British troubles in America were not over however, as the climate was set south of the border for the American Revolution.

Although British Americans won the battle against the French through raids and massacres, the Iroquois and Mohawk of the Ohio Valley were prevented from lucrative fur trading for the European conveniences that they had enjoyed.

Pontiac encouraged revenge on the Europeans, with scalping raids taking hatchets, muskets, blankets and imported goods. Realizing that the natives were losing their inherent vision of tribal culture and survival, Pontiac campaigned to rise up against the incursions of the white people. His widespread message was a new, unexpected poison to the British and American colonists.

Finally, a peace treaty was conceded with the Senecas of the Mohawk Valley in April 1764, officially ending Pontiac's War and signifying the beginning of a native confederation.

Twenty-six

Immigrant ships brought disease to Québec – Aggressive industrialization and ship building – Mondary brothers aid Carolina slave at Montréal docks – Slave comparisons back to Urbain Tessier – Scottish, Irish & French habitants recruited to logging camps – Benjamin Franklin inventions and improvements to farm life – Iron deposits at Trois-Rivières – Charbonneaus sign onto logging camp – Jean François Paquette inherits Jacques-La-Misère – Marie-Geneviève Pageau's matchmaking – Midwifery for Marie-Geneviève & birth of son – Joseph J-B Charbonneau's bobcat tale.

Industrialization and Inventions

THE BARRAGE OF SHIPS ON THE ATLANTIC BROUGHT more than immigrants, carrying rats and disease that infected habitants with influenza, typhus, and consumption. And a new hazard was created by West Indies pirate ships, plundering the Gulf of the St. Lawrence and intercepting traders.

During 1740, many merchant ship owners lost their lives or were taken into slavery defending their cargos, and that same year, one of the royal ships from France docked at Québec with a fatal contagious disease that swept the colony.

Québec was seeing change with aggressive industrialization and the progress of steam engines, printing presses, electrical adapters including capacitors for canning jars and tins, hand-powered spinning jennies, improvements to microscopes and telescopes, and bifocal spectacles.

Boat building, timbering, blacksmithing, iron forging, carriage and cutter building was adding employment to the stable economy of fisheries and trading, and expanded trade routes brought sugar and rum from the West Indies.

Besides immigrant ships arriving in droves from Glasgow, Wexford, Limerick and London, merchant ships were dispatched from European ports. Settlers on the Atlantic coast were moving westward from Nova Scotia, Prince Edward Island and New Brunswick.

"Ahoy there, matey!" Edouard shouted to the lad hoisting nets at the dock. The Mondary brothers of St. Martin, Laval, had been happy with their offers for work on the Montréal docks, as many workers were of Irish and Scottish descent and Edouard Mondary spoke with a distinct Irish lilt.

"I ain't your mate, fella; just move your arse," Tams yelled back, waving his arms to allow for the cargo net.

Edouard heard that Tams was a hired slave from the Carolinas, and held his tongue, not to put him in his place.

"Come on Tams, I see you here every day; no need to talk like you're me boss."

"I ain't your boss, and you ain't mine. Mind your own business."

Edouard was disappointed he couldn't make friends with the wiry lad, smaller than five feet. Grappling for the hoist cinch, Edouard swung over to Tam's cargo net.

"Tams! It's time we got each other's back." Edouard stretched his hand.

"The cargo boss has me in his sights." Tam allowed a conciliatory smirk, then reverted. "Put your hand away," he snapped.

Edouard, joined by Charles Garnier, heaved an unwieldy wooden crate into the netting, laden with strapped beaver pelts.

"Well, Tams, I sure wouldn't like to be owned. What happened to you that you've ended up here?" Edouard persisted.

"I'm just like that crate of animal pelts. Some people buy me and some people sell me."

"Where's your family?"

"My Mammy works in a plantation in the colonies, the ones the rich Americans own—tobacco farming. My Daddy . . . the last I saw him, he was taken away by soldiers to fight someone else's cause."

Tam looked up, horrified to see the cargo boss standing ten feet back. The whites of his eyes got bigger and the lad was taut with fear.

"Tams, there are worse places to work. Keep your mouth shut and get another load up to the deck straight away," the boss man shouted, his eyes red with fury. Spit flew and the man shook his jowls to show some power and arrogance.

Edouard had never stood between a boss and his slave. He watched the tall man in the suit and top hat straighten his arm and tighten his fist. At his side was a small crop, the kind he would use on a horse.

He called to his friend, "Hey, Charles, can you give us some muscle here? Tams and I need a hand."

With gritted teeth, he stared directly at the boss, unsure if his courage and contradiction would be punished. The Mondarys had never had slaves, and he had a strong conviction against the tradition that had come to Montréal in 1709.

The Mondary brothers stepped up between Tams and the arrogant honcho, and continued loading. They heard the snap of the whip, but didn't turn to give the slave owner the satisfaction of intimidation.

"You know, Charles, this is abhorrent," Edouard said to be heard. "But when I think back, Urbain Tessier himself was a slave to the natives, and it wasn't uncommon over the years to accept young maidens from their tribes to work in missions and orphanages. The French and Huron way is equally wrong. Now they send evil men to West Africa to bring boatloads of families torn apart to sell at auction. Some are treated well and receive education, but most are not."

"Don't heed any mind to me." Tams shrank into the folds of the cargo nets and disappeared knowing the lashings would come later. "This ain't your fight."

"Ah laddie, that's where you're wrong. We abide by our God given principles here in Montréal. It ain't right that you be treated this way. It's your boss man that's the criminal. Just you wait, Tams, he'll get his. I'll see to it."

Edouard lowered himself and glowered at the boss man.

"Don't you dare lash him for talkin' to me! If you're mad, give it to me instead. There's many more like me that will fight for what's right."

The slave owner saw the fierceness in the Irishman's eyes and stepped aside to allow Edouard and Charles to pass.

Lumbering was big business in the Ottawa Valley, with boats plying the Rideau every day. When winter ice settled on the St. Lawrence, work crews of Scottish, Irish and French habitants were recruited with a bottle of brandy to work in the logging camps.

Not since a French ironmaster assured Jean Talon in 1670 of iron deposits, had the king's attention been turned to the rich resources of New France. At Trois-Rivières, bog iron was extracted from swamps. Iron was then shipped from Trois-Rivières to the shipbuilding yards on the Saint-Charles River, to be modified and shipped on to Fort Kingston.

Labour demands exceeded the capacity of the population, resorting to hard-working Irish immigrants, exploitation of natives, and working the African slaves brought from the Carolinas. The lucky ones pledged allegiance to Britain and were granted freedom. Meanwhile, over two thousand natives, mostly Pawnee of Québec, were recorded as indentured servants.

Besides ship building, the development of smelters and foundries at Trois-Rivières was creating an industrial core, manufacturing farm implements and machinery, tools, cast-iron stoves and utensils.

The genius of American inventor Benjamin Franklin introduced Daylight Saving Time, thought as a benefit for farmers to work longer hours in their fields. His Franklin stove iron furnace generated longer and more even heat.

His brilliance was compared in the streets to Leonard da Vinci, some reveling at his fluid theory of electricity to perform as a battery. During Franklin's eight Atlantic voyages, he mapped the Gulf Stream, solving the reason the return trip was faster than going.

The theory of levers adapted to simple implements of scissors, pliers, tongs, and machinery parts, and developments in paper production and printing presses advanced communication and publication.

After 1763, the British took back the Saint-Maurice forges, converting them to crown leases, and spurring opportunities for new foundries and mines.

Lumbering on the Rideau in the Ottawa Valley

IN 1766, Jean-François Paquette, Antoine Charlebois, and Joseph Jean-Baptiste Charbonneau found winter work in the lumber camps, hewing red and white pine for the shipyards, and in the summer, they worked on log jams and floats to Montréal.

The summer camp crew was led by the foreman—the push—and the foreman's assistant—the beaver.

A crew of axmen always went ahead to mark the harvest zone and build a camp house, cookery, stock house, and crude bunkhouses that could accommodate twenty men at a time.

The camp beaver, an Irishman named Patrick O'Toole, greeted Jean-François on his first arrival at bush camp.

"G'day to you, Jean-François Paquette. I'll not be calling you that name any more, as your fancy French names don't work here. Which do you prefer Jean or Johnny?"

Jean-François smiled at the affable Irishman. "Jean will be fine. The 'J' is soft, you know?"

"Well, you know that back in Ireland, I'd be calling you Sean. Is that still your answer?" Patrick asked.

"It is." Jean-François tried to reply in a reciprocal accent. "And I'll be calling you Paddy."

Campers were in laughter as other names were sorted and mimicked. The camp boss barked from a table by the cookhouse. Tall and burly, it was apparent he was seasoned in his craft.

"Gather here men! O'Toole will post a list of names and your assignments. Work hard and don't ask nuthin."

A silent respect fell over the forty to fifty men, mostly in brightly colored flannel shirts, suspenders, and heavy boots with spurs on the toes.

Lumbermen's Camp, Engraving on wood, Artists Schell & Hogan,
Engraver H. Wolf, Picturesque Canada, Vol.1, 1882

"If you have experience as a saw filer, scaler, fitter, swamper, sawyer or roller . . . speak up quickly," the boss said.

"Sean, old boy, you're a sawyer and I'm a fitter." Antoine announced after a tiptoe peek at the list.

"What am I to be?" Joe asked.

"Charbonneau, you're a fitter, just like me."

Within five minutes, the boss returned to the cookhouse.

"You get one plate while you're here; clean it and don't lose it. Men, eat your noon dinner, then report to your team and square coordinates. Each unit has a quota. No shortfalls, you hear?"

A queue lined for split bean stew with chunks of ham and a slab of bread. The cook's assistant, a thin wisp, passed out rationed portions from his scoop.

"Save some of that bread for maple syrup after the stew." Every eye shifted to the polished tin at the end.

Working as hard as the Irish, the Frenchmen sparked competitive spirits to achieve quotas. No job was less dangerous than another, and mistakes were accepted and valued as experience.

As dusk fell, Jean-François' unit stopped abruptly at an eerie shrieking that echoed through the woods. He jumped up at the distant shouting of commands, and raced down the path. The sight was horrific—a lad didn't hear the felling call and was crushed by a giant white pine.

Branches were still falling and cracking against other trees.

"Mon Dieu, mon Dieu," Jean-François cried as Antoine pulled back on the man's arm.

"You can't help. It's too late."

The unit was ordered back to their coordinates until the gong at the end of the work day, welcome news that for the somber crew that the cook wagon was open. "They say there's no such thing as being too careful in the bush," the cook said.

Some days, it snowed so hard that workers were confined to card games in the tents, biding time with lumber songs, whittling, and shaving wood into poker chips.

After three months in the bush, the spring thaw and running of sap eased the workload at the camp, and Jean-François, at nineteen, returned to Charlesbourg to help with spring planting.

Jean François Paquette Inherits Jacques-La-Misère

On François Paquette's death several years before, Marie-Charlotte relinquished the estate of her husband to be divided amongst François's sons. Jean-François, the oldest, inherited his father's farm at Saint-Jacques-La-Misère, Charlesbourg.

The hames jingled as Jean-François hooked the harness to the barn moorings. The stable was stacked on one side with sweet smelling hay, across from two vacant stalls.

The old buckboard waited in the yard for Godfroy, his younger brother, to bring the two chestnut Clydesdales from the grazing paddock. Their heavy hooves had a soothing clomp, trailing as if in obedience.

He bridled and reined the pair, then hitched them to the wagon for his routine visit to the gristmill with his brothers.

Marie-Geneviève Pageau, was five years younger than Jean-François, and looked up to him, growing up in Charlesbourg. On her father's trips to town, she tagged along when possible, hoping for a glimpse of Jean-François. From his siblings, she knew he went to the grist mill on Saturday mornings.

"How do I get Papa to take me to the gristmill?" she calculated. "What if I took the wagon on my own?"

"Papa, I am twenty years and past my maiden years." She watched for any reaction but got none. "I'd like to go into Charlesbourg on my own. If you insist I be accompanied, I'm sure Jacques will come." Her blue eyes glazed with desperation.

"Come and sit, Marie-Geneviève. Who it is you have your pretty eyes on? I can see your heart has been borrowed by another."

"Oh please, Papa, don't embarrass me."

"I don't wish that, my dear, but I wish to protect you."

"He is a man of courage, strength and compassion. A good farmer with carpentry skills too."

"Say, no more. I know who this man is."

"He goes to the grist mill with his wagon. I thought if I went with Jacques, I could seek him out to fix our cracked wheel."

"Ah you have the determination of your father and the pretty eyes of your Ma, blessed be. Yes, Jacques will go with you."

On September 26, 1768, Jean-François Paquette married Marie-Geneviève Pageau, the eldest daughter of Charles-Joseph and the deceased Marguerite Meignin. The younger Paquette boys came to live with them to work the farm.

At the end of the next summer, Marie-Geneviève called Jean-François with urgency from the bedroom.

"What is it, dear?"

But he knew the moment he saw her fraught, and stroked her belly to ease the pain. "I'll have Josephte stay with you while I go to the Bernard place for Mother."

"That will be best, but don't be long, the baby is getting anxious."

Taking a nag from the barn, Jean-François raced bareback find Josephte Chartrain, the wife of Jean-François' brother, Pierre, on their adjoining farm. She saw the dust kicking up on the road and ran to the yard.

"Josephte!"

"Yes. It is time, isn't it?"

"Can you come right now?"

"I'll need to bring little Joseph from his nap." She returned in an instant with a bundle in her arms.

Jean-François had already hitched the nag to their two wheeled carriage. By the time Josephte arrived, Marie-Geneviève's moans could be heard from the yard.

"You go, Jean-François; get Mother right away," Josephte said. "I will stay. It's alright—this is the way of childbirth."

It was another half-hour jaunt to the Bernard's, and the ominous clouds held back the downpour at first, teasing with a drizzle. Jean-François knew the rain was imminent, and needed the best from the horse to beat the storm.

In preparation, he brought a sheet of cotton duck canvas to pull overhead. His Continental beaver hat was down past his ears and tightened at the collar, and a wool sash covered all but his eyes as the rain started. His feet were warm in sheepskin moccasin boots, and his jacket was cinched at the waist.

The buckboard jostled them as it lumbered on the pitted road and along the riverbank. On that day against the elements, it seemed like an endless journey.

Marie-Charlotte had pre-packed a basket and a stack of white linens. Her graying blonde curls escaped her cloth bonnet as she greeted her son.

My goodness, Jean-François looks like his father now, with those intense brown eyes. I remember the day when he was born, and now . . .

Jean-François caught the glint in his mother's eyes. She pulled up high onto the wagon bench and tightened her wrap, and he heaved himself up beside her.

Releasing the wheel brake, he turned the team into the yard, causing the Clydes to snort and balk. Marie-Charlotte tucked her arm in his, gripping as the wooden wheels shimmied in the mud.

Squinting through freezing rain that now pelted them on the open road, his eyes focused on the slippery ruts. His mother was deep in a reminiscent thought, her eyes fixed on smoke swirling from the brick chimney of the nearing farmhouse.

Pierre rushed from the kitchen to take the leads, as Jean-François helped his mother down from the buckboard, sheltering her from the rain.

Marie-Charlotte shooed the men to the front room while she went with Josephte to Marie-Geneviève's aid. Now pale and tired, the timing of the labour pains had intensified. Marie-Charlotte plumped up goose down pillows and cooled Marie-Geneviève's forehead with a damp cloth, then laid fresh linens beside a basin of warm water and lye soap.

"Mother, I'm afraid. Hold my hand and say a prayer for us," she whispered.

"Of course, darling." Marie-Charlotte looked into her fearful eyes and smoothed the hair from her brow.

In work britches, Jean-François paced the kitchen, but as moaning from the bedroom increased, he strutted out to the courtyard. Hardly noticing the rain and thunder claps, he regretted not sending for the circuit doctor.

But as dusk settled, the joyous sound of a newborn permeated the room, followed by excited voices and laughter. Jean-François ran inside, his anxiety worthless.

"C'est un garçon!"

Marie-Charlotte opened the bedroom door to allow the new Papa to see his wife and son, a bundle squirming in knitted blankets, to be named François after both his father and grandfather.

When Marie-Geneviève settled to a peaceful sleep, Jean-François sat by the stove with his newborn, rocking him. He hummed and whispered the sweet French lullaby, *Gentle Shepherd*.

"Little man, I promise to protect you from war. I'll share my land with you, teach you to hunt, and show you the lore of our lands. You will grow to be wealthy with love around you, and hopefully God will give you rich crops and a beautiful wife such as mine." Jean-François smiled to himself as the tiny fingers wrapped around his thumb.

In the morning, Jean-François with Marie-Geneviève, the widowed Charles Pageau, and Marie-Charlotte attended the christening at the Catholic Church in Charlesbourg.

The new father carried his grandfather's leather-bound Bible, and the priest recorded the baby's birth date in the opening pages.

Outside the Montréal wheelwright's for a repair on his rim, Jean-François Paquette ran into Joseph Jean-Baptiste Charbonneau. Augustus Renaud was inside, tightening the metal rim around the wooden hub. He set it back against the axel.

"What did you hit to crack the rim?" Augustus laughed.

"Henri, my lead horse wasn't paying attention. He cut the corner too short and my wheel caught a boulder. We could have been killed," Jean-François exaggerated, as he felt they expected it of him.

"Mon dieu, Jean-François. What road were you on?"

"The old native trail that comes past the seigneur's manor; it's seldom used, but more direct."

Joseph said, "Last week I was on that same road with my buck and my old mare, Lou." It was easier than calling her Louise.

Raising his voice and certain now that he had listeners, he continued. "Well, Lou and I were in a hurry because we'd stopped at Lévesque's and got into a bit to drink, then I realized the logging company closed at noon on Saturday. That's the fault of the new British regulations.

"Lou has a sense of smell, better than any horse I've seen. Before I knew it, she picked up the scent of a mountain cat. Lou reared up in front of me and I lost my load. Then the wagon rolled onto her side. The commotion scared the cat away, but my first concern was Lou."

Others were now standing closer to hear better from the street.

"It took a while to calm her down, but I never got her to relax those ears. The cat was watching from the trees, so I got my rifle and went face to face. She climbed a tall pine for a better look at us, but I didn't wait. With a single shot, this enormous mountain feline landed before my feet."

Joseph stopped to gauge his audience, knowing they wanted more. "I skinned her right there, righted my wagon single-handedly and rebalanced my lumber."

"Did you have the taxidermy mount her for your hearth? I'd like to come and see it next time I'm in Laval." Jean-François said, knowing by the look of his friend's face there never had been a mountain lion. But it was a tale worthy of the time spent.

Twenty-seven

Eastern Townships had 90 Seigneurs, 1712 – Siege of Québec Aftermath – The Constitutional Act of 1771 divides class & language – Liberty Bell arrives in Pennsylvania, 1752 – British colonists in America battle to preserve colonialism – Jean François Paquette debates slave auction at telegraph office– Simeon LeRoy, Poughkeepsie objects to Stamp Tax – Contingent of New England colonists attend at King George III, 1774 – First Continental Congress – Jonas Freer joins the Minutemen – Boston Tea Party– General Howe at Breed's Hill, 1775 – Paul Revere rides to Concord to warn British – Connecticut farmer burns crop seconded by American troops – Cannon ball foundry at Easton – Declaration of Independence, 1776 - Treaty of Paris, 1783.

Evolution of Lower Canada & Eastern Townships

QUÉBEC HAD NINETY SEIGNEURS BY 1712, WITH THE succession of Robert Giffard of Beauport, Charles LeMoyne of Longueil, René Godefroy de Tonnacour, Nicolas Eustache (purchased Seigneurie of Poulin de Courval Cressé at Ste-Eusache) and Pierre D'Alleboust of Terrebonne.

Even after 1763, the British allowed seigneurs to control land and raise rents, and land was allotted to parishes and municipalities for schools and towns.

After the Siege of Québec, the English took Upper Canada and the French took Lower Canada. The Constitutional Act of 1771 divided the country by language but also by a distinct class division; merchants were British, and farmers were French.

Montréal and Québec were morphed by the British language, culture and architectural styles, displacing habitants to the eastern portion of Lower Canada. In the western sector, grand mansions and Tudor manors of the English and Scots were replacing the simple, colourful French villas and country farmhouses.

Protestant and Calvinist churches provided English schools for primary education, and by the turn of the century, these multi-purpose schools doubled as Baptist churches and town hall meetings. Children fortunate to attend school often spent only three or four years in basic studies.

New England Grievances Prior to the American Revolution

HONOURING PENNSYLVANIA'S fiftieth, the Liberty Bell arrived in 1752, a ton in weight and forged in bronze in an English foundry. It presented a symbol of freedom and hope for all Americans, regardless of ancestry, and its inscription welcome as an inspiration.

'Proclaim liberty throughout all the land unto all the colonists thereof.'

While British colonists were battling to preserve colonialism, their own slaves fought for freedom. Liberty was offered to African slaves willing to follow their English masters and bear arms, but this only further sparked feelings of rebellion.

Slaves fleeing battle lines were hunted down and returned to their owners in shackles, with no movement toward abolition until many years later. The period became captivated in legends and myths, including historic writings and poems of James Fenimore Cooper and Nathaniel Hawthorne.

Propaganda and opposition to the slave trade was overheard by Jean François Paquette one day at the local office of the newspaper, Québec Chronicle and Telegraph owned by William Brown.

"Mr. Brown, good day to you!"

"And you, Jean François."

Jean François' fist was clenched and his face reddened as he read the article. "The school marm taught me to read. But about this here item, I don't know why you would post such hatred toward another man."

"I'm a business man, Jean François, and this is news that the people are entitled to know. Should I conceal facts and let the townsfolk be blind of the truth?"

Jean François' finger followed each line as he read more.

"This poor black woman from New York, Peggy and her lad named Jupiter, are to be sold at public auction like livestock. Says she's an able cook and could be bought for a hundred and fifty dollars, and the boy strong and sturdy for two hundred. If you didn't post it, they wouldn't come and it would send a message that the people of Québec don't like slave trade."

"I print news and that's my job. I don't offer my opinions to our readers, but I do respect yours, Jean François. It is your right to oppose the sale in any manner you see fit, but it won't stop more of this happening. There's what you call a human railroad, smuggling black folk out of America with hopes of one day finding freedom in the Canadas."

"Thanks for your ear, William. I'm glad we had the talk and you can pass the word, if you like, that the Paquettes had disdain for the slave trade."

"Would you like to stay for tea? I can read to you about the new King, George III, he's exerting British military strength in the New England colonies. The flag of King George was raised at Detroit."

"I never drink that stuff but I'd be happy for the chin-wag. Too bad you're British and I'm French. Then we could really get into it."

Both men laughed heartily.

South of the border in Poughkeepsie, Simeon LeRoy shared his personal fury of the English with his father-in-law, Willem Jacooks.

"It burns my britches that the British over there decide we should add to their coffers because they've overspent on their military."

"Darn right, Simeon, and the good people of New York will not stand for it much longer." Willem's voice rose, invoking his outrage. "We have defended the British in battle with the natives. We tilled the soil, and we're the hunters and farmers that create the economy of New England. Now *we* are the ones that should benefit."

Simeon said, "I refuse to buy a stamp with a tax on it for the Brits, or pay for imported tea with another tax. There'll be no end until they cease meddling in our affairs."

Willem rifled his pockets for a piece of paper. "I was in the printer's shop yesterday and read his newspaper. Folks are angry about the Tea Act and are organizing a Continental Congress for better representation for the colonies. It looks like it will soon become a vigilante movement.

"I wrote this down from the newspaper."

That they are entitled to life, liberty and property: And they have never ceded to any foreign power whatever, a right to dispose of either without their consent. ~ Excerpt from the Declaration of Rights

"The Intolerable Acts are just that. The British have forgotten what the Liberty Bell stands for!" Simeon snarled. "But Boston won't forget."

"I'm confused Simeon. Are you for the King of England or for the colonies?" Willem asked. "You have to take a side."

"Yes, father, you are wise to call me on my loyalty. Long live the King of England . . . but if he were more agreeable to listen to the very men that fought to defend him in battle, then he would be conciliatory and we could hope for peace."

Willem slapped the table in a throw of laughter

"So you'll pay for the stamp after all."

Boston Tea Party

IN LONDON, in the spring of 1774, representatives of King George III listened to a contingent of New England colonists, pleading for reinforcements for the war in the Americas. The passionate Americans from the twelve colonies included Richard Henry Lee, John Adams,

Thomas Johnson, Patrick Henry and John Rutledge, demanding the repeal of the Coercive Acts and hoping for a peaceful resolution.

John Montagu, the 4th Earl of Sandwich, came to St. James Palace to discuss the grievances sent from New York. He was accustomed to freely offer his opinion to the regent in political matters, and King George, dressed in farmer's clothes, wandered in the palace garden as they talked.

"Lord Sandwich, go ahead and speak your mind." George didn't look up but continued to clip his roses.

"Your Royal Highness, the Americas complain of not having Parliamentary representation. They object to taxes, and there's discussion of a colonial military, and the threat to rise against their King. Their petition of last year by their First Continental Congress has been ignored."

George continued to clip the thorny rose bushes. "Nonsense, I do not ignore the Americas."

He stood abruptly. "I heard from General Grant that his military can walk from one end of the thirteen colonial states to the other in a day. What resistance can a few disgruntled colonists have against the British army? Certainly discussions of it are reason to imprison offenders with charges of treason."

"A group of men insist on speaking to your Parliament. They will not go away until they are given the opportunity."

"So be it, Sandwich. We will listen."

Lee was emphatic in his declaration. "Your Majesty and members of the King's Parliament, we object to the Standing Army in the Americas collecting taxes from colonists since the end of the French-Indian War, as there was no consent by our Assemblies. Your British General insists he is the supreme power over New England. They order the fattening of naval armories and allow excessive salaries without control. The Customs Authority is ruthless in collecting taxes, now taking land from poor farmers without any rights."

The Lord Mayor of London replied speedily. "You neglect the sovereign authority that Britain has over the lands, Mr. Lee. You and your committee are respected members of the colonies, and your list will be reviewed by Parliament in time. We are displeased with the refusal to pay excise taxes on the shipments of tea that were held hostage in Boston. Some restitution must be made for the lost tariffs."

Boston Tea Party, Engraving, Artist W.D. Cooper, 1789,
Rare Book & Collections Div., Library of Congress

It was a plea the king could not ignore, as he saw fire in their eyes and a seething patriotism of a new source. Hearing the aftermath of the Boston Tea Party, George III granted the dispatch of three generals to the colonies—William Howe, John Bourgoyne and Henry Clinton—to oversee military standards and discourage groups gathering in town halls.

Endangered British patriotism in the colonies was contrasted by growing support for General George Washington of Stafford County Virginia, a veteran of the French-Indian Wars. He was petitioned be the Commander-in-Chief of the Continental Congress and negotiated on behalf of the misrepresented Americans.

Since the French Wars, British military units had seconded farmhouses at their whim for accommodations, demanding that families feed them, wash their clothes, and provide clean beds. The expense in supporting the royal armies had been dumped onto the colonists, only adding to the inferno of discontent.

In the Canadas, loyalty to the seigneur shielded habitants from the rumblings of a revolution to the south. The consensus of being a territorial bystander to the American revolts would soon cross the border to change the history of Lower Canada.

In 1775, tension escalated in America with the fateful Boston Tea Party, protesting the new Tea Act, passed in England. Demonstrators insisted that ships leave the harbour without being paid duty to the British crown.

When they refused, colonists dressed as natives descended on the docked ships, dumping their tea into the ocean and setting fire to the wharf.

Unknown to the government, this was the ideal catalyst for a powerful secret society to bring their ambitions to fruition.

A powerful passion ignited both Americans and British, including George Washington at Bunker Hill, the Midnight Ride of Paul Revere, The Sons of Liberty of Boston, Benedict Arnold, Ethan Allen and the Green Mountain pioneers, the Minutemen, the French Indian Wars and the Mohicans.

Britain continued to ignore the colonial demands until July 1775 when John Dickinson and Thomas Jefferson wrote the *Declaration of the Causes and Necessity to Take up Arms*, turning the protest into a full scale Revolution. States threatening succession were Georgia, Mississippi, Texas, South Carolina and Virginia. General Washington appointed John Rutledge, William Livingston, Benjamin Franklin, John Jay and Thomas Johnson to prepare a draft for Congress.

Minutemen of Dutchess County, NY

CAMPING ENROUTE, Jonas Freer Jr. and his companions were exhausted and thirsty, and set up camp outside town. In the morning, they would reach the Albany Land Registry to transfer the sale of Freer land that adjoined Thurber's farm in Poughkeepsie. In Albany, they'd also collect a shipment of pine cuts, and trade wheat.

"Keep our fire low," Jonas warned companions Samuel Morehouse, Peter Osborn and Reuben Willis. "We'll sleep in the bush, as the woods are crawling with redcoats."

Before dawn, the carriage proceeded into Albany, staying out of sight behind buildings, and watching a commotion outside the courthouse between British redcoats and angry colonists. The night before, the British militia dispatched a troop toward Boston and encroached on the Dunn homestead, on the outskirts of town.

"What are they saying?" Jonas asked, as his party crouched out of earshot in an alleyway.

Peter crept forward to listen and decipher, and crawled back. "Redcoats commandeered a colonist's farmhouse, ransacking a home for blankets and goods, then demanded that the woman and her daughters fix feasts for a unit of twenty men. It's Mrs. Dunn, and that's her husband yelling in the street."

"If the King of England wants his troops to patrol our farms, then he can well pay for it," Reuben said. The four edged closer, still out of sight.

"The Dunn fellow is irate. He says his family was threatened and he's demanding compensation for the abuse. This is escalating rapidly."

Dunn was a staunch Brit with unruly hair and a barbed beard. He'd become irrational and was now being dragged into the centre of the street by a pair of soldiers loyal to the king.

"What can we do about him?" Samuel asked.

"If anyone among us is a supporter of King George, speak now." Jonas said.

A rousing mumble of 'nays' came from Jonas's men.

"Dunn is badly outnumbered and the British aren't the least concerned. If we don't help him get out, they'll tar and feather him and after that they'll kill his family."

"Sam and Peter, take cover and be ready to distract. Reuben and I will careen the wagon down the road like it's a runaway, and we'll grab Dunn. Otherwise, he'll be a goner, like Schotts last week."

Within minutes, Freer's carriage rounded a turn with his horses raging, and tore through their midst. A British commander fired a warning shot to halt Freer's wagon. As they passed, Dunn was forcibly grabbed by surprise, before a lone bullet pierced the air beside Jonas's head. The horses charged onward until safely brought to a halt.

"Dunn, you alright?"

"What'd you go and do that for?" Dunn shouted.

"You were about to get tarred and feathered. Who'd look after your farm and family then?"

"Didn't you hear me? They burnt my farm and my house and took my horses. My lad tried to protect his mother and they shot him. I sent my wife and children to a relatives not far away, but I'm a hunted man because I object to the British denying us our own opinions and our destiny."

"My friends and I agree with you," Jonas said. "At Boston, a movement is enlisting colonists to join the Minutemen. Today, we have business first, then we'll be heading south to join the Continental army. Do you want to join us?"

"Aye, I am a loyalist at heart—where do I sign on?"

Word of an uprising at Breed's Hill overlooking Boston reached the Redcoats, commandeered by General Howe. The colonial militia had organized a thousand minutemen from surrounding counties, among them Jonas and Thomas Freer and a VanKleeck cousin from New Paltz, Ulster County. Lookout relays reported the aftermath of a clandestine midnight meeting at the Green Dragon Tavern in the north end of Boston where the St. Andrews Lodge Freemasons gathered.

On that dark April night, a scout listened at the window as Joseph Warren, the Grand Master, and the Mason Paul Revere planned a radical strategy to ambush British troops. From the tavern's back room, where the Sons of Liberty gathered every fortnight, the ignition of the revolution began and the American Patriots had their hero. Samuel Adams and John Hancock were sent to warn radical leaders of the British approach.

The scout jumped from his horse, antsy to share what he knew from the tavern, and ran directly to Jonas. "Revere was dispatched in haste from Clark's Wharf with William Dawes to ride through the forest toward Mystic Road, to warn of the British advance on Lexington and Concord at dawn. He didn't even have his own horse, but borrowed one from Deacon Larkin. I didn't have my horse handy or I'd have run my nag to the ground after the traitor."

"How do you know it was Revere?" Jonas asked.

The scout stammered in excitement. "I am Iroquois, and I remember the failed attempt to take Crown Point at Ticonderoga in the French-Indian Wars. I would know him by his voice."

"What did he say that has you so convinced?" Jonas persisted.

"As he rode, he called out 'The regulars are coming' and at Medford townsfolk scattered and organized an impromptu resistance. You see how we use our beacons to warn that the British are coming? Revere arranged a pattern at the bell towers enroute, hanging double lanterns when the approach was to advance by water, and one lantern to be alert and move on land. I've seen the lanterns myself."

Upon infantry sightings, high bonfires were lit on the rocky peaks and riverbanks, visible for miles around. British sympathizers with the misfortune of being captured faced torture or scalping at the hands of the natives.

"Sounds like a heroic fellow, but how can one man be the catalyst of a rebellion?" Jonas asked.

"As many conflicts begin, it's only the first shot."

Night watchmen had spotted a thousand British troops, led by Colonel Smith, wading ashore from boats near Phipps Farm at Cambridge leaving them shivering in the salt marshes.

The attack at Cambridge took a heavy toll of lives amongst the British and the Colonists.

In June, word came to the Minutemen that the British were planning to occupy Dorchester Heights, near Breed's Hill.

"We've been warned to report to Albany for a troop being dispatched to Breed's Hill," Sam deferred to Jonas Freer.

Hastily regrouping, the eager Minutemen recruits rode to the militia office and mustered to join the 43rd Regiment of Foot at the North Bridge in Concord. Wearing matchlocks and the uniform of the Minutemen, the five followed through the bush with hatchets and muskets.

Sam, Peter, Reuben and Jonas marched half-heartedly, preferring if they could to be back in Dutchess County, defending their own soil from the British army. Dunn had been tight-lipped, which worried Jonas.

Joseph Warren, Israel Putnam and William Prescott were in command of the U.S. colonies, while Sir William Howe charged the British.

"We can't wait," the Captain ordered. "More British ships are amassing off the coast of Boston. Prepare for an attack at Dorchester Heights. You'll be assigned to General Prescott to fortify a vantage point on the peninsula."

"We march tonight to Bunker Hill," Prescott announced.

In orderly haste, they marched to the farm at Breed's Hill, where the colonial militia went to work building an earthen structure 160 feet by 30 feet. By the time they realized they should have fortified Bunker Hill instead, it was too late.

A lieutenant called loudly from his telescope, "General Prescott, sir, the British frigate is preparing for assault. They're in a solid red line, emptying forty barges of soldiers."

"Spread a line across the top of the hill, and don't shoot until you see the whites of their eyes," Prescott ordered.

The British Redcoats, encumbered with heavy uniforms and equipment, marched through the farm fields and over stone walls. The colonist remained calm watching.

"Be ready to use your bayonets as our ammunition supplies are low," Prescott said.

Jonas, Sam, Peter, and Reuben lay shoulder to shoulder in the grass waiting for the order. Dunn waited with the captain.

"Fire!"

A flood of Redcoats attempted to climb Breed's Hill, however the succession of colonial muskets drove them back. They tried again and were driven back. Regrouping on the third British assault, they broke through American lines sending the colonists fleeing back up the peninsula.

"Jonas!" Sam called in horror.

It was too late. The British Redcoat bayonet snuffed out the life of the noble Minuteman, Jonas Freer, laying still with his eyes open. It was apparent he was terrified and Sam gently closed his eyelids and folded his comrade's hands over his chest.

"'Til we meet again!"

The American Revolution was in full force from the northernmost point of New York, down the Ohio Valley, the Mississippi, the Carolinas, and in all thirteen colonies. The landscape was converted to battlefields, with farmers' crops seconded to feed the Continental Army or the Redcoats, whoever arrived first.

One Connecticut farmer lived to tell that he'd received orders to harvest his wheat crop and turn it over to feed the American army. In defiance, he burnt his crop and fled the route of the Loyalists savoring sweet revenge.

Massachusetts had long established foundries. At Easton, both the Belcher Balleable Iron and the Drake Foundry were commanded to supply the American army with cannonballs. Four of the Williams brothers and two of the Churchills, Josiah and Jabez had a small ownership.

During the Revolutionary war, these foundries manufactured 2.91 caliber cannon balls, customized for the 'grasshoppers' of the Continental Army under George Washington. It was told that Washington spent the night in Easton at Benjamin Williams Tavern during contract negotiations.

Other manufacturing facilities were converted for munitions, and housewives sewed rags into flags, each person with a role.

It had been with a clear conscience in the French Indian Wars, who the enemy was that they faced. But during the Revolutionary Wars, families were divided, and the colonists had a choice to make.

The Declaration of Independence was drafted by the young solicitor, Thomas Jefferson, on July 4, 1776, stipulating the natural rights of all Americans to be protected in life, liberty, and pursuit of happiness.

The new nation evolved—The United States of America—yet the colonies were not at peace.

At the final battle of the Revolutionary War, Washington led seventeen thousand men in the Battle of Yorktown in Virginia, against British General Cornwallis and his nine thousand troops. Cornwallis surrendered on October 17, 1781, ending the War of Independence. In 1783, the new nation was recognized as free and independent, with the signing of the Treaty of Paris.

At the conclusion of the American Revolution, Mohawks followed the Loyalists into Lower Canada and negotiated on behalf of the Oka Indians at Montréal. A large contingent followed Joseph Brant into Upper Canada enticed by a promise of land. In Québec, the Mohawks settled at Oka, where descendants of Zacherie Cloutier also claimed land.

Twenty-eight

Textile production Essex County, England – Hearth & Chimney Taxes –Reaction to Boston Tea Party & Raids – Colonists loyal to King of England begin to flee U.S. – Simeon LeRoy and Wyntje Jacooks marry 1769 – American Revolutionaries search LeRoy farm – American troops burn Loyalist homes – Simeon LeRoy's family escapes along Loyalist Trail – Follow forested Gaspé route to Saint John River – U.E.L. required to join Canadian military in exchange for land – Jean François Paquette commiserates at Beacon & Stag – Québec Chronicle Posts Land Grants – Paquettes move to Sainte-Rose-de-Lima – Hudson's Bay Company challenged by North West Co.

Colchester & Ardleigh, Essex County, England

PARISHES DOTTING THE COUNTRYSIDE NEAR LONDON were growing in population and affluence. On the north bank of the Colne River, the ancient town of Colchester was transitioning from textile spinning and weaving into a centre for industrial noblesse. Cotton and textile producers were investing in machinery, with the cottage craft base disappearing from Wakes Colne. Twice a year, town clerks toured the country estates, stopping at each magnificent manor, first with an exterior assessment and a count of visible chimneys, then a knock at the door.

East-Mersea Hall was an opulent residence, with a great manor, eleven messuages[36], stables and three cottages on twelve hundred acres of arable land in the town of Ardleigh, near Colchester in Essex County.

---

[36]Messuages - Main house, outbuildings, coach houses, stables, granaries and guest cottages on a combined acreage.

Creffield Family

THE FAMILY DESCENDED from Sir Ralph Creffield, a wealthy wool draper and politician descended from Flanders in the fourteenth century, who came to Colchester via Chappel in 1653.

Lifting the iron latch, the taxman permitted himself entry past the stone walls and hedges. Cubbins raised the door knocker and permitted it to echo.

"Good day, my lady. Is the Master in residence? I wish to make some inquiries."

Willa Webster, the head housekeeper, took the clerk's hat. "Please wait in the parlour, Mr. Cubbins."

In the upper mezzanine, the sound of a spinet waffled down, then the parlor door opened and Mrs. Webster returned.

"I'm sorry, Mr. Cubbins. Mr. Creffield is at Moses Hall at the Ardleigh Estates. Barrister Weyburn in Colchester is in charge of all his estate matters and holdings; perhaps you would like to attend at his offices in town."

"Yes, in due course. Perhaps you could assist me with a preliminary inquiry, Mrs. Webster?"

"I'm not to speak on behalf of the Creffields. You understand, sir?"

"Of course, I understand your predicament. I simply want to know the number of hearths in this residence. For the Hearth Taxes[37]. You know it is legally required by Parliament."

"Indeed, Mr. Cubbins, I wish to co-operate but you understand the delicate situation."

"Perhaps, if I ask only a few questions you might enlighten me. This is of course permitted by law, when the landowner is absent."

---

[37] Hearth and Chimney taxes were introduced in 1660s by King Charles to reinforce the monarchy coffers. Each occupier paid a two shillings semi-annual fee for each hearth or stove. Taxation collection took place on Lady Day (March 25) and Michaelmas (September 29). Poor tenants were granted a certificate of exception.

Mrs. Webster felt important under the circumstances. "What do you need to know?"

"My previous records indicate the manor has seven bedrooms, two kitchens, a parlour, library, grand hall, and servant's quarters. How many fireplaces are established in the residence?"

"One to each of the family rooms and one to each bedroom. However the servant's quarters are only provided coal stoves, one cooking hearth and a wood baker's oven. There were no additions or improvements since your last accounting."

The clerk persisted. "And the cottages . . ."

"Yes, of course. One in each of the cottages."

"And the carriage house? Do a number of staff live there that use a hearth or stove?"

The head matron raised three fingers.

"Thank you, Mrs. Webster; you have been most helpful."

"You may take tea with the butler in the kitchen if you like before you leave." The house matron stepped back to open the door wider and gestured down the hall to an open kitchen door.

Any of the town clerks found these audits to be gratifying opportunities to glean information about the residents and their wealthy neighbours.

Malcolm, the butler, was more than cooperative in his opinions. "Did you hear of those audacious Americans dumping our tea in their harbour?" His voice rose and he leaned forward in full debate. "Those uppity pilgrims called the Boston Patriots refused to pay their customs taxes on three ships . . . three ships filled to the gills with tea from East India. Let them go without their tea then, I say."

Cubbins said, "As I heard it, thousands of prisoners, all of ill repute, along with natives, raided the ships and burned them while they sat helplessly in port. Serves them right that the British government closed their port."

"Yes, as a taxman yourself, I'm sure you see the outrageousness of the whole debacle. How do they expect a prim and proper British government, without paying their dues? Do those Americans expect us to provide concessions at their every whim?"

"Among the colonists, they say some remain loyal to the king, while others want to run the country by themselves. I heard some sots ran the

British off their land, tarring and feathering them. They call for independence, and I say good riddance," Cubbins declared.

"Yes, good riddance."

"Thanks for the chat man. I'll be off now."

Malcolm enjoyed his authority, and summoned Thomas Cutter, an underling and menial servant, to bring the attorney's carriage.

After tea, Cubbins tipped his hat, and left to mount his carriage to Colchester.

LeRoy Family Flees Dutchess County as Loyalists

BOTH SIMEON LEROY and Willem Jacooks were members at the Reformed Dutch Church at Poughkeepsie in Dutchess County. In their tight circle, it was natural that Jacook's eldest daughter, Wyntje, a rare beauty, could catch the eye of Simeon.

With the yield from their bountiful harvest, the local families held a market festival to exchange goods, with a barn dance and pig roast on the Schouten Farm. In the din of the festivities, with the music and jig in full swing, Simeon humbly requested a dance with sixteen-year-old Wyntje.

He was a handsome twenty-five, with medium build and a square jaw. In his nervousness, he didn't think to stop talking, but she listened patiently to every word until a stop in the music.

She stepped back, pulling her hands away and looked at him.

If only I were a few years older, Simeon might look on me differently.

Simeon LeRoy and Wyntje Jacooks married in 1769, and raised a family of three daughters in a Poughkeepsie cottage, not far from the LeRoys and Freers.

Most of the Dutch farmers built hearths with imposing chimneys from two or more fireplaces and beehive bread ovens. When they anticipated raids and retaliation to their villages by American Revolutionaries, they took refuge in secret compartments behind the fireplaces, or at the backs of cabinets under staircases, or in alcoves behind the pantries.

Sometimes a slave or wounded soldier would be hidden inside, with these discreet places known only to the builder, and unseen by intruders.

"Inside now!" Wyntje shouted. "Hear the bell? Vite!"

As the warning resounded from the steeple, there was little time for the girls to flee the yard—she knew the American soldiers were advancing to pillage or burn, just because her family was loyal to the King of England.

"Come girls, get behind the fireplace. Papa will find us soon. Remember to be still and quiet—it's an American raid."

"Mother, aren't you scared too?" Charity moaned.

"We are all scared, Charity. You're the oldest, and I know you'll be strong and quiet. Quick! Quick!"

Stiff and with cramps from standing, Wyntje was about to peek out when she heard American soldiers at her front door. First were voices, then a thunderous kick of multiple boots as the front door gave up its hinges. Knowing there was security with their mother, the girls squeezed tighter.

A heavy voice near the fireplace barked, "Come out! We know you're here. If you show yourselves, you British snakes, we will not burn your house."

Chairs and tables were thrown and thrashed, and Wyntje heard the crashing of her precious dishes. Her anger toward the Americans was growing like a spiking blood pressure.

"I'll not let them break us," she said to herself.

The sound of boots soon faded away and she relaxed her shoulders. Then a pair of soldiers returned to the kitchen and lit a fire on the floor with lantern oil. It raced up the curtains while the Americans waited. Wyntje could hear the crackle of flames and smell the wood, but felt the fireplace with her hand and knew they were still safe.

"I pray that Simeon is not harmed in the fields. He knows I will protect our children."

The three girls were frozen with silent sobbing as they clenched Wyntje. She peered through a crack of the cubby-hole. The fire was in full blaze and the men had gone.

"Thank heavens the main room is open. Come, girls, one at a time. You'll be safe wrapped in the blanket. Out the window to the grass below," Wyntje commanded with surprising calmness.

"Ma, I'm too scared," Rachel, the last out, whimpered and backed up for the run to the open window.

"Now!" Wyntje turned for one last look and charged at her daughter, scooping her into her arms. As she dove out, a blast of heat propelled her to the ground.

Orange flames lit up the sky, with the cornfields afire and the sounds of rifles echoing. As dusk descended on Wyntje and her children, she headed for an abandoned shanty where she knew Simeon would wait.

Under a full moon, with a wagon of meager possessions along the back roads to Lake Champlain, they were now refugees, hiding among corn stalks. Reaching Simeon, the horror of the evacuation was momentarily forgotten, bolstered by new courage and strength.

Simeon and his family escaped in the peace of the night, following the Hudson River up to East Hillsdale, as many United Empire Loyalists had preceded. Through the darkness, they moved north, stopping in sight of a faint lantern from a cottage near the Hudson. At a sound nearby, he covered his family behind a bush.

With a finger to his lips, he crawled close to the ground. The chirps of crickets were interrupted by heavy breathing.

A man's voice spoke in a hush. "Yo, are you friend or foe?"

"Are you British?" Simeon asked.

"I am. Come, you have made it to a safe house. We will feed you and give you comfort for sleep."

"How do I know you're not American in deceit?"

"In daylight you'd see the scars and burns on my face and wouldn't ask," the man replied.

Simeon came forward, leaving Wyntje and the girls behind the shrubs waiting for his nod.

"We are grateful for your help. Have many come this way?" Simeon asked.

"Every night, we have a patrol. Many Loyalists have come before you. I'll give you a route map where you'll be safe, but only travel in the favour of darkness."

Simeon volunteered his situation. "We have relatives in Nova Scotia, and we're facing many days ahead, walking through rocks and bushes."

Canoes and rations were at the lakeside with a Métis voyageur guide and two other refugee families, with their few treasures and rations were stowed in the bows and sterns.

The children divided between Simeon's boat and the other with Wyntje and the voyageur. Launching from the rocky bank, the paddles splashed in unison, awakening a nest of waterfowl.

Except for children, the travellers had blanket rolls tied to their backs, and Simeon strapped a rifle over his shoulder. The river guide cinched a burlap, wrapped packet at his waist, coveting rations for them of dried salted beef, peas and coffee. Wyntje's family Bible was secured in her blanket roll.

The Huron guide extinguished the lantern and directed the men to cover themselves. "Ride low as I do. Any spoken word projects over the water and bounces off rocks, disclosing our presence. Only hand signals now, or a muted sound."

He cupped his hands to mimic a cooing dove and the children silently copied.

By five o'clock, the sky brightened with a dusky hue that would soon awaken livestock and American farmers in the yawning villages. The boat glided close to the shoreline following the shadows on the banks, until they came to rest at a planned moorage with a clearing.

Silently they disembarked to stretch their aching limbs and share a modest breakfast of stale bread and cheese. From a few yards in the bush, the guide returned with a water canteen and passed it for sparing tastes.

Charity, the oldest LeRoy daughter, led the children to forage for berries within sight. The children seemed immune from reality, and in an imaginative hide and seek, whoever spoke first would be out and join the adults.

Time passed quickly for them, and they returned with wild chives and bark shards laden with currants and gooseberries, the colour of sage.

Before noon, a piercing echo of a rifle thundered from the distance, and the guide dispatched them to the water's edge.

"Bateaux, bateaux!" he said, motioning with his hands as remnants of the camp were retrieved and packed. "Sit low for balance as you did in the night. There's no reason for alarm. It is likely poachers, but still, we should move on in daylight."

The boats and crew were blanketed in scruff as they inched in shallow water. Another shot echoed from the woods.

Camping nightly beside the banks, the route followed the thickly forested Gaspé route through New Brunswick and the Saint John River, where they parted with their Huron guide.

Simeon was directed to a parcel of land in Sunbury County where the family first settled, clearing two hundred acres with river frontage before moving to Halifax in September 1782.

United Empire Loyalists fleeing from New England after the Revolution pledged allegiance to George III, and were obliged to serve in the auxiliary military. Some wealthy British landowners from New York brought with them their indentured slaves and these too were required to enlist for military service.

Simeon and Wyntje had two more girls and three boys in Halifax. George Simon LeRoy was their last child born in Nova Scotia in 1796 when his father was fifty years of age.

Coming of the United Empire Loyalists to Québec

LOYALISTS AND REBEL soldiers arrived to find relief in the brisk energy of Montréal, as factories and vineyards cried for workers. With the seigneurial system in its last throes, farmers had to reconsider their futures.

The popular place to argue controversial woes of the Canadas was in the ale houses above the wharf in old Montréal. Jean-François Paquette always found a familiar face at the Beacon & Stag, and wasn't disappointed to see some Charbonneau kin with Paul Chauvin. The lager was already well underway, feeding a festive chatter in the corner.

"Ahoy there mates, is this where I surrender?" Jean-François chortled as the door swung open. All the heads turned to him.

"It *is* the place!" Charbonneau boomed. "Do you bring a peace offering?"

"It would be better to go back to the habitant way of life and the seigneurie than be taxed into the poorhouse by the King of England. I named my horse Charlie, after the king," Jean-François joked and the men voted their delight in a chorus of roars. "But if the British found out, I'm sure I'd be taxed and sent for a reprimand in their courthouse."

"That's no joke, my friends," Joseph Jean-Baptiste added and the laughter died. "New England loyalists come to take up free land in exchange for an oath of allegiance. They have three years to clear their portion of the woods and plant a decent crop. Would you believe during those three years they're guaranteed—yes, guaranteed—rations of flour, dried meat, and whatever else they moan about?"

"I see them coming from the St. Lawrence daily, a congregation of all types of boats. Those Loyalists were tenant farmers to start, but now they're not content and insist on being freeholders," Jean-François said.

Augustus said, "So let Parliament divide Québec into two provinces, Upper and Lower Canada—that's fine with me. Let the uppity British go up. I'm happy to be with the French in the low part."

"Preposterous though, that while parliament protects the Catholic old civil code, we agree in exchange for taxation to provide our trade from the woods," Jean-François said.

"My grand-père would turn in his grave," Charlebois scoffed.

Jean-François said, "The world is changing so fast since our fathers and grandfathers. Our own shoreline now bustles with ships, looking toward the great steeples and stone mansions past Mary's Gate. I read in the Québec Chronicle of land grant postings between here and Québec. It used to be a handshake of good neighbours, but now they bring in an auction lord, and the British, Scottish, and Irish flood from all around. Americans come up the Mohawk and Niagara and scatter from Nova Scotia and New Brunswick to the Eastern townships. Some of the staunch British just go back to their motherland."

"The death of the seigneurie is not far then," Charlebois said.

"King Louis permits both Jesuits and seigneurs to acquire slaves, and the masters send slaves into battle before themselves. But the Americans still have sights on the Canadas, I say."

A tray of full glasses arrived to be clinked by the men before Jean-François would continue.

"I spent years working around the Huron reserve and I can attest that the natives have superior skills. Camouflaged in the woods, they ascend rivers at nightfall in canoes covered with brush."

Chauvin raised his glass again. "Yes, we live side by side with our Huron friends, and new generations can't forget them. I learned their scouting skills too and am sensitive to the whistling of winds and the breaking of still waters."

Habitants Adapt to New Trade Agreements

AFTER THE CONSTITUTION of 1791, the boundary between Upper (Haut) Canada and Lower (Bas) Canada ran from the mouth of Lake St. Francis to the Ottawa River, with each province vying for power in the Legislative Assembly.

Insufficient crops from the 1787 harvest left farmers hungry, and most feared the return of caterpillar infestation. Game, fish, and offerings of the woods no longer sustained a family, and unable to even feed their livestock, farmers resorted to butchering sheep and oxen to ration the meat. Every family knew tragedies of folks that didn't survive the winter, succumbing to starvation.

Jean-François Paquette and Marie-Geneviève Pageau raised thirteen children at Charlesbourg at the old Royal Bourg, farming wheat, grain, corn and hemp eking a living from the land. He often reflected on his meeting at the Beacon & Stag with his friends, but hadn't spoken a word to Marie-Geneviève about the idea of moving his family to Sainte-Rose-de-Lima near Montréal.

At the General Store, he was greeted by a shout from the store room.

"Jean-François! There's a letter for you."

Mrs. Ward heaved her ample weight and crinolines toward him, curious herself and hoping to pick some gossip.

He knew the envelope's scratch from his friend Joseph Charbonneau, from Sainte-Rose-de-Lima.

Mon cher Jean-François,

Je fais confiance dans Dieu à que vous et cher Geneviève et les enfants sont dans la bonne santé. Il est bon que les vieux amis se réunissent dans de bonnes périodes et dans le mauvais. Nous sommes tristes de l'acte de constitution maintenant nous appelle le Canada inférieur et donnant tout le loyaliste qu'il veut. Vous devez tenir cher votre terre et notre héritage pour les Anglais voudra la prendre quand nous ne regardons pas.

Marie-Catherine a eu un nouveau bébé et est beaucoup aidée par notre fille plus âgée, Marie. Nous serions les plus heureux si vous pourriez trouver votre chemin à la chambre Rose-De-Lima pour une salutation.

Mercies sont assortis à Dieu.[38]

Joseph J.B. Charbonneau

The picturesque village of Sainte-Rose-de-Lima took its name from the patron saint Isobel Flores de Olivia, meaning Rose of Lima. Jean François found it fully to his liking, charming and lined with quaint French stone cottages.

Marie-Geneviève insisted that each one should wear Sunday best clothes for the trip, not to look so much like poor farmers. After carding dyed sheep's wool, she toiled on the loom to tailor wool trousers and hand-sewn linen shirts for Jean-François, François, Sebastien and Jacques. For the girls—Marie-Joseph, Marie-Anne, Marie-Geneviève, and Charlotte— she sewed colourful Montréal broadcloth skirts and patterned blouses, each with hand-tatted lace.

The night before leaving on the long journey to Sainte-Rose, the wagons were loaded with family heirlooms and storehouse supplies. From Québec, a network of country roads connected the villages on the river and overland to Lachine.

---

[38] I trust in God that you and dear Geneviève and the children are in good health. It is good that old friends meet in good times and in bad. We are sad to the act of constitution we now call Canada Lower and giving all the Loyalist he wants. You must keep your expensive land and our legacy, for English will want to take it when we are not looking. Marie-Catherine had a new baby and is much helped by our eldest daughter, Mary. We would be happier if you could find your way to settle at Rose-De-Lima for a greeting. Mercies go with God.

The inherent rights of the Hudson's Bay Company was challenged in 1779 by the North West Company. Lead shareholders—McTavish, Todd and McGill—represented a group of Highland Scottish investors that migrated to Montréal after 1760. McTavish and Frobisher oversaw the North West Company in Montréal, and Alexander McKenzie diverted his attention to inland exploration, discovering the mouth of the McKenzie River in 1789, and conveying 20,000 beaver pelts annually.

McTavish purchased the Seigneurie of Terrebonne, adding to his massive holdings. As settlements developed, a new focus was placed on the Ottawa River for lumbering and trade. Wild animals were forced inland, including the majestic moose that were seldom seen anymore near the urban population.

The North West Company pursued trading rights for inland beaver pelts of the Michilemackinac, igniting an intense battle with HBC. The Scots prevailed over the interior routes to the Pacific, and the challenge for trading rights continued until the turn of the century. Fur trading had become a mercantile venture and no longer for hobby or survival.

Twenty-nine

Joseph Charbonneau furrows the fields at Sainte-Rose-de-Lima – François Paquette come to the aid of Marie Charbonneau's chicken coop – May Day celebrations at manor house of Seigneur of St. Vincent de Paul – François and Joseph vie for the maypole – September harvest time for feudal fealty – François Paquette and Marie Charbonneau engagement, 1793 – Simeon LeRoy has land disputes in Nova Scotia – Acadians squeezed from land by British Loyalists – LeRoys relocate to St. Andrews overland portage.

François Paquette & Marie Charbonneau

UNDER A WEATHERED STRAW HAT, JOSEPH CHARBONNEAU steered his hand plow in furrowed stripes, as Luc followed with the seed drill in the forward fields.

The pasture was fenced with cedar rails, penning four or five sheep, a nanny goat and two kids, and on the adjoining strip, two oxen and two cows grazed. His border collie circled the livestock, ensuring grazers didn't break into the low pasture's oat fields.

The Charbonneau farmhouse at Sainte-Rose-de-Lima was a one-story, whitewashed cottage with a steeped, red tin roof and colourful painted dormers. A wooden ladder from the kitchen gave access to an open beamed attic. The narrow lot ran along the river with a backdrop of deep fields, widening toward the forested hillside.

The Paquette wagon lumbered into his lane, past the now stately elms. In the distance, Marie, the oldest Charbonneau daughter, was scrambling in the garden to capture an escaped chicken with her apron.

The Habitant Farm, 1856, oil on canvas, Cornelius Krieghoff (1815-1872),
National Gallery of Canada ⑤

"Here chickie, chickie."

She hesitated in a flushed laugh as the guests came into view. Joseph Charbonneau saw the Paquettes from the plow. Cackling from the brooder house was a chorus of chaos, but Joseph and Marie-Catherine seemed not to notice as they greeted their friends.

As Jean-François Paquette released his horses, François sauntered over to watch Marie, in the hope she'd welcome his aid. Another chicken had joined the race through the wire coop, and she threw her hands high.

"Oh no! Chickens! Through the door!" Her frustration dissipated to laughter as François scooped them up, unfazed by the flapping.

Recovering some poise, Marie teased, "I didn't realize my lady chickens responded so well to a handsome man."

"Are you comparing me to a chicken, Mademoiselle?"

An awkward wink made them both laugh, and together they tied a wire to repair the gap. She stood close to watch as he secured the coop.

"There, that should keep them. Shall I come again next week to check?"

They didn't laugh, but stopped, both knowing the nervousness of the moment, unable to say the right thing. "I hope your chickens still produce enough eggs for your morning breakfast," he tried, and she nodded.

François came clean-shaven the next time, with his auburn hair tamed into place with a tad of hair pomade. He had brushed any traces of feathers, feed or sawdust from his Sunday best. With more nerve this time, Marie said he looked handsome with or without the brushing.

Visits between the two family farms became more frequent with the oxen-led drill seed plow and the thrasher at harvest.

The May Day Pole

FOR THE MAY DAY celebration at the manor house of the Seigneur of St. Vincent de Paul, François Paquette and Joseph Charbonneau selected a tall fir from the woods, to prepare a pole suitable for the competitions.

Together with Louis and Sebastian, they stripped the tree of its limbs and smoothed it to a polished surface.

At the top, Louis attached strips of material woven with ribbons, and they planted the base firmly into the ground.

"Joseph, do you really think you can beat me up this pole?" François jeered.

With mischievous eyes sparkling at the challenge, François shoved his shirt sleeves over his elbows and rubbed his palms. Wide-eyed, the two braced, then watched the other for a first move.

"Ready, Joe!" he roared.

"Me too," said Charbonneau. "1, 2, 3—Go!"

The two shinnied up, swinging and grasping to knock the other off. A crowd of farmers and children gathered quickly, with animated guffaws and laughter. Others bantered to have a go at it.

"François, I heard that Joseph Charbonneau is part Irish," an onlooker mocked, with hands cupping his mouth. "You can't let an Irishman beat you."

François shouted, out of breath. "A Charbonneau has never climbed a pole faster than a Paquette. That's a fact." It only stoked his motivation.

"Not this time, François," Joseph retaliated, and surged ahead.

The two stopped, face to face, breathing hard, and refusing to give in.

Joseph whispered, "If you court my sister, I'll let you take top hand."

Stunned by the offer, François looked at the crowd, then up at the final two yards. He nodded. The audience cheered when he made the final thrust to the top, freeing the coloured ribbons.

Then shinnying at full speed, he dropped to the ground. It dawned on him that, although Joseph yielded to him as the victor, it was Charbonneau that beat him and they would both remember that. François looked to see if Marie had seen the conquest on the maypole. She was nowhere in sight.

Joseph and François had nailed the twisted ribbon fabric in an alternating pattern at the top of the pole, letting the ribbons fall to a height about three feet above ground.

Children danced in a circle, to the music of fiddles, tin pipes and wooden whistles, threading the ribbons around the circumference of the pole until there was no more fabric.

Parents stood in a circle, dancing arm in arm in a joyeux chant.

Feu de Joie Festival at Sainte-Rose-de-Lima

BEYOND A SOCIAL event, the annual Feu de Joie, with music, cakes, wine and laughter, was a celebration of gratitude to habitants for spending two spring days planting and seeding the seigneur's farm, then two days at harvest, and two at the whim of the seigneur. Months later, in September, the celebration of Saint Michael the Archangel would be held at the same manor estate.

The Paquette wagon hobbled up the lane to the seigneur's manor at Sainte-Rose-de-Lima, maneuvering past the wagons, as others unloaded sacks of grain, and bushels of apples, corn, grapes, and coops of poultry.

A large basket lay empty, waiting for the collection of cens and copper coins to pay fealty to the seigneur.

François and Marie had been courting for months. She recently turned eighteen, simultaneous with the death of her mother, Marie-Catherine Bouchard. Her father, Joseph Charbonneau, had been left with two young sons, Joseph and Luc, and Marie to tend the household.

Marie saw the Paquette wagon at once and ran out to find François.

"I can't bear the sadness in our own house, François. I thought Papa would grieve longer since Maman died. You know I've been unhappy that he took a young wife—Marguerite is not even ten years my senior."

François pulled Marie to his side to console her. "Your papa adored your mother, but Joseph and Luc are just boys and they need a mother. Your papa thinks he is doing the best for his family."

She rested her head on his shoulder, with quiet tears. In the distance, coming across the yard, were Joseph and her step-mother, Marguerite Vanier, with newborn Ignace in her arms.

"Here we are, two grown orphans," François said. He squeezed her and she fell into giggles. "We will get in the spring planting, Marie, then we'll marry and move back to the Paquette homestead. That's assuming we will have your father's blessing. Oui?"

Marie's sparkling blue eyes looked into his. "Oui. Mother left me her wedding dress."

Marie raised onto her toes, feeling a sudden exuberant excitement. "Papa will say yes, I'm sure of it."

The magical surprise day of engagement at the seigneur's manor concluded with a dance with native horns. At the sound of the seigneur's cannon, a sequence of rifles echoed into the night air.

Loyalists Flood into Eastern Townships

ENTICED BY LAND grants, a new surge of immigrants from Britain set their sights on Nova Scotia. The British government had overruled the rights of Nova Scotians, and were squeezing French landowners, forcing many to flee to settlements in Acadia.

The Acadians were a people unjustly uprooted and persecuted for maintaining their unique French culture, but with a strong native influence. Over the centuries, Acadians had protested neutrality, being neither sympathetic to British laws nor antagonistic. When the British had the opportunity to flood Nova Scotia with its loyal subjects, they were quick to cede the land of the Acadians, leaving them homeless and without a country.

While in New Brunswick, Simeon LeRoy suffered several land disputes, and eventually sold off his farm in Queen's County for 65£ to Nathaniel Hughson. Seeking land in Québec's Eastern Townships, Simeon was enticed by Argenteuil, a Francophone community, and secured steamboat passage from Halifax to Montréal. Accompanying him were Wyntje and three sons and two daughters—William, George Simon, Henry, Sophia, and Hannah. Several married daughters remained behind, and his brother William from New Brunswick had gone ahead.

The LeRoys were recorded as the first United Empire Loyalists in Argenteuil County. Other recorded loyalists in the same area at the mouth of the North River were Martin Jones in 1788, Thomas Hyde 1792, and Henry Albright. In the 1790s, a contingent of Puritan veterans of the Revolution followed and settled nearby.

At Halifax, the LeRoys boarded a European steamboat designed by the Scot, Henry Bell. With luck, it had space for some of their furniture and possessions. Before the ice set in, steamers could ply the Rideau River, however would be land-locked from November to the melt-off in March.

Joseph Giroux met the steamboat at Montréal for the sojourn to Rivière-Rouge near Saint-André-Est, where Simeon acquired farmland in 1785. As the ongoing land portage by wagon was too rugged, the LeRoys had no choice but to sell off their furnishings to lighten the load, then to proceed on foot.

Determination brought them at last to their land, and Simeon took Wyntje's hand to savour their property.

"The North River is beautiful. Look where we are. Our land is elevated, divided by ranges on each side of a ten mile creek. We are lot 38 of the Rouge River seigneurie in the Township of Two Mountains. And William will be our neighbor on lot 37."

"It's a wonderful beginning," she said. "The agent assured that the land was well cultivated, so we can start right away to put in a spring crop."

"Indeed we will . . . perhaps I didn't tell you that every farmer in Rivière-Rouge other than us is Scottish."

The winter roads were too arduous to take wheat to Murray's gristmill, so Simeon concocted a sieve from perforated skins to make a crude home-made mill, to provide wheat for his family.

Thirty

François Paquette & Joseph Charbonneau, Hired Guides from Lac Deux Montagnes to North River – Debate with Clients over French Soil – Route follows Chemin du Roy logging road – François Paquette marries Marie Charbonneau, 1793 – Marie Charbonneau supplies General Store with eggs and pickles – Marie Charbonneau orders new Hargreaves Spinning Jenny, 1809 – Twelve Days of Christmas Feast, 1811 – Young Edouard Irvan Paquette lives with his brother – Edouard receives glimmering skate blades for Christmas – Request to live with his father, François Sr. – Edouard Irvan sets sights on a carpentry woodshop in St. Andrews.

Skiff Journey from Oka to Saint-André-Est

NATIVE SPIRIT STILL FLOURISHED IN THE EASTERN Township villages, with farming, hunting, and fishing; and river guides were in greater demand to aid British timber merchants on the Ottawa and St. Lawrence. There was no shortage of work for François Paquette, Joseph Charbonneau, and Pierre Cloutier, on the waters from Lac des Deux-Montagnes to the mouth of the North River.

François and Joseph waited patiently across the river at the Oka docks, watching for the clients who hired them to guide a camping expedition.

"They're definitely late," François said, pointing at his grandfather's watch. "Think they're even coming?"

"These people pay in generous cash . . . so we'll always wait."

In unison, two Brits barked from down the mission road. "Ahoy, matey! Are you Joseph Charbonneau?"

"Oui. Eh bien, Monsieur Ayers et Monsieur Henderson?" Joseph stepped forward to grasp the merchants' hands. "Mon ami est François Paquette de Lorette."

The British gents were pompous and equally brisk. They stepped in front of the guides and strode well ahead, assuming their proper status. Behind Joseph and François, a pair of lads carried canvas sacks of supplies and rations to the canoe.

François knelt to steady the gunwales, and Joseph extended his arm to help Ayers into the wider centre cushioned seat. Henderson was directed to crouch and step gingerly to join Ayers on the seat.

The men looked pleased with themselves, but not enough to express any gratitude.

"Welcome, gentlemen. I am as good a guide as a canoeist," François said. "We will leave right away and follow the Ottawa River. When you're tired, we'll camp."

The men were unaccustomed to canoes, and balked at the instruction to sit low to reach the safest centre of gravity. The portage lads crouched on the floor ribs against the forward and aft thwarts that ran across the canoes.

François paddled from the front, with knees on a floor blanket, and Joseph steered from the stern. The cargo was stowed without an inch to spare on the floor, and tied to the seats and thwarts.

Once settled, Henderson thought he should own the conversation, instead of enjoying the peaceful solitude of nature and the majestic silent appearances of moose and beaver.

"Mr. Paquette, do you live on British land?"

The hairs on François' neck bristled, but he knew to mind his tongue, as Marie had so often told him.

"Non, Monsieur. Ma famille has a farm on the seigneurie at Sainte-Rose. We are good farmers and have been on French soil since our ancestors came from France two hundred years ago. And you, sir—when did you come across the ocean?"

"My father claimed this land for the British during the Indian Wars," Ayers said with sarcasm. "We permitted the natives to fight for our rights alongside."

François continued paddling, but turned and looked back at Ayers without missing a stroke.

"My grandfather gave his life for France during those wars. The Hurons are my good friends at Oka and Lorette, and I learned my woodsman skills from them. They were here long before the French . . . and even longer before the English merchants."

The last words echoed and the two young lads laid low without a word.

The scenery passed for an hour, before Henderson called, "Ahoy, Captain!"

"Yes, Mr. Henderson."

"When are we going to fish?"

The canoe was steering through rough water, an unlikely place to consider fishing, but François called to Joseph.

"Joe, our guests want to do some fishing. There's an inlet at the next bay; would you agree to holding up there?"

"Sure, François. This is a good time of day for walleye, bass and maybe some pike. I know the place, we have a cache of supplies high in the trees."

Henderson's voice echoed arrogance as he moved on to political conversations with Ayers about the French Revolution and its failures, and debated the struggles of Louis XVI and his inevitable failure. It was important that he would be heard by the Frenchmen, but clearly *their* opinions would not be entertained.

"Louis had done one thing right. He abolished all those fancy titles and knighthoods, and those farms and feudal communes are going to fade away—just wait and see, Ayers. I read that he was under guard at Versailles, with the threat of an imminent execution for treason."

"Dear Lord Henderson, must we spend such a lovely morning talking of the demise of the French monarchy?" Ayers teased. "The countryside along the riverbank is as pretty as rural England, and deserving of your understudy."

"Mr. Paquette, are we following beside a logging road?" Ayers called out. "I've heard of the Chemin du Roy. Could that be it?"

At the stern, Joseph Charbonneau couldn't conceal his smirk. "No, Monsieur Ayers, but I'm flattered that you ask. The Chemin du Roy is the road connecting cities and towns along the St. Lawrence. These days, logging is done where we are now, mainly on the Rideau and Ottawa Rivers, after the pine is brought out of the thick bush."

Joseph continued to amuse the men, describing his adventures in the lumber camps and explaining how the pine timbers for their houses came to be. Turning to the lads, he hauled out a hook and bait kit from under his legs.

"Here you go, young men. Get those rods hooked and baited for our fine guests."

François and Marie Marry

FRANÇOIS PAQUETTE and Marie Charbonneau married at Sainte-Rose-de-Lima on May 27, 1793, settling in a rented cottage in the village. In their first six years of marriage, Marie had a new baby every year—three boys and three girls, then six more after that.

Marie set up a significant chicken coop at the side of the barn, and during winter months the hens were moved to a warm hay-insulated corner inside.

With the spring thaw, she rode to town more often with François or one of the older boys, with several dozen eggs and her prize pickles and jams for trade at the General Store.

Matilda Perkins, the store clerk, always received Marie well, greeting her with spirit. "Ah, my favourite customer. I had a lady in just yesterday, inquiring when we might expect your wonderful, wild strawberry confection. She gave me an order for two and asked for a dozen of your brown eggs."

"Merci, Matilda, you are in luck." Marie placed her basket on the broad counter. "I would come more often, but it is a bit of a ride from the farm. If you have orders, perhaps you could send them by with Monsieur Perkins, or one of the neighbours. Of course, I suppose it is time that I learn to drive the buggy myself." They both laughed.

"Your credit here is growing, are you saving for something special?" Matilda asked.

"I saw in your catalogue that you can order me a Spinning Jenny."

"Yes indeed, Marie. It can come from Montréal in a week. It will be delivered straight to your home."

"Oh Matilda, it has to wait, but thank you. Perhaps after harvest. For now, I'll come again on Tuesday."

Motivated by Matilda's interest in her kitchen produce, Marie sent her young children to collect wild strawberries, blackberries, pears and apples from the orchard. Jacques and Marguerite were quick to volunteer, and returned hours later with two full bushel baskets.

"Oh, my goodness! I hope you like jam too. Marguerite, come with me and you'll learn my secrets to prize winning jam; the Harvest fair is in a few weeks."

The pair set up the Clark two-gallon cast-iron pressure cooker, setting a dozen jams from each cooking. The preserves were bottled in heavy blue and clear glass canning jars with clasped lids, and by late evening, every bottle was filled.

The Hargreaves Spinning Jenny was delivered in early November 1809. Marie invited all her neighbours including Marguerite Amable Roy, wife of Louis-Antoine Tessier, and her daughter-in-law, Marie Louise Brault dit Pominville for a party, that made the men envious.

Christmas at Sainte-Rose-de-Lima, 1811

THE START of the Twelve Days of Christmas and the arrival of Père Noël was every child's most cherished time, a season of merrymaking, when grownups returned to childhood homes, and friends travelled from farm to farm with the most gracious Christmas spirit.

At the ancient church at Sainte-Rose-de-Lima, the twin bell towers chimed solemnly for Christmas Eve mass. The gongs replied twelve times, echoing to the village's far corners, muted by a new blanket of snow.

The limestone church was denoted by a Latin cross, accented with a trio of windows on the facade above the central door. Even the outside shadows of the magnificent Cathedral commanded reverence.

Beside the wagon of François and Marie at the courtyard hitching post, an empty red painted sleigh with garlands of spruce boughs waited with a two-horse team.

The night sky was breathtaking with the North Star pointing over Saint-Eustache and Sainte-Rose. It couldn't have been more perfect to gather to celebrate the birth of Jesus. In the manner that the wise men followed the Star to Bethlehem with faith, the habitants joined to rejoice in Advent. François and Marie and François-Charles and Marie-Marguerite were devout Catholics, rarely missing mass, and never on these holy occasions.

In a ceremonial black robe, the Priest opened the double doors under the oculus and released the departure of anxious children from the rituals. Ladies and young girls were adorned in long tailored coats, bonnets with ribbons and rabbit fur muffs. Men wore their smartest long jackets, cravats, and beaver felt hats.

With suitable lingering on the vestibule doorstep, Church members funneled down into the courtyard, as soprano voices sang *In Those Twelve Days* and *Let Us Sing Noël*.

The most mischievous boys and girls instigated tag in the snow and parents chased the little ones to board the wagons and cutters. Bodies and spirits were warm for the jaunts back home, with spontaneous laughter ready to break out by the old and young.

François and Marie lingered behind with the Girouxs. The Paquettes had eight young children at home, with two already married. Marie was expecting another baby in the spring, as was Marie-Marguerite.

After mass, the annual Tourtière feast and Réveillon would be celebrated at the Paquette farm. Marie never lacked enthusiasm for her traditional gathering of friends, and this year young Marie-Clémence and Marie-Geneviève begged to set the table bowls and carry the casseroles and pots.

Night lanterns hung on the curves of the sleighs, as the black Morgans pranced home. Into the darkness, voices echoed the ancient Noëls de la Nouvelle-France, *D'où viens-tu, bergère.* Every age was in hushed awe at the panorama of the stars, and under the full moon, a child pointed and asked about the Big Dipper and Orion's Belt.

At the farm, men brought in large planks to perch on a cross-stand, long enough to seat a banquet. A cast-iron casserole of boulettes and meatballs warmed on the stove, and together, Marie and Marguerite seasoned the meats with marjoram, parsley, cloves, mace, and black pepper, and prepared layers of sliced potatoes and onions sealed in a delicate, salty pastry, for the oven.

Twelve Days of Christmas at the Paquette Farm, 1815

When Marie Charbonneau died, Edouard Irvan was the youngest of the Paquette boys. Still of school age, he moved into the household of François Jr. and Marie-Louise at Saint Thérèse-de-Blainville, where they already had three children. In his senior years, Edouard's father, François Sr., still crafted his works at his carpentry bench, but led fewer game hunts, and eventually moved to Saint-Anne-des-Plaines.

Edouard cherished his father's role in family celebrations and Christmas traditions, and was sensitive to his aging years. He organized the traditional nativité scene with its crèche on the parlour table beside a pink fluted oil lamp. His grandfather had carved the figurines two generations before, and still every year, each piece would be lifted from the box and unwrapped as a special treasure.

Rosalie, Augustin, and Louis Joseph Giroux were responsible for shepherds and wise men as Edouard set up the manger scene. Stockings for the young hung on the hearth, hoping for token gifts. Edouard Irvan used one of Papa's worn-out work socks, amused at its frequent mending with unmatched wools. Yet it would still bear morning luxuries of a maple sugar cake, red orange, or a tin whistle.

As every year, the Giroux and Monderie families arrived with gifts at the Paquette's. Marguerite Paquette and Marie-Marguerite Boismenu sat with the men with tea in the parlour; Françoise, Marie-Geneviève and Marie-Louise chattered over dirty dishes in the basin and whispered about the youngest, Augustin Giroux, now stretched on the bearskin rug and overcome with fatigue.

François Jr. cradled a cherry wood pipe in his hand and lit a flint. Edouard inched closer to inhale the aroma of the rings of fragrant smoke, but his coughing soon had him dispatched hastily to the kitchen.

At four in the morning, the slumbering Giroux children were carried out and bundled into the sleigh, and boisterous exchanges of Joyeux Noël echoed through the snowy night. Marie-Marguerite Boismenu took off her shoes, and stood in silence in the empty parlour. She picked up the last Limoges saucer, and turned down the wicks.

With the room dimmed, she felt a gentle kicking movement under her apron, then knelt to touch the forehead of little Edouard under the bear skin, and covered his feet.

Sweet brother Edouard Irvan, I wish I could be more of a mother to you.

The stockings bulged on the mantle above the hearth, as François and Marie-Louise proportioned fruit, nuts and wrapped maple syrup candies. For the older boys, François had made colourful fishing lures in the ice hut, and for Edouard, his young brother, he tucked a wooden jou-jou. The girls would receive sets of pearl buttons and ribbons.

In the morning, the youngsters gathered to tiptoe downstairs in nightshirts, anxious for François to return from milking duties in the barn.

"La patience, mon peu ceux, vous devez habiller le réchauffeur et puis prendre le petit déjeuner de la maman. Nous sommes bénis seulement si nous donnons des mercis à l'enfant du Christ de ce jour et pas cherchons seulement des cadeaux. Les saints ne seront pas heureux si vous ne vous rappelez pas les. Outre de avec vous!"[39]

They bounded back to the loft, and returned moments later. Crackling corn bread and sausage were on the table, and Marie-Louise poured cold milk and steaming coffee.

Edouard Irvan exaggerated a scrunchy face, with both hands on his tummy, complaining he was still full from tortière.

---

[39] "Patience, my little ones, you have to dress warmer and then have breakfast for mom. We are blessed only if we give thanks to the Christ child that day and not only seek gifts. The Saints will not be happy if you do not remember them. Off with you."

"Ah ha, it was you, Edouard," Marie-Louise teased. "There was most of a whole pie left, but this morning, I thought we'd been robbed."

The Christmas story was read from his great-grandfather's leather Bible, passed for each to have a turn, then twelve heads bowed. François Jr. returned it to its shelf, knowing his turn would come to explain the scriptures to his own children.

"Ah, the spirits are watching," he said to himself. "I feel your presence Grand-père and Grand-mère, and my dear Mère."

With stockings opened, the boys stretched across the floor in a game of marbles, and eventually Papa got down to show how it was to be done.

Family gift exchange was reserved for New Year's Day. The air that day was sharp and biting, but no one noticed or cared. An elaborate Buche de Noël cake was served, with one bean baked and hidden inside. The lucky recipient would be King or Queen, to expect royal treatment for the day.

The parcel from Edouard's father was mysterious, and he hoped for a bow and arrow like the one Joseph Regis got at Edouard's age. François Sr. had masterfully carved the alder wood to perfection for that one, and Edouard coveted the day he too would have his.

"But this package couldn't be," he whispered out loud. As the string snapped off the burlap and the folds fell back, he shrieked, and held high a pair of glimmering blades mounted on narrow platforms with leather bindings. Without waiting, he took to the door for boots, with his imagination taking over.

Brisk wind scattered the snow to the other bank, leaving the ice like glass. François followed his brother, and young Octave lagged behind with his old blades dangling from his shoulders. Edouard fell again and again, until he found a crouched position, then the brothers moved to rollick in the snow bank, before exhaustion set in.

Grandpa François stood on the porch to watch, recalling energies of his own youth. Marie-Louise put a loving hand on his shoulder. "Ah, Papa, it warms the heart to see Edouard so happy. Some days he is a sad little boy and asks for you. He wants to go back to the Huron mission for a visit, perhaps sometime soon."

She paused, knowing the value it would be for Edouard and for her father-in-law to share those life experiences.

"Yes, I know he yearns to learn about the native culture; it's been in his blood from birth." François touched the leather string around his neck, with the bear claw earned in his youth. "He has yet to earn his own life's bear claws and porcupine quills."

"Maybe you can come more often for these visits. These years are most important for all of us, and you are always welcome here."

After the evening meal, three generations of Paquettes left by sleighs for New Year's mass. Returning to the farm, they gathered around Grandfather, some on chairs and others cross-legged on the floor. Each child came in anticipation, and bent on their knees beside his chair. François bestowed upon each of them praise for their respective qualities and hopes for the New Year.

Edouard had little patience to wait his turn, standing and squirming on his chair. Finally, he sat close and rested his elbow on his father's knees.

"Papa, my wish is to live with you. I understand that we can't always have what we want. Aunt Marie-Louise and François are very kind to me, but I dream of my own mother. I have a picture I drew from memory under my pillow. I miss you, Papa."

Edouard looked into his father's eyes knowing the impossibility of his wish. "Is it my fault that she died?"

"The day your dear mother died, you were in her arms. She told me how much she loved you. You are a strong young man for eight years, and François tells me you are doing well at school. I spend weeks at a time in the bush and cannot provide the home that you have here."

"Yes, Papa." Edouard's young strength was on the outside. The jabbing pain he felt in his heart would not surface again, as he determined never to ask for his longing.

As new settlements opened in Argenteuil and the Eastern Townships, Edouard dreamed of new opportunity. In his teens, he left the village of Sainte-Rose-de-Lima for a labour position in Saint Eustache, a short distance across the river. His sister Marguerite and her husband Michel Duperoux offered him board in exchange for helping on the farm and in the carpentry shop.

With acquired skills, he worked as a master carpenter, setting up a small tool and woodworking shop in the village. From the start, he saved what he could toward buying a small plot of farmland. His sight was on land in nearby Saint-André-Est, where many of the Girouxs and Charlebois were homesteading on the North River.

Thirty-one

Sir Ralph Creffield, Mayor of Colchester – Creffield Royal Drapers – Thomas Creffield gets tour of Looms & Skittles – Thomas apprentices with Hargrave Attorneys – Case to Catch Poachers – Prisque Cloutier takes Clémence to Brunnette's grist mill – Fascination of the Paddle Wheel – François Paquette arrives at mill with brothers – Catherine-Marguerite Jolivet worked as servant in Gilbert household – Joseph Vincent Giroux collides with Bone-Shaker – François Charles Giroux rescues Marie-Marguerite Tranchemontagne from slurs – Mondary & Jolibois brothers from St. Eustache harvest ice on Trois-Rivières.

The Creffields, Woolen Drapers, England

T HE ESTEEMED SIR RALPH CREFFIELD SR. HELD THE distinction and positions of alderman and Mayor of Colchester from 1668 to 1673.

Later, exerting his upper class influence, he arranged with John Forster for the apprenticeship of his son, Ralph Creffield Jr., as a barrister's clerk. Ralph Jr. would also become Mayor of Colchester in 1702. The generations were good to the family, and Peter Creffield, grandson of Sir Ralph, became master of Elmstead manor and the East Mersea estate in the mid-1700s.

The Creffield family continued to grow in wealth as royal drapers on High Street in Colchester, and accumulated landholdings in Essex County.

Peter's nephew, Thomas Creffield, arrived early at the Colchester establishment for his appointment to see his uncle. He paused outside to admire the building, then pushed open both double doors to the grand lobby with its brick industrial walls. The rhythmic hum of looms muffled through to the front of the building.

A stiff, middle-aged gentleman in a fine woolen suit and ruffled shirt entered the guest lobby, looking down over his monocle as if to inspect Thomas.

"Good day to you, sir. Have you an appointment?"

"Master Thomas Creffield." He offered his hand in greeting, but was ignored. "To see my uncle. Thank you."

"Yes, I see. He'll be along shortly. If you would like to take a seat, I'll bring you a pot of tea."

"Thank you, sir . . ." Thomas still waited for a proper introduction.

"Hodges," the man gave reluctantly as he left for the tea.

"Mr. Hodges, do you mind if I tour the working rooms in the meantime?"

"If you insist, I'll bring Mrs. Chase to take you through." Hodges held his breath not to huff, but Thomas sensed the imposition.

The head tailor returned with Mrs. Chase, a plump matron. Her prematurely grey hair was tight in a braided bun.

"Master Thomas, I understand you wish to see the working rooms."

"Indeed, Mrs. Chase, if it isn't too much trouble."

"Come along. We have a present order for the royals in Windsor. Lovely heavy Yorkshire wool, just now combed and ready for carding and skittling. Do you mind me asking if you'll be taking charge of the factory for Mr. Peter?"

At a slow pace, Mrs. Chase stopped at every chance to impress Thomas with sample fabrics on giant spools. Threads of silk in reds, greens, gold and blues enhanced the drapes, hanging and on tables.

"You needn't worry, Mrs. Chase. I am keenly interested in how the looms produce such exquisite fabric, but alas, I will not be taking charge of the working rooms. They seem to be in fine hands."

Mrs. Chase took it as a compliment, and smiled, standing taller.

"Then you must be here to pick up the drapery for East Mersea?"

"No, not East Mersea."

He stammered, unsure what to say next, as she was obviously expecting startling replies and information. Hodges' shadow was in the doorway with his ear extended.

"It is a personal matter I wish to discuss with my uncle."

A gust of wind from the front door stopped them. Peter Creffield's entrance in the building sent Hodges into action, and he gladly took the hat and coat of his employer.

"G'day, Thomas."

"Good afternoon, uncle."

"Well, the matter is settled. Come this way, lad."

To the others' disappointment, the pair moved to a private office, with glass windows overlooking the working room. The door was closed.

"I will do my best, sir. I have pulled all the court records regarding poachers in Essex over the past five years." He removed a folded document from his breast pocket and laid it on his uncle's desk.

"Ah, this will be the billet to be posted throughout the County. One hundred pounds, so be it. The court clerk will circulate it in Colchester, Pebmarsh and Flanders, and the culprits will be brought to justice. Hargrave's attorneys have a desk ready for you. We've agreed to a five year apprenticeship, Thomas."

To young Thomas, it sounded an eternity, but the proud-as-a-peacock look on his uncle's face helped him to muster enthusiasm.

"Yes, sir," Thomas said. "I agree that an apprentice should be knowledgeable with leg work during training indoctrination. We have a man following Pickersgill and his son. The kitchen cook complained that the men came home with fresh beef, not venison, albeit without taking time away for a hunting excursion. Sounds like we might have the guilty bird in hand."

"Good fellow."

"Thank you, sir. I won't disappoint you."

Thomas was off to the town clerk's office to take care of business, smug with his new authority, while curious eyes peered from the upper windows.

Mary will be very pleased. She was always fond of Uncle Peter.

Henry Hargrave, the Town Clerk, was conducting other business in the outer office, and excused himself from his client to greet Thomas as he arrived. A tall heavy-set man, with steely grey eyes yet a kind smile greeted him.

"G'day to you, Thomas."

"Good afternoon, Mr. Hargrave. I was just bringing the billet regarding the poachers, then I'll go to see the kitchen cook at Round House to investigate further. We shall be most interested in what she can tell us."

"All in good time, lad."

Hargrave contradicted himself by pulling a pocket watch from his vest, but as he prepared to depart, he turned back to Thomas. "Be sure to tell your uncle that Britain has just declared war on France and Spain—in the colonies."

"In the colonies?"

"Yes, Prussia will join with us. Once Britain controls the fur trading economy in the Canadas, we shall all wear beaver top hats," Hargrave said. "Our British fleet will be proud when they take those walled cities of the St. Lawrence. France needs to be taken down a peg or two."

Thomas cautioned himself.

I'll not mix politics with my employer.

Prisque Cloutier's Excursion to the Grist-mill

REGIMENTED MCINTOSH and Cortland apple trees lined the Cloutier garden in the predominantly Métis community of Oka. The spring blossoms were now ablaze in fluorescent pinks and whites. Although the perimeter of the wild grass and garden bordered the robust orchard, the total yard encompassed less than half an acre.

Prisque Cloutier had abandoned farming at Sainte-Rose-de-Lima and spent months away from home as a voyageur and river guide for the Huron fur trade.

Now back home in the village of Sainte-Thérèse-de-Blainville, he worked as a carpenter and enjoyed his orchards, and when possible, found employment at the mills.

His timber house emptied onto the main road, with a sitting room adjoining a planked porch for small talk with neighbours, an activity that Marie-Louise relished. Of eleven children she birthed, half hadn't survived infancy, a common peril at the turn of the century. Despite the tragedies, she always presented a joyful smile.

From the back shed, Prisque hauled a newly constructed wagon with three-foot dismantled barn boards on a molded iron t-frame, on four wheels from the blacksmith. Wide red planks ran down the sides and a heavy twine was anchored at the front tow bar.

A tiny voice giggled from a hiding place in the orchard. "Papa, can you find me?"

Prisque removed his hat, wiped his brow, and turned from the wagon to peer into the clouds of apple blossoms. He spied a dusty, buttoned ankle boot, high in the branches of a Cortland tree, then a glimpse of brown ribboned braids. But he pretended not to see, and continued to search the McIntoshes. The snickering grew as excitement poked at the child's impatience to be discovered.

"I'm up here, Papa," Clémence cackled. Her tanned face beamed down as she separated some branches. "Will you catch me, Papa?"

Her father braced himself in the landing position and Clémence fell into his lap. She wrapped her arms around Prisque's neck, and swung her high in the air, planting her toes on the ground.

Clémence's curiosity was drawn to the new wagon. Without hesitation, she bounded over, circling in a dizzying figure eight on the way until she lost her balance. Upright again, she looked up to her father. "Where are you going with the wagon? Can I come?"

"Only with your mother's consent. Off to the house!"

Marie-Louise followed her daughter back to the yard where Prisque waited. With approval, Clémence nestled in the back of the wagon for the trip to Brunette's grist-mill, where Prisque planned to barter with his bushels of apples and some crocks of cider.

"We'll be back in time for supper. I should be able to trade for a sack of wheat, a little rye, and hopefully some barley."

He leaned to give Marie-Louise a peck on her cheeks, and she handed him a burlap sack with bread, cheese and a jug of cider.

"Save this until you're hungry and thirsty."

"Of course, my dear," Prisque said, but he noticed Clémence had mischief on her face, with her index and middle fingers crossed.

"Yes, mother," the young child called out.

Clémence found the wagon to be bumpy and asked to join her father on foot pulling it, but soon she was running to keep pace with his long strides. Born in 1809, she was a spirited six-year-old, always the apple of his eye.

"We'll be at the mill soon, Clémas."

Ducking to peer through the light of the trees, her small voice squealed, "I see it! Oh, Papa, listen."

Clémence gasped at the tall stone mill. Through the thicket was the great paddle wheel, and the thunder of plummeting water. The creek gushed and pounded, and her tiny heart thrilled by the sight and sound.

"It is wonderful!"

Prisque and Clémence entered a single door, slanted by the angle of the stone walls that narrowed up from the fieldstone base at the water dam. He took a long breath of air, heavy with the sweet aroma of fresh pine beams. She watched, and gulped a deep breath to mimic him.

Inside was a menagerie of beams, each with a unique purpose, and large slotted wooden box trays and sieves.

Rattling back and forward in pendulum motion, husks were separated from the wheat kernels, allowing a coarse flour to sift through levels of perforations into the bottom trays.

Huge leather strap pulleys rotated in exact motion, propelled by the water. Prisque and Clémence climbed a narrow galley of wooden stairs to a lofted landing.

Monsieur Brunette was busy and had not yet taken notice of them. A row of grain sacks had accumulated along the wall below a vaulted window, with a hedge of lesser burlaps in one corner.

The whirring continued before the miller stopped to exchange greetings with his friend. Clémence, on one foot, watched shyly from behind her Papa.

"Allo, Prisque. My goodness, Clémas, you have grown. I hope you brought me some special apples. I promised Madame we would have apple pie tonight."

"Mais oui, Monsieur Brunette, you will be pleased. Your favourites are waiting in the wagon. Ma sent cider as well."

The miller winked at Prisque, then beckoned Clémence to listen closer to the rattling machine.

"Here, Clémas. Bring this empty ten pound sack and come with me to the grain chute," he said.

"Is it alright, Papa?"

"Oui, you are strong. Fill us a sack of flour for Maman."

Clémence edged between the troughs to Monsieur Brunette standing at the shaft lever.

"Hold your bag here and keep her steady."

Hanging on tightly, she waited for her little bag to fill and the chute to close. Bracing her knees and straightening her back, she was determined to bear the weight.

Monsieur Brunette drew a length of cord from a spool, and handed the tied sack to her. From ear to ear, she smiled, keeping her eyes on the fat pouch cradled in her hands.

This is like rocking one of Maman's babies.

As Prisque and the miller conversed, Clémence was absent in her imaginary world, mesmerized by the paddle wheel and the fascination it brought. Time lost its measurement, but her trance was broken by the sound of horses and the clattering of a wagon pulling into the lane for off-loading grain.

François Paquette, with sons, François Jr. and Edouard Irvan, jumped from the wagon and shouted greetings. The wagon became an instant gathering point, as they reached to hoist sheaves, throwing each one up to the shoulder, then to the wooden platform.

With the wagon empty, Edouard stood to stretch and crack his knuckles. Clémence was nearby on a bale of hay, drawing pictures with a stick on the dirt floor.

She moved a little so Edouard could sit.

"It's a lovely day, isn't it Edouard? I love to watch the workings of the paddle wheels." Clémence prattled on with gibberish, trying out big words. "The magnificent power wheels impress me."

"Yes, I agree. Do you come often?" Although senior by several years, Edouard was entertained and interested in her responses.

Winter in the Country, the Old Grist Mill, 1862 Painting,
George Henry Durrie (1820-1863), Private collection, Public Domain Ⓢ

The Cloutier sacks of grain were piled in the walking wagon alongside a wagon wheel with a broken hub for Alexis to repair. Prisque bade the miller and Paquettes farewell, but Clémas had other plans. She climbed on top of the grain, in the most awkward manner.

Edouard quickly called out, "Wait a minute. Clémence won't be safe riding in the back of your wagon, straddling this load."

Prisque shook his head in amusement about his tomboy daughter orchestrating a scene of a damsel in distress, over sacks wedged around the wheel.

He mouthed quiet words, not to be overheard. "It's not often she doesn't get her way."

Edouard turned to his brother, François. "The little one will fall or have to walk. Can we go that way and give her a ride in *our* wagon?"

"She's too young for you, brother."

"Oh, I know that, François, but it's the kind thing to do."

François nodded and Edouard went to speak with Prisque.

The wagons lumbered down the uneven trail, dodging rotting stumps and tree limbs that obscured the path. Edouard pointed out a tree swallow, a wood thrush and a yellow finch to Clémence, who was wide-eyed at his observations. She became quick with her own words.

"Over there, I see a wild cottontail, a coyote, and a red squirrel. Do you see them?"

Edouard admired the competitiveness.

"My family is from a long line of nature folk; we love to hunt and walk in the woods," he said.

"Oh, yes, me too."

Past the main avenue of Sainte-Thérèse, the Paquette wagon stopped at the weathered Cloutier house, next to the cemetery and the inn. Marie-Louise stood from her porch rocking chair, surprised to see Clémence waving from the Paquette wagon. Behind was Prisque with his buckboard.

"Boys, this is a standing invitation for summer picnics with our family, after Sunday services." Plans were agreed for the coming Sunday, and Clémence was pleased with herself, to see Edouard again so soon.

"Clémas, bring a fishing pole on Sunday," Edouard called back from the wagon. "Can you catch frogs?"

She nodded and wiggled.

Catherine-Marguerite Jolivet and the Bone-Shaker

Saint-Martin rests on Île Jésus amid low rolling green hills and flat farmlands, becoming checkerboard strips of lush greens and golden maïs. Clusters of apple orchards, and pecan and walnut groves dotted the landscape, with nothing from the land wasted.

On this day, Catherine-Marguerite Jolivet was working in the outer yard of the banker's elaborate household with a kettle over a fire. She had learned from the Hurons to pound the oil from hickory and butternuts, then boil the residue and skim off the oil for later cooking.

The Gilbert's were impressed with her skills and ingenuity and offered her the privilege of studying to learn English from a native maid. But whenever she slipped into French, she was promptly reprimanded.

"Catherine-Marguerite, we have decided you should live in," Mrs. Gilbert declared, to her surprise. "A room is available for you at the back in the servant's section; that way you can help with our new arrival. I need my sleep. You understand, don't you?"

Catherine-Marguerite was unprepared, and her immediate reaction was stunned, fumbling for words in French before her best English.

"Yes, Madame Gilbert, if that is what you wish me to do. Will there be a pay rise?" In an instant, she regretted her words.

"You will receive the privilege of living in an upper class home with conveniences, instead of your little farmhouse. We provide you with meals and uniforms, are you not appreciative?"

"Thank you, Madame. I will be most pleased."

Catherine had lost her family to a bout of dysentery when she was young. She was thin and stood a little over five feet, but had the strength of any farmer.

The Gilbert home had splendid conveniences of an indoor toilet, an icebox, and lovely kerosene lamps in every room, and Catherine thought she had turned into an English Dutchess.

Mrs. Gilbert immediately insisted that she learn to ride their new bicycle. Although they celebrated their status as one of the first families in Ste. Martin to have the new invention, the practical side enabled the lady of the house to send Catherine-Marguerite to the General Store when needed.

It was a status symbol to have a bone shaker wooden bicycle to scoot down country lanes to the villages. The first bicycle had appeared in 1766 and patented in 1790—with two wheels and a steering bar, like a scooter without pedals, before later improvements in 1812.

French gentlemen were adapting to the prestige of the bicycles, glad to be seen in the cobblestone streets of Laval and Montréal, in top hats and coats, with wooden baskets on the back carrying goods from the boulangerie and market.

On her first errand, Catherine-Marguerite found that the Gilbert's bike turned right and left when she didn't want it to, but finally went a few yards at a time, straight as an arrow. The torn elbows of her dress and scars on her knees could be dealt with later—in time it changed from frustration to satisfaction, with some delight at each degree of success.

The return was uphill, and she pedaled hard; at mid-point, she passed the Convent and stopped on the steep grade. A nun approached from the garden eager to hear news of the Gilbert household. She waved and got off to walk, but kept the conversation short as she knew Mrs. Gilbert would be waiting.

"I'll never get back to the Gilbert mansion."

The pain of new sore muscles set in as she struggled on the hill. As a wagon turned the corner, she veered and lost control, skidding to the ground with the bike on its side.

Pulling up on the reins, Joseph Giroux halted his team.

"Mademoiselle, are you hurt?" He jumped down, and reached his hand to help her up.

"No. Just my pride, I fear." But her mind was on the stranger's gallantry.

"Where are you going? I can toss the bicycle in the back of wagon and take you anywhere you'd like."

"Thank you, Monsieur . . ."

He bent his head and extended his hand. "I beg your pardon, I forgot my courtesy. I'm Joseph-Vincent Giroux of Beauport. I came to Saint-Martin to see the new grain elevator, but now I'm on my way to see relatives."

"Bonjours, Joseph-Vincent. I am Catherine-Marguerite Jolivet, but please, call me Catherine."

Joseph-Vincent Giroux married Catherine and settled at St. Laurent in a rented cottage near the Convent. Catherine-Marguerite took in sewing projects and stayed loyal to the Gilberts, keeping a few days housekeeping each week.

Joseph-Vincent's time was divided between crops and game hunting, as he'd been immersed in the language of the woodlands since a lad. But Catherine still worried when he went to the lumber camps, often for months.

Their son, François-Charles, struggled with sight to see his homework, with his nose inches from his paper, and headaches becoming common.

With money from sewing, she took him to the optometrist for a pair of bifocals, hoping a new world would open up.

"Now remember François-Charles, you must treasure those. They are costly. That means staying out of fist fights in the school yard."

"I will of course, Maman."

As a young teen, youthful confidence boosted François-Charles Giroux's energy and personality to become a fun-loving, self-declared organizer of social activities among his school friends. On a hot, summer day in 1789, he took it upon himself to plan their picnic after school at Edward's swimming hole.

Social Slurs at Edward's Swimming Hole

Marie-Marguerite Tranchemontagne sat at the front desk by the window with the younger children, and François-Charles was delegated to the last row. Flattered by a schoolyard incident in the school yard when he pulled her hair and said she could come to the swimming hole, Marie-Marguerite had begged her mother for permission.

"All I need, Maman, is a slice of bread and maybe some cheese. My swim suit covers me well and I promise not to stay long. Please—you know it's important to me."

"Appearances lead to gossip, child, and I'm not sure your Pa would approve."

"The event will be chaperoned and includes many classmates. I assure you that I behave as a lady should."

Her mother admonished, "I see the young Giroux boy watching you in church on Sundays. You must promise not to encourage advances by boys and stay strictly in a group with the other girls."

"Oh, yes, Maman, I promise. Mademoiselle Harris from the school will be the chaperone."

At the swimming hole, François-Charles couldn't take his eyes away from her, in her pink flowered swim garb and beige skin. Watching from nearby, he heard the girls' voices rising and moved closer, hoping to join. But within a few feet, he stopped, as Angélique approached Marie first.

Angélique tapped her shoulder with disdain. "You don't belong here, Marie-Marguerite. You're not French. My Pa says you are one of those Mohawks or Chippewas."

François saw the pain on Marie-Marguerite's face. In seconds, she gathered her towel and fled from the jeering girls, and he was on her heels.

"Marie-Marguerite, please stop!"

It was the one voice she wanted to hear, but now not. "I'm fine, François-Charles, you should go back to your friends."

"Friends that insult another are not mine."

She slowed to a stop and turned. Tears were streaming.

"Why did they say that, François-Charles? Have you heard things like that before? Are they true?"

"I don't know, but it doesn't matter or change anything. We Frenchmen come from many different cultures, and if you have native ancestors you should be all the more proud."

His words were soothing.

"I'm okay now. Thank you, François-Charles." She turned to leave.

"No, I was raised to be a gentleman, and I will walk you home."

At dinner that night in the Tranchemontagne home, Marie-Marguerite shuffled her fork around the plate.

"Maman, Papa? I need to ask a question."

"What is troubling you, Marie-Marguerite?" Her mother's voice was soft and patient.

"I was teased today about being a native. I know my skin is darker than some, but I see others at the schoolhouse the same. If I have native blood in me, it is my right to know."

Her parents looked at each other in an anxious pause.

"My dear, my grandmother once told me our ancestors were coureurs des bois or what they now call Métis. I asked the same questions you ask, and although my understanding is clearer, I don't know the bloodline.

"I was told that many of the Tranchemontagne families have the blood of a sauvagesse from the Pembina band. When the French soldiers came, they toiled alone before the King's Daughters came, and often were restless and went into the woods to hunt with the natives. Many of those turned their backs on France and became part native in instinct; then their children became part of a native tribe with half native blood."

"Do you know what tribes we might come from? Is it the Oka Jesuit mission at Lorette?"

"It is as you said; I have heard both Chippewa and Mohawk. Wherever we come from, we are the same under God's eyes; we are whole and instill good values in our family. Never feel ashamed. The natives and the coureurs des bois helped to make this country what it is today.

"Your arrière-grand-père was André Corbeil-Tranchemontagne from the town of Saintonge, in Charente-Maritime, France, the same as many habitants. He married a fine lady with the last name Poudrette-Lavigne. Your grand-père, Jean-Baptiste was born here in Québec and married your grandmother, Marie-Françoise. It was never identified to me where the bloodline occurred."

After dinner, Marie-Marguerite sat quietly on her bed. She removed a looking glass from under her pillow, and brushed and knotted her hair into two braids. With a strip of leather around her forehead, she stuck a duck feather in the back and looked again in the mirror.

"So it is true."

Ice Harvesting at Trois-Rivières

Seventeenth century Bishop François de Laval recognized a need to establishing seminaries for boys, then Governors Talon and Frontenac continued the encouragement of the mission schools. Built near the Grand Battery in upper town, the Laval mission overlooked the river on the north side of Île de Montréal.

Quaint churches and weathered French cottages spread across the rocky island where Mondaries, Jolibois, Girouxs and Bazinets still cultivated their farms.

As winter's arrival brought icy temperatures and blinding snowstorms, Laval depended on river access to keep residents mobile and its economy stimulated.

The Ice Harvest, Painting by Group of Seven artist Clarence Gagnon (1881-1942)

From the Lachine rapids to Trois-Rivières, the St. Lawrence freeze-up locked in fleets of merchant trading ships, with early winter hibernation from November to early January. Plates of frozen boulders and ice jams rose from the surface to settle up on the treacherous shoreline, making roads impassable.

Hazards of the ice were countered by opportunities for livelihoods from the frozen river, for those with the strength and foresight. Every winter, the Monderie brothers from Saint-Eustache and the Jolibois brothers from L'Assomption harvested ice.

They came to the river with snowshoes, travois, a toboggan or sled, and a utility wagon with shovels, pick axes, hoes, saws, chisels, breaking bar, leather belt, ice tongs, grapple hooks and tapping hammers.

Pierre teased his Vimont cousin. "Nicholas, we need a depth of eighteen inches. Do you even know what that looks like?"

"That'd be the length of your foot." A rally of quips kept their attention, away from the biting minus-forty air chill.

Pierre tossed Nicholas a wooden strip with a hook on the end.

"Our horses aren't strong enough to bring in this load, Pierre."

"Charles Giroux will be along with his Clydesdales anytime," Pierre said. "We'll have the traverse poles ready."

Nicholas pulled a heap of stretched skins from the back of the wagon, as Pierre and Martin skinned the dragging poles.

Jean Jolibois wiped his perspiration with the back of his hand and stepped back to admire their work. "This'll hold four ice blocks without strain."

Jingling harnesses announced the arrival of Charles and André Giroux. The Clydes were a sight to behold with furry boots, and snorts and breaths freezing in mid-air.

The men secured the cutting area with wooden stakes wedged and hammered into the ice, marked into fifteen inch cubes. On their bellies, they chiseled to open water to prepare a shipping channel. Long spikes were jammed every six or eight inches, the size of a cube. When cracking started, they inserted the saw to cut a clear tract, and once they had leverage, they pulled with the hooks until one end popped up.

Nicholas grappled to insert the belt around the cube, yanking it toward the open channel. The other pickers waited for the ice through the channel, then hauled the bricks onto the traverse for the horses to drag ashore.

A thunderous crack froze the men in their tracks.

"Get the horses to the bank," Pierre yelled.

"But I've almost got this last block." Martin said.

"No, leave it!"

Pierre could see Martin's feet sinking quickly into the icy current. Charles Giroux tossed a rope, and two others gripped it around their wrists. Slowly he rose to lie flat on the surface and was pulled to safety.

"That was lucky. We must have underestimated the weight of our equipment. Make sure no tracks are left for children or deer to follow," Charles said.

Every winter, the river claimed an ice man, who miscalculated the depth of the ice. With experience, the condition of the ice could be predicted by the clear blue colour and sounds.

Thirty-two

Age of Inventions & Merchant Expansion – Parisian fashion via catalogue – Grain elevators, cog wheels, and batteries improve economy – M-Marguerite Tranchemontagne buys potted ham in Durand's new tin – Grey Nuns of Montréal provide education – Separation of Upper & Lower Canada sets cultural differences – Louis-Joseph Charlebois family suffering hunger – Charlebois goes to Trading post with Louis-Antoine Tessier – Turkey in the Straw – Negotiations with English clerk for pelts – Concessions and Bartering – Friendly game of checkers.

Giroux Adapt to Inventions Lower Canada, c. 1800

RESPONSIBILITY FOR CARTOGRAPHY OF THE CANADAS fell upon the Governors and British aristocracy. Recorded in paintings and landscapes were depictions of native and new Canadian culture, with early etchings in woodcuts and oils preserved in churches and government houses.

The turn of the century unleashed new inventions beyond previous imagination, improving habitant life in comforts and efficiencies. Even waterway navigation advanced, enabling expeditions for the public with Henry Bell's steam powered boat, brought from Scotland in 1812 and then adapted to commercial steamboats.

As company on his routine Saturday runs to the Sainte-Rose-de-Lima mill, François-Charles preferred to bring along his lively young boys, for the levity of their jokes and mischief. They always ended up outside the main street barber shop.

On this day he was alone, and took his familiar chair outside, listening to the men who already loitered there, gabbing and complaining. Mostly, he wanted to hear stories and rumours of new inventions yet to come.

Before leaving town, Giroux stopped at the print shop for the weekly French newspaper for Marie-Marguerite.

"Hello, Ignace, can I have one of those newspapers? My wife loves to hear about new fashions and bargains to be had at the General Store."

"There's no point in the women trying to keep up with French fashion. They have ruffles, bustles, long fringed coats and capes with fur muffs." His hands raised to his head in mockery. "Then they've got to have one of those wide hats with peacock feathers."

"And anything for men?" François laughed.

"It's not so funny. Look here in the catalogue from Paris—tight fitting pants, vesture waistcoats with knee-length back flaps, flounced shirts and brimmed felt hats." He pretended to walk with an imaginary French walking stick.

François refused to look at the open page of cravats, neckerchiefs, puffs, and top hats from the turn of the century.

"I'm dandy with the wool toque that Marie-Marguerite knitted for me. It's a shame to throw away hard-earned money."

"I agree, but the women don't see it that way. At least someone had the good sense to design sewing patterns so the women can make their own instead of buying the imported goods."

His generation greeted the arrival of grain elevators, batteries and generators, spinet pianos, cotton gins for fabrication, and reflecting telescopes. Humphrey's electric arc was discovered during experiments to create a battery and produced a brief intense glow in glass containment.

They heard of the uproar by manufacturing firms in Montréal over the invention of interchangeable parts, not envisioned positively. Instead of mechanisms breaking down, replaceable parts made repair shops big business.

Watchmakers, clock repairs, gun part replacements, and everything dependent on a cog, wheel, nut or bolt now had repair options.

By 1810, Marie-Marguerite Tranchemontagne was buying food in tin cans, patented by Peter Durand's of England, claiming to preserve it better.

Although the can opener hadn't been invented, the practicality of the can was measured against the hammer and chisel.

At the kitchen table with an ice pick, she stabbed a hole in a can of tinned potted ham, but not big enough to get it out.

"François-Charles?"

He bounded from the larder as she threw her hands up. Before she spoke, he grasped the can. With the kitchen griddle, he came down heavily on it, splitting the sides open, but with the lid intact.

"There you are, Madame, your ham."

". . . and I know just what I'm going to do with it." Marie-Marguerite peered at him through a layer of mushy gel. Without even wiping the mush from her face, she gathered the remains of the ham and demanded that François Charles take her to the General Store immediately.

The town's millinery girl was skeptical but curious by the news of Eli Whitney's Cotton Gin that claimed to produce quality cotton by machine. The theory would become a boon to new inventions of farm equipment.

As she expounded in the Store to a cluster of ladies of her knowledge of inventions from America and Europe, the door burst open. An irate customer stormed in, her face and hair smeared with specks of meat.

"Excuse me, Ma'am. I bought this ham here yesterday and I wish to return it."

Marie-Marguerite opened a parcel of brown paper on the counter and revealed the unpalatable mess. Some ladies edged close for a good look.

"Aah! I see there was a problem," the clerk said.

"Yes, indeed, I'll exchange the ham for a yard of your new cotton gin fabrics. See the blue violets on the shelf—those will be fine."

Marie-Marguerite was firm. "Otherwise, I shall keep this parcel and show all my friends and neighbours your new tins."

"But Ma'am, it's been used."

"Put it any way you like, I am returning this and I will take the fabric. Wrap it for me." The congregation of ladies held their tongues, knowing they'd discuss it later in a safer place.

Marie-Marguerite left the General Store with a new parcel, surprised and amused at the new range of assertiveness she'd acquired.

In their St. Martin cottage, François-Charles and Marie-Marguerite raised five children—Louis, François, Joseph, Rosalie and Augustin.

Since the late 1600s, the Grey Nuns of Montréal offered medical training and education to orphans and impoverished children, and St. Mary's College and Jacques Cartier's Normal House gave theological studies, history, language, music, and master arts. During the two hundred years of the feudal system, seigneurs provided basic education. But as they did not stimulate ambitions beyond feudal farming, many Québec habitants and their families had no choice but to be illiterate.

Despite the need, traditional American school houses with country teachers didn't exist until the 1800s. At the turn of the nineteenth century, local pastors operated crude one-room schoolhouses in churches, but never during planting or harvesting season, and vacated for only two or three months a year.

Students walked or took horseback for miles into the bush to a rustic wooden building, carrying slate boards and pails with sandwiches in cloth. Parents subscribed to Protestant schools by paying a pro-rated portion of the teacher's salary, or providing free board.

The separation of Upper and Lower Canada provided for distinctions in civil codes and taxation, beginning a cultural division of the people. Freeholders or Loyalists received grants and paid taxes to the Crown, whereas feudal habitants continued to have deeded lands, with taxation by the seigneurie. It was one more divide of the allegiance of the French and British.

The ongoing influx of British Loyalists, Scottish, and Irish immigrants into Upper and Lower Canada and into the West upset the ratio of equal representation.

Trading Post Negotiations – Scot vs. Métis

THE BLIZZARD had piled the drifting snow for a week without signs of abating, and the frozen woodpile was buried.

Waking up to December's icicles and frosted windows, Louis-Joseph dreaded this morning's bitter trip to the outpost. The Charlebois household was freezing and the cows hadn't been fed for two days. Conditions couldn't wait another day for blankets, lantern oil, and feed grain, and he'd go in spite of the storm.

He dug out enough drier logs underneath to keep the potbelly stoked and satisfied, and soon the damp wood's wet spitting and hissing built to the roaring heat he wanted.

Marie lured him to the table with an oatcake on a plate. "Here Louis. You must eat before you go out into the storm."

Eight children were already at the table, and their baby slept in a rocker nearby. He looked at the faces, each seeming grateful with only a small portion of food. It pained him to see the quiet hunger in their eyes and the selflessness of his wife.

"No, dearest. Divide my portion between the children and yourself. I am not hungry," he said, overcoming jabbing pains at his stomach.

Marie and two of the children hugged Louis-Joseph at the door. A gust of wind forced the hinge open. He cleared the snow with his foot, and held it closed again, waiting to hear Marie put the latch on. The board cracks on their two-story frame house needed chinking, and yielded to the harsh whistling wind.

"Old Man Winter is most unfriendly this year," he said as he tromped through deep banks to the barn. The wide door flew out with a bang. One stall's tenant was a sleek, auburn quarter horse, and the other was a sturdy, black Morgan. They neighed as he approached, and he fed and watered both. The Morgan was agreeable at first to leave the stall, but balked as his hooves laboured in the heavy snow.

Louis backed him up to hitch to the red one-horse cutter. Painted in a bright colour, as others in the area had done, the cutter could easily be seen from a distance. Weeks before, he applied wide ski runners to the blades for travel over heavy snow.

He strapped on the leather collar, with the brass of bells draped toward the Morgan's neck. As the horse would whinny, the brass would chime with the jerking head or tossing mane, alerting opposing wagons if vision were hampered in a snowstorm.

He reined up the trappings and led Jacques into the courtyard. Throwing a thirty pound bale of muskrat pelts into the box, he mounted the driving seat and pulled the rug up over his knees.

At the Tessier homestead, he pulled in to see if Louis-Antoine would join him for the cold journey as hearty farmers were accustomed to the winter treks. The flurry was becoming lighter and the cutter glided smoothly. Although visibility was poor, smoke from the Tessier chimney cheerfully waved in sight.

Louis-Antoine was chopping wood at the back, and stopped as the jingling entered the yard. He was dressed in a heavy wool jacket and red toque, with a blue knit scarf around his head. His moccasin boots were laced with leather bindings to his knees, meeting brown wool britches.

His humming and whistling ceased and he broke into a broad grin at the approach of his good friend. His eyebrows were frozen and his cheeks red and jolly.

Louis-Antoine Tessier was distinctly Métis. His parents settled at Île de Montréal, and he married Marguerite Amable Roy in 1761. Marguerite's uncle lived a few farms over on the Roy-Pominville homestead. The Tessiers, Roys, Pepins, Pominvilles, and Charlebois were always bumping shoulders in the environs of the small town.

"Bonjours, bonjours," he called before alighting and a greeting of firm shoulder grips and handshakes.

"Come in, come in," Louis-Antoine said. "You must have a hot cup of coffee, some bread and cheese. And to see Marguerite."

"Merci, Louis. I was wondering if you have need to come with me to the trading post."

Louis-Joseph entered and shook his toque free of snow chunks. He kicked the ice off his boots, but Marguerite insisted he keep them laced.

Smelling the hominess of the kitchen, with the coffee percolator bubbling on the potbelly stove, he was overcome with guilt, ashamed for leaving his family with so little. The haunting look of his children's hungry eyes was heavy on his heart.

Marguerite set an extra place with steaming coffee, cheese, fresh baked cornbread and a pitcher of maple syrup. The enamel cups were large and almost too hot to touch, but quickly warmed their numb fingers. Pretending to eat the cornbread, Louis-Joseph stuffed it with a tad of cheese into his pocket handkerchief to take home for his children.

"Bonjours, Louis-Joseph, How is your dear Marie-Catherine and the children? We are long overdue for a visit—perhaps after the storm."

Marguerite paused with a million things to say, then waved both hands with excitement. "You must bring your family to Lachine for winter festivities. Oui, Louis-Joseph, say you will come. It will be a promise to look forward to."

"We accept your gracious invitation. Marie will be most pleased."

With a host of ideas and her French lilt reaching higher, Marguerite became animated as she started bustling about with a basket. She had seen the look of hunger in Louis-Joseph's eyes and instinctively packed a fresh tourtière, salt bacon, cheese, cornbread and a tin of maple syrup passing it to her friend with a smile.

"This is a basket I borrowed from Marie-Catherine. Please send her my gratitude." This was the Québecois way.

Before she continued, Louis-Antoine winked at Louis-Joseph and they stood in unison to reach for their toques.

"De que Maman a-t-il besoin du poteau anglais? Je ne leur prendrai pas des pommes de terre - elles aiment des pommes de terre, mais je leur prendrai la peau du loup de celle que nous avons tirée qui tuait nos poulets. Elle a eu la peau complète et je voudrais pour qu'il les observe avec les yeux mauvais. Ampèreheure, mais pas plus dégoût[40]."

"Bring us tallow for candles, flint matches, coffee and sugar if they are a fair price," Marguerite said.

Louis-Antoine called to his eldest son, Hyacinthe Amable, to keep a flame in the stove for his ma, and to milk the cows ripening in the barn.

As the cutter slid onto the road, their two husky voices sang *Turkey in the Straw*, barely audible even to them over the wind. With a rousing French rendition of song, their shoulders swayed and feet stomped.

> As I was a-gwine down the road,
> With a tired team and a heavy load,
> I crack'd my whip and the leader sprung,
> I says day-day to the wagon tongue.
> *Turkey in the straw, turkey in the hay,*
> *Roll 'em up and twist 'em up a high tuckahaw*

---

[40] "From Maman he needs the English post? I will not take their potatoes - they like potatoes, but I'll take their skins from wolf that we learned killed our chickens. She had a full skin and I would like to observe that the evil eye. Ah, but no more disgust."

And twist 'em up a tune called Turkey in the Straw.
Went out to milk, and I didn't know how,
I milked the goat instead of the cow.
A monkey sittin' on a pile of straw,
A-winkin' at his mother-in-law.

The pair stopped to gulp air and laugh before continuing –

Turkey in the straw, turkey in the hay,
Roll 'em up and twist 'em up a high tuckahaw
And twist 'em up a tune called Turkey in the Straw.
Came to a river and I couldn't get across,
Paid five dollars for a blind old hoss;
Wouldn't go ahead, nor he wouldn't stand still,
So he went up and down like an old saw mill.
Turkey in the straw, turkey in the hay,
Roll 'em up and twist 'em up a high tuckahaw
And twist 'em up a tune called Turkey in the Straw.
Oh I jumped in the seat and I gave a little yell
The horses ran away, broke the wagon all to hell
Sugar in the gourd and honey in the horn
I never been so happy since the day I was born.
Turkey in the straw, turkey in the hay,
Roll 'em up and twist 'em up a high tuckahaw
And twist 'em up a tune called Turkey in the Straw.

Their boisterous voices were now giddy, with arms flapping like ducks, oblivious to the cold. "Every Frenchmen feels this glee after a rousing chanson," Louis-Antoine roared.

Gliding and bobbing the narrow roads, sheltered by tall firs, they passed fields and farmhouses, with chimneys churning into the frigid air. Finally, the trading post came into view.

Pierre, one of the Monderie boys, was in front on a musher with his huskies and a bulk of deer hides tied to the sled's back. He greeted the men, and family inquiries were exchanged as the trio waited for the watchman to open the barrier gates.

Louis-Joseph slapped Pierre on the back and asked, "Do you know *Turkey in the Straw?*"

The two Louis' broke into laughter again at themselves, and Pierre knew he'd missed their nonsense.

A Scottish superintendent, a Métis chief trader, and an apprentice English clerk occupied the post. The Métis wore a voyageur uniform and fur hat, and the superintendent and trainee had tailored business suits, with company-issued pocket watches from their vest coats.

Pierre Monderie froze with admiration, staring toward the upper wall above the bargaining counter. A colossal buffalo head looked back down through amber beaded eyes, preventing any respect for the young moose and deer antlers mounted beside him.

"Where did you run into a buffalo? There must be a good story behind this fellow," Pierre chortled.

"Indeed, there is, but it'll cost ya!" the clerk replied.

A clatter of hooks supported multiple hides and beaver pelts beside the superintendent's office, and the side wall shelves displayed ice hooks, cutting tools, saws, tongs, ice rollers and picks. The next row had racks of yarn carders, maple syrup kettles, tallow molds, skates, snowshoes, planes, mallets, lanterns, harnesses, and lined on the floor were oak polished butter churns and buckets of nails.

"I'll have lantern oil, a sack of grain and raw molasses sugar." Louis-Joseph Charlebois threw his muskrat pelts onto the counter for inspection. "And two blankets, if you have any that are French made."

"There are no complaints with Hudson's Bay blankets. We don't have any demand for French blankets, Monsieur Charlebois."

The superintendent looked over the top of his spectacles in displeasure with Louis' inference that English blankets were inferior.

In a strained conversation in French, Louis insisted that his wife would weave a fine wool blanket, and he would not require the red and white ones on the shelf.

"These are the finest quality Hudson's Bay blankets, far superior to those locally made. However, we have taken in some home woven ones we have in the back, if you prefer."

Louis-Joseph settled on a vivid Mohawk weave that would delight Marie. Seeing that the superintendent was irked, Louis-Joseph decided in wisdom to smooth things, as he had not yet bartered with his pelts.

Fur Trader in Toboggan, Painting in oil, Cornelius Krieghoff (1815-1872) ⑨

"Superintendent, may I see your aromatic pipe tobacco. I like the cherry flavor from England; I'll take a pouch full." Louis-Joseph turned and winked at Louis-Antoine as the superintendent searched. Pierre snickered, but in silence. He had also not yet negotiated for his skins.

Louis-Antoine surveyed the match flints, agreeing on a half carton, along with a five pound sack of sugar, a parcel of coffee, and a two-gallon tin pail of tallow. The wolf hide proved to be a valuable trade, and the apprentice applied a credit to the Tessier account in his ledger.

The chief trader moved on to Pierre. "We have plenty of skins on our hands, so I'm afraid we are not dire for your deerskin."

Pierre stood taller for a better posture to tangle. "Don't you see that we've had blizzard after blizzard for the last two weeks. I don't see my friends lined at your door waiting to trade. However, I know that habitants are cold and hungry and will need much of your stores. If word gets out that you don't take trades of deerskin, what will they think?"

Both Pierre and the voyageur anticipated their barter would eventually end in a trade, but the day was long and the sport had much enjoyment and story-telling left in it.

"Well, you do have a fine collection here, but I don't know," the chief trader stalled. Pierre leaned toward the counter pretending to gather his deerskins.

"Take no heed, Monsieur, I will take my skins to the Jesuit mission. They will not be paying taxes to your King George. They are always kind and pay full value."

The trader said, "You know there is dissention between the Jesuit trade and the Hudson's Bay Company." He looked for a reaction, hoping that he had lit some concern in his trading partner.

"I am concerned only about my deerskin trade. I demand full value," Pierre insisted.

The chief trader pulled his watch from his vest. "Very well. Indeed you shall have your price today. But another day is different."

Sitting in the storeroom with a swig of brandy, they played a game of checkers—the voyageur, the two Louis', Pierre, the chief trader and the superintendent. With business out of the way, they were all friends, with time for comradery and tales.

The chief trader elaborated on stories full of adventure of the coureurs des bois that had come down from the rocky wilderness trails of the Great Lakes a few weeks before including the misfortune of the said buffalo.

Pierre knew well that on the previous visit, playing checkers with the trader, he fell innocent to the man's ploy and stories of distraction, and came away with an empty purse. Today, he wasn't so foolish, and won the game and the barter.

Thirty-three

Louisiana Purchase, 1803 – President Thomas Jefferson imposes embargos on Atlantic seaboard – John Molson get exclusive rights to operate steamboats between Québec and Montréal – Québec Mercury newspaper – Nathaniel Tredwell occupies Red House on North River – Philemon Wright brings Loyalist movement to Ottawa Valley – Tredwell buys Seigneurial claim for L'Orignal from LeMoyne – Joseph Charlebois & Hyacinthe Amable Tessier Ice Business – Mishap Hoisting Ice Blocks – Sap Run in the Maple Bush – British law requires license to be in the bush – Maple Syrup Festivals – Hyacinthe Tessier invited to Native Powwow – First Paper mill at St. Andrews, 1805 – Habitant settlers gravitating to towns – Trading posts replaced by merchants and craftsmen.

Loyalist Movement to the Ottawa Valley

NAPOLEON'S OWN WHIMS LED TO A SUCCESSION OF dramatic territorial border changes. In 1800—three years before the Louisiana Purchase—he acquired new territories from Spain, including Louisiana, Arkansas, Missouri, Iowa, Nebraska, Kansas, Oklahoma, part of Minnesota, North Dakota, Colorado, Wyoming and Montana.

Distracted with revolts and slavery issues in the Caribbean, and an ensuing battle with Britain in Europe, Napoleon was willing to discuss the sale of New Orléans to James Munro of the Americas.

By the time the agreement was penned, Thomas Jefferson was President. The vastness of the proposal would become pivotal in American history as the Louisiana Purchase signed in Paris on April 30, 1803 comprised fifteen colonial states and two provinces.

President Thomas Jefferson imposed economic embargos against European trading vessels on the Atlantic and New England seaboard, and the English took no time to retaliate with naval blockades in 1807.

In spite of the agreement, France and England maintained naval fleets, building up the importance and activity of Québec and Montréal shipyards.

A wealthy merchant, John Molson, saw the advantages of employing leisure crafts to transport passengers between the two cities. In 1810, Molson's vision of excursions included onboard libations for his clientele, and he applied to Parliament for exclusive rights to construct and navigate steamboats for the next ten years.

Community newspapers such as the *Québec Mercury* sprang up, taking advertisements for excursions and fares, and prospering by feeding an appetite for a discreet range of local gossip.

The boom in Lower Canada was not unnoticed by Americans seeking new opportunities. Nathaniel Treadwell, from Plattsburgh on Lake Champlain, was among the most enterprising Americans, occupying an abandoned trading post well-known in St. Andrews as the Red House, at the mouth of the North River and the Ottawa.

Standing tall at six feet in his finest and most intimidating business suit, Nathaniel was distinctive and turning heads as he walked on the dusty street. He had arranged to meet in front of the Red House with George Simeon LeRoy to discuss a business matter. As they were about to go inside, an unfamiliar wagon clattered up beside them.

"I'm looking for Mr. Treadwell, gentlemen. Do you know where I might find him?"

The stranger wore his hair tied back with a remarkable similarity to a young version of George Washington.

"Why would you be looking for him?" Treadwell asked, standing taller.

"My name is Philemon Wright[41]. I bring with me eight wagon loads of Loyalists. We are on our way to Gatineau and I was told that the Red House would be a suitable waystation. We are tired and also hungry."

---

[41] Philemon Wright (1760-1839), born Woburn, Massachusetts, led group of Loyalists into the Ottawa Valley and founded town of Hull. Floated the first square timber raft from Ottawa to Québec in 1806; established himself as a lumberman on the Rideau.

Treadwell relaxed, seeing a financial opportunity better than completing his trade with LeRoy. Shading his eyes from the sun, he assessed the caravan waiting on the ridge.

Treadwell stepped forward to offer his hand to Wright, then turned quickly back to George Simeon.

"Help me, Monsieur LeRoy. Open the outpost gates and let these folks in. The wagons can be tethered in the paddock."

Thomas Barron had seen the convoy passing in his outer fields and followed it to the trading post.

"Philemon!" Wright turned with a broad grin to see Thomas Barron, who had brought his cousin, Reuben Cooke, for backup.

"You are a hero, Philemon—you and your brothers, of course. Am I correct, that they are Ruggles and Tiberius?"

Treadwell wasn't certain why Wright was a hero, but promptly aligned himself accordingly. He interrupted and stepped with authority between Barron and Wright.

"Excuse me, Mr. Barron. I was bringing my guests in now for rest and refreshment."

Barron apologetically tipped his hat.

"Good day to you, Nathaniel. Well, once you have your troops settled with water and rations, I invite you, Nathaniel, and Ruggles, Tiberius, Philemon, and you too Reuben, to bring your wives to my manor for dinner this evening."

George Simeon LeRoy's face reddened with subtle embarrassment, not to be included in the invitation. At that instant, every man turned to see Edouard Irvan Paquette pulling his wagon into the yard.

"Is this a town hall meeting, fellas?" Edouard asked through the silence.

No one answered, but George Simeon left the group to step aside to meet his friend.

"No, it's not a town hall meeting. They're making fancy dinner plans."

His voice lowered to a whisper.

"And I'm not going. But I did hear them say that Treadwell bought the seigneurial claim for L'Orignal for a thousand guineas from Mr. LeMoyne."

Edouard leaned into LeRoy. "You don't say."

"Let's say we go on into town and enjoy ourselves at the hostelry," George suggested.

"Well, I was going to trade some pelts, but that'll wait. It looks like Treadwell is too busy right now," Edouard said.

LeRoy pulled himself up into the back of the Paquette wagon. "I'll come back for my rig later. Let's go."

They weren't far on the road before they liberally voiced their news and opinions.

"The British and the Americans own our seigneuries, our fur trading rights, our timber forests, and run the government. What's even left for us?" LeRoy said.

Edouard interrupted. "You know that Treadwell put up a new sawmill at L'Orignal? Now he openly invites other Americans to come and settle on *our* lands."

"Let the Americans and British go at each other," LeRoy said. "They predict we are on the horizon of another great war. If that happens, the Americans would be chased out of Argenteuil and back down the Ohio Valley."

"The Seigneurie of Argenteuil is falling apart . . . and the Crown comes to collect the taxes before the landlord asks for his fealty fees."

"Last time I was in Montréal, some bigwig came from New York City, supposedly wealthy. Not our class, Edouard! Have you heard of John Jacob Astor?"

Edouard nodded. "Everyone has heard of that rich man."

LeRoy said, "Apparently, he bought a fur depot on St. Vincent Street and exerts power and new fear into the habitant. But I'll never fear someone I've never seen."

"Can you read a newspaper, Simeon?"

"My Henry reads whenever I ask him, but it is my 'X' that goes on legal documents."

Edouard said, "I'm grateful to the Huron mission at Lorette. They took me in when my mother died and made sure I got an education."

He pulled the wagon to the newspaper office.

"Let's go inside, and I'll read to both of us about Montréal and New York."

Ice Harvesting on the River

WITH THE FRIGID winter morning so crisp, Joseph Charlebois swore that his words were frozen in mid-air. The snorts from his Percherons fogged his vision, as they lumbered home from the gristmill with barley and feed.

Near Lachine, he approached the Oka home of Hyacinthe Amable Tessier. On impulse, Joseph pulled the wagon up to the Tessier's farmhouse.

Marie-Louise answered, carrying her sleeping newborn bundle, Sophia. Her fingers were at her lips. Before he spoke, she pointed to the side of the house. Hyacinthe struggled through the hip deep snow from the back with a pair of winter grouse over his shoulder. No matter what hardship brought, he was always on for a jolly laugh.

"Well, I'll be—Joseph Charlebois. It's been a dog's age." Hyacinthe was loud and genuine. "The wild turkey was my intention, but he outsmarted me."

In his hand was a hook of thin grouse but he held them high as if they were a prized catch. "These will be feast enough."

"There's enough crystal in the air to freeze those scrawny grouse before they hit the table."

"Ah, it is true. How are Marguerite and the little ones?" Hyacinthe led him by the elbow inside to the kitchen table.

"Bonjours, Marie-Louise. Congratulations on your new baby," Joseph whispered.

She smiled with gratification, rocking near the wood stove.

"How is your own family?" she asked.

"We have three boys and a girl, the youngest just a babe like yours."

"What brings you today, Joseph?"

"Hyacinthe, the river is frozen into boulders. It's prime ice cutting time, if you ask me."

"I suppose it is. My shed has plenty of hay and splintered wood chips, so we can put a load in there. Is your wagon full?"

"A few sacks of this and that, but still plenty of room," Joseph said.

Hyacinthe pronounced, "But first some stew, then we'll go at it." In haste, they devoured the meal and were out the door. Hyacinthe walked ahead, talking incessantly. "Follow me to the shed for my cutting tools. I have two pairs of boulder forks hanging there. While we're out, maybe some fishing would bring supper." He turned and took stock. "You'll be staying for supper too."

Two of the elder Tessier boys heard the conversation and followed close, now intending to beg onto the ice fishing excursion.

With scarves covering their ears, the troop headed for the frozen waterway with two wagons, laid with beds of hay.

At the river, Hyacinthe stepped to the ice and tested the thickness of the boulders pushed ashore. "Here's a good spot."

"Olivier, bring the ice prongs and two saws," Joseph called, gripping a shovel.

"And back my wagon as close as you can," Hyacinthe said.

"I marked some squares on the ice, so you boys can start with those saws," Joseph said. His back was to them as he chipped with the pick.

Olivier and Hyacinthe Jr. worked the large saw. Getting the first square free was hardest. Young Hyacinthe pulled a strap around the block and Olivier wrapped the other end on his arm. Both boys had broad shoulders and muscular arms, often drawing a crowd at the arm wrestling table.

In unison and rhythm, they pulled and grunted. "Heave, Ho! Heave! Ho!"

"Olivier, clamp the prongs, brace yourself with your feet and lean backward. Hyacinthe, be ready to hoist it onto your shoulder and we'll shift it fast to the wagon."

"Yes, Papa," Oliver replied. His neck muscles bulged and his cheeks puffed.

"You got your grip, boy?" Hyacinthe asked.

"It's a tough one, Papa, but I can do it," Olivier persisted, but eyed the distance to lug the block to the wagon.

With the wide straps, he bent his knees with his back straight as pole, and groaned, hoisting the ice block. Keeping his sight on the wagon, he assessed every inch and balanced his feet.

Hyacinthe Jr. saw his agony and quickly put down some logs to roll the ice. It was just in time, but as the ice crashed to the ground, the logs bounced and rolled over Olivier's feet pinning him on the ground. The ice was on top and blood was oozing.

"Papa!" Hyacinthe Jr. screamed, "He's not awake."

The three men worked frantically to move the block from the log, and free the unconscious boy.

"His leg's broken and he must have knocked his head on a rock. Lift him together, and we'll get him to the doctor."

"Naw, he's a tough kid and I've set many a broken bone. Hold him steady and I'll reposition the bone at the ankle." As Oliver woke, Hyacinthe drew out a whiskey flask to numb the pain. In half an hour, he was trussed in wooden straplings and propped up in the wagon.

"You guys go on with the ice—I'll give instructions from here," Olivier said, with his humour restored.

Two months later, at the end of February, Hyacinthe Tessier Sr., Joseph Charlebois and Pierre Monderie organized their annual work party to the Saint-Eustache woods. They'd need help to clear snow-laden branches and forge a trail wide enough to pull a narrow ruddered wagon. This year, Joseph Louis Giroux, Olivier Tessier, and Pierre Monderie Jr. asked early to join the ritual.

Olivier's gimpy leg was still in a wooden brace, but his strong will overpowered the handicap. Together they packed the wagon with pails and equipment.

Hyancinthe talked proudly of his relationship with nature. From childhood, he knew about early methods of gathering sap, using vessels of birch and cedar bark, and willow skimming pans shaped like snowshoes.

Jovial Pierre could hear that his own dialect was different than Hyacinthe and Joseph, and sensed their amusements whenever he began long stories in a Parisian dialect.

He'd arrived in Québec several years before, leaving his parents and siblings in Limousin, France and still carried the Parisian vernacular. In spite of the laughter and teasing, they never really mocked each other, as they valued their respective origins.

The Sap Run in the Maple Bush

IN THEIR PASSAGE through the bush, the men took stock of the most vigorous maples and marked the tree rows with red painted crosses. Overnight temperatures were below freezing, but became pleasant by late morning with the sounds and smell of spring.

Hyacinthe stopped at the babbling brook to listen as it echoed through the stillness. Moist, heavy snow fell near him from the trees, then the crash of a branch to the ground. As the soil warmed the roots of the maples, the sap was moving through the trunk. With more minutes of sunshine each day, soon the robins would be back.

Oliver scavenged for a sumac, to slice off a handful of young, pliable branches. The soft pith was easily cleared from the reeds before whittling them into V-shaped spigots.

Hyacinthe and François-Charles drilled the trees with hand augers, passing through the crusty bark into the sap layer, leaving a small V. Pierre and the boys added taps for wooden buckets, honey pails and cans with wire-spiked handles.

A lean-to of three walls was secured from birch limbs, knotted with root twine and a canvas flap, to provide providing shelter for evaporation. Pierre shovelled melting snow into the tin vessels and wooden troughs to wash out debris at the end of the day, and placed clean, hot rocks in the melting bath to prompt fragments to rise to the surface.

In a clearing beside the sugar shack, Pierre stoked the campfire. At the crackling, they gathered close near the steaming rocks and ashes.

François propped his axe by the tree and positioned a blackened coffee pot on a rock. Joseph Louis poked the branches and added new stones into the coals, then rubbed his red hands, swollen with bent knuckles.

Making Maple Syrup/Lower Canada, ca 1837, watercolour over pencil;
Artist Philip John Bainbridge (1817-1881); Library and Archives Canada

Québecois campfires could never be quiet for long among friends, and in minutes they broke into eager storytelling and rounds of *Frère Jacques*.

"I love looking into the soul of the campfire—two are never alike. It not only warms the hands, but the heart too."

François said, "I have some rubbing paste in my sack. Put it over your swollen knuckles, and tomorrow they'll be nimble again."

"What's in it?"

"Deer tallow, honey and camphor. My wife mixed it up; it's an old native recipe."

Pierre Monderie leaned in with his broad smile. "François, shall we address you in future as Docteur Giroux?" Rounds of guffaws warmed them and some lowered their cups to clap.

"As it pleases you all," François nodded. As they joked, they became oblivious to the events of dusk around their camp.

The sound was upon them before they realized. Two Mohawk natives emerged from the bush wearing part of a British militia uniform, and carrying muskets.

"François! Mon frère!" the elder greeted the men.

"Black Bear! Welcome to our camp. What brings you to our maple bush?"

"We are scouting for poachers."

"Poachers, what are they?" Pierre asked.

"Your great leader from France, Napoleon Bonaparte, is angry with the British across the great sea. He is intent to cut off trading routes between the colonists of the south and Québec."

"I know who Napoleon is but I don't understand what a poacher is."

"Listen, frère, and you will learn."

The elder brave put his finger to his lips and leered at Pierre. "The Americans sneak across the border trade in Québec because the routes are being challenged in the Great River. The new British law requires that those crossing the river have a licence, but instead they come through the bush at night. We fear the rumblings of war will soon be upon us all."

"War! Will Napoleon be coming to lead us?" Hyacinthe jested but the pained look on the Mohawk didn't join in.

The sugar bush party talked long into the night of lore and politics until sunrise. The Mohawk braves were gone when they woke.

By six o'clock, before the sun melted the ground frost, the boys hiked deeper into the woods to restock the woodpile. The sequence of emptying sap pails and replenishing wood took them farther each day for fresh finds.

Perching heavy logs onto the chopping stumps, they took turns with their axes, thundering down with all their might, with the rhythmic motion crashing through the centre core.

Hyacinthe, François and Pierre bolstered the fires; as the sap boiled and the vapour dissipated, the liquid became sweeter, in a golden amber colour.

Thickening it to a third, Pierre filled the tin containers from the wooden crates, with tins divided for the Tessier, Giroux, and Monderie kitchens. The early batches would then be boiled again over family woodstoves until thick, then poured on fresh snow, for children to twist and twirl from sticks as sweet toffee and candy.

Across Québec in the 1800s, festivals celebrated the maple syrup season with taffy pulls and pancake events, with generous servings of maple butter, sugar cakes, granulated sugars and meat glazes.

A Tessier's Initiation at the Native Powwow

AS HYACINTHE aged in years and wisdom, he longed for earlier days when he had joined the spring celebrations of the Algonquins. He relived the day that his father, Louis-Antoine, took him to a watching spot in the bush near a circle of teepees with natives in colourful costumes.

"Hyacinthe, stand and watch the tribal chief," his father told him. "He's the tall one in the largest headdress, made from the birds of the forest. Examine the feathers of the Great Eagle, attached to the Chief's tribal staff. He is a man of the greatest wisdom and carries his ancestral spirits. Listen now. You can ask questions later, but I think what you see will be enough."

With rhythmic footwork, the Chief danced to the pounding of the drums, moaning an ode to the Great Spirit, a celebration of new life, friendship, courting and healing.

Together they watched the sacred pageantry of colour rise into smoke over the bonfire, with hours of dance, drums and healing tea. The celebration became magical to Hyacinthe, observing a young brave and his chosen maiden stepping forward for their courtship dance.

"It is so beautiful, Papa."

"Hush . . ."

A hand leaned on Hyacinthe's shoulder, and he knew it wasn't his father's.

"Young brave, come—you are welcome." A painted native led him with Louis-Antoine to the campfire. A great pipe with strong tobacco was passed his way, giving him distinction as a friend of the Algonquin. "From now on you are brother of the Powwow, you are Métis," the Chief proclaimed.

He put two strokes of paint on each of their cheekbones. "We are now brothers." Hyacinthe bowed to receive the great honor, and later told his mother he felt the presence of the Great Spirit.

The burgeoning appetite for logs evolved with new paper mills across Québec. Shipped by water, the best route to Montréal was up the Rideau, a vital waterway through the Laurentians, and a similar buildup of lumber rafts plied the Ottawa River from Hull to Montréal.

Treadwell's sawmill of 1796 was followed rapidly with John Harrington's. Then another was built at the canal and dam by James Brown and later converted to a paper mill to supply the newspaper barons. The first Canadian paper mill was at St. Andrews East, operated by Walter Ware and Benjamin Wales, two New Englanders. Their mill exported printing, writing and wrapping papers to Ottawa and Montréal, coinciding with Patrick Murray's new gristmill on the North River.

The village of Saint-André bustled as a port and hub for services under the auspices of a local council and Monsieur Pierre Louis Panet, Seigneur of Argenteuil since 1781. The Charlebois, Fournier, and Giroux families inhabited lots on the northeast corner of the seigneurie. As English and Scottish land barons filled the landscape, the town flourished, as trading posts were replaced by Main Street mercantile and craftsmen shops.

Before the county borders were established, the settlements of St. Andrews, Vaudreuil, Rigaud, Deux-Montagnes, and Argenteuil were entwined by rivers and tributaries that shared the Laurentian plateaus. This was the land of Paquette.

Thirty-four

John By builds tented village at Bytown, 1826 – Prosperity of timber trade brought improved transportation – Ecology being eroded - Lachine Rapids canal – Town talk at telegraph office – John Lewis Craig, Governor General – Cushing Coach Lines - Telephone lines across the countryside – Camerons, Hamiltons & Mears lumber merchants – Shanty towns, logging drives, canals & steamboats – Cooke Brothers from Cushing – LeRoy and Cooke commiserate over land swindling - Conflict over Great Lakes & Lake Champlain – Congregation outside barbershop – George LeRoy enquires about Dearborn lass, Asenathe Bain.

The Dying Seigneurial System of Québec

THE SEIGNEURAL SYSTEM WAS FAILING IN THE EARLY 1800s, as habitants were moving to acreages at Lac des Deux-Montagnes and Argenteuil. Habitants were tired of restrictions on livestock to pasture or deer to hunt, and disillusioned at unfair limitations on their deeded acreages in contrast to government treatment of the new British Loyalists.

The villages of Saint-Eustache, St. Thérèse-de-Blainville, St. Benoît, and St. Placide were growing as parishes of Lac des Deux-Montagnes. In Argenteuil, the villages of Saint-Hermas, Beech Ridge, St. Andrews, La Chute, and Calumet drew new settlement, with improved stagecoach routes, roads, mills, and steamboat traffic.

The river timber traffic at the Rideau and Ottawa Rivers drew John By to start a tented village there in 1826. Bytown would later become Ottawa.

Industry was expanding with investments in steel, petroleum, and Dutch windmills. At Lachine Rapids an expeditious canal was planned to be built, and in the cities, Otis ratchet and spring elevators were installed in buildings taller than they'd known.

But with progress, pristine rivers were becoming muddied and clogged with logjams, and magnificent wilderness serenity was beset with loggers and larger sawmills. As the natural habitat was corroding, many were oblivious to the decline.

A cluster of men were already outside the Main Street Telegraph office as Joseph Charlebois happened by.

"What did I miss boys?"

"Look here Joseph—the Québec Gazette is talking about building another road all the way from here to Boston."

"Balderdash! Next thing you'll be telling me is that I have to pay for it."

"No, Joseph, it's true. It says right here that Elmer Cushing knows about it—he plans to run a regular coach on it," Alderic Morrow said.

"Let me see that." Joseph moved closer to the broadsheet page posted on the wall, pretending he knew how to read.

"I don't see nothing about Elmer Cushing."

The telegraph operator stepped out to the boardwalk. "Morning gents, shall I read you a synopsis of Craig's Road?"

"You mean they're callin' the road after the Governor General?"

The telegraph operator, Soloman Burns, read from the board. "John Lewis Craig, the Scotsman, that's who. Says he plans on giving the work to the British military while they sit idle at St. Giles."

From the back of the mêlée, Martin Jones said, "I heard about some rickety lane they plan from Québec into the Eastern Townships—it'll break your wagon wheel every time."

"Better a bad road than no road," Burns argued. "The mercantile people expect the route to bring new profits."

Charlebois was sharp with acrimony. "It's time the government saw that we need road improvement, but trust Craig to see a way to put more money into British pockets."

"I've even heard rumours of a future railway connecting Upper and Lower Canada," Joseph said. "Some say even west to the mountains."

"How be a round at the tavern—to progress!" Jones said. As he turned away, the thirsty group splintered without a winner.

Morse code and the telegraph were already connecting the world, and posts with telephone lines were dotting the countryside, connecting general stores, where merchants placed calls through operators and complex wires.

Tin plate photography had found its way from Europe, and families now wanted printed photos for posterity.

Once quiet villages awakened to the presence of government agencies and post offices, blacksmiths, saddleries, carriage builders, coopers and competition by dry goods merchants.

Inns and taverns were popping up everywhere to meet social demand, and schoolhouses, bridges, and mills were under construction in every parish.

Timber Trade on the Rideau

ACROSS THE RIDEAU Valley, British and Scottish lumbermen were buying whole islands at a time, with pines, oaks, maples, and elms hewn and squared for export by the Camerons and Hamilton Brothers, who controlled the timber around Hawkesbury.

The Hamiltons arrived in Québec from Scotland in 1816 and settled at New Liverpool Cove. With overnight prosperity, they monopolized much of the forested timber on the Ottawa River or transported to Montréal for consignment to Liverpool.

But many complained that the Mears and Hamiltons were turning the countryside into shanty towns and barren land.

The river trail guide occupation had been mostly replaced with jobs as carpenters and lumberjacks for the Barrons, Cookes, and sons of Philemon Wright—Tiberius and Ruggles. A considerable contract between Braddish Billings and Philemon Wright on February 10, 1819, would process twenty thousand feet of white pine, five thousand white oak, and three thousand standard staves.

Sawmills on the Rouge and Ottawa Rivers fed the shipyards at Montréal and Québec, shepherding ancient pine logs into jams, then broken up by agile lumbermen and sent on their way again.

Passenger steamboats were caught in the jams, and memories were becoming faint of quiet river touring and the panorama of pastoral countryside. The south bank of the Ottawa River in Prescott County joined tributaries of the North Nation, Rideau, and Bonnechere; the north shores in Argenteuil County shared the Gatineau, Quyon, Coulonge and Dumoine Rivers.

As licensed agents, the Cooke brothers from Cushing—Asa, Alanson and Reuben—dragged rafts of log cribs to Ottawa, then on to Québec's markets, with journeys logged by daily entries. Through marriages, they became acquainted with the families of Thomas Barron of St. Andrews and Lemuel Cushing of Grenville.

The following logbook entries were recorded at Rivière-Rouge:

June 1, 1835 "… got out of the Sny with very little trouble on examining the raft found one Crib badly Damaged & one float of another Broke the wind heavy from the north & Drove Us ashore 2 miles below Doles the men Employed banding & repairing the Cribs at 5 o'clock PM wind fell pushed off next morning found ourselves at Hamilton wharf two men sick."

June 3, 1835 ". . . wether fine Light Breeze from the East hoisted anchor and brot the Raft to the place wher we Intended to start from hired four men, on at $12 per month, 2 at $3 per day up to the sorel and one at $4 per day and passaged to Montréal. Hired Reuben Cook for Pilot . . ."

June 5, 1835 "…Wether fair no wind started Early in the morning run two bands lost 3 Sticks two of Tiberius Wright and Christopher Columbus Wright."

Taking on lumber at Rivière-Rouge, Reuben Cooke greeted the Loyalist George Simon LeRoy from St. Andrews, who was hired on as a loader.

"How goes it, George Simon?" Reuben called.

"Well, if it ain't one of the Cooke brothers. Is that you, Reuben?"

"It is. I've got a farm not far. How's your father and mother?"

"Settled at Chatham. I work with my brother, Asa, running the timber rafts," Reuben said. "If you can't beat them—join them. That's what my father said when we were rooked out of our land, not once, but twice. First the Hamilton Brothers, then our own boarder, James Anderson, swindled our claim from under us."

"Let's commiserate at Lee's for a pint when we're done, Rube."

Barely a chair was empty at Lee's Hotel and the Beattie Inn, already filled up with stagecoach tourists. In the afternoon, more poured in from the Buckingham excursion steamboat and the train from Lachute.

As the rafts waited for men to enlist for the push up the Rideau, Rueben and George Simon rallied at the tavern, sipping spruce beer.

"Those wines are too rich for me," Simon said, eyeing some tables.

"For me too," Reuben said. "The vineyards are plentiful, but a wealthy man's craft. The boullion suits me fine while working on the river. Running the rapids at Chute-à-Blondeau today has worked up a thirst."

"Not long ago, during the 1812 war, this hôtel was a posh refugee camp as the British came up from Lake Champlain. Now that Lemuel Cushing's Stage Coach Line runs from Saint-Eustache to Grenville, its clientele has returned."

"Did you see battle yourself, George?"

"They sent me a warning to report to the British militia, but by the time I found the post, they'd left."

"Are you hunted by the military?"

"Naw, I pull up the rear," George said. "Our troops were sent all the way to the Niagara Peninsula. An unsuspecting farmer named John Crysler at Long Sault Rapids was the meetin' point."

"Me and my brother served on the St. Lawrence and many times saw the Royal Navy suck seaman and mariners from their ships into the blood waters of shipwrecks and the graveyards of the Great Lakes and Lake Champlain."

George pondered and asked, "Were you on the St. Lawrence flotilla under attack by the American . . . Wilkinson?"

"I was witness to the battle between the Chesapeake and the Leopard. Terrible! Just terrible."

"Did the Irishman get put in jail for taking your land, Reuben?"

"No, we are of good Christian spirit and believe in justice. James took advantage of our family while he was nursed back to health. We toiled to clear the timber, and planted crops to meet the government requirements to stake the claim. It took two years, and the Irishman ate our food and watched us toil. My brother went with him to the Crown Land Office in Québec and unfortunately took ill. James could not resist his good fortune and staked both our lots in his own name."

"He should be strung up for thievery," George lamented. "I say so anyway."

"With papers in hand, the man returned to our farm with proper documents, and my father complied with the law and we were evicted. However, we are Loyalists and grateful for the opportunity of free land and we found another nearby. Father went himself this time to the land office to stake our claim. They do not wish ill will against the man, and take it as a life lesson."

George said, "I hope life punished the scoundrel!"

"We can hope that. As it turns out, when we vacated the land, my mother cleaned out an olden wooden box they'd forgotten about and found handfuls of wheat seed. You'll remember she was the first woman in the township to plant a wheat crop[42], and a dandy it was."

"We lost a second farm after the LeRoy's homesteaded and vacated the farmland on Rivière-Rouge in Dutchess County. An American land surveyor from Poughkeepsie came in search of the land's rightful heirs, as it couldn't be deeded legally to American landowners without disposition of our land rights. During those years, the land appreciated in value, but we were apprehensive of any legal involvement south of the border since the American Revolution.

"Fearing retribution, we forfeited our interests. It is not an uncommon story among Loyalists, I fear," Reuben conceded.

George called to the barkeep. "Two more O'Keefes over here!"

"This is the last for me," Reuben said. "Asa will think I've gone AWOL."

---

[42] Elizabeth Landers, wife of Reuben Cooke of Ticonderoga was the first woman in the township of Argenteuil to plant wheat beginning a new farming trend c. 1808. The first crop was abundant and was the beginning of a staple crop in the community.

Commiserating over Parliament in St. Andrews, 1815

GEORGE SIMON LeRoy leaned on a horse trough outside Patrick Murray's gristmill, and within voice range, old Moise Paquette rested on his wagon bench, chewing sweet grass. Moise was engrossed in the new edition of *La Vrai Canadien* that was delivered by train from Ottawa.

One of the Barron boys, Angus, arrived from the gentlemen's estate on the outskirts of town, and slowed up in front of the Argenteuil Tribune.

A congregation of loiters were there, in debate over the day's headlines.

"Eh bien, Moise," Angus called. "I see you're reading congratulations of Louis-Joseph Papineau's appointment to the Legislative Assembly. You must be pleased. I didn't know you could read."

Moise didn't see the humour, and Angus Barron tipped his hat. He pulled the wheel brake to bring his team to a halt, but remained in his seat.

"What are you insinuating, Angus? In Dutchess County, we had plenty of good schools. I know well enough that they chartered a federal bank at Montréal, and the parliaments are discussing a forty-eighth or forty-ninth parallel to divide the Americans on their own side. No more sneaking up on our shores."

As Moise's face reddened, Angus knew his wit had gone too far. He struck to soften the situation.

"You'll have to get used to my Scottish way of pulling your leg, George. Thanks for telling me about the new bank. I guess I'll be taking my money to Montréal."

"Are you complaining, Angus? You've got enough of your Scottish kin pretending to work in our best interests. For heaven's sake, you Scots have given our quaint little French village an old Gaelic name from your Highlands. You have Irish immigrants toiling in your fields and the good farmers of Nova Scotia, who come to teach ya real farmin," George Simon said through his teeth, balancing delicately between sarcasm and insult.

"George, you know me and my uncle better than that. Our best interests are here in St. Andrews, now the heart of Canada. If you haven't noticed, it's the British and Scottish that dominate parliament. Here we have the newest gristmill right before your eyes, and an English newspaper written in French in your hand, while you sit on a grant of land just handed to you. Are you not happy?" Angus smirked and touched his vest for his pocket watch, to be on his way.

"Handed to me! I'll have you know I work darn hard on my farm. I till the ground myself and don't use no hired help," George retorted. Barron again realized he'd said too much and made a diplomatic concession to his friends.

"Well, Moise and George, it's past two. Shall we adjourn to the hôtel to debate our politics?" Angus released the brake and snapped the reins, never intending his comments to be an invitation. They watched him until out of sight.

"George, heed him no mind. He's Scottish, that's not his fault," Moise tempered with a laugh.

"Right you are. What's Murray's price for wheat today?" George asked.

"He'll tell us what he gets in Montréal and there'll be no bargaining. The Scottish aren't any competition for the best quality; they're lazy and pay folks to cut their timber. Never were ones for crop farming," Moise said.

"I've a good load with me today. Is Eustis the last load in front of ya?"

"I'm thinking so."

"Do you happen to know where the American lass from New Hampshire is working? I'm sure she said her Pa was Jeremiah."

As George contemplated, he gazed to the distance then put it together. "Ah, the Beans from Deerfield. I think she's housekeeping at the timber merchant's house across the river at Hawkesbury. You know the Hamiltons, shrewd businessmen, with a brood of boys." He hesitated. "Didn't the Hamilton Brothers try to swindle you out of your forest?"

"I'm not looking forward to seeing their faces too soon!"

"Keep your distance is all I say."

"What's the housekeeper's name? Do ya know?" George asked with some gained courage, but Moise's comments of the Hamilton's seethed inside.

"Asenathe . . . that's her name. You might know her from Nova Scotia—she came to work for those rich folk. Perhaps ask your sister,

Elizabeth, to strike up a friendship when she comes to town. I was at the general store on Monday and she was there buying eggs. Maybe she'll be there next Monday."

"Thanks, Moise. Just between us!"

George looked Moise in the eye, like a gentlemen's handshake.

Thirty-five

Courtship of Clémence Cloutier, 1830 – Edouard Paquette Portaging a load of Church Pews to Oka – Edouard clears land and builds homestead at Saint-André – George Simon Le Roy and Asenathe Bain at Argenteuil – Canal at Lachine Rapids -Louis-Joseph Papineau stirs up the Patriotes – Flood of Irish Immigrants –Extinction of Feudal and Seigneurial Rights – Wood and Mortar at Eduard Paquette's homestead readies to register claim – Marriage of Clémence Cloutier and Edouard Irvan Paquette, 1832 – Cholera Epidemic –William Lyon McKenzie Reforms –Lower Canada Rebellion of 1837 – Joseph- Louis Giroux led vigilantes at Battle of St. Eustache – Argenteuil Rangers – death of Hyacinthe Tessier in Rebellion.

The Carpenter and the Apple Girl

MARCH'S ICE RUTS WERE STILL ON THE ROAD IN, AND Edouard Irvan Paquette expected the journey to be hazardous. His wagon was cumbersome and overweight with a load of pews for the Church at Saint-Redempter.

It would be several days journey to Québec to the mission, nestled in the quiet woods overlooking the lake. The Oka Mission had used François III's master carpentry skills for window casements ten years before, and the family's reputation brought this work to him.

"Jacques and François! Come with me, I insist. We will cross at Trois-Rivières and I will carry the spare wheel," Edouard offered.

"Brother, you know the roads," Jacques said. "They're ruined with ice ridges and holes this time of year."

Edouard's hands were propped on his hips. "Eh, oui. That's why we take the spare wheel. Are you getting too old for this, boys?"

"How can we possibly pass the rapids, Edouard?" François said.

Edouard removed a folded paper from his pocket.

"Ici! I have a letter from Prisque Cloutier—that he will meet us at the barge with his wagon and exchange the load. You see, I am not only a good carpenter, but a good businessman too."

The two boys elbowed each other and turned their backs on Edouard. Although downcast, Edouard wouldn't show it, and went about his preparations.

Mon dieu, how can I do this on my own?

When the wagon was tied and tarped, Edouard returned to the house for a canteen and rations.

"Maybe you are a good carpenter, but a good businessman would have negotiated with us," Jacques laughed.

"What's in it for us?" François asked.

"Brotherly time. That's all I have to offer."

"Why didn't you say so in the first place?" Jacques and François cuffed Edouard on his back, picked up the bedrolls and camp sacks they prepared.

"You had me going; I envisioned myself with a crippled wagon, with toppled church pews. Thank you, brothers."

The wagon lumbered slowly for the first full day before stopping to camp in a clearing by a stream of running grunion.

Sleeping under the open moonlight, they counted stars. "You know our ancestors look down at us," Jacques reminded his brothers. "Grandfather once told me so."

The following afternoon, they met midpoint with Prisque Cloutier to arrange to transfer the pews. "Bonjours, Prisque. We heard about your loss of Marie-Louise. She will be sadly missed. My father sends best wishes to you and your new wife and hopes you are both well."

"Oui, Edouard. Archange knows much about you and waits to meet you," Prisque said. "You boys sure look like your pa."

Edouard looked back to the buckboard at a young woman waiting with the horses. "We are so lucky to see Archange, aussi."

"Non non, Edouard. It's not Archange . . . that is my eldest daughter. She loves a little outdoor adventure and begged to come along."

Edouard tucked his hat into his belt to improve a first impression. "Bonjours, Mademoiselle, I'm Edouard Irvan Paquette from Sainte-Rose-de-Lima. But actually now relocated to Saint-André. My parents have known the Cloutier clan for many years. We all come from France it seems, so we keep crossing paths."

"It's Clémence, but Papa just calls me Clémas."

She wore a wool skirt that went to her boots and a heavy, oilcloth coat. Pushing her scarf aside, she discarded her work gloves and swept a wayward lock that escaped her chestnut braids.

Edouard lingered while he stared into her brown eyes. "I remember you! You're the little apple girl from the mill."

"Come, boys, Archange will have a hot supper ready. I have neighbours coming in the morning to help portage your load across the chutes."

Jacques led the wagon and Edouard jumped on the back end of the Cloutier rig. Edouard was last in, and waited to help seventeen-year-old Clémence back onto the bench.

"It's been ten years," he said. "You're all grown and ready for life."

"It's been difficult since Ma passed away. My new step-mother is with child again and I feel in the way."

"I'm so sorry, Clémas. I understand very much. My ma died when I was quite young also."

"So we're like two of a kind." Clémence's laugh eased the tension.

It was dark when they reached the Cloutier house but with eager appetites they devoured Archange's dinner.

Anticipating the morning portage, Clémence couldn't sleep and rose in the darkness. By the first blink of daybreak, she was dressed and ready, with a heavy oatmeal bubbling on the hearth and coffee percolating. A basket of eggs waited on a stump by the Franklin.

The bacon aroma woke the Paquette boys, who had slept on the landing in the rafters over the kitchen.

Edouard peered over the side to make himself known. "Good morning, Clémence."

Her voice was confident, but her laugh nervous. "Coffee's ready. Are you ever coming down?"

With a step on the ladder and a jumped landing, he stood squarely beside her. "You're a fine girl, for a lucky man. You've already been to the chicken coop; did you have to wake those poor hens?"

Edouard Paquette purchased a land tract at St. Andrews East in Argenteuil County in the spring of 1832, the same year that the ship *Carrick* sailed from Ireland that brought cholera infection to the ports of Québec.

He packed enough goods for a day's ride to Sainte-Thérèse-de-Blainville, and tucked away his mother's wedding ring as an offering to Clémence. Although barely remembering Marie Charbonneau, he always froze to hear a mother singing cradle lullabies, as it remained painful to his memory.

Stretched on his back with his hat tipped to his forehead, he let a stalk of straw hang from his mouth. His upper arm muscles were feeling painful spasms and his back throbbed, and the only relief was the cool grass.

The labour was hard for them, starting before sunrises to ring and fell the pine trees. But they shared the discouragement that only one acre had been cleared after a week of chopping.

The oxen dragged the timbers from the field, to be scored and squared for Edouard's homestead at Saint-André-Est. His family and friends had pledged their help in the habitant custom of sharing to build homes, raise barns and harvest crops. Support was always there for a family member or those in need.

Edouard still found time to trek to Sainte-Thérèse-de-Blainville to visit his fiancé, Clémence. Daydreaming, he thought how she looked on the day he brought her a folded property map, how much she loved a surprise, and the glee on her face.

"Edouard, what is this?" she had said.

"It's our farm in St. Andrews. I drew a sketch of our home—here's the main room, with a new Franklin stove and a Thomas Moore refrigerator that my father purchased for us as a wedding gift."

Clémence had giggled and aahed.

"Here is the grand kitchen, with a fieldstone hearth. The stones are from our own land. And over the kitchen is a loft for friends and family. Two more bedrooms with windows looking into our wheat fields." Edouard paused to let her absorb it.

"Ah, Edouard, it is wonderful. Will it be ready before our wedding in May?"

"Ready enough for my sweet bride." He cupped her chin in his hand and planted a kiss on her lips.

With sounds of the logging crew returning to hewing, he startled himself to the present and took a sip of the cider to quench his thirst. Anchoring his feet, Edouard scored an accurate square on the log. With the sharp bevelled blade on one side of the hewing axe and a flat end on the other, he spliced from the scoring lines down a foot at a time, repeating until all four sides were clean. With the flat side, he shaved off the waste to a smooth, planed texture. At the edge of the woods, he stacked the hewn logs in an orderly pile.

The Extinction of Feudal & Seigneur Rights

"WELL, BUST MY britches, if it isn't George Simon!"

George Simon LeRoy straightened up outside the barbershop and dusted his rumpled hat. "I can tell by the booming voice, it's a Giroux," he bellowed back.

"Are you holding all those Scots and Irish at bay?" Joseph Louis Giroux joked. A serious look tightened his face. "Since the government offered free land and rations, they've been coming in droves—those immigrant ships packed to the hilt. Apparently, the grass is greener in Upper Canada. So let them be on their way."

"It's good for the timber merchants plying the Rideau, and the Scots running the railway. But for us farmers, they're just adding allegiance to the British government. I say they're trying to get us to give up our land," George replied.

"I heard that a fella named Talbot is amassing estates of land and hiring immigrants to clear the woods and grow *his* crops. Those British landowners crack the whip alright."

"How is farming at Saint-Benoit?" LeRoy asked.

"The farming has been better. Montréal is growing so fast, we can see it outside our own window. The shipyards are beginning to obstruct the view of the river," Joseph Louis said.

"Joe, where are you heading to? Time for a nip?"

"I've got business at the mill, but it'll wait." Joseph Louis put his arm on LeRoy's back and nudged him down the boardwalk.

At the saloon, George kicked a chair out from under the table and turned it so he could sit backwards, facing Joseph Louis. He let his voice travel across the half empty tavern. "Two pints here, Charlie!"

"Yes, sir," the lad called back.

"Although the war's been over for ten years, the dust still hasn't settled. The Lieutenant-Governor Ramsay and his Family Compact do nothing for the habitant. Napoleon's rule is over and the British elite feel qualified to run the whole rotten country," George grunted.

"In Saint-Benoît, some natives are part of the community and French is our common language, but the British want our children to go to English schools and speak the national language with a whiny accent. Then they want habitants to pay for it in their taxes, those that keep getting bigger every year. But we're getting nothin' back," Joseph Louis spewed. "Although I abhor conflict, I put my name in as a School Commissioner for Saint-Eustache and Saint-Hermas, hoping I could make a difference somehow for the future."

"Congrats, Joe. It's for our children. There should be more men among the French to go face-to-face with the British."

"I'll take that as a compliment, George Simon."

LeRoy snarled with resentment, "I heard there's work to be had, building a canal at the Lachine rapids. It's a convenience for sure, but they have to guard it with military so the Americans don't try to use it to bring their trade into Québec."

"Speaking of military, the Argenteuil Rangers are being located back at Morin Heights. I hear you're a Captain now, George. Blessed be, I feel much safer."

"I ordered one of those Colt revolvers, and I always have my trusty rifle when I'm in uniform. I get a telegram now and then, telling me to attend meetings. This fellow Louis-Joseph Papineau is on the band wagon, building up a team of Patriotes. You in?" George asked.

"His interests are in Lower Canada, whereas that new Scot, William Lyon MacKenzie just arrived and is making reforms in Upper Canada."

"I heard he'll be coming to Lachute later this month to organize. I'll take the Paquette boys with me, and they'll know we're at the meetin' for sure." The pair broke into laughter and stories, calling for another pint.

"Well, George LeRoy, I enjoyed that, but I got some business. Say hello to your dear Asenathe. You've got a pair of boys of your own now."

As Joseph stepped away, George leaned from the door, hoping to flag anyone he could antagonize into a political spat. He focused on a wagon coming on Main Street. "It's old François Paquette with young Edouard."

George bellowed, "Ahoy thar, Paquettes!"

"Bonjours, George Simon. What brings you into town?"

"At the docks, I saw boatloads of Irish immigrants flooding into town. The poor blokes suffered a potato famine, and now folks from Kilkenny, Kildare, and Tipperary are filling the ports at Québec and Montréal. Some say they've a better chance coming ashore here in Argenteuil."

"Here? The seigneurie isn't for sale, since Sir John Johnson bought the Seigneurie of Argenteuil some years ago from Murray," François chided.

"They'll find out soon enough and move to Lac des Deux-Montagnes," Georges spewed."

"That'll be a good place to clear. They've got the North River to the south, Argenteuil east and Terrbonne to the west," Edouard said. "But I heard men talking politics in Ottawa last week with my load of lumber. That British king, George IV, is finally going to do something good for the habitant. They talk of a bill called something like Extinction of Feudal and Seigneurial Rights. Then something else about Burthen Rights.[43]"

George's ire was up. "Any woman has birthing rights no matter where they live."

---

[43] In 1825 King George IV granted a bill for the Extinction of Feudal and Seigneural Rights and Burthens on Lands held a Titre de Fief and a Titre de Cens in Lower Canada for Conversion of those Tenures to Free and Common Soccage and other purposes relating to the Province.

Emigrants at Cork, Engraving; Illustrated London News May 10, 1851.
Note North American destinations Boston, New York, Québec.

"I think they meant something else, George Simon." Edouard smiled and tried to straighten his face, not to offend LeRoy.

The feudal system had impeded the improvement of roads, bridges, and canals, as civil laws and taxation by the seigneurie obstructed tariffs that could have benefited the community.

Although the British elite had the loudest voice in the Legislative Assembly, it would take another twenty-five years before the feudal system was abolished.

Political debates raged in the Assembly with Papineau and the Patriotes wanting seigneurial reform and opposing the British ruling elite. The Patriotes were mainly French-Canadians but gained the sympathy of Irish immigrants against the Brits and Scots.

Papineau incited nationalism, liberal government and reforms, challenging the elite in Montréal that was well established amongst the lawyers, bankers and merchants. He sought accountability from elected Members of Parliament, from Governor Lord Dalhousie, and later Sir

James Kempt. Dissention continued among the habitants in the 1820s and into the 30s, with a storm set to brew between Upper and Lower Canada.

House Raising for Edouard Paquette, St. Andrews 1832

WITH SNOW reduced to traces, Edouard arranged for George Haspach, a German mason, and Augustin Beaulne, his helper, to trawl his farm with a rock picker. As each load was weighted with fieldstones, they drove the wagon to the site for the new timber house.

The dirt cellar was excavated on a knoll near the giant maple, with a view over St. Andrews and the North River. Within days, they'd be ready to lay a solid foundation and a walk-in hearth.

The farmer's adage to make hay while the sun shines brought the men back to the field daily until planting season could no longer wait. Edouard then returned to St. Rigaud, and bunked in at the Beaulne farm to help with plowing and seeding for a fortnight, a reprieve from hewing logs.

Waiting out several days of rain before returning to the excavation, Edouard and Augustin slept on boughs under the maples, crowding at downpours under the wagon. With dry days at last, George Haspach, the mason, rejoined them for the wagon journey with more supplies.

George prepared a vat of mortar to slather the stones in the trench, secured by ridge-poles and planks around the circumference. He smoothed the walls to a mosaic of rock and plaster, and in the morning, he tapped the planks free from the mortar and placed the floor-boards. With his brothers, he raised the truss and rafter system for the steeped roof.

The logging crew came a week later to lay square timbers, horizontally pegging them to posts for the outer walls. Then a joiner from St. Andrews sealed the dovetail corners, to be ready when George Haspach would return to apply wattle to waterproof the logs.

Edouard's wedding to Clémence was only weeks away, but much work still remained. With the arrival of the Girouxs, Charlebois, and Fourniers, work sped up, to cut the windows, hang the door hung, and whitewash the house with lime to protect the timbers. The Paquettes were known for miles around, and a convoy of wagons brought men with ladders and hammers, and women and children to celebrate the house-raising.

By noon, Edouard brought everyone indoors to inspect it, and declared that the grand fieldstone and clay chimney that divided the main floor into two spacious rooms were as exquisite as he'd even seen.

In the late afternoon, Clémence arrived with her father from St. Thérèse-de-Blainville. Her father came directly to Edouard, with long strides and a firm handshake.

"Bonjours, Monsieur Cloutier." Under the circumstances, Edouard deferred to Prisque's formal surname.

"Edouard, you have been arduous in your building. Clémence will be delighted." Edouard's head turned to see her waiting in the wagon.

"Edouard, I'm wearing a new dress. Please help me down."

Blushing, he lifted her in an embrace, before putting her feet on the ground. He whispered, "You are so beautiful."

In no time, the event expanded to children's hay wagon rides and races. On pine boards set as tables, the feast unravelled as ladies placed out pots, kettles, and pies. Some brought house-warming gifts of quilts, duck down pillows, embroidered linens and preserves, and the festivity took new life on the lawn with fiddlers and a mouth organ.

Clémence was overwhelmed at all the goodness, feeling the love of a family that she'd missed since her mother passed away when she was young. Her new sisters-in-law—Marguerite Niclass, Julie Maurice, Archange Melanon and Louise Amarengher—welcomed her with Marie Charbonneau's old weaving loom and a new Spinning Jenny.

"This is too much. I can't believe how lucky I am to be marrying into the Paquette family," she squealed with tears.

"You will be seeing a lot of us. We gather for every occasion."

At the bonfire of timber scrap and stumps, the neighbours and kin kicked up their heels to lively jigs.

At dusk, wagons faded past the low tree line, spreading the adrenalin back to their homes. Edouard stood alone to watch Prisque and Clémence disappear.

Inside, he enjoyed the solitude of his walls and paced each floorboard. Before going to his bedroll, he tacked rawhide to the windows, two at the front, and on each of the end walls. Tomorrow he would order paned glass windows at Lachute.

George Haspach left him wedges and shims, to prepare wattle to fill the cracks between the logs as the wood dried and settled. At sunrise, Edouard found George, sleeping in the wagon unnoticed. With some fishing gear from the house, he roused George and Augustin, for an early morning catch on the North River. Few words were spoken.

Back from Lachute, Edouard registered his land claim at the St. Andrews surveyor's office, and returned home. Cutting a tall birch sapling, he paced out five farmer's steps, equating fifteen feet or a rod, and sawed off the tree's end. Measurements were seldom precise or never consistent as steps varied, with a surveyor's indication of a number of rods or British 'perches' commencing from a describable landmark.

From the red maple at the creek, he studied the measurements and directions on his claim. Hammering in stakes, he flipped the long sapling end to end on the borders of his land, from the maple to the creek turning west, then to the juniper and jack pine at the clearing, and back to the maple grove.

Facing north on the knoll near the timber house, he paused to envision green and gold ribbons of cornfields, golden wheat and lush pastures. His eyes followed the stream, and imagined bountiful harvests and future generations working in the fields that rose to the woodlands. His active mind placed a red barn and grain silo on the cleared crest, where he'd house his tractor plow and a carpentry shop.

He'd need to recruit his brothers to help with the first plowing. The cultivated portion wasn't smooth, and they'd face challenges clearing rocks and stumps. Potash, high in nitrogen, would be collected from the stump burning, to be returned to the fields with the furrowing, to fertilize the seeding. A modest pasture by the creek would sustain his cattle.

He sighed with satisfaction. Standing in this spot, he marked an 'X' with his boot, then pulled a tobacco pouch from his pocket and lit a cob pipe.

Edouard and Clémence married at the Church in St. Thérèse-de-Blainville on May 7, 1832, raising four sons and a daughter.

Victims in the Eastern Townships from Cholera Epidemic

AFTER YEARS at Rivière-Rouge, George Simon Sr. sectioned his land, enabling new homesteads for his sons including George Simon.

George Simon LeRoy Jr. and Asenathe Bain, cleared their land with their sons and daughters, salvaging timber for their house. Producing the required cultivated land, George secured the claim.

Henry LeRoy, his brother, purchased neighbouring property from the McMartin family.

By July 1832, old Simon LeRoy and Wyntje Jacocks had already moved across the river and retired in Hawkesbury, but remained a colorful character on the main street of St. Andrews. Returning from St. Benoit from selling a pair of horses, he stopped in at his son's farm.

Asenathe, his daughter-in-law, stepped outside as he approached on the road.

"Hello, father. What news do you have today from St. Benoit?"

He stayed back in the lane and held his arm in the air. "No hugs today, I'm afraid. Where are the boys, dear?"

"In the field, father. You're not yourself," she said. "What's troubling you?"

"Stay your distance, Asenathe. I've come from the Giroux farm and they have fallen victim to the cholera epidemic brought on the Irish ship last week." Simon's face was ashen and his limbs shivered.

"Sit and rest a while, I will burn Sulphur. I've heard from the apothecary that it should help to clear the air."

"Later, my love, I'll go and see my boys now." He waved his hand and she watched him continue past the house.

But Simon didn't go to the fields. Instead, he turned toward the sugar bush, where he was found that evening under the great red maple he adored, his hands folded in prayer and his head drooped to the side. Asenathe followed from a distance, then went to the field with the news for her husband.

"I'm sorry, George Simon. You're father came here to die and did not want to infect his family. He is with the spirits now and we must do what we can to spare our family and neighbours. I'm afraid François Charles Giroux and Marie-Marguerite Tranchemontagne had passed with the cholera too."

In the following weeks, many wagons passed to the old burial ground. Main Street shops closed and families stayed confined to their houses.

In St. Andrews, Clémence wept too as news arrived from Château-Richer that her father, Prisque, her step-mother, and several sisters and brothers had succumbed. Edouard did his best to comfort his new bride.

All of Québec was touched by the epidemic in one way or another and people were angry, blaming the government for allowing diseased ships into French ports.

The Rebellion, Lower Canada 1837

A VOLUNTEER militia began to organize in Argenteuil with talk of an unjust Canadian Constitution. The leader of the Patriote movement, Louis-Joseph Papineau, was already rousing supporters to take up arms to defend their rights and demand reform.

The Cloutiers, a pioneering family, were spread throughout the Eastern Townships with a cluster of Zacherie's descendants in Sainte-Thérèse-de-Blainville—Alexis Cloutier, blacksmith, Damase Cloutier, brewer and later postmaster, and Toussaint Cloutier, merchant clerk—all concerned with the mutiny that had arisen.

Clémas dreaded asking, but knew it was inevitable. "Edouard, will you go to battle? If my father still lived, I believe he would fight for his rights."

"It is heavy on my shoulders. I'll go to town tomorrow and settle with the temperament. You know I must stand with my friends to defend Saint-Hermas, Sainte-Thérèse, Saint-Eustache and of course, Saint-André-Est."

Assemblée des six-comtés, a painting of Louis Joseph Papineau; Artist Charles Alexander Smith; depicting the Assembly of the Six Counties, held in Saint-Charles, Lower Canada on Oct. 23/24, 1837. Musée National des Beaux-arts du Québec

She searched Edouard's eyes for truth. "Do you believe in the cause of Louis Papineau and his Patriotes?"

"We French-speaking habitants deserve equal say in government, yet our protests are ignored—they forget the passion in our blood. The government could respond to our grievances, but they continue to deny us. If we're not British or at least French elite, they turn a deaf ear."

"Yes, you talk of William *Lying* MacKenzie," Clémence said.

"Joe Giroux is holding a meeting in town tomorrow morning. Word has spread that the British plan to attack our villages and he is organizing a defence. I will go."

The Frères Chasseurs, a secret group of Patriotes, plotted surprise raids on the British, but lacking a semblance of military organization, they were defeated and retreated. Patriotes remaining in Québec were quickly hunted down and their homes burned; some caught were jailed or even hanged.

Angered French farmers rallied together with pitch forks, axes, bows and arrows, and melted tin for bullets for rusty revolvers and rifles. Vigilante groups met secretly at twilight in the woods, fields, and barns, to plot their action.

The rebellion led by the Patriotes initiated the Battle of Saint-Eustache and set Porteous Bridge—predecessor of Marius Dufresne Bridge at Bélair

Island—on fire, with the intent to slow down Colborne's advancing troops.

Then Saint-Benoît fell to the same fate, with the village engulfed, and an English garrison stationed itself strategically in Overing House.

Rebels from surrounding communities mustered to fight what became an epic battle at Saint-Eustache, with throngs joining from St. Andrews, Saint-Hermas, Lachute, Rivière-Rouge and Carillon to defend French democracy.

These were a passionate people but not normally militant, and many others chose to stay and protect their homes and villages rather than take positions on lines of attack.

The Patriotes were weakened without the front-line heroism of their leader, Papineau, who was forced to flee south with some followers. At Saint-Eustache, the British carried out a crushing defeat on retreating inhabitants.

Word spread along the road to St. Andrews that a blood-thirsty band was charging toward the village. Snow was drifting, covering tracks of horses' hooves, making it difficult for the locals to arm and track movements of the attackers.

Joseph Louis Giroux survived the attack at Saint-Eustache and organized a group of habitants to track through the woods. His plan to ambush was encouraged by Joseph Charlebois, the Tessiers, and Paquettes.

"Although we are fewer in numbers, this is our terrain," Joseph said. "We are woodsmen—we'll stay in the bush and let them pass. They will play right into our hands."

"Then we'll wait for your move, Joe," Tessier replied. He readied his bow and arrow. "They'll never hear us, we have the instinct of the natives."

Giroux's farmers numbered not more than a dozen, but rode like the famed Paul Revere, from farmhouse to farmhouse, warning of impending attacks. When the British arrived to coerce the farmers to take arms against their neighbours, they found only empty farmhouses.

During the 1837 raids, Colonel Charles McDonnell commanded the Argenteuil Rangers, defending Saint-André-Est and the villages along the North River. Legend recorded two hundred and fifty habitants joining forces on December 23 at the residence of Moses Davis who offered it as a temporary barracks: Thomas Barron Sr.; Thomas Barron Jr.; Reuben

Cooke; Thomas Barron (nephew); Jean-Baptiste Charlebois; Joseph Charlebois; Joseph Louis Giroux; Lemuel Cushing; Xavier Langlois; Hyacinthe Amable Tessier; Hyacinthe Jr. Tessier; Louis Tessier; and Edoaurd Viau.

Taking cover at the school house in St. Andrews, musket fire raged against the opposing British sentinels. While hunkered there, Joseph Giroux heard the distant resonating of cannons, and calculated the British position to be on the old Rideau Road.

Joe trudged through his own snowy woods like a brave in battle. He hid his men in the stillness, as government troops marched within arm's length, not noticing them in the bushes. As the last group of British soldiers passed, some were taken silently as prisoners, and others brought to the ground.

The rebellion advanced closer to St. Andrews in the vicinity of Giroux's own farm. Knowing that his wife, Marguerite, was unarmed with five young children, he rode alone at his highest speed on his stallion, crashing through the forests and out onto abandoned roads to reach his homestead from behind. The sound of shelling was closer and he could hear it from the house.

He climbed through a back window. "Marguerite, quickly! Get the children into the root cellar."

"But come with us, Joe," she pleaded.

"Keep the children quiet and you'll be safe. I'll defend our family and home." Joe shifted a thick rug over the latch in the kitchen floor, fearing that if soldiers entered the house, they might hear the crying babe.

Joseph braced himself at the front door with his eldest son at his side.

"Here, Marcel. Take grand-père's rifle and keep reloading for me," Joseph said as he snapped the ammunition in place. His chest was beating as if it would explode, with adrenaline raging from fear and anticipation.

A crescendo of hooves warned him of the approach, and came to a thunderous halt outside the farm. Even with the wind blowing harder, Giroux could see troops with lanterns, now lined across the road. Then a staccato order was shouted from the front.

"Halt! Take positions to surround the farm."

"Giroux, surrender your arms!" the British Captain commanded, seeing Joseph in the doorway.

He shouted from inside. "This is my land and it's my right to defend it. Six generations of Giroux lived, farmed and raised children in Québec."

"Put down your gun, Giroux!" the leader demanded a second time. "You are required to join our army to defend your government."

"*Your* government. Non! My leader is Papineau who defends the habitant," Joe spat.

"Monsieur Giroux, you do not have a choice. Join us!"

"Non! Now get off my land, or I'll shoot." Joseph stepped outside with his rifle raised, trained on the Captain.

For an agonizing, long few minutes, the Captain and Joseph stared at one another. If the rifle was to fire, one would lose their life, perhaps both. It was obvious to the Captain that Joe was not the one to concede, and he knew his personal consequences.

The Captain turned his head. "Stand down!" he commanded to his troops. "Step backward."

Conversing with others, soldiers knew that only if Giroux took the first shot, would they fire back.

"An eye for an eye, another day," one soldier said for all to hear.

Watching the last of the troops move on down the road, Joseph opened the hatch for Marguerite.

"My, dear, ready the children. We'll cross back through to my brother's farm. You will be safe with him. I must alert our friends at Saint-Benoît." He leaned to support her on the last rungs up the ladder and took the baby.

In an instant, Joseph weighed his choices—the speed of taking his quarter horse, versus the wagon on the winter roads. Across on the horizon was a blazing barn, and he turned to Marguerite and his three boys.

"Marcel and Joseph, take your ma to Augustin's farm. You cannot use the main road; go across the logging road. Marcel, you take the Colt." The boy stood before his father, feeling that he had instantly grown a foot and aged ten years. He reached for his Pa's treasured revolver.

Marcel's voice was stern, accepting a burden for their safety. "Come Maman, I'll bring Marguerite and the blankets. Quickly, Pa must leave."

Dusk descended quickly as Marcel maneuvered the stony road to the back gate of Augustin's paddock. The wagon occupants were covered in a rift of snow, but he sighed his relief that they'd made it and were safe.

"Augustin!" Marcel's voice faded into the wind as he dismounted. "Maman, you stay here. I'll get Augustin to help us with the little ones."

Joseph Giroux was a hero of the habitants of St. Andrews, Saint-Hermas, and Saint-Benoît. With only a few riders and relying on trust in the secrets of the woods, the trio charged into the army's path, sending alarms and ringing church bells as they announced the enemy's defeat.

Throughout the next few months, Joe became a vagabond on the run, only sending word back to his wife when he could trust a vigilante. Amassing eight companies of volunteers, he sent them to join the Montréal volunteer militia under the command of Sir John Colborne.

By the end of the Rebellion, St. Andrews had lost many good men who fought valiantly on either side, including the hero Hyacinthe Amable Tessier who declared, ". . . since the years multiplied, the soil is full of dead who have no face."

In 1838, the defeated Patriotes, representing Lower Canada, merged with Upper Canada under the Union Act, suspending the Constitutional Act of 1791. Lord Durham concluded in a post-rebellion report that it was the fault of government to allow French-speaking representatives to crush the power of the British government in Lower Canada.

Joe Giroux had a few things to say about that.

An admired member of the community, Joseph Louis Giroux was heralded as a hero who fought in battle without even firing his arms, inspiring a legend his descendants would bear with pride. He remained a community leader, advocating an improved education system and backed government intervention to build and grade roadways. Inland navigation to the mills was still inadequate, and Joe served on commissions for new bridges and routes through the wooded terrain.

The outcome of the Rebellion had not yet been measured at the appointment of Lord Durham, who was mandated to form a united colony under 'Responsible Government'.

In 1841, Upper and Lower Canada united under the auspice of The Province of Canada, with the British merchants being the immediate victors. Despite their minority, they waved an intimidating stick over the French Canadians, expecting they'd return to cultivation of the economy without interference. But the passionate heroes of the Rebellion would long be remembered, with sympathy and respect for the habitant rebels.

Thirty-six

Marcel Giroux, Blacksmith Apprentice – LeRoy wagon mishap – Marcel Giroux & Elizabeth LeRoy marry 1843 – Community Farming includes revolutionary steam tractors and harvesting machines – Locomotive Railway portages the Richelieu River – 1850 Grand Trunk Railway reaches Bytown.

Marcel Giroux, St. Hermas, Deux-Montagnes (1825-1902)

ONE OF THE SONS OF JOSEPH LOUIS GIROUX, MARCEL, HAD been born in September 1825. As a boy, he told school friends the legendary stories of his father's heroics in the 1837 Rebellion. Since he could walk, he'd toiled on the farm, and as a teen his physique became strong with muscles and broad shoulders, and his hands calloused from carpentry and labour.

His sister, Elizabeth, had scant memories of her father rushing them to the cellar—but telling the tales, the story grew grander with detail. Too often, Marcel came to the defence in the school yard of his younger sister, who taunted boys to take on her big brother.

"Elizabeth, you can't keep doing that," he scolded.

Her freckled face beamed back. "But, Marcel, I know you could whip the whole lot of them."

"Let's keep that a secret—until someday when you really need to be rescued from something, like a runaway horse. I can't be looking out for you all the time."

"But you'd still rescue me before Mathilde, wouldn't you?"

Marcel kicked sand at her dress, to provoke her laughter.

Aside from family homestead jobs, Marcel apprenticed as a forgeron in Saint-Hermas.

"Papa, I'll clean your guns again if you let me. In no time, I'll have it apart and together again."

"It's the Colt you want, isn't it?" Joseph laughed.

"When I'm finished with Monsieur Cloutier's blacksmithy, I'll be able to make bullets for it."

"Slow down boy, you're only fourteen, you've got three more years of apprenticeship."

"But I know about the accomplishment of creating something useful."

"Tell you what, Marcel, when you become a full-fledged blacksmith, I'll give you the Colt. My gift."

Marcel nodded, with his eyes wide and lips tight.

The searing heat and pungent air from the smoldering iron stung at Marcel's nose and an uncomfortable fullness surged in his lungs. His daily hours had become long, forging iron over the steaming anvil, under the guidance of the village master blacksmith.

George Simon LeRoy arrived at the open barn door of the blacksmith shop, lamenting that his wagon axle had found its demise in the potholes. It was a two-horse buckboard style, and the axle was dragging behind a pair of draft horses.

Marcel helped him release the horses and hammered the axle free of its wheels. George pulled their reins to the livery next door for hay and watering and arranged for their overnight keep.

Together, the men surveyed the damage and discussed the extent of the repair. "We get a lot of broken axles in here, especially this spring. There have been more than enough mud slides, since the timbermen removed our trees," Marcel said.

"Indeed, but who's going to stop them? When they've cleared the hills, they move farther inland and roll the logs out by horse and wagon."

Marcel dared to use his own judgement, in his boss's absence. "I see you have a clean break at the hub, Monsieur LeRoy. It'll take at least a day to get your rig back on the road." On returning from lunch, Monsieur Cloutier agreed with the diagnosis.

"Give us the afternoon and check at supper, but surely it looks like you'll spend the night in Saint-Hermas," Cloutier said.

John Johnson LeRoy, George's oldest son, was at the barn with his sister, Elizabeth, as the master blacksmith returned from dinner. The coals in the fire pit were still red hot, yet Marcel added another scoop from the scuttle and stabbed it to ignite a spurt of sparks.

Laying the bent axle across the metal shoe of the workbench with the damaged section on the anvil, Elizabeth caught Marcel's eye. His face flushed, hoping she wouldn't notice him covered in soot and his hands blackened and calloused.

The blacksmith sent the LeRoys for overnight rooms in the village and asked Marcel to work late so the axle could be ready in the morning. Joseph Louis Giroux was now at the barn door and apologized for interrupting. He reached with a handshake, calling him 'Simon', as George Simon LeRoy was often addressed.

One more time, Simon told and demonstrated the harrowing story of the wagon careening, nearly onto its side, and the fortune of not losing the wheels when the axle broke. He declared their luck at not being badly injured in the jolt from the buckboard, escaping with mere scrapes.

Giroux Sr. gestured toward John and Elizabeth.

"You and your family must return home with me for a hot meal and a good night's rest. Marguerite would not forgive me if I didn't invite you," Joseph Louis insisted. "She's an excellent nurse and will attend to your children's wounds too."

"How can we refuse?" LeRoy said. "You're a true and generous French-Canadian."

Recognizing Marcel's apprenticeship, Cloutier credited his business increase to the quality of his work. Late into the evening, they worked to forge and cool the iron until the axle was fortified.

At midnight, Marcel walked home by moonlight along the wagon route. A lantern flickered in the family's kitchen window, and he was reminded that he could always count on his mother's tenderness. In the back door, a cauldron of hot stew waited on the stove, still warm from embers in the chamber below. Moments later, he left without a sound, crossing the yard to the bunk in the hay loft.

It seemed that he'd just closed his eyes when the rooster crowed. With the sun filtering through the boards, he jumped down and stepped out to the morning air. At the stream, he scrubbed with lye soap, to attempt to remove soot from his hair and skin. Seeing his image in the still water, he patted down his unruly handlebar mustache, a trademark of a Giroux. With his brother's shirt off the clothesline, he hurried to the blacksmith.

By afternoon, Joseph brought the LeRoys back to town, and Marcel was ready, with the axle mounted on the wagon and prepared for the road. He straightened his shirt to look his best as they disembarked from the wagon, and again he found himself approaching Elizabeth.

Marcel Giroux completed his apprenticeship and married eighteen-year-old Elizabeth LeRoy on June 20, 1843, in a tiny church at Saint-Hermas. Marcel and Elizabeth raised eight children, the first three born there, before moving to the village of St. Andrews East. The Giroux house was opposite the river bank in the southeast corner of the seigneury, west of Barron's bridge.

Standing outside the Main Street barbershop in St. Andrews in 1852, Marcel read in the McLachlin Brothers Papers that George Simeon LeRoy had fallen on hard times with his raft and lumber business. A suit had been settled between Mr. LeRoy and his hires, Pierre Taille, George McCulloch, James Taylor, William Lamoureux, Joseph Mercella, Pascal Perant, Frances Masse and Lemment Primo for half of their wages owed.

"C'est domage," Marcel muttered to himself. "The large British lumber merchants are taking the food off the table of my friends and neighbours. Poor George, he just isn't a good businessman. I've already paid a good part of his mortgage, but blood is thicker, so I've heard them say."

Although George Simon LeRoy had lost the largest portion of his land, he still lived in the homestead, and Marcel found him at the side of his house, trying to prime his pump.

"Hello! Hello!" Marcel's hat waved in the air from his wagon at his father-in-law.

George winced and turned, anticipating another summons. But recognizing Marcel, he broke into a smile that showed some missing teeth.

"Well, well, well, if it ain't a Giroux."

"Glad to see you, George."

Marcel alit from his ride and loosened his horse to a meadow behind the barn. George's son, William Henry, had heard him arrive and stood by the house, sucking on sweet grass.

"Hey, William, I haven't seen you at the mill in a dog's age. Is it your turn to look after the farm?" Marcel tried to make small talk while hiding his sarcasm but it didn't spark a reply from William. "Come, brother, help me with my wagon."

William Henry walked briskly and helped Marcel remove a fifty pound sack of flour, ten pounds of sugar and five of coffee, a waxed box of salt pork, and a case of brown molasses beans.

Marcel looked to George, preparing to assault his rejection. Old George was silent in disbelief, and a lone tear squeezed from the corner of his eye, trailing down a dirty cheek.

"Pops George, you've been struggling since Asenathe passed, and Elizabeth has been very saddened. You should have come to us for help."

Marcel continued the loading, ignoring any gesture of hesitation by William Henry or George.

"By gosh, George, my pa says you were the light in the heart of the community all those years ago, when breaking up the land in St. Andrews started. Those United Empire Loyalists had a tough road."

George nodded a quiet appreciation and gathered back his robust nature. "I heard stories from my father too—but myself, I was born a Québecois and I've seen plenty of changes. How be we put on a kettle of coffee. I've a story or two to tell you."

The three lightened up and headed for the house with the goods.

"One more thing, George, I've a pouch of cigarette tobacco for you."

Harvest time at Saint-Hermas and Rigaud brought countless families together, exchanging farm implements and toiling in the fields. No one farmer would invest in a complete inventory, as the capital in thrashers, plows, and seeders could bankrupt one. Equipment was gladly shared farm to farm in a network of kinfolk and neighbours—the Beaulne, Lafontaine, Charlebois, Tessier-Lavigne, Brault-Pominville, Haspach, Giroux, LeRoy, Modery, and Bain families.

Painting of St. Andrews, est. 1834, showing part of the village.
From Memories of St. Andrews by Benjamin N. Wales, 1934

Marcel Giroux owned a McCormick's reaper, the type that many said had revolutionized grain harvesting. Then George Simon LeRoy III bought a new 1836 improved mowing and threshing machine from Lachute, and Augustin Beaulne co-owned a 1837 Deere steel molded plow with Georges Haspach. Across Argenteuil County, vertical silos and barn raisings were popping up, adding space for storage of grain crops and equipment.

"Hey Augustin, I heard that the Doig plow will be coming to St. Andrews for the ploughing match. Shall we give it a go?" Marcel chided.

Augustin was in.

"Yes, I heard that too; Ronald Bain and Guy Charlebois have signed up. They take the judging pretty serious now, going from farm to farm checking the evenness and how straight the furrows are. You lose points for any blade of grass that pokes through the crown. We're not likely to win a prize, but we can make that Doig fellow sweat some."

"My farm needs plowing worse than yours, so let's get some practice, Marcel volunteered. "Bring the Deere by and we'll do a trial run."

"Monday morning, I'll be at your field for breakfast and we'll start, and I'll register with the Agricultural Society on the way."

Villagers had new optimism, with no end of whistles of new steam tractors chugging in the townships, and an influx of passenger boats, barges, and merchant ships on the Ottawa River, powered by steam. Roads, canals and bridges were under construction everywhere under Lord Durham's governorship, with an abundance of jobs for those willing.

In the 1830s, Québec introduced a locomotive railway, portaging the St. Lawrence from Montréal to the Richelieu River. The Grand Trunk later reached into communities along the Ottawa, and by 1850 the Bytown railroad opened a floodgate of communication, with distribution of mail and newspapers. Travellers were astonished by the concept of speed and mileage, with touring excursions on iron rails from Carillon to Lachute now taking only a few hours.

Thirty-seven

John Creffield of Earls Colne Apprentice as Carriage Maker – 1803 Cholera Epidemic at Middlesex – Cottage Industry expands at Slough, Buckinghamshire – 1810 Enclosure Act – John Creffield II marries Susannah Brown 1812 – Rowley Co. contracts royal mail from London to Salt Hill – Flying Hawkes highwaymen attack Creffield – 1819 Princess Victoria born – Carriage Works Exposition in London – Chance Meeting of Ann Edwards at Marylebone – 1830 Susannah Brown dies – 1834 John Creffield III inherits from John Creffield of Essex and buys carriage works partnership.

Turn of the Century Prosperity in London

NEARING THE TURN OF THE CENTURY, LONDON WAS braced for a new prosperity that would more sharply divide the classes.

The distinction was visibly evident in the homes and lives of the wealthy and powerful, who were amassing luxuries, literature and art, and welcoming open social-thinking and even alternative religions.

Affluence in London increased the demand for hackneys, status symbols for wealthy landowners who were able to boast their own carriages rather than use rented drivers.

The two-wheeled carriages patented by James Bennett in 1790 were followed by the Stanhope, commissioned by Lord Petersham, and rolled out a continuous legacy of new adaptations.

The Creffields retreated from Essex and set their sights on Buckinghamshire. John Creffield, born in Earls Colne, Essex in 1789, was well positioned to apprentice with a carriage maker, as his father, Daniel, had arranged a five-year contract for John when he turned eighteen. Although less prestigious than a traditional barrister tenure, John was most satisfied when working with his hands.

The Creffield Castle at Colchester passed through marriage to the Grays and the Rounds, and John's family moved to Middlesex in London, working with a west-end coach builder[44].

John's parents, Daniel and Mary, succumbed to cholera in 1803 at Tower Hamlets in Middlesex, and John was left to be overseen by his uncles. Although the family woolen drapery business still flourished in Pebmarsh, John did not see his future in it.

Apprenticeship of John Creffield II

THE HAMLET OF SLOUGH expanded beyond farming, with new brick foundries even before the Industrial Revolution. From the seventeenth century, Buckinghamshire had been notable for its textile cottage industry, making fine lace and linens.

Slough, a manufacturing town, is bordered by Bath Road to the north, Ragstone Road south, Windsor Road on the east, and Ledgers Road west. Only twenty-four miles to the lucrative London markets, transportation at the turn of the century relied on horseback and carriages or hired wagon.

As a convenient terminus for Windsor and a pivotal way station, the steam engine traffic heightened through Slough after the Enclosure Act of 1810. Its population growth required new municipal workhouses and churches to be built in range of the eons of learning at Eton College.

At Slough's St. Mary's Church, Upton-cum-Chalvey, John Creffield II married Susannah Brown[45] on June 21, 1812, renting a humble cottage at Salt Hill.

---

[44] John Creffield is listed in Pigot's Directory in 1839 as a coachbuilder in Berkshire, Windsor.

[45] Susannah Brown, born Jan. 13, 1788, daughter of Arthur & Martha Brown of Buckinghamshire; married John Creffield June 12, 1812 at Upton-Cum-Chalvey.

The London-Farringdon Coach passing Buckland House, Berkshire, 1825, oil on canvas,
Artist James Pollard (1792-1867); Yale Centre for Cultural Art.

Their village near the Thames rested on a flood plain of marsh and bog, a thriving womb of wildlife and waterfowl. The Chalvey Ditch, a stream bordering the southern part of Upton, dwindled into the Thames below Eton.

Rowley & Co. was renowned as the respected royal coachbuilder, with accumulated patents and unique specifications that set them apart, and John Creffield knew it was a distinct honour to be chosen for an apprenticeship.

On his first day at the carriage establishment, he entered through its grand showroom. Waiting, he admired the various sizes of displayed hackneys and polished coaches, with intricate accoutrements and hand painting dedicated to each unique piece.

"Mr. Rowley, sir, I've come to begin my apprentice as a coach builder."

"Indeed, you must be John Creffield. You're just in time; we have a steel frame hanging in the factory, so you'll see the process from inception.

I used to know your father and he was insistent that I hold a place for you to make tenure. I attended his funeral some years ago in Middlesex—a fine man. And your uncle too. He says you're a hard worker."

"Indeed, sir, I will give you my best." The mention of it stung, and for an instant he felt his father's hand on his back.

"I expect nothing less," Rowley said. "We didn't get to be the King's coach builder without a standard of perfection. Prince George himself made a special request, since his father George III is in failing health. Nonetheless, we have a signed document in our lawyer's safe with the royal seal of approval guaranteeing our services."

"Of course, I fully agree. Nothing less than perfection will do."

"Did you serve the royal army during the Battle of Waterloo, John?" Rowley looked over the top of his spectacles waiting for the answer.

"Why, yes sir. Every able Englishman must be dutiful to the mother country. I served as a wheelwright and repair serviceman but unfortunately was not ordered to the front lines against Napoleon. I regret not having the opportunity to defend Britain with arms."

"It's like the cog of a wheel. Every man performs his duty and the overall unit succeeds. Tell me, John, do you have a wife?"

"Yes, I married my Susannah a few years ago. She's the daughter of Arthur and Martha Brown, but I doubt you will have met them. We have two toddlers."

"Perhaps I'll get to meet your family in the near future. Every spring we hold a grand tented picnic for all the hires and apprentices. You'll need to hone up on your three-legged skills, there's tough competition here. Something to look forward to."

"Thank you, sir." John took a gentleman's step backwards to allow pacing room for Mr. Rowley.

Rowley angled his head to look to the side toward a man suited in hounds tooth and a woolen flat cap with upturned ear flaps.

"Harris will get you settled in."

"Certainly. It's a pleasure to meet you, Mr. Harris."

"Forget the Mister, I'm just Harris. Come along."

Harris and John toured the factory, divided into sections for door panels, wheels, leather, painting, moldings, hardware, and mechanical fittings. An overhead framed pulley hoisted up heavy pieces suspended above, and a glass wall behind provided daylight into a room for painting, enamel and baking.

"I understand you'll be here for a five-year apprenticeship, so we'll be getting to know each other rather well. Mr. Rowley asked me to start you in the moldings room as we're backlogged with orders. Myrtle has overalls for you with your name embroidered, and I'll find goggles to protect your eyes."

"Thank you, Harris."

"And any questions or concerns should be directed to me. Do you understand?"

"Of course, sir."

Robbers and the Royal Mail

INCOMING CARRIAGE orders became heavier in his first few weeks, and with the additional work, the spirit among employees was high. On a summer morning, Mr. McPherson called John into his private office for a chat.

"Best to you this morning, John. I must say, the quality of your work and attention to detail is impressive. Tomorrow, I have you on a run from Paddington to Salt Hill. The government is still haggling over running the steam locomotives on the rail lines, so that's good news for our coach traffic."

"Well, congratulations are in order then, sir."

"We can seat six comfortably in our long wagon and still have plenty of room for mail sacks. Would you like to drive it?"

"I know the road like the back of my hand, but I'll need a map for the stops and schedule."

"Yes, indeed, I've prepared one. It has a few stops and you'll stay over and return the next morning. At the White Hart, ask for Charles Luff; he'll provide you a bed. When you get to Slough, find the harness-maker and stables on the east side on Peasecod Street by the name of Charles Blackmore. Also, The Cedars Inn has a livery and stables."

"Yes, I know Peascod, with its view of Windsor Castle rising at the end of the streets. But I'll stay with my folks, I won't need the room."

"Suit yourself. Kenneth Blythe, my junior apprentice will be a relief driver for your mail run. It is forty miles to Slough, John, so rest the horses every hour. You'll leave at six in the morning and should be at Luff's by four. Let Kenny try the reins when you tire, but keep a log of every stop and customer. When we carry the mail, the Postmaster General wants exact expenses to calculate into the actual cost of the postage."

Before the railway was built, the Slough road had been rutted and treacherous, but now had an improved surface designed by John McAdam, with several toll bridges.

At times it could be plagued with devious highwaymen, and unfortunately, John fell victim on the section from Paddington to the Red Cow in Upton, a fine Inn. He'd been warned to be on the watch for the Flying Hawkes, the infamous highwaymen. Rorley had described their reputation for clever disguises that appeared in their deceit without notice and with many copycats.

"Hello, are you the driver of the coach outside?"

"Yes."

The hair on the back of John's neck raised up. The man's appearance was inconsistent, with brand new boots but a tattered jacket. The bulge of a pistol caught John's eye.

"Are you carrying the Royal Mail?"

John dutifully denied his cargo. "Not today. That coach went through here an hour ago."

"Where are your passengers?"

"I'm sure it's not your business."

With only one passenger remaining on the wagon, John returned to continue his schedule for the turn-around in Slough. He braced his courage, knowing it hadn't ended.

Harnessing the horses, he sensed a shadow and reached for his gun.

It's gone.

"Is this what you're looking for, mail boy?" The abrasive man twirled John's gun in his finger. The relief driver was already in a boardwalk heap.

"What do you want?"

"I'll be off with the pouch you keep under the seat."

"I'll get it for you," John offered. Trying to maintain a frightened demeanor, he reached for the bag.

Ah, ha, weighted just right. He can keep the newspapers in that bag like Mr. Rowley said. The real mail is under the cushioned seats. You can't fool Mr. Rowley twice.

John was back on the road in an instant, quickening his pace before the thieves discovered the deception. It was a story Kenny and John told often in London, always with new praise and laughter from Mr. Rowley. But he knew he'd be riding that road again.

Creffield Family in the Shadow of Windsor Castle, c. 1819

JOHN CREFFIELD III, born at Upton-cum-Chalvey in 1813, was the oldest of John and Susannah's eight children. The family grew within sight and sound of Windsor Castle and its illustrious history.

John Sr. was nearing the end of his apprenticeship with Rowley's and took weekend work with Alston Harness shop in Windsor. He hoped to save a bit each week to put aside for investment in his own carriage company within a few years.

Curiosity brought all classes to Windsor Castle in 1819, at the birth of Princess Victoria, the future Queen, and to observe and imagine the castle renovations. Stone markers were set along the Bath Road from Paddington to Eton College, with its upper class distinction, where young men were sent for a strict education.

Victoria's grandfather, George III and his heir Duke of Kent, died on the same day in 1820. The Prince Regent became George IV, then William IV succeeded him for seven years. It was 1837 when the eighteen year old princess ascended the throne of England.

On an early morning in June, the children were lined up early at the cottage door, ready for church. "John Jr. and Daniel, mind your sisters. Ma worked hard to make your clothes clean and pressed. Absolutely no mud kicking today. Pair up and follow us into Mass. St. Mary's is just a short walk, even in the worst weather."

Peascod Street and Castle End, Windsor, watercolour Louise Raynor (1832-1924)

The Creffield family strolled together along William Street, consuming the panorama of Windsor Castle on the hill's crest. The muddy road was in poor condition as they trudged on toward the Anglican parish church.

At fourteen and keenly devoted to his father, John Jr. happily spent time in the coach factory and harness shop that his father was invested in.

"Sir, why can't we bring one of the carriages instead of walking?"

"People that buy our carriages are not working folk. They're wealthy." He paused, so as not to disrespect his own clientele. "They're . . . of a higher class. It would snub our neighbours if we behaved as though we were like that."

"Yes, Father. I don't want to be wealthy. Some seem above knowing how to have fun, go fishing, walk in puddles, and even work for their pa." They both understood and laughed.

"Besides, Walter Perkins told me that his pa won't ever buy anything that's been used. If we borrowed a carriage it would be used and the Perkins wouldn't want it."

John Creffield smiled at the foresight John Jr. displayed.

I have raised a fine boy with values. He'll do well in his future.

Young John felt slightly more mature in a borrowed top hat, black trousers and a double-breasted, grey, wool jacket. He had tied his own high collar neck scarf, and mulled over his usual clothes as a symbol of his working class status.

He was seventeen, and would take the stagecoach with his father from the Chalvey-Slough depot via Windsor on the London route.

But concerned about his wife's recent health, John Sr. questioned the wisdom of the trip at this time. "My darling, Susannah, I don't like to leave you now, when you are not in good health."

"I can send Susannah or Hannah to the neighbours, or to your sister's house by the marsh. I will be fine."

John gathered little Susannah and Kezia. "You mind your Ma, she is not well with the new baby coming."

Susannah Brown Creffield watched from the kitchen window as her two men walked toward the livery. Sweat dripped from her forehead, and she gasped with a stab of pain."

Kezia held her mother's hand. "Mama!"

Susannah rested in the rocker as Kezia read poetry to her.

"Is the baby coming soon?" Kezia asked.

With fearful and frantic eyes, Susannah consented that Kezia should run to get the neighbour.

The world seemed larger to young John than ever before, as they passed the great study halls of Eton College toward the Castle.

Carriage Works Exposition, London

THE CREFFIELDS slowed into the congestion near the great businesses of Fleet Street—Lloyd's of London, the Stock Exchange, banks, and museums—and pointed out the magnificent Gothic Churches and walled palaces. John Junior had envisioned these Victorian and Edwardian manors, and today they were far grander than his imagination.

A din of newspaper criers and bartering merchants created its own an energy as they passed. John noted that he'd return to get acquainted with the menagerie of shops of Oxford, lively with carriages and exquisite surreys, overshadowing its street sweepers and coal carts.

Mrs. Hamilton's boarding house was convenient to the Billingsgate market, near the muddy Thames docklands and the imposing iron London Bridge. The tenement house had a narrow staircase stretching up to their third floor room. It was sparse, with two metal cots, and shared a common bathroom on the second floor.

A hot steak and kidney pie was served for them in the dining room where all the boarders gathered for a simple meal. With black tea, they devoured the pie, then strolled beside the Thames, past old Davy Jones' Locker, a sixteenth century pub, occupied that night with sailors who had had been served too much ale for their best judgement.

At Aldgate and High Streets, they found the famous Hoops and Grapes Pub, reputedly with a secret tunnel to the seventeenth century Tower of London.

The front was no more conspicuous than a boarding house, with a tin alehouse sign on hinges above the door. Inside were tiny, dark rooms with benches, plank tables and fireplaces. The air was heavy with cigar and pipe smoke and a gregarious lot of blokes outshouting the other.

While crossing the room, John Sr. was bumped by a clumsy drunk. "Hey, old boy, you'll not be havin' my wallet today," John said, with his hands gripping the man.

The thief responded with a snort and collapsed to his chair under his own steam. "Blimey, ye old codger!"

In the early hours, they rose with heavy heads, but eager for their appointment at the Carriage Works Exposition. Mrs. Hamilton's oven biscuits with fried eggs and sausage drew them from their room, and every crumb was wiped clean, with profuse compliments to their hostess.

The Creffields were early for their appointment at the London Carriage Works with Mr. Felton of Leather Lane, for his demonstration of the steam carriage. Felton's warehouses on Hope Street had the latest designs and building supplies for coach and carriage manufacturers, displayed as an exhibit in this manner only once a year.

Leaving the establishment with notes and quotations, they made a brief stop at Paddington, allowing a demure young girl to board the coach. Young John, being a gentleman, took her basket and held her arm for support as she pulled herself from the mounting box through the half door.

With his best manner, he tipped his hat and offered his name.

"Thank you, sir. I'm Ann Edwards." She reached for the return of her basket, as curly, reddish-brown locks escaped from her bonnet. At first glance, he was taken with her milky white skin and rosy cheeks, but mostly her aquamarine blue eyes.

The stagecoach skirted the northwest edge of Hyde Park, the gardens of Kings and Queens, passing exotic trees, manicured gardens and gas lamps.

John pointed out the romantic rowboats on the Serpentine, with cushioned seats and parasols for courting. The resplendent scenery was soon behind as they continued on Oxford Street, then the loop along Regent to Piccadilly Circus, Ann's destination.

She pulled her lengthy cape around her shoulders, and prepared to gather her bustled, long taffeta skirt to disembark.

John and his father had arranged to be London one more night, and with a quick calculation of plans, he was overcome with a pang of missed opportunity. Before he could raise the question, his father gave him the nod.

"Miss Edwards, could I take you for a walk in the park, or perhaps a viewing of the art gallery."

She looked at John with kindness and regret.

"I'm sorry Mr. Creffield, I must decline the invitation. My employer is expecting me at the seamstress shop post haste. And after supper, I'll return to Lady Simpson. I am a char girl." From a drawn bag, she retrieved a hand-painted calling card and suggested that perhaps he would call on another visit.

Downcast, John rejoined his father, with no words spoken as they continued to Charing Cross Road, through Oxford Street to the London metropolis. He knew he would make a visit to the Marylebone address, and he placed the card in his vest.

"Naw, laddie, but we'll make it to Swan's Ale House in Windsor and I guarantee you'll see a good time—lotsa laughs and singin'. But don't let your ma know or she'll have me hide."

They laughed and teased on into the city, and John wished for many more times like this with his father.

Susannah Brown's Death, Buckinghamshire c. 1830

RETURNING TO Salt Hill, John Junior scanned the view from the hill of the familiar ivy shrouded bell tower of the patriarchal Upton Church of Saint Laurence, nestled on a terraced slope above the row of cottages lining Chalvey. As they passed the vaulted stone edifice and site that dated to the Norman era, he listened to excited voices of schoolchildren gathered at the churchyard plaque dedicated to William the Conqueror.

"We're fortunate living in these times, Father. Can you imagine history at this site centuries ago?"

"Indeed, son. I can indeed."

On sight of their house, they sped up, with an urge of panic. "Papa, Uncle Thomas's Democrat carriage is at our door and Doc Halpern too."

His father dismounted in a flash and vaulted toward the door, collecting an armful of young ones as they ran to him.

"Oh, Papa. Ma is not well. The baby is coming the wrong way. I'm so scared," Kezia whimpered.

Pushing inside, he bumped past the doctor and held Susannah's hand.

Her skin was sallow and pale, and her eyes sunken.

"I'm glad you came back, John. I thought I could do this, but I can't." She teared up and squeezed his hand. "The children need you."

John stood tall again. "Doc Halpern, what can I do?"

"I'm sorry, I need to finish delivering the babe. I'm afraid it is stillborn, and now I fear for your wife." The room fell quiet, and John kissed Susannah's forehead for the last time. John Jr. and his brother Daniel did their best to abate the grief of the youngest.

Uncle Tom and Aunt Mary came and pulled five year old Mary aside, and rounded up little Martha who was barely walking and some belongings.

"Come dears, you'll be coming with us back to Bucks."

"Papa! Papa! No, no!" Martha's faint voice echoed in John's mind.

Neighbours and church patrons picked among the remaining six children to take them in until John Sr. could make other arrangements.

John Jr. was seventeen and decided he would set out on his own, taking his brother Daniel with him. There would be no further discussion about continuing with his education and John Jr. continued working in his father's carriage factory.

Bicycles and pedestrians monopolized the congested lanes as John Sr. headed in Rowley's hackney toward the Thames with his son. Diverging onto Windsor Road, he slowed to a stop. "Over there, John—the spires of St. Mary's Church. That's Arbour Hill. And see the horses grazing in the meadow . . . beyond that is a long rambling coach factory for sale, close to the new rail depot. This is Peascod St. There are three coachbuilders and harness makers close by."

John pulled the horses up and read the note from his pocket.

"It's a Mr. Bonsey that I have to see."

John Creffield Carriage Business with Richard Coventry, 1834

THREE YEARS AFTER Susannah's passing, John wed his second wife, Elizabeth Holderway. Susannah, Thomas, Martha and Mary Ann returned to the Creffield household, adapting to their new step-mother.

John and Elizabeth had been married a few months when an officer from the London barrister's office arrived at Peascod Street.

"John Creffield?"

"That's me." He removed his painting mask and stepped down a ladder from the carriage he was coating.

"I'm from Hargraves. We have offices in Colchester and London."

John was nervous. He knew that Hargraves was a legal firm that his family had used to represent their rights in prior suits.

"Please have a seat." John pulled a stool out but the man ignored it.

"I regret to inform you that your Uncle John from Pebmarsh has passed away. The Will was read yesterday morning and he has a provision of £400 to be set aside for you."

John quickly calculated the amount to be equivalent to a year's salary for a doctor or lawyer. Locking his fists, he steadied himself.

His partner, Richard Coventry, was working in the harness room and overheard the news. By this time, John was back on his feet.

"First, please give my condolences to Aunt Sarah. My uncles have all be very kind to me," he said with a falter in his voice.

John took time to absorb the lawyer's letter. The embossed printing was impressive.

My father's inheritance went into property at Pebmarsh and on his death, Uncle John succeeded the landholdings. I never went hungry but I was taught to earn everything. Love cannot be my due.

Richard Coventry moved closer to him. "John, I overheard the lawyer. It's been on my mind to discuss with you about coming into the Coach and Harness Business in a bigger way. Perhaps this is the right time."

"What are you suggesting, Richard?"

"The railway junction of the Great Western will be coming through Slough. The biggest boon to our economy will be based on the success of the railway. Slough will grow into more than a hamlet. There's little competition in all of Upton-cum-Chalvey.

"The Eton workhouses stand in the middle of town, and without trains there is little that Slough has to offer. We are an old brick and clay industry and there's talk of more foundries."

"I enjoy my work," John said. "Together we produce a fine product with an excellent reputation. I'll need to talk to Elizabeth about this—we have thirteen mouths to feed."

"Of course. Elizabeth has a good business head. I'm certain she'll see the opportunity."

Thirty-eight

Creffield Coaches on the Bath Road – Whigs Reforms – Industrial Revolution see transportation improvements – Explosion of culture, theatre and reading houses – Introduces great writers; Austen, Byron, Dickens, Keats, etc. – John Creffield III marries Ann Edwards, 1831 – John Creffield Sr. is invited to a Pigeon Shoot at Slough.

Harness Maker & Carriage Builder, Peascod Street, Windsor

THE MOST FIT FACTORY WORKERS PEDDLED ALONG Peascod Street on bikes, with hand waves of apology for splattering mud to those who walked. But horse and buggies took little notice splashes on the less fortunate.

Creffield Coaches carried four or five passengers from London through Slough several times a day, always stopping at the Crown Inn. By 1830, sixty to eighty coaches from the industry were travelling the Bath Road from London to Slough. The Whigs were in power under Prime Minister Lord Grey, and in the memories of the working class, the violence of the French Revolution remained fresh.

John put down a copy of the *London News* that outlined electoral reforms proposed by the Whigs, with news that the Reform Bill had insufficient support in the House of Lords and would now go to a third reading.

"Richard, I believe the government is creating new constituencies so they can have more votes. If they pass the Reform bill, we'll send another representative to the legislature from Chalvey. Can't be much wrong in that," he said.

"We'll each get a vote, and in return the government asks us to pay £10 every year just to keep our land."

"I've been thinking about increasing our retail prices on the buggies. A half crown here or there won't be noticed."

"Just be sure the competition is with the same mind," Richard cautioned. "There's Charles and John Blackmore down the street and John Pasmore over on William. We'll check their prices first."

The Salt Hill livery owner gave John Jr. a meagre wage, but sweetened it enough with use of the one-room loft over the stables. At eighteen years, he was glad to take that room so near his father's house, as his step-mother Elizabeth just had another new baby.

At the morning sound of the stagecoaches, John bounded downstairs to water the horses and hang the oat bags. Despite his hard work, his wages didn't stretch far, and for every two crowns he earned, he gave half a crown to help Elizabeth, and half to pay his rent. The other went under the floor boards, that he might one day buy a livery of his own.

At dinner at his family's residence on William Street, he whispered to his father, "Let me know when you'd like a new partner, now that you've bought out Mr. Coventry."

"Creffield & Son, sounds mighty good," his dad laughed, then repeated it twice.

On a blustery March day in March 1836, John Creffield III stopped in at his own uncle's High Street office in London. The red brick factory had expanded to three floors and Thomas Creffield's office was on the third, with a view over Colchester.

"Hello, Mr. Creffield," the showroom clerk said at the entrance. "I have your shipment to Upton-cum-Chalvey ready. Do you have a truck?"

"Today, I'll just take the load for St. Mary's parsonage, but I'll be back in a few days for the rest."

"Very well . . ." The reception clerk fidgeted. "I'm sorry to hear of Susannah's passing."

Thomas Creffield rounded the corner, on hearing John's voice. "How's my nephew? I haven't seen you since the funeral. It's been three years now."

John swallowed hard. "Indeed it has been difficult for the children, but the babies have taken well to Elizabeth."

The warehouse clerk interrupted with a trolley, stacked with long boxes. "Ready, Mr. Creffield. Thanks for doing the delivery."

"Ah, St. Mary's Church will be glad to get these draperies installed for the rectory. I'm sure they will be splendid."

England's Cultural & Industrial Explosion, c. 1820-1830

WITHIN A YEAR, Creffields moved to a Victorian cottage, a stone's throw from the stables. Both Johns, Senior and Junior, worked as coachbuilders, seeing improvements in Henry Mill's luxury passenger coaches, as well as the high stepping hackneys, elegant hansoms, and the mail cargo units.

The population of every class was fascinated by the transportation advances in the country, as quoted in *The Quarterly Review*.

> What can be more palpably absurd than the prospect held out of locomotives traveling twice as fast as stagecoaches?

The Industrial Revolution in England affected everyone, mostly favourably, and the early 1800s delivered an explosion of poetic and literary works, music and the arts.

England introduced famous authors—Jane Austen, Lord Byron, Charles Dickens, John Keats, Mary Shelley, Lord Alfred Tennyson, Samuel Woodsworth, Noah Webster's Dictionary—with interest in literature spreading to the masses in every class.

But with advancements came challenges, as the steam locomotive in London was rumoured to threaten the survival of the stagecoach, as it united counties and parishes to the hub of London.

Reading houses, theatres, lectures and demonstrations were posted in local newspapers. Taking advantage of one of these occasions, John returned to Marylebone with plans to entertain Ann Edwards at a theatrical performance.

He read well in preparation and rehearsed his introduction.

"Good evening, Ann I hope you like the works of Alfred Tennyson. He's a young poet and his writing *Poems by Two Brothers* is said to be a refreshing launch into literary society."

"It will be a pleasure, John. I've heard that he is in London from Cambridge for a spell. We are lucky to be able to attend his reading."

Ann offered her gloved hand to John for assistance into the hired carriage. She wore bustles and crinolines too wide for the door and he was unsure what a gentleman should do.

Smiling warmly at his predicament, Ann said. "Put your hand at my waist to balance me and I'll hoist the skirts."

The pair smiled in amusement at their awkwardness.

By 1831, John III was earning seven shillings a week, and a factory worker was paid two and three times that of a farmer. Many factories were running twenty-four hours a day to meet demand, drawing from a work force of men, women, and children, each working twelve to fifteen hours a day. The foundry whistles blew at 5:00 a.m., earlier than a farmer's rooster.

Apprenticing with the Carriage Works Company at Salt Hill, John saved enough for rent of a humble cottage at New Windsor in Berkshire. Secure in his future, he proposed to Ann Edwards, to marry at St. Mary's Church, Marylebone, in Middlesex. Ann was overjoyed with the love of her handsome prince.

Always with a basket at her feet, Ann took in sewing, becoming known in Salt Hill for the finest French stitching and cotton point bodice work. Washboard scrubbing and a coal-heated iron were set up in the kitchen, occupying late hours after the evening meals.

In John and Ann's fifth year of marriage, they were blessed with twins, John and Anne, born in May of 1836, and followed by Henry, Caroline and Frederick.

Invitation to the Pigeon Shoot, Slough

THE POSTMAN handed the envelope directly to John Creffield Sr. It was crested vellum, sealed with mucilage, and an official stamp was postmarked November 26, 1836. He brought it inside for opening.

Elizabeth touched the embossed paper. "Curious, John. You should open it now." Moving to the desk for window light, he slit the edge with a brass opener.

"Well, it is official looking. From Mrs. Luff at the Shooting Club."

"Go on, John."

"At the White Hart Inn, Slough, on Tuesday, December 13. I am invited to a match."

"That's lovely, John, that you were selected. Who else is going?"

"There's a list of stewards: Mr. Boncey, Mr. T Brown, Mr. Burge, Mr. R. Crook, Mr. Leddel, Mr. John Creffield . . . that's me, Mr. J. Brown, Mr. Grove, Mr. Blincoe, Mr. Adams, Mr. Cooper, Mr. A. Atkins, Mr. Beauchamp and Mr. Howard.

"Furthermore, a dinner afterward at three o'clock."

"A splendid dinner too, I'm confident. You know Mrs. Luff makes money from those events."

"It seems you might be right. The tickets are 4s 6d each, at the Bar of the Inn. Don't you worry, Elizabeth, I have a small amount put away for rainy days that will cover this."

"I know you'll shoot famously. Is there a prize?"

"It's not in the prize, my darling, but in the honor of inclusion. I'll take John Jr. out to the country to help me practise. We'll find some old bottles or cans, and head out early Saturday morning before the shop opens."

The Creffield coachbuilding business couldn't ignore social changes and the demand for other modes of transportation. Without astute plans, the village could lose its place on main commuter routes.

Even with industrial advancements, Britain struggled to emerge from an economic depression with unions and battle-weary soldiers pleading for higher wages. William IV had introduced the Corn Laws to keep crop prices equitable, then labour laws to protect children under the age of nine. More workhouses were opened, and a basic schooling system was promised.

John Creffield III completed primary school, but with no resources to advance education, his future was limited to trades. Every private moment with his father was valued, especially their walks through the fields and sheep pastures from Chalvey.

At summer daybreaks, they went often in silence to the iron bridge, with John carrying the fishing pole his father had made, with a wire attached to go for gudgeon and roach. Dew worms were packed in a honey pail under a mound of dirt and moss to stay moist.

Together their legs dangled from the low bridge, crunching on apples. Cuffs of their workpants were rolled, with their feet dipping into the cool water as they watched circles repeating as they grew larger and disappeared.

John III held up a hook of brown river trout. "Do you think Ma will cook these for dinner tonight?"

"I'm sure she will, but she'll want us to clean them well first."

Looking at the jagged knife blade, John asked, "Can I do it, Pa?"

"I know a man that once cut off his entire thumb, but if you want to try, alright."

"Naw."

Young John was quiet in thought, then looked his father in the eyes. "Pa, were you a twin too?"

"No, son, I wasn't. Why do you ask?"

"Sometimes when I look in the mirror, I see Anne's shadow behind me. Was she named after Ma?"

"Yes, yer ma and yer grandma."

A suitable pair of gudgeon were hooked together and tied to the end of John's pole for the jaunt back to the Chalvey cottage. With it balanced over his shoulder, the youngest John and his father whistled and sang the country ballad *The Farmer's Boy*.

Both tried a side heel kick.

Thirty-nine

Victor Paquette episode with rifle – Disagreement with Loyalist neighbour, Henderson – Victor and the switch behind the barn - One-room schoolhouses est. by government 1840 – St. Andrews village school of Sisters of Providence – Sister Marie's Rules – Main Street St. Andrews – Milking Rosie - Sophie Tessier practises sharp-shooting – Joseph Charlebois marries Sophie Tessier 1837 – Ottawa Valley Trunk Line and Bytown Railway – Timber reforestation lacking from timber trade – Legends of Big Joe Mufferaw and Denys Demoulin – Shipping yards at Hawkesbury – Charlebois boys sign on as feller and sawyers for Hamilton Bros. – White Pine cleared from forests – Mosaic of Irish reelers enhance lumber camps.

Victor Paquette and the Switch at the Barn, St. Andrews

E VEN CHANGING THE BOUNDARIES OF THE PARISH OF St. André d'Argenteuil never altered the character of the landscape with its rich farmlands, and rivers. French farms owned miles of riverbank, while Irish and Scottish layered lands inland. Behind these settlements, pioneers laid claim to wilderness land as ancestral farms.

Edouard Irvan Paquette and Clémence Cloutier were established on farms in St. Andrews before the Rebellion of 1837. Their oldest son, Victor, was born March 14, 1833, followed by Joseph, Edouard Jr., who died at three, then Celina and Benjamin.

As a youngster, Victor frequently watched his father place the long-barrelled hunting rifle in the closet, and knew the Colt revolver was locked behind the tobacco pouch in the bureau drawer.

At four years and full of curiosity, with no one looking and silent in his pursuit, he tiptoed in his socks to the closet and retrieved the rifle. Sliding the window pane up, he pretended the enemy was in Papa's bushes. Caressing the smooth wood, he levelled the rifle to his eye and imagined a native ambush lying in wait.

Planning the imaginary attack, he was startled by a flock of ducks rising from the riverbank. Off balance, he fell backward, accidentally firing the rifle, astonished that it was loaded. His eyes darted to the door, then leaned tall over the window sill to see if anyone would be coming.

"What if I have killed a Mohawk or a British soldier? Worse, what if I killed Pa?"

Racked with fear, Victor knew his best defence would be tears for sympathy. He had no idea how Papa came so fast, and he froze at his mother's gasp in the kitchen doorway, her face as pale as the moon. Ma grabbed and inspected him for wounds, then embraced and kissed him, but he was overtaken by Papa, who had him by the ear, yelling French words he'd never heard.

His siblings, Joseph, Edouard and Celina, gathered, and Clémence shooed the smaller ones away, to stay crossed-legged by the kitchen stove.

In the yard, the neighbour's anger showed in his heavy strides toward the house, coming ashore from his canoe with his fist raised.

"Dang blasted boy, you put a bullet right through my hat. I ought to thrash you myself. Edouard, shame on you for leaving a deadly weapon loaded for children. Did you think I was an Indian? Eh, boy, what do you have to say for yourself?"

The fisherman's language and tirades worsened as his face reddened.

"Calm down, Henderson, I'll pay for a new hat," Edouard Irvan said.

The man scrunched it on his head.

"I'll be puttin' one on your tab at the general store. Now boy, take mind of your actions." Henderson stormed out the back to let the screen door slam, with Victor shaking in his over-sized boots.

His tears hadn't yet gained the support he needed.

Surely, mother will rescue me.

Indeed, Clémence's apron wiped his tears, and for the moment, he was sent to bed without dinner. But he knew that Papa was not finished with him.

Edouard came to Victor after supper.

"Boy, what did you think you were doing?" He sat on the edge of the cot. "You practically killed our Loyalist neighbour, and it would have been worse if it had been Mr. Lafontaine or one of the Delormes."

Edouard hesitated, knowing it would never happen again. "I must say it was a good shot if you were actually aiming. Were you playing that game the English play at school, cowboys & Indians?"

Victor nodded his head in agreement. "Yes, it was the English that made me do it."

Hiding his surprising amusement in the admonishment, Edouard had to make him an example, and couldn't let Clémence accuse him of being soft with the boys.

"Victor, the Mohawks have been our friends for many years. They trade with us, teach the lore of our lands, and defend us. You must never raise a rifle to them. In fact, son, you are partly Mohawk. Did you not wonder about the dark skin of the Cloutiers, and the Tessiers?

"I spent so many summers in the native reserve at Oka, learning and participating in their culture. I tell you this myself, not as a legend or story, but to instill pride in your heritage.

"And yet, Victor, you broke my trust in you. I've always told my sons never to touch my rifle. Did you not think it was the truth?"

In the seriousness of the conversation, Victor felt he grew ten years in that moment of confidence that his father shared with him. A new bond began, and they both knew it.

"Now, boy, it would not be fair to your brothers that you be spared the switch. Let's go together out behind the barn."

Edouard took the young hand and they marched out bravely. Four-year-old Victor stood steady and held back his tears. He did not want his Maman to see him cry this time.

When they were finished, Edouard patted Victor on the back and said "Maybe you are ready for hunting sooner than I thought. It is the nature of a Paquette."

"Yes Papa, I have lots more spect now."

Victor thought it over.

This has been a good day, after all.

Victor Paquette's First Day in the One Room Schoolhouse

BY 1840, the British government established a school system for both Protestant and Roman Catholics in one-room schoolhouses, with teachers paid by the provincial government. Previously, they were boarded for weeks at a time by contributing families, with their pay proportionate to the number of students.

The town flourished more through the mid-1800s with hôteliers, blacksmiths, a barbershop, boot maker, tailor, livery and stables, tinsmith, carpenters, coopers and wheelwrights. A new mercantile and hardware opened, then a carriage builder, tanner, bank, new grist and saw mills, and a telegraph office and railway depot.

As the population grew, so did the need for education services for families hungry for progress for their children.

With his nine-year-old energy in 1842, Victor Paquette skipped stones along the dirt road, passing St. Andrews Catholic Church. His younger brother, Joseph, was in tow, and together they dilly-dallied to the one-story log schoolhouse. The Church, built ten years earlier, stood on a rise back from the road, a small building bearing a cross and a suspended bell.

Of two hundred and sixty Catholic families in the population of fourteen hundred, only a hundred and twenty students were enrolled at the St. Andrews village school under the Sisters of Providence, with others at the school midway to Carillon.

With one hand, Victor swung his primer and a slate, strapped together in a leather harness, and dangled a tin pail in the other. His best school clothes were washed for today—farm britches, a checkered shirt of broadcloth with a red sash, and hand-me-down shoes from his cousin, that he dusted on the tops.

His father's exhausted brown felt hat came down over his ears, and with pride he had poked a brown feather through an old hole.

His mother said he'd be attending school with Pierre and Octave Giroux, William LeRoy and the Charlebois boys. Victor imagined games of tag, shooting marbles, catching fish bare-handed in the creek, and maybe a pull or two of girlish braids. The thought of slate boards, printing, reading, and sitting still had not entered his mind.

Cutting across the cow path, the two kicked turds to see how far they could punt, until the schoolyard came into view. The Giroux boys were climbing apple trees and a few girls in frilly skirts were playing skip rope.

As Sister Marie rang the bell, Joseph and Victor Paquette raced toward the yard and sorted themselves into a single line at the front door. With pushing and shoving, the Paquette and Giroux boys squished into the back row, four boys in two seats, with hands folded for prayer.

It didn't last, as Sister Marie insisted on more spacious seating, putting Joseph with a young Irish girl and the youngest Giroux paired with a French Métis. Victor Paquette and Jean-Baptiste Giroux were relieved to retain their post of surveillance in the back row bench, beside the potbelly coal stove.

The sister took attendance, noting ages, six to twelve, then prayer. Her rules couldn't be questioned—no talking, speak only when spoken to, stay in your seat, don't copy, and raise your hand for a question.

She admonished Victor right away to sit up straight, and his smile waned along with his enthusiasm. His attention moved to daydreams, chasing wild hares, trapping squirrels, and tug of war over the creek. He dug in his pocket for a brown baby toad, causing a small girl's shriek and a class commotion. The teacher's switch promptly made its first acquaintance, to a mixture of horror and curiosity for the rest of the class.

Victor's nose was directed to the back corner wall until dinner break, when the boys gathered under a cluster of butternut trees to investigate the tin pails. Victor and Joseph found and shared their maple ham, Clémence's cornbread, and had barely crunched into their crisp apples, when the pack erupted in a game of tag.

Understanding Sister Marie's rules better, Victor had an afternoon without incident; but glad it was over, he hurried Joseph out the door to hightail it toward the village.

School at Canoe Cove, PEI, ca 1880, watercolour. Robert Harris (1849-1919);
One room school; Confederation Centre Art Gallery. Public Domain ⑨

They skidded to a stop to throw stones at the North River Bridge, careful not to be caught by Edward Jones who built the bridge and lived within sight in the log house at the foot of the wooden causeway.

On Wales Street, as the clamour of hooves resounded from behind, he yanked Joseph to the road side by his shirt.

As the four-horse team of Cushing's stagecoach from Saint-Eustache barrelled across the bridge, the driver waved his hat to be seen. "Hey, Victor."

The boys picked up speed to keep up with the coach, but in less than a few hundred yards had fallen out of pace, resuming the urges to kick stones along the road as far as the boardwalk.

At the candy and toy store, the proprietor's clerk looked up as the bell over the door rang, amused at the boys' energy.

From his station behind an oak counter with glass cabinet, the man watched with patience as the lads crouched to peer onto the glass shelves.

The boys came here often to see it—the village's famous marionettes of Punch and Judy, resting on a velvet cushion. Punch wore a sinister grin and the red beaked nose of a vagabond, with his pointy-chinned wife Judy beside him, both in multicoloured minstrel costumes.

Often at day's end, before sunset, clerks from other establishments gathered here at the candy store, watching the Cockney and his wife perform rollicking plays with the puppets.

"Oh, please, Ma'am. Will there be a play tonight?"

"Even if there could be one, it would be past your bedtime."

Victor hung his head, long enough for the clerk to take pity and extend to each of them a piece of horehound. The lads put on their crestfallen faces to thank the clerk, and outside, their sullen looks melted as they revelled in their trickery. Neither could speak, as the long candy sticks poked inside their cheeks.

Three stores farther down the main street was their destination, Clunie Grocers & Merchants. Both Charles and Henry were on the porch on weathered pine chairs.

Henry Clunie was always glad to see Victor's big eyes of innocent mischief, and presented the boy with a broom for the outside boards and the floors. Victor worked arduously with the cob whisk, until Clunie nodded satisfaction. Paid two pence, the boys skedaddled homeward.

Clémence and five-year-old Celina were in the yard. Bear, the collie, sprinted from the knoll, almost knocking Victor and Joseph to the ground. With appropriate licking and patting, the three bounded to find their mother, stalling only to throw and retrieve a stick. She was waiting with a dish of cornbread and maple syrup for each.

Victor knew his father would be looking for him in the pasture with a pair of Holstein milking cows.

Edouard's burden was lightened by the sight of Victor, who took over the rope. Rosie, his favourite milker, bellowed as Victor prodded her into the stall for milking. He set the wooden stool and bucket beside her bloated belly, all the time dodging her thrashing tail. He knew his task well, and massaged a good yield, leaving Rosie contented and mooing.

With both hands, Victor lifted the bucket for approval. "She did well today, Papa."

"You have the farmer's magic touch, Victor."

The nanny goat was bawling from the garden behind the house. Having gnawed through the rope, she was pulling carrots at will from Clémence's vegetable patch. Victor left the barn to follow the noise, and ran through the tall grass to the garden.

"Non, non!"

The nanny saw his waving arms, but showed displeasure and continued the purge of the vegetation. Victor grabbed the remaining shreds of rope, and yanked her toward the barn. The goat wasn't peaceful in the milking progress, but produced a thicker milk that would make a creamy cheese that he knew would please his mother.

With stalls mucked out, Edouard and Victor followed the dog to the kitchen, carrying a pitcher of milk. Joseph was in his chair and Clémence was stirring a thick pea soup, yellow with chunks of ham and potato.

A loaf of bread had been half-sliced for the hungry boys, with creamy butter and slabs of cheddar on a cutting board.

Almost no scraps remained for the dog, but he was captivated by the generous ham bone that had fallen to the floor from the boys.

Joseph Charlebois & Sophie Tessier, St. Andrews

SOPHIE TESSIER was from a family of two boys and three girls, so by necessity, she knew all the farm chores equally, pitching in with plowing, tilling, and seeding chores. Although petite in stature, she was sturdy and competitive, and never shirked a test—even the physical challenge of stump clearing. Before his death during the Rebellion, her father Hyacinthe even quipped that Sophie was the third son.

"Come to the back field, Basile," Sophie urged her brother. "Let's shoot some glass." She lined up a row of broken bottles on the wooden fence rail. Under her arm was Hyacinthe's old Winchester from the closet.

Basile was reduced to carrying only the box of ammunition. He had been trained by his older brother Olivier to help Sophie with her shooting, by holding the rifle on her shoulder as she trained her eyes on the targets.

For the first few years, Sophie often appeared at the kitchen table with her left eye blackened, but her mother, Marie-Louise Brault-Pominville, never embarrassed her about it.

"Sophie, how was target practice today?" she always asked with a smirk. Basile, three years younger than Sophie, knew it as a chance to kick her under the table with his own snicker, and dodge a kick back.

"Ma, at the harvest fair this year, I'd like to join the sharp-shooting. They have some sort of clay pigeon they throw in the air. I can get Basile to throw some tins for me to improve my shot."

"It's not ladylike, Sophie, but I suppose your pa would allow it," Marie-Louise said, knowing the late Hyacinthe would have approved.

In the summer before the Rebellion, Joseph Charlebois had his mind set on the spunky Sophie, who he knew well from visits in his youth to the Tessier farm. Her family's land was near the Oka mission, letting her take lessons from native friends on camp craft and survival.

Her friend, Running Wolfe, had once taken her deep into the woods in the winter, where together they foraged under the snow for food, and to craft a bow and arrow and hunt. But when it came to having a buck in her sights, Sophie couldn't take the shot.

"Sorry, Running Wolfe. I had him in my aim, but he has a family too, and I know now the pain of losing a father."

Joseph Charlebois Jr. married the daughter of his comrade of the rebellion, Sophie Tessier, in 1837 at Saint-Hermas. Their first child was lost as a newborn, and it wasn't until the birth of their oldest son Treffle Alfred in 1838 at Rigaud that happiness returned to the home. In the next fifteen years, eleven more children filled the Charlebois household.

Railways and Legends Bring a Boon to Argenteuil, 1840-50s

ALONG THE NORTH shore from Montréal, steam engines chugged the new Champlain and St. Lawrence railway route for twelve miles on the Carillon-Grenville line. It would be a portage railroad, awaiting plans to improve routes circuiting rapids and canals, with the Ottawa Valley Trunk Line, the Montréal and Bytown Railway, and the Grenville and Carillon.

The economic balance had shifted from agriculture to the timber trade, but as railways cut through the landscape, there was no regard shown for reforestation.

France and England were far from the thoughts of Marcel Joseph Giroux, Joseph Charlebois, and Victor Paquette, when by chance they met up outside Meikle's post office in Lachute. "It's Friday afternoon," Joseph said. "Today's almost done. Who's for deferring to Cushing's Tavern?"

It wasn't hard to persuade the others, and they settled in comfort at a corner table. Meaning well, Victor couldn't help bringing up difficulties Giroux had faced.

"Well, Marcel, thankfully you survived the uprisings at Saint-Eustache. Tell me, how's your family?"

"Yes, we endured that—and Pa's stories will be retold for generations."

"I heard you and Elizabeth are expecting another baby," Jean-Baptiste teased Marcel. "That'll make old George Simon a grandpa again."

"It will indeed. He's lost count of his grandchildren."

"But he's a lucky man with so many, Marcel," Charlebois said. He waited for some hooting to quieten down across the room. "But . . . I didn't come into town for a beer to commiserate."

"How about some congratulations then, Joseph. I hear you and Sophie Tessier have a brood of little ones."

"Seven babies in ten years, mostly all boys," Joseph bragged.

"Give them a few years and you can supervise harvest from your back porch while the kids clear the fields," Marcel joked.

The tavern door burst open to an intimidating presence. The patrons fell silent as the man, an immense, brusque lumberjack, stopped suddenly six feet from the bar. He looked at the tables, ensuring he'd been noticed by every man.

Victor Paquette nudged his pals. The diminutive middle-aged barkeep trembled as the man, at least seven feet tall, approached.

The man boomed, "A round for my friends if they agree to listen to my latest accomplishments."

"That's Big Joe Mufferaw,[46]"Victor said. "He's stronger than an oxen and nimble as a wildcat."

The tables emptied toward the bar at the liquid enticement, then the crowd surged with full brews around the paradoxical, rugged woodsman. The keeper kept filling the glasses, and Mufferaw waited until he saw he had full command of the room.

"Can ye all hear me?" he bellowed.

A round of laughter and yeas echoed back.

"Well, I was comin' home the other day, and when I arrived at the Rideau rapids, I decides that ain't no good."

Joe's hand whipped around behind him and twirled a rusty axe.

"I ain't big for no purpose, I grew up in the woods. This here axe, I made myself." He flipped it in the air to recoiling gasps. "You won't meet a man in all of Québec that's mightier or more agile than meself."

The patrons dared not speak a word.

"I just completely digged the Rideau Canal with this here axe. I dug her deep enough that boats can pass. My simple efforts can be compared to two thousand Irish trench-men. I hope no one here is Irish, I'm opposed to their insults of my French comrades."

The entire bar became French in an instant.

Joe slammed his empty glass on the bar and it was refilled in nothing flat. "I've a forest to fell this morning."

Guzzling it in one gulp, Joe Mufferaw swung around and was out the door, faster than the wind.

Victor Paquette was the first to speak. "I'm surprised he didn't recognize me. We met up in the woods once."

Jean-Baptiste challenged in disbelief. "Get out of here, Victor. You as likely met Joe Mufferaw as I met Denys Demoulin."

"If we're about telling tales, I have it on good account that in Montréal, Joe planted boot marks on the ceiling of an ale house and bounded backwards to his original stance," the tender added.

---

[46] The Ottawa Valley legend of Big Joe Mufferaw (brawler, woodsman) in a popular tune by Stompin' Tom Connors eighty years later. Walt Disney did a movie where he replaced tales of Joe Mufferaw with Paul Bunyan. Paradoxical myth or legend.

With a glint in his eye, Marcel poked at both Victor and Jean-Baptiste. "If Joe Mufferaw comes back, ask him about Demoulin and the stagecoach on the treacherous road carrying the royal mail. Now Denys ain't Irish, he's a Métis Frenchman. I heard he was goin' between Ottawa and Carillon and broke a wheel, but that didn't stop him, and he jumps a giant, red pine in a single leap. He took pity on Tommy Flynn, the driver, so swifter than the eye, Denys takes each envelope with an arrow and launches it to the doorstep of the recipient."

"Now that is true. Joseph Charlebois received a letter with an arrow at his front door, all the way in Saint-Hermas."

"Unbelievable marksmanship!"

The glasses echoed as they clinked.

Roughing it in the Rideau Bush

WITH THE CANOE chock-full, Joseph and the older boys paddled downstream, fording whitewater to the Carillon Rapids, then onward to Hawkesbury and the lumber mills of the Mears and Hamilton Brothers at Chute-à-Blondeau. Expansive lumber yards at Hawkesbury partnered to build steamboats and barges, creating diverse new jobs.

Tasks clearing the woods, or as river oarsmen, rafters, and wilderness guides were gladly taken by French habitants and Métis with inherent knowledge of the land.

The Charlebois men signed on as fellers and sawyers with the Hamilton Brothers, and were given logging ropes, saws, axes, spikes, hammers, bedrolls, and even a company-issued tent for their canoe. The storehouse doled out one tin cup and bowl each, with rations of dried beans, beef brine, salt pork, molasses, coffee, and hard flatbread.

Joseph, Treffle, and Alderic Charlebois were sent to a logging site on the wooded slopes, a long day's journey inland on foot. Along the rugged horse trail, they passed the log trawlers removing rocks and stumps to ease towing and cartage to the river.

Marking Logs at Skidway, Engraving on wood, Artists Schell & Hogan,
Engravers F. Geyer, Picturesque Canada, Vol. 1, 1882

"It's a shame, boys, that moose and caribou are almost endangered, and now the black bears are displaced and the beaver dams abandoned. All for the wealth of these lumber barons," Joseph commiserated.

"Sure is! From here, I can now see the river through the woods. There was a time when Grandpa Joe talked of the forest dense with deer, and the rivers thick with bass and speckled trout," Treffle said.

"Also a time when the Hurons and Algonquins had inland villages and thrived. Now the government is pushing them into reserves," Alderic said.

The native guide, Junundat, couldn't help hearing them. "We are dispersed from our tribes and our way of life. You know there was a time when I took your grandfathers on hunting excursions, teaching them to survive in the wilderness. But it's not so easy these days."

"They call it progress, a robust economy," Joseph said sardonically.

"We have nothing to trade anymore," Junundat said. "Nowhere to hunt and nowhere to die. We have become servants, when we were born to be protectors."

The concepts of ecology, reforestation, resources and the environment were forgotten. Instead, woods were stripped of natural nutrients and irrigation patterns. Rich soils had lost their fertilizing and drainage abilities and streams were drying up, depleting the spawning beds. Wildlife no longer stayed on lands now cleared, interrupting migration, pollination, and natural fertilization, and starving the soil of nitrogen.

By mid-1800s, only the economic value of industry in Québec was a consideration by the government, selling timber limits throughout the Ottawa Valley. Even the ancient pines were stripped from the forests and sent to France as a demanded commodity.

The Charlebois' trekked on toward the distinct odor of campfire, then caught sight of a lumber crew of a dozen men easily visible through the sparse remains of a clearing section. Some wore red shirts, and brown or grey woolen trousers with suspenders. The fortunate ones had heavy English boots, while others claimed to prefer moccasin leathers.

"This looks like our camp ahead," Joseph declared to the boys.

Alderic joked, "Ah, the sweet smell of burning birch."

At the sight of them, the Irish camp boss stepped outside the shanty office. "Glad to see you fellas."

"Ready to work, sir," Joseph said.

"Settle your gear somewhere in the back. Did you bring your own tent?"

"We did, sir."

In no time, they set it up and secured their meagre belongings under their blankets before gathering at the campfire. Sophie's cousin, Jean-Baptiste Tessier, Joseph Charbonneau, and two of the Kingsbury boys were already there.

"Charlebois—that's what I'll call the lot of you, fewer names to keep track of," the boss declared. "Joseph, you'll be the lead chopper, and your boys will both be sawyers."

The boss tossed Joseph a knotted length of rope.

"The pine must be a greater measure in circumference than the rope; trees of lesser size won't be cut. Once the tree is felled, saw it in sixteen foot sections before it gets rolled, skidded, or chain-dragged by horse to the river. Understand?"

Joseph spoke for his unit. "Yes, sir."

"It's McGinnis."

Sleighs were the primary logging transport for timbers in the winter, rotating teams from the fourteen draft horses stabled at the landing site.

Joseph leaned against the fir to strap log spurs to the underside of his boots, as blades to anchor his foothold on the climb. Under his jacket, he hooked rope loops to his belt, already holding a hatchet, handsaw, and a double-edged hammer from Marcel Giroux's smithy.

He shinnied himself up from the base of the white pine, and sprung forward with the ropes and spurs. The thick, obstinate branches in the lower section were severed by handsaw, and by the time he reached the cap, the lithe branches were hacked with single swipes, falling like feathers.

As Joseph moved to the next tree, Treffle and Alderic cleaved a massive vee into the tree's north side, calculating the pine's weakening axis. Alderic held the low rope to pull to the south, and as Treffle braced for a final swing of the axe side, his voice boomed through the woods. "Clear!"

Alderic's grip could no longer hang on, and the rope escaped his hand with a stingy lash. In slow motion, the bald spire crashed to the ground in their midst, with branches cracking and the earth heaving at the thud.

With a cross-cut saw, Treffle sliced a section of bark from the lower section, slashing a mark, then a clean cut at the base and top. His hammer branded a mark 'H' for 'Hamilton Brothers', hoping to deter piracy.

Harnessed to log trawlers, the heavy horses were led back to the riverbank, where shanty men lashed the logs onto barges, each with a pilot house for sleep and eating.

With four barges loaded, the booms were set afloat on the breakneck currents and rapids down the Ottawa, with a crew of log jammers dancing and directing the flow.

White pines were the most common on the river as hardwood didn't have good floating characteristics. While the rivers were frozen, winter logging was accelerated with an accumulation held for the spring currents.

At dusk, McGinnis wailed out a lingering blast with his whistle, signaling the lumberjacks to call it a day. The cook waited with a cast-iron cauldron of unidentifiable stew, and beside it the day's bread and a blackened kettle of black tea.

"Put tomorrow's ration in the vat," the cook ordered.

Joseph placed a handful of dried beans, peas, potatoes, salt pork and a skinned rabbit into the stew. The cook appreciated it and scooped a considerate ladle of hash onto his plate, tossed on a torn chunk of bread, and pointed to the tea.

"Thank you, sir," Joseph acknowledged, coaxing a more generous portion next time.

Tales were repeated nightly, each as if the first time, often of the legendary Paul Bunyan and Babe the blue oxen. Stories became exaggerated into the night, mixed with spirited jigs of the Irishmen from Lac des Deux-Montagnes with the harmonica and fiddles.

The best logging nights had a few Irish reelers that needed no prodding, despite being less fluent in French. In turn, the French knew limited words in Irish, and mostly unkind ones. But when the fiddle got them stomping and clapping to a reel, they became kindred, with music their language.

Joseph urged one of the Irishmen, with words that adopted a comical French interpretation. "C'mon Sean! Sing of pigs, billy goats, and the lassie from Killarney."

In the shanty, loaves were by the fire for a late snack, with a platter of cold pork, and blackstrap molasses. The fire burned late, drying wet knitted mittens and toques on a rock, and moccasins laid inside out.

While all others slept, Joseph was awake, with Sophie his only thought.

Frugal and industrious, Sophie worked morning to night in the garden to harvest vegetables for winter. The one and half story stone farmhouse wasn't cramped in her opinion, but had taken on a warm and rustic charm.

She had come to value peace and solitude in her quiet evenings when the children were in bed. With her pawfoot, cast-iron sewing machine by the coal oil lamp, she fashioned their shirts, blouses, pants and skirts, often with remnants of broadcloth, checked gingham and calico.

Her daytime and evening thoughts envisioned Joseph, Alderic and Treffle, now gone for months.

Forty

Flora Simpson hires Aurelie Beaulne – Manor house conveniences include light bulbs, plumbing and mechanical broom – Victor Paquette marries Aurelie Beaulne, 1854 – Wild Turkey Shoot at St. Andrews – Irish immigrants bring white plague and typhoid, 1847 – Montréal & Lachine Railway opens 1839 – St. Andrews Roman Catholic church benevolent campaign for Irish orphans – St. Andrews annual Harvest Fair; apple butter contests, circus and tournaments – Excursion steamboats bring temperance groups to St. Andrews – Band shells & Three-Legged Race – Log Jammers Dance on the River.

Victor Paquette and Aurelia Beaulne

I T WASN'T ELIZABETH'S INTENTION TO INTERFERE, BUT she overheard Mrs. Simpson groaning from what appeared to be havoc in her household.

Elizabeth LeRoy, wife of Marcel Joseph Giroux, was in the dry goods store simply to show off newborn Elizabeth Jr. when she caught Mrs. Simpson's lament. Her husband, Robert Simpson, was a magistrate and tanner in St. Andrews, and their family was well respected, with five children from infants to school-aged rebellious boys.

Elizabeth interrupted her, "You shouldn't have any trouble, Mrs. Simpson. There are many young girls in the Charlebois, Giroux, Paquettes, Tessiers and LeRoys in need of a disciplined position such as yours."

At first, Mrs. Simpson took an affront to Madame LeRoy's proposal, then latched onto the suggestion, giving a second thought to the words 'in need of a disciplined position'.

"Do you have a specific suggestion, Madame LeRoy?"

"Well, a young girl at church on Sunday recently came to St. Andrews from Rivière-Rouge on the stagecoach with Treffle Charlebois. Poor dear lost her father in the Rebellion and her ma to the fever. He'll know where she got out. It's a close-knit community and word travels as quickly as the steam train."

Mrs. Simpson was suddenly informal and patronizing.

"Dear Elizabeth, as you can see I have my hands full. Would you be a dear, to find the girl and ask her to come by the house for a chat?"

"Indeed, Flora."

Elizabeth put emphasis on Mrs. Simpson's given name then took the opportunity to insinuate indebtedness.

Aurelie's parents, Augustin Beaulne and Marie Lafontaine, had settled near Sainte-Madeleine de Rigaud. When she was three, her father fought in the Rebellion with the Argenteuil Infantry, and her mother worked as a laundress. At ten, Aurelie began scrubbing floors at the seamstress shop, and didn't have the privilege of attending the country schoolhouse.

"Ma, I overheard the Charlebois and the Paquettes on Main Street," she had prodded. "They lowered their voices when I came near, but I heard them say my Pa died in the Battle of Saint-Eustache. Was he a hero?"

"Yes, my dear, he was young and handsome, but especially a hero. You have his eyes and passionate soul."

Aurelie treasured those words nightly, envisioning her father and what he might have been if fate hadn't taken him so young. Then her mother, Marie Lafontaine, died in Rigaud when the cholera epidemic ravaged the community, leaving young Aurelie an orphan at fifteen.

At seventeen, she received room and board in return for services at the long, brick house. Robert Simpson was twenty years older than his bride, Flora Jones, who became step-mother to the oldest boys, Robert and George. Aurelie was close in age to the others, Moses, Emily and Leister.

"Such a blessing to see the conveniences in this luxurious house, and I mustn't take them for granted. When I marry, I expect it will be to a farmer's wife on a rugged homestead."

Aurelie's thoughts were lost in that fantasy as she dusted by the window, gazing through the tall first-floor paned window that overlooked the drive.

"Mademoiselle Beaulnes!" George snapped.

"Oui, Monsieur George."

"I need to ask you to pick up a delivery at the General Store. Write down these items right away."

Aurelie made indiscernible scratches on a scrap of paper, and looked up with relief to see that Mr. Simpson had gone.

I can't let them find out I can't read or write.

Marcel Giroux congratulated himself and Elizabeth LeRoy for the match-making of Victor Paquette and Aurelie.

Victor married his twenty-year-old bride on September 18, 1854 at St. Andrews. Starting as a young boy, selling toads and frogs to his friends, he saved every penny through his youth, and his frugal savings enabled him to purchase a portion of land from his father.

Building a log structure on the homestead with plans for expansion as the family grew, Victor and Aurelie settled beside Edouard and Clémence and shared the farm work.

Flora Simpson wasn't prepared to lose Aurelie, but compromised with permission for her to live outside the Simpson manor at night, stretching two more years. The Simpson children had bonded with Aurelie after six years, and continued to visit her home.

Victor and Aurelie had seven sons and five daughters—Victor, Edward, Urgel, Alexander, Dollard (Adelard), Medas (Hormidas), John, Marie, Adelle, Valerie, Deline, and Sara.

Wild Turkey Shoot in St. Andrews

VICTOR'S WORK as an oarsman and game guide was split between the Murray Manor House on the left bank, Reverend Abbott's Priory two hundred acre estate, and the famed Red House, a mile west of the manor.

Proudly, he was also self-appointed leader of the Wild Turkey Shoot in the hills beyond St. Andrews, held in the spring mating season, at a choice time for male turkeys to strut and be heard. By late winter, anticipation of the shoot was exhilarating for the village, with excitement building to a pitch in the spring as townsfolks prepared to cheer on their men.

As every year, the front of Wales Store would be the starting line. Mrs. Wales was assiduous in detail and discipline, ensuring that each hunter was properly registered, and given red flags to wear on their backs. The crowd started appearing at dawn forming a semi-circle outside the store.

Mrs. Wales stood on a chair to be heard. "There won't be any mistaking the hunters," she declared above the revelry. The assembled included the Smiths, Bradleys, Todds, McGregors, McGowans, Turners, Fletchers, Watson and dozens more, mostly with full families in tow.

When Victor Paquette climbed to the chair to speak, the crowd hushed.

Then Mrs. Wales caused a commotion, raising more cheers as she struggled to pin the red flag on his back. "Just in case, Victor, you must wear this."

"If I can have a kiss, I will." Victor leaned over and puckered for the sake of his audience.

"Hogwash, you old goat. I don't know how Aurelie puts up with you."

John Barron stepped forward, wanting the chair now and shouting over the participants.

"Gentlemen! May I remind you about the Rules?"

"Ha, John, we ain't got no rules," Justis McGinn howled, sparking more merriment.

"You beat me to it. The only rule is that the first hunter back to Wales Store by six o'clock with at least six wild turkeys wins. That was the record from last year."

"Easy as a piece of cake," Felix Paquette called out.

"We'll see about that," John Barron said. "Here's a fine bottle of whiskey. I'll put up this prize, adding to the booty."

"You'll have to share it with the lot of us," Blanchard snorted in laughter.

"A bottle of whiskey and 50£. Quit your jibber jabber and throw in a pony and I'll be joinin' you all," Simon LeRoy boasted from the sidelines. "Last year, Victor tied me, but my time was slower. Not this year!"

"George Simon, how about one of my old porkers instead of the pony?" Charlie Anderson shouted.

"Ah, that'll keep my larder full for a while. Charlie, I'll take that as a promise. I'm in!" Simon jumped from the railing and headed into the store to make things right for Mrs. Wales.

"Come on, George, you're holding up the hunters," a ranger chided.

The crowd cleared the street to watch the competitors spread in a line to wait for Barron's whistle.

"It's all in how acquainted you are with your rifle," Victor taunted the rest, while fondling the long wooden barrel. "My Daddy's old rifle has the finest shot. Best of luck to the rest of you men."

Victor's brothers, Benjamin and Joseph, and the Cloutier cousins were only a small part of the town's contingent of hunters. They headed into the woods north of the Priory, to the hills over the old Seigneury and the Red House. Benjamin wore a Huron bow with a bag of hand-made feathered arrows across his back.

Victor fumbled with the cloth and knotted its corners to his suspenders.

"I'd say Mrs. Wales' red flag might save a neglectful woodsman his life, so we'll wear the fandangled rags. It will be a calling card for our chase victims. It's those bumbling Englishmen I worry about."

"No one knows these trails like you and Pa," Benjamin said. "Too bad he decided to sit this one out. I heard him say it was time to pass the torch."

From the hill, Victor eyes scanned the closest bush with his hand cupped behind his ear. As a game hunter, he was aware of the habitat of wild fowl. He wore his duck hunting jacket, and his woolen hat had a pair of turkey feathers in the side. Joseph teased as they waited. "Don't flap your arms, you could be mistaken for aviary game."

The others laughed and Victor gestured with a salute. "Farther north, the only birds are squab and quail. The Hurons take a spit of dozens at a time of those tiny birds over a fire and feast, without forgiving their hunger. They won't do for today."

"Blanchard's group is trailing us to the east!" Joseph breathed, his finger at his lips.

"Stay down and quiet until they pass," Victor nodded. Their party of five hushed, low under the huckleberry growth.

Whispering, Victor leaned toward his brothers.

"When we catch the Great Wild Beast, I'll be plucking his dandy feathers and make myself a Mohawk headdress. Wait until we hear the first strut and gobble of the birds—they're usually over there."

They all turned toward a cluster of bushes fifteen yards northeast.

"The coast is clear, Pa."

Victor rose. Folding his thumb into his fingers, he made a calling whistle.

Caaaw . . . cccucaw . . . Caw . . . Caw. Caaaaaaw.

Across the way, a reply came. "Grggle . . . grgle." In seconds, a span of heavy wings tried futilely to raise into flight.

"Race is on, men. Two to the right and two left; I'll come through the middle."

The crashing brought out two wild, red-bearded gobblers. Their breast hairs were extended for defence, with wings flapping violently in the spurt to flee the barrage of hunters. Joseph was the first within reach and took a dive at the fowl.

"Stay with him, Joe!"

"Keep low and run your fastest; you'll see the brown and black feathers are up and rustling. They are communal, so if there's one, there's up to a dozen more," Victor cautioned.

Benjamin took a position on the left flank, steadily lining up his bow. With a ping and the whistle of disrupted air, they listened for a distress call of a big Tom.

"Je l'ai! I got it!"

Victor sniped at a pair on the run with the long barrel, striking the largest one. "Cette chance!"

Joseph Paquette and Jean-Baptiste Cloutier were in a heap, pinning down the awkward flapping wings.

"What do we do, Victor?"

"Hold his legs, but you know he has thorns." Victor watched the debacle, but before he could say more, Tom escaped with a deafening cry.

"It's too late now. Give the birds a rest and be careful of the nests."

At high noon, their party returned to a camouflage position in the sumacs and huckleberries, and Victor slid a whiskey flask from his vest. "We'll at least celebrate our count of two successful captures."

"Uncle Vic! How many did you bag last year when you won?"

"We'll need four more, but in a new nesting area. We've caused these birds enough grief that they won't nest again for a few days."

At the Beech Ridge Road, a rifle echoed from the north. "We'll cut away to the east; it must be Brown up ahead. See where I notched the maples on the way to the creek? Stay in that line and we'll come across another nesting ground."

By five o'clock, the five musketeers marched down Main Street with burlap sacks over their backs and the heads of two magnificent male turkeys flopping on the canvas. Over Victor's shoulder, the dust of LeRoy's wagon was making a charge, but it would be in vain.

Aurelie watched from the finish in a new calico, with newborn Adelle in a baby sling, and three toddlers—Victor Jr., Edward, and Marie Aurelie. Marie, no longer the youngest, swung for attention on Aurelie's arm.

"Ahoy, Barron, the whiskey's mine!" Victor yelled out over the laughter of the crowd, starting a merriment that wouldn't die down until midnight.

Grosse Isle Québec & Irish Immigration, 1850s

AT THEIR POINT of desperation, evacuation from the Irish potato famine seemed a solution after years of infertile soil. With as many as a million in Ireland were dead, orphans were fleeing as stowaways from Warrenpoint, Sligo, and Newry.

The tragedy precipitated a mass immigration in 1845 to Grosse Isle in the Gulf of the St. Lawrence. On ships arriving in Canadian waters, more than thirty percent died enroute from rampant diseases including white plague and typhoid, with many others kept in quarantine for years.

In 1847, French-Canadians feared the disease spreading in their midst, once again expressing alarm that the government would fail to intercede.

In many eyes, the Irish were thought to be a lower social class, taking labour jobs on railway lines and iron and limestone quarries. When the Montréal and Lachine Railway opened, rumours spread that beleaguered Irish immigrants would be sent to build a railway coast to coast.

Victor Paquette sympathized with the new immigrant populace, more than the Brits and Scots. At Sunday mass in St. Andrews, he observed Richard O'Callaghan in the back row with other Irish folks. The French and Irish had some affinity with the Roman Catholic faith and attendance.

In a fine mood, Victor walked to the back to put a smile on their faces.

"Hello, Richard. How's your family?" he greeted.

"It's nice to see you, Victor, but these aren't my children. Their parents all died of typhoid on the crossing and they have no place to go. I took pity on them at the docks."

Victor perused the deep eyes of a young boy, face-to-face with misery and tragedy in such a short life—too soon to be bitter and defiant. Beside him, a wee girl desperately clung to his hand, and next to them were two frightened adolescent boys.

"Hello, boy. Is this your sister?" Victor spoke slowly but gently. Aurelie had moved up behind, and bent to take the girl's hand.

"Richard, how would you and your orphans like to join us for Sunday dinner?" Aurelie said. Her mind spun, wondering what spare clothing and shoes she could offer.

The wee girl looked up at Aurelie. "You're a nice lady, but we ain't orphans, we're immigrants."

"Richard, wait when mass is over and follow us home. I have folks I need to speak with."

Victor vanished into the throng of the congregation for a mental note of wealthy families that might take in the children.

Maybe Ladouceur, Ferguson, Barron, Johnson, Dewar or Morrison.

At the front, he pinned the officiating priest, Father Michaud from Notre-Dame du Portage, about the urgency of aid for the Irish orphans and the spoken word of 'do unto others as you would unto yourself'.

After the ceremonial rituals of mass, the priest raised his hand.

"Please parishioners, don't leave. In our midst are a number of new Québecers from Ireland. Our duty, as a church and community is to open our hearts and homes to those that suffer. We have children and homeless adults in need right now—in need of a Christian hand at this time of dire need. If you can help, see me in the rectory, or if you are in need or know of someone. Go home this morning with benevolence in your heart."

Victor closed his eyes. He squeezed Aurelie's hand and his lips mouthed a silent prayer.

From that day onward, Father Michaud freely called on Victor and Aurelie as orphans passed through the congregation and the community of St. Andrews. A warm bed and hot meal were always provided with a bag full of clothing. Aurelie kept a box at the back of the church for patrons to leave used clothing for the less fortunate.

St. Andrews Harvest Fair, 1869

WITH A NEW sawmill at Carillon, and another at the Beech Ridge port on the Rideau, local employment was surging. Other mills were expanding to meet demand in Argenteuil County, including McQuat Brothers on Lachute Road, Meers Brothers of Prescott, and John Hamilton of Hawkesbury, just over the bridge.

Brown's Creek was a favourite meeting place, luring every age for a dip on humid summer days. Victor's family were masterful swimmers and were almost always at the swimming hole for Sunday picnics.

The water was murky but cool, and no one truly knew how deep it was. When Stanford's boy drowned there five years before, many men dove deep, trying to recover his body in futility. Weeks later his remains were found floating near the beach.

Before daybreak, the Paquette's wagon was loaded for this Friday trip to the Market Square, with extra sacks of corn, potatoes, and garden vegetables.

"Get cracking, kids," shouted Victor. "We need to get on the road early to set up next to the Girouxs and Cloutiers."

Aurelie had glass jars of apple butter and preserves, and Clémence carried on her lap a basket of prize brown speckled eggs and sweet butters. Rev. Mackie had agreed to allow the displays to be set up in the church. After the judging of her apple pies, she'd display them for sale on a pine board. They were always good sellers—cinnamon, maple, and deep dish.

"Look, Papa," said Edward. "Watch those leaves on the yard; I think they're dancing in the wind, the red ones and the oaks." He gathered a fistful of crimson maples for school.

The younger ones were packed together in the cargo box—Marie-Aurelie, Adelle, Edward, and Urgel—and the toddlers, Alexandre and Valerie, sat wiggly on Aurelie's knee. The rig lumbered toward town with their shepherd dog zigzagging behind.

"Come on boy," Victor Jr. egged. The kids hooted and snorted, holding on to each other over bumps as they dared to stand for a look.

"He's coming. Socks is still behind," one yelled. Undaunted, he lagged near the wagon all the way at the beckoning of the children.

A cricket tournament started in the park, followed by baseball, and a lacrosse challenge came from a team from Oka that bragged about their adept feet. That only made the locals laugh, and in making fun, it drove up their own competitive spirit.

The corral, beside the livery and stagecoach yard, was transformed into an impromptu circus ring, with magicians, acrobats, and a black bear that could spin a ball on its snout. Victor Jr. dragged his father to it.

"I know I could teach Socks to spin it."

"No way, Victor. Those bears have trained all their lives. They're on a tour across America and Québec. No spinning the ball or antics, or you'll break your leg."

Half an hour later, Marie's soprano voice raised above the crowd. "Papa! Papa! Victor's hurt."

I knew it!

The celebrations cranked up around the bonfire. Maynard's Brass Band from the United Church set up first, with the crowd calling jibes to players they knew, and Hawkesbury's Eilemann's Band stepped in next. By noon, people of East Hawkesbury, across the shared bridge, joined the festivities as if it were its own. On the boardwalk, an Irish ensemble warmed up a squash box with buttons and bellows. In the wings, square dancers waited in flouncy skirts, practicing allemandes and do-si-dos.

Joined end to end, tables overflowed with platters of smoke-house and honey hams, headcheese, salted pork, and pails of maple syrup and buckwheat honey.

Steamboat Wharf 1843, Port of Montréal in 1850, lithograph with beige tint stone and watercolour, Artist James Duncan (1806-1881) National Gallery Canada

Children lugged boxes and cages of rabbits, puppies and kittens, ruffled cockerels and squawking hens. In the shade of the band shell, a circle of tabletops showed off prized needlework, beaded moccasins, log cabin quilts and woven willow baskets.

Every head turned at the clatter and fanfare of the excursion steamboat docking from Montréal, with an overloaded temperance group with horns and tambourines, all dressed in conservative hats, skirts and cravats. A rush of children crowded the wharf to welcome them in jubilation.

The tourist boats, *Buckingham*, *Gatineau*, *Vermont* and the *Catherine*, graced the boardwalk, with Ottawa passengers waving as if they were going abroad for a year. Like Morse code at sea, the boat masters laid three short whistles on arrival, two as they turned right, and one toot to the left.

Displayed on the boardwalk in front of the Glasgow-Manchester Warehouse were Mr. Farrish's selected dry goods. Next door, William Catton's store showed its most expensive lace, satins and silks to a bevy of young ladies. Across the way, Thomas Fenner's bench had Lee and Barclay hand-made shoes, and Blanchard and Wales boasted the latest tools and hardware inventions to reach town.

A hand-cranked music box echoed from the toy shop, pulling the boys there first. Having touched everything they could reach on the shelves, Victor led Edward Jr., Urgel, and Alexandre down to explore the new fire engine house. Wee Deline was perched on Victor's shoulder. One by one, they were lifted aboard by the volunteer water brigade crew, to try out the steam whistle.

Echoes shook the fire building with each blast, bringing in more from the street. Toot! Toot! Toot! Finally, with a sustained whistle, a colossal ball of steam produced a hiss and an eruption of giggles, and a final exhausted sigh from the engine.

In the afternoon, the festivities spilled to the oarsmen at the boat races. Close to shore, log spinning gathered an audience, ready for the usual challenge from the Rideau lumbermen, J.R. Booth and Alanson Cooke. Defending St. Andrews were the Monderie brothers and Jean Charlebois.

Choice smooth pine tree trunks were hoisted to the water, as two jousters bragged of mastering it in bare feet, with balance poles. At the shot of the pistol by Captain Shepherd of the Ottawa Navigation Company, they were running. Like cat and mouse, they spun and re-spun, relying on the poles to navigate. Beyond the cheering of the crowds, Sean Mulligan fiddled the Irish Log Jammers Dance in tune with the frenzy.

"Go Jacques, Go!" yelled Simon Giroux. His sister Cecilia echoed out, "Take Alanson now, boy. You've got him backing up."

The log dance brought elation as the crowd mimicked and swayed, but agony for the loggers, engaging at times in arm wrestles—two men, face to face, with pride at stake. Some said it was the best festival ever, with villagers reunited from all of Deux-Montagnes and Argenteuil and beyond.

Establishments were festooned with decorations, flowers, and hanging boughs of purple, red and yellow Indian corn. Burlap and straw dolls with pumpkin heads stared back at curious kids. Blue ribbons were awarded for baking and condiments, and prized cattle posed for proud junior farmers. Children released strutting hens, and men of all unqualified occupations excelled at shearing sheep, sawing logs and tossing horseshoes.

Grown men became adolescents as they donned overalls to climb greasy poles and stretch for the cherished flag on top. Blacksmith rivals challenged vets like Le Diable, Palliser, and Tommy Bristol, and audiences cheered at their adeptness and anvil speed.

In the bandshell, musicians tuned up with a medley of plucking bows and trumpet trills. The ensemble was dressed fashionably, with men in vested tailored suits, starched shirts and wide cravats. Their hair was trimmed short, with jaw sideburns and waxed moustaches. The few women wore ribbon and taffeta skirts, puffed, ruffled blouses and silk bonnets, with parasols to shade porcelain complexions.

With nightfall, the teepee-style bonfire at the square was reduced to embers and coals, for layers of corn cob husks to steam on the red ash.

Aurelie and Clémence pulled the youngest Paquette children back from the sparks, and settled on picnic blankets under elm trees. Victor and Victor Jr. collected a feast of roasted corn to roll in sweet butter, and from the hamper, Aurelie brought out a jug of cider, cold ham and molasses bread, buttermilk rock cakes, and Clémence's shoo fly pies.

With their pipes, Victor and Edouard retreated in search of their hunting buddies to congregate at Lee's Tavern for a taste of Smith's fermented root beer.

When the band struck up *When You and I Were Young, Maggie*, the square flooded with partners, kicking heels, with flowing skirts, waltzes and twirls.

Forty-one

Marcel Joseph Giroux weds Elizabeth LeRoy, 1863 – Visit to Lamb's Post Office & discussion of Confederation – Fenian Raids (1866-1870) – Queen's Own Rifles March on Ridgeway – J.B. Cooke, Ensign with Toronto Militia – General Grant expels Fenians – Royal Assent given for new Dominion, 1867 – Sir John A. MacDonald becomes first Prime Minister – British North America Act – Celebrations across Eastern Townships, July 1, 1867 – John Abbott of St. Andrews proclaims to be future Prime Minister – 1881 Census of Argenteuil – Victor's Carpenter Bench.

Pre-Confederation in St. Andrews

AT SIXTEEN YEARS IN 1863, ELIZABETH, DAUGHTER OF Marcel Joseph Giroux and Elizabeth LeRoy, married Treffle Alfred Charlebois at Saint Hermas, beginning a family of twelve. Large families were common and although Elizabeth bore her first son Joseph in 1864, her own mother, Elizabeth LeRoy (Giroux), had two children after her daughter's marriage.

Treffle banged on the door of Lamb's Post Office first thing in the morning. With movement inside, he knocked harder for the supervisor.

"Monsieur Lamb. Are you open?" he called repeatedly.

His purpose was to see if a wire had arrived from Elizabeth's sister Rachel in Montréal. Mr. Lamb hadn't opened yet and was sweeping, but unlocked the door and stepped officially behind the high oak counter.

"Bonjours, Monsieur Lamb. How is your wife today?"

"Merci, Treffle; she is fine. And tell me about your Elizabeth and the young ones—are they well?"

"Her health is excellent, but her family keeps her on her toes. You understand. There's always a maiden aunt, or a deficient niece in need of nursing."

"Ah, Treffle, I know that well. My wife's mother will arrive from Montréal in a few days. She always reminds me that my Sarah could have done better." He grimaced, then forced a laugh. Treffle enjoyed the humour, but his thoughts sympathized.

"Is there news of this so-called 'Confederation'? The gatherings in Ottawa seem more serious by the day," Treffle said.

Lamb reached for a script of newspaper, written in French.

"George Cartier, from Montréal, claims to have been working for seven years to make us a whole country. And the Macdonald fellow has gathered a group larger than our Sunday congregation. Too many voices and they can't agree."

"It is certainly not what the King of France was hoping for two hundred years ago," Treffle replied.

The door opened and Basile Tessier poked his head in and tipped his hat. "Hello, Cecil. Is yesterday's news posted yet?"

"Before Lamb could speak, Treffle interjected, "It's tomorrow's news we're commiserating about—this talk of Confederation."

Mr. Lamb's broadsheet newspaper was now unfolded and his finger ran down the page leaving a black smudge from the fresh ink.

"Let's see. Since that meeting in Charlottetown a few years ago, the group has grown to somewhere over thirty, but only a half dozen represent Québec. There's Cartier, of course. Then Tupper, Tache, McGee, Langevin, Galt and Chapais. I'm afraid they'll get doused by the Ontario government."

Treffle said, "There are too many issues to resolve including Louis Riel stirring up Manitoba. Really, what's the difference between a native and a Métis?"

"Oui, oui, the fire of the Métis, they don't back down." Lamb interjected. "They are fiercely passionate about their distinction in society."

"Here we sit in our helpless town watching and waiting." Basile sneered.

Before leaving Main Street, Treffle Charlebois visited Blanchard's store to satisfy Elizabeth's tastes, as she was craving sweets again.

"Already one boy and one girl, maybe this will be another boy."

The family of Treffle Charlebois moved from St. Hermas before the Census of 1881 to the village of St. Andrews, next door to James McQuat. Treffle and Elizabeth lived in the village for the next forty years.

The Fenian Raids, 1866 -1870

ORGANIZED BY THE IRISH Brotherhood, the Fenian Raids divided not only Canadians, but even Irish Catholics against Irish Protestants. Those loyal to Québec's heritage gathered old militia uniforms and created new ones from old clothing, providing troops of mosaic colours. Nonetheless, they were known as soldiers 'wearing of the green'.

Intending to break from British rule, an Irish militia would invade from the American side of the Niagara. A plan to take Fort Erie failed, but disrupted the railway, cutting telegraph lines and burning ties.

The Proclamation of the Fenian Brotherhood rallied weak support in Upper Canada:

> We come among you as foes of British rule in Ireland. We have taken up the sword to strike down the oppressors' rod, to deliver Ireland from the tyrant, the despoiler, the robber. We have registered our oaths upon the altar of our country in the full view of heaven and sent out our vows to the throne of Him who inspired them. Then, looking about us for an enemy, we find him here, here in your midst, where he is most vulnerable and convenient to our strength . . . We have no issue with the people of these Provinces, and wish to have nothing but the most friendly relations. Our weapons are for the oppressors of Ireland. Our bows shall be directed only against the power of England; her privileges alone shall we invade, not yours.[47]

The Fenians offended the Loyalists and British, who prepared an offensive at Fort Niagara, including soldiers from Toronto and Ottawa.

---

[47] Fenians Proclamation was written by T.W. Sweeney, Major General of the Irish Militia. Sourced at History of the Queen's Own Rifles of Canada.

The Irish marched toward the Welland Canal, however the Queen's Own Rifles amassed troops from Toronto to intercept.

Loyal British troops were shipped from Toronto along Lake Ontario's shore to Port Dalhousie, where Colonel Booker's column joined with Colonel Peacock at Stevensville. Unfortunately, the whistle of the train coincided with the charge to assault, warning the Fenians of the approach.

The Queens Own Rifles and the 13th Battalion of Hamilton marched north to Ridgeway alongside the York Caledonia Rifles Company. Habitants tried to warn the British that the enemy had camped at Black Creek, however Peacock's troops turned toward Chippewa, leaving Booker's line vulnerable.

Booker divided his troops into five columns. Through the morning mist of July 2, young James Barron Cooke marched with Company No. 5 as a volunteer from the Toronto Militia. They stayed low as they advanced. The cornfields provided cover, but were less than full height and thickness and could expose the troops in the rising sun.

When they made it to Garrison Road, Company No. 5 came under a full assault by the Fenians. The Queen's Rifles pushed forward, causing the Fenians to retreat. Adrenaline rushed through the British and their first encounter with battle—the war had begun.

J.B. Cooke muttered a prayer, loaded his Enfeld musket and marched up from the rear guard of Booker's lines, as six other units followed the advancement pattern, many with Spencer repeating-rifles.

Gunfire took a heavy toll on both sides, and Ensign McEachern was hit in the stomach. Cooke looked at the soldier on his knees, now doubled and holding his gut. He shuddered, and listened to the man's sombre wish, "Dear God, take me from this evil place."

He sat upright, remembering teachings from his youth, and reached for the Ensign's hand.

"McEachern, this old body is damaged and in pain. Allow the angels to release you and let the Lord lead you. In Heaven there will be no war, no morning and no night. Take his hand and wait for me. May the Lord rest your soul."

In his dying words, the wounded soldier whispered, "Tell me that it is my death that wins the war. I go victorious to my grave; don't weep for me. It's been a good fight."

Life was whisked in a gust of wind to the Heavens, leaving J.B. holding a cold palm. McEachern was gone.

With gunfire closing in, his strength surged and he raised his rifle at the line of Fenians, barricaded behind fences. Ammunition was low when Booker called for the Cavalry formation and ordered relief columns to advance. The orders sent confusion to the troops, giving the advantage to the Fenians, and the Toronto militia were forced to scatter and regroup.

The Fenians turned their sights on Fort Erie, leaving seven dead soldiers of the Queen's Rifles: William Smith, Mark Defries, Malcolm McEachern, Anderson, Tempest, McKenzie and Mewburn. Twenty-one others were wounded.

Battle-scarred Fenians were ordered by Colonel John O'Neill to cross the Niagara River at Buffalo, from their American base. A first attempt of sabotage failed when the USS Michigan, a side-wheel gunboat, was deployed. Munitions and supply routes to the Fenians on the Canadian side were cut off. Conceding that victory would not happen, the Fenians released their prisoners and retreated across Lake Ontario to Buffalo.

The Québec circuit riders, similar to the Pony Express of the Wild West south of the border, returned news by riding day and night to St. Andrews and villages along the rivers.

Subsequent to the Fenian attack at Fort Erie, General Ulysses S. Grant and General George Meade agreed that the U.S. could not harbour or encourage the Fenian group and enacted laws against their formation.

Elizabeth Giroux's Visit to Doctor's Office

WALKING FROM their nearby home, Marcel Joseph Giroux and Elizabeth LeRoy arrived early at the Catholic Church in Rivière-Rouge to take a front seat at the christening of their granddaughter Victoria Charlebois.

It was the year before Confederation, but politics was far from their minds. Their attention centred on their new addition, Victoria Marie, born February 19, 1866, the third child of Treffle Alfred Charlebois and

Elizabeth Giroux. Rossana leaned to the cradle and kissed her dark, soft cheek. As she touched Victoria's curly, brown locks, the baby's brown eyes opened, sparkling in everyone's view.

"She's beautiful—like you, mother, but she cries too much."

Elizabeth fretted with sleepless nights and hastened to visit Dr. Ladouceur a week later.

"Good day, Elizabeth. How is your wee one?"

"It seems she's got the colic, I think that's what it's called."

Their small talk wasn't yet over when the doctor's door flew open and a wailing child was carried in by Victor Paquette.

"Doc, his arm's broke right through. I've set a few bones myself, but this is more than I can handle."

Victor suddenly understood he'd interrupted Elizabeth Giroux's consultation with the doctor. "I'm so sorry, Elizabeth, I didn't realize . . ."

"By all means, Victor, you go ahead. Victoria is asleep right now."

Victor carried Edward Jr. over to a table and laid him prone. "Now boy, calm down and lie still."

With young Edward quiet, Dr. Ladouceur turned to Elizabeth and gave her a bottle of peppermint. "When the baby's upset, give her a drop of this and she'll settle down. Come again next week to see how she's doing."

The moaning across the room intensified and Elizabeth Giroux delayed her exit, curious to hear what story they'd give about Edward this time.

Victor said, "My boys were taken with the thrill of log rolling at the fair, and set about with their own logs on the North River. But jousting with poles, things got out of hand. The logs got spinning so fast."

Victor's eyes squinted and his cheeks cracked with laughter as he spit out the story. "Their feet were faster than you'd believe. For a minute or two, they displayed a lot of talent, and I say that Edward here had the upper hand."

He looked up, hoping for a reaction.

"Incredulous," Docteur Lacouteur said, holding back enthusiasm.

Elizabeth remained spellbound, waiting for the moment of clarity.

"We heard a roar from underwater, then with a crash, the poles were launched into the sky with my boys after them. Of course, I dove in and dragged them out of the drink barely conscious. I knew the wounds were worse than I usually deal with, so I brought him straight away to you, doc."

Elizabeth shook her head at the door.

"I've always told Treffle those Paquette boys are accidents waiting. He'll hear the truth from me. Then when he goes to town, he'll hear Victor's tale again, but far larger from life.

Royal Assent to the Dominion of Canada, 1867

QUEEN VICTORIA gave royal assent on March 29, 1867, and when the Dominion of Canada was formed on July 1, Sir John A. MacDonald was proclaimed Prime Minister. A federal mandate was passed to build the Intercontinental Railway of Canada—with rail joining the Maritime Provinces to Québec and Montréal, and the western line of the Grand Trunk Railway connected from Rivière-du-Loop. It was agreed that the new government would extend the railway to Halifax as a priority.

Manitoba was established in 1870, and a year later, British Columbia joined confederation on the promise that rails would be built to the Pacific coast, extending it across the vast country from the Atlantic.

In 1867, the first Fathers of Confederation included Sir John A. McDonald, George Brown, Alexander Campbell, George-Étienne Cartier, James Cockburn, Sir Étienne-Paschal Taché, Jean-Charles Chapais, Alexander Galt, Hector-Louis Langevin, W. P. Howland, William McDougall, Thomas D'Arcy McGee, and Oliver Mowat, and another twenty-three signers for Nova Scotia, New Brunswick and P.E.I.[48]

The rich province of Ontario, under Premier John Sandfield MacDonald, claimed the old government at Ottawa, promising better trade and railroads, ships on the St. Lawrence, progress in schools, and strong communities. Québec's Premier was Pierre Joseph Chauveau.

---

[48] Others represented: Adams Archibald, N.S.; F. B. Carter, Nfld.; Edward Barron Chandler, N.B.; George Coles, P.E.I.; Robert Dickey, N.S.; Charles Fisher, N.B.; John Hamiltlon Gray, N.B. & P.E.I.; T.H. Haviland, P.E.I.; Wm. Henry, N.S.; John Johnson, N.B.; A.A. Macdonald, P.E.I.; Jonathan McCully, N.S.; Peter Mitchell, N.B.; Edward Palmer, P.E.I.; W.H. Pope, P.E.I.; John W. Ritchie, N.S.; Ambrose Shea, Nfld.; Wm. H. Steeves, N.B.; Samuel Tilley, N.B.; Charles Tupper, N.S.; Edward Whelan, P.E.I.; R.D. Wilmot, N.B.

Fathers of Confederation at the London Conference, 1866. Painting J.D. Kelly (1862-1958). Six delegates from Canada and four each from Nova Scotia and New Brunswick drafted a final version of the Québec plan. Library and Archives Canada.

The first British North America Act of 1867 became the core of Canada's constitution, enacted by the Parliaments of Canada and Britain. The plan would unite the Province of Canada with New Brunswick and Nova Scotia, and maintaining a British hierarchy in the legislature.

Eighty percent of Québec was of French heritage at Confederation. Of Canada's entire population of nearly three and half million, Québec represented a third, Ontario close to half, and New Brunswick and Nova Scotia the rest. Before Confederation, trade and barter commerce was conducted in bank notes or French coins.

Farmers still carted grain and livestock to town to exchange for boots and shoes, or services of the blacksmith or wheelwright, and along the way, it was common to encounter a travelling merchant from the city or an elixir wagon.

At Blanchard's, opposite Wales on Main Street, Victor mulled about Aurelie's grocery needs. He'd be frugal with cash, as a carpenter's wages were barely over $2 a day in the new Canadian currency. But he was still welcome to barter with grains, eggs, maple syrup or firewood, a preferred method in the Paquette household.

In a basket, he gathered musconado sugar, table butter and a gallon of molasses, then secured a hand wagon for a bushel of oats, a barrel of mackerel and one of grist wheat.

The once quiet streets now throbbed with morning songs of robins, drowned out by horns of tug boats, and the whirr of the mills and clopping of horses. Townsfolk marveled how fast it had changed, remembering one hotel and schoolhouse, a single hardware, and a mercantile and dry goods.

"So this is what they say is progress," Victor muttered. "Pshaw."

He scuffed his boot on the boardwalk, hiding the worn opening under his toe.

July 1, 1867 – A Day to Remember

PASSING THE PRINT shop at St. Andrews' Market Square, Treffle Charlebois stuck his head inside to see who had already joined the morning debate. On the street, a marching demonstration of cavalry was practicing for the celebration parade.

"Mornin' Edwin. I've come for your editorial on the Confederation." Treffle winked with amusement.

"I've a few things to say about Sidney Bellingham and John Abbott but they say I can't print it without getting my business burned to the ground," Edwin Harrison, the proprietor of the shop bemoaned.

"You don't say, Edwin. It must be true or you wouldn't have such a fire in your belly."

"You know the Abbott family has a big foothold on the town, don't you, Treffle?"

"Sure do," Treffle egged Harrison on, getting a rise from setting off the British rancor.

"Well, Abbott's running to represent us in the Legislature and he'll no doubt win. He's the same man that signed the Montréal Annexation Manifesto urging us Canadians to join up with the United States twenty years ago. Have folks all forgotten that?"

"It don't matter much, Edwin, there too many British and new confederationists. They'll hang you out to dry, and no doubt you would lose your business."

"Ain't that the truth? I heard his daughter say that someday soon Sir John Abbott[49] plans on being Prime Minister."

Stewardship of Paquette Carpenters, 1881

BY THE TIME of the 1881 Census, Clémence had been recently widowed and lived next to her oldest son, Victor. Her niece, Harriet Cloutier, lived at the Paquette farm as a boarder and companion, and the family remained close with Celina, Clémence's only daughter.

Victor's temples and his beard were now peppered with white. On the streets, his character inspired his friends and village folk, and his uncanny storytelling held his grandchildren wide-eyed.

"Urgel, I need more pine timber today from the saw mill at Rivière-Rouge. The front and side panels should be pine, but my stock has bowed."

He wiped his hands on his canvas apron, smeared with sawdust, and pointed to the pine logs by the wall.

"Take half a dozen of those and wait till they're cut."

In mid-afternoon, Urgel rolled back into the lane of his father's farm. Victor was over the carpentry bench, sanding and admiring it like a piece of art. On the barn floor, the maple frame of the cabinet stood bare like a skeleton. The smoothest, honey-coloured boards waited on the sawing bench for inspection, and planks with bird's eye knots were set aside.

---

[49] John Abbott of St. Andrews village in Argenteuil was the third Prime Minister of Canada between 1891 and 1892.

Victor took one end of the bow saw and Urgel the other, creating a rhythm and silent harmony.

Victor spoke quietly as they worked, tutoring Urgel on use of the ivory-tipped plough plane and ebony ultimatum brace that he reserved for the finest of cabinet work. Under their stewardship, the pine logs from their own back woods were given new value, set with fine tongue and groove.

After sanding, Victor rubbed and re-rubbed a homemade concoction of beeswax from the back orchard into the boards to produce a soft luster.

On the lower back of the cabinet, he etched the craftsman's signature, 'Paquet'.

Forty-two

Coronation of Queen Victoria, 1837 – Union Jack incorporates England, Scotland & Ireland, 1801 – Wave of popularity for new Queen – The Great Western Railway, 1838 – Royal Reception at Salt Hill, Buckinghamshire – Carriages & Coaches being replaced by trains – Queen Victoria Marries Prince Albert, 1840 – John Creffield II worked as Coach Builder on Peascod – Creffield Summoned to Court of Relief for Bankruptcy, 1847 – Sarah Webb & her daughters enter Berkshire Poorhouse – John Creffield III marries Clementina Webb, 1859 – John Creffield works as Hired Hansom – A Dickens Christmas Carol – Old Curiosity Shoppe.

The Victorian Era, London

NO ONE COULD ANTICIPATE THE EXCITEMENT THAT swept the country, when the eighteen year old princess royal was crowned Queen Victoria on June 20, 1837, ending the joint monarchy of Britain and Germany.

New visions and aspirations peaked for Londoners caught up in the Coronation, as royal insignias and flags topped government buildings, ships and even private houses. The Union Jack embodied three prior flags from an 1801 proclamation—England's red cross of St. George, Scotland's white saltire cross of St. Andrew, and St. Patrick's red saltire of Ireland.

Banners flowed everywhere, from lamp posts and shops, as Britons breathed in an enhanced level of patriotism.

The emergence of Wheatstone and Cooke's telegraph lines rattled with ferocity across the Atlantic, and newspaper criers scrambled to meet demand on the streets of the towns and villages.

The London Times and newspaper barons of the United Kingdom were hungry for information of the new royal couple. The public, craving any glimpses, were appeased by the photographic process by W.H. Fox Talbot that was quickly applied to newsprint techniques.

The first trains of the Great Western Railway steamed into service in 1838, with the expected ado. The grand opening excursions on May 31 were packed from Hayes to Maidenhead on the North Star, with festivities at both ends, and a cold luncheon for 300 people under a tent in Salt Hill.

Chalvey and Salt Hill were ramped up in anticipation of seeing the royal couple arrive at the rail depot.

"John, we need more cases of champagne from your brother's wine shop in Wakes Colne. Can you send someone this morning?" Ann asked.

"Better still, I'll send one of those new magnetic telegraphs and get a shipment ready. The railway has a tab there, and I can add another order. I've too much to do here but Thomas can bring it."

A number of men grappled with posts for an immense tent on the rugby field. Long tables were set with white linens, to magically convert the austere, worn grass patches to an ambiance of elegance fitting for the railway managers. White chairs were placed in rows, and a raised dais divided the head table.

Ann was dizzy with her thoughts, knowing it lagged behind schedule. "The ladies from St. Mary's and St. Laurence are not finished preparing sandwiches at the rectory. We should send a truck to wait for them."

John nodded. "The crowds are overflowing, and the railway directors have already filled the inns at Slough and Salt Hill. Perhaps Thomas and his driver could stay here."

"The Crown Inn too? Of course . . . they sell the train tickets."

Royal staffers arrived ahead of the royal couple to inspect the food and beverage. The luncheon was an elegant affair with the finest silver and flowers, never before seen to this extent in Chalvey. Within an hour and a half, the food was devoured and dignitaries returned to the coaches for the return to Paddington.

Months after the opening of the railway, the Emerald Stage Coach was the first business fatality, as they were replaced by trains.

John began to worry about his investment in coach building.

Queen Victoria & Prince Albert Ride to Slough, 1842

QUEEN VICTORIA married Prince Albert in 1840, the same year the awaited broad-gauge railway was completed from London to Slough station.

Enthusiasm was heightened for zealous entrepreneurs over the pioneering vision of the prolific engineer and inventor Brunel. Newly prosperous businessmen jostled to buy speculative railroad stock, creating a frenzy at the London Stock Exchange.

The station depot near Wellington Street, at the cross section of Slough and Salt Hill, was ready to provide open rail service for the Great Western Railway, north through Eton and Berkshire, and the west end of London at Paddington Station.

The Windsor link extended to the royal castle in 1842, celebrating Queen Victoria's maiden train excursion from Slough to Bishop's Bridge at Paddington.

At only six years, John Creffield III sat tall and motionless, hoisted to his father's shoulders to see the robust Queen.

The House of Hanover royal entourage rolled to a stop in front of him, in polished, black Rowley carriages, with a team of identical liver-chestnut black prancing horses, festooned in brass and the royal standard.

The band played *God Save the Queen*, as the royal couple stood beside their coach. An assembly of dignitaries fidgeted and waited, starched into cut-away morning coats, cravats and silk top hats. Finery and fashion was respected among the elite, and for many that pretended and aspired to gain status as upper class.

The telegraph master paced at the window, prepped to send a telegram to Windsor by Morse code, at the moment of the train's departure.

The Queen's royal locomotive was accented with luxurious red velvet, seats of soft tufted leather, hand-polished mahogany panels and gleaming brass rails.

Marriage of Queen Victoria and Prince Albert, 10 February, 1840. Engraving from 1886 book "True Stories of the Reign of Queen Victoria" by Cornelius Brown.

The jovial, little monarch allowed the dignitaries to be presented by name, patiently acknowledging each bow and curtsy.

Her satin empire gown bore the red and gold sash of Victoria's standard. It was beyond anything commoners could imagine, with puffed sleeves, lace trim, ribbon rosettes and stunning gems and jewels. Her wide brimmed hat held ostrich plumes, lace and beads, and her brown hair looped in braids over her ears.

Victoria's personal standard of red, blue and gold was flying in the royal tradition, wherever she was in residence or travelling. An official appointed photographer was on hand early with a tripod camera on the platform to catch a pose of the Royal Saloon before embarking.

John's twin sister, Anne, was firmly in her mother's grip as the pair squirmed and wiggled through the crowd for a better vantage. The cheering crowds pushed and waved as lightsome pick-pockets collected coins and watches.

With a labored hiss, the giant cast-iron arms of the steam engine began in a slow grinding rotation. Crowds leaned to watch the giant wheels move and clang as they inched on the track.

Then, flapping in its chimney, the whistle gave one final blast, enough to scare folks back from the tracks.

With arms in the air, John and Anne balanced on the rail, watching the royal train disappear, becoming a black dot swallowed into the hills.

Forever, they repeated the story of Queen Victoria's train at every family occasion, and no one tired of it.

Creffield Coach and Harness Closed

JOHN CREFFIELD II found supplemental work as a porter at the riverside train station in 1845 when the family moved to 66 Peascod Road. His carriage business was bearing financial distress since the railway took control of traffic in Slough.

Directors of the railroad had influence and power over the success of coachbuilders, even creating hardships with supplier contracts in obtaining factory parts and wheels.

John muttered alone at his accounting desk. "I should have invested in hotels or an inn. They are always full on weekends, but as for me—I can barely pay my workers."

Knowing that Ann would be waiting for him to come for dinner, he gathered his coat. He'd be noble. "Ann, I'm thinking we should consider taking in a boarder or two." He swallowed on his guilt. "Nothing to worry about, dearest, but my material costs have risen faster than my revenue."

Ann maintained an even, matter-of-fact tone.

"John, I was a young charwoman when you met me and I will do that again. In the meantime, we'll post a 'room for let' sign in the shop window."

"Thanks, Ann. I'll go out for some fresh air." She gathered his woolen cap for him, knowing it was his favourite.

Standing on a hill, John viewed the majestic Windsor Castle and imagined the comings and goings of the royals. He loved the sounds and smells of the trains and the bustle of passengers, remembering that day when Queen Victoria came to Slough.

"My father before me built coaches. It's a family business that I hoped I could pass to my own son. It seems I have lost my vision and the world is passing me by."

In May 1847, John Creffield II, was summoned to the Court of Relief for Insolvent Debtors in Aylesbury. Declaring the claim of his Assistant, who had not been paid according to the apprenticeship agreement, Creffield Coach & Harness formerly of Slough, doing business as a coach painter, smithy, wheelwright and harness maker was closed permanently.

Widow Sarah Webb & Daughters, Berkshire Poorhouse

THIRTY MILES from Chalvey Slough, in Berkshire, the small Webb family had fallen on misfortune with the loss of the young father, John. At twenty years in 1840, Sarah Elizabeth began a brief widow's life, and her tiny daughters took refuge in a children's orphanage at Hatcher Lane— Clementina at five years, and Louisa two.

Before falling into ill health herself, Sarah worked as a house matron at the orphanage to stay in the lives of the two girls. It was also home to a dozen more children and another matron, Harriet Squelch. Eventually, Sarah died in a poorhouse in London.

When Clementina Eliza Webb was fifteen, she gratefully accepted a servant's position with the Seymour family at 12 Terrace Street in Berks, Wargrave. She was satisfied at such an age to advance to the station of servant rather than orphan.

On a late evening, Clementina was awakened by a ruckus in the Seymour house, and downstairs found Mr. Seymour's sons in the kitchen, behaving rowdily for such an hour. The men all worked in the family business as harness makers.

Clementina gathered the nerve to hush them, before discovering they'd brought friends from the shop, John Creffield III, Robert Elsworth and William Foster. The roughhousing stopped at her presence, and John was the first to remove his hat. The workers' eyes shifted back and forth, then to Clementina as John spoke.

"I'm pleased at your acquaintance." His head bowed halfway as she stayed in his sight. "I'm John Creffield. We're sorry for the disturbance."

Her lips formed to dispense a sharp piece of her mind, but she stopped. Sizing up the young man, she admired his tall, lean build and curly, light brown hair. She felt he was afraid now to look *her* in the eye.

"Thank you, John Creffield. The children have been put to bed. Please take your noise outside."

Clementina's eyes followed John as the door closed to the lane.

Creffields Move to New Windsor, 1859

JOHN CREFFIELD III married Clementina Eliza Webb of Winkfield, Berkshire in 1859, the daughter of John Webb, a sawyer from Wargrave, and Sarah Elizabeth Griffin.

In the year of their marriage, they rented a flat on Bexley Street, then moved to 2 Carter Street, New Windsor in the shadows of Windsor Castle. When employment with local coach builders waned, John worked as a railway porter and Hansom cab driver, while dabbling in his brother's wine merchant business on the side.

Clementina worked as a laundress and charwoman as they raised seven children in the following eleven years—Annie, Percy, Clementina, Frederick, Louise, Georgina, and Eliza.

The Metropolitan underground locomotives started service to London at Bishop's Road in Paddington in 1863. John's position as a hired Hansom driver was in demand as the mode was the choice of gentlemen, passing wooden wagons on the streets as their nags carried workers to the factories and wares to market. Yet for distances in the city, every working class household depended on bicycles.

With the evolution to trains, John took night work as a porter and redcap at the rail depots between Slough and Windsor, with days free to start a vintage wine shop near their home. He regretted not having the foresight to compete with omnibus stagecoaches and by 1861, trolleys on rails provided public transportation. Although only affordable by upper and middle class, it enabled a commutable population in the suburbs.

By 1871, they had moved to Charles Court, providing John work in nearby farms. That Census recorded the family name again as 'Criffield', with only four living children. Louisa, Georgina, and Eliza Louise had died within months of each other during the London cholera outbreak, and losing three children in as many years was heartbreaking for Clementina.

A Dickens Christmas in Victorian London

SOCIETY'S APPETITE for culture was insatiable for middle and upper class Londoners, led by literary portrayals of Victorian England by Charles Dickens in the veritable *Oliver Twist*, *Pickwick Papers*, and *A Christmas Carol*.

Dickens reverberated an amusement that woke up British society in characterizations of the Old Curiosity Shoppe on Portsmouth Street near Lincoln's Inn Field. Family values were rekindled and communities rallied to shame the intolerable conditions that they'd always been aware of in the poorhouses and children's workhouses.

At Christmas, Dickens-like stories played out in real life on the streets, and seasons' greetings were on the lips of even the poorest.

Charities provided more for the underprivileged and coal rations increased. Dickens inspired the exchange of Christmas cards and a one penny stamp on yuletide mail. Streets bustled with shoppers, and passengers crowded terminals and coaches with armloads of parcels.

Dashing between street traffic, John leapt the street puddles toward Clementina who waited at the carriage depot with Annie, Percy, Clementina, and Frederick. The two youngest stretched on their toes, watching through the sleet, but squealed and waved as John appeared.

The Old Curiosity Shop, 1897, from 'Home School of American Literature', author Birdsall, William (1854-1909) and ed. Jones, Rufus (1863). Library of Congress.

Clementina embraced her husband with a sigh. "John, I have one more laundry parcel to deliver in Berkshire. Can we do it now, then to Paddington for the tube?"

"Don't worry, Clemmie; I'll flag a bike courier."

With a whistle and a wave, a bicycle came to his aid.

"Ensure this is delivered in Ashgrove straight away. If I have your assurances and your personal address, I could be convinced to provide a generous gratuity."

"Indeed, sir." In an instant, he was off.

The Creffield children had taken the Paddington train to London, but were now in fits and giggles for the new adventure on the underground Metropolitan and a first ride on the double decker trolley that ran the rails in Central London.

Their mother had teased them daily for weeks, building up to today's visit to the Old Curiosity Shoppe. At last the excitement was upon them, to be dazzled with the glitter and magic of Christmas toys.

Out of the Metro, they ignored the disorderly laughter at the mug houses and pubs, but slowed at the fabled Magpie & Stump of Dicken's fame.

John motioned to circle him. "I hope you'll remember this place; I've known it since a boy—in a book I read over and over, *Pickwick Papers*. In the year our gracious Queen was crowned, Mr. Dickens wrote it in nineteen parts, as his first novel."

Near the Old Bailey, the imposing wrought iron gates of Victorian barristers' houses segregated their privileged lives. Farther along were limestone and redbrick gabled townhouses, separated by gothic churches.

Streets were lively with carriages, led by sleek, high-stepping horses bedecked in brass bells and holly wreaths. The clomping of hooves created its own beat, drowning out strolling carolers until they passed within a few feet. As if on cue, the rain changed to fluffy snowflakes, and Clementina mouthed the words to the soprano choir voices trilling, '*Here We Go a Wassailing*'.

Frederick's tongue reached for a wet flake on his cheek and his hands felt for more to gather on his hat and jacket, hoping for a handful to throw. At his feet, the snow was melting on impact at the cobblestone, washing into the day's puddles.

Clementina grasped his shoulders. "Frederick, I'll not tell you again to stay out of the puddles. Keep your shoes dry."

Their faces pressed to the first shop window, wide-eyed at the painted wooden rocking horses, tin-plate model trains and musical pop-up minstrels. Percy and Annie drew with fingertips on the frosted glass, and others peered beyond to the lure of shadow puppets, teddy bears and porcelain dolls. They crowded inside to the imagined treasures of cast-iron trucks and ornate dollhouses. Great shelves at the back heaved with rare literary books.

At last, they reached the Curiosity Shoppe. The tallest china cabinets brimmed with antique china, alabaster music boxes, and pearl ivory dresser sets. In the children's fantasies, the magical nutcrackers and sugar plum fairies marched and danced, fully alive in this wonderland. Each was given a silver three-pence and a copper half penny to spend, creating a conundrum of choice.

Anne watched the clerk wrap a stand-up paper doll of the Queen, and reached for a lemon twist to carry outside the package. Percy was in line with a rolling gyroscope, and Frederick was still in a different world at the back, working a flat wooden sailor with legs and arms and a floating button on a string. Young Clementina stood with her mother, with wooden clackers and a sarsaparilla stick.

By afternoon, dark nimbus clouds were spreading. In the gusting winds, a unicycle moved from post to post, lighting the gas streetlamps with a stick. Undaunted, the carolers huddled closer, protected by sweeping tweed coats and fur muffs, and gentlemen wrapped plaid scarves under their top hats.

The family walked past red pauper kettles of coins organized by William Booth of the Christian Mission in East London, and Frederick gulped a momentary pang of regret for buying the peppermint stick. In his pocket, he found a thin half-farthing for the pot to relieve the guilt.

John and Clementina scurried against the wind toward the station, for the 4:50 to Paddington, then Chalvey station. The lights of London faded as the scant flicker of farmhouses and village life swirled past the train.

Forty-three

Creffield Christmas at Chalvey Grove - Parish of Hemel Hempstead & St. Albans, Hertfordshire – Henry Turner's family Christmas ride from Frogmore to St. Lawrence Church – Henry Turner weds Jane Turner, 1859 – Paper Mills Major Employer – Industrial Revolution led to Rise in Paper Linen Industry – Corn Law repealed in 1846 improves Wages – Henry Cole & Prince Albert Organize Great Exhibition of European Works, 1851 – Many Literary Guests invited to Crystal Palace – Education Act of 1870 requires all children to attend school.

Christmas Eve at Chalvey Grove, Buckinghamshire

IN BERKSHIRE, JOHN LEFT CLEMENTINA AND THE CHILDREN outside the mercantile to stop in at his wine shoppe. He chose a Christmas brandy from his stock to package in parchment, and a crimson ribbon with a twig of holly for his father and new step-mother, Elizabeth. From the wine racks, he picked a sparkling German for his own dinner.

As his clerk rolled the wine in brown paper, John reached into his breast pocket for the man's bonus and greeting card.

"Merry Christmas, Bennett. Go ahead and close up at five o'clock and get home to your family," John said.

Back at Chalvey Grove, he greeted the carriage of his father, John II, with Elizabeth and their four toddlers—Isabella, John, Ada and Helen. Ann Edwards[50] had passed away eight years before. John Sr.'s brother, Henry, a bachelor, was at the door momentarily, and struggled to hold all the adoring tots in his lap at once.

Sleigh bells blew in the wind gusts as Frederick's Aunt Caroline and her beau, William Wegg, burst through the door, ducking the mounted holly swags.

In a key pitch too high, she started up *We Wish You a Merry Christmas*, joined by others without hesitation, and soon building to laughter and embraces. To everyone's applause, she dragged William to the mistletoe in the foyer.

Fragrances of the impending feast wafted through the house, with essences of salmon slivers and lemon tartar sauce, turkey with apple, leek and sausage stuffing, and whole roasted chestnuts. Vegetable bowls were topped with roasted potatoes and caramelized onions, parsnips and celery, and butter turnip with nutmeg. Crystal dishes brimmed with homemade cranberry sauce and spiced pear chutney.

Young Percy was unaware his tongue was swiping his lips from his full concentration on constructing table crackers of coloured paper, wool and ribbon. A spruce was garnished with bead strings, hand-sewn snowflakes and peppermint canes shaped like shepherd hooks. The children added gingerbread men, garlands of dried juniper and cranberry, tin designs and baubles, and Clementina surprised them with a box of brilliant German hand-blown balls.

"Ah, mother, the tree looks pretty!" Annie chirped. "I'll get the candles for Louisa, Georgina and Eliza—we can't forget our sisters."

Clementina set her bowl on the table, and Annie saw a tear in her eye. "I'm sorry, mother, I didn't mean to make you sad. We can shine a light so they can see us from Heaven."

The main table seated all the adults including boarders John Muggins and Henry Wiggins, and the children's table was hosted by Clementina Jr., Percy and Annie, and included Frederick, Isabella and young John.

---

[50] Ann Edwards died 1861 at Windsor, Berks. Five years later John II married Elizabeth Adamthwaitee-Newbold raising four more children between 1865 and 1877.

Christmas Tree Family, Victorian Christmas, 1858;
Etching by J. A. Pasquier, from Illustrated London News

Frederick begrudged not sitting beside his father, and before the meal, he stood beside him as hushed voices listened to the legend of Prince Albert's gift to Queen Victoria in 1841, of the first Christmas tree entirely decorated in colours of the Queen's standard.

"But the true gifts were brought to symbolize the birth of Jesus," John II emphasized.

As the room folded in around him, Frederick sought to escape the din of impertinent adult questions and mistletoe kisses; but when grandfather invited the children to join a circle around his over-stuffed arm chair, his interest in the sack of wrapped parcels was renewed.

When it was Frederick's turn to sit on grandfather's lap, he bristled up against the old gentleman's beard.

Fingering the creases of the green tissue wrapping, Frederick clutched it close to his heart. He was certain it was a book and let his fantasies rule until it was his turn to tear the wrapping.

"Stuart Little! Oh thank you, I've wanted this for so long." As the carriages and sleighs departed, he needed no coaxing for bed.

"First, I'll put out my old wool sock. I borrows the bottom stair post."

The Turners of Hemel Hempstead, Hertfordshire

TWENTY MILES northwest of London, the parish of Hemel Hempstead nestled itself in the chalk hills of the River Gade, a scant seven miles west of St. Albans.

The Gade converged with the River Bulbourne at Two Waters, on the south side of Hemel by the Grand Canal that links the Thames. Sprinkled beside scenic rivers and railways were charming hamlets, lush farmlands and grazing sheep pastures.

The village, long incorporated by the grace of Henry VIII to honour a bailiff who licensed the people of Hemel, boasted of High Street markets and village fairs, some grander than many in London. On Wednesdays and Saturdays, farmers, locals and Londoners intermingled in shops, arriving by bicycle, wagons, carriages and locomotives.

Ample two and three-story stone cottages with thatched roofs and wide dormers opened from the planked walkway, many in rows of six or eight that surrounded a communal square, sharing pumped water.

Hemel's skyline was spiked with tall brick chimneys, both stout and skinny, scattered steeples, and an assembly of paper mills. From the Church spires, the day's chimes echoed the message of Christmas. The bell ringers of St. Mary's Church pulled ropes of heavy cast bell weights, causing gongs to peal eight timed tones far from the reaches of High Street.

At the house of Henry Turner, the children waited to be loaded into a hired polished Whitlock Canterbury coach, with festive boughs and ribbons attached in the price of the livery rental.

A longtime neighbor, Thomas Rolphe, was bolstered up from the carriage step to the front seat. The five children bundled into double seats, then Henry hoisted his wife to the front bench and joined her. Holding the team's reins on the ground, the driver at last climbed to a single, partially suspended seat, towering over the snorting and pawing horses.

The three mile ride took half an hour, across the ancient, stone bridge, passing Bricketwood and Providence Retreat near the railway on Kindersley Way, and on toward the castle turrets of Abbotts Langley Church.

On special occasions, the Turner family made this trip southeast from Frogmore to the vine covered St. Lawrence Church where Henry's parents worshipped and were included in Tithing Rolls. Abbotts Langley was a deeply religious community for both Catholics and Protestants, as the birthplace of Nicholas Breakspear, Pope Adrian IV.

Henry Turner, born in 1840 at St. Albans, Hertfordshire, was married in Buckinghamshire in 1859. Henry and Jane first resided at Hemel Hempstead near their mutual employment at Paper Mill Mead, before settling in Buckinghamshire. Jane advanced to the position of Envelope Borderer at the mill, and Henry worked as a Card Finisher.

Since 1840, the Industrial Revolution required mass production from England's mills of woodcuts, engravings and personal watermarked parchments.

Publishing houses competed to deliver sewn book bindings, and society's etiquette now expected calling cards, hostess and tea cards, invitations, and formal announcements.

The Turner flat was near the mill, and daily before the closing whistle blew, Alice Jane left home on her bike toward the worker's queue to meet her mother. A horse-drawn lorry streamed past the workers, with bundled deliveries on the truck's flat back.

Jalopy horns and street commotion seemed excessive at the end of the day to young Alice Jane, who preferred the peace of her tiny village.

"I love my village," she said to herself, "but why can't things be quiet and peaceful every day, like Sundays?"

Alice's mother stopped at her neighbor's house to collect her smallest child. This was Friday, when workers received their pay envelopes, and she knew that Henry would also bring home a can of kippers for a treat.

She heated the fry pan with bacon grease, and started sliced potatoes and onions. When they became crisp, she added a tin of canned corned beef into the hash and a canned vegetable. After devouring their meal in silence, they came alive in conversation of the day's events.

The Great Exhibition, Crystal Palace, London, 1860

THE CORN LAWS of the early 1800s brought challenges of high tariffs to manufacturers, including the Hempstead paper mills of John Dickinson and the Fourdrindier Brothers. In 1846, the law was repealed, enforcing limited liability and improving wages for labourers in Hertfordshire.

Rumours of the Great Exhibition of European Works of Industry were spreading by 1851, with London's entrepreneurs and social community preoccupied in anticipation.

Organized by Henry Cole and Prince Albert, it would bring fourteen thousand world exhibitors to London, displaying technology, silver designs, Doulton Lambeth stoneware, architecture and manufacturing. In Hertfordshire, as in every town, the exhibition was on everyone's lips, especially factory owners and managers.

On the day it was announced, Henry Turner rushed home in the evening to share the news he'd heard. At dinner, the children watched him eat quickly, so that he could tell them something big was coming.

Finally, he blurted it. "They say the great Crystal Palace will have a million square feet right at Hyde Park for the Exhibition." The young faces were blank.

"It sounds quite big, father," Alice said. "Is that a lot?"

"Big indeed. Imagine a glass building that goes from our house to the mill. That's how long it is—a third of a mile."

Henry went on with news from the factory. "Every imaginable invention will be there. I want us all to go. Jacquard looms will demonstrate punch cards to set patterns—we'll see that for certain."

Front of the Crystal Palace, London that housed the Great Exhibition of 1851.
Originally from Tallis' History and Criticism of the Crystal Palace. 1852, uh.edu ⓢ

"Queen Victoria will be there on the first of May," Jane said, "and many important people, even Dicken himself, Lewis Carroll and Alfred Lord Tennyson. Fees are too dear at first for our family, but maybe better by the end in October will be better. The opening will unveil a spectacular musical organ to pipe in the Queen's procession. Can you believe it all?"

The economic boom created a renewed demand for workers, ultimately legislating child labour in factories and coal mines, and a designated work week. The Education Act of 1870 required all children under thirteen to attend at parish schools in a public school system overseen by an elected Board, for a level of mass education never before seen in English society.

The Turner family enrolled Agnes, Arthur, Alice Jane, Eliza, and Lilian, envisioning a better future for them. Alice Jane thrived in school, but by the age of twelve also apprenticed at dressmaking to help with expenses at home. By fifteen, she took High Street employment as a servant in the Mole and Jones household.

Privately, Alice Jane set her sights on the greater opportunities that were luring her generation to London.

Forty-four

Folklore of legendary Swamp Creature – Joseph Charlebois Caught in a Trick – Steamboats Competition for Grand Trunk Railway – Ships built on North River at Hawkesbury, 1870 – Charlebois Sisters shop in Montréal – Urgel Paquette seeks Victoria's favor – Urgel Paquette marries Victoria Charlebois, 1887 – Victor Paquette's Wilderness Prowess – Cooke Brothers Lumber Pilots on Rideau for J.R. Booth – Izaak Walton Hires Victor as Wilderness Guide – Victor Claims to be a Half-breed – Victor Paquette dies by his Canoe, 1906 – Urgel Buys new Home Sunshine Range from Chicago – Coal mines of Québec – Invention of the Bell telephone, 1870 – Ice Jam on St. Andrews Bridge – Urgel Saves the Beaver Lodge.

Legendary Bisso, Tales of the Rivière-Rouge

FOLKLORE TALES PROLIFERATED IN RIVIÈRE-ROUGE OF a mysterious man called Bisso, who had ridden years before on the country roads along the river. Losing control of his horse drawn carriage, he was swept over the bank and plunged into the deep swirling rapids.

Years later, hunters recounted the vision of a husky, aquatic creature meandering on the banks. Avoiding humans, he sought refuge in the woods, hunting voraciously, then slipping into the river's dark whitewater.

With the mischief allowed to an older brother, young Joseph Charlebois never missed a chance to scare his sisters, and couldn't pass this opportunity as they hiked the red silted, sandy path.

As the girls skipped rocks to the river, Joseph made his move, creeping in the rustling bushes, creating a commotion fitting to the son of Bisso. Victoria, Rossana and Blais dropped the stones and fled to the road.

Joseph chased them to taunt more. "I see his eye, Victoria. He's watching you."

"I'm scared, Joseph!" Victoria cried, then froze.

"Look—there's Bisso," she screamed. Across the water, floating debris swirled in the current, with the tip of a stump floating and bobbing. Eyes of an ogre peered over the log, fixed on the children.

"Run, everyone, run!" Joseph took off in the lead, never to tease of the creature again. In time the girls mocked back about the mirage of the driftwood, but the legend of Bisso remained to be told to generations.

Charlebois Sisters, River Rouge to Montréal, c. 1885

VICTORIA WRAPPED a package in the St. Andrews millinery shop and stepped out to the wooden walkway to take a few moments in the morning sun. She had become a refined, young lady, long grown from when young Urgel Paquette had teased her, pulling her braids.

Hats were in vogue, and the shop bustled on the weekends with tourist boats from Ottawa and Montréal. Steamboats stopped at St. Andrews and Carillon for passengers to board trains to Grenville, then another steamboat on the Ottawa River.

Victoria listened as the Buckingham excursion steamer echoed its horn, drawing a gathering of townsfolk to North River wharf. Within minutes, it would deliver affluent clientele to the street and to the hat store.

The river steamers displayed an opulence envied by many a villager, offering garish saloons, comfortable state rooms, and wide decks for fashion promenades. A fare of three dollars included exotic dining with chandeliers and fine china, proper English high tea, poetry readings, cards, and a temperance band and moonlight orchestra. Steerage passengers waited to eat later in less formal dining rooms, at a dollar fifty fare.

Well-to-do merchants and managers preferred first-class river travel when possible for business, but more often for amusement and to be seen, flaunting a perception of wealth and stiff etiquette.

Most ships were built at the mouth of the North River and the Mears shipbuilders at Hawkesbury. Each boat flew the flag of the Royal Union until 1870, then raised the Union Jack, with conflicting emotions of pride or resentment.

At the dock, Captain Augustin Delorme's crew unloaded crates for stockrooms of the street's merchants. The Captain, who built and ran his own boats, conveyed them from Lachine, with products from snuff-boxes and flint-lock muskets to grandfather clocks. His four-ton capacity bateaux were propelled by sails and brawny-armed oarsmen.

Steamboats remained relevant with their slow and pleasurable pace, but were perceptively nudged by competition from the Grand Trunk Railway, between Carillon and Bytown. Nearing the late 1800s, rail was successfully depressing the domestic passenger steamboat industry.

The Charlebois sisters had saved their wages to take the steamer to Montréal for a Christmas shopping trip. Their mother, Elizabeth, cautioned them not to come home poor.

"Oh, mother. You know I'm frugal with my money. I am setting aside for the day when I need a lace and satin wedding dress," Victoria said.

Urgel Paquette Courts Victoria Charlebois, 1887

HIS LONG-BOX wagon rambled along the dirt ruts of the Rivière-Rouge Road, past a row of fifteen clapboard houses, with the clatter echoing from the adjacent brickyards near the sawmill. It was still a distance to the canal, and lugging three large pine logs and a maple, the wagon heaved and creaked with the weight.

Urgel Paquette slapped the reins to encourage the horses uphill.

"Come on boys!"

A girl in Rivière-Rouge had caught his fancy and he prided himself on securing a first date. Urgel daydreamed of the look of Victoria—her dark brown eyes, and her hair in braids as a crown of shiny brown curls.

Her demeanor might be abrupt, but it will only be a challenge.

Mr. Hooker helped Urgel unload the unprocessed logs from the wagon, and set the saw for quarter-sawn lumber. The fragrance of fresh-cut pine and pungent cedar engulfed the mill house, as the turbine churned through a log, spitting out smooth, golden boards.

Urgel watched the sawblade whir, and minutes later loaded the planks back into the wagon, minus a few selected by the miller as payment for his services. A half-hour down the road, he pulled to the edge as the hay wagon of Treffle Charlebois approached. Urgel was already moving slowly to avoid rocks and fallen branches, as a broken wheel would mean a camp out until help came.

The two exchanged opinions on the Farmers' Almanac crop. As Treffle gave his weather predication, Urgel nodded but his eyes had moved to Victoria's.

He tipped his hat. "G'day Ma'am. You must be a fine help to your father, to be on the Rouge Road today."

Treffle huffed and answered for her. "I don't mind the company; and she's a good help with the younger children."

Victoria nudged his arm. "Pa, couldn't you give me a compliment?"

Treffle saw the point and fumbled for words she'd like.

"She's a mighty fine girl, Urgel. Victoria's got spunk, and of all my girls, she has the prettiest brown eyes—like her ma."

Urgel looked at the ground. "Well, I don't often see her eyes, but I'll take your word at it."

The men eyed each other's loads, and Urgel traded a broad width maple plank ideal for a table, for a sack of wheat, a spare wheel hub, and a spool of barbed wire.

He looked back at Victoria as Treffel's rig disappeared behind.

If Monsieur Charlebois invited me to visit Victoria, I would have given him the better maple plank. Next time.

When Urgel Paquette arrived at the Charlebois door to court Victoria, he carried flowers and sweets, and wore his Sunday suit as his sister suggested. Victoria was swept away, but early on suggested he take her on a steamboat excursion.

"My goodness, you have a big family," he remarked, trying to recount names and numbers of siblings.

"It's a blessing, it really is, to be close and unified. Ma has a new babe every year or two and we all help her. Joseph and Rossana have left to make their own homes. But it's hilarious at Christmas, when we're filled to the rafters, with all the boys sleeping in the barn."

Urgel was instantly at ease by her offhanded nature.

"Well, Mademoiselle Charlebois, shall we go to Lee's Inn for a fine dinner?"

His hand supported her back as she stepped into the carriage, and she felt a thrill to the toes. When he was up beside her, she stole a glance at his Paquette brown eyes.

When Urgel and Victoria married in 1887 in St. Andrews, some of his older siblings already had families in the area. At twenty-two, he was a proven hunter and oarsman of the North River, continuing the passion from his heritage.

Family support mattered and Urgel remained close to them, especially his sister, Sarah Azilda, ten years his junior. Victoria maintained a similar bond with her sisters, Assenath and Regina, although ten and twenty years younger.

Victor Paquette's Last Voyage 1906

FAMILY LIVED no more than a holler from the kitchen, as the Paquette farm was divided between Victor's sons. Both were settled on the banks of the North River, a short skip for any of them for duck hunting or fishing.

Over hectic a town life, Victor would always choose refuge on a log at a campfire, on a stump outside his cabin with shavings of carved sticks or tobacco residue at his feet.

In his children's eyes, his harmonica was magic, and they stayed glued to his deliberate contortions as his cheeks drew and puffed, before he started up his stories and ballads. The eager young listeners were spellbound at his feet.

The Paquette, Giroux and Charlebois hunting grounds extended to the bushes of Deux-Montagnes, with black bears and moose. Aurelia relented to allow a mounted buck, over the hearth, as proof of Victor's prowess.

Victor's raft waited for an easterly breeze, then hoisted the anchor as the last four hired men boarded. Up ahead, he knew the distant silhouette to be Reuben Cooke, a lumber pilot of the Old Rideau. Their tent was set up at the head of the Jones River with a vista over the Grand. Below, at the basin of the Ottawa River, were tugs, freighters, logging drives and excursion steam boats, and a few canoes and skiffs that dared to be there.

Piloted river boats, operated by the company of J. R. Booth, a lumber merchant from Ottawa, directed a log jam up river below the cliff.

Victor received a request from his friend, Izaak Walton, to guide a wilderness vacation, with the event documented.

Izaak Walton had no more ardent devotee than Mr. Melanchthon Seymour, of Montréal. A familiar scene on the North River was the old gentleman seated in a cushioned chair under an ample sunshade, in the stern of the Harrington skiff; and always Victor was the guide and oarsman for a day's fishing. Their return at sundown often meant a fish dinner for village dames, for Mr. Seymour was very generous with his trophies.

It was Victor who kept these memories from fading, for our party was never complete without him. Victor was half Indian by descent, and altogether Indian by instinct. He loved the haunts of nature, and he knew its secrets—the eddies where the lusty bass and pickerel could be caught, and the coves where the wild ducks could best be decoyed. To have Victor with us meant a holiday to be remembered, for he was an expert in camp craft. What couches he could prepare with evergreen boughs, where we could rest, inhaling the balm of cedar and fir tree! What savoury bouillon he made for hungry hunters!

One summer day, in later years, the old man was missed, sought for, and found lying beside his canoe on the bank of the North River; but his spirit had fled. With lamentations he was carried to his grave by his seven sons, but his burial casket should have been his canoe for voyaging to the Happy Hunting Ground of the spirit world. Dear old Victor! Requiescat in Pace.[51]

---

[51] Memories of Old St. Andrews and Historical Sketches of the Seigniory of Argenteuil by B.N. Wales, Watchman Press, Lachute, Québec. P. 119-120. (1934).

It was usual to be gone for day to the bush or in the canoe, and when possible, he took a son, most often Urgel, who was ten years behind the oldest, Victor Jr.

Urgel yearned to adopt his father's wilderness instincts. Victor claimed his skills were inherited, proudly insisting he was half-breed, with his mother from the Oka tribe and claiming Métis ancestors.

His jovial nature was transparent through heavy whiskers and a rugged physique. In smoky hunting skins and hand-sewn deerskin moccasins, he took long strides with his bow and arrow across his back. With a hunting flint in his sash, he pulled back his wool toque high over his brow. At the water, he launched and paddled into the current, whistling a rousing *Alouette* to stir his imagination of returning home.

The fabled hunter, Victor, died in 1906 alone beside his canoe. On a still night, under the moon and stars, a whisper drifted through the trees, and many said it was Victor's voice in song. His seven sons carried him to his grave, with his funeral was witnessed by his twenty-two grandchildren. Grief-stricken, Aurelie passed away a few years later.

Victor's legendary wilderness stories were passed on as inspirations to descendant generations, fortifying his memory as a hero to his family and those he touched.

St. Andrews Home Life and the New Sunshine Range

THE PEGGED carpenter's bench in the barn was brushed clean of sawdust and shavings, with wooden screw vises anchored by Urgel at one end, and a pole-turning lathe at the other. An overhead shelf lined his planes and spoke shavers that he organized meticulously. A lower board held loose boxes of iron and wooden pegs, nails, cotter pins, and spikes.

Two bow saws hung near the door, one from the departed Victor Paquette, and the other a pride from the local auction. Urgel always valued the carpentry tradition of the family, with the same tools that had passed from grandfather to father to son, for two hundred years.

Atelier du Menuisier (Carpenter's Workshop),
Marie-François Firmin-Girard (1838-1921) France

He inhaled the aroma of the pine and the touch of the planed oak bleeding its character. In the barn rafter, his father's old canoe preserved his memories with old Victor in the woods.

Papa, there will be many generations of master carpenters just like you.

Urgel brushed his hands on a leather apron with pockets of tools, then set his stance over the sawhorse.

Victoria accepted that her hands would be weathered forever from farm labour and daily chores, scrubbing washboards, gathering wood, digging potatoes and toiling in the garden. The callouses on her hands from the rugged life gave way to a mother's patience and tenderness, as she brushed and braided her daughter's hair in the mornings and before bed.

When the house was peaceful at night, she sewed beads and buttons and repaired clothes. Life for the children included cuts and scrapes, encounters with barbwire and tree climbing, and Victoria nursed each mishap, fever or illness.

She woke earlier this morning to check on little Felix. She hadn't slept much, worrying into the night. The doctor said it was a case of croup, with the fever relentless and the boy fitful. She remembered her own mother giving her peppermint when her tummy was upset, and reached for a bottle from the apothecary at the back of her shelf.

Joseph Jr. was the next awake, and before he left for the yard, she sent him to Blanchard's Mercantile for camphorated oil and laudanum. If they weren't open yet, he could knock on their door in this emergency.

Finally the fever broke a day later; but the croup had spread to two other children, and Victoria knew it was a blessing she'd been spared herself. Thankfully her sister, Assenath, came from Ste. Hermas for a week-long visit, a godsend to Victoria, baking bread, milking cows, and collecting eggs from the henhouse.

Urgel was still away, hired by the Caulfields and Wellingtons to find prized game. With Assenath leaving, Victoria was feeling the exhaustion of work and family.

When Urgel finally came up the lane, she ran to his arms from the herb garden before he reached the house, and embraced him with all her strength. As she leaned to his ear, his head tilted brushing against her warm cheek.

"You know you smell like smoked venison?" she whispered. He roared with delight at her quip, then again at her quiet snicker. Content to have him home, she rubbed the dirt and bark from his rough hands.

Urgel rose early. "Victoria, after chores, I need to go to town on business. I won't be long at all."

On the camping trip, the Caulfields had raved about new work-saver stoves in Montréal and pitied the woman without one.

The Lachute General Store was the agent for Chicago's Sears Roebuck, with picture books of all kinds of newfangled appliances, claiming to be the Cheapest Supply House on Earth.

I can look over the pictures in the store, and order one to be brought all the way from Chicago to St. Andrews.

"Hello, Kenneth! I've come to order Victoria one of those six-burners from the new Chicago picture book."

Home Sunshine Range, 1897 Sears Roebuck Catalogue

"We've a mighty fine selection, Urgel. Do you plan on burning wood or coal?"

"Wood, of course, I ain't got no coal."

"Might I recommend the Home Sunshine Range? Burn's hard or soft coal and wood too—a good square oven, fire box, ventilated flutes, and very ornamental."

Urgel peered into the catalogue. "Well, I don't need the musical instrument, just the stove. How much without the flute?"

Kenneth reserved any fluster. "There's no charge for the flute. It'll let out the hot air. Delivered, it's $21.75."

With his cash counted out, Urgel added a pouch of tobacco, and at the door, he stuck a pinch in his bottom lip.

Even in anticipation, the countryside and village streets bustled for the ladies' bees in St. Andrews—apple-coring at harvest, quilting ones for brides, and knitting or needlepoint socials. Victoria knew they were an excuse for a gathering, and that was fine with her. She hugged the women as they arrived as if they hadn't seen each other in ages.

The men declared no interest in these events, but still appeared, some with coring knives, enticed by rumours of meats, cheeses, pies and cakes, and cider and English teas. Victoria insisted that the ladies come in to the long oak table, and she wasted no time showing off her Sunshine Range.

A card game in the corner escalated to laughter, songs and dancing late into the evening, stopping only when voices were hoarse and the moon was summoning folks back to the farms.

Although modern conveniences made their way into the homes of St. Andrews, Urgel and Victoria were content with a flicker of a few light bulbs, pumped water, and the outhouse beside the barn.

Farming Gives Way to Lumbering & Industry

AFTER THE 1906 Depression, log cabins disappeared, replaced by ample houses built from milled woods. Large agricultural farms diminished, as sections were severed into hectares, then hectares into acres. Practicing tradesmen forsook farms for urban employment, and labourers were enticed by timber merchants to the woods and rivers for months at a time, to meet the demand for lumber.

A new industry was providing energy for manufacturing and transportation—coal mines!

In Québec, as in England, Wales and Cape Breton, the mines sent lines of men deep into the bowels of the earth. Coal had been discovered in the 1700s at Trois-Rivières, Val D'Or and Rouyn-Noranda in the east, and nickel was found at Sudbury in 1883.

With men labouring from the peep of sunrise to the last glimpse of the moon, it was common for single women to run farms on their own and take in work until their husbands returned.

Professor Melville Bell's telephone invention was promoted in Québec by Dominion Telegraph in the 1870s, with later modifications patented by his son, Alexander Graham Bell, in Ontario.

In St. Andrews East, word got out of the new wooden crank phones, used by the Montréal Telegraph Company, the Grand Trunk Railway offices, The Argenteuil Advertiser and The Watchman newspapers.

Telephone orders were fulfilled quickly, modernizing communication for shipping yards, government agencies and aspiring businesses.

Urgel's shop beside the barn was acquiring the latest carpentry inventions as they became available. At every chance, he demonstrated his new hand-cranked American table saw and boring machine. Although expensive, the machinery was the meat and potatoes of his household.

The signature 'Poquet', often used by Urgel, became a familiar mark on many fine carpentry pieces around the village of St. Andrews.

Back from hunting, Urgel's arms couldn't carry the weight of his spoils. Victoria rushed from the house to greet him and lifted the partridges and grouse tied to his back. "The boys can come back to the canoe with me," he said. "Two deer are there, and as many fowl as the boat would carry."

Victoria cleared a table to truss and clean the squab, rabbits, ducks, and fish. On a flat board outside, the larger game were quartered and hung by Urgel with the help of his brothers; then with burlap and butcher's paper, he wrapped the salted meat for winter storage. Urgel lowered the ladder to the cellar under the latched floor slab of the back kitchen. Piece by piece, the meat was handed down to hang in the musty, dark room.

The shelves below were already stocked with baskets of apples, bags of potatoes, glass jars and crocks of pickled vegetables, and salt barrels down one wall. On the opposite side, large hooks hung from the ceiling beams to support the heavy meat.

During the winter, Victoria and Urgel fed their family from the rewards of the cellar, and even when they scraped the bottom of the barrels for soft apples or potatoes, nobody complained.

Ice Jam on the St. Andrews Bridge

EVERY RESIDENT was aware that a collapse could come, with the river's high current and the age of the bridge. In most opinions, it was a matter of time before the old pilings would begin to shift.

Urgel's neighbour galloped to his lane, on a circuit of arms to alert every family of the urgency. His voice was hoarse and he was out of breath as he shouted from outside the house.

"The North River has jammed up! It's at the St. Andrews Bridge on the point of tragedy."

Urgel took off to town on his horse. Others were arriving too, and he gathered with a group of men, surveying the resilience of the bridge supports. With a chain of hands, they lowered one man down the slope to the water to examine it.

Stafford stood at the top, dressed in style, ready to take charge. "It seems that some beaver chomped at the tresses near the river bank."

He raised his walking stick high in the air and peered over the top of his glasses. He was proud of his pomposity, and the others were silent, withholding guffaws.

"First of all men, let's clear this beaver dam and get the ice chipped apart. Unfortunately, the lodge is fully occupied so we will have to relocate the vermin," Stafford pronounced.

"Make a coat out of them," Simon yelled from the bridge.

John Barron spoke quickly. "Urgel, you have skills with this sort of thing. How do you propose we attend to this?" The crowd murmured and craned necks as John slapped his friend on the back.

"I'll get my ice fishing waders from the wagon," Urgel said. "Anyone else care to join me? The more hands, the quicker this will be."

Stafford quietly stepped back.

A few of the more agile helpers were lowered down the bank, and some older men leaned from the bridge to give advice. One of the youngest fellows got to the dam first, and pulled away boughs and logs from the congested pile.

The first appearance of a beaver head in the open water created a hush. Quickly it dove, returning a few minutes later, irritated by the intrusion. A man, crouched beside the lad, leaned over to assist.

"Ahoy there, mother, you're going to have to move, darlin'."

The large female beaver stopped in the water ahead; looking back in distress, she raised her head hissing, then flapped her tail with startling force.

"It's March, the poor girl is likely pregnant with her next litter," someone called out.

William LeRoy had arrived on the bridge now to give an opinion. "Now that the mother is out, be cautious—the male may still be around. The way beavers hibernate, there might be sharp gnawed saplings that can spear you." The men nodded all around.

"Don't harm him," Urgel said. "Beavers are monogamous; his family needs him for the lodge to survive. His ancestors were here before ours. No guns or arrows!"

Urgel planted his feet firmly in the water, prepared that the icy temperature would instantly numb his feet. With heavy gloves, he grasped at the largest of the saplings and tossed them on the bank.

"Hand me some rocks fast, to fill up the den."

Three or four men formed a line, tossing the rocks down to Urgel until it was full.

"Now we need some construction men to put in new pilings under the bridge. What's here is going to collapse."

A man from the St. Andrews Road Company had already gone for help and returned with a crew to secure the bridge. With barrels of Aspadin's cement mixture, they filled the troughs.

Soaking from the ice water, Urgel Paquette climbed into his wagon after applause broke out from his cronies, and every man returned home to describe to their families how they had helped in the restoration.

Forty-five

Turner Christmas at Frogmore End, Hertfordshire – Twelve Days of Christmas Pageant – Boxing Day, Alms for the Poor – Clementina's Poorhouse Memories – John Creffield III dies at Berkshire – Frederick Creffield Meets Alice Jane Turner – Frederick Works in Chalvey Foundary - Death of Henry Turner – Frederick Creffield weds Alice Jane Turner, 1891 – Clementina Eliza Creffield (nee Webb) becomes Laundress in Wargrave – Frederick Creffield's family increases by five – Youngest William Creffield dies, 1911.

Turner Christmas, Hemel Hempstead, 1872

ACROSS THE ATLANTIC, THE HENRY TURNER HOUSE WAS dressed. With only five days until Christmas, it teemed with excitement and noisy laughter in the streets and shops.

Bundled for the biting air, Jane bustled past shoppers on the village's main market on High Street, now vibrant with the highest spirit of the season. Near the market, she stopped at the twelfth century St. Mary's Church of Norman to reflect on the season.

Alone in the sanctuary, she breathed in the peace and serenity, and from the back pew, she admired the architecture and masterfully painted glass stands.

"I must do this more often," she whispered. "It's an escape from the distracting commercial life that's tempting our townsfolk."

The broad avenue wound uphill from Market square through Lower Hemel and Broadway, offering The Rose and Crown Public House and more Tudor-style pubs and inns.

The Village Church, 1886, Old Christmas Sketchbook of Washington Irving,
Illustrator R. Caldecott (1846-1886), Public Domain

Stores and trades of all kinds graced the street—with Salter's Basket
Shop, Palmer's Straw Plaiters, a bowl turners shop, the linen draper, and a
leather currier. Across were the whitesmith tin maker, the Penny Post and
letter carriers office, and a wool stapler. The surgeon and bone-setters'
rooms were next to the barristers' house, and at the end were a saddlery
and farrier, the miller, butcher, and the wheat mills.

Patrons crowded outside the Vintner's and the dry goods, stocking up
for social events and holiday dinners. Jane's intention was to add only a
few last minute items. After the stationery store, she visited the millinery
house, dressmaker, and the bookseller for special family gifts.

As bells rang across Hemel Hempstead on Christmas Morning, only a
few carriages trotted through the silent streets. Long columns of white
smoke spiraled from chimneys, and the morning peace was finally broken
by the London train whistle on its approach to Midland Station.

Henry Turner returned his family from St. Mary's Church, to his home
amongst a row of Tudor and Georgian cottages on Frogmore End Road.

"Merry Christmas, my good man," Henry nodded, dismissing the
driver. The children ran ahead through the picket gate, then into the
wonderland parlour decked in colour.

"Oh, the aroma of a succulent roast goose and mince pies," Henry
declared. With no formalities, his hat sailed to land on the front door rack.

"In good time, Henry!" Jane replied, joining him in the parlor. "Have a nice cuppa tea."

Knowing he'd be ready, the tea tray was already laid and Jane dunked a Twinings bag until the colour was suitably amber. Henry languished in his leather Morris chair as she sat nearby on a tapestry settee with her knitted shawl.

The four girls stayed in their Sunday best, with buttoned laced boots, eyelet-trimmed pantaloons settling at the calf, and drawstring calico dresses and petticoats. Jane had tatted lace collars for each of them, with hand-sewn satin bows for their tresses.

They settled near each other on the floor for the most special day of their year. "When can we start the Christmas Pageant, father?" Eliza asked.

"You mean 'The Twelve Days of Christmas'?"

"Of course father, we've been practicing for weeks," Lilian added, placing a copy of the script in Henry's lap.

As Henry announced the first, a partridge in a pear tree, Lilian entered with coloured feathers in her hair, and holding a paper pear high. From rehearsed enunciation, she recited from Matthew and Luke.

Then under the door's garland, Alice Jane and Eliza walked up on their toes, with flapping arms and white paper hats with drawn faces of turtle doves.

Arthur and Agnes paraded behind, cackling like French hens that started the room into contagious laughter. Henry laughed so hard that he almost collapsed to the floor in fits.

Finally, Jack the befuddled spaniel was led in, and Lilian attempted to explain that he was somehow addressing the virtues of faith, hope and love with a simple tail wag. Minutes later, the dog was back with a paper hat with a bird face, with the girls representing the evangelists Matthew, Mark, Luke, and John.

The five children held embroidery hoops as golden rings, with the sixth in Jack's mouth. At that point, the play went awry, with chaotic charades of laying, milking, dancing, and leaping. At last, drumming of pots wound up the twelve beliefs of the Apostle Creed.

The audience of just Henry and Jane stood and clapped as the children took bows. "Excellent play! Bravo!" Soon everyone cheered but Jack, curled in the corner.

Boxing Day and Alms for the Poor

THE YOUNGER Turner children were confused every single year about the reason for Boxing Day after Christmas, and Jane knew they'd ask again. She gathered them in the parlor.

"Queen Victoria started Boxing Day," she said. "It's to gather boxes of gifts to donate to churches and poor houses in the spirit of charity."

"What can we gather?" Eliza asked.

With pride, Jane nodded. "Go to your belongings and find something other children would like. And come right back so we can do them now."

Each brought back a meaningful piece of clothing or keepsake, and decorated their boxes with drawings or scraps of fabric and paper.

Alice Jane had knitted blue mittens and a scarf, and added a sweet orange and a slightly-used hair bow. She stuffed a cotton bag with roasted chestnuts, and gave up the peppermint candy cane from her Father Christmas stocking.

With the boxes tied, Henry set them by the door for the priests to collect and redistribute to the needy.

From the window, Lilian watched as an entourage of priests campaigned the streets collecting gifts. A lump filled her throat, feeling pride yet a sense of loss, as she saw her own box taken.

Clementine Tells of the Orphanage

IN NEW WINDSOR, Christmas started in the wee hours before sunrise for Clementina Eliza Creffield. As the household slept, she cooked and fussed alone in the kitchen, and finally woke her husband, John, to share her plan.

"I need to tell our children and grandchildren how grateful we are for our home and our family. They should be told today of our own memories and experiences, and about our heritage."

The family was poor from the loss of the carriage business, but their strength endured in a more simple life of non-material values. John and Clementina had two sons, Percy and Frederick, and five daughters, while living on Bexley Street.

At breakfast, after saying grace, the children chorused, "Amen."

"Children," he said, "Your mother will tell you things today to carry in your memories and tell your own children when it's time."

Young Percy John spoke up. "Mother, my own children, your grandchildren, will know the truth of your childhood then."

Clementina came to his chair and embraced him, then walked in the kitchen as she spoke, with all the eyes following her.

"My mother was Sarah Elizabeth Griffin and my father's name was John Webb. You wee ones share a part of them. You see, for the last hundred years, there have been poorhouses and workhouses in the parishes of London. Thank goodness, you'll never see the likes of it.

"As it happened, when I was five years old, I went with my mother and baby sister, Louisa Sarah. All Ma had was a carpet bag with a few clothes, and barely a tuppence hidden away. We knew what 'poor' was and I was scared."

"I'm sorry you had to be scared, grandmother," Martha Jane said, and began to walk beside her.

"Thank you, my dear. We were not alone. There were many orphans, old people, cripples and some just plain penniless, like us. The priest at our Church sent my mother and me with my sister to a big wooden house. I wondered why we had given up our flat and even more why Pa hadn't come home.

"My father was loving and kind, but he developed the factory cough and we couldn't afford the medicine. I heard mention of a workhouse where sick and old people went and died. I think that's what happened to Pa.

"We learned not to ask too many questions of Ma. She sobbed in the lonely hours of the nights, and during the days she worked at scrubbing floors, making gruel, and whatever the head matron demanded of her."

"Where did you live?" Frederick asked, sitting cross-legged at her feet.

"We were given a small corner with only one cot at the Orphan House. Since I was older than six, I was sent to labour, sometimes weeding the church cemetery and other times at the big house. We were given three meals a day—breakfast a pint of mild porridge and a few ounces of stale bread. In the afternoons, I was sent to learn to read and write. I'm thankful as that was lucky for me.

"As children, we lived near poverty level, not yet in poorhouses, but couldn't pay the parish fees required for education. Ma didn't have to pay for Sarah or me while she worked in the orphanage."

"What did you get for lunch, grandmother?" Martha Jane asked.

"A pint of beef broth and bread, but I looked forward to supper when we got cheese with the bread. On Saturdays, the cook always had a plum pudding made of suet and raisins."

"Yuk, Yuk!"

Clementina laughed at the reaction, and the children joined with giggles.

"You children are spoiled but spared, as I have never cooked a plum pudding since." Clementine paused.

Little Martha Jane looked up sadly. "We won't let you ever go back to the orphanage. You can always stay here with us."

"Yes, I know, dear. I wanted you children to understand how privileged you are to have a home and family."

Martha Jane took Clementina's hand and led her to an armchair. With her thumb in her mouth, Martha snuggled in comfort.

By 1891, Clementina was a widow of sixty-seven living with her son Frederick in the duplex cottage at Berkshire. Frederick worked as a plasterer and labourer, wherever he could find work.

Percy John, the eldest son, married at twenty-three to Emily Lovelock from Lambourne, settling at Myrtle Cottage in Chalvey Slough, Bucks where he became an iron molder in a local foundry.

As Percy and Emily's family grew, they moved to Wellington Street, Upton-cum-Chalvey, raising six children—Martha Jane, Percy John Jr., Frederick Charles, Henry Thomas, Jane Beatrice and Charles George Creffield.

Frederick Creffield & Alice Jane Turner, 1891

HEMEL HEMPSTEAD was only twenty miles from London, but seemed a slow train ride connecting by the Old Windsor Road down to Upton-cum-Chalvey.

Hertfordshire flourished as a farming community, close enough to supply the London markets with daily corn, wheat, and watercress through the summer and harvest season. Employment for men was mostly in labour at the brick fields, malting, gravel pits or iron foundries. Women could find lighter work in textiles of straw plait and silk, or the paper mills.

The foundry whistle woke the town every morning but Sundays, and within minutes the street teemed with bicycles. Frequently, as an open stake truck passed, the most able men on foot clambered on board.

Frederick Creffield lived at 4 Wardour Place with his mother Clementina and his sister, Clementina Eliza, at Chalvey Slough. He was lithe and his body lean and wiry, and his determination and ambition drew him to always look for something bigger with more promise than his foundry job.

Before the blast of the whistle, Clementina prepared him a full breakfast of bangers and mash, eggs and toasted whole wheat, when the budget could squeeze it. Against Frederick's wishes but at her insistence, he took a gulp of black tea and a cough elixir to keep the foundry worker's disease at bay.

She'd make sure he'd never forget.

"Mother, just wait and see," he boasted. "I'll make foreman at the factory before long." With a mixture of pride and humility, he tossed his pay envelope into Clementina's lap.

"As long as you're happy, that's all I want for you, son. They talk of unions coming, and they can be nasty times, Fred. You'll watch yourself, I know."

Frederick met Alice Jane Turner when she was visiting her ailing father in Berkshire. She was a devout Anglican and devoted to her mother.

Alice noticed that her mother's prayer was longer on this visit, and observed the sinking of Henry's eyes, with the sallow look that she knew came before death.

Her mother pressed Henry's father's pocket watch into Alice Jane's hand, and she nodded back her understanding.

"Mother, I need a few minutes to walk on the street."

She looked for a bench to compose herself. The rain had reduced to a drizzle, and Frederick couldn't miss seeing her as he passed toward the railway depot. Her hair was auburn and her eyes blue, but soaked with tears. She knew her father's time might come today and was racked with the grief.

Frederick stopped to offer assistance as she rose to walk. She touched her face with her scarf, and he tipped his hat with an awkward greeting.

"Pardon me, Ma'am. May I carry your satchel for you?"

Strolling near the depot, they eased through introductions, but it was impossible to hide her emotions behind emerging tears. Frederick was scarcely at a loss for words, but in this circumstance, he was stricken.

"Can I do something to help, Miss Turner?"

"No . . . I'm sorry. I just visited my father in his feeble health, and the prognosis is poor; but really, my emotions shouldn't be blubbering all over you." Her blue eyes looked up. "Forgive me."

"Please, no apologies. But let me take you for a cup of tea until you gather your strength. A Twinings sign is up ahead."

"You are so kind, Mr. Creffield; and yes, that sounds just right."

Frederick led her by the elbow as she dabbed at her eyes. His memory flashed to a discussion Clementina had with him so many times—'Always open the door and pull out the chair for a lady'.

"Please, Alice Jane, I'll get the door."

Frederick felt responsible and official as Alice poured out her heart and concern for her mother, over a pot of Earl Grey and watercress sandwiches. They parted at the train station, and Frederick whistled a tune on his way home.

On July 4, 1891, at the parish church in Upton-cum-Chalvey, Frederick married the elegant Alice Jane Turner from Hemel Hempstead.

Their mothers were respectively ushered by Frederick—Jane Turner, recently widowed from Henry, and Clementina Creffield widow of John.

A lawn reception gathered in the shade of the trees at the backyard of Frederick's cottage at Wardour Place. Alice Jane was radiant in her mother's simple wedding dress, with a piece of tulle as a veil.

Salt Hill, beside Upton-cum-Chalvey in Slough, was a half day's train journey from Hemel, Hempstead. With Jane Turner settled in rented rooms in Buckinghamshire, Alice Jane and Frederick arranged to set up their own household nearby.

Clementina moved to Wargrave, Berkshire in 1892 as a laundress and seamstress. Her daughter, Clementina Eliza had married and moved beyond Berkshire, but still in the Slough Parish, they always met on Sunday mornings.

Frederick and Alice Jane raised three girls and two boys, Alice May, Clementina Eliza, Winnifred, Frederick Playdell, and little William, who died as a wee boy. After his death, the family moved to Eton, Buckinghamshire in 1906.

London had taken on a new modern face, with automobiles, double-decker trolleys and underground tubes absorbing its surging traffic. Piccadilly Circus was drawing patrons for nightly theatre and vaudeville plays, but also home to a darker parallel of gambling houses, thievery and even murder.

Forty-six

Eruption of Mt. Vesuvius, 1906 – 1908 Olympic Bid for Naples Moves to London – Olympics bring construction boost – Labour Unions were attempting to fight lung disease in foundries – U.K. Labour Party – Peter Walker, victim of consumption – Creffield's Charity to Widow – *The Darkest England the Way out*, William Booth – Bernardo Boy's Homes, 1870 – Campaign to send orphans to Canada & Australia – Railway boys roundup – Alice Jane Creffield Adheres to Anglican Faith – Alice May Creffield, b. 1892 – Creffields move to Cowley Farm, Cuddington – Clementina Eliza Creffield convalesces in Aylesbury.

1908 Summer Olympics Defaults to London

THE DAY'S HISTORIANS EXPECTED MT. VESUVIUS TO erupt every twenty years, and on April 4, 1906 it satisfied their predictions. Over four days, the volcano opened its vents around the mountain, spewing molten ash to the shores of the Bay of Naples.

At three in the morning on April 7, the rim of the volcano roared like a lion, releasing spirals of gas and ash high into the sky. Some said the flames looked like a stem with flowers, dropping petals as it grew. The eruptions repeated for two weeks, levelling colossal damage on Naples and the surrounding villages and landscape.

The World's Olympic Committee had given Naples the 1908 Olympics bid, and construction crews were already underway with stadiums, pools and tracks. With structures shaken by the eruption, Naples conceded to be unable to recover for the games.

Reviewing the second highest bid, the Committee declared the games should instead be in London. With luck, they were already equipped with world class facilities and venues, but nonetheless it created a boom for construction and transportation industries.

The unions had settled down, and the Boer war, from 1899 to 1902 in South Africa, was now a distant past. For most Londoners, it was a time of celebration and joy.

London in 1908 was resplendent with regalia, as streets of banners and flags heralded the summer Olympics in the city and at Henley-on-Thames, for the regatta and rowing events. The labour class from Chalvey, including many Creffields, quickly found extra work.

Coinciding with pressure on the British government to take care of the burgeoning poor class in England, the Canadian colony was desperate for labourers and domestics. Even farming in the western provinces lacked enough labour for basic agricultural chores.

In Montréal and Québec, a growing and affluent upper class created a demand for household services, and the U.K. saw it as an opportunity for a mass exodus of homeless children and domestics to Québec and Ontario. After all, the colonies still 'belonged' to the British—it was their inherent duty to shuffle the population as it suited them.

Labour Union Struggling at Chalvey Foundries

AT THE BLARE of the noon whistle at Chalvey Slough, workers found their familiar corners on crates and barrels. Frederick perched on his usual spot and unsnapped his black lunch box for his thermos. The men's boxes were no longer shiny metal, but had turned to dull black from the factory soot that was taking its toll.

"Look Frederick—my wife gave me this brand new lunch box for Christmas. But now just six months later, it is pure black."

His co-worker's finger rubbed at the smoky surface with no change, meaning to make a joke of it.

"What's worse is that it matches all of yours, too."

"Jake, old boy, what are you? Thirty, forty?" Frederick asked.

"No, I'm twenty-five."

Frederick turned his head away to avoid looking at Jake. There was silence among the workers, who ate as they listened.

"I hear union folks talking about making things better for us. If my lungs are as black as this, I'm worried," Ainsley said.

"Maybe we should go to that meeting tonight," Frederick said.

After a thirty minute break, the whistle blew and the queue resumed, with most men somber and quiet.

Frederick decided on a bit of alehouse gibberish to lighten the mood.

"Hey there, Jake, hold up. I've got a joke for ya."

"Well, get to it quickly."

"As me buddy told me at the bar last night. A drunk staggers into a Catholic Church, enters a confessional booth and sits down but says nothing. The Priest coughs to get his attention but the drunk continues to sit there. Finally, the Priest pounds three times on the wall. The drunk mumbles—Ain't no use knockin, there's no paper on this side either."

"Fred, you told me that one yesterday, and the day before that."

"Well then, at the bar tonight we'll get us some new ones."

The majority of able Chalvey men worked at foundries, with conditions forcing life spans of only forty to forty-five years. In the dangerous air quality, men coughed through shifts without dust masks or ear plugs. Families faced the grim prospect that years of a breadwinner would be taken early in return for honest hard work.

Labour union buzz was rampant, to force a way inside and promise better conditions. Frederick hoped for improved health and the day when he'd get some kind of pension. His pals at work were uniting in their anger, and he now found it building in himself, against his nature.

The United Kingdom Labour Party was forming from the rumblings of trade unions, and the enraged populace was becoming vocal in joining riots and uprisings to have sanctions of the 'Railway Servants Act' repealed.

On the first day his friend Peter Walker was missing from his workbench, Frederick didn't worry. They'd worked side by side for ten years, and neither had missed days before. A week passed, then several. After work one night, Frederick turned toward the Walker house. A drizzle ran down his face as he passed the tracks to the row housing district.

Frederick knew the Walker house well, and tonight it was dimly lit on his approach, with the garden overgrowing the walkway. Peter's wife, Elizabeth, answered the knock.

"Frederick!" Elizabeth said in surprise. "Come in, come in—it will brighten Peter's spirits so much to see you."

A voice mumbled from near the window, and from an armchair, Frederick heard his name. He lowered the blankets from Peter's face.

"Peter, what has happened?"

Elizabeth moved a kitchen chair a few inches closer to Peter's side.

"Frederick, please stay and visit. I use this chair to stay by him in the day, and I even slept in it sitting up last night," she admitted boldly. "I'll make a strong pot of Red Rose for the two of you."

Peter watched her speak and turned his frightened eyes to Frederick. They remained speechless for a few moments, both knowing the truth. Peter's throat gurgled to speak and he gasped for air enough to be heard.

"I won't be coming back, you know."

"Yes, I know, dear friend."

Peter lurched forward in a violent cough, grasping a large rag he'd used for a handkerchief. When it was over, the cloth was splattered in blood.

"What can I do? Please let me help," Frederick pleaded, his mind now vacant and grasping.

"You will check in on Elizabeth and the children from time to time, anything to keep them out of the poorhouses."

A tear appeared on Peter's face, and the tea was taken in silence.

"Peter, the factory workers are trying to get a Union for better conditions and also pensions; I even heard mention of a widow's pension."

Frederick gulped, having actually said the word 'widow'.

The wheezing started again, and Frederick rose to thank Elizabeth, then gave Peter a gentle hug. He crumpled his hat in his hands and stopped before the door.

"Dear Elizabeth, I wish I could do something."

"Perhaps you can help the union get into the foundry, and save others."

Frederick smiled and nodded at the magnificent burden placed on him. His insides pained for his friend, as he walked home the long way.

Peter passed away a few days later, and Frederick and Alice attended a humble funeral. No one else from the factory came.

On pay days, Frederick stopped by to see Elizabeth Walker on his way home. Elizabeth insisted she would make do with her sewing and char work, but saw that the cupboards were bare. She wouldn't take money, but he brought back a parcel with a tin of dried milk, a box of tea bags, potatoes, dried peas and a bundle of sausage.

He felt he was blessed himself, and left a package weekly outside her front door, a solution that became acceptable.

To keep in shape, he was faithful to the Cricket Club of the Thames Valley, meeting weekly in the field off Chalvey Road behind the Catholic Boarding House for Wayward Women. As a rough sport for his age, Frederick left with bruises after each match, and Jane noticed they didn't always heal well, leaving black bruises he covered with turtlenecks and a hounds tooth cap.

"Frederick, we've been granted a longer life than many. I'll never take it for granted, you know."

"It's true, dear Jane," he said, knowing his health was no longer secure.

From time to time, Jane sent Elizabeth Walker knitted mitts and woolen hats, and at Christmas she sent a prayer shawl that she had started when Peter passed away. Thereafter, Alice Jane and Elizabeth remained devoted and supportive friends.

Orphans & Poorhouses

AT THE TURN of the century, England was overwhelmed with poverty, flooding the workhouses, poorhouses, orphanages and infirmaries. But a movement was afoot—expounded in *The Darkest England and the Way Out* by William Booth—proposing three new societies of city, farm and overseas.

In 1870, the Bernardo family sponsored a government project, British Home Children, with good intentions to take in orphans and non-orphans whose parents couldn't care for them. Youngsters could be placed in an institution and schooled with a focus on farming and domestic positions, then to be sent to farms and homes in Canada and Australia.

The idea was not new. Previously, in 1826, a police magistrate in London had proposed to an emigration committee a solution for the swelling population of orphaned children.

"They beg on the streets and sleep in the gutters. It will serve Britain best to send surplus children to the colonies to work as labourers where there is a great need."

William Booth renewed this charitable option, envisioning a new territory for his mission work. Unfortunately, few of the children were adopted into homes, as feeding and clothing was an additional burden, and many simply became cheap labour. But it seemed to be the charitable thing to do, understood as similar to rescuing Oliver Twist from the gutter.

Booth thought he could overcome this image, and set up vigorous campaigns to seek endorsements in Europe, the United States and Canada. His founding organization, the Salvation Army, always gathered crowds to hear its bands and rallies, and many offered funds to the campaign.

Meanwhile, Thomas Bernardo, an Irish philanthropist, established the first Boys Homes in London in 1868. The operation grew and extended to Australia and Canada.

Before leaving London, each boy received a peaked cap, rubber-soled boots, slippers, two night shirts, two pairs of wool socks, underwear, two shirts, two handkerchiefs, braces, a belt, wool and needle for repairs, a boot brush, New Testament, and the book *Pilgrims Progress*.

Boatload after boatload brought children aged four to sixteen years to Québec or Montréal, and onward to Toronto, then shipped by rail to farms as far as the prairies and western Canada.

Britain felt it was their right to populate the Canadian colony according to their convenience, sending more than a hundred thousand children. Many of the orphaned children were denied any knowledge of their ancestry or living relatives.

On his way to work before sunrise, Frederick Creffield slowed on his bicycle at a commotion under the railway bridge. He got off and eased closer to hear what was going on. Around a burning oil drum were half a dozen vagrant boys, hungry and dishevelled. Several policemen had a pair of boys each by the ear, while a parish priest tried to calm them.

"Boys, boys! We are not here to harm you. You will be taken to a safe place with a warm bed and supper every night."

"We're just fine here lookin' out for each other," the one named Billy boasted.

"Winter will be upon us soon enough. These officers will take you to the East End of London where the Bernardos have a home especially for boys—those without a home of their own."

"We don't need no hand out." Billy's kick flew high at the officer.

"It's not up to you, Billy. The government has decided you will be best taken care of by Mr. Bernardo. If you are lucky, you'll be put on the ships to Canada and sent to the Agricultural Farm in Manitoba where you'll be trained with a skill."

"Are you arrestin' us, father?" Billy chided.

"Yeah! *Are* you?" a pair of boys chimed in.

"Put it however you like. You are all minors and under the authority of the government. The poorhouses and workhouses are full with destitute lads, the likes of you all."

"Poorhouses, father! That's where you sent me Mom and she withered away and starved to death."

"That won't happen to you boys, I promise."

By this time, the half dozen boys had been cuffed and loaded onto a wagon with walls of metal bars to confine them.

"Father! I'll pray to God that he forgives you for this terrible thing you do," Billy spat from the wagon.

Frederick was frozen, and still watching in the stillness from the bank.

Those poor lads. I best talk with Alice Jane. Perhaps we could take in one or two of the railway kids to save them this fate.

Alice Jane Turner, a Stalwart Anglican in England, 1910

ALICE JANE rose before the sun and sat alone in the kitchen. She dunked her tea bag and stared out the window into space, mourning and drinking in the silence and solitude. Frederick was suffering and she saw him looking paler than usual, that his blue eyes were now a distant grey.

"I have to tell him the news of the baby, but perhaps not just now."

Frederick's and Alice Jane's oldest child was Alice May, born in 1892. From an early age, she was responsible to help her mother with her younger siblings, Clementina Eliza and Frederick Playdell. Little William had been born in 1901 and his frail body didn't survive his first year.

Alice Jane was in her second trimester when Frederick noticed her waist thickening. At the kitchen sink, she felt his arms gently wrapping around her from behind.

"Is it a laddie this time?"

Alice Jane turned and wept as they held their embrace.

Her thoughts went to tiny William. Frederick blamed himself for the ill health of the child. It must have been consumption, but the Creffields had been unable to pay for medicine and hospital care.

"Oh my dear boy, Willie." Frederick lowered himself to his knees, asking God to take care of his precious son in Anglican heaven.

Jane Turner was raised an Anglican. Her parents had been devout church goers, and she missed and yearned for spiritual comfort. Although Frederick had little confidence in God, he never stood in her way on Sunday mornings. In his own way, he was refreshed to see the spirit in which she returned home, smiling with renewed strength. He admired her faith and thought it a good thing that she read the Bible to the children.

At Christmas in 1908, Alice Jane invited Frederick to come to the Anglican Church with the children. He feigned ill health, but it occurred to him that there was no harm in sitting in the back row; perhaps God might notice his suffering. Humming the tunes *I Surrender All* and *Amazing Grace* gave him some peace, and he decided he'd come again if Alice asked.

Frederick left the medical office, eager to tell Alice of the doctor's positive observations, that his cough wasn't as prolonged. He bounced in the door, laughing with the news, and she welcomed his optimism, ready to share his new outlook.

Just after their fifth child, Winnifred, was born in the spring of 1905, Frederick admitted that he'd developed the dreaded foundry cough. For a few weeks, he'd noticed a loss in his weight, and now had less strength.

Alice Jane was out walking with the children, and he settled at the kitchen table for a strong cup of tea. So many questions gathered in his mind—foremost, who would take care of Alice, his girls and the lad?

When she returned, they sat by the coal stove.

"Frederick, I know you're not well. We'll trust the doctor and get through this. And God too, you know."

"You're right; I haven't lost confidence. If I don't go to work, I won't get paid . . . we have many mouths to feed and now another on the way."

"Frederick, the parish priest asked if you'd accept an offer of medicine from the church benevolent fund."

"It is not right for a man to take what he should give to his children. Your God has given us poverty to test our endurance. There are others in greater need; like the orphaned boys under the railway bridges."

Jane arranged to take in more sewing, and put her name in with the monsignor for extra work cleaning the cathedral.

"Alice May, you are old enough now to help with the sewing and cleaning. You're an excellent scholar, but I must depend on you for more."

Alice May was enthusiastic at the suggestion. "Of course, mother. I can tat lace and do embroidery as well. Don't worry, we'll be alright."

Young Alice May slipped to her room and returned with a £1 note.

"I want you to have this. I know father is too sick to work right now, but I pray to God at night and I'm certain he will get better."

Fresh Country Air at Cowley Farm, Cuddington

FREDERICK'S COUGH was discharging blood and he was overwrought as he couldn't justify sick time. Visiting the doctor, he learned that he did indeed suffer from consumption, later called tuberculosis.

"Unfortunately, Frederick, you know there is no cure and it is inevitably fatal," the doctor said with compassion. "And there are institutions where you can be cared for."

"How long?" Frederick asked, and the answer did not please him.

"Who will take care of my family? I fear their destiny is in the poorhouses."

The doctor didn't offer medicine for Frederick, but the prescription was to get out of the foundry and into the country air. Frederick and Alice commiserated about moving near Aylesbury, where his mother lived. She was getting on in years, and they wanted to be closer too.

Driving to Aylesbury, they passed a farming facility called Cowley Farm at Cuddington. Frederick found the manager outside one of the barns, and learned that they needed a cowhand. The man sized up Frederick and asked what weight he could lift.

"I can lift my wife," he fibbed a little. The barn manager wasn't sure, but laughed and said he would give him a chance. Back at the road, he winked at Alice Jane, prompting her giggle of delight and a hug.

"You look like you're in need of some fresh air and sunshine. Are you sure, Fred, that you can do this?"

"I'll give you my best."

The children stayed at Eton while Alice and Fred dropped in on his mother, Clementina. It had been a few months since he'd been to Aylesbury to see her. Her condition had deteriorated and it seemed like hospital care would be a long term solution. She declared at first that she was perfectly comfortable in the boarding house and still taking in small sewing jobs, but they knew her mind was feeble.

"Perhaps, Frederick, you could bring the little ones by sometime to see Grand-mama?"

Clementina *1stared into his pale eyes. "Are you not well, Frederick?"

He was afraid of how his words might sound.

"Dear Mother, God is watching over me in his own time, but we are coming to the country to get better air."

Alice pulled a chair closer. She knew that Clementina's fragile state of mind might be best treated at an institution.

Clementina said, "At my age, I deserve to be with my children. Alice May will be leaving your home soon and I would like to join your household. I'm still useful in the kitchen and can sew and wash clothes."

Alice Jane turned to Frederick and saw a fleeting glimpse of happiness.

"Of course, mother. We are looking for a place to rent in the country where the air is fresh for Frederick." Jane kissed her mother-in-law on the forehead.

Forty-seven

England's General Election, 1906 – Winston Churchill – Old Age Pensions and Minimum Wages – Salvation Army Rally Coming to Chalvey – William Booth campaigns to send poor children to the colonies – Death of King Edward VII, 1910 – Coronation of George V, 1911 – Alice Creffield Trains for Royal Banquet at Eton – Tensions high in Europe over Austria-Hungarian annexation of Bosnia & Herzegovina – Churchill Reforms lead to Pay Equality – Royal Fusiliers of London Recruits Soldiers - Women's Domestic Guild of Canada Recruits in London – Alice Creffield attends Info Sessions for British Domestics – Alice is Recruited by Mrs. Francis to travel on White Star line to Montréal, May 1913.

Old Age Pension & Trades Dispute Acts, England, 1906

SUPPORTED BY WINSTON CHURCHILL, THE 1906 GENERAL Election passed the Trades Dispute Act, allowing collective unions in disputes to be immune from civil law sanctions. It led to widespread social reform, with the Old Age Pensions Act for retirees and the Trade Board Act that guaranteed a minimum wage.

Frederick read about it at the pharmacy, as he unfolded the broadsheet *The Daily News*, his favourite paper. Started by Charles Dickens in 1846, he liked that the newspaper was bought in 1901 by chocolatier George Cadbury to campaign for old age pensions.

He hoped he would be able to collect his ten shillings pension, counting on reaching seventy. He asked the clerk if he could take the page, and with care, he clipped the article to read the good news to Alice Jane.

"Thank the Lord, Frederick, you can retire on a pension now," she said. "It's such a blessing, this will give you the chance to stay rested and get better. Peter Walker would have be pleased."

"Frederick, there is a rally coming to Windsor next week. Those Salvation Army folks are bringing their bands and hosting food lines; all you have to do is listen to a short sermon."

"Alice Jane, you go and take Alice May. I've heard that the Booth fellow is looking to take children and domestics to slave in the Canadas. He holds huge rallies in the United States with cavalcades of cheering folks, parades and fanfare. Perhaps that's a better future for Alice May."

"I'll talk to her."

When Alice May came in that evening, the sun had already gone down, and her mother was prepared, with a pot of tea, a broth and a biscuit.

"Come here, dear, I want to talk to you. Have you heard about the Salvation Army rallies?"

"Yes, I have, mother." Her voice hushed. "But I didn't want to upset father by suggesting that I attend one."

Changing of the Royal Guard, George V Ascends Throne

BY MIDDAY, word of mouth had spread the news in factories and schools and onto the streets. It was May 7, 1910, and the country was in tears at the death in the night of King Edward VII, son of Queen Victoria and Prince Albert.

The king, affectionately known as Bertie, died of pneumonia at Buckingham Palace, after royal service of nine years.

Alice Jane heard it at the post office.

"He was a good king," the postmaster said, and showed her the broadsheet daily. "We have much to be grateful for during his reign. London has seen buses, taxis, and even production of Ford automobiles. Your Frederick would look good in one of those vehicles."

Alice knew it would be unlikely, but agreed politely and excused herself. "I must get home to tell Frederick about the king."

She brought him in from the garden and called Alice May from the stove for the important news.

"The Daily Graphic says that the coronation of King George V will be on June 22, with the open carriage procession to run from Slough through Eton and on to Windsor Castle. Eton College will host a royal luncheon and they're asking to hire proficient cooks and servers from the local community."

Young Alice May was exuberant.

"I can cook, Mother; it would be grand to be part of that. Imagine serving the King and Queen of England. It's minutes from here, and I'll ride my bike with my application."

Six weeks later, Alice received an official letter from Eton College granting her a position as a General Cook for the aforesaid luncheon. She showed her father, and they both pinched the linen stationery and the engraving at the top.

"It says I must present myself with my passport at the Dean's Office for training."

An embossed card fell from the letter, naming her training slot to start in the following week. She was to wear polished black serviceable shoes in good repair, a laundered and ironed white blouse, and a black skirt that must hang to mid-calf.

"My hair must be pulled into a tight bun, and I'll be given a hairnet and cap from the College."

In a grueling day of menu reviews and tasting, the candidates were rated throughout, with a warning that only a degree from utmost excellence would be deemed acceptable.

More than half the class was dismissed before training was complete, but Alice remained, more determined to make a pass worthy of serving the king.

At the end of the day, she burst into the kitchen, eager to relay her experience to her mother.

"Oh Mama, it was such a good day. I will be working on the Chef's line, preparing casserole of partridges stuffed with morel mushrooms. Then I'll move to assist the Pastry Chef in a line, prepping Baba cake steeped in kirsch and maraschino, served with bananas. We make a Sabayon sauce ourselves that we learned today, from white wine, egg yolks and sugar. It is marvelous."

The irony couldn't get past Jane, as she burst into laughter.

"Sorry love, all I have for you tonight is English sausage, potato hash and broiled tomato."

"Ah, but I get to have it with my mom. What more would a girl want?"

Only three days later, Alice Jane knocked on her daughter's bedroom as she prepared for her job at Barber's house. Her hands were flat, holding out a pleated black wool skirt and her own white Sunday blouse, with a new lace collar.

"This should do you fine, Alice."

"But Mama, that fabric for the skirt was to be for your winter coat. You shouldn't have been so generous."

"I will get more pleasure seeing you looking so fine. After all, it's not every day you get to prepare lamb cutlets for the king. I will fold the clothes in proper lingerie tissue to keep them crisp."

With a restrained smile, her daughter left their tiny rented cottage, with visions of the king and her mind on the future.

But she needed more time to try her next ideas with her mother.

Rumblings of a World War, 1912

AUSTRIA-HUNGARY, Germany and Italy signed a compact in 1882 called The Triple Alliance, to oppose Russian influence in the Balkans, as the Ottoman Empire was disintegrating. Emperor Wilhelm II's agreements with Germany's Chancellor Otto Von Bismarck were falling apart, weakening Russia's alliance.

Counteracting The Triple Alliance was the Franco-Russian pact in 1902, and two years later Britain and France inked the Entente Cordiale. The temperament in Europe was tenuous and thrust Britain into signing the Anglo-Russian Convention.

The monkey in the middle of military aggravation was Britain, starting a naval building war, culminating in the Triple Entente. Allied countries set their attention on strengthening naval forces, and Britain launched the HMS Dreadnought to solidify their advantage. The arms race between Britain and Germany was in full swing.

In 1909, Austria-Hungary annexed Bosnia and Herzegovina, angering Serbia. Britain was on tenterhooks and recruitment offices popped up in London to build an auxiliary military force and train volunteer cadets.

The gruff politician, Winston Churchill, knew the rumblings of War and encouraged all women of working age to sign up at factories, many refitted overnight to manufacture weapons and war supplies.

In 1897, the National Union of Women's Suffrage was formed, and in 1912 women were promised equality in wages and politics.

Women demanded equal pay, an apparent achievement that had taken over a hundred years. Protests marched at London government buildings, and sceptics said the inequalities might continue another hundred years.

Some weeks after the king's Eton luncheon, Frederick's brother Percy and his wife Emily journeyed from Twickenham for a Sunday night family dinner.

"Congratulations, Alice May, for your contribution to our monarchy," Uncle Percy beamed.

"Thank you, Uncle Percy. It was indeed an honor that I will always cherish."

Chatter continued about the new royal family and Britain's hope of the qualms of Europe settling without war on the horizon.

Percy levelled with his brother, "You know, Frederick, my boys Percy John and Frederick Charles are eager to wear the British uniform. I'm indeed proud, but as a parent I do lose sleep."

"Yes, my Frederick has been talking with your boys and they are convinced there's safety in numbers. Thank goodness, Frederick is not yet sixteen. Myself, I've never touched a gun, whether to hunt an animal or kill an enemy. Of course, the pigeon shoot in Chalvey doesn't count," Frederick said.

"The Balkan Wars will be over soon and maybe that will be the end of it," Emily said, placating herself. In quiet thought, she returned to meal preparations.

"We have no idea what's ahead," Percy said. "For now, the boys will simply show up in Manchester to convert an old amusement centre into battalion barracks for training. They'll be drilled from 5 a.m. until dark seven days a week."

"And without a day of rest, no doubt," Frederick said.

Women's Domestic Guild of Canada Recruits in London

"WE NEED to talk, mother. I'm thinking I should work in the munitions plant—it's the one converted from Whittackers' old shoe factory."

"Alice May, you have a secure position at the Barber's house. It's close to home and with no board."

But she knew it was time for her daughter to spread her wings.

"Myrtle, Georgie and Rita plan to apply too, and it would be nice to work with friends."

"That appears to be good, but talk to your father too. He'll tell you what it's really like to work in a munitions factory. You won't have time to visit with your friends, nor will you be on the same assembly line."

"I can feel the agitation of war on the horizon and it scares me, but I feel my patriotism."

"Uncle Percy's boys—Percy John and Frederick Charles—signed up with The Royal Fusiliers in London. They have their papers, uniforms, and weapons. God forbid they be killed or kill someone else. Poor Aunt Emily, her heart is breaking at the thought of it."

"Have they left Langley already? I'd like to go around and see them."

"Percy Jr. has already joined the 5th Battalion," Alice Jane said.

"I wish I'd known."

Alice May grabbed her coat and bag and ran toward the big houses of High Wycombe, stopping at number 52. At the wrought iron gate, the number was carved in enamel on the stone post. With a skeleton key, she unlocked the padlock and passed the gardenias and white lilies on the path.

At the house, her mother's words echoed once more, 'You have a nice position at the Barber house'.

Entering at the back kitchen, she brought in a metal dairy box with quarts of milk, salt butter, and a pint of cream.

Mabel, the cook, tilted a plate of scones toward her. "I've got a fresh pot of coffee brewing. There are always pastries left too after the Barbers have had their fill."

"It does smell good indeed."

"Alice . . . it's our patriotic duty to sign up for factory assignments, but if we both left, the Barbers would be in a spot."

"If that is my decision, I'll agree to come round and make their dinner and put the children to bed. That should help. Besides, Mrs. Barber herself will be expected to do war work too. The rules for sign up don't have leniency for class status."

"Lands sake. I can't see the ladies of gentry applying themselves to operating machines," Mabel snickered. The next week, Alice Jane Creffield and her two daughters, Alice May and Clementina Eliza, went together to the silk weavers' office to take war assignments.

The converted factory was recruiting women to sew uniforms, linens, bandages, and the British flag, or on the munitions assembly line. Those forced into the workforce received meager pay, working for older matron supervisors able to be strict and keep a tight ship. Men in management were paid a higher wage, which seemed acceptable to many.

"So much for suffrage," Alice Jane mumbled. The newspaper was spread in front of her, and the second page advert by the Women's Guild of Montréal caught Alice's eye.

> British Domestics urgently needed in Canada. Opportunities for young single women between the ages of 16 and 25 in lovely Québec homes to work as nannies, housekeepers, cooks, seamstresses and general duties. Good wages for good references. Reasonable passage fares on White Star Dominion line accompanied by matron, Mrs. Emily Francis, in sponsorship with the Women's Domestic Guild of Montréal, Canadian Immigration and the Department of the Interior, Salvation Army, The East End Immigration Fund in London and the Department of British Emigration. Loans for passage available.

"I heard the girls talking about this, Mother."

She looked for a reaction, and grinned with clenched teeth, hoping the issue wouldn't be distressing.

Alice Jane said, "You know my world has never been larger than London; but with advancements in travel and now these Canadian opportunities, I see it better. I've always understood a time will come when you'll want to see more of the world."

"It says there is a meeting in Frogmore this weekend. Would you mind if I went with my friends to investigate?"

"You're twenty-one, Alice. You don't need your parent's permission," Alice Jane said unconvincingly.

By 1913, the global war was stirring throughout Europe, incited by imperialistic foreign policies, with two grand alliances—the Allied Powers of the United Kingdom, France and Russia opposing the Triple Alliance of Germany, Austria & Hungary, and Italy. Italy then took offence from Austria & Hungary, and later signed with the Allies.

Laurentic Sails to Montréal, White Star Line, 1913

ALICE MAY and Mable Preston ran through the downpour toward the Salvation Army Citadel in Eton. Their brollies fought the wind, and they took cover under an awning. They hardly ever missed a Sunday night meeting and would carry on when the weather let up.

"Mable, do they have this much rain in Canada?"

"I've heard it is all blue skies and fresh air."

"Mrs. Francis said she could easily find me work with a respectable family in Montréal. In Québec, they have factories and farms, but not enough workers. I'm sure they'd be grateful to have a British girl add status to their homes," Alice teased.

"Us? Girls of status?" Mable laughed. "Just because we speak English and require tea?"

"You can make a loan from the Salvation Army for passage and repay it over time when you're in Canada. We travel third class steamer for £5 plus we have to show proof of £2 10s on hand for local transportation and personal sundries on arrival. Besides, they promise £1 landing money when you go through Mr. Marquette at Québec Immigration."

"It would be difficult to say goodbye to my family, but I know they could rent out my bed to a foundry worker and they'd be better able to put food on the table," Mable said. "Mrs. Francis talked about the Guild girls in Montréal having parties, evening classes and weekend gatherings, to keep a British girl from being home sick."

Alice had no interest in being sent to war. Work was hard to find in England, and the parish poorhouses struggled to cope with demand.

"I'm already a nanny and housekeeper; I can do the same work in Montréal," she said. "I'll go to the recruitment rally, Saturday, at Frogmore. It's at the Citadel."

"I guess I can spring for train fare," Myrtle agreed.

Alice's anticipation kept her awake that night, planning her new life.

Mabel and Alice were welcomed at the door by Mrs. Francis, who invited them to find comfortable seats as the room would be full. She'd address the audience shortly with details of the Canada program. They took the remaining chairs in the front and observed the other young women filing into the hall.

Mrs. Francis was from the Women's Domestic Guild, affiliated with the East End Immigration Fund of London. She was also organizing children from orphanages and parish poorhouses for the Boys Farmers League, similar to other groups in England that were shipping boatloads of immigrants to Canada.

At the first signs of war, passenger lists filled quickly for Montréal and Québec, then with rail passage to Toronto, organized by the Children's Aid Society, Salvation Army, Boy's Leagues, and Waifs and Strays Society. From 1906 to 1920, hundreds of ships sailed from Liverpool to Canada.

Mrs. Francis stepped to the podium. "Welcome to your new life of opportunity. As you sign up, you will receive a pamphlet stating the requirements and duties in your post, and explaining your employer's expectations and your rights. Many of you will be granted employment in upper class homes, with the finest of convenience not yet seen in your own parishes. They have electric brooms, and running water inside pipes coming out of taps in the kitchen and the bathroom."

Oohs and chatter rose and eased from the crowd.

"The Domestic Pay Booklet outlines your pay, ranging from £6 to £12 per month, with your own room and three meals from your employer. Read the leaflet on baggage allowances, and if you intend to take your own sewing machine, we will make special arrangements for it.

"In Québec and Montréal, many organizations will provide support and social connections with others of your standing, including the Traveller's Aid Society, the Salvation Army Cathcart Lodge in Montréal, the Women's Guild of Canada, British Immigrant Society for Domestics and others on the pamphlet."

Alice whispered to Mable. "Sounds better than what we can expect in Britain. My grandma poor last year and my own dad isn't well enough to work. We are imminently at war, and England is overgrown with the poor and sick. I'm going to do it."

The line to sign up with Mrs. Francis buzzed with nervous impulses and laughter. Alice was next and took a deep breath.

"Yes, Mrs. Francis, I would like to take a domestic position in Montréal. What positions are available for me?"

Mrs. Francis opened Alice's envelope of her employment and character references, and sized her up silently by height and demeanor.

"I see you were a cook at the King's Luncheon in Eton. You would do well in a position with the Emonds, as long as your references check out. Mr. Emonds runs a local haberdashcry and his wife needs cooking and housekeeping in the home. Let's see . . . there are three children, an infant, a three year old and a five year old."

As Mrs. Francis took a few minutes with papers, Alice May scanned the growing line behind her, satisfied this would be the best thing.

"Very well, Alice. I've made arrangements for you on the Laurentic of the White Star Line." Her finger followed along the paper for Alice to see. "You'll depart Liverpool on April 26 with a group of English domestics and labourers. It's just eleven days ocean travel and you'll disembark in Montréal. Make sure you have your passport declaring you as a British national."

"I won't have the full passage, Mrs. Francis. I will need a small loan."

"That will be arranged, but you're aware that repayments to the Guild must be on time from your earnings in Québec." Her eyes sized Alice a last time. "Hopefully we'll have confirmation of your employment before you depart from Liverpool. Otherwise, the Salvation Army Immigration office or employment agents will get you settled."

Mrs. Francis initialed the application and waved down the line. "Next!"

Walking home, Alice was distant in thought. Far off, she saw her home, with the night light waiting in the window.

Mother will pretend to be sewing or something, but I know she's waiting for me.

"Mother, you should be in bed, it's late."

"I had to get this done for Mrs. Preston. Let me make you a cup of tea." Alice Jane rose stiffly out of her chair.

"Mother, your arthritis is getting worse. I'll make the tea. How be we try that new Market Spice I got in London."

Alice pulled a chair up beside her mother and took her hand.

"I was at the Salvation Army meeting tonight. I have news that I didn't expect so suddenly."

"I heard about what they are doing," Alice Jane said.

"Britain is waiting for a war, and I don't want to be in a war-torn country. I'll go and see how it works out. If I don't like it, I'll get a ticket right back."

"Wasn't that great ship Titanic from the same shipping company you mentioned—White Star?" her mother asked.

"That was a freak accident, with an iceberg. It won't happen again."

"Then you must go. Your decision is made."

"Mother, you are the most precious gift in my life. I will miss you every day and pray for you every night. I'm counting on that. With your fiftieth birthday, you'll now be getting old age pension. That makes me glad."

"We will be fine. Frederick Jr. is still at home to help and I'll be taking in a few boarders as well."

"I'll be leaving in three weeks, Mother."

Jane forced a smile. "Well then, we must pack you a steamer trunk filled with English delights."

Every inch was needed—the bottom with aprons, work clothes, two pairs of button laced shoes, and a woolen coat from her mother. She folded a black, taffeta skirt carefully. "Maybe this will be for special occasions," she said to Alice Jane.

Tight in the trunk were bolts of cotton, gingham, broadcloth and a small amount of silk, and between the fabrics, she tucked Grandma Jane Turner's Bible, wrapped in tissue. Her mother stood behind, with extra hairpins to keep her braid in place, and a crisp, white lace blouse. She packed and repacked, padding her delicate English tea set, and stuffed corners with teas, cotton sheets, her sewing box and English soaps. The trunk seemed almost full, and they laughed and hugged as she puzzled about fitting her church hats.

"You can only wear one," her mother teased.

Frederick counted down her remaining days as he went to the yard in the mornings. In his frail health, he knew what it meant, and spent every moment with her, to talk about her youth and his own.

Forty-eight

Alice May Creffield's preparations for Departure from Liverpool, 1913 – Emotional Separation from her Windsor family – Encounter with other British Domestics assigned to Québec – Joining the Salvation Army contingent for departure – Two Weeks aboard the Laurentic – Mrs. Francis has Rules & Regulations – Arriving at Vieux Port, Montréal – Transfer to Drummond Street – Meeting Miss Bull – Gus, a Friendly Hackney makes an Introduction.

Atlantic Crossing - Liverpool to Montréal, 1913

THE DAY OF EMBARKATION CAME QUICKLY. WITH THE anxiety, Alice was extra kind to young Frederick who was just fifteen, talking more openly than before about his work at the Cuddington Farm. She told him he looked like Pa, and that he'd be so much taller when she'd see him again.

On the second last day, the Ship's porter service picked up her trunk for the Customs House dockside. Alice wasn't sure if she should tip the fellow, and with embarrassment forced five pence into his hand.

The morning's farewell was difficult. Mother's voice quivered, knowing it was unlikely they'd ever see each other again, and Alice May promised she'd write every week.

When Alice May waved with her satchel in the lane, tiny tears streamed down her mother's cheeks.

She knew her mother and father would stand outside until there was no further sign of her at the road, and she nerved herself not to look back.

Print of postcard from R.M.S Laurentic, serving Liverpool-Canada.
British ocean liner of the White Star Line.

Percy offered to drive Alice to the White Star pier, since Frederick was in poor health. Alice was dressed for a good impression, with a round pill-box burgundy hat cocked on the side of her head and black gloves.

Uncle Percy and Aunt Em lived close by in Berkshire, with three sons of enlistment age, and their Frederick Charles already enrolled. Aunt Emily was worried about her own, and now Alice May too. "Life is burdensome, Percy. Is there an end to these troubles?" she often asked, and each time he renewed her confidence.

"Uncle Percy, thanks for bringing me. I'll write you and Aunt Emily often, and I'll ask for a letter in return. I'll pray for safety for Percy and Frederick too. Mother and dad worry about me, so please stop by to see them now and then."

Alice May heard her inner voice. *I'm asking too much.*

"Emily will see your ma on Monday mornings, and I'm here to help your dad. They're welcome for Sunday dinners and I'll pick them up."

Alice set her bag down and gave her uncle a firm embrace and kiss on the cheek. "I'll never forget your kindness."

Excerpt from Passenger Manifest, SS Laurentic
Registering Alice Creffield, second name on the left.

Quickly, she blended into a queue, recognizing some from the recruitment meeting: Annie McDowell, a machine operator; Lizzie Shelley, Nettie Jamieson, and Agnes Mitchell, all domestics; Mary Adams, a tailoress; Catherine Smith, a typist.

A young lady, Harriet Lewis, noticed and spun to greet her. "I remember you from the Citadel meeting." Awkwardly clutching their bags, they shook hands and laughed at themselves.

The din of voices and porters relieved her as she was nearing the desk. With a push of the line from behind, she adjusted her foothold and caught her heel between the boardwalk planks. Raising her arms for balance, Harriet steadied her elbow.

"Can't be 'avin you going to Canada with a broken ankle, can we?" Harriet smiled sweetly. "I'm from Buckinghamshire too."

"Thanks 'Arriet. I'll keep me eye out for ya and return the favor." She smirked at her own humour.

The ship's list recorded Passenger No. 3137622, Alice Creffield, 21 years, Domestic, born in England, travelling with the Francis contingent as part of a Salvation Army group.

A file notation beside Alice's name stated a bonus was allowed to Mrs.

Francis, as a recruitment fee by the Superintendent of Immigration in Canada. Mrs. Francis accompanied the entourage as a chaperone, to escort the domestics safely to Québec and Montréal.

Mrs. Francis, and others like her, were building a business of shuttling British girls across the Atlantic, with bonuses and fees from multiple sources, making her a rich woman during the next six years. She was not alone in her enterprise as there were many others like her.

"Hello, Alice. Your loan for passage was approved by the Women's Domestic Guild of Montréal. Your earnings with the Emond family will be £8 to start, with a rise to £10 in three months. You should have no trouble repaying your loan."

"Yes, Ma'am."

"Once we are settled at sea, I will send a note to your cabin of a meeting to review your Canadian entry procedures."

Mrs. Francis peered to the luggage row without focusing on anything in particular. "You marked your bags, I presume."

"Yes, they're labelled to the address you provided."

"Good girl. Once in Montréal, avail yourself of the services of the Traveller's Aid Secretaries for advice or concerns. Now, if you have no questions, proceed for boarding. Congratulations, Alice Creffield."

Porters and carts pushed alongside a throng of passengers in search of boarding depots. The emblems for White Star and Laurentic caught Alice's eye, and she jostled with the crowd that flowed in that direction. A porter's commissionaire at the front door reviewed her ticket, and pointed to a line under the Third Class sign.

Mrs. Francis paced outside a rope line stanchion, getting names and checking her manifest.

"May I see your tickets and passport, Alice?" Her name was ticked off the list of British immigrants, without even looking at her face, as a tiresome, methodical chore for Mrs. Francis.

"Checking twice is better than checking once," she said to Alice. "That's a lesson in life. Here's your cabin number. Your roommates are Maude Simmons, Harriet Lewis, and Jean Crookshaw. They are part of the Salvation Army Corps too."

"We are all going to Montréal?"

"Yes, indeed. We can count on you to do a good job. Correct, Miss

Creffield?"

Two hours later, she ascended the gangplank, securing her footing on the wooden slats, gripping the handrail. The boards opened into the bowels of the great ship to a uniformed purser. The official reviewed her vouchers and directed her to a security desk with her passport.

Two Weeks on the Laurentic, May 1913

ALICE LINGERED over the railing, as the ship pulled out from Liverpool. She watched and listened as some next to her waved and called out family names to those on the dock. A few enterprising passengers tossed rolls of coloured paper strips, cascading in mid-air to the water.

The clamour and excitement faded as they moved out of voice range, hearing only faint echoes of 'Bon Voyage' and 'I love you' from the distant harbour. She knew her own parents would have been there if they could.

They understand why I'm stepping out into the world this way.

A light ocean spray refreshed her face. Watching the coastline disappear, Alice wondered about Ma setting the table for dinner at home today, with one less setting. A pang of loneliness overwhelmed her, but she knew to expect that.

Soon after, Mrs. Francis arrived on the deck.

"Move along to your cabins, girls." The hostess quickly turned into a commander. "You all go down below to Steerage."

Each narrow hallway was dimly lit, with arrows redirecting at each turn and at the bottom of each staircase. Alice's cabin door was ajar and two voices were already inside. She stepped high over the rise of the doorstep and glanced at the daylight from the porthole.

"This is very nice," said Harriet, still with adrenalin from the deck. "We'll have so much fun. This is Maude, and we're missing Jean Crookshaw still."

Two outside cots had been claimed, with belongings scattered on top, but the two inside were empty. Alice's trunk was at foot of one, and she sat on the hard bunk. The headboard shelf had sliding doors for toiletries and a glass lantern at one end.

She excused herself to queue up at the common washroom down the hall and signed the waitlist sheet for a 6:30 a.m. shower in one of the four stalls assigned to her cabin sector.

A megaphone echoed on the decks, instructing passengers to report to muster stations with lifejackets. Alice ran to the cabin for hers, and a lighter outfit.

She halted Harriet in the corridor. "I saw them unlock the grate for Steerage passengers to get to the upper deck. It's faster."

"Just for the muster day, I'd say," said Harriet, "or for a real emergency, I'm sure."

An officer, with a rollcall and checklist, led the safety drill and within an hour they were back in the cabin.

A printed menu was on her pillow, with a meal schedule card—Table #27, Third Class Dining (buffet style), 7:00 P.M.

"Look at this. It's truly elegant," Harriet said. "After hors d'oeuvres, it's Consommé Fleury or Potage à la Sidney, then main course of Fillet of Halibut Duglere with Macaroni a la Sugo, or Roast Haunch of Mutton."

"Ah, this is how British chefs like to confuse us," Maude sighed.

"There's more; it says accompaniments of wax beans, yellow squash, caroline rice or boiled potato, and we pick from fruit jelly or ice cream. Ah, dinner, of course, would not be complete without properly steeped tea."

"Let's simplify the menu, girls," Jean said. "Looks to me like consommé or potato soup, fish or macaroni or yukky mutton, beans or squash, rice or potato, and jello or ice cream. Forget the French description."

"I liked it better in French," Alice said to everyone's pleasure.

Maude loosened them up with more. "I have a sea worthy joke, girls. Where do fish go to borrow money?"

"To the cod shop?" Alice guessed.

"No, silly. The prawn broker."

As giggles became laughter, the ice was broken, with wit flying until Maude could barely hold her sides.

In relaxed exhaustion, Alice said, "My father always came home from the pub with a joke. His favourites were Pat and Mike tales. Irish, I think."

It occurred to her that the four of them just might become long-time friends. She hoped so, as this day had started so well.

The girls dined together, and Harriet declared that it was the sea air that made them ravenous and tired. After the meal, Alice strolled the upper deck to smell Harriet's sea air. At the railing, she stared at the ocean, then at the third quarter moon. She reminisced of times debating the moon's phases with her father, whether a half or third quarter, and he set her straight each time.

She thought of Ma, sitting tonight on her porch under this same white moon, and the connection felt close. She removed the pocket watch from her skirt and caressed it, imagining how it had managed her grandfather's time for so many years of his life. Her mother insisted she take it to remind her of home in Berkshire.

That night in her nightgown, she wrote in her diary by the lantern, recording the people she met, her feelings about home that night on the deck, the anticipation of her future in Québec, and the friendship of Maude, Harriet and Jean.

Enjoying her British pals helped fight the loneliness, and Maude always eased things with a repertoire of humour. But late that night, Alice and Jean noticed that Maude slipped out in the evening and came back smelling of liquor.

Alice's mother had enforced in her to avoid gossip, but this was reason to be concerned for Maude. She envisioned the stern matron.

"Mrs. Francis wouldn't be liking that much," she said to Jean in the morning.

At seventeen knots an hour, the Laurentic was on schedule, powered by its triple-expansion, reciprocating steam engines. The centre funnel and two masts rose high above three full passenger decks, for First Class, Second, and the lowest for Third and Steerage. Partial decks stored life boats, sails, and mooring equipment. A sheet on Alice's door required that Third Class passengers use the designated dining facilities for their cabin.

On the second day, Alice and her cabin mates were summoned to a meeting by Mrs. Francis, to outline what she called 'Woman's Work in Canada' and the expected responsibilities of British domestics.

Mabel complained to the others, "I've looked after my family's home for years, yet they want to give me Canadian instructions."

Alice said, "I've heard there will also be a variety of speakers and demonstrations of duties at the Guild in Montréal."

Settled in the main dining room before 10 a.m., they waited for Mrs. Francis. Alice hadn't met most of the others in the room yet.

"Good morning, Ladies. Please collect the handouts at the door, explaining the use of equipment in a Canadian household. Many of you will be in urban, middle-class homes with modern appliances. Gone are iceboxes, replaced with electric refrigerators and ranges; no more boiling water for bathing or laundry as many homes have hot water taps at their fingertips.

"Most important, remember your place. Household staff are to remain in the kitchen or performing housekeeping duties. Otherwise, you do not eat with the family, nor do you make friends with them. Separate dining and sleeping quarters are assigned to you, usually at the back of the house. If you need comradery, you should go to the Women's Services offered in many locations."

"My goodness, Alice," Mabel elbowed, whispering her irritation. "We've been put in our place."

"I remind you that you'll be paid with Canadian dollars, and the equivalent of £5 is $25 of that money. And set aside funds every week for warm winter clothing, as the climate is severe."

A Salvation Army deaconess interjected, "We encourage you to open an account at The Bank of Montréal for your savings."

Alice reviewed the pamphlets, only raising new apprehension. The commercially printed brochure included legal jargon in the finest print, outlining a licensing agreement of the Guild and its services to the girls. She was surprised that the girls would agree to 'nonspecific deductions from their pays to cover membership costs, etc'. The etc. was not further explained, even with questions raised by another girl and met with frowns from the podium.

With a smooth, full week behind, the Captain came on with a weather announcement of changing conditions.

"The ship will passing through a gale today, and all passengers should batten down luggage and breakable items. Food service is suspended throughout the duration, other than tea and biscuits and hot chocolate in the galley."

Within hours, the ship lurched into mountainous slow motion swells, then surging back up and into another. The megaphone demanded that everyone don life jackets immediately until other notice.

The ship's jacketed staff rushed the decks to secure furnishings and doorways. High waves, splashing onto the decks, seeped with pressure under the doors and poured down staircases. Confined to their quarters, the girls stayed on their beds as the ship rolled.

Alice's lips moved with her whisper. "Blessed Mary, make the mighty power of the ocean beneath me calm, and release my fear. My head is spinning like a merry-go-round and my stomach wants to move into my throat."

Holding the wall, Harriet crossed the floor toward the tiny porthole. "It's churning with tumbling water," she said. "The white splashing is reaching our window." She staggered back to the cot. "We're fortunate as some have no daylight at all."

"If we keep our minds busy, we might not get sick," Jean said. "Maybe sing old English ditties, or even a good ole Irish one."

She tried to start one with Alice, but gave up as Maude retched into a chamber pot. Alice rinsed a washcloth in the basin to sooth Maude's forehead.

"Come on, Maude," she said. "We're missing your jokes and outrageous tales."

Maude moaned with a feeble smirk. "All I got for you today is 'When the Ship Goes Down, Pray to God, but Swim for Shore'."

Hours later, the swell eased back into a calm rhythm.

"We must be over the worst, girls. As soon as the Captain takes back his threat, I'm to the loo, then a stiff cup of coffee and fresh air," Jean said.

But fresh air was denied, as the Steerage gate was locked in place holding the lower passengers below deck until it suited the Captain.

At last, the megaphone bellowed, "Passengers may remove lifejackets, but be careful on deck. The wash has left the floor slippery."

The ship's nurses were providing bromide drinks to the sea-sick, and the girls found their way up the steps. Maude was capable of walking, and accepted a dose.

Waves were still high but Alice found the rhythm soothing.

In a small library, Alice joined an English Scrabble game, partnering with Harriet. Across was a game of checkers, and a table had an abandoned puzzle. Alice returned to the library frequently, meeting different people each visit. In the afternoons, she watched shuffleboard after tea-time.

Absorbed in a daily routine, she lost track of the days. Sunday morning found her relaxed in a foldout wooden lounge, watching the crest of the waves and shapes of clouds in the blue sky. Her eyes followed a convoy of seagulls that stayed with the ship, some bravely landing on deck, but others patient for any food remains at the disposal chute that dumped into the frothy wake.

The final days passed quickly, with some mornings bringing a heavy fog, and others with blue sky and sunshine that shimmered on the water. No matter what the weather brought, the sea air was invigorating. Occasionally, but rarely, a distant ship or freighter came into sight as a dot on the surface.

She knew her waistband had tightened.

I'll lengthen my strolls. The food's not that good. In fact, it is bland as the English will have it.

With two days to port, a faint landscape appeared at times. Maude joined her on deck, talking incessantly.

"Oooh, the coastline is magnificent—they said it's Newfoundland. Look at the boulders rising from the ocean." Others gathered at the rail in disbelief at the magnitude of the icebergs.

"Girls, look!" Alice said. "A pod of humpback whales are keeping pace."

"We'll likely never see this view again," Maude said, unsuspecting the irony of her words, as only a rare group of British domestics would chose to return to their motherland.

In the morning, the Laurentic docked at Québec, but Alice would continue to Montréal. She felt a bit of giddiness to see her first sight of Canadians on the shore.

Imagine this. And back home they're having dinner now.

Breakfast had more generous choices in the last days, with grapefruit or stewed prunes, rolled oats or cornflakes, fried fillet of Whiting or broiled sausage with savory rice, and Wiltshire bacon with fried or poached egg. In addition, the same staples were there that always appeared: Saratoga potato, French and Graham rolls, toast, derby and griddle cakes, preserves, tea, coffee, and radishes.

Passengers disembarking at Québec had to vacate their rooms by 10:00 a.m., three hours before docking. The commotion started before sunrise, with porters collecting luggage, and maids cleaning walls and cabins. At noon, all departing passengers were called to the dining room for instructions.

The next day, Alice had the same drill. As the horn blared nearing Montréal, a claw in her stomach poked at her, pondering what her real life would be like.

On the dock at Vieux Port, Montréal, the domestics were welcomed by a Salvation Army band, playing lively tunes on accordions and tambourines as they sang.

Perhaps I'll give the Sallies a try. Mother would be displeased for me not to find a good Anglican church, bless her heart.

In Search of New Life in Montréal

STEPPING TO THE wharf, the reality gripped her. Although governed by the England she knew, Montréal was uniquely French, more than she had expected. It occurred instantly that the King she served weeks before near her home was the same man that ruled this very French new land.

Alice could hear voices from the Market Square, beyond Mary's Gate and within sight of the Wharf, and a new excitement welled in her. The city was beautiful, but voices surrounding her spoke a language she'd never heard.

I assumed my employer would be English, but perhaps they are French or Canadian speaking.

Mrs. Francis was on guard, reverting to her militant attitude.

"Single file girls, stand erect and no talking!"

Under her breath, Jean muttered, "They treat us like prisoners."

Emily Francis heard the quip.

"Jean Crookshaw, go to the back of the line."

Dazed and tight-lipped, she complied, and the others stiffened. Alice showed no emotion, but she grappled with why they would be admonished this way.

The queue moved only inches at a time, as Mr. Marquette checked documents, first for the girls, then the groups from the Boys Farmers League. One by one, they reached his office to fill his forms, then identified their trunks for David Bridges of Traveller's Aid Society for transport by truck.

Marquette spoke in English. "Welcome to Montréal, Miss Creffield. Please proceed on your right, and the luggage and local transportation will be arranged."

The girls ahead of Alice were met with cheery pleasantries by Mrs. Francis, with a promise to meet at the Women's Guild.

But at her turn, it was different.

"Alice, there's a mix up with your transfer. You can line up over there and wait for me. Tonight, you'll stay at the Guild House, and Gus will take you in the morning to your job. Report to Miss Bull when you arrive."

Alice joined three other girls on the concourse. Mrs. Francis didn't come as promised, but together, the girls were shoved through the back entrance of an electric trolley car for a half-hour trip to Drummond Street.

On the wooden transit bench, she weighed everything.

Everything is so different than I imagined. Mother and father will be in their cold damp parlour, while I am here, uncertain of the very next minute. Wet shoes running to the Barber's house doesn't seem so bad after all.

Near an English-style residence, the driver announced their stop. From the doorway, a matron in a grey wool suit called to them. "Good day ladies. I'm Miss Bull, come in." Her voice was deep, and she forced a smile.

The four were assigned to a humble room with two double beds. "The house rules are simple," she said. "It's tea at ten and two, and supper at five with self-service from the buffet."

Alice raised her elbow with a query.

"No questions, missy. You'll wash your own dishes, but no more than two in the kitchen with the cook at any time. I won't allow gossiping or wandering the house."

Her scowl went away for an instant. "Ladies, you may have use of the back garden if you wish."

Alice's appetite wasn't fully satisfied by her first Canadian supper.

The cook rationed out hipped beef, mashed potatoes and mushy peas, with enough guarded for another day. Miss Bull entered again as they finished. "Join me in the parlor and take up knitting squares for refugee blankets.

By 8:30 p.m., the sky was dusky and Alice wanted to crawl into bed. Hungry and scared, she cradled her arms around her shoulders and cried from the inside.

Tomorrow has to be better.

The sun was up before six, and so was Alice, with her satchel at the door. "Who's Gus?" she said aloud to herself, anticipating a better start.

Out on Drummond Street, a grandfatherly hackney waited by the curb.

"Mornin' miss. Why the sad face, luv?"

Alice delighted in the sound of his voice.

"Goodmorn', you must be from London. Is it Gus, by chance?"

He lowered his tweed cap. "I'll be taking you in the GMC today to Westmount. That's a lovely suburb of Montréal. A little uppity for me, but with all the convenience a British lass will appreciate. Don't worry about your trunk; Harold will bring it along later."

"Thank you. When shall we leave?"

"My orders from Mrs. Francis say promptly at nine. But I must say, Miss Alice, you're looking a bit forlorn. I see that a lot when the girls first arrive, but after the probation period, not even a handful choose to go back to England. You'll see things differently before you know it."

"I hope so."

"Chin up, Alice, and if it don't, then come lookin' for Gus and I'll take you to a real proper English pub. There ye can meet British guys and gals."

He is a godsend. I expect I'll be seeing Gus again.

Gus produced a small notebook. "Alice, give me your full name and I'll jot where you'll be. Sometimes, ladies that made friends on the ship look to reacquaint with their travel mates. Sooner or later they find me."

Alice laughed at his enthusiasm and wondered how many homesick girls he had brought a smile to. "God bless you, Gus." At 9:00 a.m., Mrs. Francis came outside with the delivery address and her face was kinder.

"Alice, if you need assistance at all, go to the Cathcart Lodge; it's at No. 24. The Emonds are ready to meet you now, and I'm sure you'll have a grand time in Montréal."

Forty-nine

Urgel Paquette holds Ad Hoc meeting at Barber Shop – Mimicker & Story Teller – Local Railway Chatter – Emile & Joseph Paquette Sojourn to St. Eustache – Commiserating over Cider & Cards – Attack of the Bobcat on Beech Ridge Road – Donald Loynachan to the Rescue – Another War Brewing - Parliamentary Discussions at Moise's – 'Conscription' raised by Robert Borden – Two Bullets through the Streets of Sarajevo, 1914 – Germany Declares War on France – Britain Retaliates declaring war on Germany – Québecois Conundrum over Britain's War & Conscription – Paquette & Charlebois Households Discuss Allegiance.

Moise's Barber Shop, Main Street

URGEL PAQUETTE WAS QUICK TO VOLUNTEER TO GO for the latest issue of *The Watchman*. It should have been a twenty minute stroll to Main Street, but it always took him the full morning, with visits on the way and often an odd carpentry repair in his impromptu social visits.

Main Street in St. Andrews always thrived with morning activity; the favoured meeting stoop was outside Moise Paquette's Barber Shop, with the men at the mismatched chairs there or in front of the hotels. On most days, these were his destinations.

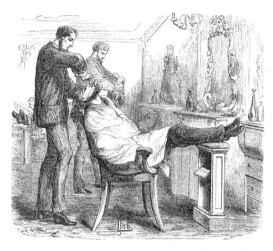

Chez le coiffeur/ At the barber's, Artist Léon Job-Vernet, France, ca 1830,
Wood engraving, from L'Illustration, Publisher Paris: Bubochet & Cie, 1857.

Leaving the house, he asked Victoria if she needed kitchen basics, and she knew it helped him justify the urgency of his outing.

Victoria had refused to let Urgel arrange for a wall telephone to be installed at the farm. "It's just a waste of money. Next, they will arrange that we won't have to walk anywhere."

Before he could answer, she predicted his plan. "No, Urgel, you can't buy your brother's old Ford."

In recent years *The Watchman* of Lachute had overtaken The *Argenteuil Advisor*, a weekly publication in French only. Local French-Canadians thought it was useless to provide news to the Anglophones, some even suggesting they were misguided and didn't appreciate local goings on.

Many daily and weekly papers came and went in the surrounding communities, struggling with the same French and English dilemma, and struggling for advertising money to survive.

Familiar faces gathered on the verandas, perched on chairs, benches and railings. The barber shop was owned by a distant cousin of his, yet the Paquette name itself could draw a crowd worth joining. The barber chair inside was empty and Moise stood at the door in a white apron. He recognized Urgel's silhouette approaching in the morning sun.

Urgel always had his pipe, and was most comfortable in weathered whiskers, and his grey wool cap. Whenever it got left behind in town by mistake, it inevitably found its way back home. He settled in a wooden chair in the middle of the group.

"Allo Urgel, come inside," Moise said. "I know more about these gents on my step than they know themselves."

The four or five listeners laughed and applauded, and Moise Paquette added a husky chortle. Urgel leaned forward in his chair on the pretense that he was about to rise, then sat again, and they all roared once more.

"Well, Moise, I was startin' to tell mes amis about my pa's adventures. At the moment, I have their full attention."

"Oh, they've heard them all before, Urgel. Believe me, they'll still be in the same spot when you're finished your haircut."

Moise looked at the men for agreement.

"Oui, Urgel, we will wait," one said, and two others nodded.

"Urgel, come to the chair *now!*" Moise said. "An Englishman is coming this way. You don't want to wait for an Englishman to finish, do you?"

"Man oh man, that'll be the day."

Moise ambled inside; behind him, to the amusement of his pals, Urgel mimicked his bowed legs and jolly belly. Snickers came from his audience.

Removing his cap, Urgel exposed unkempt curly hair and hung the grey cap on the hook.

"You'll be wanting the same cut?" The common style for a French-Canadian male was a part down the middle and bangs pushed to the sides, with clean shaven neck, cheeks, and chin. If it were to a man's liking, a mannered moustache was in vogue.

Urgel leaned back to let Moise attach a bib and hot towel over his eyes. "Relaxin' ch?"

"I'm tinkin' of takin' a nap even," Urgel muttered.

"By golly, my business is more exchanging information than the actual haircut. You can't deprive me, Urgel."

"What did the last Englishman you had in here have to say?"

"Thomas Barron was here a few days ago, lamenting of the traffic congestion caused by the new bridge over Cruise's Gully. You know where it runs along St. Andrews Road? Seems the horses aren't taking too well to the new Reo he bought in Montréal."

"What's a Reo?"

"It's a two-seater putter made in St. Catharines. You'll be surprised; it looks miniature, like it's meant for kids."

Urgel laughed at his own scenario. "I'd never get all my family into a two-seater, even if I piled the lot of my kids and grandkids onto Victoria's lap."

"Yesterday, outside my own window, I saw a band of Irishmen singing old railroad songs on their way to the depot. Seems they were sent here to work on the railway joining Lachute to St. Andrews." He snorted as he laughed, "Since the first one didn't work."

"Well, they don't call the Ottawa Valley Railroad the 'Get Out and Push' railway for nothin'."

Shuffling his feet back to the Paquette farmhouse, Urgel sang *I've Been Workin' on the Railroad*, a tune he learned from a pair of Irishmen in the tavern.

Urgel marched in animation with the tune until a cartage carrier barreled down the road kicking dust in his mouth.

"Urgel waved his hat in disgust. Slow down there, Emery."

Joseph & Émile Paquette's Stopover in St. Eustache

EVEN FOR A DAY'S visit, the vibrancy of Montréal was invigorating. With his sons, Joseph and Émile, Urgel left to get there early to negotiate a tender for work on the Ottawa River.

The bells of Notre-Dame Cathedral tolled overhead as they wound through cobblestone streets, past the stone foundries. Soon their own talk was drowned out by street sounds of vendors' voices at the bustling carts.

They were quick getting to the city this time, and Joe slowed and then stopped at the Wharf.

"What are you doing?" Émile said. We don't have business here."

"But we can afford to stop, Émile, and there's no better place than the docks for energy."

The men walked on the pier, admiring the massive ropes and hanging anchors on the overseas ships, freighters and lumber tows. Joe plugged his nose at the pungent algae washing, and they decided together to get on with business.

They both dressed well whenever they came to Montréal. It was expected of any respectable businessman, a contrast to the comfort and familiarity in St. Andrews.

By two o'clock, they left the meeting and loosened their vests with relief. They wound out of the city, intent on arriving early to spend the night at St. Eustache, to see their Giroux and Monderie cousins. At Uncle Georges' farm, they'd trade this rushed pace for lush strips of farmlands and crops, visible for miles.

The contrast from Montréal struck Joe especially this time, even from the dusty road. The air here was calm, with silence broken only by crows over the fields.

Émile pointed to the field as they approached. "They love their complicated thingamajig equipment," he said. Uncle Georges was moving at a steady pace, harrowing the cornfield with his steam tractor, and one of the sons followed with a Hill Seed Spreader.

Joseph's stories were bigger than life, and kept his cousins captive around the dinner table, elaborating on his grandfather, Victor.

With animation, he jumped from the chair, to act out encounters in the deep woods, whether an angry ram, a head-butting elk, hungry black bears, stalking wolves, or especially the attack of porcupine quills. Each time, the stories were embellished with greater drama, and his voice inflections became more comical, traits he acquired from Victor.

Georges brought out his best cider and a deck of cards, easily luring the men to play long into the night.

"Uncle Georges, you beat me again. You know this means either you have to come to St. Andrews or we'll be here again for a rematch."

"Anytime, Joe, I'll always take you on."

Marie-Louise was up before sunrise, preparing breakfast, aware the men had barely slept, but knowing their pending appetites. She packed a lunch for the Paquette boys, and filled a burlap sack full of baby clothes that would not be needed on the Giroux farm.

It was the spring of 1912, and Joseph was a young man of twenty-three living at home. His mother, Victoria Charlebois, was hard-working at forty-six and due to give birth to her eleventh child. Joseph graciously accepted the sack from Aunt Marie-Louise, and felt empty-handed that he had nothing to offer in return. For Marie-Louise, his hug was ample.

Attack of the Bobcat on Beech Ridge Road

FAREWELLS DRAGGED on to the lane, and with a sandwich in hand, Joseph maneuvered the wagon onto the road toward Saint-André-Est. An overnight rain left the road muddy and slippery, and halfway home, Joseph thought he felt his left lead horse coming up lame.

Both men dismounted and found the horse had thrown a shoe. Joseph was bent over inspecting the hoof, when something made the hairs on his neck raise. He raised his hand to Émile, at the rustling and crackling of underbrush. News had spread in town the week before that a bobcat in the area had killed a dog and a foal. Joseph's senses now gave him a sick feeling.

His index finger was to his lips. "Cougar . . . no fast moves." He pointed to the lead horse's reins, and Émile silently unhitched Chester.

Joe hitched the wagon to the other horse, and Émile got up to drive. "I'll walk Chester," Joseph said.

A crackle of twigs was closer, and Joseph saw the movement of brush keeping pace.

"He'll go for my lame horse," Joseph decided. "If he doesn't go for the horse, he'll go for me."

Émile could see nothing but a tragic ending. "Joseph, leave the horse and get up here! We can race down the road and save ourselves."

"No. Don't underestimate the speed of a cougar or bobcat or whatever has latched onto us. The road isn't good, and we won't get any speed."

Joseph was even with the driver seat and reached for his pa's new Colt hammerless breach-loading rifle. They always said he saved money where it didn't matter, but for hunting guns he always got the best. Joseph drew the lame horse over to the protected side of the wagon. With the rifle to his shoulder, he found a straight view from under the bench.

"Surely, the cougar will sense our fear," his rationale said.

There—he saw the eyes of the stalker staring from the bush, arched and poised to lunge.

Whoosh! A sudden flutter of birds evacuated the shrubbery.

"Émile, get the Smith-Wesson revolver, and maybe the hunting knife in your other hand."

Joe knew they'd be easy prey, at least one of them. The horses were skittish and rearing, taking all the boys' strength to control them and hold a line of defence. Joseph talked later about the trauma he felt at the instant he saw the cat's open jaw and teeth.

With a sustained growl, it crashed through the woods toward the horse. Émile fired, but the wounded cat kept coming at breakneck speed.

His sight stayed on its eyes in mid-air, and in precision measurement, he fired again. The second from the Colt brought down the ninety pound bobcat. Struck and writhing in flight, the torn cat gripped the neck of the lame horse.

The horse screeched, with claws ripping her neck as the cat slid to the ground. With a final bullet, the bobcat was motionless.

Fearing a runaway, Émile's reins tightened to steady the wagon horse. "Steady! Steady! Whoa boy!"

Joseph stayed with the lame horse. "Easy boy, easy!" He rested his arms on her to calm her, then leaned his head whispering into its ears.

The two boys stood speechless, then broke into a feeble laugh to break the tension, then howled until they were weak.

"Shall we go back and tell Uncle Georges about this one?"

"I'll stay with Chester." Joseph tore his sleeves to soak in the creek, then dabbed the wounds.

"Émile, you go for help."

The good horse, Warden, was untethered from the wagon and Émile got on, bareback.

At the first farm on Beech Ridge Road, he found an English farmer with a horse trailer.

"What is it? You're one of the Paquette boys, aren't ye?" the farmer, Donald Loynachan, asked.

"Yes, sir. We came under attack of a giant cougar. My brother is down the road with a lame and wounded horse. She can't walk."

"I've had my share of lame ones, lad," Loynachan said. "I'll take a team and my trailer to find your brother. Just go on and get your pa."

Marcie, Émile, and Victoria waited on the steps for the horse-trailer to come into sight in the dusk. They'd see it pass under the light of Murray's gristmill just before the farm, and were finally at ease when the shadow appeared.

Victoria shrieked at Joseph's blood-soaked shirt and muddied face. She was quick for a pregnant woman, wringing her apron in her hands, and lurching at her eldest son.

"Mon dieu!" She embraced him and touched the surface of his scratches with her fingers.

"He looks strong enough to me," Urgel said. "We'll get him washed and bandaged soon, but let's see the horse now."

Joe's face lit up, and led his Dad to the trailer. A blanket over her back was already drying and sticky, and Urgel checked the wounds in the light.

"I'd say that with a new shoe and time to heal, she'll return to health, Joe. We'll have the vet stop tomorrow; there could be infection, or worse, rabies. The bobcat was at the back of the wagon covered in spruce boughs, preserved for the taxidermist.

After hushed words, Urgel approached Mr. Loynachan and offered him payment for his services and a gracious handshake.

"Thank you, Monsieur Paquette, but there's no need to hire me. If it were my boys, I'd hope for the same. Perhaps, though . . . it's dark now. Could I offer a bunk for the night and hear the story of this great adventure?"

The Englishman's hat was folded in his hands anticipating the first-hand Paquette tale. Joseph and Émile grinned at the brief heroism status.

"But, of course, come join us for supper," Victoria said. "We'll be more than glad if you stay now, and any other time you come to St. Andrews." She directed him inside to the wash basin by the kitchen door.

The next day, Urgel was anxious to go to Moise's Barber Shop to tell the story of not one cougar, but a cougar *and* a bobcat.

He languished in the attention and the barber insisted today would be a free shave.

St. Andrews and the Brewing Great War, 1913

THE OTTAWA CITIZEN'S Editor was reporting on the doom and gloom of the war brewing in Europe, with anarchy between Austria and Hungary drawing lines among their neighbours.

France consented to join the Allied nations if tensions were to result in war. There had never before been a Great War, especially one that drew the attention of St. Andrews East.

Shops and shoppers in St. Andrews ground to slow motion as the gravity became clear. What had been rumour and caution was now fear as the candid reality was presented by Prime Minister Robert Borden.

At the barber shop, Urgel heard about the newest Parliamentary discussions about recruitment and enlistment of young boys. Some on the chairs outside said the papers had even used the dreaded word 'conscription'.

Georges Giroux said, "It seems wrong. Some say the pressure to send volunteers is Britain's issue, not Québec's. Why are we involved in European matters?"

Fortunat Charlobois chewed on a straw. "And what about lost labour here, if men enlist? That will be a burden for our families too."

Urgel brought the concern of conscription home in his thoughts, concerned for the boys' safety, more than the labour.

He chose the dinner table to discuss both issues.

"Ah, this is much ado about nothing," Joseph said.

"Let the British fight for their own Imperial Country," Victoria added, with her new babe asleep in her arms.

Urgel added, "Borden says everyone will need to work . . . whether it's across the seas, or at home in the factories. Well, Victoria, I guess that means you too. Means you knit or fight."

She didn't laugh at all.

"I have my own full detachment here in this house. Don't you think for one minute Urgel Paquette that I don't work? I'm fifty years old, and no

Robert Borden's going to tell me what I should be doing."

The boys looked at their father.

"I was teasin' you, love, come rest your weary bones. Desneige and Marcie will look after the kitchen."

The Spark that Ignited the Great War, 1914

TWO BULLETS echoed through Sarajevo. The crisp morning of June 28, 1914 was broken with the shots, assassinating Archduke Franz Ferdinand, first in line to the Austrian-Hungarian throne, and his wife. On that day, they'd been invited to join General Oskar Potoriek, Governor of Bosnia-Herzegovina.

Unknown to the Archduke, plans were afoot by the Black Hand to remove him from interfering with concessions to the Southern Slavs impending independence, with support from the Chief of Serbian Intelligence, Dragutin Dimitrijevic.

Three of Dimitrijevic's men stepped forward for the clandestine suicide mission that morning at Sarajevo. In the first attempt to disrupt the royal party, a bomb was thrown under the approaching car. Several were injured, but Duke Ferdinand and Sophie escaped in the second vehicle.

When the Duke insisted on returning to visit injured dignitaries from the blast, one of the escaped men of the Black Hand, eighteen year old Gavrilo Princip, took advantage and jumped out in front of the Duke's open car on the bridge. In an instant, he fired the shots that killed the royal couple, sparking the powder keg and World War I.

On July 28, 1914, the war began. On August 3, Germany declared war on France. The next day, England's Foreign Minister, Sir Edward Grey, exhausted himself with demands that Germany retreat from its invasion of neutral Belgium. He was summoned to meet with King George V, and on August 5, Britain declared war on Germany.

"It's all happening too fast," Urgel told Victoria. "In town, they say our soldiers are being trained at Valcartier, near Québec. It's too close to home in my mind. Georges says Canada can send thirty-five thousand volunteers. He reads every line of the paper, so it's true."

"Urgel, how can Wilfrid Laurier ask French Canadians to go to Great Britain to be trained in battle to settle squabbles overseas? It's asking too much," Victoria said. Her knitting needles worked rapidly reflecting her ire and adrenalin.

Urgel tried to appease her. "Politics is greater than the village of St. Andrews, dearest. Pay no mind to the British until they order our sons to fight their battles."

"I don't have a good feeling about that."

With a deepened and more serious voice, Urgel continued, "The Lachute paper quoted exhortations from King George V, British Prime Minister Asquith, and Sir Edward Grey about terrible losses. Look at the great heroism of Canadians—just in October, we sent more than thirty thousand troops, thirty transport ships and seven thousand horses."

"Land sakes, Urgel. Should we fear for our own sons?"

"Britain has sent navel escorts to the Gaspé for our troops but that is little consolation to Québecers."

"I feel so helpless. Last week I saw one of those military jeeps heading along Main Street. The only time they're seen in town is when they are delivering a death notice. Did you hear who it was?" Victoria asked.

Burdened by the war, Joseph was conflicted by the conundrum between English and French Canada, then his duty to his family and community.

"Should my allegiance be to the French-Canadian people, or the British government that serves the whole of Canada?"

He considered a fast trip to Montréal to sense the heart of his people and to find his allegiance. But first he'd find his grandfather, Treffle Giroux; his opinion would count.

Joe's maternal grandparents had been close to him since the day of his birth as they lived a stone's throw from Urgel's house. Treffle Charlebois and Elizabeth Giroux greeted him in the yard. Aunt Assenath was in the kitchen, as she was when he stopped the week before.

"Joseph, it's always so good, but you still don't come often enough," Assenath said. "Sit now; I have an apple cobbler right out of the oven and Ma has the coffee pot brewing."

LARGEMARCK
ST JULIEN
FESTUBERT
GIVENCHY

New names in
Canadian history.
More are coming —
Will you be there?

ENLIST!

Make us as proud of you
as we are of him!

WWI Recruitment Poster, 1914-18, offset lithograph, 69.8 x 52.0 cm,
Author Patterson, C.J.; Printed Lawson and Jones; Library and Archives Canada

After two spoons of sugar and a dribble of cream, he blew the rising vapour from the steaming coffee.

Joe said, "The rumblings in St. Andrews are concerning. Everyone has a political opinion. I'd like to go to Montréal to find out for myself what all the worry is about, grandfather."

"You can worry here or you can worry there. Does it matter, son?" Treffle asked.

"Yes, Grandfather, it does."

Joseph looked into Treffle's brown eyes. "I can see that you've experienced much of Québec and lived its history. I need to have my turn too. It's one thing to raise a rifle to an animal in the woods, but quite another to set your target on a human being."

Treffle straightened his back against his chair.

With thumbs in his suspenders, he said. "I'd forgotten that the spirit of the Paquettes dwells in you, and I'm not one to stop you from seeing the world. Will you be enlisting with the Van Doos?"

"I don't see that the government gives me a choice. And at least France is one of the Allies I'll be defending. I've got time to mull it over, Grandfather. They're just talking conscription, but the process through parliament will take a long time."

As Joseph got up to leave after their pleasant visit, Elizabeth, came to give him a hug. At the same time, she feebly shoved a ten dollar bill into his hand.

"Ah Grandmother, you know you're my favorite, but not this time." Joe folded her arthritic fingers over the bill and squeezed her hand.

Fifty

Alice Creffield Takes a Position in Westmount, Montréal

AFTER A TOUR OF THE KITCHEN AND LARDER AT THE Emond's residence in Westmount, Alice was led to the back room she'd share with the housekeeper. The sun shone onto the wall above her bed through the small window. "I'll like this room," she said, and looked out over the manicured lawns.

The house was a rectangular stone mansion, with a curved centre hall staircase. Fresh flowers in Ming vases on pedestals framed each corner.

At the outset, Mrs. Emond showed little emotion. Alice noticed her to be a handsome woman, always with a stern face. She took a glance at her burned amber bouffant.

"Here's your schedule for today, Alice. This afternoon, I'll sit with you to go through your menu for the next week. We do it early so the butcher and grocer can be notified. Oh, and Bradford detests lamb and rice pudding." Her face lightened with that.

"In the mornings, take a basket and walk with Guthrie, the gardener.

He has a vegetable patch yonder behind the red maple, and likes to know what you remove from his beds."

"I hope you'll feel welcome, Alice. Take note that lunch will be served promptly at noon." With that, she turned and Alice assumed she was dismissed.

Alice spent some morning time alone in the spacious kitchen, getting oriented to the appliances and cupboards. From her baggage, she brought out a collection of folded papers detailing the ship's menus, glad she'd been particular.

Taking account of the larder, she decided today would be a clear consommé, handmade salmon cakes with slivers of chive, potato croquettes and a green gruyere and pear salad. For dessert, she had time for an apple tartlet.

Surely I can't go wrong with this. We'll see if the plates are cleaned.

The lunch was a resounding success and Mrs. Emonds smiled warmly. "Your recommendations are indeed well deserved."

Millicent, the housekeeper, was in charge of Alice, but was easygoing and glad of the companionship.

At the end of the first week, Millie suggested that Alice attend the Salvation Army citadel, since she had Sunday morning off.

Matchmaking between St. Andrews & Montréal, 1914

JOSEPH'S MOTHER brought the mail in. "One for you today, Joe." He read slowly to himself first.

"It's from Cousin Elizabeth Giroux," he said. "She says an English woman in Montréal can arrange a few days' bed and breakfast. Her name is Louise Callaghan, and I assume she's with the Salvation Army as it's on their paper.

"Elizabeth says I'm to wear a red handkerchief in my breast pocket so Miss Callaghan can recognize me. That's funny, but I guess she'll pick me from the crowd at the railway station."

"Is it soon?" his mother asked.

"Thursday at four o'clock. I'll reply yes."

Joe's English was broken, but he had no difficulty being understood. He'd listened to the English gents on Main Street plenty of times. Looking forward to the comradery, he got a shave at Moise's, dressed his best and put on an ascot.

Louise found him without difficulty and removed his handkerchief. Her face flushed for a moment before she extended her gloved hand.

"Pleased to meet you, Mister Joseph Paquette."

"Thank you, Miss Callaghan, for meeting me and arranging my accommodation. I am grateful. The train ride was scenic and Montréal looks beautiful today. I have been many times to see old friends, but I see it in a different way."

Joseph thought he'd heard that you take the lady's hand with his left, bow ever so lightly and kiss the top of her glove. He felt awkward with it, but she didn't notice.

Louise tried to break the ice. "It seems our grandmothers are acquainted through cousins and whatnot."

"Well the Girouxs do have many cousins in the Townships."

Joseph hailed a hansom cab at the train depot, and Louise gave the driver an address for the boarding house.

"It's across town, but not far. The Montréal Tramways run trolleys and electric streetcars along main routes throughout the city. If you don't have plans this evening, Mr. Paquette, you are welcome to join me and my friend at a Literary Meeting. She works as a cook in Westmount—she's British." As badly as he didn't want to go, he hid it in his acknowledgement.

Louise and her friend, Alice Creffield, rode the tram and walked on foot to the boarding house, to accompany Joseph to Lindsay Hall.

This all seemed peculiar to him. He sat next to Alice, as a dissertation from Henry Wadsworth was read. After a buoyant discussion, members took an intermission for tea and mingled about the room. Miss Callaghan went directly to the speaker for an intellectual discussion.

Joe noticed Alice's fine buttoned shoes and the bit of lace at the top. She was shy, but courteous. Her accent captivated him, and he encouraged her to speak about her home in New Windsor and the voyage to Canada.

Still sitting, he took glances up at her face as he dared, observing her fair skin and blue eyes, even her fine nose; her hair was pulled back with combs and Joseph noticed that she wore tiny pearl earrings.

"How did you meet Miss Callaghan?" he asked in broken English, hoping it wouldn't offend her.

"I signed onto a Salvation Army group back home to travel. Mrs. Francis, our chaperone, arranged employment for all the girls over eighteen. I'm assigned to a Dry Goods Merchant and his wife with three lads, none yet in school."

"Well, I'm glad you made the decision to come to Montréal."

"I do miss my mother, but I am making friends slowly. It's good to get out to events, to meet others in similar situations. An enormous number of girls like me were sent through the Army. The house I'm at has a boisterous lot of boys, so it's refreshing to get out and talk 'adult'." They both laughed.

"I'm afraid I don't know much about the Salvation Army, but I know a lot about a house full of boys. I'm the oldest of eleven children and my ma just had a newborn last year."

"My gosh!" Alice raised her gloved hand to her lips.

"Oh no, it's nothing to be sorry about. We have a lot of fun, the more the merrier."

"If you are still here on Saturday night, you can come with me to a meeting. You'll like it, I'm certain."

Alice showed intrigue and deep interest as Joseph talked about his family and small town St. Andrews. His effort to speak English charmed her.

"Sounds lovely to get out of the big city," she mused.

As if Joseph read her thoughts, he asked, "Do you perhaps have a calling card? I may come back soon and I'd be happy to take you and Miss Callaghan to my town for a visit."

His voice trembled slightly. "The Fête de Dollard in honour of Queen Victoria will be celebrated in a fortnight. If you'd like to come, I'll make train reservations. My mother loves to have company."

"That is a lovely offer, Joseph," Alice said. "I can't speak in French, so I hope they'll like me anyway."

Louise and Alice whispered, before accepting Joseph's invitation.

At the boarding house, Joseph tipped his hat and bade them adieu. "They'll like her," he repeated to himself.

The next morning, he strolled Montréal's Market, and watched from Mary's Gate as enlisted troops converged from different parts of Québec, noticing that many were just young boys, not even out of school. Although the minimum enlistment age had dropped to sixteen, they must have turned the other way, for surely some of the lads were not more than twelve or fourteen.

Urgel and Victoria took the news of the Montréal girls with chagrin.

"Why, Urgel, can't Joseph court one of our own? The Charlebois girls are lovely, the Monderies spunky, the Girouxs hard-working, or the LeRoy sisters or Cloutiers that he went to school with. Any of those girls would be good prospects. You don't need to go farther than Lachute or Carillon."

"Ma chère, it will be alright. He's twenty-six years old and yearns to set up his own farm. We should give Joseph credit for going out of his way to bring this girl to St. Andrews."

"Do you think she speaks French? I really don't like that hoity-toity British whine."

"Now, now, Victoria. Don't speak like that."

"You're right, Urgel. I'm sorry, I went too far."

"Just count your lucky bridges Joseph isn't listening."

Joseph borrowed the family buggy early Friday morning, scrubbed it clean and buffed it with wax. The seats were polished and the floorboards swept. Urgel watched from the house and reminded Victoria this British lady must be special.

The final inspection came from his sisters, Agathe and Aurore.

"You've already been to the barber this morning," Agathe teased and felt his smooth, shaved face. She tightened the bow tie and gave Joseph a peck on the cheek.

They chuckled in delight, at the first time they'd seen Joe nervous about a girl.

"I'll bet we'll be having at least one sister-in-law before the year is out. Émile is also sweet on Olivina Larose over at St. Hermas."

Guests for Victoria Day Celebrations in St. Andrews

JOSEPH'S BUGGY was at the St. Andrews train station a full half hour early for Alice, and he sat outside the teller's wicket, passing time with the clerk and chewing sweet grass. Their conversation was lengthy, but Joseph remembered little of it as he watched past the man and down the track. At last, the whistle of the engine blared its arrival.

The two weeks passed quickly since he'd seen her. St. Andrews was revved up for Victoria Day celebrations, with British ensign flags draped over hotel railings and proudly identifying stores owned by Brits or Scots. Patriotism was already on display around the world, stoked by stories of the nations' courage at war.

Joe offered his arm to Louise Callaghan first, then to Alice, as they stepped from the railway car to the boardwalk. Locking eyes with Alice, he noticed her blush. She extended her hand for assistance again on the walk, wearing the same lace top boots with pretty buttons.

Loose strands of curls framed her oval face, and Joseph noticed for the first time that the sun caught gold beams in the reddish brown tresses. As her kind blue eyes watched him, he was tongue-tied for a first time.

The porter reached to Joseph with two large satchels, and he tucked one under his arm, and gripped the other handle. By the time the girls were in the buggy and bags stowed, he worried that a trickle of sweat might show on his shirt.

The stone farmhouse had never looked more beautiful to him than today. He was seeing the welcoming homestead through the eyes of a stranger, and realized he had never before appreciated it this way.

"La maison est très agréable, Joseph," Alice declared, to his delight.

"Oui, oui, très jolie," Louise added.

Victoria sat on the porch, pretending to be mending from her basket. Urgel knew though that she was ready to see the Anglican girls, and he came right away from the barn to join her.

Victoria found herself taken by Alice. She put forth her best effort at English, and Alice reciprocated with practiced French words. Within moments, any tension was gone and they chatted and laughed at Victoria's stories of Joseph.

Nobody was excluded in the introductions, as his siblings lined up, scrubbed and polished to impress Joe's friend. One by one, they reached to touch or shake Alice's hand—Emily, Regina, Émile, Aurore, Desneige, Marcie, Agathe, Felix, Rosemary, and finally Rose Anna Marie and Philippe, both under five.

Aurore and Desneige led Louise and Alice to their accommodations. The room had two double iron beds, and Desneige teased that as guests they would be using the best one, as the other had an irritating sag in the mattress.

"That is so kind of you, girls. I had a bed exactly like that back home in Berkshire. It had been in the family for a long time," Alice said.

"You'll need to mind your head on the slanted roof, but you'll also find it interesting," Desneige said. "Some guests who stayed in that bed have written a note for us about their visit. We'd be obliged if you would too."

Alice instantly knew what she would write later. 'Ask and you shall receive.'

Habitants Ode to Jubilee on the North River

JOSEPH WAITED downstairs. He'd borrowed a skiff from Mr. Fournier, fitted with a double bench and cushioned seats, and a canopy for shelter. In the afternoon sun, he surprised Louise and Alice with a leisurely drift on the North River, and Louise said right away it was one of her best days.

Barefoot and in cotton dresses, they were cool under the awning, letting their fingers idle in the water through lily pads.

Joseph's paddle always left the water without a splash, and they followed two mother ducks with their flocks close.

At the dry goods store, Joe had found a posting of the *Habitants Jubilee Ode'* and had written out the words for the occasion. It took him most of a week to memorize the first part.

I read on de paper mos' ev'ry day, all about Jubilee
An' grande procession movin' along, an' passin' across de sea,
Dat's chil'ren of Queen Victoria comin' from far away
For tole Madame w'at dey t'ink of her, an' wishin' her bonne santé.

An' if any wan want to know pourquoi les Canayens should be dere
Wit' res' of de worl' for shout "Hooraw" an' t'row hees cap on de air,
Purty quick I will tole heem de reason, w'y we feel lak de oder do,
For if I'm only poor habitant, I'm not on de sapré fou.

Of course w'en we t'ink it de firs' go off, I know very strange it seem
For fader of us dey was offen die for flag of L'Ancien Regime,
From day w'en de voyageurs come out all de way from ole St. Malo,
Flyin' dat flag from de mas' above, an' long affer dat also.

De English fight wit' de Frenchman den over de whole contree,
Down by de reever, off on de wood, an' out on de beeg, beeg sea,
Killin', an' shootin', an' raisin' row, half tam dey don't know w'at for,
W'en it's jus' as easy get settle down, not makin' de crazy war.

Sometam' dey be quiet for leetle w'ile, you t'ink dey don't fight no more,
An' den w'en dey're feelin' all right agen, Bang! jus' lak' she was before.
Very offen we're beatin' dem on de fight, sometam' dey can beat us, too
But no feller's scare on de 'noder man, an' bote got enough to do.

An' all de long year she be go lak' dat, we never was know de peace,
Not'ing but war from de wes' contree down to de St. Maurice;
Till de las' fight's comin' on Canadaw, an' brave Generale Montcalm
Die lak' a sojer of France is die, on Battle of Abraham.

Dat's finish it all, an' de English King is axin' us stayin' dere
W'ere we have sam' right as de 'noder peep comin' from Angleterre.
Long tam' for our moder so far away de poor Canayens is cry,
But de new step-moder she's good an' kin', an' it's all right bimeby.

"There's more of the story too, do you want to hear it?"
"Yes, yes." The girls clapped and laughed.

If de moder come dead w'en you're small garçon leavin' you dere alone,
Wit' nobody watchin' for fear you fall, an hurt youse'f on de stone,
An' 'noder good woman she tak' your han' de sam' your own moder do,
Is it right you don't call her moder, is it right you don't love her too?

Bâ non, an' dat was de way we feel, w'en de ole Regime's no more,
An' de new wan come, but don't change moche, w'y it's jus' lak' it be before.
Spikin' Français lak' we alway do, an' de English dey mak no fuss,
An' our law de sam', wall, I don't know me, 'twas better mebbe for us.

So de sam' as two broder we settle down, leevin' dere han' in han',
Knowin' each oder, we lak' each oder, de French an' de Englishman,
For it's curi's t'ing on dis worl', I'm sure you see it agen an' agen,
Dat offen de mos' worse ennemi, he's comin' de bes', bes' frien'.

So we're kipin' so quiet long affer dat, w'en las' of de fightin's done,
Dat plaintee is say, de new Canayens forget how to shoot de gun;
But Yankee man's smart, all de worl' know dat, so he's firs' fin' mistak' wan day
W'en he's try cross de line, fusil on hee's han', near place dey call Châteaugay.

Of course it's bad t'ing for poor Yankee man, De Salaberry be dere
Wit' habitant farmer from down below, an' two honder Voltigeurs,
Dem feller come off de State, I s'pose, was fightin' so hard dey can
But de blue coat sojer he don't get kill, is de locky Yankee man!

Since den w'en dey're comin on Canadaw, we alway be treat dem well,
For dey're spennin' de monee lak' gentil-hommes, an' stay on de bes' hotel,
Den 'Bienvenu,' we will spik dem, an' 'Come back agen nex' week,
So long you was kip on de quiet an' don't talk de politique!'

Yass, dat is de way Victoriaw fin' us dis jubilee,
Sometam' we mak' fuss about not'ing, but it's all on de familee,
An' w'enever dere's danger roun' her, no matter on sea or lan',
She'll find that les Canayens can fight de sam' as bes' Englishman.

An' onder de flag of Angleterre, so long as dat flag was fly--
Wit' deir English broder, les Canayens is satisfy leev an' die.
Dat's de message our fader geev us w'en dey're fallin' on Châteaugay,
An' de flag was kipin' dem safe den, dat's de wan we will kip alway![52]

---

[52] The Habitants Ode to Jubliee, written by William Henry Drummond (1854-1907), Canadian poet.

The ladies applauded Joseph for his courage, telling him his dialect was brave and appealing. Feeling confidence and responsibility to entertain, on the way back he sang *Frère-a-Jacques*, and after the first round, the girls joined in.

"Such a beautiful story. Your French accent is delightful, Joseph!" Alice praised.

"It's not an accent, Alice. Dats de way I talk."

At the dock, Joseph steadied the skiff. As Alice stepped nimbly from the skiff, she touched the back of his hand for balance. She already knew this day would be special.

The circular pine table was set all around, and soon the dinner was embellished with family tales and exaggerations. Over the laughter, Urgel said, "There's no such thing as a quiet meal in this house."

At dusk, they gathered on the front lawn on blankets for fireworks, voting to skip tonight's finale of the torch procession through town.

As Alice looked up to the sky, Joseph admired her silhouette, finely boned with high cheekbones, oval porcelain facial features with a shy captivating smile. It was a contrast from his own long face, squared forehead and thick brown hair parted in the middle, and a flip of a wave. His eyebrows were thick, and eyes brown.

Finishing breakfast, Urgel and Émile hooked up the stake-wagon for Saturday's festival. The kids piled on top, chattering about the picnic, mostly of the sack and three-legged races and pole climbing. The St. Andrews Band would start the revelry on Main Street, triggering all-day park competitions of greasy pig, skeet shooting, horseshoes, tug-o-war, and ending with boat races.

Joseph brought the buggy to the side to escort Louise, Alice, and his mother, each carrying picnic goods. Alice and Louise begged to hold the toddlers—Rosa Anna Marie, newly walking, and Philippe, still in arms.

As runner-up in the greasy pig contest, Urgel smelled rather bad, or at least they wouldn't miss the chance to tease him. Agathe and Rosemary managed second in the sack race, and Victoria got a blue ribbon for apple pie, a title she'd coveted for five years. Her sister Sophie, from St. Hermas, was a close rival, taking second place. After supper, Joe tried pole climbing, but couldn't catch Jimmie Ferguson.

Louise and Alice confessed to exhaustion as soon as dusk fell, pleading that their stamina just wasn't as good as the rest. "Must be an English thing," Louise said, getting laughter all around. Fatigue had caught up to the rest too and others gave in to go home.

"I'll take the buggy back to the farm," Joseph said.

"We can watch the fireworks from there," said Alice, but that was just a guise, as the ladies both slept as soon as the buggy rolled. Alice woke to thank Joseph for the wonderful day, and closed her eyes again. Later, when the midnight fireworks began, he tapped on their bedroom door but only heard gentle snoring.

When Alice let her head relax on her pillow, she thought, "What a beautiful place, and such a lovely man," and she gave in to a deep sleep, ignoring the distant sounds from the heavens.

Visits between St. Andrews and Montréal became frequent for Joseph and Alice, with her life becoming integrated with their family celebrations.

Before arriving in St. Andrews for Christmas, Joseph had been to the jeweller in Lachute, and carried the velvet box in his pocket, to reserve for Christmas Eve.

Fifty-one

Alice May Creffield & Joseph Paquette's Engagement – Alice Agrees to Catholic Conversion classes, Lachute – Pang of Homesickness for Buckinghamshire – Alice Jane Turner's Bible in the Trunk – Joseph & Urgel Paquette search for Property – Lots 438 & 440 need many repairs – Grandmother Giroux's Minnesota treadle is set by the garden window – A Mother's Touch – Joe Tries Out the Decrepit Bakery – Joseph Paquette & Alice May Creffield Marry at Montréal, 1916 – Barrel of China from England – London News of air raids – Alice learns to Fish – Bell's speaker box arrives.

Reappearance of Jane Turner-Creffield's Bible

URGEL AND VICTORIA were jubilant about the impending marriage of their eldest son and his lovely Alice May Creffield.

Alice consented to attend conversion classes at the Roman Catholic Church in Lachute. She did it begrudgingly, conscious of the importance to Joseph and his parents of a Catholic wedding.

Never has a Paquette married outside their faith. It's my obligation to do this.

Months before the wedding date, she was baptized by a Catholic priest, and consented that any children born in this marriage would be raised Catholic. Alice laboured in thought over such a life-changing commitment, and wrote to her mother in Buckinghamshire, asking for guidance and understanding.

Nevertheless, she continued diligently to study the Catechism regarding the Blessed Trinity, Ten Commandments, Incarnation and Resurrection, Destiny of Man, Purgatory, the role of Mother Mary, the Sacraments, and obliged perfection. Contrary to some beliefs that she was raised to respect in the Anglican Church, she continued with the readings.

On three occasions, she met with the Monsignor for paperwork and to document her family's history at the Anglican Church in Buckinghamshire. He was kind in his guidance of the requirements for her conversion.

She didn't claim to be a devout Christian—that would be Alice Jane, her mother, who gave her every opportunity as a girl to strengthen her commitment.

One evening, after a long session, she returned home and went directly to find her mother's Bible, wrapped in her trunk. How ironic, she thought to herself. What would mother say?

Here I sit in a French-Canadian country, with your Bible in my hands, Mother. The same Bible that your own father held in his last moments. I feel the power and protection within my hands. As you have taught, the good Lord will continue to be a lamp unto my feet.

Two weeks later, a letter came from Alice-Jane Turner-Creffield. Alice recognized the English scrawl and the small envelope imprinted 'AJC'. Her mother sympathized, but encouraged her to respect her husband's wishes.

She read the last paragraph over and over.

> . . . It is a ritual, my dearest Alice. Your heart can never be changed, once you know 'The truth, the way and the light'. You must keep your heart faithful, and all will be right with the Lord.

Engagement of Joseph and Alice

AS ALICE decided wedding plans in Montréal with Louise's help, Joseph and Urgel searched St. Andrews for a property Joseph could afford.

At Moise's, they learned that Arthur Fournier of Carillon had a property now for sale, some distance east of mid-town. The two hastened by wagon out on Rue Principal, to lots 438 and 440.

House of Joseph and Alice on the North River, St. Andrews

The two-story wood frame and stucco house impressed Joe on sight, even before seeing the attached bakery with brick bread ovens, pump, and a set of scales. A barn was converted into a large garage, with a path to its own docks on the North River and a vacant lot with an orchard.

"Look, Pa. I can fish every morning!"

"So you can, Joe, and I'll join you in the ice shanty when the river freezes over."

"Come with me," Joe said.

His legs stretched to pace the woods behind the barn and his father followed the same. "There's a creek here with spawning smelt, and nests of duck and goose eggs along the river's edge."

Urgel pointed at the corner patch. "And over there, I see wild rhubarb, cabbage, pumpkin and who knows whatever else is under the soil. You'll feast as soon as you move in."

On a cursory tour inside, they examined the rooms and walls. Urgel observed, "A foot thick of plaster . . . that's good winter insulation."

"It's a lovely home, Joe, for you and your bride. Perhaps you'll want to put in electrical wiring and a few repairs to the roof. There are indications of a minor leak over the kitchen," Fournier suggested.

Urgel and Joseph found a ladder in the barn with a broken rung, and Urgel started up.

"It won't hold the both of us. I'll go, Pa; you stay and hold it."

Joe's nimble footwork on the roof nudged a few shingles loose. As they tumbled onto Urgel's head, he was torn between laughter and concern. "Will you be needing these back or are they spares?"

Descending, Joseph conceded, "Well, we definitely need a new roof, and also the bricks are crumbling at the chimney over the bakery."

In spite of the repair calculation, Mr. Fournier wouldn't budge, staying firm at $1,600. Joseph had savings of $1,000, and Urgel offered to put up a $600 mortgage on the property. The deal was struck that day by a handshake, with instructions to be sent to both lawyers.

"You have a fine property, Joseph. As a gesture of goodwill, I'll send me boys to help you when you put on the new roof," Fournier said.

With the agreement registered, Joseph returned to explore it again. The front door hadn't been used for some time, and didn't open easily.

Inside to the right, a door led to the dining room. At the end, he unlocked one to the bakery, and surveyed the long wooden tables and brick ovens. He inspected some bread pans from the racks, and wondered how he could revive the business.

I know how to make bread, that's for sure. Perhaps I'll convince Alice to let me have a go at it.

The sitting room on the left had a central potbelly stove for heat, and two side rooms were brightened by single-paned windows. The skeleton of a pair of iron bed frames remained with a lopsided wooden bureau.

"I'm a carpenter. Would be a shame not to fix these up."

Joe stood in the kitchen by the wet sink, eyeing the rusting cast-iron oven and boiler. He primed the pump and waited for its gurgles and splashes. "Mr. Fournier was right. Everything seems to work."

Some flour and sugar bins had mouse droppings, and a decrepit pie shelf fell to the floor for no reason he could see. He took them to the woodpile beside the barn. An alcove upstairs would fit a cot or crib, and more iron beds were in storage in the main bedroom. A hall space would suffice for a child's room, and beside it was a room with a slanted roof.

It's plenty for a large family.

Urgel came with him the first morning to assess the work.

"With five months to September, Joe, it will be in its finest shape for your bride. Émile and I will pitch in, and even Felix will help. The summer days are long and we can work till sunset."

Joe said, "I know Felix is just twelve, but I've seen him handle a hammer like the rest."

"Well, I'll say you one thing, Joe. A carpenter can't make do with these rusty tools in the barn. I'll bring some spares from the farm."

The next day, he brought all the tools Joseph would need. On the weekend, he returned with the wagon and unloaded a new workbench.

"Let's find a place in the barn for your new workshop," he said.

Urgel respected his heritage as a master carpenter as far back as the Paquettes in France. Most of the ancient tools of Étienne Pasquier had long ago met their demise, replaced by modern saws, planes, and axes.

In the second week, Urgel brought Victoria, with little Rose Anna Marie and Philippe in tow. On a blanket, Victoria set out a picnic hamper with ham sandwiches and pie for the family, and a jug of lemonade. Joe was out when she toured the kitchen and made her own mental list.

"Urgel, Grand-mère Giroux's old Minnesota treadle sewing machine is in good repair. It would sit nicely at the back window overlooking the North River."

"I'm sure Alice would like that," he said.

"Urgel, you should make one of those pie shelves with the glass doors, and put on dainty china knobs like you did for the Abbotts."

He nodded. "I could, with that new pine board."

"Myself . . . I'll go to the hardware store. Last week they had a sale on oilcloth flooring. All those pretty patterns and only fifty cents a yard."

Victoria made careful measurements with her shoe so there wouldn't be too much cutting. "Remember now, measure, measure, measure so we don't waste." A racket outside brought her to the door, where Joseph was unloading his wagon.

"Look Ma! I passed the old parsonage. They've been rebuilding since the roof caved in, and I salvaged this old English buffet. I wasn't thinking of anything in the dining room now, but this is perfect, don't you think?"

"Oh, Joseph. Lovely, yes. I hope you got a good price."

Joseph T. Paquette and Alice May Creffield, at engagement.

"What I pay for my wife, is my own business, Mother." He laughed alone and gave his mother a silent hug.

Victoria measured the front and back windows, then the sitting room and dining pane, writing it down this time.

"Nottingham Lace Lambrequin curtains are twenty-seven cents a panel in Sears' catalogue," she said. "They'll make a better impression than plain windows. You want Alice to have privacy from the street. Besides, in England these niceties would be more important to the lady of the house."

Joe listened, with no promise. He knew his mother's strong will, but also that Victoria truly wanted to please Alice, her first daughter-in-law.

The foundation was sound, and the boys replaced roof tiles and secured the chimney bricks. The only chimney was from the bakery and it raised the question again. "Could I make bread and sell it?" he asked. "What would Alice think?"

"It looks pretty crude, Joe . . . but I'm sure you can make something of it. You should see what Alice says."

One day by himself, Joe swept out the bakery, washed down the bread kneading counters, and fired up the old brick oven. He had taken yeast, lard and flour from Victoria's kitchen, enough to try his hand. Relieved to achieve success with two golden loaves of bread, he laid a clean tea towel over the top crust, and placed it in the wagon. He was ready to show Alice.

The Wedding of J.T. Paquette & Alice Creffield, 1916

IN JUNE, Alice came by train from Montréal. She hadn't visited for a month, and Joe planned to surprise her with the house on the way back. It looked pleasant enough from the street, and he knew the expanse of yard would impress her. He was right as she first noticed the white blossoms in the apple orchard of their adjoining lot, then squealed and kissed him.

"Oh my, Joe. You've done all this for me."

"It's for us and our family."

Through the front door, she breathed in the aroma of freshly cut pine, and clasped her hands to her mouth at the Nottingham Lace curtains.

"Oh Joe, they are like ones Ma had in her cottage in Buckingham." Together, they continued the tour of the rooms, saving the kitchen for last.

At the treadle, she let her foot smoothly waffle back and forth and scanned the view of the North River. "There's such peace in this spot," she said. "I'll spend so much time here."

Joseph was less confident entering the kitchen. With no running water, she'd have to draw from the pump. A galvanized icebox cabinet backed to the wall in lieu of an electric refrigerator, but Alice didn't make an issue.

"Joe, perhaps someday soon we'll get an electric fridge." She knew she'd been spoilt with conveniences from the Westmount house. She admired the linoleum, giving the room colour, and the curtain below the sink.

"Émile excels with the wood lathe, Alice, and he's already started to make shapely chair legs for dining . . . and Dad will set up a pie shelf with new pine and polished knobs. I hope it is all fine. And my mother wants so much to help make it perfect for you."

"Oh, yes, I can see a woman's touch. Tell her I do love the curtains."

Inside, Alice fought a jealousy, that the Paquette family had been coming back and forth making changes to *her* house at their pleasure. In her head she wrestled with it, knowing Joseph worked hard to please her.

Always be kind and appreciate a gift. Indeed this is a labour of love, forgive me Lord for my hasty judgement.

Summer passed quickly, with carpentry repairs of the highest standard. Alice asked that the iron bed rails be painted white to match a crocheted bedspread received from her aunt in England, and Joseph ordered a new cotton ticking mattress from Blanchard's, with assurance it would arrive before the wedding.

On September 25, 1916, Urgel and Victoria Paquette boarded the Ottawa Railway in their Sunday best. Joseph had gone to Montréal a few days earlier and would meet his parent's train.

Louise Callaghan, the maid-of-honour, helped Alice into a crispy, white fine linen blouse with delicate lace on the collar. She removed the cameo broach from the box she'd opened from Uncle Henry in England, and examined its brilliant, tiny diamonds set around a pearl cluster.

Louise said that all in white, she looked more beautiful than the finest angel. Over her white pleated skirt, Louise wrapped a satin sash around her waist and tied it in a flowing bow at the back. Her auburn hair was pulled up loosely into a bun, and her wisps of curls were set to frame her face.

Louise said, "I don't think I've seen your eyes sparkle this way."

"They're my father's eyes," Alice laughed. "He'd thank you if he were here."

A polished black carriage waited to bring them to St. Michael's-Archange Roman Catholic Church in Montréal.

Joseph waited by the rectory door on Rue Saint-Viateur with Urgel, his best-man. Victoria was ushered to the best seat in the front row, beside Joseph's grandparents, Treffle Charlebois and Elizabeth Giroux.

The groom wore a brown wool suit, and a white, high-collar shirt with a fine pin-stripe. He fidgeted with his black silk shield tie, tucking it into his vest.

His left hand clutched a bouquet of red roses with a delicate trail of green ivy for Alice, and his right held a boutonniere.

Stepping from the carriage, she gazed toward Joseph at the door and felt a surge of tears and longing.

Those dark brown eyes are kind, compassionate, loving and I pledge my life to him.

Monsignor Avery waited in the rectory as an altar boy led the group to his chambers. Urgel and Louise stood as support at the simple ceremony, with family members and a couple from the citadel as witnesses.

As Louise was about to throw rice, the altar boy intercepted. "Please, there is mass tonight and the janitor is off."

The wedding party moved to a reserved dining table at Place Viger, which served as a hotel and railway station. As a reminder of Buckinghamshire for Alice, the chef prepared a proper English meal of traditional Roast Beef and Yorkshire pudding, with mashed potato and maple glazed carrots.

Jane Creffield-Turner sent a barrel full of bone china that had been a gift by the Turner family on the occasion of her own wedding to Frederick. Alice fingered each piece with emotion of her family in England, and with a cotton cloth, she dusted aside the wooden packing chips.

"It's the Roxbury pattern, of royal porcelain made in England, and enough for twelve . . . my great-grandmother's prized Staffordshire. Isn't it beautiful, Joe? Imagine all the family meals it's served."

"It's mighty kind of your ma." Seeing the happiness the china brought her, he picked up the platter and his finger ran over the etched gold and sage green ferns.

With fresh appreciation, he worked to embellish his words. "I think it's the finest I've seen; we'll save it for special occasions so it is preserved for our children."

Three shades of green edged the pattern, with roses and cascading sweeping fern, and gold accents on the contoured edge. On the way home, Alice asked if Joseph would find her a dining set with a china display cabinet to house the full setting.

The next Saturday, a celebration party in St. Andrews brought together their family and friends. Joseph's Irish, Scottish and British pals wouldn't miss it.

"This'll be a grand party, once you put an Irishman and a Scot in the middle," Joseph said. Then he shouted for the crowd at the back to hear, "Alice, I hope you brought some dancin' shoes!"

Couples nearby leaned in to hear them better.

"My English shoes will do just fine, Joe. Are you planning on giving me a twirl?"

"I am, my love. We'll be spinning around these fine folks."

He called out, "Start up the accordion and fiddle!"

Every voice cheered, with glasses raised high.

Joe and Alice, Early Married Life

ALICE'S FIRST letter from home in Buckinghamshire, England came a week after the wedding.

> October 1, 1916
>
> Dearest Alice,
>
> I was sorry to miss your wedding, but with warships in command of the British coastline, travel is restricted for civilians. The passenger ships are converted to hospitals and supply boats. Percy and Emily are worried about the boys working with artillery. Frederick Charles looks pale and was hospitalized for a few weeks, but is now back at the front. Our own Frederick Playdell has been commandeered to Manchester for mandatory training.
>
> As soon as it falls dark, we are asked not to turn any lights on. The London air raid makes a horrible sound with shelling and bombing going on for hours. The other day, I was bringing in my laundry from the clothesline and a full squadron of fighter jets swooped too close to the ground.
>
> It's becoming a regular occurrence for official army jeeps to drive by. We've learned that they are the bearer of sad news. Prime Minister George is warning that conscription will continue as long as it takes. All boys over sixteen years must report for duty.
>
> The munitions factory at Faversham exploded, killing over a hundred workers. The Irish Republican Brotherhood is kicking up a farce that England doesn't need in the middle of this eternal war.
>
> I won't belabour you any further news of war developments, but I have put in the front page of the London Times in case you're interested.
>
> For your sake, Alice, I am glad you are in Québec. This is a happy time

for you and Joe. I trust the china arrived in good shape. When I heard your voice on the transatlantic call, it was cracking up badly, but I knew it was you, my darling.

All my love to you both,
Mother Creffield

In the first autumn of their marriage, Alice came face-to-face with a contrasting culture, adapting to new habits and French-Canadian customs.

She was curious about fishing, and willing to try it for herself. On the North River, Joseph helped her hook a chubby river trout. Alice tried to reel it in, but as it flapped uncontrollably in the air before her, she ducked and swung it toward Joseph.

"Joe! Grab it before I get hit."

Joseph took over her rod. "Now, now, my sweet English lass. You'll have to learn to do this yourself."

"Oh, no, that's what I married you for," she chided.

"Since you are dressed with such a pretty blouse, I'll clean the fish this time, but next time wear a pair of my old dungarees."

"For my part, I'll do the cooking and you do the fish cleaning. That's that," Alice humpfed sternly.

On his regular hunting trips with his father and brothers, Joseph returned with snared rabbits for stew and skins, squirrels, grouse and pheasants, and deer meat to be shared with Émile's family.

The first time, Alice insisted that he hang the meat in the old barn, far from her kitchen, and small game would stay there a few days before moving to the root cellar. Knowing that Alice would protest if he put a massive hind quarter of venison in the cellar, he thought it best not to mention it. Several days later, he regretted his silence.

Alice shrieked toward the yard, "Joe! Help! There's a bear in the cellar!" He ran to the house with a slow realization of the problem. He found her locked in one of the side rooms, fearing for her life.

"It's okay Alice, it's our winter meat. Sorry, love. I should have told you about it."

She unlocked, but spoke through the door.

"Now Joseph! I laid down the law about my kitchen."

The fall garden was full, with herbs and root vegetables; with a new interest in canning, she lined her cellar shelves with mason jars and glass vinegar jugs for winter preserves. The first orchard yield was more than plentiful for apple pies, and applesauce was served at every meal as a sweet staple. She wrote out her tested dessert and cider recipes to trade with Victoria and her sisters-in-law.

But pregnant with their first child, she became despondent, as Joseph was maintaining his old hunting life and frequent absences.

One day, she wrote to Jane, saying that she longed to come home.

Alice seeded the garden early the next spring, with peas, beans, squash, tomatoes, carrots, radishes, green onions, and beets. By late spring, she was due to deliver her first child, and tending the garden was difficult. Joseph took over the outside chores and gardening.

Sensitive to her needs, he pampered Alice with whatever she wanted. His parents burst with pride on the arrival of the first grandchild, Marjorie, with dark and curly hair, and brown eyes like her father. Victoria rushed from the truck to see the new infant, and Urgel followed close behind with a rocking chair.

"Alice, you use this now; I'm too old for birthing more. Philippe and Rose Anna will go to school soon, and it's time for me to focus on my grandchildren. Philippe is our last and he's almost six now."

"It's an heirloom we will treasure, Ma."

Joe paused. He had news he hadn't yet told Alice.

"The time has come for us to install one of Mr. Bell's speaker boxes in the kitchen," he said.

Alice held back her enthusiasm at first.

"That will be wonderful, Joe. Mother Paquette can call me anytime she plans to stop for a visit."

Her heart pumped a bit faster, satisfied that she'd been kind, yet assertive enough to request notice.

The Bell Telephone Co. strung wires to poles stretching to the road from the house, and then to the next. The Paquette's phone was given a special ring, its own designated sound. Alice's French improved and she could gab almost like any Québecois housewife.

Fifty-two

Canadian Expeditionary Forces established – Royal 22nd Regiment recruitment exclusively for Québecois – Patriotism Building – Letter from Aunt Lucy – Red Cross in Canada Solicits home sewing program – St. Andrews Red Cross Auxiliary Meet at Old Harrison House – Alice and Sarah Azilda Paquette Join the Abbott Workshop to sew Bandages – Marjorie Paquette, newborn of Joseph & Alice Paquette – Sarah Azilda drives Amadee's Tin Lizzy – Day of the Draft June 5, 1917 – Van Doos Regiment (the 22nd) take Passchendaele – Victory Bonds raise war funds in Canada – Joe faces death in Passchendaele bunker - Joseph Roussin, a Mohawk Hero – Official Army Letter delivered to St. Andrews – Joe Paquette, wounded – Armistice Day Parade, November 11, 1918.

Canadians Pitch in during the Great Warm, 1916-18

C ANADA WAS CALLED ON BY THE BRITISH PARLIAMENT to send troops and munitions support. Robert Borden declared it in the papers in town.

It is our duty to let Great Britain know and to let their friends and foes know that there is in Canada but one mind and one heart and all Canadians are behind the mother country.

The staunch declaration did not sit well with Francophone citizens in Lower Canada, where the population ratio was overwhelmingly French.

"How can the British assume that England is the mother country for all Canadians?" Victoria said. "Indeed, France will *never* be forgotten in Québec and our house."

*Québec's famed 'Van Doos' 22ⁿᵈ Battalion resting in a shell hole on their way
to the front line, September 1917. Library and Archives Canada*

Revolts and protests continued for months on Montréal's streets, with
lives lost, but the government didn't back down and known activists were
jailed.

The Canadian Expeditionary Force sent battalions as land troops to the
front line, and before 1917, the 1st to 5th Canadian Divisions built a
reputation as the finest of the Commonwealth.

Although French-speaking Canadians balked at conscription, over
3,500 aboriginals were eager to enlist for Canada. The toll on troops at
Somme and Vimy reduced the overseas troop numbers significantly, and
new enlistment dwindled in response.

Urgel returned from town sullen, as Georges had just shared the
headlines to the barbershop gathering. Urgel then picked up his own paper
at the postmaster's. It was the dreaded announcement.

Joseph was at the carpentry shop at their house, and Urgel called him
in. Victoria read it silently at first, her hands shaking, then repeated it aloud.

Arthur Mignault will command the Royal 22nd Regiment of Canada. Consequences of the objections of French-Canadians, this regiment will hold enlistments only for French Canadian males over the age of 20 years. Enlistment will be mandatory. Recruitment offices are found in every port along the St. Lawrence.

The citadel fortress at Québec will be the headquarters for the 22nd. All eligible men must carry enlistment papers on their person at all times, or punishment effected accordingly. All men eligible report to their local recruitment office.

She looked up at the end and gasped in horror.

"My goodness, Joseph. That includes you and your brothers."

"I wonder if I'll be shipped out right away. Perhaps Felix and Émile will go with me from St. Andrews. I know Alice will be pleased for me to fight for her country."

Patriotic songs echoed in the streets from sporadic groups in the military drills. Minutes later, they would board trains to Québec to be assigned to units and warships.

In 1917, as the Third Battle of Ypres in Belgium was in jeopardy, Alice received a letter from Lucy Creffield, her dear sister-in-law in Buckinghamshire.

Dearest Alice,

We fear for our boys in the muddy trenches of horrific battle. Both Percy and Frederick are with the Royal Fusiliers; Percy is a Lance Corporal and Frederick a Sergeant facing the German machine guns and mortar. We were so proud of Percy when he was wounded last year saving the life of his comrades but once he was able they sent him back.

Frederick is struggling with epilepsy and has requested a discharge for medical reasons. It's shameful how people judge his manhood for such a thing. When the boys have leave, they come home with a haunting gaunt look in their eyes having seen horrors we can't imagine.

I am glad, dear Alice, that you are spared the air raids of war, I but beg for your prayers. Mother Alice-Jane is stoic but I know she worries too. But my Percy says little.

Forgive me for prattling on of war when you are a new bride in a new country. Send us a note when you can.

Yours with love,

Lucy & Percy

Alice felt her heart. Joe's time for conscription was imminent. As a new mother she was exempt from factory work, but accepted a home sewing assignment of bandages for the Red Cross.

Sitting with her ankles crossed on a footstool, her fingers rapidly stitched cotton rags into proper medical compresses, according to specifications in the pamphlet.

It wasn't long ago that I sat with my mother doing this very same thing. It was on that day we saw Mrs. Francis's advert and here I am.

When she wasn't sewing, the guilt of idle hands was consuming. Even in town, as women lined up for rations, wool was unravelling from handbags, with needles clicking to produce blankets.

Maude Abbott's campaign to collect supplies for the Red Cross convened at the old town hall on Monday mornings, and on Thursdays at the Old Harrison House.

Alice took young Marjorie in tow and went to sort bandages and supplies, packing them in standardized tin boxes with the Red Cross identifying mark, the international symbol for First Aid.

Joe's aunt, Sarah Azilda Paquette married Amedee DeNault and settled on a large property down the road. She was only thirteen years older, and a new bride three years earlier. As their gravel business prospered, they purchased a used 1913 Model-T Ford roadster.

The jalopy horn announced Sarah's arrival, and in seconds she bounded through Alice's door with her own two toddlers in tow. "Are you ready?" she called up the staircase. "Let me help. I'll put a sweater on the baby."

Alice gathered a bag of morning supplies.

"How'd you do with the sewing, Sarah?"

"Thank heavens for thimbles, but I managed to complete my box. Miss Abbott will have us working hard today, packing and sewing uniforms."

"I suppose you're right. The Vicar has allowed us to use the priory basement and the Red Cross shipped a dozen Singers. Robert Borden and Sam Hughes should be pleased with themselves."

"Joe would have a few words for you, Sarah, if he heard that. He's not pleased at going to Britain's war."

"I'm not much for nationalism when it comes to sending my brothers to fight in France, either," Sarah said. "Anyway, come along dear."

Alice stowed her bags under the front seat and slid to the leather bench with Marjorie on her lap and Mila and Cecile tucked between. With a crank of the engine, the Tin Lizzie motored toward town.

The church basement was packed with eager sewers, many with toddlers at their knees.

Maude had prepared a place for everyone, and when they had all arrived she began, "Ladies, specific instructions from the International Red Cross need to be followed for sewing uniforms. Miss Hoyt and Miss Draper of New York travelled to the front lines and it's imperative that there be continuity. Once the machine sewers have done their work, the uniforms will go for hand stitching, then to the packers in the corner.

"However, I do have good news. The tents are being made up in Montréal, so we won't be assigned those."

She stopped to allow some giggles and sighs of relief.

"If we do a good job, Alice, they might ship us to Montréal to work in the factories," Sarah laughed.

The two were assigned to Singer treadle machines and the room became a hum of rhythm, lulling Marjorie to sleep in her basket. At ten o'clock, Miss Abbott announced a tea break in the upper foyer. "Mind your time, ladies, to be back at your station in fifteen minutes."

"It is good to stand up. Next time remind me to bring my cushion."

"Ha, and mine too."

It was the morning of June 5, 1917, forever known as the Day of the Draft. The new black Ford puttered into Joe's lane on Main Street, with Urgel at the wheel, wearing the famed grey wool cap.

Church bells pealed over St. Andrews East, calling able-bodied men from their fields and homes. Residents and curious onlookers came out onto the streets, applauding the brave men streaming toward the trains waving flags.

"Okay boys. Time's up," Urgel hollered. "I'll drive the lot of you to Lachute, to the headquarters of the Argenteuil Rangers."

Wearing work clothes, farm boots, and with new gunny sacks over their shoulders, Joseph, Felix and Émile shuffled to the car with Felix Charlebois.

"I heard at the barber shop that King George V made a personal request for the Paquette boys of St. Andrews," Urgel persisted in a best effort to be jovial.

"Yes, Pa, you're right. They've set up an entire French Canadian Regiment—the 22nd of Québec."

"Vingt-deux! Oui, they say the Van Doos has a nice ring to it, Émile."

"I'd rather the Van Don'ts."

Urgel raised his cap to Alice standing at the back window, with Marjorie at her feet. Her pained half-smile said more than he could bear. Turning away, he wiped a tear from his eye.

"Let's get on the road so you boys will be in Montréal for lunch."

The drive was painful to the men, struggling to be brave. Queues of men walked, and some rode on horses or hitched rides. By the time the jalopy arrived in Lachute, a band of brave men clung to the side on the running boards and bumpers of the Ford, as Urgel couldn't turn any away.

"Pa, we'll write as often as we can," Joseph said. "You'll look in on Alice and Marjorie won't you? The new baby's due soon."

The 22nd Regiment takes Passchendaele, 1917

CANADIANS WERE offered government Victory Bonds in an effort to raise $150 million to support the troops. For a guaranteed return of 5.5% over ten years, many depleted their savings. The campaign was successful, exceeding $398 million, with further programs reaching the billions.

Urgel's family gave up what they had saved, not knowing that before the ten year return was due the country would be in economic turmoil.

Private Joseph T. Paquette became a new recruit in the Québec Infantry from St. Andrews and Carillon pushing toward Courcelette. The French town had been under German control since 1916 during the Battle of the

Somme, and as the Canadian Expeditionary forces neared it, enemy troops secured tactical positions.

On October 26, 1917, the Canadian troops under Lt. General Arthur Currie began their offensive. Below grey skies, they forged across muddy flat terrain, shelled every inch of the way. The invincible Private Joseph Roussin, a lumberjack and Mohawk from the Kanesatake band, was in the group within sight ahead.

On the battle's eve, the heroic tale of Roussin spread through the platoon; two months before, at the Battle of the Hill in France, he'd fearlessly attacked a group of eight enemy soldiers. Thought to be lost in battle, he then appeared through the mist, with three prisoners tied to each other and five others dead on the battlefield. His patriotism returned him to the front lines close to the Van Doos.

Roussin turned to shout back in their direction, "Vive les Canadiens!" Then, seeming to be without fear, he waved his rifle toward the line of fire and charged on foot through the artillery smoke, maneuvering barbed wire, mines and airborne mortar. In off-key baritone, Joe's voice added to an impromptu francophone chorus of victory. As more added volume, the sound of courage and determination boosted the troops.

> Amour sacré de la Patrie
> Conduis, soutiens nos bras vengeurs
> Liberté, Liberté Cherie
> Combats avec tes défenseurs!
> Sous nos drapeaux que la victoire
> Accoure à tes mâles accents
> Que tes ennemis expirants
> Voient ton triomphe et notre gloire!"

The Van Doos suffered heavy losses from the German attacks, and in driving rain on October 30, the French Canadians joined the Allied forces on the front line pushing toward Passchendaele.

Shelling came closer than Joseph had seen before, exploding within yards, until he found sanctuary in a water-filled bunker.

A man sat alone there, dazed and bleeding. When smoke drifted up, he saw it was Louis Bégin, separated from his group.

"Hang in there, Bégin; help will come soon."

Joe's eye was focused down the barrel of his rifle and bayonet, counting at least four Germans heading toward the bunker.

Unbeknownst to Paquette, Joseph Roussin doubled back, seeing the same break-off group of Germans rushing for the French Canadian occupied bunkers. He flashed a look toward Joe who was firing at the enemies in rapid succession.

As if in slow motion, Joe saw the close-up eyes of a young German lad not more than sixteen, charging with his bayonet. He grabbed Bégin's arm to wake up, but his sight stayed on the boy, now only feet from the bunker. At first the lad was frightened, but then his eyes went wild, going for the kill. Three more were behind him.

Joe's weapon jammed as their bayonets met. The German's eyes rolled and Joe stared at death in the instant the boy dropped. From the back, Roussin felled the other three.

Later, Joe recalled that Roussin dove into the trench. Then his own legs became rubber, and his head spun, throwing his vision upside down.

As faces loomed over him, their voices echoed as if distant, in a dark moment he'd never forget.

"It'll be alright, Joe." Roussin patted him, then diverted his attention to Louis Bégin, in convulsions.

Joe recalled a searing pain as senses abandoned him before he collapsed.

"Joe, Private Paquette . . ." A young French woman stood over him dressed in white.

"Am I in Heaven? Are you the Virgin Mary?" Joe mumbled.

"No, sir. My name is Evangeline; I'm one of the nurses in the field tent here near Passchendaele." She spoke softly in French.

"What? How?"

"The Mohawk soldier, Roussin, carried you to safety. You took a bayonet that pierced your lungs. You've lost a lot of blood. If it hadn't been for your comrade, you'd have died."

"Where is he?"

"He has already returned to the front. He insisted he could better serve his country on the front line. We need more courageous men like him."

"I owe him my life . . ."

On November 6, the Winnipeg 27th Battalion joined the Van Doos, and the 5th Canadian Mounted Rifles stalwartly forged against enemy lines to capture the town of Passchendaele. On that day, Canada lost four thousand men and retrieved twelve thousand wounded.

Many became heroes on battlefields during those two weeks, with Victoria Crosses for valour granted to Christopher O'Kelly, George Mullen, George Pearkes, James Robertson, Colin Barron, Cecil Kinross, Hugh McKenzie and Robert Shankland, the last two posthumously.

Stories of the bravery of Private William Cleary, a Montagnais and lumberjack from Point-Bleue and Private Joseph Roussin would become legendary in the Van Doos.

Other Canadian heroes were Billy Bishop, nicknamed 'Hells Handmaiden', who downed 72 German aircraft, William George Baker, an Ace Flyer and top Commonwealth Flyer, and comrades Mullock, Stearne and Brown. It was Brown who downed the German Red Baron.

Tens of thousands of unnamed heroes never returned.

Far Away from Passchendaele in St. Andrews, 1918

EACH WEEK, Alice received the *London News* headlines from her mother and a scratchy letter from Joseph. She longed for someone to share her agony of waiting, and on many evenings she paced the road to be with Urgel and Victoria.

"Father Paquette, come listen to this," she beckoned, reading from her news clipping.

"King George V has declared the Order of the British Empire, uniting Scotland and Wales with England. It's about time."

Alice sensed no reaction, and paused to look up at Urgel and Victoria. "Can I go on?"

"Yes, please. My patriotism is growing with the Alliance."

"They've started daylight raids on English towns on the outskirts of London, killing civilians. The British got turned back at the Battle of Gaza by seventeen thousand Turks; then they took Turks captive in November.

"For the life of me, I don't understand what the Turks are doing in England's war. Next, we have Germany attacking under the sea with U-boats, and on land they're experimenting with a vicious gas they made called chlorine, that's killing soldiers by the air they breathe."

"I heard about that, Alice," Victoria said. "A munitions factory in Montréal is making goggles to filter the poisonous air. In Émile's last letter, he said they wore special goggles to breathe in the trenches. Maybe they use the Canadian ones."

"One more thing, and this is the bee all and end all. Londoners have to use food ration stamps for butter and lard, meat and sugar. Mother takes sugar in her tea at least three times a day."

"I'm sorry, love. I wish we could just bring her here."

"Yes, but Winnifred is still at home, and Mother is afraid to travel; especially since so many ships have sunk."

News of the war hung over Alice as it seemed that every day another British warship or hospital vessel was finding its way to the ocean floor. She thought constantly about Joe, and fretted about her cousins in the British Army.

"Alice dear, try not to worry so much—it will make your baby anxious. Tomorrow, we'll bring supper to your house so you won't make the walk with Marjorie. Mothers-in-law are supposed to pamper their son's wives and children."

"Thank you, Mother Paquette. I do tire."

The next morning, Victoria was at Alice's door before ten.

"Alice, please sit down."

Her face paled as she collapsed into a chair.

"What is it? Is it Joe?"

"I don't know dear. I'm coming from the post office; this envelope came addressed to you. I'm sure it can't be bad news, or someone would have come to your door with a telegram."

The envelope was official, with a thin parchment envelope marked 'Air Mail', and a return address of the Allied Army Headquarters in Piccadilly, London.

"Please open it. I can't . . ."

Dear Mrs. Paquette,

Joseph T. Paquette is being returned to Canada under medical treatment. He was wounded on October 30 outside Passchendaele and has been in a field hospital these past weeks recovering from a battle wound. Unfortunately, he has had slight nerve damage from the chlorine gas used by the Germans and a discharge has been effected for medical reasons. We will refer him to the hospital in Montréal. The doctor there will discuss his future care with you.

It ended with an indiscernible government signature.

"Thank goodness . . . Joe's alive and coming home."

Victoria was glad too, but concern wouldn't let her show it.

"I'll prepare a sick room on the main floor for Joe. The stairs will be too much. One of my Charlebois cousins came home with symptoms of the gas and developed pneumonia."

"Of course you're right; I didn't think of that."

"Urgel will go to Montréal and get Joe. You are looking peaked. I can see you wincing. Is it labour?"

Joe had already been on the ship, and arrived home the next week.

Dr. Allier assured her he'd stop by every few days to check his cough and temperature. On the first day, he prescribed liquid medicine and refreshed the gauze dressings.

"Alice, ensure he takes this every morning and at bed. He should be up and around soon; he needs some exercise but not too much to labour his breathing. I've seen much worse cases come home from England. Call me if he gets jaundiced or the headaches are too bad."

"Thank you, Dr. Allier."

"Before I go, I'll check on you too. Is the baby kicking yet?"

The End of the Great War

IN ALL, CANADA immobilized over 620,000 troops, losing 67,000 in battle and bringing a quarter million home wounded. Most significant were the Battles of Somme, Vimy and Passchendaele where the Canadians had fought as units.

The Canadian flag flew at its proudest in every Québec town on Armistice Day, November 11, 1918. Germany was forced from their trenches and began a line of retreat under a cease-fire with the Allies.

The war had raged in the air, at sea, on aircraft carriers, boots on land, by horseback, in the trenches, with tanks, and towards the end of the war by submarine.

Nightmares and shadows of war would never leave. Cenotaphs, naming the fallen, stood in each community. For soldiers left in Flanders Fields and who died at the beaches and towns of Normandy, the Cenotaphs became lasting memorials before a wall of remembrance was built in Ottawa.

Slowly, factories returned to commodities of shoes, clothing, furniture, machinery, and food supplies, instead of bullets, arms, walking canons, and aircraft.

The declaration of victory to echo over the next thirty years was, 'The Great War was the war to end all wars'.

But in Québec it was 'je me souviens'.

For its veterans, all of St. Andrews stood to observe a solemn but celebratory parade at the end of November.

"Come Joe, we're ready. Your pa's in the driveway," Alice called.

In the parlour, he admired his khaki wool walking out suit. "Alice, can you fix the collar? It's supposed to stand up."

She patted the two front pleated pockets and tightened the seven brass buttons. "You've lost weight, Joe."

"Well, you've plenty of time now to fatten me up."

The brass band and drum corps marched in precision down Main Street. Joe knew in these moments what it truly meant to be a Canadian, not just a French-Canadian.

He walked proudly with his brothers and comrades to the sound of drums, bugles and horns. In thanks, he lowered his head as he marched beside some with missing appendages.

It could have been me. I remember Joseph Roussin crawling ahead of me out of the dugout. Overhead the sky was a blaze of smoke and artillery. No one knows the fear I felt. The stench of death turned me inside out. Common sense told me to hold steady.

As his feet moved in the parade, his mind was at war. Pain throbbed in his shoulder where shrapnel had been. He whispered, "Thank you." It was for the strong arms of Joseph Roussin that carried him to a medic.

As fresh as yesterday, he knew Louis Bégin's lasting face, as mortar tore into his back. It wasn't consolation that Bégin's mother received a Purple Heart in memory of her heroic son. Joe had never felt so unified with another soul on earth as the moment Louis was taken.

The victory parade ended at the Argenteuil Armories, and Alice waited, surrounded by other wives, parents and siblings.

"Joe, are you alright?"

"I'm no hero, Alice. It was the men that lost their lives who sacrificed."

His face was taut and his jaw clenched, and she was unsure how to comfort him.

"Thank goodness, Joe. We couldn't bear to have lost you."

Joe said nothing, allowing the guilt to remain, and the images of Louis Bégin and Joseph Roussin lingered. The scars on his shoulder burned, but it was nothing compared to what he'd seen.

Fifty-three

Roaring Twenties & Rise of Vaudeville – St. Andrews village Auxiliary Firefighters – Fireman Paquette Challenges Captain to Arm Wrestle – LeRoy's house Ablaze – Joseph Paquette Rescues Prize Setters – Joe & Alice Welcome another daughter, 1919 – Treffle Charlebois dies, 1919 – Frederick Creffield dies in England – Transatlantic Call – Three more daughters complete the Paquette family – Household split between Anglican and Catholic, Dorothy persecuted at school – Ink Stained Blouse – Urgel Paquette dies in 1929 – Hotly Debated Funeral discussion.

St. Andrew's Volunteer Firemen, 1920s

EXPECTING TO RESUME THE JOBS AND LIVES THEY LEFT, soldiers instead faced unemployment, strikes for unionization, and economic hardships.

Patriotic songs and sentimental ballads told of broken hearts, followed by the rise of vaudeville and Tin Pan Alley. Big bands drew throngs to nightly dance halls, and the *Roaring Twenties* were on the cusp, ready to bring needed financial prosperity and social expansion.

The population growth was creating community pressure for more services, and Joseph, Felix and Émile volunteered for the Fire Roster of St. Andrews Auxiliary Firefighters.

On his first day, barely in the door, Joseph went to the engine house to find the Captain.

"Can I drive the Reo? Or am I one of the water pump runners?"

The man burst into laughter, splattering his coffee. "Volunteers don't get to drive, Joe. You and Felix will be ladder runners, so you'd better get in shape."

Joe lightened it. "I can take any man here in an arm wrestle."

"You're on, Joe."

Captain Andrews settled into a wooden armchair by the table, his elbow planted firmly with an amused smirk on his face.

"With all due respect, Captain, you don't think a Paquette could forfeit his reputation in a momentary challenge," Joe chided.

"You're forgettin' Joe, it's the British that allow you immigrants to farm on our sovereign soil." Andrews knew his comment would rile Joe.

"Sovereign soil indeed. It's the land of the great Frenchman, Jacques Cartier, who first planted the flag of France. You Englishmen have such foggy memories."

Joe's eyes twinkled, enjoying the banter, but a wise voice in his head that sounded like Alice said, "Now Joe, remember your place. There's nothing to be gained in shaming your superiors because of *their* ancestry."

"C'mon Joe . . . you can take him," his French buddies cheered.

A jovial English accent echoed from across the room. "Now sir, remember the pride of the British is at stake. Take him now!"

With cackles and a wink, Joe wouldn't embarrass his commander and feigned a collapse to rounds of applause and boos. Some had just settled into a card game over the station house, when the dreaded bell started clanging incessantly.

Joe grabbed his coat and gun boots as he stumbled to the fire pole.

"It's LeRoy's house!" Felix yelled.

When the belly of the water pumper was dry, the firemen could do nothing more than stand back to watch the timbers crash in a heap of charred debris.

Out of the crowd of spectators, a reporter stepped to the front.

"Hello, Joe! Can I have your words to describe the loss of this fine house?"

With a glint, Joe removed his heavy helmet and displayed a row of white teeth and eyes, a stark contrast to the black soot on his face.

"Joseph Paquette of St. Andrews . . . if it's going in the papers." In case of a photo, Joe ran his hand over his wayward hair, parted in the middle with an even row of bangs.

"What was the scene when your fire truck arrived?"

"The new Mack Truck is the finest in Argenteuil, but the house was engulfed when we arrived and the pumper ran dry. But I'm keen to my senses and my first instinct is for safety and the lives of my friends.

"LeRoy and his family were on the lawn, but I knew they had a pair of prized setters not accounted for. By myself, I crawled the circumference of the house, listening . . . and there they were, hiding in the cellar. I went in by the coal chute and brought the pair out before the floor gave way."

"Monsieur Paquette, if there is a hero today, it would be you."

"Mighty kind of you to say."

A few days later, the picture of volunteer fireman Joseph Paquette was on the front page of the newspaper, posing with two Irish setters.

Alice sat giggling with her shoulders shaking, looking at the photo.

"Joe, you look like a miner. This is definitely not your good side." It was her way of saying she was proud.

The Paquette Family in St. Andrews Grows

WITH CURIOUS fingertips, two-year-old Marjorie pushed the cradle of her new sister, Dorothée, born to Joseph and Alice in May 1919. With delight, she squealed as Joe joined her to play on the floor, and she erupted in giggles by his animated faces. It escalated as he flapped his elbows, teaching her to clap to a perky French chanson.

"Joe, I wished you'd met my mother. Dorothy has her fair hair and blue eyes. Marjorie is like the Paquettes, with chestnut hair and brown eyes."

"Not just like 'er grandmoder but like her own Ma."

"Pshaw, Joe. Mother is sending a christening shawl for the service at Paroisse de Saint-André. Monsignor Luce Langpre wishes to officiate."

"That'll be grand." he said. "Are we agreed that Dorothy's godparents will be Amadee Denault and my Aunt Sarah Azilda? I've invited them to attend and notified Monsignor Luce."

"Oui, oui, Joseph. Sarah is excited to be chosen."

"Just as happy were Grand-père Charlebois and Grand-mère Giroux to be my godparents."

He stretched again on the floor to play patty-cake with the girls, then sang in his deepest bass, surprising them in an exaggerated falsetto. Over and over, he sang his favourites, *Rosie O'Grady*, *For Me and My Gal*, and *K-K-K-Katy*, with animated actions as the girls clapped and kicked.

That September, Treffle Charlebois faced his death bed in Saint André, widowed eight years before. His grandson Telesphore had phoned Joe from Treffle's farm where he lived and was a labourer.

"Allo, Joseph? Grand-père Charlebois has asked for you today. He is failing quickly and I've summoned Father Luce for last rites."

"Tell Mother I'll come straight away."

Joe and Alice got there in time with the children. Victoria's sister, Virginie, was in St. Andrews for a few weeks and agreed to stay longer.

"The house seems so dark in this silence," Alice whispered to Joe. "We'll start bringing the girls to your parents' farm more often to brighten your mother's spirits."

She carried baby Dorothy across the room to Victoria, asleep in the rocker. Her eyes opened and she began to rock, with her arms wrapped around the infant. She felt Dorothy's tiny fingers, smaller than her own thumb. A tiny shriek and kicking foot reminded Victoria of the blessings of this new generation, and she stayed transfixed on Dorothy's wide eyes.

Transatlantic Call from Windsor, England, 1920

ALICE JANE wasn't at the Windsor market long, needing to rush home to Frederick. He'd been too weak to keep his balance and seldom left his bed. In the quiet house, he stood and fumbled through the bureau for Alice's Bible. He looked to the door, hoping she'd return.

Some loose pages at the back fell to the floor, and he leaned on the wall to gather them. He read the first lines of a sonnet she used to sing.

Quietly, he let the words roll through his mind.

Gonna lay down my sword and shield;
Down by the riverside, down by the riverside, down by the riverside;
I ain't gonna study war no more,
Ain't gonna study war no more, ain't gonna study war no more;
I'm gonna try on my long white robe . . .

He burst into a sob, deep from his heart. With a peacefulness, he sat down at the kitchen table, laying his head into his folded arms.

When Alice Jane walked in, she clenched her hands over her closed eyes and sobbed, then sat beside Frederick's lifeless body and said a prayer she had dreaded so often in his failing years. Gathering composure, she went to Frederick Jr. with an envelope and led him to Frederick's bicycle.

"Go quickly to Uncle Percy and Aunt Emily's house and give them this envelope."

By suppertime, Percy and Emily returned with Frederick Jr.

"Don't you worry, Jane; you are surrounded by a loving family. I'll call the Monsignor," Percy said.

"God bless you for your help. I suppose I'll go to the Post Office in the morning and send one of those transatlantic telegrams to let Alice know."

"Jane, write out what you want to say and I'll have it sent. You have much on your mind for now."

The following day, Alice May was preparing porridge for Marjorie and Dorothy when the wall box started to jingle.

"Joe, my hands are full. Can you get the phone?"

He listened, and put his hand over the receiver, then on his heart. "Yes, she's here." He looked at Alice.

"What is it? No, not from England?" Alice could tell from his face it was bad news.

"This is Alice Creffield . . . a telegram for me from Windsor?"

Joe placed a kitchen chair by the phone for Alice.

"Yesterday? He's in Heaven. Funeral is when? Yes, you can put the notice in the post." Alice lowered the receiver to her lap.

"Father."

She rose and went up to the bedroom to weep. "Poor Mother!"

Then There Were Seven

SURELY THE THIRD would be a boy, Joseph thought. In February 1922, they welcomed Gladys, then Kathleen two years later. All the girls had Paquette brown eyes except Dorothy, with blue like Alice.

With four little ones under six, Marjorie and Dorothy became willing helpers with the younger ones. Daily, after supper, Dorothy climbed up onto Joseph in the big rocking chair, holding baby Kathleen in her lap until she slept.

In the fall, the older two started school, a touchy issue as Urgel and Victoria encouraged Alice to send the girls to the Catholic school to learn the language and sacraments, and Joseph sided with them.

With his best diplomacy, he tried to convince Alice. Three to one, were not the true odds, as Alice was strong-willed and fought back, determined that her daughters not go to the Catholic school.

"They *must* be schooled in English," she said, and so it was when possible. But the girls still moved between French and English schools.

During primary years in English schools, the girls faced religious persecution and name-calling. They cringed without understanding when they were called 'frogs', but the tone and teasing too frequently brought the youngest to tears, with the others defending her.

When switched to the French school, Dorothy was considered English and was at times under the instruction of an unsympathetic sister.

Dorothy sat in silent humiliation when Felixiphore Girard dunked her braid in an ink well and leaned to whisper insults to her. Coming to referee, the school marm saw Dorothy's braid smearing ink on the back of her blouse.

"Please, Ma'am. Can't we fix it? My mother will be unhappy with me."

"Well, Dorothy, this isn't entirely uncalled for," the sister replied. "There *is* an English school not far away for Anglican girls. Your mother must find fault where it is due."

Dorothy had a fleeting look at Marjorie, who stayed clear of it. Walking home, Dorothy knew the ink had dried and the panic was setting in.

"Mother will be so angry with me. But if I can find the bleach, I can wash it out in the river."

But Marjorie ran ahead and squealed, and there was now no time to fix it in the river. Without dinner, Dorothy sat by the galvanized water pail with a glass of water, lye soap and the Pears scrub board, until her knuckles hurt. But the ink was still there.

"I'm so sorry. I'll sew a new blouse by myself," Dorothy said, fearing to look into her mother's eyes. Sometimes they were sunshine blue and happy, but other times grey and distant.

Marjorie was eleven and Dorothy nine, when Joseph and Alice had their fifth daughter, baby Gertie, in March 1928, with brown hair and eyes.

Supplementing the carpentry jobs, Joseph fished or hunted every day to feed the family of seven. The small orchard provided bushels of apples, and Victoria regularly sent sacks of potatoes and bags of corn in the harvest months.

Alice became ill and more spent hours resting, with less interest in the household. Joe saw Alice's indifference about the girls, and knew he should shelter them from worry about her health, lethargy and disinterest.

He took the girls for a stroll in the orchard one evening. "Girls, mother just needs her rest. After school, it's sometimes best that you play outside or at Aunt Desneige's or Aunt Sarah's house with your cousins."

"We understand," Marjorie volunteered.

Alice's condition wasn't lost on the girls, and arriving home after school, they watched for clues. If the curtains were drawn, mother was resting and they'd play outside until father came home. If they saw the wash hanging on the line or Alice meddling in the garden, it was better day.

Marjorie and Dorothy had always handled chores since pre-school, but responsibility for their siblings now grew progressively, especially with the infant, Gertie.

"Come on, Gertie," Marjorie said after school. "Time to ride around the yard on my shoulders."

Urgel, Joseph's father, died suddenly in October 1929, predeceased by two of his children. Victoria gathered at a private Mass with the remaining ten sons and daughters to mourn his passing. Alice and Joseph attended, but the five girls stayed home at Alice's strict instruction.

"Joseph, you know I don't like the Priest telling my girls that they won't go to Heaven unless they pray to the Virgin Mary."

"They are getting confused by religion, Alice. It's asking Mary to pray for us. My family has been Catholic for centuries; this is not the time to make an issue. I've turned my head the other way when you slip out to the Anglican Church in Lachute with Marjorie and Dorothy."

"So be it, if your family wants to pay the Church so that Urgel's soul is received at a higher level of respect before God, I'll not allow you to put in a penny."

"Alice, this is my father. I will do whatever I feel is right."

"Very well. What time will the family be going to the Church?" Alice conceded.

"Two o'clock, Alice."

"I'll be ready to go with you, but the children stay home." Alice turned her back and left the conversation.

Joseph gathered the four oldest girls and told them to dress in their Sunday best, and make sure Gertie was bathed and dressed in her white frock.

"But Pa—Mother said we wouldn't be going to Grandfather's funeral."

"Yes, Marjorie, she did say that you wouldn't be going to the Church, but she didn't say anything about you girls coming to the cemetery. You be ready and I'll be picking you up on the way. If Gertie gets too fussy, Cordelia from down the street said she would come and sit."

The girls looked at each other, knowing that Joseph would bear the brunt of an argument later.

Early Saturday morning, Marjory filled the laundry washtub and added pots of boiling water. With small hands weathered from scrubbing the washboard, she passed each piece to Dorothy to rinse in the next tub and hang on the clothesline across the yard.

Inside, with the dust mop, Gladys skidded through the main floor, making a game of the work. Sometimes, they put down a tea towel and sat Gertie on it.

"Hold on tight, Gertie. I'm taking you for a fun ride," Gladys said, knotting the corners into a make-shift hammock.

Gladys dodged the furniture with Gertie tied by twine to the towel and then to her waist. Buckling over in laughter, they camouflaged their bruises, uniting to overcome their young hardships.

Fifty-four

Stock Market Crash of 1929 – Bennett's Work Camps – New Generation of Boxcar Hobos – Hunger on Main Street – William Fitzgerald finds Hope with Joseph Paquet – Teach a Boy to Fish – Share & Share Alike; an Apple a Day – Desperate Québecois go into bush camps – Prosperity starts to return 1930s – Government Sponsored Trans Canada and Air Canada Airlines – Moise's Barbershop Gatherings – Paquette girls take in Sewing – Punishment for Dot – Marjorie Paquette leaves St. Andrews, 1933 – Chautauqua comes to St. Andrews – Search for Council Candidates finds Joe Paquette – Table Manners - Sweet Singing of *Alouette* – Alice agrees to see Dr. Allaire – Dorothy Finds the Forbidden Trunk.

The Great Depression of 1929

IT STARTED A YEAR BEFORE, WITH WHEAT PRICES plummeting to 15% of their marketed value. But the October 1929 stock market crash hit harder than one could envision.

Men left in droves, chasing after work anywhere—on the railway, logging, manufacturing or mining. Many travelled to Bennett's Work Camps, and some as far as British Columbia and northern Ontario. Despondent mothers watched as young boys of twelve were sent to find work to help put food on the tables, with many families in St. Andrews were torn apart.

For five years, the drought left families starving and without crops to harvest; then the country was hit with reduced demand for timber and manufacturing. No one coast-to-coast was spared the suffering, with thirty percent of the labour force unemployed and needing government relief.

Hobos hitching rides on rail boxcars made room for desperate businessmen. At night, farmers near the tracks guarded their crops, as shadows crept the fields scrounging abandoned potatoes and young corn, and escaping back to the rails. Local policing authorities refused to lay theft charges on those even caught red-handed.

During the Great Depression, Joseph managed to survive on his own land. His visits with cronies to the Main Street barbershop were chances to find simple pleasure with friends, although they saw their numbers depleting and the shared stories were becoming tragic.

"Joe, are you going to town this morning?" Alice asked.

"Sure am, Alice. I'm taking a chair I repaired to Robbie Barron. He'll give me something as a barter."

She winced. "It's been a while since we've seen a dollar bill and the root cellar is getting thin."

"What do you have need of most, Pet?"

"I haven't had a spot of English tea in weeks. I know flour is expensive, but the bakery ovens need it."

Joe felt the anguish of seeing his wife in need.

"Have your kettle ready for when I return; you shall have your tea."

Ah, the Barrons are Scottish to the core, surely they'll trade some tea for the chair and enough to pay my bill. The Wales and the Blanchards aren't keen on keeping a credit in these times, but I'll do what I have to for the flour.

"Alice, I'm going to help young Leland with his fishing before I leave." Living on the North River gave Joe a sanctuary of escape from life's stresses, and never a disappointment to the larder.

A good stout rod and some shiny tin and the trout come calling. They don't have an economy in the river and don't have to mind the British.

He laughed at his random thoughts. Donning his tattered cap, he was out the door with a hook and reel. Half an hour later, Alice peeked from the kitchen and saw him jaunting off toward town with a bulging sack over his shoulder.

"Don't forget the chair," she called out.

On the Main Street boardwalk, Joseph settled into his chair, hoping for some cash. At his feet was a bushel of Paquette apples and a half dozen loaves of bread from his own bakery oven.

In a stone crock were posies of hand-picked wildflowers for those that came by in desperate need. His benevolent nature didn't always give him the sense to hold back a few loaves for his own family.

What the Lord giveth I give away too.

Across the dirt street, a queue of hungry folks lined outside the hotel for soup and dried biscuits. A man brought stiff coffee out as they waited, and Joe could smell it from his chair.

The hotel had become a community stop off. If there were rumours of jobs, they'd be known there; and if not, the neighbours would lend a hand whenever they could.

Joe stood up at the sight of William Fitzgerald maneuvering his car down Main Street. William waved and pulled up outside the barber shop. His pride hid his feeling of hopelessness, but Joe sensed it from his face.

Joe scratched his chin. "Why Willie, what are you doing pulling your car with your horse?"

"What else can I do to get around? There's no market for my wheat and that means no pay for me. I saw a fellow in Lachute driving one of these. They called it the Bennett buggy because R.B. can't see to fix the economy. That means I can't afford gas. I took the engine out."

Joe got up to look under the hood. "How's your family coping, Will?"

"Margaret does her best to spread what we have at supper, but it's harder each day. Do you know where I can find a bit of work, Joe?"

As they talked, Joe bagged some apples and wrapped a loaf of bread in butcher's paper. He walked it to William's front seat.

"I'll keep my ears open, Will . . ."

Joe stopped, and raised a finger as he formulated his thought.

"Will, bring your Bennett buggy by my house in the morning. The fish in the North River don't know about the economy. Come fishing with me and you'll feed your family to a feast tomorrow night."

Fitzgerald sat up straight. Joe had given him faint hope for the day, and he had no quick reply. He looked at the ground, then across at the queue of hungry men, then at Joe. When he spoke, his voice cracked.

"Would you mind if I bring my boy? I haven't been much of a father, worrying about each day. If you could teach him to fish, it would mean much more than supper, Joe."

"Come early, before the sun comes up. We'll catch them when they get up for breakfast—it's the best time. If your boy would like to clean up the rotten apples from the orchard, you can treat your horses too; they're no good once they hit the ground."

Two days after they'd fished, Joe told a story at the barber shop—not the truth, but a tale of the giant mackerel that got away, and what a hero William Fitzgerald had been in hooking it.

On the weekend, two men walked with hesitation to the Paquette's river dock and cast a reel of hope.

Another man come alone on Tuesday, and two more Wednesday. Joe always offered a welcome, and when they could spare bread or apples, he left a basket by the dock.

Alice's poor health didn't keep her from coming out when able, to greet those at the river.

She walked back with Joe to the house, with an empty basket to fill. "Joe! When will this stop? We are becoming like your barber shop."

"Alice, no one knows when there will be jobs again. We are blessed to have the fruits of God's earth. I am thankful every day that I have been spared the fate of some men who have given up hope. Maybe one day soon, the Bennett government will help the needy instead of putting money into manufacturing and new fandangled transportation ideas."

Joe was buoyed by the companionship of the fishermen, and told Alice he was even inspired by the discussions with these men and boys. His fables of old St. Andrews gave assurance and hope in return.

With no notice, winter stormed in with two feet of snow packed against the house. With apples finished and scarce carpentry work, Joe went into the bush camps, vying for a logging job with many others, and was soon promoted to Assistant Camp Boss.

North River at St. Andrews East, Québec

But by the end of the first week, Boss O'Malley berated him. "The Hamilton Brothers will pay a good price if we meet quota, Joe, but you'll have to crack the whip harder to keep your men on target."

"Crack the whip over my men?"

"Yes, you heard me. Don't get soft, Joe."

"I did hear, and you can keep your whip. I'll not treat my friends that way. Find one of your Scottish mates to do it for yer, I quit."

By the next Monday, Joe was back in St. Andrews, trying to organize hunting excursions, and doing carpentry repairs in exchange for staples at the dry goods store and a bit of gas for the car.

In the Dirty Thirties, Bennett's Conservative government established the Bank of Canada in Montréal, then the Canadian Wheat Board, seeking foreign markets and a fair price for prairie farmers. It took eight years for wheat prices to stabilize before they set their sights on transportation. Montréal opened an international airport at Dorval for commercial flights, and with tax dollars the government sponsored two airlines, Trans Canada and Air Canada in 1937.

For Canada to keep pace militarily, funds were spent on research and technology, with advances in bombers and surveillance. A small Canadian manufacturing sector of Avro began development of interceptor crafts. Finally, sectors were seeing new jobs and financial relief.

Spring came early in 1937 and the summer was warm and sunny; some said it was a predictor of a return to prosperity.

Through the window, Moise Jr. watched Joseph socializing in animation outside the barbershop. He excused himself from his patron Loynachan, and poked his head out. It was the same question as yesterday, "Hey, Joe. How's Alice today?"

"This morning she's gathering sweet peas. This bright sunshine will do her good," Joseph replied.

"Come into the shop before you leave. My wife sent some sewing for the girls and a basket of blueberry muffins for Alice."

"That's mighty nice of your wife, Moise."

Donald Loynachan's face appeared from under a hot towel in the barber's chair.

"Hallo, Joseph, do you really have a cougar's head over your fireplace? I'd be surprised if your wife allowed it; I know mine wouldn't . . ." Donald almost choked in his laughter.

Joseph enjoyed the quip and lived for these Main Street exchanges.

"Well, hello to you, Donald, and it's not really that funny. It's been too long anyway. Alice and I always have cold cider in the stone crocks; come by for a chin wag anytime."

"I just might sometime soon. We were talking the other day—Louise wants a pine trunk like that one you did for the Barbers. Are you still doing carpentry?"

"Of course! You ask a Paquette if they are still doing carpentry, you'd be askin' a dead man. Ha. My hands are full right now, but the kids will be in school after harvest and I can get 'er done fast then. I still owe you for saving us, so you can have a good price."

"Hey, Joe, I almost ran you down with my new Ford last week, but instead I put on the brakes. Does that give me a good price too?" Claude Billings spurted from the street.

A roar of laughter came from the railing outside, then more stories of rescuing Joe. He stepped outside again, seeing the audience ripe.

"Well, I guess it's time I read you this clipping of a real joke my mother-in-law sent me from the London newspaper the other week."

"Tell it fast, cause Loynachan's almost finished his cut. You're next," Moise said.

"Well, it seems Pope Pius XI was driven from the airport to meet the Queen. He tells the chauffeur to speed up as they've fallen behind. But the driver insists on the speed limit."

Between puffs of smoke, the laughter broke out, until Joe hushed them. "Wait, hear me out, there's even more to it.

"So the irritated Pope says, 'Pull over, you get in the back, and I'll drive.' A pair of policiers stop them and the older officer tells the young one to write them a speeding ticket. But the junior comes back."

"He says 'I can't do it. The person in the back is too important.' The senior cop gets mad."

"Well, who is it?" The old cap says.

"I don't know, but he must be important. The Pope is his chauffeur."

Roars of laughter picked up again, with snorts and guffaws. "Hey, Joe, we don't want to offend the Pope," Claude spurted.

"And Joe, you earned yourself a free cut." Moise pointed to the chair.

Hearing more stories through the open door from the rail outside, Joe was restless to get back out, and finally returned home in time for lunch.

"Alice. Alice," he called.

"Shush, Pa. She's asleep in the garden hammock," Kathleen said.

"Well, I'm just going to get her up."

He scurried to the garden at the back, leaving parcels in the kitchen.

"Come dear, sit at your window table."

"What's so important, Joe?"

"I was in town. Louise Paquette, Moise's wife, sent you this basket of fresh muffins. From the money I saved on a haircut, I bought you Anjou pears and a clump of red grapes. I know how you like those. And look— some Lord Grey." Alice's smile was weak but genuine.

"It's Earl Grey, and thank you. Joe. Do you mind putting on a pot of coffee and we'll have the muffins? I'll sip with the Earl later."

Dorothy and Gladys had arrived at the top of stairs.

"Girls, I have a basket of sewing from Louise Paquette. She'll pay you your take-in rate. I'll bring her basket back next week when I see Moise."

Several other neighbours gave them small mending and ironing jobs, and on rare occasion babysitting and housekeeping. Alice was becoming more withdrawn, with her bouts of illness and frequent fever. She was confused and frustrated, with her behaviour unpredictable from day to day.

That afternoon, she seemed dazed and flustered that her collar had not been ironed properly. "Dorothy, you didn't do this right," she said calmly.

"I'm sorry, Ma, I'll do it again."

"I'll give you something to remind you." Without explanation, Alice picked up Dorothy's hand and placed it flat on the hot pot belly stove.

Dorothy's shrieking brought Joseph to the house. "Gracious, Alice. What are you thinking?"

Alice was unresponsive, sitting upright at the table and staring to space. With lard, Joseph lathered the red, blistering skin. "Dot, when you feel up to it, soak your hand in cold water. It will help the swelling." As Joe kissed her forehead, his coarse fingers wiped the streaks of tears.

On Alice's better days, she used the swing at the oak, and wandered about the wild flowers along the riverbank, lifting her skirt hems to walk barefoot on the shore. On windy days, she enjoyed the freshness of the air, watching her sheets flap in the breeze on the clothesline. On warm evenings, Joe took her in the rowboat and they'd drift until she was sleepy.

The girls skipped into the yard on a Saturday morning, racing and laughing with school friends. Alice was on the old swing, so Dorothy left the girls to join her. "Do you want a push, Mom?"

"No, leave me be," Alice said. No solution was clear to Dorothy how to help, and she rejoined the girls as Alice swung in silence.

No one in town knew how the girls suffered, as they always projected a joyful image. Together they were able to absorb the impact of Alice's mental state, with healthy escapes to swim, or fish with Joe, pick apples or skip to their grandmother's house.

In 1933, Marjorie left home at sixteen, and her sisters knew it was to break away from the childhood memories. She found work in Montréal and wrote the first week to her sisters, but the letters became rare and then stopped, with no letters or phone calls again for many years.

Dorothy felt some abandonment, but the void was overshadowed with her responsibility to protect young Gert as she still faced years at home.

Joe, Gert and Alice in the boat on the North River

Québec after the Dirty Thirties

FRENCH-CANADIAN spirit returned in bounds to St. Andrews and Lachute. Sunday afternoons were dreamy for townsfolk, languishing on lawn blankets at the band shells, sponsored by the Molson's lager company. Belanger's brass band drew standing-only crowds, dancing on the lawns to swing tunes like the big bands on the radio. No one talked of the Great Depression any more, and citizens were showing revived beliefs of optimism.

Concerts and theatres were springing up in even the smallest towns with local productions, and often promoters took a chance on bringing big-name drama talent. The Chautauqua experience even came to Argenteuil.

Lachute's Rex Theatre had burned to the ground before the depression, but then its owner, Monsieur Fassio, built a larger theatre in the 30s during the heyday of the big screen.

The motor club trials started in 1934, and subsequent years built arenas for curling, boxing, and hockey. In 1939, the French Cycling Club came to Lachute. With towns burgeoning, demand grew for larger public facilities, road construction and sponsorships.

Hoping for a feisty political debate, Joe was heartened that Robert Barron and Jack LeRoy were at it already at Lafond's barbershop. Before they even saw him, he pulled up a chair.

"G'day Joe! So what about council in town?" Robert spurted.

Joe let on he was up to speed.

"Oh yes . . . council. That's a problem now, isn't it?"

Robert grunted, "We need better candidates for the next Town Council." His hands waved high as he ranted. "St. Andrews is growing in leaps and we need a proactive mayor."

"And councilmen too," said Jack.

Joe nodded quickly. "What are the issues?"

"Taxation," Jack replied.

"I don't agree with it at all," Joe spurted.

"C'mon Joe, we're serious, you know. The Paquette name is one of the oldest in St. Andrews, and people listen to you. Council will be the same for you as the barber's boardwalk, except you'll wear a suit and with a lot more people listening. I've never seen a Paquette deny an audience."

"You're pulling my leg. Council is made up of merchants and aristocrats," Joe said. "St. Andrews has sent many fine politicians to Ottawa. There are good men in the wings."

"Come with us to the Town Hall meeting tomorrow night, Joe. Have a listen before you rush to judgement," Robert asked.

"If I'm there, I am—if I'm not, I'm not."

The girls took the usual route past Aunt Desneige's and Rose Anna's house after school, a short walk from Main Street. From Desneige's, the four collected a sack of laundry for their job, and graciously accepted a basket of muffins and a raspberry pie for Alice.

In the kitchen, they jostled in fun over their alternating stove duties. "Dot, I'll cook the fish if you peel these shiny potatoes," Gladys said. "Gertie, gather two handfuls of peas from Ma's garden, and don't eat them on the way back."

Alice came to the table at precisely six, rested from the afternoon.

"Thanks for making supper, girls." She breathed deeply. "I could smell this delicious aroma upstairs."

On the rare opportunity to enjoy a congenial family dinner, Gladys and Kathleen leaned on their elbows over their plates.

"Well girls, I see it's time you learned some manners. In England, I was raised to behave and act with respect and gratitude at the supper table."

They braced for a scolding, but their mouths fell open as Alice began a soft tune. Her voice was a surprise to them, a high soprano and sweet to their ears. Dorothy said later that it gave her a thrill to hear that hidden gift that she never heard again.

> Mabel, Mabel strong and able,
> Get your elbows off the table,
> This is not a horse's stable.

The girls were so enamoured with her voice that they didn't listen to the words. Alice noticed and continued.

> Mabel, Mabel strong and able,
> Get your elbows off the table,
> We told you once, we've told you twice,
> We'll never tell you more than thrice."

Dorothy poked Gladys until she sat back in her chair.

"That was lovely singing, Alice," Joe remarked.

"Perhaps you girls will remember the words. Whether rich or poor, young or old, my girls will learn to have English manners."

Crisis with Alice and the Forbidden Trunk

ALICE'S HEALTH brought new alarms to Joseph, and against her wishes, he summoned their family doctor, Dr. Allaire II, to hasten to the house.

The doctor was calm, and his compassion encouraged Alice to speak about her symptoms. They began by talking gently about the family, and she spoke openly about her love for them. But at an early point she stopped, as her own words brought her to tears.

"Alice, your family loves you and are concerned that you may not be healthy. Let's talk this over and see what we can do to make you feel better."

"I feel trapped here in this house with all my children. Yet, I love them and it pains when I'm not being a good mother. Joseph thinks I'm Catholic, but really I'm Anglican. I have pain in my stomach now and my back. Mostly dizziness and sadness in my head."

"This is good to talk, Alice," Dr. Allaire said. "I think you could be open in telling Joseph your symptoms. We are going to take some tests. Would you be willing to stay in the hospital overnight, so we can get everything done all at once?"

"What do you think is wrong with me?"

"I don't like to speculate, but I know that you're a woman that needs answers. By the pallor of your skin and eyes, and the swelling in your ankles, my first suspicion is renal insufficiency causing toxic poison. That means your kidneys aren't doing their job. You could also be suffering from long-term depression. Now that's not a bad thing, Alice, and we can help with medications."

"I would like to be a better wife and mother," she said.

Alice mulled over the hospital. "Just one night then!"

Dr. Allaire determined it to be depression and tired blood, with advanced stages of uremia. The toxic overload would be terminal if she didn't stick to her medicine. Joseph tried to explain it to the girls, asking for their patience.

But it was too late. Marjorie was gone and Dorothy was anxious to leave too. Joseph had never raised a hand to his girls or used an angry word, but Alice kept a switch for them behind the barn.

Alice sat motionless on the swing at the giant oak overhanging the river. A stream of Canada geese passed overhead broadcasting their journey south, and a soft autumn breeze brushed her flushed cheeks.

Ah, Mama and Papa, why did I leave my home? It has been difficult in a country where I worship in a Church where I was not baptized, a new language, and now I have a family to care for. I didn't know it would be so hard."

She tried to hold back the tears welling in her eyes. After a while, she jumped down from the swing and sauntered along the river bank searching for water lilies. With a pinkish one tucked in her hair, she rolled her skirt up high to morph into pantaloons. Her Oxford shoes and nylon ankle stockings were placed meticulously on the dock. Easing herself down, she let her legs dangle in the river, oblivious to nature around her. The water was cool and forgiving and tiny ripples caressed and soothed her legs.

Alice was unaware that she had started to sing a song she heard so often from Joseph's jigs. Joe heard it from the yard, and came closer to listen to the sweetness of *Alouette* as he had never heard before. His thoughts went to the day he first took Alice and Louise for a drift on the river.

He found Alice's shawl and strolled to the dock. Holding hands, they sat in the peace of the evening.

The Paquette master bedroom was usually darkened with window shades, and the girls knew it was forbidden to enter—especially never to open the English trunk in the corner of the bedroom, behind the wooden dressing fold.

Curiosity lured Dorothy there when Alice was out of the house at a doctor's clinic. Her heart pounded as she stood over the trunk, flooded with emotion and guilt. She turned to go back, then looked at the door.

What if I find something I don't want to know? God knows I'm dealing with enough.

The heavy hinge creaked. There, on top of Alice's wedding gown, was an old Bible. A release came over Dorothy.

This is Alice Jane Turner's Bible from England. Do I dare read it?

Deciding she had a few minutes, she sat on the floor reading the Psalms, then memorized two lines from the Book of John.

> I came that they might have life,
> And might have it abundantly.

She whispered out loud, "I'll come back here."

One day, Alice caught her reading at the trunk. Dorothy got a whipping with a buckled belt, and a stern warning. But it didn't deter her; she would be more discreet, to read and memorize it when she could.

In her mother's books, she found a scrap of paper with an address in Buckinghamshire. Saving pennies for postage, she wrote to Alice Jane Creffield-Turner, her grandmother in England.

Gertie and Dorothy shared the small upper bedroom across from her parent's room, with Kathleen and Gladys in the other. At night, Dorothy talked of all of them getting across the ocean to their grandmother. "Somehow . . . someday."

"Is that far?" Gertie asked.

"Yes, it's almost half way to Heaven to get there, and maybe God would see us." She gave Gertie a goodnight kiss.

Oh how wonderful it will be when I get to Heaven.

A deep bond grew and always remained between the odd pair.

At the mailbox one morning, Alice held the envelope high. It was her mother's handwriting; she recognized it instantly, but the letter was to Dorothy. Alice erupted in anger and ripped it open. "Dorothy's been sending mail behind my back," she ranted.

"Dorothy!" Alice yelled.

"Yes, Mother."

Alice waved the envelope. "What's this about?"

"Is that from Grandmother Creffield?"

"You know it is. It says in here how Grandma is delighted that you are reading scripture. God isn't going to make your way through life. The dice decides your fate and you're stuck with it. I forbid you to correspond further with *my* mother."

After that, Dorothy went daily to check the mailbox first, hoping for another letter from England. One day in late 1936, a small envelope came, marked 'AJC', full of love and hope, and more special scripture. A few months later, another came addressed directly to Alice. The writing did not look like Grandma's.

Giving the envelope from England to her father, Dorothy waited on the stairs to hear the news. He fingered the envelope, then took it to Alice. Dorothy was scared that her continued secret relationship had been revealed, with punishment to bear.

She listened at the staircase at loud wailing from Alice's bedroom. When her father came down to see her, he looked sad and not angry at all.

He drew Dorothy to his side and squeezed her hand.

"Your Grandmother Creffield went up to Heaven. You would have liked her so much. Your own mother has her pretty face, as do you." Joe cupped Dorothy's face in his rough hands and kissed her on the forehead.

She was no longer a little girl, but knew she could only stay a while longer, needing to be close to her father. Her heart ached for her mother, yet she yearned to walk her own path in life now.

That night, Dorothy and Gertie knelt by their bed and prayed for Grandma, for Mother, and for Father; then for help and hope.

Fifty-five

Dorothy Paquette leaves St. Andrews for Montréal, 1937 – Painful separation for the Paquette sisters – Joe is Heartbroken – Dorothy Finds Employment with Simpsons Downtown Store – Germany invades Poland, 1939 – Britain & France Declare War on Germany – Dorothy transfers to Toronto and begins Bible College – Alice Agrees to Thanksgiving Dinner at Desneiges – Eyes Glowing in the Darkness – Bandit Heaps Havoc on Alice's Garden – Joseph determined to trap the vermin – Night Watch from the Chaise – Barn Roof Patched as Alice sees Joe heading for town wearing a new coon hat.

Dorothy Paquette goes to Montréal

DOROTHY WAS EIGHTEEN, AND IN THE FALL OF 1937 SHE decided that her time had come. In the evening, she took Gertie to their fishing spot to break the news.

At ten, Gertie had known it would happen soon. Before they reached the river, she stopped Dorothy.

"You're leaving aren't you? That's what we're doing, isn't it?"

Her eyes filled and they hugged before Dorothy could reply.

"Sweet Gertie, I promise I'll prepare a way for you to come when you're old enough to leave school. I've saved a little money for the train to Montréal and to share a flat until I find a job. Then I'll go to Bible School when I'm able."

Gertie's small arms clung to her and wouldn't release. They sobbed together in the darkness, draining any strength.

"Does Mother know?" Gert asked.

Dorothy's mouth formed the silent words, "Not yet."

"I will write every week," she said.

Sitting close on a stump, Dorothy pointed to the clear sky that twinkled with stars that night.

"When we are not together, Gert, look up at the stars like this. I'll be watching them too, from wherever I am. Our hearts will be together. I'll pray for you, and for Mother and Father every day."

Gert wiped her tears. "I'll always do the same."

Dorothy knew that Gertie would be taken care of by Gladys. At sixteen, she was showing responsibility for many chores and caring for Gert too. She knew they'd share laughter, playtime and a similar bond.

A few days later, she told Joe.

"Father, it is time for me to go out on my own. An inner voice is telling me that I belong in Bible College and I need to go to Montréal."

"I knew this would come, Dot. But nonetheless, I am sad."

"Father, I'll miss you so much and I'll write every week. You'll always be in my heart."

Dorothy allowed the embrace to linger with her father, inhaling a smell she wanted to remember forever. The feel of his bristly whiskers, his tear stained cheeks and the aroma of his pipe. It was the embrace that Toussaint gave to Étienne three hundred years before.

Two weeks later, Dorothy left with her bag.

Standing tall, she took a deep breath as she walked through the polished doors of the downtown Simpson's store in Montréal. It was an unfamiliar and illuminated world and she was determined to enter it with confidence.

Dorothy stopped inside to listen to the carollers' voices that carried through the main floor. She passed small children at the toy sections, and marvelled at luxuries that she and her sisters hadn't known. It was a fantasy world.

Management was recruiting for the Christmas season and she was hired on the spot for the glove department. On her second pay day, she sent small Christmas gifts back home—suede gloves with tiny buttons at the wrist for her mother, and a fine silk bow tie for Joseph with a red elastic to go under the collar.

As an exemplary employee, Dorothy was granted her request to transfer to the Toronto store, where could enroll at Eastern Bible College. She found a place on Jones Avenue to share with her college roommates, Ruby and Estelle. With her expanded life of work, studies and choir, she hadn't been back to St. Andrews since last Christmas.

On September 1, 1939, the Germans walked into Poland, and the Nazi party had the world on tenterhooks. As Canada prepared to join Allies in Europe, the Québec factories were retrofitted for munitions again.

"It's like a clock turning back," some said.

Manufacturing innovations ground to a halt, returning communities to basics of woodstoves, iceboxes and coal furnaces, with reminders of the depression.

Two Alliances emerged—the Allies (Britain) and Axis (Germany), involving over a hundred million people and thirty countries, from North Africa across the Atlantic to Hawaii and north to Hiroshima, Japan.

St. Andrews had not forgotten the Great War and the depression, but this time the news was more vivid, as it was broadcast daily into every home. In the first week of September, updates of the Battle of Westerplate in Poland began, announcing the loss of lives to the Alliance. Germany invaded Poland overnight and soon took the battle to the Atlantic.

Bandit & Thanksgiving in St. Andrews, 1942

BACK HOME, Desneige doubled her visits to Alice in an effort to add enjoyment to her routine, and observe her health. But her concern continued as she watched Alice's progressive despondency. Gladys had gone from the house, then Kathleen left for a caregiver position in Halifax, with only Gertie remaining.

"Alice, my dear, with my boys overseas, will you, Joe and Gert come on Sunday for Thanksgiving?"

"I don't know, Desneige. You know I haven't been outside for weeks."

"All the more reason, Alice. Please come."

On the ride home Sunday night, Alice realized how glad she was that she'd gone, and that Desneige had insisted.

"Isn't the sky beautiful, Joe?"

He pulled the jalopy into the drive and helped Alice from the car. "Listen Alice, can you hear the loons biding adieu?"

"I do . . . it's been a lovely evening. My best for a long time."

Alice stayed at the screen door looking toward the river. Joe had gone to sleep, and she wandered in the kitchen and outside. Far in the back garden, she watched two twinkling lights like someone staring at her.

"Joe! Joe! Come down!" she called. "Something is in the yard. I heard banging too."

Without a word, Joe retrieved his shotgun. In his slippers, he silently opened the kitchen door and walked the yard. Alice waited inside in fear.

"The coast is clear, Alice. Perhaps the eyes of a wandering deer passing through the yard, Love. Now, off you go to bed. I'm right behind."

In the morning, garbage was strewn from the barn to the bin, and Alice joined him to see the disarray.

"Joe! You should see my garden—it's been demolished. Who or what would do that?"

He instantly knew the culprit. "That darn Bandit. It's the raccoon that roosts in the barn rafters in the winter. Sometimes he sets up house in the hollow of the big willow by the river."

"Can't you do something to keep him from my garden?"

"I'll set traps and another by the garbage can. A chicken wire fence should keep him out."

The next morning was the same, with the garden gone and garbage spread. "I'll rig a string to the dinner gong. Tonight, Alice, he'll trip the wire and I'll be at him with my gun in an instant."

At well past midnight, the gong echoed through the house, but by the time Joe got out, Bandit was out of sight.

"That dang vermin!"

Exasperated, Joe set up post in the wooden chaise in the yard.

"I'll sleep with one eye open."

"Don't fall asleep, Joe. Your snoring will warn the coon."

A quarter moon created silhouettes, and Joe's eyes adjusted to watch for shadows.

Rustle! Rustle! Bang!

Bandit approached, then tore into the chicken wire. Joe inched forward and sat upright. The sound moved behind him and he made a sudden jerk.

He jumped to his feet. "Blah, blah, blah!" he shouted. With his arms waving and feet stomping, he banged on pots and pans, and showed his best grotesque face.

Running across the yard was Alice, shrieking and white as a sheet.

"Joe, help me, Joe. Something is attacking me." She'd been on her way to the outhouse.

"Oh Alice, you poor dear. I'm sorry, I thought you were the coon."

She slumped with her hand feigned over her chest. "I think I'm having a heart attack, Joe."

He eased her into the chaise, and in the darkness, he caught a glimpse of Bandit standing on his hind legs rubbing his hands together, clicking. His eyes glowed with iridescent light and Joe said later that the coon was gloating.

"Cursed coon! I'll outsmart him if it's the last thing." For two weeks Joe slept in the chaise.

One morning, Alice looked out as Joe headed off to Main Street, whistling with a skip in his step. Instead of his weathered cap, he sported a coon tail hat.

The barn roof had a patchwork of repairs from foot holes and buckshot, and the willow hollow smoldered from burning to a char.

Alice shook her head.

"Yes, that's Joe," she said with a smirk he'd never see.

Fifty-six

Ice houses on Lake Simcoe, Ontario – Cooke Family Operates General Store & Post Office, Big Bay Point, 1938 – Lester Cooke Ice Man – Compute from BBP to Keary Coal Co. in Toronto – Across the Street is Dorothy Paquette's flat on Jones Avenue – Recruitment Active for World War II – Lester appeals for Militia Service on the Niagara River – Army needs C.F.B. Borden supplied with ice – Les Cooke applies for Ice Contract – May 8, 1945 Germany Surrenders, followed by Japan months later – Winston Churchill's 'V' for Victory - Dorothy waits at Union Station for Gertrude's arrival – Dorothy Phones Joe 'I've met a wonderful man' – Lester Cooke and Dorothy Paquette Marry, 1947 – Being Raised in a Make-Do Environment, Dorothy uncomfortable with Mink Stole – Public Utilities Desperate call on Christmas Morning – It's Better to Give than Receive.

Days of Ice & Coal, Toronto, 1944

AS THE ICEHOUSE DOOR OPENED TO A COOL BREEZE, FOR a moment the heat of the summer day was forgotten. Les Cooke's faithful friend, Old Dan, pressed his Collie nose in to nudge the door open. Les shooed him with a pat and returned to load the '34 GMC, its weak floorboard creaking under his work boots and brawny 185 pounds.

Harvested from Kempenfelt Bay on Lake Simcoe north of Toronto, the ice blocks were crystal clear and easy to haul to his customers at Big Bay Point. In February and March, he had cut them from the lake, to store under sawdust until summer. The icehouse smelled of the woodchips packed around the blocks, still stacked on wooden skids and separated by layers of burlap.

With tongs, he grappled with a fifty-pound block and heaved it to his shoulder—then another and another. Sweat trickled from his face, staining his white undershirt.

Les Cooke's parents first summered at a Big Bay Point cottage across the lake from Barrie's railway depot, then ran the General Store. With the post office inside, they knew every name and face at a glance. The family's history started there in 1870 when his grandfather, J.B., owned a two hundred acre farm on Rockley Beach on the 14th Concession.

Years before, in 1933, sixteen-year-old Lester rode a twenty-year-old bike with wooden rims to the cottages with grocery deliveries from the store, then was out again by supper with the Toronto Evening Telegram. At doorsteps, he heard complaints that fuel companies were getting out of home ice delivery.

"Dad, I see opportunity. It might be small, but I hear it over and over."

"But not on your bike." Silby, his father, grinned. "What's the plan?"

With his savings, he made a deal on a 1929 GMC two-ton stake truck and rode to Toronto on his bike to make the transaction. In the early winters, he look lumberjacking jobs in Northern Ontario before the ice harvesting, and in summers took other hauling jobs besides ice.

In 1938, without abandoning the ice business, Les delivered gravel and coal for Keary Coal on Jones Avenue in Toronto. At five foot eleven, he was strong from physical work, with dark hair and black brows over brown eyes.

Dorothy Paquette left her shared room at 477 Jones Avenue in Toronto's Riverdale section, with no attention to the Keary Coal truck parked across the road. Nor did she see the delivery man, Lester Cooke, setting the chute for a coal delivery.

Finished in Toronto for the day, he took deliveries to the iceboxes of Big Bay Point back up north, depleting his daily load of over a thousand pounds. With an ice pick, he severed some to fit into family iceboxes.

In the spring, tensions in Austria were at a breaking point, and the Canadian Army was opening recruitment offices. Lester saw the ad, to apply for army service at the Royal Canadian Mounted Police detachment in Orillia.

The Sergeant passed him an application and health questionnaire.

"Fill these out, then down the hall for fingerprinting."

Time passed as he waited for a roll call and reporting assignment. First it was weeks, then months, with nothing until August 21, 1939. But the letter was a shock to his self-esteem, and he read it several times.

On the basis of a visual defect, the department renders you unfit for engagement in this Force.

He refolded the letter to its envelope and stuffed it into the desk drawer. *My sight. Although I haven't had vision in my left eye since I had scarlet fever at six, I've compensated and I am equal to any man.*

The next day, he appealed to the Department of Defence. Within weeks, an offer came for military patrol at Niagara-on-the-Lake. Les took the assignment, rather than not serve at all, but inside, he longed to join his friends and relatives across the ocean to defend his country.

The post office notice was up for only a day when Lester heard that Canada's Munitions and Supply Department was accepting contract bids to supply ice to military bases.

With penciled calculations in a notebook, he ran his financial figures over coffee in the kitchen.

This is right for me in many ways. If I get this, I can add trucks and start a cartage business. Even hire local drivers. Mother could handle dispatch and the books to start.

"There's a vacant office and warehouse on Essa Road," he told her. "Bert Warnica says he'll help haul ice from Toronto with his Fargo. If I can contribute to the war by supplying army bases, there's reward in that."

His mother, Agnes, said, "You know that your Dad's service in the Great War left him incapacitated. Then with the Depression, it broke his heart to lose his own cartage business. Listen to your heart."

"Who knows how long the war will last?" he said.

He spread the front page of The Telegram on the table.

"There's a meeting this week in Québec City with Churchill, Roosevelt and MacKenzie. That suggests that Canada will play a big part in this war."

Les reached for the cornbread and maple syrup, and added the figures again.

"I'll call Mrs. Leslie about the warehouse right away."

Germany's surrender came on May 8, 1945 and Japan's on August 15. With the end of World War II, the Cold War began between the United States and the Soviet Union.

Winston Churchill's 'V' two finger symbol became famous in his photos, as a rallying emblem for freedom and victory. His speech was heard around the world, and in the households in Ontario and Québec— 'Never in the field of human conflict was so much owed by so many to so few.'

At the end of the war, demand for ice in Base Borden diminished and Les turned to piano and furniture moving.

Matchmaker for Lester Cooke and Dorothy Paquette

LILLIAN PEEVER knew them both—her cousin Les at 27 and Dorothy 25. It seemed ideal in every way, even long before she took it upon herself. She knew Dorothy from the College; another cousin, C.B Smith was the Dean, and other relatives taught classes.

"Les, you must meet my close friend, Dorothy Paquette. She's from St. Andrews near Montréal and is perfect for you."

They both laughed at her teasing. But as the summer weekend approached, Lillian insisted that he come to the family cottage in Cobourg, on the site of a cluster of relative's cabins on Lake Ontario.

"Dorothy will be with me at the cottage next to your parents," she said. "You won't be sorry. She's funny and shy too."

Les grinned, but with demands of business, declined. She didn't let it go and urged him continually until he relented.

"Alright, Lillian. If there's a campfire singalong at C.B.'s cabin, I'll bring my guitar. Perhaps your friend would like that. Mind you, it's tossing the poor girl into the midst of our clan."

"She won't mind at all. Lester, she has a heart of gold. I know you love to tease girls to make them blush, but don't do that with Dorothy. At least not at first."

His arms crossed in sarcasm. "Anything else I should know, Lillian?"

"I love you, cousin, and I feel in my bones that this is the one for you."

Dorothy planned to ride on the bus, but Mrs. Griffin from the College insisted she go with them. As they'd stay on, Dorothy could take the bus back. On the first day, Lillian kept close watch on Lester, certain he was smitten.

"Dorothy, do you have family in Toronto?" he asked.

"Well, the college staff and students are family now, I suppose."

"You've met my parents; besides me there's just my sister, Joyce." He paused at the noise of the throng around him. "Oh yes, and I have all these cousins too. They're everywhere here." As they laughed, she flashed to her own cousins in Québec.

"Where did you come from?" he asked.

Dorothy squirmed, dealing with the question. "Montréal—well, a little town south of it."

She brightened with thoughts about Gertie. "My little sister, Gert, is coming to Toronto in a few weeks. The Lachute Salvation Army set her up with a citadel on Dufferin Street. I can't wait for her to arrive."

After Sunday lunch, Dorothy prepared for the afternoon bus to Toronto, but fumbling in her purse, she discovered her funds would be too close for the fare. Lester saw it and stepped in.

"Dorothy, is there anything I can help with?"

Her blue eyes squinted through her blush. "Les, I am so embarrassed—I'm short fifty cents for my ticket."

His warmth and charm stepped in. "If I loan it to you, then I'll have to see you again to be repaid."

She placed her fingers gently on his arm. "I'll definitely repay you when I see you again."

Les reached for her hand.

Perhaps Lillian was right.

Toronto's Union Station echoed the arrival announcements. Dorothy waited on a bench in the Great Hall, unsure which train would bring Gertrude. The polished floors reflected the sunlight from the four-story arched windows. It seemed magical to her today, a wonderful place to bring her little Gert. The giant clock ticked slowly, waiting for the twelve o'clock from Montréal.

The time and track number suddenly changed on the board, and Dorothy ran with others to watch the train chug in. As the throng filled the platform, she scanned the crowd from her tiptoes, looking for her favourite brown hat.

"Gert! Gert!" She waved her gloves, hoping to be seen.

Gertrude had never been out of Montréal. At sixteen, contemplation of such a distance and the lights of another grand city thrilled her.

Dorothy wrapped her arms around her. "I can't believe it's you."

"Oh, Dot!"

"Father must have been broken hearted to see his last—and I believe his favourite—daughter leave home," Dorothy said.

"Aunt Desneige drove me and Dad to the train to see me off, and she promised to check in on them. She's very kind to Mom."

"Dear Aunt Desneige. She was always intuitive when we needed help."

"Well, tears *were* running down Dad's cheeks. From the train window, I saw him on the boarding ramp and pressed my hand flat to the glass. I hope he saw me. It was heartbreaking. Mother will be lonely too."

"You're bunking with me, Gert, and I've planned a good weekend. You brought walking shoes, didn't you?"

Gert pointed at her solid black, laced oxfords with a sensible heel and brown socks.

"The Sally Ann loaned them to me," she said.

They both burst into laughter.

Dorothy Paquette & Lester Cooke Wed, 1947

"HELLO, DAD. It's me, Dot." Joe pulled a chair close to the kitchen wall phone.

"I'm so glad to hear your voice," he said. "Are you okay? Did Gert get settled in?"

"Yes, she's with me, and we spend every weekend together. I won't let her out of my sight, you can be assured."

Dorothy paused. "Dad, I've met a wonderful man. You will like him, I'm sure of it. He asked me to marry him."

"And what did you say?"

"I said yes."

Joe's heart leapt. "You're the first of my girls to get married, you know. What's his name?"

"Dad, his name is Lester Cooke. He has a trucking company north of Toronto in Barrie. I was hoping you and Mother could come for the wedding. We've set a date; May next year."

"Well, I don't know if your mother will be up to travelling. Let me talk with her."

"Is she doing well?"

"She's resting right now. We're going to Desneige's for supper tonight. I'll raise it then."

"Give her my love, and also Aunt Desneige and her family. I miss you terribly, Dad." With a lump in her throat, her eyes began to sting.

A few weeks later, she received an envelope from St. Andrews. *From Mother.*

She took it to her room to read. "It's a note from Mother," she said to Gert, who was lounging on a pillow. "I'm afraid she's going to say 'no'. You open it, Gert."

Gert didn't need to read it aloud, as Dorothy watched her face sober to a frown.

"They can't make it. I'm so sorry, Dot. But you have me."

Reverend Ratz agreed to give Dorothy in marriage in the absence of her parents. Gladys and Gert would be bridesmaids—Gladys in a deep rose satin gown and Gert in soft pink silk.

On May 10, 1947, Dorothy entered the church, with a hush at the sight of her white satin gown and floor-length veil, and a trailing bouquet of red roses and baby's breath. In a slow walk down the aisle, her eyes scanned the congregation of her expanded family and new friends.

Her life was so different now, but would never erase the memories of her roots back home.

At the moment of her vows, she was most beautiful in her soft reply.

A Lesson in Charity

SETTLING IN BARRIE, north of Toronto, Dorothy and Les became active in church and charities, and later he served on City Council.

He slipped through the back door with a box from Straussmans' store and beamed with pride as he led her to the table. "For the City Council Inaugural next week, I have a surprise. Dorothy showed little expression as she lifted a mink stole from the box and felt the softness of the fur."

"It can replace your wool coat," he said. "It's more elegant, and dressy for the reception. As the Mayor's wife, I'd be honored if you wore it."

"Thank you. Les. It's thoughtful of you to treat me this way." Her mind flashed to her humble life as a girl that her parents still knew.

For Inaugural, Dorothy planned her pink brocade dress, and a hat with a black veil. Les put the stole around her shoulders and she was gracious again in appreciation.

"You know this isn't me," she said and he understood.

The standup reception was formal, greeting distinguished guests and members of parliament. For Dorothy, the social formalities and conversations were most enjoyable with the spouses of Lester's peers.

But to her shock, a woman she didn't know singled her out privately with an insulting remark. It cut Dorothy and she turned away, but the woman persisted.

"Mrs. Cooke, you have everything you could want including a mink stole. Too bad you've never known what it's like to be poor."

In an instant, Dorothy removed it. "Here, I want you to take this and enjoy it with no hard feelings. I much prefer my wool coat—I'm really not one for fancy things. I do want you to have this now." Stunned, the woman put out her hands. Dorothy wore a borrowed coat home from lost and found, and there was never another discussion about a fur coat.

The phone rang very early at Cooke's house. It was Christmas morning in 1959, and Les was on the emergency call list for the county.

"Mr. Cooke, it's the Utilities Commission. Sorry about this today, but we have a situation. With the deep freeze, it's come to our attention that a family in a house in Angus needs help. They were too proud to put their name forward for a Christmas hamper, but a concerned neighbor called the help line. Someone suggested you'd know what to do."

"Are there children?"

"Yes, four. I have their names and ages."

Dorothy sat beside Les as he wrote notes from the call.

"Mr. Cooke, it's not just the hamper . . . their electricity and heat were turned off for non-payment."

"Can a crew turn it on this morning? Put the charges on my household bill."

"Thank you. I just needed some authority."

"Good man. We'll take care of the hamper."

Dorothy tapped her index finger as she listened. When the phone was hung up, they hugged each other without a word.

Their three daughters were now up and pacing to check their stockings and Santa presents. Dorothy sent them for their housecoats, then to the kitchen.

"What's the matter, Mom? Ruth asked.

"Sit at the table and we'll explain."

The Christmas story was open at Luke Chapter 2. "For unto us is born this day, in the city of David, a Savior who is Christ the Lord."

"Ruth, please read the next one, then Shirley. Mom will read for Lorraine."

With the story told, Les asked the girls, "Isn't it better to give than receive? We have all our needs met."

"Yes," they said in unison. Les told the story of the Angus family and read the list of children.

"This Christmas, your stockings can be packed for these four children. Our gifts can be opened and together we'll rewrap them. Mom has the turkey ready for the oven, and you girls can help get the vegetables ready."

Dorothy was always frugal, ingrained never to waste or want and as an adult taught charity over material.

"When the dinner and the presents are ready," she said, "Dad and I will take them to the family in Angus."

"Can we come?"

"No. Do you understand what pride is?"

"I think so."

"We can make presents for each other, right?" Ruth said.

"Yes and they're the best kind."

Turkey, trimmings and Dorothy's gravy and pumpkin pie were packed into containers and delivered hot. The afternoon was spent with board games and watching *It's a Wonderful Life* on the black and white RCA.

It was the best Christmas ever for this author. I'll be eternally thankful.

Dorothy (Paquette) Cooke at about 20 years;
Pencil sketch by Sara Burton.

Epilogue

Alice Paquette was my grandmother, and Dorothy my mother. Alice passed away in 1960 after a long struggle. She had the pleasure of meeting her grandchildren on several occasions during visits to St. Andrews East.

Joseph travelled to Barrie for the first time in 1961 for Christmas with the Cooke family. It was a busy time of year, yet Joe delighted to soak in the laughter of the children's concert at the Grove Street Church, and a Christmas party for families at the trucking company.

With his 'Dot' and the girls, he stood on the wintry day with crowds on Dunlop Street, clapping to bands of the Santa Claus Parade. With my father, Lester, he cheered the Barrie Flyers hockey team and attended an Armory Park veterans' dinner.

The house grew in love when Gladys and Gert brought their families to see him—Gert with her beau, Wilson Simms, and an engagement ring. As a child, I saw a tear in Grandpa Joe's eyes. Perhaps he was reminiscing, missing his Alice, seeing his family love and this joy of reuniting.

Joe died of lung cancer in 1965. There was talk of Mirabel Airport wanting to expropriate his land, but that never happened. The old house on Main Street was demolished by the City of St. Andrews in 1970.

Although this line of the Paquette name came to an end when Dorothy died in 1984, the lineage remains strong.

In 2013, I travelled to Dissay, France, the town where the line of Étienne Pasquier commenced in this story. Driving on a country lane through the cornfields near Poitiers, we saw the first glimpses of turrets over the treetops—a castle with a blue-grey tiled roof, breathtaking and astonishing.

Transfixed, I stood at the moat drawbridge, knowing this was the Castle of Dissay, in the town where my ancestors, the Pasquiers, lived.

For me at that moment, it was sacred ground. In genealogy research, I had traced ten generations of Paquettes and Pasquiers to the Bourg D'Issay, now the quaint communal town of Dissay.

Following the road uphill from the Castle, I stopped at the Church of Saint-Pierre and Saint-Paul, where Étienne Pasquier attended, was married and buried.

"Incredible," I thought. "Could it be the same church from 400 years ago?" Well it was, and had survived centuries of war. I asked a man in the parking lot for directions to the church's old cemetery.

"I'm afraid you're standing on it. It fell into the ground over the years." But he sent me to the nearby Mairie office, for old church records. The old stone building was welcome relief, as a records clerks brought a great cloth-bound book from the archives. His name was Sean Bource—I'll always remember that.

Before me was the handwritten name of Étienne Pasquier, logging his funeral at the Church of Saint-Pierre et Saint-Paul on May 21, 1638, in this French village of Dissay, thousands of miles from St. Andrews East.

It was not the end, but the beginning of a long journey.

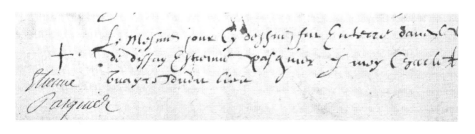

Shirley Burton at the Château de Dissay, Poitou, France.
Castle of Pierre d'Amboise, granted from Charles VII, 1484.

Chronology

1129	*Hugues Chaumont, son of Suplice I d'Amboise, died in Religious Crusades.*
1162	*Henry II ordered the murder of Thomas Becket for questioning the supremacy of the ecclesiastical courts.*
1337-1453	*Hundred Years' War, England and France.*
1348	*Creffield ancestors from Flanders, Normandy to Chappel near Colchester, England.*
1405	*Birth of Pierre d'Amboise, son of Hugh III of Chaumont & Jeanne de Guenand.*
1415	*Death of Hugh VIII of Chaumont at Battle of Agincourt.*
1422	*Pierre d'Amboise defended Meaux in Seige of 1422, establishing royal favour.*
1428	*Pierre d'Amboise married Anne de Beuil, takes residence at Castle de Meillant.*
1429	*Pierre d'Amboise, under command of Duke of Alencon, defended King Charles VII's Residence of Château de Chinon. Joined the French troops at Siege of Orleans, under Jeanne d'Arc until her capture in 1430.*
1431	*Jeanne d'Arc convicted of heresy, condemned to death at the stake, Rouen, France.*
1434	*Pierre d'Amboise, Governor of Touraine, designated Chamberlain to King Charles VII. King ordered Castle of Dissay to honor military service of d'Amboise.*
1450	*Pierre D'Amboise III born at the Château Chaumont-sur-Loire. Became Bishop of Poitiers.*
1473	*Death of Pierre d'Amboise II at Castle de Meillant, age 68 years, buried at Bourges.*
1497	*John Cabot, Italian navigator, staked Nova Scotia for King Henry VII of England.*
1519	*Leonardo da Vinci lived and died at his vineyards at Clos Luce Manor, part of the Château d'Amboise. Buried at the Chapel of Saint-Hubert on the estate.*
1520	*Jacques Cartier married Catherine des Granches, daughter of Jacques-Honore Guyon des Granches and Françoise Du Mast, at St. Malo, France.*
1528	*Death of Giovanni Verrazano, Italian explorer who chartered coast of Atlantic from Newfoundland to Carolinas.*
1529	*Birth of Étienne Pasquier, son of Stephen Pasquier of Ferlandière, Brie. Notable as future philosopher, writer and King's historian.*
1533	*Jacques Cartier is recommended to King Francis I for commission to New France.*
1534	*(April) Cartier departed St. Malo, France for Labrador coast, on Grande Hermine.*
1534	*(May) Grande Hermine ran aground on the cod banks of Newfoundland.*
1534	*(July) Cartier met the Micmac Chief Panounais in a spirit of friendship.*
1534	*(August) Cartier negotiated with Chief Donnacona to take two of his sons, Domagay and Taignoagny, back to France for education and to study the French way of life.*
1534	*(October) Cartier's ships, Grande Hermine & Petite Hermine, returned to St. Malo.*

1535	*Stephen Pasquier of La Ferlandière at Brie becomes a Court Justice; meets Pierre d'Amboise in Paris.*
1535	*Cartier departed St. Malo with Grande Hermine, Petite Hermine & Émérillon.*
1535	*(October) Cartier's men captured Chief Donnacona to take him back to France.*
1536	*Grande Hermine returned to St. Malo, Brittany, France; new commission postponed.*
1539	*Stephen Pasquier defended François Labertine of Poitiers at trial for stealing milk.*
1539	*Chief Donnacona died in France.*
1540	*King Francis I of France commissioned Cartier for a new expedition to New France.*
1541	*Cartier, with 1500 men, arrived in Charlesbourg, Québec, to establish a settlement.*
1542	*Jacques Cartier ordered to return to Saint-Malo, France.*
1557	*Cartier settled at Limoulou estate with his wife, Marie-Catherine. Contracting typhus, he dies at his home.*
1557	*Étienne Pasquier, the writer and court justice, married widowed client, Françoise Belen de Montmaine.*
1558	*Étienne Pasquier's first son, Theodore, was born in Paris.*
1562	*Étienne Pasquier became ill, convalescing away from Paris at d'Amboise and Brie. Began to write Les Recherches de la France.*
1569	*Admiral de Coligny led Huguenot army through southern France, attacking town and Castle of Dissay, leaving it badly damaged.*
1574	*King Charles IX was succeeded by Henry III, the corrupt King. Étienne Pasquier exiled from Paris.*
1574	*Samuel de Champlain born at Brouages, in Bordeaux, southern France. Parents Captain Antoine de Champlain and Marguerite LeRoy.*
1585	*Birth of Étienne Pasquier, at Dissay, Poitiers, Poitou, France.*
1589	*Birth of Jeanne Poussard(e) in Paris, France.*
1589	*Assassination of King Henry III after tumultuous reign.*
1590	*Françoise Belen died at family residence in Château d'Amboise in Loire Valley.*
1594	*Under King Henry IV, Pasquier was returned to the Court of Justice, opposing the Jesuit Order.*
1595	*Samuel de Champlain serves in battle in Bretagne (Brittany), France for three years.*
1598	*Champlain joins Gravé de Pont on commission to Gulf of Mexico and Mexico City.*
1603	*Champlain joins Gravé du Pont to Tadoussac on fur trading expedition.*
1603	*Champlain meets Membertou, Micmac Grand Chief, on Annapolis Escarpment.*
1604	*Étienne Pasquier resigns at the Court of Justice in Paris; retires in Ferlandière.*
1604	*John Duval, of Champlain's crew, is tried and hanged for plotting the assassination of Champlain.*
1607	*Champlain's winter camp moved from Saint Croix to the Bay of Fundy.*
1608	*Champlain's crew built the first Church in Lower Town at Québec. Foundation was laid for the Château of St. Louis and the First Habitation.*

1609   *Champlain's party joins with Algonquins, Wendat and Hurons in an ambush on Mohawk and Iroquois raiding parties.*

1610   *Champlain marries Hélène Boullé in 1610 in Paris. By agreement she remains with her parents for several years before joining Samuel in Québec.*

1611   *During the Beaver Wars, Henri Membertou caught dysentery; has a Christian burial.*

1612   *Samuel de Champlain was appointed Governor of Québec.*

1614   *Étienne Pasquier meets with historian Étienne Pasquier at Black Stag, Poitiers.*

1615   *Historian Étienne Pasquier dies at Ferlandière, age of eighty-six. Étienne of Dissay receives inheritance and royal cape.*

1615   *Champlain is recalled to France.*

1620   *Marriage of Étienne Pasquier and Jeanne Poussarde, at Du Bourg D'Issy, (Dissay).*

1620   *Hélène Boullé accompanies husband Samuel de Champlain to Québec. Adored by the natives she was called the 'White Princess'.*

1621   *Baptism Étienne Pasquier, son of Étienne Pasquier & Jeanne Poussarde, at Dissay.*

1624   *Hélène Boullé again accompanied her husband to Québec*

1624   *Baptism Mathurin Pasquier, son of Étienne Pasquier & Jeanne Poussarde, Dissay.*

1624-1626 *Second Habitation began construction at Québec.*

1627   *The Company of One Hundred formed to control trading monopoly in New France.*

1627-1629 *Under Charles I of England, the Anglo-French wars raged throughout Europe.*

1628   *Seige of La Rochelle ordered by King Louis VIII to suppress protestant movement.*

1629   *British cut off supply ships to the French in the St. Lawrence. The Kirke Brothers granted a monopoly on fur trade.*

1632   *Treaty of Germain-en-Laye returned illegally British-occupied lands in Cape Breton, Québec and Acadia to France. Kirke Brothers received control of Newfoundland.*

1632   *Black death plague invaded Normandy, France.*

1633   *Death of Jeanne Poussarde, buried at Church of Saint-Pierre et Saint-Paul, Dissay.*

1634   *Robert Giffard left Mortagne, France, to become Seigneur de Beauport, Québec.*

1635   *Samuel de Champlain fell ill during the building of Québec and died among his people.*

1636   *One of earliest passenger ships left La Rochelle, France, to Acadia and Québec.*

1636   *The Hébert family produced the first crops at Charlesbourg.*

1636   *King Louis XV decrees an annual two-day festival with bonfires, singing and dancing in the streets. Celebrations took place in both France and Québec.*

1638   *Death of Étienne Pasquier, spouse of Jeanne Poussarde, at Dissay, France.*

1642   *Foundation laid at Québec for Hôtel-Dieu, mission hospital run by Jeanne Manse.*

1645   *Habitants of Québec established their own Community of Habitants, opposing the trading monopoly of the Company of One Hundred in Montréal.*

1647   *Henriette Marie Rousseau born, daughter of Jacques Rousseau and Jeanne Arnoult.*

1648   *Zacherie Cloutier signed as an engage at Château-Richer, Québec.*

1648   *Urbain Tessier voyaged to Montréal, married Marie Archambault of Aunis, France.*

1649   *Jean Brébeuf, Jesuit priest, was burned at the stake by Iroquois.*

1650   *King Louis XIV of France ordered the first census of Québec; population 750.*

1651-1657 *Jean de Lauson became Governor of New France.*

1653   *Creffield family established at Colchester, Essex County, England as woolen drapers.*

1654   *Hélène Boullé died as an Ursuline nun 'Saint-Augustin' outside Paris.*

1654   *Toussaint Girould married Marie Godard in Montréal. Land deeded at Beauport.*

1659   *Adam Dollard defended fortress at Long Sault for five days against 700 Iroquois.*

1662-1689 *England collected Hearth Tax based on the number of chimneys per residence.*

1663   *King Louis XIV declared New France a royal province.*

1665   *King Louis XIV names Jean Talon Intendent of Québec, priority King's Daughters.*

1665   *Étienne Pasquier enlisted with Carignan La Motte Regiment on L'Aigle D'Or; departs La Rochelle, France for Charlesbourg, Québec.*

1665   *Hudson's Bay Company, formerly the Company of One Hundred, and granted authority for overall trade monopoly by Charles II.*

1666   *Census of Québec listed Étienne Pasquier, single habitant, 45, jardinière voluntaire.*

1667   *Henriette Marie Rousseau sent from St. Nicholas parish, Paris, as King's Daughter.*

1667   *Étienne Pasquier deeded plot of land at Seigneurie Petite-Auvergne at Charlesbourg.*

1667   *Simeon LeRoy dit Audy signed as engagé and master carpenter, Seigneury St. Joseph.*

1667   *Louis XIV ordered construction at Fort Pointe-a-Callière of the manor of Saint Gabriel for the King's Daughters when they arrived from France.*

1668   *Henriette and Anne Rousseau sail from La Rochelle to Québec as King's Daughters.*

1668   *Simeon LeRoy married Claude Blandina DesChalets, from Poitou, at Charlesbourg.*

1668   *Étienne Pasquier signed contract with Françoise Barbery. Cancelled weeks later.*

1668   *Étienne Pasquier marries Henriette Rousseau at Notre-Dame, Montréal.*

1668   *Several hundred Carignan returned to France after a long bitter winter.*

1668   *Seigneur Robert Giffard died, with Seigneurie de Beauport ceded to his son, Joseph.*

1668-1673 *Sir Ralph Creffield is Mayor of Colchester, Essex County, England.*

1669   *Étienne Pasquier and Henriette experienced first Iroquois raid in Charlesbourg.*

1670   *Étienne and Henriette had their first child, Anne Pasquier.*

1670   *Iron deposits discovered at Trois-Rivières.*

1671   *Étienne and Henriette had second daughter, Étiennette Marie Pasquier.*

1673   *Philippe Pasquier born to Étienne and Henriette at Bourg-Royale.*

1673   *Marie Anne LeRoy, daughter of Simeon LeRoy, born at Charlesbourg.*

1675-1676 *Massasoit, Chief of the Wampanoag, adopted English name of Philip. King Philip's Wars were named for him.*

1676   *King Louis XIV decreed a ban of fur trade with the coureurs des bois in New France.*

1681   *King Charles II granted land in Pennsylvania and Delaware to William Penn.*

1681   *The family of Simeon LeRoy removed to Montréal from Charlesbourg.*

1681   *Thomas Creffield born at Wakes Colne, Essex, England.*

1682	*Family of Simeon LeRoy moved from Montréal to Albany, New York.*
1682	*Louis de Buade, Governor Frontenac recalled to France for seven years.*
1683	*Frans François LeRoy, son of Simeon LeRoy, born at Albany, New York.*
1685	*Jean Charlebois dit Joly at age 20 joins volunteer forces of Marquis de Crisafy to thwart 800 Iroquois attacking the fort at Sault Saint-Louis.*
1685	*Recruits of French soldiers arrived in New France to help quash marauding Iroquois.*
1689	*British incited Iroquois to attack French villages, leading to Lachine Massacre.*
1689	*Frontenac recalled to France, replaced by Cavelier de La Salle.*
1690	*During native uprising at Battle of Coulée Grou, Jean Girou burned at the stake.*
1690	*Étienne Pasquier died at Petite-Rivière-Saint-Charles, Charlesbourg, Québec.*
1690	*New England troops captured Port Royal in Acadia, relinquished by Frontenac.*
1690	*Lower Town Québec began building batteries with stone walls to protect the city.*
1695	*Philippe Pasquier trekked to high country to rescue natives with scout, Hiroons.*
1697	*Wilderness adventure of Philippe Pasquier with fabled Huron guide Ononthio.*
1697	*Hurons and Wendat abandoned Jesuit mission and longhouse village at Lorette.*
1697	*Philippe Pasquier courts M-Jeanne Genevieve Brosseau, daughter of Julien Brosseau.*
1698	*Marriage of Philippe and M-Jeanne Genevieve at Saint-Charles-Borrommée.*
1699	*Huron braves befriend Henriette Rousseau at Petite-Auvergne, Bourg-Royale.*
1701	*The Great Peace Treaty of Montréal signed between the 40 native nations and Louis Hector de Calliere, Governor of New France.*
1702-1713	*Queen Anne's War raged between France and England and native allies.*
1704	*French forces with native allies attacked and destroyed Dearborn, Massachusetts.*
1712	*Thomas Creffield apprenticed in law firm of Henry Hargraves.*
1713	*Treaty of Utrecht gave more economic control to British.*
1713	*Sir Ralph Creffield knighted by Queen Anne.*
1714	*First Census of Dutchess County, NY, has slaves owned by Frans François LeRoy.*
1715	*Joseph Pageau married Madeleine Boesme at Saint-Charles-Borrommée.*
1716	*Jacques Charles Charlebois married M- Françoise Danis in Montréal, Québec.*
1716	*Philippe II, regent for King Louis V, granted economic rights to gambler John Law.*
1720	*François Paquet born, son of Philippe Pasquier and M-Genevieve Brosseau.*
1720	*John Law's Bank-issued Mississippi script was destabilized.*
1723-1725	*Jean Tessier-dit-Lavigne and son, Louis, encounter grizzly.*
1725	*Thomas Creffield, Jr. born at Pebmarsh, Essex England.*
1727	*Marie-Charlotte Valin born, daughter of Charles Valin and Louise Darveau.*
1728	*First List of Freeholders, Ulster County, New York, mainly German & Dutch.*
1728	*Philippe Pasquier returned to wilderness experience with son, François, and friends.*
1731	*Vincent Girould, son of Toussaint, farms on Seigneury Jacques de Chambly, Québec.*
1731	*Louis Roy Portelance took daughter, Marie-Catherine, to clockmakers in Montréal.*
1731-1737	*Chemin du Roy (King's Highway) built between Montréal and Québec City.*

1732	*Shipbuilding yards established at mouth of the St. Charles River, Charlesbourg.*
1732	*Valin and Paquette families shared Fête de Noël at Saint-Jacques-de-Misère.*
1732	*Death of Toussaint Girould at Beauport.*
1734	*Great Fire of Montréal destroyed over one hundred homes.*
1735	*Philippe Pasquier died at Saint-Jacques-La-Misère, Charlesbourg, Québec.*
1739	*Simeon LeRoy, son of Frans François LeRoy, married second wife Blandina Freer.*
1740	*St. Jean de Baptiste Day celebrated throughout Québec, ordained by King Louis XV.*
1740	*Stone grist mill built at Charlesbourg on the Charles River.*
1740	*Slaves, imported from the Carolinas, frequently sold in Montréal.*
1740	*Iron extracted from bogs around Trois-Rivières sent to shipbuilding yards on Charles River and Kingston. The site named Les Saint-Maurice Forges.*
1741	*Benjamin Franklin secured patent for the first open hearth stove.*
1744-1748	*King George's War raged throughout North America.*
1745	*Jacques Ambroise Charlebois married Marie-Catherine Roy Portelance.*
1745	*François Paquette married Marie-Charlotte Valin at L'Ancienne Lorette.*
1745	*Joseph J-Baptiste Charbonneau married Marie-Anne Chartrand, at Rivières-des-Prairies.*
1746	*First son, Louis Joseph, born to Jacques Charlebois at Montréal.*
1748	*Death of Marie-Catherine Roy Portelance in childbirth, wife of Jacques Charlebois.*
1750	*Unrest on the St. Lawrence and Ohio Valley led to mandatory recruitment of habitants to defend Québec, Montréal and the Chemin du Roy.*
1750	*Benjamin Franklin patent for the invention of lightning rods attached to barns.*
1752	*Joseph Jean-Baptiste Charbonneau saved wounded wolf cub he named Lucius.*
1752	*Liberty Bell arrives in Philadelphia, Pennsylvania.*
1754-1763	*French Indian Wars fought in North America.*
1756-1763	*Seven Years War in Québec and the St. Lawrence Seaway.*
1756	*Louis-Joseph de Montcalm appointed commander over the French regiment.*
1758	*James Abercrombie organized British and American troops to attack Fort Carillon, then Louisbourg and Kingston; then Britain declares war.*
1758	*Wilderness expedition: Pageau, Tessier, Charlebois, Paquette with Running Bear.*
1759	*Battle on the Plains of Abraham at Québec. François Paquet, son of Philippe Pasquier fights in battle as a Private. Wolfe and Montcalm both mortally wounded.*
1759	*Siege of Québec City victorious by British troops, who raised their flag.*
1760	*King George III ascends the British throne.*
1762	*François Paquette in killed in battle near Charlesbourg.*
1762	*Frans François LeRoy's death divides family lands at Poughkeepsie.*
1762-1763	*Chief Pontiac attempted to expel British by mass attacks on British forts.*
1762	*Simeon LeRoy, son of Frans François, inherited land and slaves at Poughkeepsie.*
1763	*Treaty of Paris signed at Versailles returned fortresses taken back to the British.*

1763   *British seized Saint-Maurice forges and leased out crown mining opportunities.*

1763   *Seigneuries still collected taxes throughout Lower Canada.*

1763   *Joseph Vincent Giroux married Catherine-Marguerite Jolivet.*

1764   *The Sugar Act imposed taxation on sugar and coffee in New England.*

1764   *Prisques Cloutier of Château-Richer married Marie Reine Langlois.*

1765   *The Stamp Act imposed taxation on newspapers, documents, and imposed licensing.*

1765   *Daniel Creffield born to Thomas and Mary Creffield at Pebmarsh, Essex, England.*

1766   *Jean François Paquette, Joseph Jean-Baptiste Charbonneau and Antoine Charlebois go into lumber camps for winter work.*

1768   *Jean François Paquette married M-Geneviève Pageau, daughter of Charles-Joseph.*

1769   *François, son of Jean- François Paquette (dit Bernard), born at Loretteville.*

1769   *Simeon LeRoy of Poughkeepsie married Wyntje Jacooks of Dutchess County, NY.*

1771   *Constitutional Act divided Upper Canada to British and Lower Canada to French.*

1774   *Contingent of Americans took grievances to King George III of England.*

1774   *François Charles Giroux born, s/o Joseph Vincent Giroux, at Île de Jésus.*

1775   *The fateful Boston Tea party dumped three shiploads of English tea into harbour.*

1775   *Midnight ride, Paul Revere and William Dawes, to Concord warn British of ambush.*

1775   *Jonas Freer of Dutchess County, NY, joined the Minutemen.*

1776   *The Declaration of Independence drafted by Thomas Jefferson.*

1778   *Prisque Cloutier born at Château-Richer, descendant of Zacherie Cloutier of Perche.*

1779   *Fur trade rights of the Hudson's Bay Company challenged by the North West Co.*

1781   *Monsieur Pierre Louis Panet became Seigneur of Saint-André and Argenteuil.*

1783   *Benjamin Franklin negotiated The Treaty of Paris, ending Revolutionary War.*

1784   *Evacuation began of American colonists fleeing to Québec, with land grants and one year's free rations in exchange for allegiance to Britain.*

1784   *Benjamin Franklin proposed the theory of Daylight Savings Time in a Paris journal.*

1785   *Simeon LeRoy's family escaped American soldiers at the end of American Revolution. Fled to Nova Scotia with the Loyalists movement, then moved to Rouge River.*

1785-1800 Loyalists from New England colonies flood into the Eastern Townships.

1785   *Daniel Creffield married Mary Nixon from Spitafields, England.*

1787   *Crop failures in Québec created hardship and hunger for habitants.*

1789   *Mouth of the McKenzie River discovered to access inland fur trade.*

1789   *Daniel and Mary Creffield have son John born at Earls Colne, England.*

1789   *François Vincent Giroux defends the honour of M-Marguerite Corbeil for being teased as a Métis at school.*

1790   *Winter rendezvous at Trading Post: Louis Joseph Charlebois, Louis Antoine Tessier and Pierre Mondery.*

1790   *James Bennett patented the first two-wheel buggy in England.*

1790   *First bicycle patented with two wheels and steering bar, referred to as 'bone-shaker'.*

1791-1796 John Graves Simcoe appointed the first Governor of Upper Canada.

1792   *Feu de Joie; François Paquette-dit-Bernadon meets Marie Charbonneau.*

1792   *Hyacinthe Tessier-dit-Lavigne married Marie-Louise Brault-Pominville at Lachine.*

1793   *François Paquette weds Marie Charbonneau, d/o Joseph J-Baptiste Charbonneau.*

1794   *François and Marie's first son, François, born at Saint Martin, Île de Jésus.*

1794   *Thomas Creffield Sr. died at Pebmarsh, Essex.*

1796   *François Charles Giroux married Marie-Marguerite Corbeil-dit-Trachemont.*

1799   *Joseph Louis Giroux, s/o François, born at St. Eustache, Deux Montagne.*

1800-1840 Boon of inventions: elevators, batteries, spinet pianos, Cotton Gin.

1802   *Merger of Hudson's Bay Company and the North West Company.*

1803   *Daniel Creffield, son of Thomas Creffield Sr. dies at Middlesex, England.*

1803   *The Louisiana Purchase signed in Paris, encompassing thirteen New England Colonies and two provinces.*

1803   *Thomas Moore granted patent from President Thomas Jefferson for the refrigerator.*

1804   *Family of Reuben Cooke flee from Ticonderoga with influx of Loyalists to Calumet.*

1804-1820 Hamilton and Mears brothers control timber industry in Argenteuil and Grenville Townships, including Hawkesbury Island.

1805   *Prisque Cloutier married Marie-Louise Guyon at Ste. Rose-de-Lima.*

1805   *First paper mill built at St. Andrews by Benjamin Wales and Walter Ware. Patrick Murray built the first gristmill.*

1806   *Edouard Irvan Paquette born to François and Marie at Ste. Rose-de-Lima.*

1806   *Philemon Wright floated the first square timber raft from Ottawa to Québec.*

1806-1817 Edouard Irvan Paquette spends his learning years in Huron village.

1808   *Elizabeth Landers, wife of Loyalist Rueben Cooke from Ticonderoga, planted first wheat crop in Argenteuil.*

1809   *Hargreaves Spinning Jenny sent from Sears to Marie Charbonneau.*

1809   *Joseph Louis Papineau elected to the Legislative Assembly with Liberal views.*

1809   *Clemence Cloutier, d/o Prisque Cloutier, born at Ste. Redempteur Mission at Oka.*

1809-1816 Death of Marie Charbonneau at Ste. Rose-de-Lima.

1810   *The Enclosure Act in England brings steam engines through Windsor to Slough.*

1810   *Molson began serving libations on excursion boats on the Ottawa and Rideau Rivers.*

1810   *Marie-Marguerite Tranchemontagne's experience with Durand's tin can invention.*

1811   *Commencement of the Twelve Days of Christmas at Ste. Rose-de-Lima.*

1812   *War of 1812 is fought along the Niagara Peninsula in Upper Canada.*

1812   *Henry Bell's steam powered navigation used on commercial and excursion steamboats.*

1812   *John Creffield, Earls Colne weds Susannah Brown, Upton Bucks, Buckinghamshire.*

1812   *John Creffield II apprentices with Rowley & Co. as a coach builder.*

1813   *John Creffield Jr. born, s/o John and Susannah Brown, at Upton Cum Chalvey.*

1814   *Seigneury of Argenteuil sold by James Murray to Sir John Johnson.*

1815   *Joseph Louis Papineau appointed Speaker of the Assembly.*

1816   *Prisque Cloutier takes Clemence to the grist mill, meeting the Paquette wagon.*

1816   *Hyacinthe Amable Tessier, François Charles Giroux, and Pierre Mondary repeat wilderness adventure, joined by sons Joseph-Louis, Olivier and Pierre Jr.*

1817   *Edouard Irvan Paquette lives with brother, François, at St. Thérèse-de-Blainville.*

1817   *George Simon LeRoy, s/o Simeon LeRoy and Wyntje Jacooks, marries Asenathe Bain, daughter of Jeremiah Bain of Deerfield, New Hampshire.*

1817   *The Irish Potato Famine brings influx of immigrants from Tipperary, Kildare, and Kilkenny to Montréal and Québec.*

1819   *Princess Victoria is born to Prince Edward, grandson of George III, and German born Mother Princess Victoria.*

1820   *George Simon LeRoy, son of Simeon LeRoy, is born at Terrebonne, Québec.*

1821   *Work began on the Lachine Canal to bypass rapids.*

1822   *Joseph Louis Giroux married Marguerite Monderie (Mondery) at St. Benoit.*

1825   *Marcel Joseph Giroux, s/o Joseph Louis, born at St. Hermas, Deux Montagnes.*

1825   *King George IV abolishes Seigneurial system, converting tenure to habitants.*

1826   *Tented town on Ottawa River started by John By, renamed Bytown (later Ottawa).*

1829   *Carriage Works Exposition in London.*

1829   *Susannah Creffield (nee Brown) died at Upton Cum Chalvey, Slough.*

1830   *First locomotive railway portaging the St. Lawrence River to the Richelieu River.*

1830   *William IV was King of England. Lord Grey, from the Whigs, was Prime Minister.*

1830   *John Creffield of Upton Cum Chalvey apprentices as coachbuilder with Carriage Works Company of Salt Hill, Buckinghamshire.*

1830-1864 *Legends of Big Joe Mufferaw, strongest French-Canadian alive, thrive in Canada.*

1831   *John Creffield married Ann Edwards of Lewes Sussex at Marylebone, London.*

1832   *Edouard Irvan Paquette weds Clemence Cloutier, d/o Prisque Cloutier of Ste. Redempteur, followed by house-raising bee.*

1832   *Cholera epidemic arrives on Carrick from Ireland, ravaging the Eastern Townships.*

1833   *Victor Paquette born to Edouard and Clemence Cloutier at St. Andrews.*

1835   *Rueben and Asa Cooke pilot lumber barges on Ottawa River for Philemon Wright.*

1836   *Hascall's improved mowing and threshing machine comes to Lachute.*

1836   *John Creffield Sr. invited to Shooting Club's pigeon tournament at the White Hart.*

1836   *John Creffield and Ann Edwards have twins born at New Windsor, Berkshire.*

1836   *The Champlain and St. Lawrence railway opened running on the shores of Montréal.*

1837   *John Deere's steel moulded plow became part of the machine co-op in Argenteuil.*

1837   *The Rebellion triggered attacks through Argenteuil. The Battle of St. Eustache incited Joseph Giroux. Many died including Hyacinthe Amable Tessier.*

1837   *Joseph Charlebois of St. Placide married Sophie Tessier-Lavigne, d/o Hyacinthe Amable Tessier at St. Hermas, Rigaud.*

1837   *Princess Victoria, niece of King William IV, is crowned Queen Victoria. Coronation the following year.*

1838   *Treffle Alfred Charlebois was born at St. Madeleine, Rigaud.*

1838   *The Great Western Railway opened in England from Hayes to Maidenhead.*

1838   *After the Rebellion, Lower and Upper Canada merged under the Union Act.*

1840   *Queen Victoria married Prince Albert.*

1840   *The Québec government provided one-room school houses for both French and English.*

1840   *Blanchard and Wales Grocery stores in St. Andrews sold a barrel of grist wheat for 4 shillings and 3 pennies, while muscovado sugar was 6 pennies.*

1841   *Upper Canada and Lower Canada unite as The Province of Canada.*

1841   *Prince Albert presents Queen Victoria with first Christmas tree decorated with candles, shiny keepsakes and red and gold ribbons, the colors of the Queen's standard.*

1842   *John Creffield inherits £400 from his Uncle John Creffield of London. Buys out Peter Coventry from the Coachbuilders & Harness Makers on Peascod Street, Slough.*

1843   *Marcel Joseph Giroux married Elizabeth LeRoy, d/o George Simon LeRoy and Asenathe Bain, at St. Hermas. Marcel completed blacksmith apprenticeship.*

1845   *Irish Potato Famine brings a second exodus of immigrants to Eastern Townships.*

1847   *John Creffield, of Coachbuilder & Harness Makers of Slough, declared insolvent.*

1850   *Bytown railway opens floodgate of communication – telegraph, mail and newspapers.*

1850   *Touring railway excursions ran from Carillon to Lachute in a few hours.*

1851   *The Great Exhibition of European Works of Industry takes place at the Crystal Palace, Hyde Park, London.*

1852   *George Simon LeRoy, of River Rouge, falls on hard times and declares bankruptcy.*

1854   *Victor Paquette, s/o Edouard Irvan, weds Aurelia Beaulne, at St. André Est.*

1850   *John Creffield III marries Clementina Eliza Webb, d/o John and Sarah Webb.*

1861-1865 *American Civil War between Confederate army and Union Cavalry resulted in Confederate victory and freedom to slaves.*

1864   *Frederick John Creffield born at New Windsor, s/o John and Clementina Creffield.*

1865   *Fourth son of Victor Paquette, Urgel, born in the village of St. Andrews East.*

1866-1870 *The Fenian Raids take place in Upper Canada, the voice of the Irish immigrant.*

1867   *Confederation creates Dominion of Canada under PM Sir John A. MacDonald.*

1869   *St. Andrews Fall Harvest Festival celebrated at St. Andrews and Hawkesbury.*

1870   *Education Act of the U.K. requires mandatory enrollment for school-aged children.*

1870   *Royal Union flag of Canada is replaced by the Union Jack.*

1870   *Professor Melville Bell's telephone invention lauded by Dominion Telegraph, Québec.*

1871   *Census of Québec lists Paquette descendants of Edouard Irvan and Victor.*

1871   *Census of U.K. lists Creffield family living at Charles Street, Buckinghamshire.*

1872   *Turner family prepares for Boxing Day collection of alms for the poor, a tradition started by Queen Victoria in England.*

1880   *Victor Paquette and his sons attend the Annual St. Andrew's Turkey Shoot.*

1883   *Nickel discovered at Sudbury, Ontario. Coal found years before in Québec at Trois-Rivières, Val D'Or, and Rouyn-Noranda,*

1886   *Depression strikes Eastern Townships of Québec.*

1887   *Urgel Paquette marries Victoria Charlebois, d/o Treffle Alfred Charlebois and Elizabeth Giroux at St. Andrew's East.*

1887   *St. Andrews East and Carillon become independent communities.*

1889   *Joseph Treffle Paquette, s/o Urgel Paquette, is born at St. Andrews East.*

1889   *John Creffield III of Eton, Buckinghamshire dies.*

1891   *Frederick John Creffield weds Alice Jane Turner, d/o Henry Turner of Hemel Hempstead.*

1892   *Alice May Creffield, d/o Frederick/Alice Creffield, born, Eton, Buckinghamshire.*

1897   *National Women's Suffrage was formed.*

1906   *Woodsmen and guide, Victor Paquette, found dead beside his canoe.*

1906   *General Election supported by Winston Churchill supports the Trade Disputes Act.*

1907-1913 *Clementina Eliza Creffield is admitted to care residence at Aylesbury.*

1908   *Olympics default to London, England.*

1909   *The Trade Board Act introduces Old Age Pension and minimum wage England.*

1910   *Frederick John Creffield takes work as farm labourer at Cowley Farm, Cuddington, Aylesburg, a short distance from Chalvey.*

1912   *In England, women were guaranteed wage equality.*

1913   *Alice May Creffield departs on Laurentic, White Star, from Liverpool to Montréal.*

1914   *Archduke Franz Ferdinand, first in line to the Austrian-Hungarian throne, and his wife assassinated by a Black Hand assailant.*

1915   *Joseph and Emile Paquette stalked by wild bobcat.*

1916   *Joseph Treffle Paquette purchases Fournier land on Lots 438 and 440, Main Street, of St. Andrews East.*

1916   *Marriage Alice May Creffield to Joseph Treffle Paquette at St. Michael's, Montréal.*

1917   *Mandatory Conscription ordered by Canada for all able-bodied men 20-45, for enlistment during the Great War.*

1917   *French-Canadian reaction to Conscription led to riots on Montréal streets.*

1917   *Joseph Paquette and his brothers enlist with the Van Doos of Québec.*

1917   *Marjorie Paquette born to Joseph & Alice Paquette at St. Andrews.*

1918   *Armistice Day brings the Great War to an end.*

1919   *Dorothy Stella Paquette, d/o Joseph and Alice Paquette, born at St. Andrews.*

1919   *The Great Winnipeg strike during post-war economic depression.*

1922   *Gladys Hilda Paquette born to Joseph & Alice Paquette at St. Andrews.*

1923   *Kathleen Alice Paquette born to Joseph & Alice Paquette at St. Andrews.*

1928   *Gertrude Marie Yvonne Paquette born to Joseph & Alice Paquette at St. Andrews.*

1929   *The Great Depression begins with the Crash of the Stock Market.*

1933   *Marjorie Paquette, oldest daughter of Joseph Paquette, leaves home for Montréal.*

1934-1939 Economy begins come-back, with bands, music, theatre, hockey, motor clubs.

1937   *Canada government boosts commercial flights, contracts in aero manufacturing.*

1937   *Dorothy Paquette, second oldest daughter of Joseph Paquette, leaves for Montréal.*

1939   *German tanks invaded Poland overnight. Warsaw capitulated seventeen days later.*

1942   *Dorothy Paquette moves to Toronto, enrolls Eastern Pentecostal Bible College.*

1942   *Ice and coal delivery business operated north of Toronto by Lester Cooke.*

1945   *End of World War II, troop withdrawal; start of Cold War, USA and Russia.*

1947   *Dorothy Paquette marries Lester Cooke, Toronto, Ontario.*

1960   *Alice May Paquette (nee Creffield) dies, buried at St. Andrews East, Québec.*

1965   *Joseph Treffle Paquette dies of lung cancer at St. Andrews East.*

1984   *Dorothy Cooke (nee Paquette) dies at Barrie, Ontario.*

2012   *Shirley Burton (nee Cooke) visits Dissay, Poitou, France, to the 16th century streets of the Pasquiers, the Church of Saint-Pierre et Saint-Paul, and the Castle of Dissay.*

Bibliography

The Annual Pigeon Shooting, White Hart Inn, Slough; November 26, 1836. Windsor and Eton Express. Bucks Chronicle and Reading Journal, 2008.

Barber, Marilyn J. *Below Stairs: The Domestic Servant* – Vol. 19. Ottawa, ON. Carleton University; 1984.

Barber, Marilyn J. *The Women Canada Welcomed: Immigrant Domestic Servants for Canadian Homes,1870-1939.* Ottawa, ON: Carleton University, 1980.

Bedore, Bernie. *The Shanty: a story from the Ottawa Valley of Canada, Big Joe Mufferaw.* Toronto, ON: Mufferaw Enterprises,1975.

Berton, Pierre. *War of 1812.* Toronto, ON: Anchor Canada Publishing, 2011.

Boyd, Julian P. (Editor*). Declaration of the Causes and Necessity for Taking Up Arms. Papers of Thomas Jefferson, vol. 1, 1760-1776.* Princeton University Press, 1950.

Canadian Census records 1851, 1861, 1871, 1881, 1891; UK Census records 1841, 1851, 1861, 1871, 1881. Latter Day Saints Research Library. Salt Lake City, Utah.

Champlain, Samuel de. *Des Sauvages, Voyage de Samuel Champlain, de Brouage, fait en la France Nouvelle, 1603.* Edited by C. Heidenrech & K. Ritch. The Champlain Society. Monograph, 2013.

Chaumont, Pierre (Father). *Wendat Versions of the Lord's Prayer.* Wyandot Org.

Cohan, Ray. *How to Make it on the Land.* Toronto: Prentice-Hall, 1972.

Cooper, Janet (Editor). *A History of the County of Essex: Vol. 10, Lexden Hundred (Part) including Earls Colne and Wivenhoe.* London, UK: Victoria County History, 2001.

Crowder, Norman K (Edited). *Early Ottawa Valley Records.* Ottawa: Ontario Genealogical Society. 1988.

Drouin, Claude. *Répertoire Alphabetique Des Mariages de la Famille Roy de 1608.* Ottawa: Drouin Collection, 1989.

Eccles, W. J. *The Canadian Frontier, 1534-1760.* Albuquerque, NM: Holt, Rinehart and Winston, Inc., 1969.

Fahmi, Magda. *Ruffled Mistresses and Discontented Maids: Respectability and the Case of the Domestic Service, 1880-1914.* Ottawa, ON. Social Services and Humanities, 1997.

The Farm of Etienne Pasquier and Ferlandière, a scholar of the sixteenth Century (1529-

1615). La Société d'Histoire du Châtelet-en-Brie. Mairie, Le Châtelet-en-Brie, 1995.

Fournier, Marcel. *Paquette-Pack-Pasquier Genealogy.* Montréal, QC: Drouin Genealogical Institute, University of Montréal.

Francis, R. Douglas. Jones, Richard. Smith, Donald B. *Origins, Canadian History to Confederation.* Toronto: Holt, Rinehart and Winston of Canada, 1988.

Fraser, Maxwell. *The Rise of Slough 1196-1916.* Slough, UK: Slough Corporation 1973.

Garneau, R. D. *Canadian History a Distinct Viewpoint: 1600-1614, 1663, 1694-1699, 1719-1724, 1800-1849.* Edmonton, AB: 2015.

Germ, Jean-Marie (Researcher). *Etienne Pasquier and Jeanne Poussarde.* Québec Federation of Genealogical Societies, 2013.

Gill, Lesley A. (transcribed by). *1851 Census, St. Andrews, County of Two Mountains, Québec.* Pointe Claire, QC: Québec Family History Society, 1999.

Grant, George Monroe. (Editor) *Picturesque Canada; The Country as It Was and Is – Volume 1,* New York: James Clarke Publishing, 1882.

Grassmann, Thomas. *Dictionary of Canadian Biography – Manitougatche. Kiotseaeton, Le Crochet. Vol. 1.* Toronto & Montréal. University of Toronto/University of Laval, 1966.

Greenough, William Parker. *Canadian Folk-Life and Folk-Lore.* NY: George H. Richmond, 1897.

Graymont, Barbara, edited by Porter, Frank W. III. *Indians of North America – The Iroquois.* NY: Chelsea House Publishers, 1988.

Howison, John, Esq. *Sketches of Upper Canada.* London: G.&W.R. Whittaker, 1821.

Hearth Tax in England and Wales. Salt Lake City, UT: Familysearch.org. Latter-Day Saints Library.

The Historical Directory of London, Essex, Kent & Suffolk via the Pub Inns, Taverns & Beer Houses History and Trade Directory. 2008.

A History of the County of Middlesex: Vol. 2. – Coach-Making. London: Victoria County History.

History of Salvation Army. Archives. Salvation Army of Canada, 2015.

Illustrated Historical Atlas of the County of Carleton including Ottawa (1897). Toronto, ON: Belden, H. & Co.

James, J. L. Beaumont. *The Story of France 1814-1914.* London, UK & NY: Thomas Nelson and Sons, Inc., 1916.

Jenkins, Kathleen. *Montréal, Island City of the St. Lawrence.* New York: Doubleday & Company, 1966.

Jette, Rene. *Dictionnaire Généalogique des familles de Québec.* Montréal: University of Montréal, 1983.

Jury, Elsie McLeod. *Dictionnaire Biographique du Canada – Savignon*. Toronto. University of Toronto, 1966.

Kauffman, Carl. *Logging Days*. Sault Ste. Marie, ON: Sault Star Commercial Printing, 1973.

Keating, L. Clark. *Étienne Pasquier*. New York: Twayne Publishers, Inc., 1972.

Kolle, David. *Surname Index to Robson's 1839 Directory of Buckinghamshire, A-F*. 1994.

King's Daughters & Regiment. La Société des Filles du Roi et Soldats du Carignan, Inc. Chantilly, VA: 1994.

Laliberté, Serge. *Mariages de St. Eustache 1769-1979*. Ste. Jerome, QC: Société Généalogique des Laurentides, 1987.

Laforest, Thomas J. Simeon Le Roy dit Audy; *Our French Canadian Ancestors. Vol. III*. Lisi Press, 1984.

Leboeuf, J. Arthur. *Complement au Dictionnaire Généalogique Tanguay – Premiere Series*, 1957.

Lepage, Louise. *Mariages St. André Est 1833-1984, Vol. 6*. St. Jerome, QC: Societé Généalogique des Laurentides, 1989.

London Metropolitan Archives. *UK, Poll Books and Electoral Registers, 1538-1839*. London.

Mendel, David. *Québec, Birthplace of New France*. Québec: Commission de La Capitale Nationale, 1995.

Miner, Horace. *St. Denis A French-Canadian Parish*. Chicago, IL: University of Chicago, 1939.

Montgomery, Noel Elliot. *The Central Canadians Directory 1600-1900, Vol. 1&3*. Toronto: Genealogical Research Library, 1994.

Moore, Christopher. *The Loyalists, Revolution, Exile, Settlement*. Toronto: McClelland & Stewart, 1984.

Moyles, R. Gordon. *William Booth in Canada*. Edmonton: AGM Publications, 2006.

O'Callaghan, E.B., M.D. *The Documentary History of the State of New York*. Albany, NY: Weed, Parsons & Co, 1850.

Ouimet, Germain. *Généalogies de St. André Est, Québec, 1600-1900*. Montréal: Editions Bergeron, 1981.

Page, Johann and Poulin, Nancy. *Mariages de Lachute – Argenteuil, Volume 7-2*. Québec. Société Généalogique des Laurentides, 1988.

Paquette families in Québec. Genealogical Research Library. Niagara Falls, ON: 2003.

Pigot & Co.'s Trade Directory of 1830. Pigot's Trade Directory. Berkshire (Eton), 2008.

Reid, Richard (edit.). *The Upper Ottawa Valley to 1855, A Collection of Documents*. Toronto: The Champlain Society in Cooperation with the Government of

Ontario, 1990.

Rigby, G. R. *A History of Lachute*. Lachute: Giles Publishing, 1964.

Rivest, Lucien. *Mariages du comte de Argenteuil, Vol. II (L-Z)*. Montréal: Société de Généalogie de Lanaudière, Joliette, 1972.

Rutherdale, Myra. *Public Discourse and Salvation Army Immigrant Women and Children 1900-1930*. Toronto: York University.

Sanders, Carol. *United Kingdom: The Bernardo Boys*. London: Winnipeg Free Press, 2012.

Savage, Marie. *The Incredible Adventures of the Fearless Fur Traders*. Canmore, AB: Altitude Publishing, 2003.

Schroder, Gary and Tuesdell, Carol (Compiled). *Lachute Protestant Cemetery, Argenteuil County*. Pointe Claire, QC: Québec Family History Society, 1992.

Schwartz, Seymour I., *The French and Indian War 1754-1763 – The Imperial Struggle for North America*. New York: Simon & Schuster, 1928.

Sparks, Sadie Greening. *The Family of Urbain Tessier dit Lavigne*. 2014

Speed, Peter. *Shire County Guide, Berkshire*. Buckingham, UK. Shire Publishing Ltd, 1992.

Stacey, C. P. *Québec, 1759, The Siege and the Battle*. Toronto: MacMillan Company of Canada, 1959.

Sulte, Benjamin. *Recensement de 1666 en Nouvelle-France*. Laval, QC. 1977.

———. *Histoire des Canadiens-Français*. Laval University. Montréal. 1977.

Sweeney, T.W., Maj. Gen. Irish Militia in Upper Canada. *Fenian Proclamation*. The Queen's Own Rifles of Canada, 2nd Airborne.

Tanguay, Cyprien. *Québec, Genealogical Dictionary of Canadian Families (Tanguay Collection) 1608-1690*. Provo, UT.

Tanguay, L'Abbe. *Dictionnaire Généalogique des Familles Canadiennes, Vol. 6*. Montréal: Eusebe Senecal & Fils.,1889

Thomas, Cyrus. *History of the Counties of Argenteuil, Québec & Prescott, Ontario: From Earliest Settlement to Present*. Montréal: John Lovell & Son, 1896.

Thwaites, Reuben Gold (Editor). *The Jesuit Relations and Allied Documents in New France 1610-1791*. Le Jeune's Relation, 1633. Vol. V. Cleveland: Historical Society of Wisconsin. The Burrows Brothers.

Trigger, Bruce G. *Dictionary of Canadian Biography – Erouachy, Vol. 1*. Toronto & Montréal. University of Toronto/University of Laval, 1966.

Trudel, Marcel. *Catalogue des Immigrants 1632-1662*. Cahiers du Québec Collection Histoire. Editions Hurtubise, 1983.

Varney, Jack. *The Good Regiment, Perche, France to Charlesbourg, Québec 1665*. Montréal: McGill-Queens University Press, 1991.

Vital Statistics for Province of Ontario. Archives of Ontario. Compiled by Ian

MacDonald. Toronto, ON: Queen's Printers, 2001.

Wales, B. A. *Memories of Old St. Andrews and Historical Sketches of the Seigniory of Argenteuil.* Lachute: Watchman Press, 1934.

Wallace, Paul A. W. *Dictionary of Canadian Biography – Dekanahwideh. Vol. 1.* Toronto & Montréal: University of Toronto/University of Laval, 1966; revised 1979.

Weaver, Emily P. *Canada and the British Immigrant.* London: The Religious Tract Society, 2016.

Booklet of Agreements in regard to British Domestics in Canada. Women's Domestic Guild of Canada. Montréal.

93524662R00378

Made in the USA
Columbia, SC
11 April 2018